The King and Queen of Swords

Second Book of
THE OROKON

Also by Tom Arden

The Harlequin's Dance
First Book of THE OROKON

The King and Queen of Swords

Second Book of THE OROKON

TOM ARDEN

VICTOR GOLLANCZ

LONDON

First published in Great Britain 1998
by Victor Gollancz
An imprint of the Cassell Group
Wellington House, 125 Strand, London WC2R 0BB

© Tom Arden 1998

A catalogue record for this book is
available from the British Library.

ISBN 0 575 06371 8

Typeset by SetSystems Ltd, Saffron Walden, Essex
Printed in Great Britain by
St Edmundsbury Press Ltd, Bury St Edmunds, Suffolk

98 99 5 4 3 2 1

The Swords Song

Everything is lemon and nothing is lime,
But even the truth shall be revealed in time:
Then we shall drink from the mocking-tree gourds,
And sup with the King and Queen of Swords!

Everything is hidden and nothing is known,
For even the truth is like a cur's old bone:
Come, let us kneel at the mocking-tree boards,
And pray for the King and Queen of Swords!

Everything is water but nothing is wet,
And even the truth is like an unpaid debt:
What, you would anger the mocking-tree lords?
Still, you may lie with the Queen of Swords!

Everything's a pebble and nothing's a stone
When even the truth is left to lie alone:
Fool, you would plunder the mocking-tree hoards?
Then die with the King and Queen of Swords!

Everything is falling but nothing will fall,
Though even the truth will vanish when you call:
Come, let us take all that mocking affords –
Come, let us live in the Land of Swords!
Come, let us dream in the Land of Swords!

Players

JEM, *the hero, seeker after the Orokon*
CATA, *the heroine, robbed of her memory*
UMBECCA VEELDROP, *their scheming great-aunt*
POLTY, *a villainous young army officer*
VLADA FLAY ('AUNT VLADA'), *a remarkable old lady*
RAJAL, *a Vaga-boy, friend to Jem*
MYLA, *a Vaga-girl, sister to Rajal*
XAL, *'Great Mother' to the Vagas, a mystic*
ZADY, *a simpleton, cousin to Xal*
GOVERNOR VEELDROP, *Umbecca's ailing husband*
EAY FEVAL, *her spiritual advisor*
NIRRY JUBB, *her long-suffering maid*
HARLEQUIN OF THE SILVER MASKS, *an elderly entertainer*
CLOWN, *his long-time companion*
WYNDA THROSH, *an elderly bawd*
ARON THROSH ('BEAN'), *her son, friend to Polty*
'JAC' BURGROVE, *handsomest bachelor in Varby*
PELLI PELLIGREW, *an innocent young lady*
WIDOW WAXWELL, *her Duenna*
FRANZ WAXWELL, *a fashionable apothecary*
LORD MARGRAVE, *a loyal civil servant*
HEKA *and* JILDA QUISTO, *society-girls*
STEPHEL, *a coachman, father to Nirry*
'HARION CORNFIELD' *and* 'BEERJACKET', *soldiers*
QUALITY-FOLK, SOLDIERS, VAGAS
DRUNKARDS, HARLOTS, PRISONERS
&c.

IN AGONDON:
EJARD BLUEJACKET, *the unrightful king*
TRANIMEL, *his evil First Minister*
MATHANIAS EMPSTER, *a noble lord, guardian to Jem*
JORVEL OF IXITER, *Archduke of Irion, great-father to Jem*
CONSTANSIA CHAM-CHARING, *society hostess*
JELICA VANCE, *a young lady of fashion*

PELLAM PELLIGREW, *brother to Pelli*
SIR PELLION PELLIGREW, *his elderly great-father*
ELSAN MARGRAVE, *friend to Lady Cham-Charing*
FREDDIE CHAYN, *scion of a worthless principality*
MISTRESS QUICK, *headmistress of an exclusive girls' school*
GOODY GARVICE, *her faithful assistant*
COLONEL HEVA-HARION, *a supercilious Bluejacket*
'JU-JU', *Duenna to Jelica Vance*
MADDY CODA, *a red-headed actress*
JAPIER QUISTO, *Agondon's finest gentlemen's tailor*
WEBSTER, *of coffee-house fame*
BERTHEN SPRATT, *a maid, also called* ELPETTA *and* VANTA
THE ARCHMAXIMATE *and other* MEN OF THE CLOTH
THE REJECT *on Regent's Bridge*
COURTIERS, SERVANTS, RABBLE
&c.

IN ZENZAU:
'BOB SCARLET', *a mysterious highwayman*
LANDA, *a beautiful young Zenzan girl*
DOLM, *her father, steward of Oltby Castle*
ORVIK, *her betrothed, a foolish prince*
MORVEN *and* CRUM, *Bluejacket soldiers*
HUL *and* BANDO, *Redjacket rebels*
RAGGLE *and* TAGGLE, *sons to Bando*
PRIESTESS AJL, *Keeper of Viana's faith*
CORPORAL OLCH ('WIGGLER'), *betrothed of Nirry*
SOLDIER ROTTS, *friend to Wiggler*
SERGEANT BUNCH, *their company sergeant*
SERGEANT FLOSS, *sergeant in another regiment*
LORD MICHAN, *colonial governor of Zenzau*
LADY MICHAN, *his wife, the former Mazy Tarfoot*
A lazy FRIAR
ARMIES, ZENZANS, REBELS
&c.

OFF-STAGE – OR DEAD:
EJARD RED, *the deposed king*
SILAS WOLVERON, *father to Cata*
GOODMAN WAXWELL, *a wicked physician*
BARNABAS, *a magical dwarf: now missing*
LADY ELABETH, *mother to Jem*
TOR, *mysterious uncle to Jem*

ULY *and* MARLY, *Aunt Vlada's cousins*
UNCLE ONTY, *their ambitious father*
PELLEAS PELLIGREW, *brother to Sir Pellion*
HARTIA FLAY, *Diva of Wrax*
MISS TILSY FASH, *the Zaxon Nightingale*
MISS VYELLA REXTEL *and other* MISSING PERSONS
THE LADY LOLENDA, *who may yet return*
THE PRINCE-ELECT *of Urgan-Orandy*
GAROLUS VYTONI, *Zenzau's greatest philosopher*
LADY RUANNA, *sister to Umbecca: a famous novelist*
SIR BARTEL SILVERBY, *also a famous novelist*
MR COPPERGATE, *a famous poet*
DR TONSON, MR EDDINGTON, *and other* AUTHORS
PROFESSOR MERCOL *of the University of Agondon*
HEROES *and* VILLAINS *in Silverby's novels*
HISTORICAL FIGURES *from Ejland's past*
&c.

GODS AND STRANGE BEINGS:
OROK, *Ur-God, father of the gods*
KOROS, *his first-born: god of darkness*
VIANA, *goddess of earth*
THERON, *god of fire*
JAVANDER, *goddess of water*
AGONIS, *god of air*
TOTH-VEXRAH, *evil anti-god: formerly* SASSOROCH
THE LADY IMAGENTA, *his daughter, who shall return*
THE HARLEQUIN, *who may or may not be Tor*
THE SHOPKEEPER OF WRAX
MAN OF GREEN *and* MAN OF GOLD, *in Bando's song*
THE KING AND QUEEN OF SWORDS
EO, *an intimate of Myla*
PENGE, *an intimate of Polty*
'BOB SCARLET', *the bird of that name*
RING *and* RHEEN, *metamorphs*
THE FINE GENTLEMAN *in the Shopkeeper's story*
THE VARBY, *inhabitants of a mysterious cave*
THE VICHY, *a monster made of mud and leaves*
Other CREATURES OF EVIL
&c.

The Story So Far

It is written that the five gods once lived upon the earth, and the crystals that embodied their powers were united in a circle called THE OROKON. War divided the gods and the crystals were scattered. Now, as the world faces terrible evil, it is the task of a boy called Jemany Vexing to reunite the crystals.

In *The Harlequin's Dance*, First Book of THE OROKON, it was told how Jem was born a cripple, but gained the power to walk when he found the first crystal. Brought up by his wicked Aunt Umbecca, Jem's prospects were bleak until he fell in love with the wild girl Catayane. Gifted with mystical powers, Cata helped Jem realize his destiny; learning of his quest, Jem learnt too that instead of being a 'Vexing', or bastard, he was in truth the son of Ejard Red, the rightful king deposed by the Bluejackets.

Now, urged on by the harlequin, his secret protector, Jem must leave behind the world of his childhood. His village has become a Bluejacket base, and Umbecca, married to the military governor, Veeldrop, has found a wider stage for her wickedness. Cata's father, Jem's mother and his beloved Uncle Tor have met with terrible fates – all owing to Umbecca. Meanwhile Veeldrop's sadistic son, Polty, has delivered Cata too into Umbecca's clutches. Robbed of her memory, scrubbed and civilized, the wild girl has become a lady. Cata recalls nothing of her powers – or of Jem.

As his new adventure begins, Jem is a renegade from Bluejacket justice. Disguised as a wandering Vaga, he makes for the city of Agondon. There, in the house of a certain Lord Empster, he is fated to begin the next stage of his quest.

But Jem's old enemies are closer than he thinks.

And so is Cata.

PART ONE

The Varby Wait

Chapter 1

A WINDOW IN VARBY

Dearest cousin—
Or should I say, my once dearest cousin? You are a deceiver,
Miss Jelica Vance – or rather, Her Royal Highness that is soon to be!
Is it right that I should hear from Aunt's maid that my best, my most
beloved friend has captured the heart of one of the most desirable
bachelors in all the Nine Provinces? False creature, it is not to be
borne! When we parted at the gates of Mistress Quick's, you assured
me through your tears that we should be separated only in body.
Packet after packet should fly from the groves of Orandy; in
imagination (so you promised) your beloved puss-cat should float
beside you like a phantom through all the fragrant walks of that
southern clime. Whisper, whisper, would go her phantom-skirt
through the cool corridors of the white, low houses; and when the
harvest-balls began, would not the phantom puss-cat be twirling,
whirling, beside her beloved Jeli as she took to the floor with this
dashing suitor, and that? Poor puss-cat! How was she to know that
her Jeli should take to the floor (and more?) with none other than the
Prince-Elect of Urgan-Orandy, and that all thought of her best, her
dearest companion should fly from her fickle mind like chaff? And can
the betrayed puss-cat be blamed if she calls to mind some lines of Mr
Coppergate's—

> *The northern suitor must take proper care,*
> *But southerly ladies? Easier fare!*
> *As hot as the sun, their eyes shine on all:*
> *So Lexion lands see many a fall.*
> *How soon the citadel, hard to invade,*
> *Falls in Orandy's cool colonnade!*

I am, my dear, your much aggrieved—

The young woman scratched out a florid squiggle and sat back,
satisfied.

But only for a moment.

A furrow creased her brow. Uncertainly she looked back over what
she had written. Was it quite the thing? Beside her on the writing-table
lay Mr Coppergate's *Poetical Works*, open to the lines she had quoted;
she had spent some time searching, and was proud to have found them.

But no, something was not right.

She crushed the letter and flung it on the fire.

The young woman paced the carpet. Decked out in little-girl flum-
meries of lace, she was locked in her room for Luncheon Slumber. Each
day it was the same: when the mid-meal was over, her aunt would
jingle impatiently for the maid and demand that her charge be taken
upstairs. *Really, I'm not a child!* the young woman would protest, as the
maid helped her out of her morning-gown. *You're a Wait-girl. Still a
Wait-girl*, the maid replied sagely, as if nothing else must needs be
said.

The young woman's name was Miss Catayane Veeldrop. She was a
tall, willowy creature with alabaster skin and abundant black hair, worn
'down' until her Entrance, that fell about her shoulders in a rich cascade.
Her eyes were of a deep green, like a cat's, and her lips, quite without
the aid of paint, were the colour of red roses.

She was not beautiful – rather, she was striking, imposing. There was
something a little harsh in the set of her features, something unyielding
that might give one pause. Her cousin Jeli, with her yellow ringlets and
laughing blue eyes, was what men would call beautiful. But Cata did
not want her cousin's sweet, passive features. One day, she sensed, there
would be things more important than beauty – though what they might
be, she was not yet quite sure.

Cata often had the strangest thoughts.

She returned to the window. A haze of rain still filled the sky. Parting
the thick masking-scrim, she looked out on the wet world.

She gasped with pleasure.

Her window hung above the Square of the Lady, central meeting-
place of the opulent resort-town. In the rain the square had become a sea
of umbrellas, blue and red, green and yellow and purple, stretched wide
beneath the soaring façade of Varby Abbey. Defying the rain and the
ending season, all the quality-folk were out for their mid-strolls. The
colours, sleekly wet, were magnificently bright. Beneath the umbrellas,
Cata glimpsed a trailing shawl with cloth-of-gold 'Wrax trim'; an
avenue-hat of heaped silvery gauze; a soldier's dress-uniform in bright
'Ejard blue'. A little lap-dog in a jewelled collar trailed distractedly
behind a great lady's skirts, and weaving through it all were the
hurrying forms of servants, black and white and drenched in the wet.

For a moment Cata too longed to run in the rain, dashing bedraggled
through the stately crowd.

She saw her aunt.

The fat form was unmistakable. Sheltering in the archway beneath the
Foretelling Clock, Umbecca Veeldrop inclined her head in eager converse
with the Prince of Chayn. The fat woman's little eyes rolled about

merrily and she flung back her hands, exclaiming over the raillery of the handsome gentleman.

A wave of misery swept over Cata. In the afternoons her aunt would venture out alone, meeting all manner of fashionable people. It was so unfair! Cata had challenged her, begged her to be allowed just a modest freedom, but the woman would have none of it.

Freedom, indeed!

'How ever is a girl to be honourably wed, if she goes about meeting *gentlemen*? And child, the danger – the danger!'

There was always the danger. At any time a young lady's virtue might be in peril, but in the last seasons the spa-town had been plagued by a spate of abductions. What had become of young Lady Vantage? No one knew. Miss Mercia Teasle? Who could say? Only a moonlife ago the sudden disappearance of Miss Vyella Rextel had shocked all Varby. Betrothed to Sir Turvy Badgerback, courted by Lord Aldermyle, loved hopelessly – so all knew – by the Marquis of Heva-Harion, the 'Gorgeous Vy' had long been the subject of heated interest. When Vy vanished, no other topic was discussed on the meeting-greens for at least the length of an entire day.

The 'Varby Vanishings,' as they were known, had followed a curious pattern. In each case, the victim was a beautiful young heiress; in each case, a ransom was demanded – and paid; but in each case, too, the victim was never seen again. What was most alarming, perhaps, were the ransom-notes. They were not signed, but written across the bottom of each, where the signature should be, was instead the legend (this and no more):

THE VARBY WAIT

What could it mean? No one knew.

There was a tickering at the glass. A bird, a little bird with a bright red breast, had alighted on the window-ledge. Cata looked down, smiling, into the pinprick eyes. Often she felt drawn to birds – other creatures, too. It was as if they called to something deep within her, some memory perhaps – some buried memory.

Quizzically, the bird blinked back at her through the glass. In Ejland, such a bird was called a 'Bob Scarlet'. Cata thought he was a Koros-season bird, and wondered what he was doing here at Equinox-time. The thought came to her that she must ask him, as if a bird – as if any dumb creature – could talk to her as a human might.

A foolish thought!

But Cata pulled up the window-sash. Scratchily the bird clambered on to her wrist, and his little eyes stared intently into hers. It was the strangest thing. For a moment it seemed as if he could indeed see into her mind – but only for a moment. When she tried to draw him back through the window, the little bird seemed alarmed and fluttered away.

Cata sighed. She flung herself down across her curtained bed. She rolled on to her back, breathing deeply, gazing up at the rich fabric of the canopy; idly her eyes followed the stitches that formed the shape of a flower, a stem.

She thought again about Jeli.

The day before, Cata had fallen into a doze over an old novel; she had been lost in a dream when all at once there was a thunder on the stairs and the door of her chamber had burst open. It might have been Lord W—— in the novel, come to ravish the fair Donnabella.

It was Aunt Umbecca's maid.

'Miss Cata! Miss Cata!' Nirry laboured to catch her breath.

Fire? Murder?

No, no: marriage!

The story was this: Nirry's friend, Lady Somebody's maid, had heard from Miss Somebody's Duenna – who had heard it, it seemed, from Miss Somebody Else's – that Lady Somebody's cousin-by-cousin had contracted the most spectacular match . . . And who was Lady Somebody's cousin-by-cousin?

Nirry drew herself upright, her bright eyes almost bursting from her head.

Miss Jelica Vance, that was who!

Fresh waves of envy surged through Cata. She scrambled off the bed. Once again she took up her pen, scratching rapidly in blue Sosenican ink:

> *False friend!*
> *Can it be that this is, indeed, a world without honour? For so it must be if the pledges of my Jeli – even my Jeli! – are to be rated at naught. What promises you made! What protestations! What has become of that friend who was to loom like a fond phantom over my shoulder, each time my sad visage gazed into the glass? I fear she has faded like a mist on the mirror.*

Last night Cata had barely slept, thinking of Jeli's great adventure. At Mistress Quick's, her friend had been a model pupil. On passing-out day she was commended in speeches, more fulsomely than any girl for many years; leaving the hall, she carried with her not only the Regency Memorial Award, the Cham-Charing Cup and the Ejard Certificate, but a heavy gilt prize-copy of Coppergate's poems, presented by the elderly Coppergate himself.

Really! What a prig!

But not until now had Cata's resentment overflowed. Until now, she could think that Jeli, at least, was not allowed in Varby. They had kept her away, locked in a confinement worse than her own.

So it had seemed.

Cata stared glassily ahead of her for a moment, chewing at the feathery end of her quill.

Then: the inspiration.

> *But I banter.*
>
> *Poor Jeli! You are a naughty girl – but how dull it must be for you in that hot province, if even your pretty little pen-hand is unstirred! My sympathy for you is boundless. How well I imagine the cool, white villa where your great-father resides, the beautiful hills, the groves of lemon and lime – but oh, the society! Who was that fellow who called on you once at Quick's? The 'Prince-Elect' (was it?) of Urgan-Orandy, or some other worthless title? In any case, a frightful, clodhopping boor! You must tell me if you have any more comical encounters with him, my dear – though I hope for your sake you don't! Still, one could almost wish to see the creature released from his misery. Perhaps in time some sallow old maid with a cleft palate and smallpox scars might accept his hand, do you think?*
>
> *Oh, the provinces!*
>
> *My dear, I must fly – I pen this only in the interstices of dressing, dressing, for tonight's assembly. (If I could begin to describe my gown!)*
>
> *Must go – C.*
>
> *(Pity your poor puss-cat – her head is reeling!)*

Cata's mouth set hard. She waved the letter in the air to dry, then creased the creamy paper into two swift folds, running a sharp fingernail down each edge in turn. She melted a red blob of sealing-wax and squashed it flat with her uncle's seal.

SHIAM: Service of His Imperial Agonist Majesty.

'So, she's not a sleepy girl today, then?'

'Aunt!' Cata started. Absorbed in her task, she had not heard the fat woman labouring up the stairs. She turned, smiling airily. 'I've just been writing to Jeli. To congratulate her.'

'Hmph.' Aunt Umbecca looked dubiously about the room, frowning at the open window, the billowing masking-scrim. 'It will profit you little to keep up correspondences with giddy girls who fling themselves away on the first available suitor – a *province-wedding*, indeed! Child, if I thought you should not be better matched, I should fling you out on the streets this instant. Now where's my tea? Really, a woman could starve to death, waiting for that wretched maid! Nirry! Nirry!'

23

Chapter 2

A WOMAN IN GREEN

A woman in green. A man in black.

In a room across the square from Cata's window is a woman resplend-ent in a green gown. For a time she has gazed out into the afternoon, watching the twitchings of Cata's gauze scrim. The woman turns from the window, but not before she reaches for a little creature, a certain scarlet-breasted creature, that has fluttered back to her.

Smiling, she pets the tame bird.

The man in black is an image in her mind.

The woman sits at a dressing-table. Wryly, sadly, she studies her reflection. If her face is barely lined, still it is not the face of a woman in youth. There is something ancient, something immemorial in the set of the brow, the curve of the jaw – a noble face, yes, but more than noble.

More, perhaps, than human.

Through the window falls a slant of light, refracted goldenly through the drizzling rain. From time to time the light flashes, catching a band of emeralds at the woman's pale neck. But her eyes, her extraordinary eyes, glow with a greater greenness.

The looking-glass shimmers and her image disappears.

In its place is the man in black.

'My greetings, old deceiver.' The woman smiles.

Far away in Agondon, the man smiles too. In his eyes, in his face, is the same ancient mystery. 'So you are with them now, in Varby?'

'Indeed, I am far from home – too far.'

'But the scheme is afoot?'

'Shall we say I have secured my first possibility?'

'Possibility? I had thought the scheme was firm.'

'We knew I must shuffle them, did we not? Like a deck of cards? Again and again the girl speaks of her friend – I begin to think the friend may interest me more.' The woman indicated the scarlet bird, that hopped before her on the dressing-table. 'Ring has been investigating, haven't you, Ring?'

Intently the little bird eyed its mistress.

'Investigating?' said the man in black.

'The friend. Whether *she* is the one we seek, I cannot yet say. It may be that there is something . . . *extraordinary* about her.'

'Ho! So you favour, instead, a commonplace girl?'

'Droll. Shall a commonplace girl be Queen of Ejland?'

'None better.' The man in black smiled. He drew back on an ivory-stemmed pipe. Visible behind him was a luxurious chamber. 'But Priestess, this plan troubles me – it is too little, too late.'

'You have no faith in my feminine ways?'

'I say only that your plan is desperate.'

The woman gave the man a sardonic look. Her door was ajar, and padding into her fine boudoir came a magnificent black cat. Luxuriantly the cat buffed his big head against the green satin of her gown. She reached down, petting his ears. There was pleasure in her eyes, but her voice was earnest.

'In these dark days, everything is desperate. There must be a wedding, must there not? I tell you, if there is to be a Queen, I shall control her. She shall be mine!'

'But only a Queen! Priestess, how can you believe in her sway, when the King himself is the merest puppet, jigging on the First Minister's wires?'

'The King has not the power of my sisters behind him.'

'Sisters? Are you not forgetting, Priestess? Slipping into the past?'

'I forget nothing! The power of my sisters resides in me still, for all that they may have been taken from me. Shall Hara, guardian of Viana's faith, be cowed by the accursed Tranimel? By the machinations of your vile Brotherhood?'

'Call it not mine! I am an infiltrator, that is all.'

'But you go tonight? Ah, I see it in your eyes – you go! Do you not fear you may contaminate yourself?'

'Priestess, you forget that I, too, have powers!'

'I do not forget you are a man – or rather, that you have in you the weaknesses of a man.'

The mysterious figure would have replied, and sharply. Instead, he looked down, his eyes growing sad. Ah, he knew his weaknesses well enough! The Priestess leaned back, lighting a tobarillo. Sinuously, blue smoke writhed around her temples.

'Their ceremonies, I imagine, are of the crudest?' she bantered.

'Orgies of shrieking and spurting blood.'

'I knew as much.'

The Priestess smiled again. By now, the bird she had called Ring had fluttered to the floor. By the hearth he was hopping, twittering, pecking at crumbs, when all at once the black cat pounced. With a smile the Priestess glanced down, making no effort to intervene, as sharp claws ripped open the bright red breast.

She turned back to the glass. 'But the boy? Where is the boy?'

'Soon – soon now – he shall be with me.'

'And soon his quest shall begin?'

'There is time yet, a little time. The boy is green—'

The woman's eyes flashed. 'The crystal is green!'

'And he shall find it – and the others, and the others . . . Ah, but I fear there is much he must learn, if he will be man enough for all that lies before him.'

'Man enough!' The Priestess had to laugh. 'And how do you propose to ensure that?'

'Let us say I have found a teacher. Your young charge has a brother, does she not?'

'Ho! I see there is a pleasing symmetry in our affairs.'

'Priestess, yours was a symmetry I always found pleasing.'

'Deceiver, deceiver! Had I given myself to the passions of love, still I know that another would have been first in *your* heart.'

There was a silence. 'Hara, do not speak of things that can give me only pain.'

'How can I not, if I am to speak at all? Evil rushes upon us, beating in the air like the flying serpent that, until now, was its most terrible manifestation. This talk is idle. The time of reckoning is coming to these lands, and we must think only of the campaign before us.'

'You speak truth, Priestess.'

'Call me not Priestess. Like you, I am known now by another name.'

'But of course – "The Remarkable Vlada Flay".'

'An amusing identity, is it not?'

'A notorious one – if there are any, here in Ejland, who remember that woman. But pray, what has become of the *real* Lady Vlada?'

Again the Priestess smiled. The black cat leapt up into her lap, purring loudly, and she stroked his furry head. 'You have heard,' she said, 'of a highwayman who has terrorized my native land? A certain Bob Scarlet?'

'Like the bird? I know he is an intimate of yours.'

'I am intimate with no man,' said the woman coolly. 'All I say is that the highwayman knows what has become of Vlada Flay.'

'Priestess, I fear you have become a cruel woman.'

'Crueller than you? But call me Vlada. Have I not absorbed her essence into mine?

'The projection must be hard to sustain.'

'For one who still bears with her the powers of the Sisters?'

The man might have made some cutting reply, but at that moment there was a commotion at the door. Swiftly, the Priestess – or rather, Lady Vlada – turned away from the looking-glass. Behind her, the magical image swiftly faded; before her, breathing deeply, stood a pinch-faced crone, dressed in the black garb of a Duenna.

Evidently the crone was in some distress.

'Widow Waxwell!' The pretended Lady Vlada smiled pleasantly. 'And pray, where is your virtuous young charge?'

'Oh Lady Vlada—' the Widow struggled to catch her breath '—your wicked niece has . . . has slipped away! She has gone off in a carriage, with . . . with Mr Burgrove!'

It was shocking news, or should have been. But Lady Vlada registered no shock. Instead, she laughed airily, 'Why, Widow, of course. I allowed it – commanded it.'

'Allowed it? But—'

Then the Widow saw the dead bird, and screamed.

'Lady Vlada' only laughed again.

Chapter 3

TOBARILLO

'Heka, I'm slipping!'

'Oh Jilda, take my hand, do!'

Through drizzling rain the Misses Quisto hurried, shrieking, back towards the tea-house. In a moment, no doubt, their Duenna would upbraid them, and the silly little minxes would giggle breathlessly, exchanging secret glances. Bewailing the mud on their dainty shoes and the raindrops that rolled down their taffeta skirts, Duenna Quisto would hardly guess that the girls – all ribbons and ringlets and pink, plump cheeks – had almost ruined rather more than just their clothes.

As they vanished round a curve of the woody-walk, a handsome young fellow with black lacquered moustaches was watching them and smiling wryly, knowingly, to himself. Dressed in the uniform of a captain of dragoons, the fellow had just emerged – in a fashion more leisurely than the little minxes – from the darker recesses of the walk. Now, sheltering beneath a sturdy arch of branches, he shook the raindrops from his three-cornered hat and smoothed the rumpled contours of his costume.

What a pity about the rain, he thought ruefully. The spatter of droplets through the thick treetops had been just the excuse for the Misses Quisto to scurry back to safety. The pretty one, Miss Jilda, had been eager for more than just a tight-lipped kiss, too – he was sure of it. If he could get her away from that drab sister, who knew what bastions she might not yield? Just before she broke from him, the captain had implored her, in a hot whisper, for another assignation.

Here. Canonday morning. First thing. Alone.

Ah, what pleasures he would teach her then!

The captain sighed, adjusting the formidable bulge in his breeches. In the rain, the avenues were almost empty. There was no one about, but he would wait a few moments, just a few moments, before he followed the girls. One could not be too careful. Gossip, after all, was rife in Varby: it was that sort of place.

In Theron-season, when they came to Varby, quality-folk would exclaim how pleasant it was to escape the heat and stench and pall of lassitude that overcame the capital during those hot moonlives. And in the spa-town there were no curfews, no mutterings of war, and superstitious fears, inflamed as the thousandth Cycle of Atonement drew near, were banished. All was forgotten in a round of gaiety; yet if the Varby-revellers only looked upwards, to the hills that rose above their stately streets, they might see reminders enough of the grim affairs of the day.

All through that Theron-season of 999*d*, Holluch-on-the-Hill had been readying itself for the next Zenzan war. To the sound of thud-thudding drumbeats, regiments from Lexion and Orandy and the Western Inner had filed through the valley to the garrison-town. Sounds of drillings and target-shots drifted down from the hills. Off-duty soldiers, descending to the spa-town, were frequently to be seen in its elegant walks. But in Varby, gunshots were only syncopations beneath the rhythms of the Quadrant Dance, and the bright uniforms of the Bluejackets only colours in the gaudy, passing parade.

The young captain reached inside his jacket, drawing forth a silver tobarillo-box – a gift, as it happened, from a certain lady famed through all The Inner for her shining virtue.

Of all the world's illusions, its manifold deceptions, the one the captain found most contemptible was that of female virtue. A woman's honour! Why, only that morning, calling upon the betrothed of one of his brother officers ... He licked his lips, remembering the bobbing head, the jiggling curls. What price a lady? A woman of the streets would have demanded five, even ten crowns to indulge in such depravity. Beneath their fine silk and lace, the flowers of society were no better – worse! – than the pox-ridden tarts who trailed after the King's regiments, offering themselves to the men of the ranks. It was not virtue that ladies cared about, it was reputation. Any bold fellow could have them for free – so long as no one knew ...

The rain was easing. The captain tapped his unlit tobarillo on the gleaming lid of the box. A tinder-strip flared, briefly but intensely, in the dripping dimness of the woody-walk. Smoke clouded the air behind him as he sauntered back towards the gates of the park.

Now where had his idle side-officer gone?

Ul-ul-ul-ul-ul!

A high burst of birdsong sounded across the green. It was a beckoning-bird, a rainbow-feathered Wenaya dove, swooping high over the heads of the Misses Quisto.

'Heka, it's the Swords Play—'

'Sister, no! We must get back—'

'Oh, let's watch, Heka, just for a little! You've always loved the Vagas, I know you have—'

'Sister, really! A dirty little street-troupe—'

29

But the older sister took her place cheerfully enough amongst the fine ladies and gentlemen who braved the rain in the park that day. With the authority of their parasols and rustling taffeta, the sisters pushed through the idle footmen and parlourmaids and nurses with tethered infants who loitered, craning their necks, behind the quality-folk. Giggling, they squeezed between a lady's hooped skirt and the wickerwork bath-chair of a gouty old gentleman. A young Bluejacket, with a polite tilt of his hat, moved back to permit them a better view.

Jilda eyed him. Tall, but not handsome: and only a lieutenant. With a little shiver of excitement and fear, she thought back to the brief but intense pleasure she had enjoyed with the captain. Now there was a man! She must keep their assignation, she must! Canonday? Why, that was tomorrow! The last Canonday before the Season was over – her last chance. Jilda closed her eyes and almost moaned, there in the crowd, imagining the tender, sweet caresses of her lover . . .

Ul-ul-ul-ul-ul!

The beckoning-bird alighted on its perch above the Vaga-round, cawing out a final sharp summons before settling its beak into its bright chest and falling instantly, contentedly asleep. The little crowd looked expectantly to the platform. The Vaga-round, one of many in the spa-town, stood at a confluence of the smart walks that criss-crossed the wide expanse of Eldric's Park. A peaked roof, painted like the plumage of the bird, surmounted a small rotunda, like a miniature bandstand, raised on a stone plinth above the level of the paving. Raindrops dripped steadily from the curving eaves and a thick blue curtain, spangled with stars, billowed between spindly moss-furred columns.

From behind the curtains came a hollow, heavy resonance: the tolling of a bell. The gouty old gentleman in the bath-chair sighed, as if the reverberations were strangely soothing. Jilda giggled; Heka said she was bored. Only the young Bluejacket remained silent, watching thoughtfully as a long-fingered brown hand emerged from between the curtains, drawing them slowly back. Inside, light streamed from an ornate lamp, suffusing the dank air with a haze of gold. Incense wove upwards in fragrant smoky trails.

In Vaga-shows, the curtains often remained partly drawn, making it difficult to see what passed within. A fine lady arched back her heavy, bewigged head; Jilda craned her neck, peering into the shadows. The Vagas stepped forward. First, as always, came the Purple Player, dressed in velvet of the deepest sunset shade.

But something was wrong. The Player should have been elegant, even ethereal; instead, he was a big, bull-necked fellow, with a hulking gait and a foolish grin. A bushy black beard covered his cheeks and jaw.

30

There was a ripple of guffaws as he took his place, squatting gracelessly at the back of the stage.

Equally disappointing were the rest of the troupe. The Gold-and-Green, the singer of wisdom, was a plump little girl; Destiny Blue and his opposite, the Scarlet Endeavour, were two willowy boys of the awkward age, quite lacking in the required dignity. As for the Lingering Pierrot, the Black Guard, the Jumping Jongleur and all the other roles of the Swords Play, there were none to fill them. There were not even Imperials, not even Beholders, to swarm forth and dance through the crowd with linked hands.

'Hmph!' The gouty old gentleman stirred uncomfortably. Heka rolled her eyes; her sister sniggered. They had seen the best troupes the empire had to boast, at the Volleys, at the Wrax Opera, at the Ollon Pleasure Gardens. Why, only last season the famous Silver Masks, five hundred strong, with fifty monkeys, a horn-horse, a leaping-lion and a thousand trained birds, had been the highlight of Lady Cham-Charing's Festival Levee. Street-Vagas, it was true, could hardly offer as much; but even a little avenue-band should be worthy of its licence! This shabby lot, thought Jilda indignantly, were hardly fit to play before quality-folk.

The quality-folk, it seemed, agreed. Many drifted away. There were restless murmurs, even among the servants. But still the young Blue-jacket watched the stage intently.

A hollow, sudden sadness overspread his face as the Swords Play began.

Vagas, as all knew, were an idle, dissolute race, wandering heathens with a propensity for all manner of vice. Worshippers of the dark god Koros, in many parts of the empire they were outlawed entirely. Only in the southern counties of The Inner were they tolerated as conjurors, dancers, actors; but even here there were some who thought they should be driven into exile, or kept in special camps. The young lieutenant was not one of them. He watched the Vaga-troupes whenever he could, and liked them. He would like even this one. In their very shabbiness they reminded him of his childhood and the Vagas who had come to his village green.

How long ago it seemed!

Tears pricked at the young lieutenant's eyes as the big ungainly Vaga-man in purple, oblivious of the retreating crowd, stared upwards, stretching his hands above his head. Swaying over him, just within reach, were hanging ropes, like jungle vines, braided into spirals of many bright colours. The hands reached into the vines and gripped. The lieutenant brushed his eyes. The tolling of a mournful bell came again, then another, concealed in the roof of the Vaga-round.

The clangings came six times, each from a different bell: one for each of the five gods and one for the Ur-God, Orok. Then, at first slowly, the single sonorous clangings gave way to a stately carillon, *clang-clang, clang-clang, jangle-jingle-jangle,* two bells together, bells overlapping, bells resolving themselves into a melody. Soon what was single had become multiple, what was simple had become complex, but all was controlled with an unexpected grace by the hulking fool, rising slowly from his squatting position until the vivid vines of the bell-ropes surrounded him like leaping, luminescent prison-bars.

The blue boy advanced, then the boy in scarlet, each holding aloft a weighty golden sword. The young lieutenant followed them with his eyes. In truth, he knew the swords had in them no weight at all, nor were they made of gold. Colliding, they would give forth only the dull clack of wood; yet, gilded with radiant Vaga-paint, they seemed in the unearthly light of the booth to be possessed of a curious magic. Stealthily, on cat-feet, the boys circled each other, but if they were enemies they were enemies without passion, readying themselves for battle without fury or fire.

The golden lamplight mingled with the glimmering light of evening, twisting on the air like the perfuming incense; then the Gold-and-Green, the girl, began to sing. Her voice had in it an extraordinary purity, like the high vibrating hum round a rim of crystal.

Each boy made first one, then another, slow swooping pass. In moments, the young lieutenant knew, the magic would begin. Wooden swords would clash and reverberations, as of cold metal, would seem to fill the air. Perhaps then the curtains would billow back; phantom shapes would flurry from the haze and the rainbow patterns on the roof would shift and spin, streaming out like brilliant ribbons. Then perhaps the duellists, writhing with the ribbons, would prance among the crowd, prodding into being with their blunt sword-tips the rich silk handkerchiefs, the glittering coins, the fluttering coloured birds that would bring forth exclamations from all who were gathered there, quality-folk and vulgar alike.

But no.

Of course not.

These things would not happen, not today. The young lieutenant had slipped into reverie. While he gazed, enraptured, at the glittering swords, the crowd around him had vanished almost entirely. More and more of the fine ladies and gentlemen, even the maids and footmen, had gone. There were catcalls, hisses, from those that remained. The gouty old gentleman, waving a stick, signalled his servant to wheel him away.

The young lieutenant bit his lower lip. The sadness returned, pressing heavily at his heart. He looked back at the Swords Play. No, there was no magic, no prospect of magic; only two clodhopping boys in silly costumes, playing at fighting while a fat little girl burbled out a cater-wauling mantra.

Then all at once the scarlet boy was jumping about the stage. Abandoning the stylized passes, he played incongruously at the part of a savage warrior, flicking his wooden sword back and forth, back and forth in the blue boy's face. Whether he was impatient at the blue boy or at the apathy of the audience was hard to say; in any case, it was curious behaviour for a Vaga.

The blue boy was angry. Everyone knew that blue, not red, was supposed to triumph. First he tried to fight back, then he leapt out of range; when the scarlet boy would not leave off, his partner flung down his sword in fury.

There were jeers and a scattering of ironic applause.

Miss Jilda Quisto had had enough. 'Oh Heka, let's go—'

'No, Jilda, just a—'

'Heka, really! You don't mean you *enjoy* this vulgar—'

A third voice intruded, 'Ladies, just leaving?'

The young lieutenant turned. He saw the deep bow, the solemn countenance, the respectful doffing of the three-cornered hat. To think that his friend should have learned such arts!

Miss Jilda Quisto giggled, swiftly releasing her sister's sleeve. All at once her cheeks were flaming. Awkwardly she endeavoured to compose herself, smiling and permitting the handsome young man to touch his lips to her glove, just for an instant, before she swept away, twirling her parasol, trailing her sister reluctantly behind.

But the brief moment was enough. The captain's eyes flamed. He knew it now: he was sure of Miss Jilda! Tomorrow morning, in the shadows of the woody-walk, he would be waiting – waiting eagerly.

Oh pray, pray that it did not rain!

'Hard to believe such girls are yet Unentered. Wouldn't you say so, friend?'

The young lieutenant looked admiringly at his companion. The captain's lacquered moustaches glimmered darkly in the golden, waning light. Uninterested in the Vaga-troupe, the handsome fellow was sucking back on his burning tobarillo, gazing after the departing girls with a frank, sensual relish. On the hand that held the tobarillo there glinted an amethyst ring.

'Ardent enough,' he mused. 'The young one especially. Lexion-blood: you can see it in the eyes. How does that rhyme go?

> *The northern seducer must take proper care,*
> *But Lexion girls? It's easier there . . .*

Something like that. Perhaps, friend, when I succeed with Miss Jilda, I might set you up with the sister?'

A prim protest broke from the young lieutenant's lips. The captain laughed and took his side-officer by the arm, drawing him, unresisting, away from the Vaga-round. When he spoke again his voice was soft, wheedling; perhaps ironic, but who could say? The captain was all pleasantry, and even as he murmured to his lanky side-officer he was careful to catch certain looks, certain smiles, from passing promenaders on the arbour-walk. Ladies tossed their heads. They fluttered their fans.

'You judge me harshly, friend,' the captain was saying. 'There is an undiscovered country beneath Miss Jilda Quisto's skirts. Soon your dear friend shall be its first explorer. But so long as the fair Jilda is mine, should I begrudge a plainer conquest to my faithful, my loyal—?'

'Oh no, that wasn't what I—' Like Miss Jilda, moments earlier, the poor lieutenant had flushed scarlet.

'Friend, I know!' The lieutenant was not sure what his companion knew. 'But now it is yourself you estimate harshly! You are equipped as I am – well, not *quite*. But many a pretty rogue would moan beneath you willingly enough. Think of the chances you let slip by!'

The lieutenant had thought of them often enough. But somehow, thinking did not do much good. Once, emboldened by ale, he had told his friend that he respected ladies, respected them too much, and vented himself – that was his expression – only with common women. His friend had merely laughed, and called him a fool; but the claim, in any case, was not quite true.

In fact, not true at all; and the captain, of course, could tell.

'Dusk is falling,' he said now. 'Time for a little evening nectar, would you not say?'

The lieutenant brightened, but as the young men strolled towards the gates of Eldric's Park, the captain returned to the old theme, his voice sweet as honey.

'Friend, there is no shortage of receptacles for our lust. Why, for a few dirty coins the lowest man in the ranks may repair from latrine-duty to the arms of a willing wench. There are sluts enough for all! Oh friend, you are failing in your duty as a man!'

'I know, Polty, I know!' the lieutenant wailed miserably.

But at this the captain gripped his side-officer's arm and, spinning back to face him, brought a finger to his lips. 'Bean, really! How many times must I tell you? Remember I am Foxbane, Captain Foys Foxbane. And you are Lieutenant Bage Burry.'

Poor Bean only sank deeper into misery.

Chapter 4

LASHER

'Hup!'

Stephel gave the horses a flick of his whip and the carriage began its stately progress round the Circuit. Each afternoon in the Varby Season, as the blue-white light reddened and waned, quality-folk would drive through the smart streets past the Royal Assembly and Eldric's Park, then out through the city gates and along the tree-lined banks of the Riel. Filling the gap between day and evening, the Circuit-ride was for some a particular pleasure, a time when, with the merest glimpse of eyes or flicker of a fan, the most subtle and intimate understandings could pass across the air between one carriage and another.

For Umbecca, the ride was Cata's daily 'airing', and much to be preferred to the alarming promiscuity of a walk in the avenues or the meeting-greens. An Unentered girl could safely drive with her aunt – if, as her aunt insisted, the windows of the carriage were covered in thick gauze, like the masking-scrim in Cata's room. It did not occur to Umbecca, though perhaps it should have done, that a 'gauze carriage' would only inflame the curiosity of some – especially when the carriage in question was one of particular finery, and emblazoned with the arms of an imperial governor.

Idly Cata stared through the gauze. There were not many on the Circuit that day. The rain had thinned to a mist, but all over Varby the sense of the Equinox was gathering and growing. Leaves were falling from high pollarded trees and darkness was drawing in earlier now; already the kindling-boys were lighting the lamps all along the curve of Eldric's Parade.

Umbecca was saying, 'A very forward sort of girl, I've always thought. Rash.'

'Hm? Oh, Jeli,' said Cata distantly, as if it were not to be expected that she might still be thinking about her cousin. But she roused herself and added, 'One always thought dear Jeli would contract a hasty, ill-considered match. Mistress Quick often said she was an impulsive girl. Of course, she always flirted outrageously with any gentlemen callers.'

'Gentlemen callers?' Umbecca pursed her lips. 'There weren't *gentlemen callers* at Quick's, surely?'

35

Cata laughed, 'Oh, aunt, you are a silly! Some of the girls had ardent lovers – they could hardly be kept from storming the gates!'

'Child, really!' Umbecca was shocked. She knew the story was a lie, of course; what shocked her was that her young charge should tell such a lie. It hardly bespoke the virtue of a Quick-girl; and virtue, as all knew, was the watchword of Quick's.

The academy was a place where quality-girls were groomed in the necessary accomplishments of their sex – deportment, embroidery, polite conversation; but most of all, in that disposition of purity which was, so all agreed, a girl's most vital asset. It was the boast of Mistress Quick, and her little joke, that a Quick-girl was guaranteed a quick match – as Miss Jelica Vance, it seemed, had proven. For the length of almost two gens – though it might have been for eternity – all the best quality-ladies of Ejland had been Quick-girls; and when each year a new crop made their Entrances, invariably it would be said of the finest of them that they, too, had passed through the portals of Quick.

One could *tell* at once.

The year when Cata had lodged at Quick's had been a year of secret despair for her aunt. Umbecca may never have been a Quick-girl, but she knew the academy well enough. In her girlhood she had often taken walks by the big neat house across the Ollon marshes, staring up wistfully at the tall whitewashed walls. How it inflamed her to think of Cata, revelling in the privileges her aunt had been denied!

But it was for the best. All for the best.

When Chaplain Feval first proposed the scheme, Umbecca had been appalled. Then, slowly, she came to see his point. What use could there be, keeping the child in Irion? The governor seemed to think his son would marry her, but after all, the poor old gentleman was senile. No, suggested the chaplain, there was a better use for little Miss Catayane. They had hoped, had they not, that Umbecca's poor husband would be made a lord? Alas, that their hopes were all but dashed! Yet now, might not a second path be open to them, in their quest to escape provincial ignominy? Miss Cata was a striking child, was she not – exotic? Why, many a fine gentleman – many a lord – would pay dearly for so fine a maiden! If the girl could be married, and married well, think what advantages this might bring!

Of course, all this had been but hinted, implied, by no means stated boldly. By now, perhaps, Umbecca even believed, sincerely believed, that the scheme was an altruistic one, a noble act of philanthropy, all for dear little Cata's own good.

But still Umbecca burned with darker passions. First would come the tides of greed, the vaulting ambition.

Then the doubt – the resentment.

36

Silas Wolveron's daughter – at Quick's?

An ominous rumbling came from the sky.

'Oh dear me, listen to that!' said the fat woman briskly, glad of the distraction. 'No Vosper's Loop for us today, my dear!'

'Aunt, that's not fair! You haven't taken me on the Loop for days!'

'Come, child! Is the weather my fault? There's a storm coming, I'll be bound!' Umbecca rapped at the ceiling of the carriage. 'Stephel! Turn back at the gates, do you hear?'

Cata pouted. Vosper's Loop was the part of the Circuit that lay outside the city walls, the band of cinder-road that curved off the highway and down by the river. On a fine day, it was a splendid thing to gaze on the reedy water and the verdant meadows beyond, draped in languorous willows. In high Theron-season there were wreathing flowers, and the fragrant air would insist itself even into their closed carriage, subduing the heady redolence of polished wood and leather.

It was intoxicating; but how glorious would be the river under a rain-burdened sky! Cata imagined a lashing storm, suddenly overwhelming them. She would fling herself from the carriage and dance in the rain.

Oh, how she would dance!

Sometimes Cata was filled with the strangest desires, desires she knew would shock her aunt – and all the girls from Quick's, too! And Mistress Quick. And all the ladies in society. And the gentlemen – especially any gentleman who might want to marry her . . .

What could be wrong with her?

Oh, but she longed for *some* excitement!

'Aunt?' she began, and hummed a little tune – a Varby waltz.

Umbecca sighed. She knew what was coming. The Equinox Ball! But the fat woman would never let the girl have her way. Not for the world, Umbecca thought, would she allow in herself the laxness which some now thought permissible. Her young charge could watch the Vaga-play and the fireworks, but must leave, as an Unentered girl should leave, strictly on the stroke of the Fourteenth.

No Equinox-gown, no Quadrant Dance, no Lexion Revels, no Holluch reel.

And not a single Varby waltz!

Really, why had they come into the great world – for pleasure? Gentlemen might dally with giddy girls but what would become of giddy girls, when their bloom was rubbed away? Married to a trades-man's son, if that! Umbecca shuddered at the very thought. They must follow the rules, and follow them to the letter. Only a girl of the strictest virtue could secure an earl, a marquis, a duke – a prince!

'Pelli's staying,' Cata attempted.

'What's that, my dear?'

'Pelli's staying – at the Ball.'

It was Cata's best argument. That season Miss Pelli Pelligrew, though she did not know it, had become for Cata almost a prop and stay. *Such a nice girl*, Umbecca would murmur, as she thrust her young charge into Pelli's company; though Cata did not agree, she had come to be glad of this unwanted companion. Pelli, after all, was a Wait-girl like herself, and in the charge of a guardian worse than her own – far worse. Pelli, too, was quite lacking in charm, drab and dull and silly: her inferior, thought Cata, in every way.

At the academy, Pelli had been one of a set of girls that Jeli had amusingly dubbed *the dowries*. With her dun-coloured hair and oily skin, only her substantial dowry seemed to ensure a future for drab little Pelli – so said Jeli, with a superior laugh, and Cata, delighted, had agreed. Soon they flooded the academy with jokes about Pelli's dowry, its beauty, its virtue, its feminine grace. *How long*, the girls giggled behind their hands, *shall Pelli's dowry remain intact?* It was a marvellous game, made all the more marvellous on that night in Sorority when the girls surrounded Pelli in a tight circle, chanting *Dowry! Dowry!* and reducing her to tears.

'Miss Pelligrew?' Umbecca was saying. 'The Equinox Ball? Really, child, you must be mistaken. Miss Pelligrew's Duenna feels as I do. She would never permit—'

The exchange did not go on. All at once came a sound like thunder, but not the thunder of the expected storm. It was a rumble of hooves and rolling wheels. Quality-folk would not drive at such a pace!

Umbecca's eyes darkened; Cata's flashed fire.

A 'Lasher'!

She knew the sound well. On dreamy afternoons at the academy Cata had often leaned from the window with Jeli, gazing at the pale road that lay across the marshes. They were world-weary girls, or so they told themselves, yet the advent of a fine equipage would soon belie the claim. A coach-of-state, bearing the royal arms, would fill their heads with visions of palaces and princes; the barouche or landau of some noble lord would summon chimerical balls and banquets and fine marriage settlements. Even a humble post-chaise would set the girls dreaming of the world beyond their walls – but most exciting of all was a 'Lasher', a light open carriage modelled, it was said, after the racing-chariots of Unang Lia. Only the sharpest young blades would drive them.

Cata swept the window-gauze aside.

'Child!'

It was shocking behaviour, positively ill-bred; but when her young charge twisted back towards her, Umbecca saw that Cata had been shocked, deeply shocked, in her turn. The girl's mouth hung open and her face was white.

'Child! What is it?'

'Aunt, it's Pelli!'

'Miss Pelli Pelligrew?' What could the girl mean?

'Whoa!' cried a jaunty masculine voice. There was a snort of horses as the 'Lasher' drew beside them. Umbecca was aghast. The driver was Mr Burgrove, a most immoral young man – and sitting openly on the box beside him, flagrant and laughing, was Miss Pelli Pelligrew!

'Dear Miss Veeldrop, my greetings!' Mr Burgrove raised his hat, scattering raindrops – of course, inadvertently – over Umbecca's bonnet.

The fat woman shrieked. Of all the gentlemen in Varby that season, the one she feared most was Mr 'Jac' Burgrove. Indeed, he was barely a gentleman – everything about him showed his want of breeding, from the cloth-of-gold cravat that burgeoned at his neck to the over-emphatic buckles on his gleaming shoes. At their lodgings, the maids were instructed to tell Mr Burgrove, politely but firmly, that Miss Veeldrop was not home. Let the insolent fellow turn his attentions elsewhere, Umbecca had thought – but had not thought that he would turn them to little Miss Pelligrew.

She had foisted the girl on Cata because she was sure the girl was safe – a good influence!

Umbecca's brows darkened with rage.

Jac Burgrove's horses stamped and steamed.

'Catty, it's the most awful fun!' Miss Pelligrew was calling – shouting in the street! 'Jac's taking me round the Circuit. We're going fast as fast can be! We're trying to make it back before it rains again!'

Pelli giggled and twirled a parasol.

Cata was almost fainting, white with anger and envy.

'Catayane, close the window!' Umbecca boomed; then, twisting confusedly from one girl to the other: 'Miss Pelligrew, what do you think you're doing? Where's your Duenna?'

'Join us, Miss Veeldrop?' cried Jac Burgrove, gesturing expansively to the box beside him.

'Catayane, sit down!' Frantically Umbecca rapped for the coachman. 'Stephel! Drive on!'

The carriage lurched and Cata fell back into her seat. There were hoots of laughter from the young people in the 'Lasher'. Jac Burgrove cracked his whip and they thundered away, outpacing in moments the trundling formal coach.

Cata's cheeks were burning. Hot tears brimmed in her eyes.

'Poor Catty,' a braying cry drifted back on the air, 'she's such a little goody-goody!'

Chapter 5

FIVE LETTERS

Dearest, dear madam—

Your last lies before me on the escritoire as I write. Since your last, but last, has anything more precious ever lain there? Perhaps I could recall a day when your hand – your dear hand itself! – lingered but for a tender moment, as you paused beside me in the days (but how far-off they seem!) when distance, cruel distance, made no bar between us! But would I risk the merest hint of disrespect to a lady who floats like a diaphanous wraith above all that is merely of this fleshly realm? Oh, let not such coarseness even flutter for a moment through a breast in which each of the Five Virtues is alike spelled B-E-C-C-A!

Your epistle has taken me on a passionate journey. Could the Great Wheel itself, that arcs through the air of the Ollon Pleasure-Gardens (ah, that we could be together in the capital!) flood my being with sensations at once so painful, yet exquisite? In your imagined company have I not shared first laughter, rage, then (oh most delightful!) tears, delicious tears, that blot your page until (but alas!) your sweet ink unfixes itself and runs? With what wit, what style do you describe the Varby Round! Could the pen of Coppergate himself, that inky rapier, have etched more finely the drolleries of the Pump Room, or the Royal Assembly? Then (now, sound the stentorian chords!) with what justice do you expose the evils, the depravities that eat like greedy cancers at society's very heart! How brightly burn your zealous fires! (Has Duenna-dom, and its attendant evils, been castigated more roundly, more righteously?) Dear lady, were you of the stronger sex, your declamations might ring across these lands like a clarion-bell, calling this kingdom back to those paths where all should walk meekly, with downcast eyes, in the footsteps of the blessed Lord Agonis! Why, you should be the soul's teacher of all Ejland, and who but a blockhead would fritter away his time with Dr Tonson's Rover, with Mr Eddington's Speculator – nay (but do not tell!), who would attend to the Archmaximate himself – could he take his moral ration from a masculine B-E-C-C-A?

But thanked, oh greatly thanked be the Lord Agonis, that the sweet secret teacher of my soul is indeed of the tender sex, for who but that most awe-inspiring of creatures in creation – I speak, of course, of a VIRTUOUS WOMAN – could flood my heart with those compassionate tears that flowed when I read of your concern for your young charge, your more than daughter? But dear lady, fear not, I beg you, for must not all be blessed that lies within the aureole of your formidable radiance? The girl's origins are unfortunate, it is true, but has she not now been coaxed, curbed, trained like a writhing vine round the stiff stem of righteousness? You tremble for the sanctity of that virgin-knot, which the wicked boy Jemany would have violated so barbarously, but think – only think! – that your more than daughter reposes now in the protection of that bosom which spells out all virtues – charity, chastity, godliness, generosity and love – in the five letters B-E-C-C-A!

    But hold, your dear husband calls me to his side again, and I must away.

    I shall resume forthwith.

        With all respect,
            In the love of the Lord Agonis,
              I am, dear lady,
                  Your humble spiritual servant,
                      E. Feval

Postscript.
Can it be true that a new round of 'Varby Vanishings' has terrorized that fine town, where once I passed such carefree days? Say it is not true! But (alas!) in this far province, the Gazette *comes too late. I pray all is well when you receive this, and that these dark rumours are the merest tittle-tattle.*

Dearest spiritual companion,

    Your fine words have touched my heart. What comfort, what joy to know that even in these depraved and degenerate times there is one, at least one in this world, to whom a simple woman may open, as it were, the innermost recesses of her being. If only we could be together again, enjoying once more the daily intercourse which for so long gave us such fervent, such sweet satisfaction!

    My dearest, Catayane still troubles me. That she is a girl of uncommon parts is clear, but other young ladies lodge at Quick's for a full cycle before they reach the time of Entrance. Can the elapsing of a mere five seasons eradicate all traces of her early life? You say the girl has been curbed, moulded, but Eay, more and more I glimpse her headstrong nature; often now, I see traces of the girl she once was. Her eyes flash defiance. The maid reports she has troubled dreams. Could she be slipping back? Pray, pray that she may not be lost to us, before we settle her in some noble house!

    True, she is no worse than many of her contemporaries. In my green years my privations were greater than any these 'Wait-girls' are called upon to endure. My beauty was left to wither into the sere, unseen, unloved! But did not faith teach me to endure my fate bravely, stolidly, grateful only for the small blessings that had fallen to my lot? What virtue can we expect of girls who cannot even endure, with common patience, the trivial discomforts of the Varby Wait?

But I am weary, and can write no more. Ask me not about these 'Varby Vanishings'! I am fearful for my Catayane, it is true, but never – like some slattern of a Duenna – shall I permit my vigilance to slip for a moment. There are some things, at least, that I do not fear.

O Eay, that I could throb once more to the rhythm of your litany – thrill, as I did, to the firmness of your rectitude! Write to me, my dearest, of the affairs of the province, that I might imagine us in my chamber in Irion. For though I long for the heady air of Agondon – so long unbreathed by me – I know it shall be a bitter air without you beside me.

Curse these duties, that keep us apart!

Dearest, I am for ever

Your

U.

Postscript.

I have received the enclosed, from our dear Poltiss – a poor correspondent, as he admits, but such a simple, good boy! I fear for him in the wilds of (can it be?) Zenzau, but trust he will distinguish himself in the Imperial service; trust, too, that he will be rewarded more fulsomely, more generously, than some have been!

But I must not fret myself on that distressing subject.

(Under same cover)

Honoured MOTHER-of-my-heart,

Excuse, I pray, the elapsing of long moonlives since last my pen has stirred. Yet why should I beg excuse, since no neglect of one so dear may ever be expunged from the Book of Vices? There it must remain etched beneath my name, and I can but pray that my Virtues shall grow longer! But dear MOTHER, here in these far-flung wilds, what can your poor HEART-SON imagine but that all his life before was a fond dream, no more! Yet (as you, and my HONOURED FATHER have taught me) must I not endure this pain, that our glorious EMPIRE may bring – to places, even places the most benighted – the all-merciful love of the blessed LORD AGONIS?

You understand I cannot say where I am (only – this you know – that I am far, far away!). Let me but insinuate that one hears rumours (yet what are rumours?) of a fresh Zenzan campaign. Could it be true, that the rebels are gathering – a 'pitchfork army', so it is told – even now, on the steppes of Derkold? O, barbarous! But tremble not for me, mother, as I struggle in my turn to tremble not for the trials of

my DEAR CATAYANE. (How I fear for her in the world of fashion!
Can it be true, these tales that reach my ears – even here, *dear*
MOTHER – of 'Varby Vanishings'? Pray, pray that my HEART-
SISTER shall be safe, from all who would bruise so tender a plant!)

How I wish we need never have wandered! Might not our dear
FAMILY be together again, one fond day, in the fastness of
Irion? Your poor SON can only wish it might be so, and that soon,
soon – but duty enchains him! – he might clasp again to his fast-
beating bosom his dear MOTHER, his SISTER, and (but how I
tremble for the poor gentleman) most HONOURED FATHER, to
whose faded eyes you – you, *dear MOTHER – have brought such joy!*
I remain
     Your loving—
       POLTISS
(O kiss, kiss for me, our DEAR CATAYANE!)

Cruel madam!
– For what can these epistles do, but cause me pain? Ah, my
dear, but it is a sweet pain, as all must be sweet that flows from so fine
a lady. A LADY, I say, in the true and full sense, for in spirit is not a
certain B-E-C-C-A a lady as much as the grandest, the proudest
Baroness, Countess, Duchess in the land? (Finer, to say no more, than
that pompous dowager, Constansia Cham-Charing?) And do I not
vow that one day – one day *– what is acknowledged in the hearts of*
those who love you shall be acknowledged by all, in outward show?
Say not that you have been left to wither—

    'O break, my heart, break, that this could be true!'

Dear lady, the way before us may be hard, but the time of your
ascendancy is approaching fast, I know it!
Yet I am touched by your womanish fears. The girl, it must be
admitted, was always a risk, but can we say it is a risk that may not
yet prove worthwhile? Calm your fears, my dear, and cast the girl on
to the sea of society! What becomes of her may yet be of great – oh,
immeasurable! – advantage.
But hold, I am called to the Glass Room, and must break off.

        (Resuming)

You ask me to write of country matters, but how – to you, dear lady –
am I to expatiate on sheep-rustling in the Dale of Rodek, a raid at the
Lazy Tiger, a Vaga-hanging on the village green? To a lady pent long
within the walls of fashion I could, perhaps, embroider these themes

with a pastoral charm; but to one of such unaffected and exquisite sensibility, what could I convey but disgust and lassitude?

And yet, there is a matter it behoves me, perhaps, to bring to your attention. Dear lady, it is your husband. Alas, his decline has not been halted. Seldom does he stir from the big bed that now fills the clearing (as I may say) in that room from which I have but lately returned. The army surgeons are useless, knowing no cures but leeches, purgatives and the saw. As I write, the old man has blown up like a bladder, dropsical and pus-filled and ready to burst. I pray that a little local easing may make him tolerable again for a time – for after all (dear madam, heed my words) if his elevation is yet to come, it can only come while still he lives! (Did I say that I have written again to the Under-Secretary? O pray that our hopes may not be dashed again!)

But dear lady, how I must pain you. How desolating for you, to be from his side! That one with no thought but for her womanly duties should be thus divided, riven between the callings of wife and mother, is a tragedy worthy only of the pen of Coppergate!

Dear one, now and always,

   Your

   Eay

(My poor, poor commander! My poor, poor lady!)

Chapter 6

THE VAGA-DOOR

Clack-clack! Clack-clack! went the wooden sword, dragged along the railings of Eldric's Park. It was one of those from the Swords Play, and it trailed from the hand of the boy in scarlet. Nonchalant, humming a little tune, he sauntered along the wide curve of pavement.

The Blue Endeavour, some lengths ahead, turned back and called, 'I think we should hurry.' There was anxiety in his voice. The little party had no night-stamp and had to be out of the gates by dark. It was dusk already and the lamps were lit.

The scarlet boy skipped ahead, wielding his sword. 'To the breach, to the breach!' Gold paint flashed in the aqueous sunset. 'Draw, Sir Rajal!'

His companion did not, and only hissed, 'Nova, stop it!'

Quality-folk, leaving the park, turned to look at them. Others could see them from the windows across the street. What did it say, Directive No. 3? *Children of Koros must negotiate public thoroughfares silently and with eyes cast down, endeavouring at all times to abate the offence caused by their presence.* It was printed on their permit, clear as could be. Oh, why did Nova have to be such a fool? It was bad enough that he had spoilt the play. Didn't he know it had to be the same every time?

One day he would get them all in trouble.

There were four of them, making their way back to the Vaga-camp – five, if you counted the beckoning-bird, as Myla liked to do. Myla was Rajal's baby sister, the little girl who played the Gold-and-Green. Her legs, like the rest of her, were short and fat, but she was eager to keep pace, and strode doughtily just behind the boys. Perched on her shoulder was the bird, whose name was Eo.

It was the Purple Player who was the true straggler of the party. A curious sight, the hulking fellow was as much a cause of remark, one might have thought, as the exuberant Nova. When he forgot himself, the big man would linger and gaze lengthily at the grass between the cobblestones or the green spikes of the railings or a thick elm-branch that jutted overhead. With his face vacant and his hands hanging, he would watch entranced as a sere leaf, perhaps, detached itself from a twig and fluttered slowly down.

'Zady, come on,' Myla called from time to time, skipping back and tugging at his hand.

'Poor Raj!' Nova was saying. 'All you ever say is *Nova, don't*. Just one time, wouldn't you like to say, *Nova, do?*'

'I can't imagine it.' Rajal strode forward purposefully. 'Now come on everyone. It's going to rain soon.'

Nova twirled on the balls of his feet, flung his sword up in the air – and dropped it.

'Nova!'

'Garnish?' said the Keeper at the Vaga-door.

Wizened fingers twiddled impatiently as Rajal, half turned away, fumbled with the drawstring of a little leather pouch. He was annoyed. Usually he got the garnish ready before now, but tonight Nova had distracted him, damn him.

Two sentries stood by – or rather, slouched. They should have been disposed on either side of the door, their faces expressionless, their muskets slung back stiffly. As it was, they were sniggering and smoking tobarilloes. One of them had neglected to shave; his chin was stubbled like a Harion cornfield. The other had stained his jacket with a brown slosh of beer.

They were only on Vaga-duty, after all.

'Hurry up, scum,' said Harion Cornfield, prodding Rajal with the point of his bayonet.

Rajal flushed hotly. Myla was humming a silly little tune and he wanted to tell her to shut up. His fingers slipped and a bright rush of coins clattered to the cobbled ground at his feet. At once Nova and Myla were beside him, scrambling with him in a muddy puddle.

The sentries guffawed. *Scoop, scoop*, went the brown hands. *Pick, pick*. The sleepy bird on the girl's shoulder opened its eyes and gave a little squawk.

Burning with shame, Rajal shoved a coin towards the Keeper.

'Hmph,' said the Keeper.

A second coin.

A third.

At last the old man shifted wearily and opened a drawer beneath the counter of his booth, retrieving the permit the little party had surrendered that morning in order to gain entrance into the city. He glanced at it, clicked off the Vaga-count on an abacus – one, two, three, four – sniffed, and let the permit fall.

The sentries guffawed again as Rajal dived for the crumpled card, plucking it swiftly from the slimy puddle.

'Good takings, Vaga-scum?' said Beerjacket with a sneer, as the little party were about to slip through the door.

Rajal cast down his eyes. *The pig's goading me, that's all.* Within the Varby walls it was forbidden for Vagas to speak to Ejlanders. To reply, Rajal knew, would mean a pulling of his hair, a cuff across the ear, a kick up the arse.

Something like that.

'I said, good takings? We saw your takings, boy. Garnish, garnish.'

Rajal suppressed a mute protest. Hadn't he given enough? Besides, their takings were nothing: loose change, flaky little bronze and copper zens and jits and fives. Barely a crown in the lot, let alone an epicrown. What did the pig think they were, the Silver Masks? They were strolling players: they were robbed on the roads, their camps were raided; the law did not protect them, but they were taxed without mercy; wherever they went, pale Ejlander palms, like this pig's, were held out demanding garnish, garnish ... But Ejlanders, Rajal knew, thought all Vagas were rich, with wads of Blue Ejards sewn into their tunics and secret pockets stuffed with silver and gold, gleaming epicrowns and sovereigns and tirals and swirling-patterned therons ... Rajal could have laughed. The only theron he had seen had been made of clay, and crunched into bitter dust between his teeth.

He was reaching again for the little leather bag when Nova nudged him sharply.

'We've paid,' Nova hissed.

'What's that, Vaga?' With a grin, Harion Cornfield turned to the boy in scarlet. 'Cocky little beggar, this one, eh?'

Rajal offered up a silent prayer. *Koros of the Rock, hear your child. Make Nova shut up. Please.*

Nova did not. His eyes flashed boldly at the sentry. 'I said we've paid.'

Beerjacket snorted, 'Vaga-brat, you haven't *begun* to pay!' He stepped forward, raising his musket. All at once there was a guttural cry and the musket fell skittering to the ground.

'Get him off, get him off!' Beerjacket gasped.

It was Zady: suddenly the big man had lunged forward, clamping his hands round Beerjacket's throat. Harion Cornfield struck out sharply, striking the attacker with the butt of his musket. But this time, no one dared to intervene.

Zady fell.

Harion Cornfield kicked him in the head.

'Oh, stop it, stop it!' Myla wailed. 'He's only a Simple, can't you see? Oh, leave him be!'

'Shut up!' spat Harion Cornfield, though whether to Myla or to his moaning fellow-sentry was not quite clear. He eyed the Vagas viciously. Myla, on her knees, was comforting Zady, helping the big man to

47

stagger upright; above their heads, the beckoning-bird fluttered nervously.

A low cunning overspread the stubbly face. They could have arrested the Vagas there and then, marched them off to the lock-up.

But would not.

Harion Cornfield held out his hand. Quickly Rajal ripped the coin-pouch from its fastenings beneath his tunic and thrust it clumsily towards the expectant sentry.

Laughter rang behind the frightened Vagas as they blundered through the door, clutching each other. Only the old man in the booth was silent, looking on sourly, hooking a claw-like finger into a nostril.

In a moment he would demand his share of the purse.

'Damn, damn.' Rajal kicked the stones of the city wall. 'Everything we've earned. Everything we've got. Gone.' He turned viciously on his companion, his partner, his brother of the sword. 'Satisfied now, Ejlander? Have you made your protest felt?'

'Raj, I'm sorry. I know it was wrong. It was the way that pig looked at you, I did it for *you*—'

'For me!' Rajal spat. He pushed Nova in the chest. The boy in scarlet staggered back. 'Ejlander, next time you feel like doing anything for us, don't. Just don't. We don't need you, we can get along without you perfectly well—'

The rain was falling again, and Myla, meanwhile, was anxious about Zady. Concussed, the big man could only stagger weakly, his legs wobbling.

'Brother Raj, help him, do!'

But her brother wasn't listening.

Grimly, Rajal pushed ahead, trudging down the muddy track that led back to the camp. Outside the city walls, the world was a churning mass, black and green and grey, brown and purple and blue. Above, the ominous sky massed darkly over the hills; at the base of the valley, the River Riel churned tempestuously, brimming over its banks. They passed through a thick line of elms that screened the Vaga-camp from the Varby walls.

'Get along without me?' Rajal span round; Nova, sloshing behind him, had grabbed his arm. 'Yes. Like the way you got on in the ambush at Jarl. Or the raid at Lake Lygar. What do you want to do, Raj, spend your life getting kicked? Licking arse, and saying thanks for the favour?'

'I'm not the one who nearly got his face smashed in—'

'I'm not the one who grovelled on the ground—'

Myla wailed, 'Brother Raj, there's something wrong with Zady—'

But Rajal's eyes were fixed on the boy in scarlet. He laughed bitterly, 'Yes, I grovelled. Disgusting, isn't it? Disgusting that I don't want to give up all our takings – only some of them, because that can't be helped. Disgusting, not to spend the night in the lock-up, with a whipping in the morning thrown in for good measure. Disgusting, not to lose our permit and be sent back north to the prison camps – disgusting, really disgusting. But of course, I'm forgetting. You've never been in a prison camp, have you, Ejlander?'

'Oh, Raj, Raj,' the scarlet boy muttered, his teeth gritted and his forehead screwed tight. As the assault went on, he sloshed slowly round in a circle; twice he punched his fist into his hand. Rain was dripping from his ears, from his neck; soon the dark dye in his hair would run.

Rajal plunged on, 'Oh, I don't know what you've done, I don't know why you're running. But you've come far enough now, haven't you, Ejlander? The Valleys of the Tarn are a thousand jels away – why not just wash off that elberry juice and go back to your own kind? They'd love that white skin, that haystack hair. Why don't you go for a soldier, hm? A Bluejacket, why not? Easy life. Slouch in a piss-stinking doorway all day with your hand held out, saying *Garnish, garnish*—'

Nova had turned away, as if he didn't want his friend to see him; now he swung back suddenly, his fist slamming into Rajal's face. In the next instant the boys were rolling in the mud, scrambling, punching, kicking. An instant later, Nova broke away, running blindly, directionlessly in the rain. He crashed back through the screen of elms, and was gone.

Rajal slumped limply on his back in the mud. His nose was bleeding and his chest was in pain.

Oh Nova, Nova.

Big heavy raindrops thudded on his face.

Myla shook him.

'Brother Raj, it's Zady. He can't walk. He's not moving, Brother Raj. Oh Brother Raj, help him.'

Chapter 7

THE CURE

'Zady . . . dear Zady.'

Wrinkled hands smoothed the bloodstained hair. His breathing laboured, the big man lay on one of the long couches that ran down each side of the cluttered van. The gash in his forehead was deep and wide.

'He's not dying, is he, Great Mother?'

'Girl-child, no!' The Great Mother turned back to the centre-stove, where a little brass pannikin was heating on a trivet. 'Cousin Zady's had a knock on the head, that's all – enough to make any fellow's wits all hither and yon. But then, my poor cousin's wits were already hither and yon, long before he ventured through the Varby-gate today, weren't they? Hm?'

With a smile the old woman plucked the pannikin from the heat, brought it up to her nose and inhaled deeply. There was hardly any need: already the rich aroma filled the van, a potent compound of herbs and spices, potions and powders that the Great Mother, calm in the emergency, had swiftly assembled from her many mysterious bottles and pouches, canisters and phials. Unmindful of the heat, she scooped up a handful and smoothed the potion thickly over Zady's wound.

The bird on Myla's shoulder blinked expectantly, confident, it seemed, of the Great Mother's power. So was Myla. Her eyes were wide, filled with love and awe. *One day,* she thought, *shall I too have the powers of the Great Mother? Shall I be a Great Mother in my turn?* It was a question the child did not dare ask; but oh, how she hoped it would be so!

It did not occur to her that perhaps, by the time this came to pass, Great Mother Xal would be with her no longer. Myla was a child given to large, solemn notions, but this was too large, too solemn. How could she live without the Great Mother? How could they all? To the Vaga-kind, Myla knew, the old woman was special, for in her lay the key to the destiny of their race.

At first, when road-Vagas had spoken in awe of the old woman, saying that it was she who had *struck the blow,* Myla had not even known what they meant. Irion Day, which would live on in Vaga legend and lore, would remain to the child, who had been there, no more than a blur, as if it were only a story she had heard. Could it be true that the wizened old woman, so placid and gentle, had started the great battle?

50

In any case, the story spread; Vagas who had never been near the Tarn would speak in hushed tones of Irion Day, and bow down in reverence to the Great Mother. How Myla longed to do the same! But the old woman only told her not to be silly.

The bird ruffled its feathers. Zady began to moan; at any moment he would open his eyes.

Rajal sat in a corner. He was sullen. Wrapped in a bright blanket, he might have been just more of the garish clutter that filled the van almost to bursting. All around the little party it pressed, burnished and shifting in the swaying lamplight – the cooking-pans, the ladles and spoons and knives, the bolts of rich fabric, the draping beads and curtains, the urns and bottles and cases and sacks, groaning and clinking, creaking and juddering.

It was a wild night. Tonight, all the Vagas would be huddled in their vans. Tonight there would be no camp-trade, no Ejlanders eager for the stronger magic that could flourish outside the city walls, the strange medicines, the prophecies of the future, the liturgies unheard in the temples of Agonis. No glittering coins would change hands, in return for this or that exotic bounty; tonight there would be no campfires, no chanting, no dancing, no beakers of scalding Elixir of Jarvel passed, with broad grins, from hand to hand while breezes rustled softly, warmly in the trees.

They might have been at sea, deep in a ship's hold. Rain drummed unrelentingly on the wooden roof of the van; they heard the wind whipping through the trees beside the camp and the turbulent rushings of the river below, rolling and tumbling headlong from the hills like a prisoner, freed suddenly from implacable chains. Yes, it was a wild night; so where, Rajal wondered, could Nova have gone? Anger with Nova fought in him with alarm; should he be out again, a lantern in his hand, calling hoarsely over the tumbling rain?

But the Great Mother only said, *No, leave him be. Leave your brother be.*

My brother! thought Rajal with contempt, and then felt ashamed because he had felt contempt, not only for Nova, but for the Great Mother. After all, what she said must be true; but, oh, how difficult to believe it sometimes!

It had been one bright morning on the edge of the Wildwood, deep in the northerly Valleys of the Tarn, that Rajal had first met the boy they would call Nova. Long seasons had passed since then, but Rajal still remembered that day. Then, there had been only the four of them – Rajal, Myla, Zady, Xal – on the run from Irion and lying low.

The night before Nova came, they had holed out in an empty farm-house, one of many that lay about the valley like hollow shells in the

51

aftermath of the Siege. Disguised as peasants, driven from the land, they were heading south, following the Pale Highway. Untold dangers would await a lone Vaga-band, crossing the vastness of the Harion lands. But there was nothing for it: they must head for The Inner, where Vagas could at least be licensed singers, conjurors, dancers.

In the Tarn, stray Vagas would be rounded up and shot.

That morning, Rajal had been off with Myla, foraging for wood-meat and sweet leaves and berries. The Great Mother had warned them not to be long, but they wandered far and deep into the woods. By the time they found their way back to the farmhouse, the sun was already climbing high in the sky and Zady's cart was ready to go.

Unsurprised, unalarmed at their lateness, the Great Mother turned to them. Rajal's arms were filled with sweet tree-roots and Myla's skirt, held up at the hem, was heavy with leaves, berries and nuts; but the roots and leaves and berries and nuts fell in a slow cascade to the ground as the hidden stranger revealed himself to them.

Slowly he stepped out from behind the cart. He was gaunt-faced and wiry, dressed, as they were all dressed now, in peasant-garb. That first day he was shy, and cast down his eyes, but Rajal had seen already that they were coloured bright blue. A head of tow-coloured hair surmounted the pale form.

'This boy is called Nova,' the Great Mother said. 'Take him to your hearts as your brother, my children, for he is to be as a brother to you.'

Rajal was horror-struck. 'Great Mother, have your eyes failed? This boy is not of our kind. He is an Ejlander – a worshipper of the smooth-tongued Agonis! Have you forgotten already the carnage of Irion Day? Have you forgotten the gallows on the green? For if you have forgotten your son, Great Mother, I have not forgotten my father.'

At this, Rajal would have strode forward, striking the pale Ejlander to the ground; instead, he stumbled and fell into the dust. He gazed up at the Great Mother, sitting beside Zady on the box of the cart. How easily she could subdue him! With a sharp throb he was aware of the Vaga-mark, like a wound, that was spreading secretly on the inner flesh of his thigh. He was becoming a man; he had sought to speak as a man.

But his voice had been high and cracking and his resolve had faltered quickly.

The pale Ejlander offered his hand, but Rajal spurned it and scrambled up alone. Shame-faced, he would have turned then and run, flailing helplessly across the ruined pasturelands. But he could not. He looked at Myla. The girl-child squatted obliviously on the dusty ground, snatching spilt fruit from the ardent nuzzlings of the beckoning-bird.

The Great Mother said kindly, 'Child Rajal, how could I lose the memory of your father? Each day my heart bleeds again for the one fruit of this withered womb I had thought would thrive, when I at last had passed beyond the Realm of Being. But in you, Child Rajal, I know that my son lives on, and in you I know he shall live nobly.

'This boy, too, is the enemy of our enemies, and were he to stay here in the Valleys of the Tarn his life would be no safer than yours or mine. Look beyond the surface, Child Rajal. The Rapture is not strong in you, as it is in your sister. But can you not see that mere skin is beguiling?'

She drew the stranger close to her, rolling up his sleeve; the white flesh of the forearm dazzled Rajal's eyes.

'His body is of the pallor of sunlight, and though he has grown almost to manhood, still he shall not bear the mark which distinguishes the men of our tribe. No, this child is no Child of Koros, but as we travel through the Harion-lands, there shall be times when his whiteness is to our profit. With him it shall seem that we are all of paler face; and later, there shall come a time when we in turn shall conceal him, staining his skin and hair with the dark juice of elberries.

'Oh my children, there shall be many debts; but all debts in time shall be repaid. Time passes: but in time, the meaning of all things shall be revealed to us.'

And Rajal had shut his eyes, pressing back tears, for he had known, of course he had known, that what the Great Mother said was true.

Zady's eyes opened.

'Cousin Xal . . .' Trustingly he looked up into the wizened, kind face.

'Dear Zady . . . hush, hush.' With gentle restraint his cousin bade him be still, but Xal knew that her remedy was working. A little smile flitted across her lips and the old woman picked her way carefully round the centre-stove. Pushing aside a heap of bright garments, parting a curtain of beads, she slid up a panel in the back wall of the van.

'Great Mother, the pattern-music?' Myla's voice was an awed whisper.

'It is part of the cure. The vel-viscidity is but the first part; this is the second, and there shall be a third. But perhaps you know that already, Myla-child? You shall know it in time, when The Rapture in you is stronger.'

Myla's heart swelled: she *had* known it. She reached up, smoothing her bird's bright feathers, as carefully, gravely, the Great Mother's gnarled hands drew forth the second part of Zady's cure. First she had to unwrap a thick blanket, then successive layers of gossamer cloth. A hollow sonority rang on the air; delicate varnish glowed with its own fire in the golden, glimmering lamplight.

'Zady-cousin, come,' the Great Mother murmured, placing the instrument gently into his hands. It was a triple-gittern, one of the rarest products of Vaga-craft. Three spindly many-stringed necks protruded from a brittle, rounded sounding-bowl, decorated elaborately with symbolic carvings. Only at the most solemn times was it played, and it was only Zady who ever played it.

In the big clumsy hands the strange instrument might have been about to shatter at any moment. But the hands instead were surprisingly tender, picking out a melody which had in it all the grace that the player, at first, had seemed to lack.

Slowly in the beginning, then faster and faster, the fingers plucked ever more complex patterns from criss-crossing sets of jangling strings.

Xal closed her eyes. She knew what was to come. Beneath the pattern-music and the drumming rain she heard the burble-burble of running muddy rivulets, swirling beneath their wheels, sopping dangerously into the loose clods of soil. From the distance came the whinny of a frightened horse. In a moment, breaking through the complex web of sounds, a thumping, rapid and urgent, would shake the door of the van.

Who could it be?

But Xal would know. Cousin Emek, with a warning: the river was riding high, too high. They must move the vans; they must harness the horses.

To Rajal, sloshing out into the rain again, it would seem impossible, a nightmare. Lurid in guttering lantern-light, the world would seem only an evil, precipitous ooze, and the camp, with all its vans and carts, its horses and children and dogs, its spangle-cloth, its incense and beads, destined at any moment to slither into the river. Shouting and straining, they would struggle uselessly; Cousin Emek would be all in a flurry; but just as the collapse would seem about to come, at the moment when it would seem that all was over, calmly Zady would take his place beside them, planting his strong legs in the liquid ground.

Afterwards the fragrant balm would be washed clean from his forehead; his wound would be gone; and the girl-child, looking on with a growing understanding, would know that the big man had completed the third part of his cure.

But this was to come.

Zady played; Myla sang. At first her song was wordless, the melody strangely undulating; at last it turned into a doleful folk-tune that Rajal remembered hearing on the road, somewhere, sometime.

A man might love a lady dressed
In finest silk and lace,
But if she did not love him, too,
He'd run a fruitless chase—
Ladies fine, Ladies fair

54

'The girl-child's voice grows prettier, does it not, my young warrior?'

But Rajal was barely listening. Serenely, Xal struck a match on the centre-stove, lighting an ornate curving pipe. Clouds of sweet smoke filled the cluttered van as she took up her place beside her huddled great-son. She looked at him sadly and her voice was a husky whisper, almost lost beneath the music and the rain.

'My poor child, do not resent your brother in your heart. Oh, I know of the pain which has passed between you. One of you looks into the eyes of the other – what does he see? Here a rash fool, teetering on gable-ends; there, a coward creeping low on the path, hiding in holes when footsteps sound. And each in his heart hugs his contradiction. Says one, *Rash? I am brave where he is weak.* Says the other, *Coward? A calumny; I shall thrive when he is dashed to the ground.*'

> *A knight might seek a secret prize*
> *That glitters bright as gold,*
> *But should he lose his honour, then*
> *That prize he'll never hold—*
> *Spirits fine, Spirits fair*
> *Dance about him in the air,*
> *But are they more than pictures drawn in sand?*

'My child, each of you shall thrive only together; and this, as time passes, is a lesson you must learn. See no weakness in the Ejlander-child. He is strong like you, but his is a strength of a different kind. Turn back now to the friend of your heart, for without him your destiny shall be for ever lost to you. Your story is but beginning; this night shall pass. Embrace the Ejlander like the brother you must be, and think of the future.'

> *A King might come in glory, bound*
> *To claim back his lost crown,*
> *But should he fail his secret trust*
> *His foes will strike him down—*
> *Kingdoms fine, Kingdoms fair*
> *Rise and wither in the air,*
> *But whither, whither goes this sacred land?*

The shifting mud burbled beneath the floor. Still the rain was falling harder, harder; inside, the strange music swirled on the air, at one with the smoke, the lamplight, the myriad glimmering things.

'But Great Mother,' said Rajal, 'where has Nova gone?'

There was no time for an answer. An urgent thumping shook the door of the van.

Chapter 8

HARLEQUIN OF THE SILVER MASKS

After Jem had broken from Rajal, he had sloshed obliviously through mud and soggy grass; he had flailed along the curve of Vosper's Loop; he had run and run and kept on running. All he saw before him was a grey-brown murk and all he heard was the rain, swishing, swirling.

The 'Lasher', bearing down on him, he did not see, did not hear until the sudden frightened whinny of a rearing horse, the girl's shriek, the single sharp *crack!* of the whip.

Jem crumpled.

'Vaga-scum, I'll warrant!' Harsh laughter rang above the rain as the 'Lasher' vanished round a curve of road.

Jem lay on his back in a ditch. He barely cared. The whip had made a cut across his cheek; he was bleeding, but could not yet feel the pain. His head was full, thinking of the quest that lay before him. He knew it was fear, the terrible fear inside him, that had burst out in his foolish fight with Rajal. Until now, Jem's destiny had seemed safely in the distance. Now it was closer, almost upon him. In days, the Vaga-band would arrive in Agondon – and Jem, in days, must leave them.

You shall go to a street called Davalon Street, the harlequin had said. *To a house with golden scrolls at the windows and doors. It is the house of a gentleman who is known as Lord Empster. You are to go to him, Jem, and he shall receive you.*

By now, perhaps, with Agondon so near, Jem should have struck out on his own, scrubbing his skin of elberry juice, setting out on foot. But he could not do it. To travel alone was dangerous, too dangerous – and how could the Vagas leave Varby, before the season was out?

Jem knew he was a cowardly fool.

Shuddering, he gripped the crystal he wore in a leather pouch around his neck. Sometimes an aching filled his heart as he thought of the crystals that must still be found. How huge it was, the task before him! As a child, he had longed for adventure, and adventure had come to him, thick and fast, in his long journey with the Vagas.

But now, as a greater and more dangerous adventure loomed near, Jem often wished he was home again. How he dreamed of Cata, dear Cata, and the love they had shared in the Wildwood! But that seemed so long ago, so hopelessly long ago – and Jem knew he could never go back.

If only the harlequin would appear to him again, filling him with strength for the quest that lay ahead!

A coach came rumbling along the road.

'Coach-person, I say!' An imperious voice rang over the rain, accompanied by the *ding!* of an ingenious little bell. 'Do stop, do!'

Another voice, lugubrious, came, 'What is it, oh, what is it? Already we are far behind the rest of our party. Can't we hurry? One shall catch one's death – one *has* caught one's death. One is dying, old 'panion, dying.'

'You are not dying. Really, can't you think of others? A young person, I suspect of the masculine gender, is sprawled in the most fetching fashion by the roadside.'

'In the rain and mud? Undoubtedly he is dead.'

'No, but he may be hurt.'

'Oh I say, I shan't look. Is there blood?' *Ding!* 'Coach-person, do drive on!'

Ding! again. 'No, stop!' A head leaned out intrepidly. 'Muddy he may be, but he is dressed, one observes, in the garb of the Scarlet Endeavour. We cannot leave him. Young person, young person in the mud, I say—'

Jem sat up suddenly. He drew in his breath. He had never seen a coach like this before. It was painted a deep blackish purple, with the royal arms in gold on the door. Four handsome black horses, like the drenched coachman, were garbed in the same livery, but it was the face staring at him from the carriage window that arrested Jem's attention.

The face was concealed beneath a silver mask.

'Are you hurt, young person? Can you walk?'

Jem scrambled up. His gaze remained fixed on the mask.

'Your poor face! Oh, to tend to it with my cambric handkerchief . . . Fear not, young person, we are of your kind. Come, let us take you into our protection—'

The door swung open.

'Are you mad, old 'panion? This child is no more than a rogue, a vagabond! Oh, we shall be murdered—'

Ding!

Ding! again.

'You forget, we are all of us rogues and vagabonds!'

Hands reached out and Jem was hauled into the interior of the purple-black coach. The bell rang again and he looked about him. Inside, too, the coach was remarkably plush, with rich deep quilting of the same dark shade, ornate cushions strewn liberally about, and thick patterned rugs, in one of which Jem's wet form was immediately enfolded.

He blinked and swept back his dripping hair.

A little lamp swung from the ceiling and in the warm, soft light Jem saw his new companions properly for the first time. If one wore a mask of metal, the other wore a mask of a different sort. The lugubrious voice, Jem saw now, issued from a face plastered thickly with make-up. It was white, dazzlingly so, except around the mouth, where a pair of painted lips were turned grotesquely downwards. The skin beneath the make-up was sagging, scored with lines; it was a face to haunt the dreams of children, the face of a clown who could not laugh.

Suddenly Jem felt a sense of danger. He was not only muddy, but cold and bruised. Weak. Vulnerable. Why had he got into this strange coach? The mask, staring down at him, had beguiled him, he knew; it was a mask he had seen before.

But no. It could not be.

The clown was saying, 'Vagabonds we may be, but we are no mere wastrels! The boy is a common road-Vaga, no more. Come now, old 'panion, put him out, put him out.'

'Clown, where is your compassion? This Vaga-boy has been set upon by thieves, I'll be bound . . . That nasty cut! Now where, where is my cambric handkerchief—?'

'Set upon? He probably *is* a thief.'

'Nonsense. One can tell at once he is a lost innocent.'

'Old 'panion, you are too romantic.' The sad face turned towards Jem. 'Tell us then, Vaga-boy, what is your story?'

Jem's heart thudded hard. In the last moments he had realized a remarkable thing. His strange companions were wrapped in dark cloaks; he could not see the costumes they wore beneath, any more than he could see their true faces. But perhaps the purple-black of the coach was clue enough; perhaps the rugs and fabrics, the familiar rich patterns . . .

'You're Vagas!' said Jem.

There was a silence. Mask looked to Clown, Clown looked to Mask; Mask erupted into pealing laughter. Jem bit his lip. They *were* Vagas, they had to be – but how could they ride in this magnificent coach?

Then he remembered.

Rajal had spoken often of the Silver Masks, the celebrated 'Royal Vagas'. They were the stuff of Vaga-legend. Licensed under the hand of the King himself, for epicycles the company had performed at the highest levels of Ejland society. To be chosen for the Masks, some said, was the highest goal a Vaga could attain; in the Masks, the lowest juggler or dancer enjoyed privileges unknown to common Ejlanders, let alone to the ruck of Vaga-kind. The stars of the company lived in luxury, like quality-folk; Blajir Harest, the great Pierrot, was said to have been the most valued courtier of the Holy Empress.

The Masks were the stuff of Vaga-dreams, and Rajal, Jem knew, thought fondly of a day when he too might join their number.

They were coming to Varby for the Equinox Ball.

MASK: Vagas! Well.
CLOWN: You'd prefer 'Children of Koros'?
MASK: No, no. The innocence is charming.
CLOWN: Boorish ignorance!
MASK: Come Clown, you must see—
CLOWN: See what? My eyes fail.
MASK: This child is the one we seek. Well, the latest.
CLOWN: No, no. He is a mere provincial.
MASK: The provinces have their prizes.
CLOWN: Pish-pash! Would you have us play the depths of Down
        Lexion, the furthest valleys of Varl? Quality, old 'panion,
        is an aspect of geography.
MASK: Of birth, surely.
CLOWN: Birth! Ah, had I but been the heir of—
MASK: Heva-Harion? Vantage? Irion?
CLOWN: Droll, droll. But Irion, yes. An ancient title—
MASK: Provincial.
CLOWN: What, provincial? The Archduke is a leader of society—
MASK: His title derives from the furthest province—
CLOWN: Pish-pash! One dreams not of his title, but his place.
MASK: One is nothing without the other.
CLOWN: Is that so?
MASK: Clown, you are a fool.

Bewildered, Jem looked down. Idly he had been rubbing the skin of one hand, from knuckle to wrist, from wrist back to knuckle; suddenly he stopped and folded his arms. The potion that stained his skin was strong, but the storm, he saw now, had been too much for it; the rubbing had smeared the colour away. There could be little left of his Vaga-disguise, and now the strangers were looking at him intently.

CLOWN [continuing]: Fool, you say? That is a compliment to a
        clown. You see, I take you kindly. Others would not,
        were you to call them fools.
MASK: You have one in mind?
CLOWN: Our young friend here?
MASK: Oh, no! [To Jem:] Fool, fool! See, he does not respond.
CLOWN: Then indeed he is a fool.
MASK: Cruel Clown! He is young. A babe in arms.
CLOWN: Arms! The child is not armed, is he? With every year
        the roads become more dangerous.
MASK: Not so much droll, as drab. But old 'panion, you must
        know that this is the boy.

59

CLOWN: The one we have sought? I mean, the latest.
MASK: But of course. It is clear to me. Can't you see it?
CLOWN: I said, my eyes fail. He *is* muddy.
MASK: We shall wipe the mud away.

Mask, as he spoke, had begun to fumble beneath his cloak, searching, perhaps, for the promised handkerchief. At last he drew it forth, but Jem's attention was all for something else; for in the moments when the cloak had been parted he had glimpsed the costume beneath, bright with the particoloured diamonds of a harlequin.

Could it be?

A hand reached out, dabbing the handkerchief at Jem's hurt face. Jem caught the wrist. *Embrace me now, my child,* a voice had once said, *for long seasons must pass until you see me again.*

Entranced, Jem sang softly:

> *Hey, ho! The circle is round!*
> *Where can its start and its end be . . .*

He trailed off. The harlequin's hand hung suspended before his eyes like a dead thing, and in the swaying lamplight Jem saw that it was old, terribly old, the skin stiff and spotted and lined.

The moment was broken.

Sharply the harlequin pulled away. 'Do you mock me, boy? You are of our kind. Do you not know that song is the harlequin's, the harlequin's alone?'

'I thought—'

Jem could say nothing. He had been a fool. This was not the harlequin, not *his* harlequin – this was the Harlequin of the Silver Masks.

He closed his eyes. He must command himself, think only of what mattered now.

He must go back to camp.

Now, at once.

'The King!' came a chorus of gruff, respectful voices. They were passing through the arch of the Varby-gates. Stiff-backed sentries saluted, as they must, a coach bearing the royal arms.

'I've got to go—' Jem lurched forward, reaching for the handle of the quilted door. He would leap out, run back through the gates, swiftly, swiftly.

Mask grabbed his arms. The grip was hard and sharp like talons. 'Come, Vaga-boy, where are you going, suddenly all a-haste?'

'The curfew—'

'Curfew? Who do you think we are? For us there is no curfew – no licence, no garnish.'

Jem struggled. 'What do you want from me?'

A high laugh. 'You are the merest young wayfarer, are you not? A traveller, dare I say, with some lowly troupe, grovelling for jits in the public ways? Put that life behind you, my child! With us, you have entered a new sphere!

'Soon we shall arrive at our luxurious quarters; soon we shall be dining on Varby-eel and venison, served by obsequious Ejlander-servants. Why, we shall quaff the finest Varl-wines, the sweetest Tiralos. Perhaps even Clown shall smile; but oh, Vaga-boy, I know *you* shall! Tonight you shall sleep in sheets of silk—'

'I've got to get back—'

'Importunate child! As our friend, you shall wear the finest clothes, ride in our coaches, learn our manners! Clown and I have had many such friends, have we not, Clown? Ah, child, think of the world that is opening before you—'

'I said I've got to go!' cried Jem, writhing and bucking. Violently he broke from the restraining grip. He lashed out, kicking the harlequin in the shins.

'Oh! Coach-person, oh!' burst out the harlequin, half in pain, half in delight, scrambling urgently for the driver's bell.

Ding! Ding-ding!

Too late. An instant later, Jem had wrenched open the quilted door, flinging himself out into the street; by the time the driver drew the horses to a halt, the boy had gone, vanished into the murk of the rainy night.

CLOWN: A cold Equinox we're having this year.

MASK (*rubbing his shin*): The seasons are not what they used to be, Clown.

CLOWN: Nor, alas, are the starving wayfarers.

MASK (*sighing, a sad, old man's sigh*): But the boy was promising.

CLOWN: Oh, most promising! He reminded you, perhaps, of a boy we have met before?

MASK: A special boy.
(*Pause.*)

CLOWN: Our pet, our prop and stay, our little lost 'prentice?

MASK: Old 'panion, you know me too well! (*Sighs again.*) But ah, could a boy like *Tor* come more than once in our lives?
(*They rattle on towards their luxurious quarters.*)

Chapter 9

LADY FINE

'There are few things,' Umbecca would say, 'that disgust me more than a *Duenna*. What could be more depraved than to thrust a tender, innocent girl, trembling on the brink of womanhood, into the care – if care it be – of a *hired servant*? For long cycles, did I not see to the spiritual, moral and physical well-being of my poor niece Ela? Could I – should I – have seen her parted from my bosom? Now, as another frail vessel of virtue has come into my care, am I to entrust it to an uncaring hand? Why, the mere thought is monstrous!'

Umbecca could say more in this vein, and often did; but for all that she execrated the Duenna-class, still there was one for whom she made an exception.

'You understand, my dear, my comments can have no application at all to – *you*.'

This was as well, since the Duenna in question was the principal audience for Umbecca's tirades. It was her old friend from Irion, the Widow Waxwell. After her husband's tragic death, the Widow had lived on for some moonlives at Blossom Cottage, tended only by her doddering maid. But it was clear – so Umbecca insisted – that her friend was unhappy. Could Berthen endure those lonely rooms, denuded now of her dear husband? That she declared herself content was neither here nor there; grief must have turned the poor woman's wits. So it was that Umbecca, drawing upon her power as governor's wife, had Blossom Cottage closed, the servant dismissed and the Widow taken into the governor's household.

This compassionate act was much applauded in the village, especially after Eay Feval made it the subject of a Canonday address.

For a time the Widow lived happily – so all were convinced – as her dear friend's companion. It was therefore with some surprise that the villagers heard she had *taken a situation*. When Theron-season approached, she would depart for Varby, to become Duenna to a certain Miss Pelligrew. For a moonphase or more, the gossips had no other topic. Some felt deeply for poor Madam Veeldrop, professing themselves shocked at the Widow's ingratitude; some deplored the thought of paid employment; some pointed out, not without bluntness, that the Widow was hardly suited to her new career.

After all, she had only one hand.

Umbecca's reaction came as a surprise. One might have expected her to forbid this new folly; on the contrary, she was sanguine about the Widow's prospects. It was as well that Berthen adjusted herself to her new place in the world. What dignity could there be in living on charity? What shame in respectable employment? If Duennas there had to be, was it not as well that they be women like Berthen Waxwell, of the highest moral character?

If Umbecca had a regret, it was only that her dear friend should lavish her talents upon the child of another – the child, let it be said, of a virtual stranger. Shortly Miss Cata too was to make her Entrance. One might have hoped that in common gratitude the Widow would have seen where her responsibilities lay. But then, Umbecca would sigh, perfection was hardly to be expected in this world, and after all, one must make allowances for a woman crazed with grief.

When the Widow left for Varby, Umbecca was beside her.

'Nirry!' the fat woman screamed, as they burst back into their lodgings.

Umbecca's maid came running, alarmed that the mistress had returned so early. By the time she had taken her orders, the girl was exhausted. Put away those dresses, put away those jewels! Look at this place! Was Nirry keeping a harlot's parlour? Why, the tea-things weren't even cleared away! Why hadn't the fire been made up yet? They would take supper in their chambers, and take it now!

Only an early and massive repast could assuage the fury in Umbecca's heart, and enable her to gird her loins – so she put it – for the confrontation to come.

The repast was gruesome. In public, Umbecca was all decorum, all dainty gestures and correct forks and knives; huddled over a tray before her own fire, she stuffed her cheeks to bursting with cakes and cold chicken, custard and kidneys, lattice tarts and salt-pig, in no particular order. With greasy fingers she tore at her food. Between mouthfuls she called down curses on the wicked Widow Waxwell, who had deserted her duty so grievously, so cravenly.

She would not get away with it!

Up and down the stairs poor Nirry ran, raiding the pantry again and again.

Cata only pushed her food about her plate. Her aunt upbraided her, then snatched Cata's plate away and scooped up the contents, ramming the meat, the mashed pumpkin, the slices of beetroot into her own mouth.

Rain seethed behind the drawn curtains.

At last Umbecca reared up from the fireside. Before the meal, her huge bulk had trembled, shivering like a monstrous jelly; now she faced the world with the solidity of a rock, her pinprick eyes blazing in her bloated face.

'Bed for you, my girl!' she boomed, and called to Nirry for her umbrella and cape.

Cata protested, 'Aunt, it's so early!'

'Early?' Umbecca swept her niece aside. 'Do giddy girls who moon after the likes of Mr Burgrove deserve any better? Answer me that!'

But Umbecca did not wait for an answer.

'Now into that room with you! Nirry, the key!'

Locked in her room, Cata soon sprang up from the bed. Impatiently she pushed the curtains from the window, gazing into the darkness. All round the square the lamps were lit; reflected fire shimmered on the wet paving-stones. Between lurid pools Umbecca strode, her umbrella like a shield, a doughty warrior crossing the square towards the lodgings where Pelli, until this evening, had endured the regime of the Widow Waxwell.

Whatever could have happened? Frequently Cata had heard the Widow's praises. Berthen Waxwell, Umbecca would say, was a perfect specimen of Duenna-kind, keeping her charge tightly on the leash, brooking no opposition – so unlike the lax, liberal Duennas of today!

Cata turned from the window, miserable. In her mind she saw again a laughing girlish face, high up on the 'Lasher' beside Mr Burgrove. Envy bubbled inside her like bile. She wrapped her night-shawl tight about her shoulders and slumped before the fire, hugging herself. To envy Jeli – beautiful, popular Jelica Vance – was one thing.

But Pelli Pelligrew! The ignominy!

Wind was rattling at the window-panes and there was a heavy, steady drumbeat of rain.

Pelli, Pelli, it seemed to say.

Jem's heart beat hard. Sheltered beneath a high gable-end, he was doubled over, breathing deeply, in an alley somewhere behind the Royal Assembly. After leaping from the carriage of the false harlequin, he had darted blindly through the evening traffic, plunging into the darker recesses of the city. What an end to the day! He was cold, wet, filthy, and trapped for the night within the Varby walls.

He looked up miserably. From one end of the alley came the haze of a street-lamp, lighting the way back into the brilliant regions; the other end was darker, snaking out into a different Varby, hidden from the eyes of quality-folk. This was a Varby of huddled backstreets, where servants and cabmen and men of the ranks, released temporarily from the bondage of duty, indulged themselves in their own entertainments. From the first Varby, under the *plunk!* of rain, Jem heard the ripplings of a harpsichord; from the second, a muttered oath, a snatch of coarse song.

His way was clear. In the warren of lanes behind the Royal Assembly, could even a shivering Vaga-boy hide himself for the night?

But no. Soldiers were everywhere.

Jem held cupped hands into the rain and sluiced his face. The broken skin on his cheek stung cruelly, but he rubbed vigorously at his Vaga-stain.

Then there were his clothes.

There was a noise close by, a rapid gurgling. In the dim glimmerings, Jem made out a swaying human form. It was a servant-boy, pissing; somebody's page, in a cloak and feathered hat.

Jem sprang. 'Sorry, friend!'

The arc of piss skewed wildly up the wall.

Moments later, Jem's cloaked form emerged into the shabby recesses of The Revels, as the other Varby was called by those who frequented it. Sewage and smoke and aromas of roasting mixed and mingled on the lowering air. Jem adjusted his new-found hat and looked about him. How could it be, he wondered, that such a place was here, when perhaps a hundred lengths away, or less, through a few thicknesses of wall, quality-folk were gathered in their finery?

A ragged creature staggered past, holding up a gin-bottle. 'Your health, young fellow!' the creature slurred, and took a swig; then, turning back, with a hand on Jem's arm, 'The young fellow would be, perhaps, a little lonely?'

The hand tightened its grip and Jem saw that the creature was a woman, dressed in the remnants of what once might have been a fine lady's gown. A sour stench rose from her skirts and even in the dim light Jem could tell that her face was wizened.

'I'm sorry, I—'

The tavern-door beckoned, suddenly inviting. Jem shook his arm free; as he made his escape, the harlot cackled after him, 'Drink your fill, young fellow! I'll still be here when you've nerved yourself up!'

The tavern was low-beamed, smoky and crowded, the floor a mush of battered straw, sticky with slopped ale. On a fine night, the revellers would spill out into the lane; tonight they were clustered in the foetid indoors, swaggering Bluejackets, emboldened grooms, footmen and kitchen-hands crushed tightly together. Pot-boys weaved like wraiths between them and the only women were harlots, more harlots, with beauty-spots drawn grotesquely on their cheeks and breasts bursting from tightly-laced gowns. From somewhere amongst it all came the sound of voices raised in ragged unison, bellowing out bawdy songs.

In the page-boy's pocket, Jem found a couple of zens and jits. He pushed his way to the bar.

'Friend!' There was a shout behind him and a hand clapped on his shoulder, spinning him round. It was a young man in a tunic of yellow plush, eager-eyed and smiling. His smile faded swiftly when he saw his mistake. 'I thought you were—'

Jem thought quickly. 'He's not coming. Double duty—'

'But who are you?' The young man gestured to the livery Jem wore. 'I thought I knew all the Prince's servants—'

'A big household, my friend!' Jem muttered with a throwaway smile. He shrugged and turned away, a pang of guilt assailing him. In his mind he saw the page-boy, crumpling to the ground. The poor boy would have a headache in the morning; still, he would probably have had that anyway, and now, at least, he would have a story to tell.

Moments later, bearing a tankard, Jem struggled to a free space of benchtop, the only one he could see, at the back of the mean tavern. Candles dripped perilously from a brace above his head and, in a corner close by, a party of Bluejackets, gathered in a circle with arms draped round each other, launched into another of their favourite songs.

On the choruses, they swung their tankards lustily back and forth.

DRINKING SONG

He'd wiped himself on handkerchiefs
Of finest Varby lace,
But till he met that pretty miss
He'd run a lonely race—
   Oh, Lady Fine, Lady Fair,
   Ran her fingers through his hair
   And smiled and took an eager boy in hand!

He'd aimed his gun at all the game
That run and leap and trot,
But till he met that pretty miss
He'd always missed his shot—
   O-oh, Lady Fine, Lady Fair,
   Ran her fingers through his hair
   And smiled and took an eager boy in hand!

He'd been to parks and palaces,
He'd been to gilded halls,
But till he met that pretty miss
He'd never been to balls—

O-ooh, Lady Fine, Lady Fair
Ran her fingers through his hair
And smiled and took an eager boy in hand!

Now all you lonely soldier lads
Standing stiff and straight,
Find yourself a pretty miss
To help you pull your weight—
O-oooh, Lady Fine, Lady Fair
Wraps her fingers way down there
And smiles and takes an eager boy in hand!

The song ended in laughter and lewd gestures. Jem turned away, his face hot. Poor Jem! In many ways he was still an innocent; he did not know that the passion of love wears, and must wear, many different faces. He closed his eyes and thought again of Cata. What they had done was fine and noble. What they had done was pure.

Tears, hot and bitter, welled behind his eyelids.

Jem was raising his tankard to his lips when someone knocked his elbow. He turned, annoyed, but was met only by a cheerful grin. The owner of the grin was a burly fellow in a coachman's cape, sucking on a pipe. Jem relaxed; at least the fellow was a servant, not a Bluejacket. The coachman gave Jem a wink of acknowledgement and made a remark about the miserable weather.

'Bad cut on your cheek, lad,' he added. 'You'd be in the Prince of Chayn's service, then?'

Jem nodded. 'And you?'

The coachman pointed to a crest embroidered on his cape. Jem took a gulp of ale, pretending disinterest. But his heart was beating hard again. For a moment he had not recognized the fellow before him.

In Irion, Stephel had been a shambling drunkard.

Jem said cautiously, 'Irion?'

'Aye, he knows his nobility. Now that's vital in our class of people, lad. In my day we learnt the liveries, crests and mottoes of all the Nine Provinces and the Deliverance, too. Learnt them by heart, we did, or had them beaten into us.'

Jem smiled politely, but in his heart he cried out, *Stephel, don't you know me?* For a wild moment, Jem wanted to give himself away, but the moment ended when Stephel looked at him curiously and said, 'Eh, lad, haven't I seen you somewhere before?'

Jem blanched. Suddenly he was frightened. Wasn't he supposed to be lying low – travelling in secret? With pretended nonchalance he adjusted his stolen hat, drawing the brim down over his eyes.

But Stephel answered his own question. 'Hah! What am I thinking of?

For a moment, you reminded me of another lad. Now that lad would hardly be a servant, I think. Besides, he's dead!'

'Poor lad!' Jem thought it best to say no more. A strange feeling stole over him, compounded at once of euphoria, sadness and fear. Yes, he was dead, dead to them all back home. To Stephel. To Nirry. To Aunt Umbecca. To Polty.

To Cata. I'm dead to Cata, too.

Jem shook himself, fighting off the waves of emotion. He smiled again at Stephel. He knew he should have excused himself, leaving the old man.

But something made him stay.

'You're far from home,' Jem attempted. It was a sly remark. A startling possibility had just occurred to him. 'They say the white mountains are a staircase to the sky. Is that true?'

The coachman grunted, 'I wouldn't bother about white mountains, lad. The green hills of Varby are bad enough on the horses.'

'But you're from there? The mountains?'

Stephel did not quite answer the question. 'I'm not a one for moving about, I'm not. Not a one for change. If everything were like it was when I were your age, lad, I dare say I should be happy. In my day, everyone was in his proper place. Why, these days a man doesn't know his master!'

'He doesn't?'

'I said to my daughter, aren't we in the Archduke's service? And where's the Archduke today, I ask you? Agondon, and won't come home! Here's the Tarn, in the hands of a stranger – now here am I, a Tarn-man, in Varby! Ooh, what a topsy-turvy world I've lived to see!'

Stephel might have said more, but realized, perhaps, that his thoughts were running in a dangerous direction.

One could not be too careful.

He sighed again, 'It's this young ward, you see. That's why I'm here. The young miss – and her mistress.'

A comical sourness came over Stephel's face, and Jem pretended to laugh. Desperately he wanted to ask about the young miss, but restrained himself.

As if for luck he touched his chest, feeling the secret burden in the leather bag.

Softly, softly.

A hand clapped on his shoulder, hard. 'There you are, hiding in corners!' It was the young man in yellow plush. Evidently he had been drinking, but was still seeking the page-boy. 'Oh, it's not like him . . . Who did you say you were? I thought I knew all the Prince's servants . . .'

Jem turned away decisively.

'Say, pot-boy!' Stephel had drunk his tankard dry and Jem bought him another; the coachman thanked him and called him friend.

'Your master,' Jem attempted, 'I've heard he was the one that caught the evil king.'

'Aye, a great man, my master, that he be.' Stephel paused and continued woodenly, 'In league with the Zenzans, he was.'

No, one could not be too careful.

'Your master?'

'My master? The red king, boy! If the red king had his way, we'd be just a province of Zenzau now – instead of the other way round. Revived the Agonist faith, he did.'

'Ejard Red?'

'No, Ejard Blue! By the Lord Agonis, lad, you're green. Without the blue king, where'd we be now, I ask you? Sunk in a sty, sunk deep in a sty!'

A tankard crashed to the floor behind them as two Bluejackets, haggling over a whore, descended to blows. Some gathered to watch, shouting and laughing; others, oblivious, were downing bumpers of ale to the accompaniment of whistles and whooping cries.

Only Yellowplush was apart from the fray. *'Nasty cut you've got there,'* he hissed in Jem's ear.

Jem ignored it and leant closer to the coachman. 'The young lady—'

'She's a whore, lad!' (Close by, the subject of the fight was squealing excitedly.)

'I meant *your* young lady—'

Stephel bristled and his hand darted upwards, clutching Jem's throat.

'You're calling my young lady a whore?'

Jem realized that Stephel, for all his smart livery, was still a drunkard.

'No, no.' He prised the hand away. 'I meant, she must be a creature of uncommon beauty.'

'That cape doesn't fit you well,' came the hiss in Jem's ear.

Stephel lapsed back into his accustomed demeanour. With a studied air he sucked on his pipe, producing a prodigious, enveloping cloud. Behind them, a flying chair collided with a tray of glasses; Jem struggled to fix his attention on the clouded figure before him.

'Aye, she'll make a fine match. Fit for a king,' Stephel was saying. 'They say the dark are finest, though the fair are fairest.'

Jem sighed, 'I should like to see so fine a girl!'

It was a risk; the coachman might have flamed into anger again.

This time, he only laughed.

'Ah, lad, she's not meat for your table! Offal like that—' he gestured to the harlot '—is all that's left for the likes of us. Why, you'd have a hard time even to *see* my young lady! What with the Vanishings, you can't be too careful. '

'Vanishings?'

Stephel swigged back his ale. 'Lad, where've you been? Didn't you hear about Miss Vyella Rextel?'

Jem would have asked about the Gorgeous Vy, but at that moment someone seized his arm.

'Yes, I knew it!' Yellowplush again, drunker now. Squinting through the fug of smoke, he inspected Jem's cape. His fist lashed out. 'What have you done to him, what have you done to him?'

'Eh, steady on, lads!' Stephel cried.

But the coachman was forgotten. A moment later he had vanished and Jem had crashed to the floor, rolling and writhing in the grip of Yellowplush. To others, it must have seemed just part of the first fight, the fight about the whore, that by now was spreading to involve half the tavern. It may as well have been: Bluejackets, whores and servants alike, ostlers and footmen, even the tavern-boys joined eagerly in the fray, whooping ringingly as Yellowplush held Jem down in the straw, pinioning his chest, clutching at his throat.

Jem struggled for freedom. He didn't care if they thought he was a coward. All he wanted was to escape. He wrestled free, but a Bluejacket grabbed him, flinging him back; he was free again, but Yellowplush rose up rapidly and pulled him down once more. Only the third time, when a Bluejacket and a pot-boy had come to blows – more exciting blows – beside them, and a bored whore tripped up Yellowplush as he rose, did Jem at last break away.

Moments later he was back in the darkness, weaving through the filthy alleys in the rain.

Chapter 10

DEATH-DREAM

Midnight.

Now, as deepest darkness descends over the land, let us turn our gaze briefly from Varby to another and greater city. It is the city where Jem is bound, that crouches in wait for him like a great spider, huddled darkly in the centre of its web.

Agondon, capital of Ejland.

Our scene is set on Regent's Bridge, spanning the broad expanse of the Riel. Mournfully on the darkness come the fifteen tollings of the bells to end the day. Midway over the bridge a man in a dark cloak pauses, perhaps uncertainly. Shadows obscure the face beneath the broad, plumed hat.

'It is fated.'

Speaking to himself in a whisper, hoarse and urgent, the man in the cloak is trying, perhaps, to convince himself of something, to compel his own assent. Behind him, on the south side of the bridge, lie the fashionable squares and terraces of Agondon New Town; before him, on the steep rise of The Island, the dark labyrinth of the old city huddles mysteriously about the Great Temple of Agonis.

Soon it will be time for The Summoning to begin.

'Yes,' comes the whisper again, 'it is fated.'

The man in the cloak rests a hand on the parapet, gazing sadly into the waters below. Like a vast serpent the River Riel slithers through the city, rippling on silvery scales. Theron-season is almost over. It is as well: when fiery air rolls up from the far kingdoms of the south, Agondon's river becomes a hideous thing. By day, a dank putrescence steals its way skywards, hovering over the city in an evil shroud. At the height of the heat the beguiling waters shrivel away like a discarded skin, unveiling the festering sludge beneath.

Dead dogs. Garbage. The flowings of the sewers.

Now, a skein of cloud dissolves in the moonlight. The lapping waters shimmer more intensely. How beautiful they seem! How entrancing! But then, the lady in the moon has always been a deceiver. Perhaps that is why, in the time of Hornlight, it is forbidden to stare her in the face.

The man in the cloak lifts his eyes. Pox-like ravages disfigure the gleaming disc. An old story says that when the earth was new, the

71

moon's face was fair and shone full each night; now, when the earth has grown older, becoming sick and rotten, so the moon-lady, too, has decayed. Her face is ruined. In her wounded vanity she strives to turn away, and this is why her light will wax and wane. But she can never turn away for good. She is tethered in place, for it is her lot to witness what passes on the darkened earth.

Some say that one day, when this ruined world is redeemed, so the moon-lady, too, will be restored to her beauty.

> Moon-lady, moon-lady,
> Come back alive:
> But through the power
> Of the Crystals Five!

With a wry smile the man in the cloak intones the old rhyme.

But now comes another voice, a wheezing croak:

'Hornlight.'

The man in the cloak turns his head slowly. He has not seen the Reject huddled in rags, at the base of the statue in the centre of the bridge. The curfew is long past; the Reject should be hidden from view, sequestered beneath the dank arches of the Embankment or in the doorways of dark, narrow alleys. Here, on the bridge, the Watch will soon find him.

And kill him.

The Reject has risen and shuffled forward on feet bound in strips of filthy sacking. A hand reaches out brazenly, palm upwards, expectant. A stiff claw, the hand might belong to a twisted old man, but the face beneath the wispy beard is young – too young.

The voice comes again, a deathly rattle:

'Hornlight.'

It is a demand that had not been heard for many seasons in the Empire of Ejland. Since the crowning of the Bluejacket king, the soliciting of 'Hornlight alms' has been outlawed.

The man in the cloak sighs. With a smooth, elegant gesture he reaches for a coin, a gold tiral, and holds it aloft in his gloved fingers. It flashes in the moonlight. A tiral, just one, might keep the Reject in hot rolls and ragout for the length of half a moonlife, or at the gin-shops for a full euphoric day. But there is no eager grasping, no broken-toothed grin. The ragged figure seems already to have forgotten where he is, and what he has begun.

This must be one of the worst ones, thinks the man in the cloak. One of the Chronics, who has lost his wits as well as any rightful place in the world. The gloved fingers relax and the coin falls to the cobblestones, clinking and spinning.

The man in the cloak turns away.

But now the Reject grabs his arm and with a little dancing step swings round to face him. Foul breath gusts through a rotten mouth. The man in the cloak shudders in disgust. He would break free but the Reject grips him tightly, staring at him with goggling, crazed eyes as he struggles to form what seem to be the words of a song:

> *Everything is . . . and nothing is . . .*
> *Everything . . .*

The Reject is overcome by a fit of coughing, but will not relax his grip. The man in the cloak purses his lips. He knows the song. It is an old Zenzan air, brought back from the colonies in the time of the Holy Empress. In those days, minstrels had sung it as a round, and it had been popular at court; now it has declined to a nursery-catch, crooned in whispers to soothe sleepless infants. Perhaps it will soothe the Reject; perhaps the ruined young man is longing to be soothed.

Now it is the man in the cloak who grips the Reject tightly and intones, his lips close to a scabious ear:

> *Everything is lemon and nothing is lime,*
> *But even the truth shall be revealed in time:*
> *Then we shall drink from the mocking-tree gourds,*
> *And sup with the King and Queen of—*

'Yes! Yes!'

A smile comes to the Reject's lips and he would sink to his knees in gratitude, but when, a moment later, he slithers to the cobblestones, it shall be for a different reason. With the same smooth elegance that has brought forth the coin, the man in the cloak now produces a second object. This time the object, though it is sharp and shiny, does not glint; for now its owner stands with his back to the harsh moonbeams, and now the two figures are enfolded, as in an embrace, inside the cloak. There is a kind of ecstasy on the Reject's face, an ecstasy that seems not to diminish, but rather to spread and glow, as if with its own light, as he slowly registers what is about to happen.

The dagger lances his midriff like a boil.

Moonlight, harsh and glittering, catches the wild whites of his eyes, but at no time does the Reject cry out, not even when the blade thrusts probingly up through his thorax, then slashes rapidly back and forth inside him, shredding the interior of his chest to tatters.

It is over in an instant.

The man in the cloak sighs, satisfied, as the spindly body goes limp in his arms. Why has he killed the Reject? Perhaps compassion, urgent as lust, has suddenly overcome him, compelling him to remove such misery from the world. He draws the blade out cleanly. Efficiently he bunches the beggar's rags over the wound, containing the dark spurtings of blood; then gently he gathers up the frail corpse and carries it, lightly and easily, to the parapet.

The splash is strangely muted on the turgid air.

The man in the cloak hurries on, his boots clicking sharply across the cobblestones. Ahead of him, narrow streets rise steeply upwards towards the Great Temple; behind him, the gold tiral lies, glittering, where it has fallen.

Yes, it is time for The Summoning to begin.

Rajal could not sleep.

How he wished the night had been warm! In high Theron-season they had slept outside, in a stillness perfumed by a thousand fragrances. Then, the river-sound would be only a languid burbling, at one with the creeping of this or that insect, the distant call of an owl, the quiet crumbling of a dying fire. In the cool softness of the grass, he would lie looking up into a brilliant darkness, its immensity alive with winking lights.

Not tonight.

They had moved the vans out of danger at last, further up the sloping ground towards the city walls; the camp now clustered hard against the trees that hid it by day from the Pale Highway and the snaking, raffish curve of Vosper's Loop. The river could not reach them here, but Rajal's heart still thudded hard. Miserably he wrapped himself tighter in his blanket, shifting restlessly from side to side. Above him the rain kept thudding down, beating out its rhythm on a frail ceiling of canvas. How he envied his sister that night, huddled in the Great Mother's warm van! On shelter-nights the boys had to sleep in Zady's wagon, a dingy affair of splintery timbers and prodding nails.

To Zady it was home; in all weathers, curled up on sacking, he slumbered contentedly in his shabby quarters, his breath rising and falling evenly like a dog's. How strange, thought Rajal, that Zady should be a hero. Saviour of the camp, and not for the first time. Was he, perhaps, the one true hero among them? Yet in the morning, the big man would remember nothing, nothing at all that had happened that day. It was terrible, tragic.

Or was it?

Sometimes Rajal found himself wondering whether it would really be so bad to be a Simple. Perhaps it would be better. Much better.

Plunk! A bead of moisture, yet another, detached itself from the clammy canvas and spattered his cheek.

Cold as ice.

Rajal thought of times on the road, in their long journey down from the north, following the route of the Pale Highway. How many times had they lain in hayricks, forests, plains of grass, fields of corn? There was the night, somewhere in the Harion-lands, that they had spent in the branches of a veriol-oak, fearful of the prowling plains-wolf below. There was the night they had spent on the waters of a lake, floating on the flesh of immense lilies. One night they had concealed themselves in a field of sunflowers; in the morning it was like waking in a world gone yellow, with yellow daylight and yellow shadows flickering back and forth as the petals above them shifted on a breeze.

It's like magic, Rajal had said.

It is magic, Nova had replied.

Sadly Rajal looked over to the place where Nova should be. Would he come back? The sunflower-morning had been one of the good times, one of many. But the good times always seemed outweighed by the bad.

Rajal thought again of the fight the day before. He knew it was wrong, but how could he have stopped himself? Nova was a fool, a hot-tempered fool. What happened to Zady at the Vaga-gate had been Nova's fault, there could be no doubt. Yet still the Great Mother said nothing against him, only commanding them to live in bonds of love.

Poor Rajal! Again and again he would say to himself, *I shall love him as my brother.*

How hard it was to do!

But when Nova was gone, Rajal missed him sorely.

Of course we must return to the man in the cloak.

Inside the temple, the dark-garbed murderer moves rapidly through the cavernous nave. There is not much time, yet still he pauses, with an accustomed air, gazing up at the sacred altar. In the Hornlight rays, eerie and chill, glows a vast Circle of Agonis. He stares levelly at the golden, bejewelled symbol, making no obeisance. Then he lifts his eyes to the window above. In the moonlit pallor its splendour is only shadowy, yet still there is a hint of its daytime radiance. The work of Ejland's greatest craftsmen, the vast mosaic of coloured glass depicts the figures of a man and woman, naked and holding hands.

The Lord Agonis.

The Lady Imagenta.

Beside the altar, looming high, is a lectern of carved stone, bearing the burden of a huge El-Orokon. Only in the parchment of the sacred pages have this man and this woman been united like this – it is a scene that has never been real, a scene only foretold. When at last the Lord Agonis

75

finds the lady he has lost, the lady for whom he has been searching, then will come the redemption of this world – so it is believed.

At least, by those of simple faith.

Others speak of the Crystals Five.

A smile comes to the murderer's lips. But this is no smile of superior contempt.

'Imagenta,' he breathes sadly. 'Oh, Imagenta.'

Only now does he make his obeisance, sinking in homage to the sacred lady.

Behind him, the long lines of pews, the mighty pillars, the ancient plaques and effigies stretch away into the darkness. The temple is the largest and most magnificent in all the world – at least, in all the world that Ejland knows. Here lie the tombs of a hundred kings and queens. Here is the place of a hundred royal weddings. Here, for generation upon generation, voices have rung high to the vaulted ceilings in times of lamentation, in times of joy. If the being of a race could be distilled into an essence, that essence is here, embedded in the ancient timbers and stones. If a place can hold, as in a chalice, the promise and meaning of a faith, this temple is that chalice.

Who would dare violate the sanctity of such a place?

The murderer recovers himself. He must hurry, hurry. At the back of the altar, he clicks open a panel in the wainscot. Down winding steps he descends to the temple's deepest vaults. Flaming torches burn against the dank, sinister walls.

Deep in the vaults lies a subterranean chapel. But this is a chapel very different, it is clear, from those to be found in the temple above. Oh, there are pews. An altar. A congregation, too. But who – what? – is worshipped here?

Cowled heads turn towards the new arrival. With a wry look the murderer's eyes flicker over the assembled black-garbed figures.

Ten . . . fifteen . . . twenty . . . twenty-four.

He is the last of the Brotherhood to arrive.

Quickly the murderer dons his cowl and takes his place in a pew at the back.

His name?

But of course, it is the man who calls himself Lord Empster. Lord Mathanias Empster.

That night Cata had a vivid dream.

She was often troubled by dreams. In the dreams, she saw herself in the strangest places, acting sometimes in alarming ways. Many times she would be running through a forest, barefoot and dressed in the flimsiest of rags. Brambles and briars scratched her arms and thighs, but she felt no pain, only a welling joy. Sometimes she dreamed of a petal-strewn bower, where birds, bears and foxes would come to her like friends. In the dream it seemed she could speak to them, and they could speak to her.

Once she dreamed of a mysterious stripy creature, flashing in and out of the undergrowth; then that the creature – a fearsome tiger! – had nuzzled into her arms and she had stroked him, kissed him. For several nights this foolish dream came; then one night the creature was a tiger no more, but a strange boy who lay beside her, naked, a boy more fair than any she had ever seen before. In the dream she caressed him with a passion that shook her, that brought her to choking, gasping sobs.

For a virtuous young lady it was a shaming dream, but when she awoke, Cata's shame subsided swiftly, and she longed only to return to the passionate fantasy.

But sometimes the dreams were frightening, too. Once – no, more than once – Cata had dreamed of an old man who wore a heavy cowl to conceal his head. Through the forest she would run to him, her heart swelling hugely; but when he pulled back his cowl her joy turned to terror, for where the old man's eyes should have been were only seared, empty pits.

But tonight, Cata's dream was different.

Tonight, she dreamed of Pelli Pelligrew.

In the dream she was back in the gauze-carriage, rumbling rapidly through sloshing streets. The wheels made long sibilant splashes and the horses' hooves were unnaturally loud.

Stephel cracked his whip.

Faster.

Then Cata realized: they were chasing the 'Lasher'!

There was a *boom!* of thunder. They plunged through the arch of the city gates. At once the wet valley was upon them, glowing emerald-green in the twilight. Cata took in the high hills above and the rapid running of the river below; she saw the walls of Varby behind them and, ahead, the willows whipping back and forth in the wind. They lurched on to the steep downward slope of Vosper's Loop. Her aunt's face was frantic. Urgently she rapped for Stephel.

Faster, faster.

Cata was thrilled. She leaned dangerously from the window while her aunt, who might have pulled her back, only huddled into herself like a fat black chicken, jogging ridiculously up and down.

Then a squawk: 'Child! Can you see them?'

At first Cata could: there was an impression of Pelli's parasol twirling whitely; then, all at once, the 'Lasher' had vanished.

They could not go on. Thick mud was splattering beneath their wheels. The road was a medium viscous as the clouds, churning, black, ominous. The horses whinnied. The carriage shuddered sharply.

'Stephel?' screeched Umbecca. 'Stephel?'

'Mistress!' The wizened brown face was suddenly at the window, hanging upside down like the muzzle of a bat. 'Mistress, we must turn back . . . turn back . . . turn back!' The voice became a squeal, the words a meaningless chant.

Cata barely heard. Gazing beyond the bat-face, out into the rain, she was watching something – someone. It was a figure by the roadside, a woman, twirling round and round with arms outstretched. The woman's hair was plastered to her skull; a sodden gown cleaved to the orbs of full breasts. Enraptured, the woman held her face up to the sky, her mouth yawning wide as if to drink in the rain. She might have been a vision; she might have been a portent. Moments passed before Cata saw the truth.

The figure was her own.

Distantly she heard her aunt calling her: *Come back, come back.* But she would not – could not. Cata was delirious. Purple-black, the sky churned above her like a maelstrom. Round and round she whirled until her swishing hem, grown heavy with mud, caught between her feet and she slipped and fell. She scrambled up, laughing; she kicked off her shoes. How gloriously the black mud squelched between her toes!

Then came the horseman.

Cata was running; she stopped still. The horseman – at first she thought it was Mr Burgrove, but no, it was a soldier – came struggling through the rain, supporting across his mounted form a heavy human burden. Cata felt her heart, huge in her chest, tolling tolling like an insistent bell. Over the noise of it, and the noise of the storm, she could barely hear the horseman's shouted words:

'There's been an accident—'

Awkwardly the horseman dismounted, sloshing forward, the burden in his arms. Cata only looked on wildly, unable to think or feel. But she knew at once what had happened, of course she did. The figure in the soldier's arms was female, and dressed in a muslin tea-gown.

Blood was flowing over the chestnut hair.

Who is the god the Brotherhood worship? Deep beneath the temple, the secret crypt writhes with the frenzy of an evil chant. Feet stamp the floor. Spittle flies. Hideous echoes boom and boom again.

Lord Empster, like all of them, mouths the words – then shouts them, shrieks them in a desperate mantra.

O mighty one, we await your coming!
Mighty one, consume this world in fire!
Mighty one, sink this world in flood!
Mighty one, swallow this world in mire!
Mighty one, bathe this world in blood!
   One who came as Sassoroch,
   Come to us as TOTH,
   Come back into Being,
   Burning with wrath!
O mighty one, we await your coming!
Mighty one, destroy this world in fire!

On and on it goes – then suddenly it is over.

Standing at the altar, arms outstretched, is a lean, charismatic figure, dressed in white. No, not the god, but the cult's leader – yet he, too, might be some evil divinity. A glare, stronger than the flames of the torches, surrounds the pale form with a mysterious radiance. Hanging behind him is a pair of thick curtains. From time to time the curtains billow, revealing a huge looking-glass. Soon, it is clear, the figure in white shall turn back, tearing the curtains away.

But first he must speak. He flings back his head. His face is a dazzle of brilliant white.

'Brothers,' he cries, 'again we gather here when the moon-lady burns like a beacon in the sky. What is her vigil, what is her pain, but a longing that one day she may welcome again the true god of this rotten world? For what is the moon but a looking-glass child, waiting, waiting, dejected and forlorn? And what are we all but children like her, forsaken and hideous, hanging in the darkness? When the Dying Fool, the Ur-God, set about his creations, striking the Rock of Being and Unbeing, what care had he for the creatures he created? None! What aim had he, but to bring into Being one shaped as he was, blank-faced and smooth-tongued, echoing back his words, as he drifted through the long stupor of his dying? So it was that only Agonis, false Agonis, he took to sit by him in the golden palace. But the Ur-God and his fool son reckoned not with the powers they had rejected! No, they reckoned not with mighty TOTH!'

The leader swings round to face the curtains. By now, the billowing is wild, as if a wind were blowing, deep underground. Urgently, the dark fabric sways, pulses, jerks with the energies that flow from behind the glass.

In the darkness at the back of the chapel, the man who calls himself Lord Empster looks on, astonished, ardent, appalled. For all this ritual has yet to bring – the sacrifices, the screaming, the spurting blood – this is the moment, this moment coming now, that makes his heart hammer the hardest. How many times has he seen it before? It does not matter. Always, he is left burning, eviscerated at the first sight of the anti-god.

Any moment now, any moment now, Toth-Vexrah shall be revealed to them again, crying out from the horror that is the Realm of Unbeing.

The leader cries, 'O mighty one, many times and in many guises you have slipped your way back through the Gates of Being, passionate to resume your place in this world! GREAT ENCHANTER, whose magic destroyed the vile delusions of the Vale of Orok, casting the false Agonis into despair, return now to complete your task! BANISHED OF OROK – you who should have been the GREATEST OF GODS, but instead was the child suffered not even to skulk in your father's vilest corridors – the time draws near when you shall return to us, unleashing all your power! Yes, O FIRST OF REJECTED CREATURES, the Time of Atonement hurries to its close! Come to us, come to your Brothers-in-longing, sweep us into the flames of your cleansing fire! Pray it be soon, O pray it be soon, O mighty, O greatest, O blessed TOTH-VEXRAH!'

With that, the leader tears the curtain away. Acrid smoke billows from the altar. Hideous discords sound on the air. And now, almost bursting from the magic glass, comes the image of a huge and hideous face!

Sobbing, crying out, the Brothers abase themselves. But the god, if god it be, will not be appeased. From the looking-glass, his execrations fall like lashes over the backs of his cowed worshippers.

'Fools, vile fools! Mired in luxury, wallowing like pigs in your sty of sloth, you dare dream of my coming? What care you for my suffering? Have you forgotten that I am imprisoned in Unbeing, locked in this abomination of a form? Have you forgotten that until the Key is found, I can have no release? Where is that Key? Bring it to me, bring it to me!'

The leader cries out, 'Great One, still the Key eludes us! How can it be otherwise, when the Crystal of Koros, flung to the skies by the Father of the Gods, has been lost beyond all power of men to find it? But does prophecy not say the Key shall be revealed to us, that soon, soon, the Key shall come? Even now, so it is foretold, the Child of Destiny has embarked upon his quest! Even now, perhaps, there is one who walks this world who carries with him the Crystal of Koros!'

An agonized shriek almost shatters the glass. 'What care I for your prophecy? What care I for your promises? Are you traitors to my cause? Were you true to me, you would tear this world apart, drain every river, raze every mountain, that you might bring me the Key to the Orokon! If I have but that Key, I can escape this bondage! If I have but that Key, I can assemble the crystals! Then my power shall be limitless and eternal! Then, all creation shall bow before me! Destruction shall rain over all works of Orok and his five vile children! Fools, the Key! Bring me the Key!'

It is always this way: always the anti-god pours forth his wrath, execrating his followers as if they were his enemies. Desperately, the leader tries all in his power to appease the wrath of the enraged god. Prayers, supplications are to no avail. Rapidly the sacrifice is bundled forth.

Bound and gagged, the child is dragged to the altar. It is a small boy, some beggar-urchin snatched from the streets. The white-garbed leader rips off the bonds, then tears away the child's rags, exposing his nakedness. Inferior Brothers, garbed in black, hold the child down as the brutal leader whips forth a dagger from the folds of his robes. Hideous in their terror, hideous in their pain, the shrieks of the child pierce the evil darkness.

With a dazzling flash the blade stabs down, slashing open the tender young flesh. Reeking, steaming, the coiled intestines spill from the ripped abdomen. Glistening kidneys, lungs, a liver, rise in the leader's dripping hands. At last, triumphant, he offers his god the quivering infant heart.

But when the flashing dagger has clattered to the floor, when the leader's robes are crimson and blood runs from the altar, still the face in the glass will not be appeased. There was a time when the anti-god would have rejoiced, at least for a moment, in the evil energies unleashed by the sacrifice, seeing in them a prelude to his own coming reign.

No more. 'Fools! This child is nothing! Is this the Key to the Orokon?'

'Sacred One, it is but a matter of time!'

'Time? I have had enough of time!'

Sobbing, the leader sinks to his knees. 'But only a little, only a little more! Before the seasons have passed another cycle, your return to this dimension is ordained. Destiny is working, even as we speak! But a few moonlives, but a few moonlives more—'

But now the face in the magic glass is shrieking more terribly than the sacrificed child. Wildly it cries that it is dying, that they are killing him, wildly it cries for the one thing it wants:

'Fools, the Key! Bring me the Key to the Orokon!'

Chapter 11

THE REMARKABLE

'Miss Cata! Miss Cata!'

Cata was awake. Nirry's hand was shaking her shoulder and the maid's face loomed above her, furrowed in concern. Cata rubbed her eyes. She was stiff and cold, slumped in an armchair before an ashen grate. Pale sunlight slanted between the curtains and from the square came the pealings of the abbey bells.

'What were you thinking of, sleeping in a chair? Ooh, I should have checked on you! Come, Miss Cata, you'll be late for Canonical!'

That morning Cata dressed as if still in a dream. Her composure was odd. Ever since they had been in Varby, the young miss had bemoaned her abbey-costume. It was ugly, she would say; it was old-fashioned. Other girls were not forced to wear the black canonical-gown, the coal-scuttle bonnet, the golden Circle of Agonis.

Nirry, though she sympathized, could only tut-tut. Besides, the bonnet wasn't really like a coal-scuttle, and wouldn't Miss Pelligrew be wearing one just like it? *Come, Miss Cata,* Nirry would often say, *you're a respectable young lady, and must dress like one – a respectable, demure young lady.*

Cata was often a trial to the maid. Sneakingly, Nirry admired the girl's rebellious spirit, but she tried not to show it. Already the girl would ask the most awkward questions – *Nirry, will you tell me about when I was little?* or, *Nirry, before my illness . . . what was I like?* Ah, what answers Nirry could have given! But no – impossible. *Under no circumstances,* the mistress had boomed, *must the child be reminded of her sordid past! Do you understand me, girl?*

Sometimes Nirry longed to spill out the truth. But the risk was too great. The mistress – fat old cow that she was – would dismiss her if she knew. Then what would become of her? Without references, Nirry would never find respectable work again. No, she must lie. Nirry had a young man in the army, and one day hoped to marry. She must work, keep her reputation, and save for the future.

But her lies left her uneasy. When the wild girl first came to them, the maid had been alarmed. But rapidly she had grown to love the girl, love her as much as she hated her fat, greedy mistress.

Sometimes she dreamed they would run away together.

A dream, of course. Only a dream.

'There, Miss Cata. Ready!'

'Hm? Oh yes, yes.' Like a sleepwalker, Cata clutched her little leather-bound Cantorate. Really, what was wrong with the girl this morning?

Even Umbecca seemed oddly subdued, not at all her imperious, bustling self. They descended the stairs in silence. Outside, a lemony sunlight shone cleanly and the carillon of the abbey-bells filled the morning, swelling and bursting, bursting and swelling. Carriages crowded the square, disgorging quality-folk who bustled in bright lines through the high, gargoyled doors of Varby Abbey. Blankly Cata gazed at a lady in a hoop-dress, at a smiling taffeta-girl, at a Bluejacket with glittering gold epaulettes.

With equal blankness she saw a page-boy in dishevelled livery, stepping towards her as she crossed the square. For a strange, entranced moment the boy stared at her, stared at her directly; then slowly, disappointment overspread his face. Perhaps this boy, too, had been a dreamer, whose dream was now over. In his hand he held a feathered hat that he had removed, as if in ardour, from his head; the ardour over, the hat dropped from his hand, rolling slowly over the gleaming paving-stones.

Cata's face remained blank. At another time, there might have been some stirring, some jarring of memory. Now, though she saw, she did not understand.

What she did not see was the woman in green, standing in a window on the other side of the square. It was the window of Pelli Pelligrew's lodgings, but the woman was not Pelli – or the Widow. The formidable figure focused her gaze upon the boy, as if aware of him, suddenly, obscurely, as a danger.

Her eyes glowed greenly, and the moment ended. All at once came a shout through the crowd – *There he is!* – and the forlorn page, alarmed, took to his heels. Pursuing him were a servant in a tunic of yellow plush and his companion, dressed only in a flapping blanket.

'Really! Such vulgarity!' murmured Umbecca, who had barely glanced at the bedraggled boy.

Only Nirry, lingering in the rear, had seen even a glimmering of the truth. That boy – why, he looked so like Master Jem! It gave her quite a turn.

But of course, poor Master Jem was dead.

On the abbey steps, Cata turned back towards the square. There was no sign of Pelli. On Canondays, Pelli and the Widow would join them on the steps; then they would all go in together. Today only the Widow appeared, her eyes downcast, her face more than usually sour and pinched.

Cata said, 'Where's Pelli?'

There was no answer. The canonical was beginning. Majestically, the thunder of the organ rolled from the open doors as they filed to their pews. Alleluias rose to the vaulted ceiling. Dreamily Cata held her Cantorate aloft. She gazed towards the altar.

> *Praise her! Praise her!*
> *All praise the Lady—*

A memory flooded her. She saw herself in another temple, far far away; she saw herself turning slowly, watching as bearers brought a long gleaming box ever further down the aisle towards her. That was soon after Cata's illness, and much was still vague to her. Inside the box, they said, was the Lady Elabeth, but Cata did not know who this lady might be. She knew only that she was sad, deeply sad.

Now a new sadness possessed her. She turned again, and just before she turned she seemed almost to see another coffin, Pelli's coffin, making its stately progress to the altar. Poor Pelli! It had been a stormy night; the Loop was unsafe. For a moment, until the strange delusion passed, Cata could almost have believed that she had been there, witnessing the tragedy.

There was a commotion at the doors. When she turned, what Cata saw was not a funeral procession. There were murmurs – gasps. Two fine ladies, late for Canonical, were sweeping imperiously down the aisle. One wore luxurious emerald satin and a dark veil, depending from a fantastical hat. In the crook of an arm she held a fluffy white lapdog that would yap from time to time.

The second lady was light where the first was dark, and not, after all, so imperious as she may at first have seemed. Diaphanous in lime-green, shot through with silver threads, she had about her the air of a novice, following imperfectly the pattern of her mistress. In truth, she was a little insipid; yet it was this lady, the younger, who most astonished Cata.

She was not a lady. She was Pelli Pelligrew.

Eldric's Park.

Not all quality-folk were at the Canonday service. In the dripping darkness of the woody-walk, Polty – or rather, Captain Foxbane – drew forth the timepiece from his pocket, his lips twisting impatiently. He smoothed the dark wig, the sleek black moustaches that formed his disguise. What sort of minx was little Miss Quisto, to keep so fine a suitor in suspense? Surely by now she could have slipped away.

Polty felt a troublesome swelling in his breeches. Last night he had dreamed again of Catayane – dear little Catayane, so close and yet so far. Time and again he had thought that 'Foys Foxbane' might insinuate himself into the girl's company, but it was difficult, too difficult – dangerous, too. Oh, but how he longed for his dear heart-sister! After Waxwell had performed his dark magic, Polty had thought the girl would be wholly his. With past outrages wiped clean from her mind, how could she doubt he was her virtuous brother? Fondly he imagined how lightly he would lead her – *Come, sister, come . . . come through the labyrinth* – to a new and delicious consummation.

It had all come to nothing. How he cursed that fat old cow Umbecca! What madness was it, to turn the wild girl into a society-lady? Sometimes Polty could have laughed himself sick, thinking about his heart-mother's delusions. How she would blanch, blanch and moan, if she knew the truth about her sweet little innocent! Sometimes he longed to tell her everything, to watch the fat face redden and burst as she learnt how, time and again through a long season, her virtuous heart-son – a novice, then, in the ways of love – had repaired to a little room above the Lazy Tiger, where good old Wynda Throsh kept her finest child-whore.

Of course, he had not known at first that 'Dolly' – so Wynda called her – was in truth none other than Wolveron's spawn, the little half-Vaga who used to run round the village, barefoot and in rags. They used to throw stones at her. She crawled with lice and fleas. Her nose ran with snot. But when he knew the truth, Polty knew something else, too. He knew it didn't matter. He knew he didn't care. His lust was only harder, harder and fiercer.

After they sent the girl away, Polty wanted only to escape from Irion. In the end it was easy; the transfer came through and in a matter of moonlives his old life might have been chaff in the wind, blown away behind him. He would forget his heart-sister; for after all, as he had urged to Bean, the world was full of girls, many much sweeter, the willing, and – yes, especially delightful! – the not-quite-willing that a man must conquer.

But seeing his heart-sister again in Varby, Polty had felt waves of new and more urgent lust. It was not that he lacked for conquests. By now, he had tasted every joy the fair sex could provide. And yet – Polty could barely admit it to himself – had he ever found a girl he wanted as much as his dear, dear sister? But how was he to have her? Outright rape, yes – but that was never Polty's way.

So he told himself as he awaited Jilda.

He sighed. He paced. He lit a tobarillo.

And as he walked across the green
The rays of love were brightly seen

Soaring high
In flaming dye
Into the forehead of the sky—

Massed voices rose ringingly to the vaulted ceiling, borne aloft on the swellings of the pipe-organ. Cata's cheeks burned. Jammed tight against Pelli's glittering gown, it was as much as she could do to open and shut her mouth, as if in obedience to the surging melody. Twice she almost dropped her Cantorate to the floor.

There was a nudge in her ribs. 'Catty! I told you Aunt Vlada was coming, didn't I?'

For some moments, pretending to a sacred rapture, Cata could ignore the eager whisper. Then canticles were over and Pelli's little-girl voice was squealing excitedly, 'Oh, Aunt Vlada, this is my best, my very best friend . . .'

'Miss Veeldrop? Charmed, charmed . . . my little niece has told me *everything* about you.'

The elegant woman had not raised her veil, but the voice that drifted from the gauzy shadows was kind. In a daze Cata felt the pressure of a soft, gloved hand; then in the next moment the party were seated and the Doma of Varby was gazing down over the assembled ranks, intoning the day's text from a huge El-Orokon, tethered to the lectern by a golden chain.

'. . . Then the long Theron-days give way more easily, ever more easily, to the conquest of the dark. A chill, creeping stealthily, has come upon the air, and we know once again that a time when we have lived, a time when we have loved has passed and gone by . . .'

It was the Equinox Lesson, from the Book of the Five Seasons. But Cata heard little. Her mind was reeling. The Doma, becoming expansive, spoke of falling leaves and gathering winds and the rustling footsteps of the goddess Javander. Cata could think only of Pelli Pelligrew – and the exotic creature who sat beside her.

Yap! went the lapdog.

'Ring, *shh*.' There was a sound of kissing.

Dimly Cata recalled Pelli mentioning an aunt. But Aunt Vlada was hardly what she had expected. Cata ached with envy. Gone was the tenderness of moments before, when, like a fool, she had thought Pelli was dead.

'. . . And again we are standing as at a crossroads, and it is a crossroads where we have been before. Whither shall we wander?' the Doma asked. 'But we know, as we knew before, that there is but one way. At this dying of the season, let us look to our own dying, and the virtue which

86

alone shall sustain us as we totter, our steps ever-faltering, towards the judgement which, we pray, shall not be visited too heavily upon us . . .'

A snort came: 'Stuff and nonsense!'

It was Aunt Vlada. The protest was a soft one, a mere gust of breath; the Doma, high above, could not possibly have heard. That did not matter: Cata was amazed. To mock the Canonical! Her own aunt, glowering blackly beside her, had always insisted on full, rapt attention. At Mistress Quick's there had been heavy penalties for girls who whispered, girls who smirked, girls who turned their eyes from the altar.

'At last!' cried Aunt Vlada, as they rose for Litanies. 'The fellow does *go on*, doesn't he?'

Only the renewed surge of the organ disguised her words from the pews behind. Trembling, Cata tried to fix her eyes ahead, but turned almost against her will towards Pelli's aunt. Beneath the veil she glimpsed curiously bright eyes, bright as gems, and saw with a start that they were gazing back at her.

Aunt Vlada leaned across her silvery niece. 'Dear Miss Veeldrop, I'm positively parched – and poor Ring . . . You'll join us in the Pump Room, when this *stuff and nonsense* is over?'

There are false gods and true gods, but which are which, not all shall agree. Polty had no doubt which god was the truest. It was a secret god, a god called Penge.

He had not always known that Penge was a god. At first he thought of Penge as a general, intrepid in war; then he decided that, no, Penge was a king – did he not wear a glistening crown? Now, in Polty's fond contemplation, Penge was endowed with all power to create and destroy. He had to be a god.

There had been a time when Penge barely existed. Before the magic, if magic it had been, that made him into the man he was now, the part Polty called Penge had been very different. In those days, Polty's entire body hung heavy with swathes of dough-like flesh, yet Penge – Penge, as he was now – was nowhere to be seen. Beneath the pendulous whiteness of his belly, between the swollen mounds of his thighs, Polty had possessed only the merest shrivelled nub. But when the great change had overtaken him, when the dough-like flesh grew lean and hard, it was rather as if some prodigal fate had decreed that Polty should yet possess one place, one part of his person, consecrated to fleshly excess.

Polty flung down his tobarillo. By now, his secret god was throbbing, throbbing hard. Where was Jilda – where was she, damn her? Had he not told her that Captain Foxbane was bound for Zenzau with his regiment, leaving as soon as the Equinox had passed? There would be no more furtive meetings like this. Yet still to keep him hanging here! Why, Penge would be merciless if the girl came now! There would be no concessions for virgin delicacies – no patient nuzzlings, no concerned enquiries. By the time Penge was through with Miss Jilda, the royal surgeons would swear on their hearts that the child had lost her innocence long, long ago.

Furtively Polty drew back deeper into the dank, dripping shadows of the woody-walk. The madness was upon him. With rough, impatient hands he tore open his breeches. How boldly Penge sprang forth!

Carefully he slid a hand over the veiny vastness, permitting himself just one, just one little shudder of pleasure – no more. This was Polty's code: deeply thankful for the blessing Penge had been, he had vowed never to squander his gift. Would Penge go unaccommodated, like a poor wayfarer, laying down his burden in the trees and grass? Were Penge a god, would this not be blasphemy?

But now there comes a rustling in the coppery leaves that strew the long avenues of the woody-walk. Now there comes a susurrus of whip-whipping skirts, of rapid little feet in spangly pumps; then an eager little breathy cry, *Captain, my Captain? Captain, are you here?*

What happens next will be Cata's fault, all Cata's fault – so Polty tells himself. All night Penge has ached for her; by now, his lust is boiling. It will not be denied. Little Jilda is a second, a poor second.

But she will just have to do.

'Come, my darlings!' The last chord of the anthem had barely died away when Aunt Vlada burst into the aisle like an imperious great ship, surging on the tide. Eagerly she tugged at the two young girls. Splendidly the trio filled the aisle, their long dresses trailing, catching, trailing.

Umbecca cried, 'Lady Vlada, I don't think—'

'Servants. So tedious,' Aunt Vlada whispered, loudly this time, and Cata, delighted, could barely restrain a little, wild whinny. Her heart exulted. Just when she had been about to mind, and mind bitterly, about her dull, pious costume, suddenly Cata did not care at all. Aunt Vlada's arm was linked in hers. Every eye in the abbey was upon them. Upholstered matrons, taffeta-girls, Bluejackets and their fine erect ladies all hung back, startled, letting them pass.

'Lady Vlada! I am not a servant! Really, Lady Vlada—'

But even Umbecca was powerless against the mysterious woman in green.

At the altar, the Doma turned with pursed lips to his young Cantor Lector, observing dryly, 'The remarkable Vlada Flay.'

'Your worship?'

The lips smacked together. 'My boy, really! You have not heard of the great courtesan? The Zenzau-blood who scandalized all Agondon, two gens ago? They married her off to some colonial in the end. *Shh*-money, if ever ... In any event, one thought The Remarkable had been safely consigned to the colonies! Now, one gathers, she is widowed, and returned to her old haunts.'

The Cantor Lector's eyes were wide as he gazed after the courtesan. 'A widow, your worship? But where are her weeds?'

The elderly Doma could only laugh, in his best imitation of a man of the world. With friendly condescension he squeezed his young colleague's arm.

'Weeds? You forget, my boy, we are speaking of the *remarkable* Vlada Flay!'

In the aisle below, Umbecca was staggering, clutching at her breast. Rage reddened her face, but her strength was gone – sapped away, as if by some swift, sharp spell.

O glorious Penge!

Turning, Polty is ready for the fair sacrifice. His leer he swiftly replaces with a smile; Penge he drapes – merely drapes – in a flap of blue jacket. With a finer lady, a lady of any consequence, one might trouble to conceal Penge more, cramping him hastily into the darkness where he must hide; but today, Penge will tolerate no such indignity, and little Jilda, for all her airs, is only the child of a rich tailor. No, such precaution would be otiose; on Canonday morning, no curious eye roves through these deserted walks; no staying hand will intervene to save the virtue that in moments shall be lost.

Jilda, my Jilda! A honeyed call; then quickly, urgently, Captain Foys Foxbane folds the innocent child into his arms. Hotly, brutally, he smothers the sweet mouth, crushing the tender little petal with his kisses; in moments, when he pushes the child to the ground, a firm hand shall contain the screams that would burst so breathily from the fluttering lungs.

Fool, little fool, to slip away, repairing to a gentleman alone and in secret! Ah, Polty knows these minxes right enough. On the morning before he is to leave Varby, she comes to him for a tender moment, an exchange of fine sentiments, a promise to write; filled with proud thoughts of her feminine charms, does she not think of him – *my Captain*, indeed! – as some love-struck fool, fluttering after the lace at the hem of her gown? What would she offer him – butterfly kisses, the twining of fingers? Fool, giddy fool, to toy with his heart, thinking she can evade the tax she has incurred!

Jilda struggles. Pushing up her skirts, Polty exults in the victory to come. First his sharp fingers feel the way, forcing open the chasm of Penge's glory.

O dauntless Penge! O Penge the lion-hearted!

Soon, too soon, it shall all be over, and little Jilda's pride shall be humbled in the dirt.

In the moment of conquest – for of course, it comes – could not a man almost laugh aloud, at the follies of these girls, these feeble-minded children? How droll, that they should primp and preen at their charms, fussing and fretting over a length of muslin, a lacy front, the spangly beads on a little shoe! Then, what of their pathetic accomplishments – their litanies, their samplers, the inept little pieces they would tinkle on the harpsichord, to goad polite applause from a drowsy drawing-room? Their jealousies, their rivalries, their pratings of love? What did it all come to in the end, all this costly panoply of vanities – what did it mean, when all a man wanted was to rip his way through these gauzy webs, forcing his way to the one thing, the one part of a woman that had any value?

Thus were Polty's thoughts as he took his pleasure.

O Penge the Valiant! O Penge the True!

The great plumed ship that was *The Remarkable* sailed back triumphantly through the gargoyled doors. In the portico, Aunt Vlada released her two young charges and swelled forward, gliding down the many steps. She turned back, lifting her veil, to look up at the girls. She might have been an artist, contemplating a picture. Behind her, sunshine sparkled in the puddles of the square.

'But of course, you are lovers. I could see it at once!'

'L-lovers?' Cata stammered.

'Ah, the bliss of girlhood! Miss Veeldrop, not a word – no, no words are needed!' Aunt Vlada held up a restraining hand. 'What is a word? A leaf on the wind! Can mere words add to the pictures painted (such charming watercolours!) in the sketchbook of my mind? Pellicent, darling, take your friend's hand. You must walk together.'

The girls complied awkwardly. As they made their way down the steep steps, Aunt Vlada turned from them and strode across the square, expatiating to the sky with a gesturing glove, 'I see you, my darlings, on your half-holidays, taking long rambling walks in sun-speckled woods, brushing against wildflowers and fronds of ferns! I see you on chill Koros-evenings, huddled together in your dormitory-room, toasting mushrooms at your little fire. Such innocent pleasures!'

She turned back suddenly. 'Yet ah, how you have chafed in the Bondage of Uly!'

Cata gulped. Uly? What could it mean?

Expectantly she gazed at Aunt Vlada, but Aunt Vlada only let out a high, horsy laugh. 'Come, my darlings! Let us be first in the Pump Room! It's good luck, don't you know?'

Now it is over.

Polty sighs deeply. It has cost him little effort; if force was necessary, it was nothing untoward. But alas, he fears that Penge is not pleased. He quizzes him a little – tries to reason with him. *True, Penge, this was not the sister you wanted; but have we not redeemed our loss, just a little, in the sweet theft of* this *child's innocence?* But why does Polty even ask these questions? Chaff, merest chaff. Will Penge be beguiled? He has been given ease for a time, that is all.

Another, and another must fall, soon enough!

Polty rolls off the ruined girl. Sadly he wipes Penge on a skein of petticoat, before returning him to his warm home. An immense boredom and contempt fills him. On another day, he might tend to the girl – say something, do something, to end her sobs. He would plead that his passions had overcome him, that never before had he let himself be so carried away. Should she turn on him, he would be quick to anger, berating the fatal beauty that had brought them both to ruin; if her sorrow would not end, he would sorrow beside her, mingling his tears with hers as he stammered forth regrets, vows – vague talk, that the little fool would construe as a promise of marriage.

Afterwards he would never see her again, or if he did, would pretend not to know her.

There was no time for these niceties today. The minx had been late, and he must repair to the Pump Room. He needed time to don his next disguise. With a contemptuous snort Polty departed, looking behind him only to fling down a few worthless coins. Should someone find her, they would constitute evidence – evidence, that is, that the girl was a whore.

Coppery leaves fell from the branches and fluttered down slowly over the moaning, bleeding girl.

Chapter 12

THREE SISTERS

Only when looked at from a certain angle is the Square of the Lady dominated by the façade of Varby Abbey. Turn your back on the abbey and its dark arched windows, its spired towers, and you will see instead a temple of another kind: the cool, spare, high-columned edifice of the Pump Room. This, not the abbey, is the heart of the fashionable town, the true source, the fountainhead of all its pleasures. If the rituals of the Canonday disrupt these delights, they do so only briefly. Soon the elegant halls will be thronged again with the fashionable – and the rather less so – come to partake of the Varby waters.

Aunt Vlada tossed back her head, draining her glass in one smooth, silent motion. Fascinated, Cata watched the rippling throat. Aunt Vlada's neck, like the face beneath her veil, was surprisingly soft for a woman of her years. How many years, Cata did not know, but suspected they were more than one might think.

'Boy!' Aunt Vlada snapped her fingers and a footman in magnificent livery rushed to fill her glass again.

'Catty, isn't it marvellous?' came Pelli's voice.

All around them was a hubbub of life. They had descended to the hall called the Lower Promenade. Unceasingly, laughter and raised voices rebounded from the marble of the walls and floor. All society was there: and if there were bath-chairs and walking-canes, if there were wooden noses and withered cheeks, plastered thick with paint, so too there were the most fetching exhibits of humanity the spa-town could afford. *This* lady's blush was no product of powder; *that* gentlemen's calf, curving in its stocking, was muscle, not wood!

Reclining on a curving, many-buttoned sofa, Aunt Vlada's little party could smile happily at passers-by; but look down, too, over an elegant balustrade to the sunken, almost boiling bath just below them, where folk in simpler garb were intent on a different 'Varby cure'. It was only the first of a chain of baths, part of an immense subterranean complex.

'Catty, look,' said Pelli eagerly. The girl, it seemed, held something in her hand, nursing it secretly so that no one else could see.

She was excited, but Cata did not look.

Aunt Vlada smiled, half-listening to murmurings nearby:

'I say, fine creature, what?'

'The Remarkable? Or do you mean the doggikins?'

'The new young creature. Pert little thing in the black canonicals—'

'My dear! A mere academy-girl. Quite Unentered—'

'Unentered? But is that not the charm?'

'Hm. Indeed. Yes, indeed.'

They sounded like actors in a bad comedy. The speakers, powdered and primped and squeezed into the finest silk and lace, were a pair of old bucks from the time of the Regent Queen. The first wore a wig of excessive height, that teetered alarmingly on his trembling head; his companion stared, blinking wetly, through the glass of a thick lorgnette that with each remark he would flick, like a reproving fan, at his friend.

'A girl's Entrance! How one should like, just once more, to—'

'Your condition, my dear. Think of your condition.'

The reply was a glugging of Varby-water.

'Catty, you're not looking,' Pelli hissed. She nudged her friend and huddled close. Her hand, first clasped at her breast, sank into her lap and she opened her fingers. Black-red spheres, plump and glowing darkly, lay in her palm like a bunch of cherries. Cata drew in her breath. What Pelli held was a necklace, a magnificent ruby necklace.

Pelli giggled, 'Aunt's so kind.'

'Put your baubles away, Pellicent – hm? You aren't at the Equinox Ball yet, reeling in Mr Burgrove's arms!' Aunt Vlada laughed, a high, unexpected laugh that lasted a little too long, until she broke off with a snap and added, 'Ah, if *Uly* could see you girls now!'

Cata's brow furrowed.

'Dear me, Miss Veeldrop, but I have made you curious! But surely, Pellicent, you have told Miss Veeldrop about *Uly*?'

Cata coloured, but she was not sure why. She looked back and forth between Pelli and Aunt Vlada. Then she looked only at Aunt Vlada, staring into the emerald eyes. For a moment it seemed as if the bustling room around her had faded, stilled. She was alone with Aunt Vlada and the gentle, clear voice was washing over her like soft rain.

THE STORY OF ULY

'There were three of us,' Aunt Vlada said. 'Uly, Marly, and me. Often I think of us, as we were then. I see us in the schoolroom on long lemony mornings, yawning as the light slanted over our copybooks. I imagine us, innocent in our white muslin, gauzy and dappled as we wandered in the woods above my uncle's house. Through trees we looked down at the house below, laughing at how small it seemed . . .'

Aunt Vlada paused – perhaps blinked away a tear.

'Your lovely sisters!' Cata said dreamily. 'How I should like to have a sister!'

The story of Uly would proceed no further.

Not now.

'*Sisters?*' A harshness entered Aunt Vlada's voice. 'You are unaware, Miss Veeldrop, of my origins? Or do you seek merely to be provoking?'

Cata was confused. In that moment she would have looked again, questioningly, into Aunt Vlada's eyes, but instead felt her gaze diverted by the intent stare of the fluffy little lapdog. A sense of strangeness possessed her, a strangeness and a chill, creeping fear. She snapped her attention away from Ring. What was happening?

It was as if the dog could see inside her mind.

'Aunt Vlada?' she whispered.

But only a laugh came in response. Swiftly, like a woman many years her junior, Aunt Vlada gathered up the mysterious Ring, and sprang up impatiently from the many-buttoned sofa.

'Darlings, come – let us promenade,' she cried, swivelling fragrantly into the steaming hall just at the moment when a new voice accosted her:

'Lady Vlada? But no, it is a vision!'

A cloth-of-gold cravat burgeoned before them, serving up, as if on a platter, the handsome head of that debonair, if rather *louche* young man-about-town, Mr 'Jac' Burgrove. In 'fast' fashion, he wore his own hair, which was thick and curly. A splendid pair of whiskers, shaped like mutton-chops, offset the fellow's immaculate ears.

Aunt Vlada smiled coolly, extending a gloved hand. Mr Burgrove pressed the fabric to his lips, then rose again, offering the same honeyed gallantry to the lady's young companions.

'Like sisters,' he whispered, 'three beautiful sisters.'

Cata suppressed a rush of embarrassment. Pelli, bright pink, squirmed with delight.

Aunt Vlada began to walk.

Swish, swish.

'We failed to see you at the Canonical, Mr Burgrove?'

'My lady, you shame me!' (Mr Burgrove showed no shame.) 'But would you have me bestir myself from dreams of your beauty?'

'Ho, Mr Burgrove!' The gem-like eyes glinted. 'And would you spend, upon a woman stricken in years, that which should be saved for one somewhat younger?'

'Stricken in years?'

'*Old*, Mr Burgrove!'

'I see no old woman here – Miss Veeldrop, do you?'

It was, perhaps, an unfortunate moment. To one side, a pair of shrivelled crones, their faces thickly plastered, hobbled up and down in pathetic finery; to the other, a wheezing dowager and her rickety accomplice tottered, relieved, to the vacated sofa. For every handsome girl, there were two – three, four – broken-down widows, decrepit spinsters; there were tribes of companions and black-garbed Duennas, woman after woman, old, old, old.

Elderly sufferers from many diseases boiled like lobsters in the baths below.

Cata suppressed a laugh; but then, at that moment she did not know that somewhere in the Pump Room a particular *old woman*, her strength returned in force after her nasty turn, had pushed her way past an obstructive porter and was blundering back and forth indignantly through the crowd.

Buzz, buzz, blunder, blunder, like a huge, bloated, black fly.

Poor Cata! The Umbecca-fly would settle on her soon.

Pelli was saying, 'Oh, how I long for the Last Reel!'

'Miss Pelligrew, you startle me. You would wish the ball away?'

Pelli giggled, 'Mr Burgrove, no! But when they open the shutters, when dawn floods the hall—'

Aunt Vlada gave Cata a wink. 'Spattered candle-wax? Exhausted dancers? The pallor of painted faces in the light?'

Pelli was oblivious. 'I shall struggle, Mr Burgrove, to contain my emotion—'

'I shall struggle, Miss Pelligrew, to contain *mine*.'

'Admirable, Mr Burgrove,' declared Aunt Vlada. 'Wit is the first requirement in a man, would you not say? Well, perhaps the *second . . .*'

Cata might have laughed, but instead lurched, sickened. At the Equinox Ball, when the Last Reel ended, it was customary that a gentleman-dancer might petition for the hand of his lady partner. How many marriages had thus been made? Lurid as life, she saw Pelli, her neck circled redly by rubies, her programme filled with Mr Burgrove's name.

And shortly that name would be Pelli's, too.

'Oh, Catty, I can't believe it's nearly upon us! Can you believe it? Can you wait?' Pelli, clutching her rubies again, grabbed Cata's wrist and gave a little jump.

Cata thought, *You bitch!*

But she only smiled sadly, 'Alas, I apprehend—'

'Apprehend nothing, dear Miss Veeldrop!' Depositing her dog on a startled Mr Burgrove, Aunt Vlada swished forward. First she withdrew Cata from her niece's grasp, then linked her arm in the black-garbed girl's, swinging her round to face their companions.

Others, the decrepit and desirable alike, looked on, intrigued, at the display that followed.

Cata barely saw them. She could only stare at Aunt Vlada's glove, gesturing slowly before her eyes; though there were murmurs from those who watched, even the odd exclamation, Cata heard only Aunt Vlada's voice.

'Miss Veeldrop, I see you freed of this garb of girlhood, stripped of these habiliments of humiliation—'

'I say,' said Mr Burgrove, blinking, shifting the squirming burden of Ring.

'For too long, you have lived in a cell, dank and dark, gazing through the bars at the brightness, the life, the lushness of the world beyond your window—' The voice, like steam, seemed to hiss in Cata's ears; yet Aunt Vlada's words were loud, like lines declaimed from a brightly lit stage.

'Aunt!' Pelli hissed. 'You're embarrassing me!'

Her aunt, evidently, did not care. 'The Bondage of Uly is over, Miss Veeldrop—'

Uly! Was the word a magic charm? The chain round Cata's neck gave way suddenly. She gasped, clutching at her Circle of Agonis, just as it was about to clatter to the floor. Gently Aunt Vlada took it from her hands, spiriting the symbol of piety away.

'Gold! Yes, Miss Veeldrop, but at the Equinox Ball I see you instead in a golden *coronet*—'

Swiftly she tugged at Cata's bonnet-strings. The bonnet fell away like a discarded shell, releasing a cascade of dark tumbling hair.

Swish, swish, went Aunt Vlada. Ardently she scooped up the tresses, heaping them high, her fingers splayed upwards like the stars of a crown.

'Aunt! What are you doing?' Pelli clung to her rubies like a charm, desperately wishing the scene to end.

It only got worse.

The tresses tumbled again; now the golden gloves ran over the black dress. In a moment the bodice was unbuttoned, peeled back to expose a radiant whiteness.

There were gasps – a wail from Pelli.

TEETERING WIG: By the blessed Lord Agonis! Let me bury my
    head in those orbs—
LORGNETTE (*alarmed*): Your condition, my dear!
TEETERING WIG: Bugger my condition. That girl is a vision!

And she was.

Aunt Vlada's glove darted like a glittering serpent, striking at Mr Burgrove's neck. Like a trophy, she plucked off the cloth-of-gold cravat.

In an instant the cloth was waving over Cata – here, there, here, there – billowing like a sail before her bodice, her hem, like some magic garment that flickered first in, then out, of existence.

In, out.

Here, there.

'. . . A gown that glitters in the candlelight like stars and faces down the sun when the dawn breaks at last. A gown that is the envy of all who see it, and elevates its owner to the pinnacle of beauty. Such a gown shall be yours, Miss Veeldrop. Child, fear not. You shall come to the ball. And you shall be the *belle*—'

'Aunt Vlada,' Pelli was almost sobbing, 'Oh, Aunt Vlada!'

Her protest was lost.

Eagerly the watchers broke into applause. There were calls of *Hear, hear!* and *Well done, what!* All eyes were upon Cata. It was as if at that moment she were really dressed in the golden gown. None – certainly not Aunt Vlada – had a thought for Pelli, nor for Mr Burgrove, naked-necked with Ring squirming awkwardly in his arms.

The applause stopped suddenly.

'Catayane!'

The cry was like a thunderclap. Enraged, Umbecca burst through the crowd like a spirit of vengeance, unleashed from The Vast. There were nervous titters, anguished wails. The vision in gold was suddenly gone, and Cata was once again an Unentered girl, standing in the Pump Room with her breasts exposed.

Umbecca grabbed her.

So did Aunt Vlada.

There was pulling. Tugging. A *rrr-ip!* of fabric.

'Give me my girl, you Zenzan harlot!'

Aunt Vlada laughed. To her it was a game, a hilarious game.

'She's a good girl! A moral girl,' Umbecca gasped, imploring the help of all who stood by. Some turned away, others only watched. Harassed footmen intervened in vain.

LORGNETTE (*urgently*): Shouldn't one *do* something?
TEETERING WIG: Watch, my friend! Watch and enjoy! Mm, just
        look at those bouncing orbs!

Ring, too, was enthralled by the fray. Yapping furiously, the little dog struggled harder to free himself from Mr Burgrove.

'Keep still, you little beggar—'

'Oh Jac, the shame!' A weeping Pelli collapsed against his shoulder.

'Damn!' He staggered, and Ring scrambled free.

Now it happened that Ring was the smallest of dogs, the smallest of dogs and one of the frailest. But all dogs, even lapdogs, were once wild wolves. Ring's bones were brittle as a chicken's, but he was fearless – he was fierce. And his little teeth were razor-sharp.

'Ring! Ring!' Mr Burgrove was on his knees.

Here and there, hither and yon, Ring scurried through a dangerous forest. There were gleaming shoe-buckles, white-stockinged calves, hemlines billowing back and forth. At any moment a foot would shift; then would come a yelp and a crunch of bone.

'Ring! Ring!'

But his fate was decided. Before him swayed the hem of a certain lady's gown; and though the gown, it was true, was the drabbest in the vicinity, Ring hardly cared. Disclosed in the billowing was the most succulent ankle he had ever seen. So fat! So juicy!

Ring charged.

It was the work of an instant. Perhaps Ring had been seeking more than merely a meal. Perhaps, like a gallant knight, he had sought to serve his mistress. If this were so, his plan went awry. Sure enough, his little teeth sank in like a snakebite – Umbecca screamed.

But as she screamed, she staggered back.

There was a piteous howl; startled, Aunt Vlada let go of Cata's arm.

It was the fatal moment. Pelli, in her despair, had been torturing her necklace, twisting it this way and that in her hands; suddenly the chain snapped. Red rubies spilled to the floor and rolled in all directions, just as Cata cannoned back into the wailing form of Umbecca.

Winded, Umbecca felt herself toppling, and in turn could only clutch her young ward tighter. Locked together, skidding on rubies, they collided into the two old bucks who had watched them so intently. Desperately, LORGNETTE struggled to right himself, but a ruby – just one – rolled beneath his shoes.

Cries rang out as the bucks – LORGNETTE, TEETERING WIG and all – fell into the bath with a mighty splash, Cata and Umbecca tumbling after them.

Chapter 13

HOLLUCH-HAWS

'Squelch, squelch! Squelch, squelch!' Myla cried happily, stomping up the slope of the soggy hillside.

'Sister, wait!' Rajal laughed. The girl was so eager; but then, she had not spent most of the night struggling with frightened horses in the rain!

They were out on a mission. Before they left for Agondon, the Great Mother wanted certain berries that grew only in the Holluch hills. Rajal kept his gaze upwards, looking to the place where the valley's green pastures gave way to woody uplands. Watery sunlight sluiced through the clouds and arcing over the trees was a vivid rainbow. A splendid sight – but still Rajal's steps were a little leaden, and so was his heart.

Where was Nova?

And why did he care?

'Come on, slow-carriage!' Myla called, and she looked so happy that her brother's spirits lifted. There was nothing Myla liked better than a berry-mission, and it looked as though her brightly-coloured bird agreed. Eo sailed after her in big looping circles, from time to time descending and prodding muddily into this or that clump of weeds or crumbly mole-hole, or capering playfully about Myla's feet. Then, delighted with each other, the girl and the bird would dance, hopping absurdly, left-foot, right-foot, until the bird in his exuberance spread his wings wide, soaring again like a rogue scrap of rainbow.

Rajal had to laugh. How he loved his little sister!

'Wait!' he called again, struggling up the hill. On the brink of the woods, catching his breath, he turned and looked back over the wet valley. On the rise below them, the town of Varby lay fast within its walls. Sonorously on the air came the Canonday bells; but tonight, Rajal knew, was Equinox night. There would be no rest in the spa-town today, and little prayer. Carriages, delayed perhaps by the wild weather, rumbled purposefully towards the city-gates; at the cargo-doors at the back of the city, a long line of traders' carts was banked up, waiting.

There was also something strange. Weaving out suddenly from the line of carts came a figure in bright livery, running, a cape billowing out behind him like a sail. Traders looked on curiously, then turned away, shaking their heads, as the figure first skittered some lengths along the cargo-path, then cast himself down on the wet hillside, breathless and laughing. What a way for a page-boy to behave! But ah, who knew what they did in Varby?

Suddenly Rajal was scrambling back downhill.

'Nova!'

'Hello, Raj. I gave them the slip.' The voice seemed carefree and Nova's blue eyes gazed up cheerfully at the Vaga-boy who stood over him, outraged, arms akimbo.

'Gave who the slip?' hissed Rajal, yanking his friend up roughly from the ground. Swiftly he pulled him out of earshot of the traders. 'Your face is all white again! And what are you doing in that costume? That's the Prince of Chayn's livery, isn't it?'

Rajal had the unsettling thought that he was speaking to someone who was slightly mad. Something had happened to Nova, something upsetting. But all he said was, 'Raj! Have you been studying to be a coachman, too?'

'I don't know what you're talking about. Come on, we're looking for Holluch-haws. Come with us, hm? You'll only get in more trouble if I let you go now.'

'Good apothecary, what shall become of her?'

The fashionable druggist was a plump little man in a powdered periwig, of a style rather too gentlemanly for a man in trade. He had turned away and was snapping shut the lock of his smart bag when Umbecca reached forward, grabbing his sleeve. He turned back with a professional smile.

Wrapped in thick rugs, the fat woman had sunk deeply in an armchair by the fire, a leg propped on a footstool, revealing an ankle swathed in bandages.

'Now, my lady, I think it is more a matter of what shall become of *you*. Your young ward is a girl in her prime. Yours, I am afraid, is the more precarious constitution. Exertion such as you have exhibited this morning can do untold damage to the radical heat – its flow, its fluidity, its fluctuations. To say nothing of the radical moisture. Rest, good lady, and swallow your medicine. All shall be well by Canonday next if only you rest, rest . . .'

'Canonday? But we must leave Varby! We must leave at once! Oh, my poor, poor girl!'

The apothecary offered up an urbane laugh, as if in response to a joke that was not funny, but which politeness obliged him to appreciate. In like manner he addressed Umbecca as 'my lady' or 'good lady'; of course, the woman was nobody – the wife of some provincial administrator, no more – but the apothecary had learnt it was as well to treat his patients according to their pretensions, as opposed to their actual place. It did wonders for trade. Besides, Madam Veeldrop was ambitious – very ambitious.

He knew her game. Pretending to a strict morality, she kept the girl on the tightest leash. All through the length of the Varby Season, no fellow was permitted more than a sniff of her. The girl would chafe, the fellows howl. But by Season's end, the indulged young misses, let loose from the strings of liberal guardians, would be looking a little shabby, a little faded already. At 'First Moonlife', when the girls made their Entrances, what fellow would want to give them so much as a look? Then came Madam Veeldrop, dangling fresh bait. In a moonlife – less! – the marriage-settlement would be secured, and a fat one, too. Why, perhaps as fat as Madam Veeldrop!

Now she was terrified that a single morning had destroyed the work of a full Varby Season.

The apothecary permitted himself just a hint of irony. 'Lady, you would leave now? On the brink of Equinox? Oh, barbarous!' With an expansive hand he gestured to the window, where sunlight filtered palely through the gauze. 'Tomorrow the darkness over Eldric's Park shall explode into a million stars. Brightly coloured figures in masks of silver shall pirouette and prance like spirits unchained, turning all in their midst to magic. Oh my lady, it shall be an enchanted night! Would you not look from your window, at the least?'

To Cata, standing by the window in question, the apothecary's words were sweet music. She turned back towards him, eyes aglow. For a moment, it seemed, she forgot the shame that had consumed her since her departure from the Pump Room. For a moment, perhaps, she imagined that she might really go to the ball.

Umbecca was unswayed. Sedated heavily, her mind already muzzy, she struggled nonetheless to wail out her protest. 'Good apothecary, you know not the shame that has descended like a shroud over my young charge! Oh, that wicked harlot, Vlada Flay . . .'

There was more in this vein, much more, until the fat woman trailed off at last. Kindly the apothecary patted her hand, and droned what he imagined were comforting words.

'. . . Now, as I say, rest is vital if the humours are to regain their proper balance. Oh, and a very *sparing* diet. I shall instruct your maid to prepare you a thin gruel for luncheon; for supper, a boiled egg and a slice of dry toast . . .'

Umbecca moaned piteously before she passed out.

Cata laughed.

The apothecary turned to her sharply, wryly. The girl was dressed again in the black garb of piety and her still-wet hair was swept back from her face in a ribbon of charming silky blue. Her sudden immersion had done her nothing but good, it seemed; her skin glowed.

How innocent she looked, how demure!

Alas, he had missed the incident in the Pump Room, but already the apothecary had heard two accounts of it, first from the maid who had summoned him, then from a brother-in-trade who accosted him laughingly in the Square below. *Ah, Franz, if only you had been there!* The brother-in-trade had to wipe his eyes as he blurted out the ludicrous details of the scene. *That fat old bitch hauled from the bath like a big black whale . . . those old bucks thrashing in the steaming water . . . but oh, the girl!* At this, the brother-in-trade ceased his laughter, and pleasure of a different sort glowed in his face. He leaned close to his intent listener, whispering hotly of the dripping gown, clinging to young, firm breasts *. . . But Franz, is not the Veeldrop girl one of your round?* The apothecary had only to say that indeed this was so, to hold up his bag with an indicative air, and bid a hasty farewell to his suddenly envious colleague.

He eyed the girl.

Had he not thought of her as a dull little thing, tied to her aunt's leading-strings? But she was a hot-blooded one, he was sure of it now. What a pity he had done no more, in all the time she had been in Varby, than check the throbs of her heady little heart, and administer spoonfuls of sugar-orandy! In the course of his duties the apothecary would often treat certain of his feminine patients rather more extensively. Many a fine lady had moaned and shuddered in time to the rhythm of his exploring fingers . . .

The aunt had always been there, that was the trouble!

The apothecary suppressed a surreptitious smirk, and with the aid of further reflections on radical heat, radical moisture, and the balance of the humours – such was his arsenal of expertise – assured the young miss that her aunt would be well again, entirely well again, but could hardly expect to travel so soon as she might wish.

He was glad of it.

So, he was sure, was the girl.

'Alas, Miss Veeldrop, there are other calls I must pay, but be assured I shall return soon, *very* soon, to check on the patient . . .'

At the door of the little drawing-room he bowed, briefly gripping the girl's hand; dimly Cata was aware that his manner towards her had acquired a new gravity, a new air of respect. Was he mocking her? Flushing, she looked down at his hands.

The nails were beautifully clean and filed.

'I say, these are awfully good,' said Nova, licking the berry juice from his fingers.

'You're not supposed to eat them, you idiot!'

'Why ever not? Are they poisonous?'

'We're saving them for the Great Mother.' Rajal dropped his voice, gesturing to Myla, as if the little girl would particularly disapprove of his friend's latest thoughtlessness. They were in a grove of dripping pines, their pockets stuffed with Holluch-haws. The sun rose high over the woods, stabbing bright needles of gold through the branches.

'I'm afraid I've eaten quite a few of mine,' Nova whispered back. 'In fact, all of them. I haven't had any breakfast, you know.'

'Breakfast! Well, you'd just better find a few more, hadn't you? But I don't think you'll be in the mood for breakfast soon, Nova.'

Rajal could not resist a knowing smile. Holluch-haws were for magic, not eating.

'By the way, what happened to you last night?'

Still Nova's manner seemed a little too lively, his gaiety forced. 'I slept in a doorway. I got into a tavern-fight. Oh, and you won't believe it, Raj, but I nearly joined the Silver Masks.'

Now it was Nova's turn to smile.

'*What?*'

But the conversation got no further. All at once a high, pure sound rang out on the air. It was Myla. The girl-child was standing a little way off, her wispy hair shining in a shaft of sunlight, her mouth open and her hands outstretched. What issued from her lips was without melody, without words, but rang on the air like the reverberations of a tuning-fork. The sound was hypnotic, and as it went on the brightly coloured bird began to flutter in slow circles about her head. The boys could only listen, fascinated and a little frightened; then, in a voice that was not her own, but deeper, graver, Myla said:

THE VARBY WAIT

That was all, but then she said it again, turning to her companions with eyes strangely glazed, yet glowing:

THE VARBY WAIT

Chapter 14

THE HUMBLE CAPTAIN

Cata paced back to the window when the apothecary was gone. Restlessly she pushed aside the gauze scrim. Sunshine was returning, but only uncertainly. In the flutter of a kerchief or a milliner's plume a hint of chill was still evident in the air; in the quality-folk sporting Theronfinery there was, perhaps, a defiant folly, as if the season, after all, were not manifestly dying.

Her gaze scudded reluctantly, inevitably, to the portico of the Pump Room. But a fifteenth before, and for all to see, she had been borne down those steps in the arms of a footman; Umbecca, clawing at the footman's arm, had sloshed beside her, screaming that her poor child was dead, dead, and it was all the fault of the harlot, Vlada Flay. A crowd had gathered round them; there were looks, laughter; by now, all of Varby would know what had happened. Umbecca's caterwauling had not ceased until she collapsed at last, exhausted, on the threshold of their lodgings.

Three men-servants had to carry her upstairs.

Cata's cheeks burned crimson. Curse her aunt, curse her! What use was it to dream of the Equinox Ball? Umbecca, in one thing at least, was right. Cata's career in society was over, over before it had begun.

Grunting snores erupted from her aunt's stricken form. For a moment Cata could cheerfully have grabbed a cushion and held it down firmly over the quivering mouth and lips. Instead, she cast herself down on the sofa. Hot tears burned in her eyes.

There were footsteps on the landing.

Quickly Cata composed herself, sitting up sharply just as Nirry intruded, 'Please, miss, there's a gentleman—'

'Gentleman? What gentleman?'

Had the apothecary come back so soon?

But the visitor was a new one, a handsome young Bluejacket in dress uniform, with bright eyes and black lacquered moustaches. Displacing the maid with a swift polite pressure, the stranger was at once across the threshold. Doffing his three-cornered hat, he bowed deeply, his cane and white gloves clutched beneath his arm.

'Ladies, you will pardon this precipitate appearance, but—'

Wildly Cata looked at her aunt. Should she wake her?

No!

Cata turned back, smiling, to the guest. With a gracious hand she indicated the sofa, hissing to Nirry to take the gentleman's things.

The maid hovered, departing only reluctantly, her brow crumpled into a worried frown.

Artlessly Cata gazed into the stranger's eyes. He spoke softly, so as not to wake Umbecca.

'Miss Veeldrop, I am afraid I put you at a disadvantage. Your identity is known to me; mine not to you. But perhaps, on the contrary, you see the resemblance?'

'I'm sorry, sir, I—'

Like a conjuror, he passed a hand over his face; when he drew the hand away, his countenance for a moment seemed to have assumed the semblance of an old man's, with rheumy eyes, withered cheeks, a pendulous goitre. Cata was puzzled; then the visitor pointed to the air above him, wobbling his head from side to side.

The girl giggled. A teetering wig!

'My – ah – uncle, I'm afraid, is a little indisposed. Oh, nothing serious; like your own dear protectress, he merely needs a little rest, I've no doubt. But Miss Veeldrop, you may be assured that he is *most* solicitous to discover your fate – and let me say how pleased I am that my report shall be a positive one.

'My uncle is a gentleman of the old school, Miss Veeldrop; pray, do not for a moment imagine that he would prefer not to call upon you in person. Were it possible, he would have done so; but may I beg you to accept, in his place, not the noble Earl, but the humble captain?'

It was Rajal who broke the enchantment. He darted forward, snatching his sister from the shaft of sunlight. A moment later she was struggling in his arms, demanding indignantly that he let her go.

'What is it?' said Jem. 'I don't understand.'

'An *attunement*,' Rajal said. 'Something in the air, speaking through her. It's evil—'

'Of course. It's happened before, hasn't it?'

Troubled, Jem recalled the last time Myla had gone into a trance like this, and the explanation the Great Mother had given.

The Rapture is strong in her, but Child Myla has yet to gain full control of her powers; too easily, she becomes a conduit for the dark beings that long to resume this world, Rejects of Orok that rustle and scratch at the parchment-skin dividing us from the Realm of Unbeing . . .

Jem shuddered. Many times he had heard the girl burbling and mumbling.

As an infant in swaddling-bands, she spoke the words clearly. Often she was sick for many days, and we feared for her life . . .

'The presence here must be strong, to cast her back into the helplessness of infancy.' Tenderly, Rajal stroked the little girl's hair. 'Hush, Sister Myla. You're all right now . . .'

'I was all right before!' Myla broke free, turning on her brother. 'Don't you understand? Brother Raj, The Varby wanted to speak. They wanted to speak – through *me*. Now they've gone and you've made them angry!'

'I've made *you* angry,' her brother said, abashed.

'What's she talking about?' said Jem. 'What did she mean, *The Varby Wait?*'

'Nova, don't you know anything? Remember the first night we arrived in camp here? The song the Great Mother sang round the fire?'

Jem remembered a long, droning ballad, half of which seemed to be in the old Vaga-language. It was not unpleasant, but Jem had fallen asleep long before it was over.

'That was the Threnody of Placation,' said Rajal. 'The Great Mother says we must respect the presiding spirits. The Varby were the Dominants of the valley below, long before the tribes of Ejland came; even afterwards, long afterwards, the springs that now lie beneath the city were theirs. The peasants of old understood The Varby, and lived at one with them; not so the Agondon-folk, who drove them away. Now in the hills The Varby mourn their lost waters, and dream of the day when they shall resume them.'

Jem's brow furrowed. He had picked up a little of the history of Varby. It had been in the reign of the Holy Empress, Elabeth the First, that quality-folk first began repairing to the springs. The military governor, General Lord Milander, found to his delight that the Varby waters brought him relief from the pain of his gout. In his gratitude he endowed Varby Abbey, and as time passed the abbey – or rather, its attendant springs – became a place of pilgrimage. In Agondon, fashionable physicians would recommend 'a course of the Varby-waters'; but it was not until the Zenzau-plague of Cycle 970, when Eldric the Eighth removed his court to the spa-town, that Varby's destiny was sealed. The plague passed, but quality-folk continued to flock to Varby, not only for health but for pleasure.

Jem had never heard of the creatures called The Varby, but even in the religion he had learned in Temple there was talk of evil beings these lands had once contained.

He thought of the serpent Sassoroch, and shuddered.

Myla, wandering a little away from them, was staring into the shaft of light where she had stood a moment before. Was it Jem's imagination, or had it grown brighter? It hurt his eyes. Rajal, too, gazed into the brightening light, then at his sister, then at the light.

Jem resumed, 'You said they were evil.'

'They're angry,' Rajal replied solemnly, 'and anger, be it ever so just, turns swiftly to evil.'

It was something the Great Mother might have said; but then of course she had said it, a few moonlives ago, after one of the innumerable fights between the boys. Jem had to laugh, but his laughter was stilled when Myla turned back to him, muttering in her own voice, but a voice stripped of childishness, 'I can't think *you* have cause to laugh, Prince Jemany.'

At that, the beckoning-bird, perched on a branch, gave a loud *scree!*, as if of assent. Myla took to her heels, the bird to his wings, blundering through the green spiky caverns of the pinewoods.

'Sister Myla! Come back!' Rajal called. He started forward, then left off, swivelling round, kicking at a clump of ferns. The girl-child was fast, and had gone far ahead.

Savagely Rajal turned on Jem. 'What did she call you?'

'I don't know.' The shaft of light was fading. 'Some nonsense, I expect.'

She knows, thought Jem.

'Sister Myla doesn't talk nonsense.'

'You said she babbled. Babbled and burbled.'

'That's not nonsense.' Rajal grabbed Jem's arm. 'She knows, doesn't she?'

Of course she knows. She's Xal's heir, isn't she?

'Knows what?'

'Who you are. Your real name. Am I to believe you were just some peasant-boy, found by the roadside? I don't think so.'

It was a thought that had tormented Rajal before. Resentment surged through him. He loved his sister, he loved the Great Mother – but how they had excluded him! How they had lied to him! He slumped miserably on to a mossy log. The boy they called Nova had turned from him again, gazing into the fading light.

Say nothing, thought Jem. *Just say nothing.*

Rajal thought, *What a fool I have been!* There were times when he had almost convinced himself that Nova was a Koros-child like himself. *My brother.* But brothers would be of the same race, and to Nova, thought Rajal, the Koros-race was just a stain, a stain to wash away. With a sharp clarity it came to him that Nova would soon leave them. All this time the stranger-boy had been making his way to Agondon, sheltering like a coward under the Great Mother's mantle, and when he got there the Ejlander would vanish into a new life – some life of ease, Rajal spitefully imagined – with the dispatch of Myla's bird, fluttering from one side to the other of a high, spiked wall. *I was a Vaga once,* he might say one day, laughing urbanely to some pale companion as he passed a party of Koros-children clattering their wooden swords against the railings.

Then Rajal thought, *But I shall always be a Vaga.* Oh, he could conceal the gash that discoloured his inner thigh, the crimson scar all Vaga-men bore in the place where Theron had stabbed the dark Koros. There were some, he knew, who bore no other sign; safe from all but the most virulent Vaga-purges, such 'pallor-children' could pass as Zenzans, even Ejlanders. But Rajal was a Vaga, a Vaga beyond doubt.

A pain throbbed in his reddened thigh-flesh. He had heard that the Vaga-mark, the *membrance,* would hurt while it was growing, spreading through the years of his fourth cycle; some said it hurt throughout a man's life. Rajal cursed the dark Koros. Why should he be punished for the folly of a god? Why should all his race be punished? But the El-Orokon said the Koros-children must suffer, for their god who had ruined the creation of this world; and if there were those, like the Great Mother, who believed that a time was coming when their race would suffer no more, who could believe it?

They had always suffered.

The question came into Rajal's mind, 'That wasn't true, was it, about the Silver Masks?'

Jem, still gazing into Myla's light, thought of the times Rajal had spoken of the troupe, of the marvels of their talents, of their envied fame and wealth. They might as well have been a race of gods. An irritable desire stirred in him to tell the truth, but something checked him. It was not quite tenderness, more a species of caution. A shape – but it must have been only a pattern, say, of hovering spores – seemed to be churning in the shaft of light.

Jem did not turn.

'I saw them coming,' he mumbled. 'From a distance. A splendid equipage, Koros-coloured with the royal arms on the side, progressing like a vision down Eldric's Parade—'

Rajal's eyes shone. 'From a distance!'

The Masks had always been a fantasy to him; now they seemed real. In that moment, perhaps, the determination was forged in him: *he would join them.*

But how?

Rajal rose from the mossy log. 'And how did you get back into the city?'

'The cargo-gate. Where you met me. It's easy there, Raj. The Bluejackets, they defend things a lot less well than you'd think. They're not frightened of anyone—'

'Not the Zenzans? There's talk of a new war—'

Jem's voice was soft. 'Something is coming. But I don't think it's Zenzau.'

Rajal stepped close to him, touched his arm. In the seasons they had spent on the road, his friend had grown taller, leaner, assuming rapidly the lineaments of manhood. This was something else Rajal might have envied, but did not, not now. After all, soon they would part.

My brother.

'What do you mean? You know something, don't you? Tell me who you are—'

The sound of drumbeats thudded through the foliage.

'Bluejackets!' Jem's eyes flashed. Were they not so deep in the woods after all? But of course not. A road ran close by, winding up from Varby to Holluch-on-the-Hill. 'Where's Myla?'

Ul-ul-ul-ul-ul!

And where was the bird? Eo's call was high and strained, echoing alarmingly, unreally on the air.

'Quick!'

It was Jem who moved first. They plunged away through the pine-woods and the grove was left empty, silent again but for the drippings of drying branches, the creakings of wind in the treetops, the *tock-tock!*, here and there, of a beetle beneath the bark.

But they had gone too soon, and only a squirrel, arrested in its stealthy, intermittent scuttlings, was there to see the shaft of light brighten slowly again, and to watch intent with large, dark eyes as the phantom faces formed inside the light, mouthing with strangely shaped lips the words:

THE VARBY WAIT

The music of Umbecca's snores resumed again, more loudly; Cata barely heard. She looked wonderingly at her strange visitor, more than a little thrilled at his smooth mode of address. The thought came to her that she was, to all intents, alone with a gentleman.

What would Jeli say?

An amethyst ring flashed on the captain's hand. Reaching inside his jacket, he drew forth a small, flat, silver box. He flipped up the lid, drawing forth a rolled tobarillo. 'You don't mind, Miss Veeldrop?'

Cata shook her head.

'Beautiful, isn't it? Would you like to see?' The captain held out the box and Cata took it gingerly, tracing her fingers over the ornate design, feeling for the catch that made the lid flip up. On the underside, engraved in fine scroll-script, was the following rhyme:

I who have opened my secrets to thee
Give you this box in remembrance of me:
Its many columns shall pleasure you less
Than you pleasured me with just one, I confess.

Was it a riddle? Cata did not quite understand, but smiled knowingly nonetheless. She was beginning to feel frightfully grown up. Was this what it was like to be an Entered girl?

Grey-blue smoke clouded the air.

'Ah, Miss Veeldrop, I see what you are thinking.'

But the captain did not.

'My name – my uncle's name – is one you do not know. Such is fame! Miss Veeldrop, you are young – oh, delightfully so – but did the years lie more heavily upon you, perhaps you might recall my uncle's glory days. You think of him only as some painted old fool—'

'Captain, no!'

'Miss Veeldrop, yes – no need for sweet lies.' Smiling, the captain took Cata's hand. 'Let us face one another with trust in our hearts. Youth, Miss Veeldrop, is a swiftly fading flower. Had you seen my uncle in the time of the Regent Queen, you would have seen a man who was the toast of Varby. Alas for the poor gentleman, but there must be those whose glory lies behind them; for after all, there must be those whose glory lies ahead. Before me, perhaps, I see one such?'

There was a mischievous glint in the captain's eye, and for a moment, drawing back on his burning tobarillo, he held Cata's glance.

At once the girl leapt up. A sob caught in her throat.

'Captain, you mock me! Your uncle, you said, has told you what has happened?'

She paced back to the window, feeling the tears start. But then the captain was behind her, clutching her arm.

He span her round.

'Dear Miss Veeldrop, you are young, so young! Can you believe the work of one foolish day shall blight the happiness that is certain to be your lot? My intercourse with the great world has been, I dare say, more promiscuous than yours. Hear me, dear girl, and dry your tears. For now, you are the talk of Varby, but soon, sure as the sun shall rise tomorrow, some new folly, equal in evanescence, shall engross the attention of all the great world. No, Miss Veeldrop, that world lies before you. Reach for it now, with arms open wide!'

But Cata, by now, could do nothing with her arms, for the captain had crushed her tightly against him. His eyes glinted; his lips sought hers. Suddenly Cata was frightened; the lacquer of the black moustaches

110

smeared against her face. She might have struggled, but at that moment came a violent interruption.

'Madam Veeldrop! Madam Veeldrop!'

There was a hammering at the door.

The captain released the girl and they sprang apart – just in time. All at once Umbecca's eyes were staring wide, her fat neck swivelling in alarm. On seeing the captain she gasped, and for a confused moment thought he was the source of the affray.

'Sir! What is the meaning of this?'

The door burst open.

'Widow Waxwell, please!' Helplessly Nirry tried to restrain the visitor who pushed past her, forgetting all decorum.

Sobbing, the Widow collapsed to the floor.

'Oh, what now?' Umbecca boomed. 'What can have happened?' Wincing at the pain in her bandaged ankle, she struggled up from the depths of her chair.

The captain went to the prostrate form. 'Dear lady, what ever can have distressed you? Pray, tell us, what ever is the matter?'

All that came forth was a stream of incoherence; but then, bobbing on the tide of tears, the ominous phrases *She's gone, she's gone* and *My poor, poor Pellicent!*

Umbecca wailed, 'Oh, something dreadful has happened, I know it!' Painfully the fat woman slumped to her knees, pinching and slapping the Widow's face in mingled alarm and rage. 'Berthen, Berthen, tell us what it is!'

The poor Widow could say no more, but all was clear a moment later when the captain extracted a crumpled note from the distraught woman's hand:

> *Miss Pellicent Pelligrew is in our custody.*
> *10,000 epicrowns or the girl dies.*
> *Details, &c., to follow.*

THE VARBY WAIT

Chapter 15

CABIN IN THE WOODS

'A Tarn regiment.'
  'Irion?'
  'The Fifth.'
  'They've come a long way.'
  'Something's up.'
  'I told you it was Zenzau.'
  'I wonder.'

Jem's voice was a tight, dry whisper; Rajal's replies came through gritted teeth. On the brink of the pinewood, the boys lay in the undergrowth, peering out on the road as muddy boots slapped in time to the rhythm of fife and drum. Coldly the sun glimmered on buckles and buttons and the silvery steel of bayonets. 'You men there! Keep in step!' came a bawling voice. Blue pennants fluttered on the breeze and in the rear of the procession, straining against the gradient, weary horses dragged juddering, laden carts.

The Fifth Royal Fusiliers of the Tarn were making their way up the hill to Holluch.

'But where's my sister?'
  'Crossed the road. She must have come this way.'

Only when the last cart had trundled by did the boys break cover, darting from one screen of trees to another. On the other side of the road the wood was darker, thicker, the ground steeper, rising sharply towards the rocky crest of land where Holluch-on-the-Hill looked down over the valley. Through pungent greenery, the fife and drums faded invisibly on the air.

Then came the caw of the beckoning-bird.

'This way,' said Jem.
  'Myla? Sister Myla?'

They came suddenly upon the log cabin. Hard against the hillside, the little hovel was almost concealed beneath a web of draping vines. It might have been abandoned for long years, but a curl of smoke was rising from the chimney.

From above the door came the sound of chimes, stirring in the wind.

'There he is,' said Jem.
  'Eo?'

Jem pointed. On a branch of vine above the cabin door sat the beckoning-bird, silent now, his beak tucked neatly into his bright breast. It was the posture he assumed when he had done his summoning – when it was time for the play to begin.

'But where's my sister?' asked Rajal again.

'The door's ajar.'

They were both still whispering as they weaved their way forward. The undergrowth about the cabin was thick, but a track nonetheless had been beaten to the door. Flattened grasses showed signs of carriage-wheels.

'Sister Myla?'

Rajal went first. The door opened with a low groan of hinges, like a ground bass beneath the chimes. Inside, the fire had collapsed into smouldering embers and only a little of the green forest light seeped through the slats of the window shutters. But even in the gloom the boys could see that this was no woodcutter's cabin, no gamekeeper's hut.

The place was filled with rich, ornate furnishings.

'Look at these things!' They crept forward wonderingly, running their hands across a long, curving chaise longue, over the backs of chintz chairs, over surfaces of marble and marquetry and giltwood. Somewhere an olton-clock ticked rhythmically. Thick carpets covered the crude floor and the golden glimmerings of picture-frames hinted at the portraits that hung about the walls.

'What is this place?'

Jem pushed back the shutters. A little more light fell into the room and they saw it more clearly. If the first impression had been of wealth, the second was of a certain raffish squalor. The furniture was strewn about higgledy-piggledy, and all of it was old, worn and faded – the chintz threadbare, the lacquer chipped. It was junk-shop stuff, knocked down, perhaps, at the auction of some broken nobleman and battered about thereafter with a carefree disdain. Sticky trails of wine ran about like blood. Remnants of a feast – gnawed chicken-bones, half-eaten chunks of cake – covered several little inlaid tables and the buttoned surface of a sofa. Picking his way between chairs, Jem kicked a dish cover, upended on the floor; it let out a low resounding, like a bell.

He reached down, stilling it.

'Myla?'

There was a giggle.

'Myla?' Rajal said again.

After the giggle came a rat-like scratching.

'We know you're here somewhere. Sister, don't be silly!'

The scratching again.

Jem whispered, 'It's coming from the wall.'

It was true; between hanging bolts of red rep, thick with mould, was an expanse of wormy panelling. Jem traced his fingers lightly over it. Standing close, he could hear Myla's breathing on the other side. His finger slipped suddenly into a ragged hole.

'Ouch!' came a wail.

'What is it?' said Rajal.

Jem turned, laughing, as the panelling juddered stiffly back and Myla was revealed to them, rubbing her eye indignantly. Raised high above the floor, she was squatting on the mattress of a bed, concealed in the wall.

'A chava-bed,' said Jem.

'You'll be sorry, Prince Jemany,' Myla hissed, blinking tearfully. 'Remember all those Holluch-haws you stuffed down your throat?'

'Holluch-haws?' Jem echoed, then wished he had not. The name was like a charm. At once he felt an alarming, liquid churning in his bowels. He slumped against the red rep, holding his belly. 'Excuse me,' he said with an absurd politeness, like a spinster proposing to take a little air, 'I might just step outside for a moment . . .'

But Rajal was not listening.

'Shh!' He grabbed Jem's arm. From outside came the whinny of a horse, a jangling of reins. Then voices: a man, a woman. 'Quick!'

Rajal scrambled up beside Myla in the chava-bed, hauling Jem after him. There was just time to force the panel back into place before the man and woman, approaching rapidly, stooped beneath the lintel and pushed open the door.

'Raj, I'm going to shit myself,' Jem muttered.

'Shh!'

And Jem could only screw himself up into a ball of clenched agony, willing himself not to writhe or cry out, as they looked on through the holes in the panelling at the curious scene that followed.

The players were two young people of fashion, the gentleman a dandy with a cloth-of-gold cravat, the lady a flouncy creature in the finest silk and lace.

'Jac, what is this place?' She was lingering in the doorway, looking about uncertainly.

'You don't know, my love?' Her companion strode forward, lighting a lantern, flinging a log on the dying fire. 'I thought a girl like you would know at once.'

'I don't understand.'

Squatting by the fire, the gentleman applied himself vigorously to the bellows. His cravat glowed golden in the light as he laughed and said, 'I think you do.'

'Jac?'

He set by the bellows and rose again, turning, opening his arms.

'Jac!'

'Pelli!'

She blundered towards him. He took her in his arms, stroking her hair. 'Yes, I think you know this place, my love.' He kissed her neck. 'What can it be, but love's bower?'

'Oh, Jac!' Struggling free, the girl slumped on to the chaise longue. She grabbed a cushion and hugged it to her breasts. 'You're not getting all silly again, Jac, are you?'

'Silly?' The young man knelt beside her. He tried to take her hand but she snatched it away. 'You know what we've talked about, darling. Well, here's where it begins.'

Fear glimmered in Pelli's eyes.

Then she laughed loudly. 'Oh Jac Burgrove, you had me believing you! Now come on, why did you bring me here, really?'

But there was no hint of laughter in Mr Burgrove's reply. Eagerly he wrested the cushion from Pelli's grip. He took her hands in his, gazing into her eyes.

'Some other fellows and I, darling, we have a little club. This is, you might say, our meeting-house. A place where we bring certain young ladies—'

'Oh, Jac!'

'No, no, darling. I mean *ladies*—'

'What ladies?' Pelli writhed in his grip.

'Remember Miss Vyella Rextel? Or young Lady Vantage?'

'Jac, what do you mean?' A sudden horror overspread Pelli's face. 'They were kidnapped! The Varby—'

'Hush, my love. They weren't, you see. You knew, you must have known, that the young Master of Heva-Harion was burning with . . . with *love* for the gorgeous Vy – for Miss Rextel. And hadn't you seen how the Earl of Varl was looking at Lady Vantage, in the Abbey, in the Pump Room, at the Assembly? They were lovers, darling, lovers like us, kept apart by a harsh world. But now they're together.'

'Jac?'

Horror fought in Pelli with excitement as Mr Burgrove told her of The Varby – or rather, of the club that called itself by that name. With shining eyes she learnt that she would soon be on the road, bound for the furthest tip of the Deliverance. Behind her she would leave her reputation for virtue, undiminished as it had always been. Another – yet another – victim of The Varby, she would inspire no execration, only sympathetic tears. But for Miss Pelli Pelligrew, in truth, no sorrow lay ahead, only the joys of virtuous marriage, and a new life in a far, freer land . . . Mr Burgrove's voice was a hot whisper, and between the ardours of his promises he cooled his lips against her neck, her breasts.

'I don't believe a word of it,' Rajal hissed.

'The Ejlander has the countenance of a liar,' said Myla.

'I can't hold it!' Jem was writhing urgently now, rocking dangerously back and forth on his haunches.

Pelli's face clouded suddenly. 'But the Equinox Ball—'

Laughter was all that greeted the protest. 'There will be balls enough to come! Forget your old life! Darling, they have kept you like a prisoner in chains—'

'That's not true! Aunt Vlad—'

'Your aunt? Only another kind of gaoler. What is she but a Zenzan harlot, who shall succeed only in dragging you into her own abyss? Look what she did to Miss Veeldrop – the work of one morning . . .'

But Pelli was not listening. 'Jac, I'm not in chains! Don't you see, my life is just beginning? I'm going to be Entered—'

'Entered? Cruel Pellicent, I thought you had found already the man you loved!'

'Oh Jac, it is you who are cruel! Am I never to see Agondon again? Or my great-father? Or my brother – my dear, dear brother?'

'Brother!' spat Mr Burgrove. 'What deception is this? Pellicent Pelligrew, do you take me for a fool? You say you love me, but I see it now – you seek another, amongst the fops of the court who know nothing of virtue, only of venery—'

'No, Jac, no! You don't understand! My heart is yours, but we must go by the way of the world—'

'The world? That is no way! My father's trades have made him a man greater than half the lords of this land, but still it is title, title, that counts with the ladies—'

'That's not true!' Poor Pelli sank to the floor with her lover, embraced him, stroked his hair. At last she began to shiver and sob. 'Oh, let me go back, just let me go back—'

Mr Burgrove let out a sudden, sharp laugh. 'Ah, but dear Pellicent, that cannot be. I'm afraid your Duenna already has the letter.' His face crinkled into a smile and his eyes widened as he intoned:

THE VARBY WAIT

'Jac, no!' Pelli would have collapsed in tears, but she did not have the chance. Mr Burgrove's mood had changed. Roughly he grabbed the girl again and clutched her to him, telling her that nothing mattered, nothing

116

but their love. Hotly his moist lips sought hers; with rough hands he squeezed her breasts and thighs.

'Darling, we're wasting time. Did I not say, this place is love's bower?'

Pelli struggled. It was no good. Impatiently he hustled her across the room, blundering into the cluttered furniture, dragging her towards the chava-bed. His hand fumbled behind him, patting at the panelling, feeling for the handle that would slide back the screen.

'Let me prove my passion to you now, let me – oh, Pelli, let me—'

'Let me go!'

There was a flurry of alarm behind the screen. Rajal, repelled and frightened, scrambled towards the back of the bed, as if there could be any hope of concealment. *I'm a coward, a coward.* But Myla was beside him, clawing and tapping at the wooden wall.

'Brother, help – there's a way!'

'What?'

Meanwhile, Jem's agonies had reached new heights. By now, his rocking shook the bed and his breath burst from him in pained gasps. *Pelli, Pelli,* came a voice through the screen, and *No, Jac, please!* Mr Burgrove filled Jem with loathing; there and then he would have burst from the bed, striking the seducer to the floor, but for the churnings of agony inside him.

Curse Myla, curse her!

He bit his lips, dug his nails in his palms, anything to keep his burning buttocks clenched tight, tight.

Myla tapped at the back of the wall.

There was a rattle at the front. Swollen with damp, the screen was sticking, but it would be only a moment before Mr Burgrove forced it back. Jem felt a fresh liquid lurch inside him. There was nothing for it. He tore suddenly at the fastenings of his breeches and there on the bed, in one swift, unstoppable rush, voided the scalding lava from his bowels.

'What's that?' Mr Burgrove's brow furrowed. He sniffed. It was Pelli's chance. She broke from him, flinging herself back across the cluttered room.

'Pelli!' Mr Burgrove was after her, grabbing her, but she was desperate now. Chicken bones and gravy sprayed the air as she swiped up a silver plate from a table and bashed it, hard as she could, against his nose. He staggered, crashing into a chair.

Pelli plunged back through the cabin door.

In the bed, Myla whispered, 'I've found the way—'

There was a second screen. With a sharp wrench from Rajal, the screen was open. Then it was closed, and in the instant between, dragging Jem

117

with them, the brother and sister had vanished into the blackness beyond.

Alone now, Mr Burgrove sprawled on the stained carpet. Blood streamed from his nose. Moaning, staunching the flow with his cravat, he struggled upright. *Pelli, Pelli . . . oh, damn the little bitch!* For a moment he would have pursued her again, but what was the good?

She was gone.

He must lie down.

He forced back the chava-screen and flopped down on the bed.

Chapter 16

EO'S RAINBOW

'Remember, my dear, it is all a matter of rest, rest.'

'Theirs, you mean?'

'Hm. Theirs. For you, some medicinal orandy. Perhaps a little Varl-wine, just a little. To relax. Or some mild exercise – something gentle. Truth to tell, my dear, I fear for the balance of *your* humours now. Who knows when the radical heat may rise too high? Who knows when only an infusion of radical moisture may restore a lady's balance? Especially a *young* lady's.'

The apothecary, on the brink of his second goodbye, was holding Cata's hand, clinging to it for just a little too long as his neat fingers massaged the palm, the wrist. He leaned close and whispered – but why was he whispering? – 'My dear, I suspect you need a *thorough* examination.'

Cata blanched. By the fire, not one but *two* old women now slumped, insensible, beneath thick rugs. What new trouble could assail her now?

Feeling for Cata's pulse, the apothecary had just the hint of a smile – or was it a leer? – behind his smooth professional air.

'Just something gentle to begin with. Hm?'

'Sir, I am not sure I favour your prescription—'

'No?' An eyebrow arched beneath the perfumed periwig. 'You have felt, my dear, certain shocks. Tender and delicate filaments have . . . jarred. Now, a little stimulation in *another* direction . . .'

The girl's countenance clouded, then cleared as he hurried on, 'One might go so far as to suggest the participation in certain proceedings . . . pertaining to the Equinox?'

'No!' Umbecca cried from the haze of her sedation, but whether her negative was to be applied to the ball, or to her condition, or to the loss of Miss Pelligrew, could hardly be determined.

For long moments – it had seemed an age – both Umbecca and her friend had alternately keened and moaned, crying out *No!* and *It cannot be* and *Curse this vile world* until the apothecary's new and stronger prescription took hold. The Widow, overwrought, even threatened to leap from the window, struggling with her single hand to fling up the sash. Umbecca, hobbling on her bandages, had to restrain her, tugging at the capacious skirts until her old friend gave it up and they fell to the carpet in a ludicrous black heap.

There was a rapping at the door and Nirry appeared.

'Miss Cata, a gentleman—'

'Gentleman? Another?'

But it was one Cata had seen before. Dressed magnificently in the style of the Regency, the gentleman – a very *old* gentleman – stooped his head beneath the door-frame, permitting the passage of his teetering wig. Now it was the apothecary's turn to blanch. 'My lord—'

The rheumy eyes paid him no attention. 'Child, I had to come! Oh, you must be frantic, frantic. My nephew has told me of the tragedy—'

'But Lord Foxbane, you're not well! Good apothecary, a chair—'

The apothecary's countenance clouded darkly, and he fetched the chair with little grace. How fondly the girl gazed on the withered old man! Eagerly she sat beside him now, rehearsing the details of the day's events as the old fool shook his head, muttering *Oh, monstrous!* and patting her knee.

The apothecary permitted himself a sharp *ahem!* and beckoned Cata back to him. With furrowing brow he consulted his fob-watch. 'A professional man must pay his calls, and alas, there are others I must visit now,' he murmured. 'But be assured, my dear, there is no call I would pay – or should I say *court*? – rather than to *you*.' He leaned close and whispered, '*The Equinox Ball.*'

Cata sniffed. Did the fellow think he could beguile her when Lord Foxbane had come to call? Gazing fondly on the uncle, the girl could think only of the handsome nephew.

Like the young man, the old one wore an amethyst ring.

'Good apothecary, a word.'

The old buck shuffled forward, supporting himself on an ornate stick. The apothecary brightened. For a moment he forgot the luscious girl, and essayed his best professional smile. This old buck had never been on his round; indeed he was unsure which of his colleagues tended to the gentleman. But imagine! A Regency buck would need bucketloads of pills, shelves of potions, powders. Regular leechings and treatments with mercury.

Hm, yes.

'Good apothecary, there is a service I would do for you.'

'For me? My lord, I should regard it as the highest—'

They had turned from the girl, and with a lurch of shock the apothecary was aware that the old buck's hand – the hand that wore the ring – was playing, *toying*, between his thighs.

Well, really!

At once flattered and alarmed, the apothecary was uncertain what expression to adopt, when in a single, startling moment, the playful hand leapt up, clenching and twisting.

The apothecary felt a sharp infusion of radical heat.

Radical moisture sprang to his eyes.

'My lord . . .'

The poor fellow could barely retain his decorum. It was all he could do not to cry out as he beat his hasty retreat from the room, gasping and doubling over as the door shut behind him.

Pelli blundered through the pinewoods, her eyes blurred with tears. Branches slapped at her, pine-needles pricked her; her hair was dishevelled and her gown was torn. She lost one of her shoes, but hobbled on, snuffling. At last something sharp, some spiteful stone, gashed through her stocking and she could go no further.

She slumped miserably on to a mossy log. The resinous, thick smell of the pines filled her nostrils and a pale shaft of light was shimmering before her. She rubbed her foot, smearing the stain of blood beneath the gauzy heel of her stocking.

What could she do? She was lost, alone and frightened. Only a day had passed since Aunt Vlada came to her, permitting all freedoms. To Pelli, it seemed an age. How she longed to be at home again, smothered in Pell's tight embrace!

Her brother would never have let this happen.

Vividly Pelli recalled a day when they were little, when their nurse had taken them to the Ollon Pleasure-Gardens. Excitedly they had watched the flame-tigers and the Blue and Red Play, and Pelli had ridden on the roundabout until she was nearly sick. Then darkness fell and it was time for the fireworks.

Pelli had never seen fireworks before. Her brother, with the superior wisdom of two extra years, had told her they were very beautiful, lighting the sky brighter than the moon and stars. But he had said nothing about the frightening noise. When the first meteors showered above them, filling the darkness with a kaleidoscope of light, her brother flung up his arms, exclaiming joyously. At the same moment his terrified little sister rushed away, blundering tearfully through a forest of human forms.

Hey little girl.

Why so fast, little maid?

Child, come back.

She was found aeons later, huddled amongst sacks at the back of the muffin-booth, shivering and wide-eyed, her thumb in her mouth. How she recalled her joy when Pell rushed towards her, a joy so great that it could only spill in tears. *Hush sister, we've found you! Why are you sobbing? Dear Pell! Dear brother!*

On the mossy log, Pelli's grief burst forth afresh. She fumbled in her pocket for her handkerchief, but all she found there were rubies, unstrung, glistening like cherries in the forest light.

She flung them into the undergrowth.

That was when the voice came, *Hush, sister, hush.*

Pelli looked up. 'Pell?'

She brushed away her tears. There was no one there, of course there was not; yet it seemed to the girl that the shaft of light descending through the pines had grown more intense. Disturbingly, the thought came to her that she was not alone, not really.

There was a scuttling close by.

Only a squirrel, squatting on a branch, watching her with dark unblinking eyes.

But there was something else. Someone.

Pelli looked about her, to the left, to the right, but always her gaze returned to the eerie column, blazing in the centre of the grove. Its light, it seemed to Pelli, was brighter than the sun's, and all at once she knew it was a brightness she had sought. Had her destiny arrived, so soon, so suddenly?

The voice came again and the phantom face called to her only three times – *Come, child* and *You belong with us* and *Let us take you* – before Pelli rose from the mossy log and hobbled the few steps that would lead her to her fate.

The brightness flamed into a searing column, and in the last moment, before it consumed her, Pelli was aware only of the words:

THE VARBY WAIT

The squirrel looked on for a long moment, then scurried suddenly, urgently away.

'It's dark—'
   'Ouch, that's my foot!'
   'Pooh, somebody stinks!'
   'Whose fault is that?'
   'Who scoffed the Holluch-haws?'
   'What is this place?'
   'Ouch!'
   'What now?'
   'I hit my knee. On a rock.'
   'It's all rock—'

'It's a cave—'

'What?'

'It's a cave,' Myla said again.

Rajal groped about him. A cave: it was true. But how could they get out? Clinging together, they had blundered some distance from the panel in the back of the chava-bed. Even to find it now would be difficult; besides, they could hardly go back that way!

'Sister Myla?'

'What?'

'So what do we do now?'

But Myla only began to hum.

'That girl,' Jem said. 'Do you think she's all right?'

'Sister Myla? Why are you humming?'

'No,' said Jem. 'That girl, Pelli. Do you think she's all right?'

'Really, Nova! I'm surprised you noticed her.'

'I would have saved her! If I could.'

Rajal sniffed loudly. 'Some hero!'

'Some coward,' Jem shot back. But he did not want to bicker. Miserably he squatted on the rocky cave-floor, aware of the stench that rose around him.

Myla broke off her humming briefly. 'You did save her.'

'What?' said her brother.

But it was true, wasn't it? The girl had got away. No doubt about it, Jem was a hero – of sorts. His spirits lightened, and it was almost with pride that he ripped a length of cloth from the tail of his shirt, scrubbed it energetically in the cleft between his buttocks, and fastened his breeches again.

'Now, let's see about getting out of here. Myla, why *are* you humming?'

'He will come to us. He will come if he can.'

'Who?'

But a moment later, the answer was clear. The dark air was filled with a flutter of wings.

'Oh no! A bat!' Rajal covered his eyes.

'No, Raj. Look.'

'I can't, it's dark—'

'Open your eyes—'

Ul-ul-ul-ul-ul!

It was an extraordinary sight. Fluttering before them, the beckoning-bird illuminated the darkness. Coloured lights shone from his feathers, arcing in bright streams above them like a rainbow.

'But he was outside! How did he get here?'

'The cave, Brother Raj. It has an entrance.'

They had discovered the secret of the cabin in the woods. Epicycles ago, the rich counties of the Inner had been burdened with heavy taxes, unknown in the hinterlands. Smuggling flourished. In Agondon, the docks were under constant siege; patrols terrorized the coast. But Ejland, after all, was not an island. So it was that from the Holluch hills, illicit supplies of Jarvel and tobarillo, orandy and rum, Varl-wine and Tiralos made their way southwards through the rich valleys that surrounded the capital. The woodcutter's cabin was a smugglers' base, built hard against the cave that served it like the sub-cellars of many a low tavern, dug in secret in the depths of night, or the doors behind the bookcases in grander establishments where they kept the best wine, the best Jarvel.

There was little profit in smuggling now: holding sway over all of northern El-Orok, the Bluejackets had made all its peoples equal, equal in taxes, equal in tyranny. The smugglers of old had long gone, leaving the cabin in the woods to rot. They had been evil men – but how innocent, how inept they would have seemed, against the party of seducers who had commandeered their base for their own, rather different trade!

But the cave had yet another secret to reveal.

As the little party scrambled back to the world outside, following the bright trail of the beckoning-bird, Jem called suddenly, 'Stop!'

'What is it?' They were climbing ever higher; evidently the cave wound upwards through a hill. Rajal, helping Myla, turned back irritably. In the weird luminescence of Eo's rainbow, their faces were a flicker of orange, purple, green.

They had to laugh. 'You look bilious!'

'So do you! Raj, listen. That girl! I just saw her—'

'Girl?'

'The girl called Pelli—'

'But that's absurd—'

'No, she was here – just for a moment—'

Jem strained his eyes, trying to focus, but nothing was clear in Eo's strange light. That was when he became aware of a mysterious feeling of burning in his chest.

'Come!' cried Myla. 'Eo is tiring. His light will not last—'

'Wait!' cried Jem. 'Look—'

He flailed towards the cave-wall, barking his shin against a shelf of rock.

'Ouch! Look—'

'Look at what?'

The cave-wall was scored with smugglers' graffiti, crude squarish initials and dates, cruder drawings and diagrams.

Rajal flushed hotly. 'Myla, come away—'

124

But Myla would not. She whispered, 'The Varby—'

'You see it too?' said Jem.

'Of course I see it!'

'See what?'

Rajal tugged anxiously at his sister's hand. Eo's light was beginning to flicker, they must hurry . . .

But then he too saw the shapes, the older, graceful shapes – not quite animal, not quite human – that curved beneath the thousand coarse hackings on the wall. The pigment, it seemed, had seeped deeply into the rock, yet the figures showed only in certain slants of light, dancing out in some, not others, of Eo's changing shimmerings. Cave-paintings, that was all they were, defaced long ago . . . except that the animal-people were *moving*, prancing triumphantly round the walls.

Still Jem felt the burning in his chest. But it was worse now.

'Wh-what are they?' said Rajal.

Jem breathed, 'She was with them. I saw her—'

'You think you saw her—'

'Raj, I did—'

'They're not human.'

Myla intoned:

WE ARE THE VARBY
THE GIRL HAS JOINED US

'But what can that mean?' Jem's teeth were gritted and he clutched his chest.

Rajal pushed past him.

'Sister, snap out of it!' He shook her roughly and turned her face away, breaking her attunement for a second time. For a moment he thought she would scream at him in anger. Instead she clung to him, shuddering as she blurted, as if voicing his own thought, 'This place is evil—'

'Yes. Hurry, Eo's light—'

'The Varby want us. *Us*. They want our *power*—' Myla's voice was different now, a child's voice, frightened. 'Brother Raj—' She was pleading with him, but he could do nothing except hold her, grip her tight as her shudderings grew more violent and she screamed suddenly, a terrible piercing cry.

Ul-ul-ul-ul-ul!

Eo cried out too; wildly the rainbow patterns whirled about the walls and the prancing shadows cavorted so grotesquely that they might at any moment have burst from their pigment-world, assuming a new and terrible reality. In their ecstasy they had lost their grace, writhing into hideous new forms, blending obscenely into one another and into the

125

many marks that overscored them, taking up and discarding in vertiginous couplings the monstrous breasts and phalluses and gaping vaginas that bored boys, eternities ago, had scored into the rock.

'They're coming!' sobbed Myla. 'They're coming, I know it!'

'The Varby?' said Jem.

'The Creatures of Evil! But Prince, you know it. They want *you*, *you*. We must go—'

'Prince? What do you mean, Prince?' said Rajal.

'Hurry!' said Myla.

There was no time to say more.

Ul-ul-ul-ul-ul!

Eo whirled round and round about their heads, struggling desperately to maintain his power for the long moments until the terrified party emerged at last, panting, scratched and dirty, on a windy hillside high above the valley.

He slumped, exhausted, at Myla's feet.

'Eo, poor Eo—'

The wind scurried impatiently, contemptuously about them. Bluejacket drums sounded in the distance. Grimly Jem looked down at the valley below. The burning, the terrible burning at his chest was subsiding. He clutched the hot crystal beneath his tunic and whispered, almost to himself, 'Yes, they're coming. The Creatures of Evil—'

Rajal took his arm. 'Nova, she calls you Prince. Tell me who you are. Please, tell me—'

Myla cradled the beckoning-bird. 'Shh, shh—'

Jem said nothing; Rajal turned away. What did it mean? A fresh surge of anger filled his breast, anger and a terrible, corrosive envy. The scene in the cave felt suddenly unreal to him, as if his sister and the boy she called Prince had been, in truth, tormenting him, deceiving him with tricks.

Oh, Myla, Myla!

And he thought she had loved him, she at least!

Jem's eyes flickered over Varby, over the valley, over the winding course of the Riel.

'Look below!' he said suddenly. 'The camp! Something's wrong—'

Rajal turned back, sorrowing, and would have uttered bitter words, as if he had been certain that this, too, was some trick, but was arrested by the distant sight of flames, scattered carts, hurrying human forms.

'The Bluejackets!' he cried. 'There's been a raid!'

Chapter 17

FOXBANE

'You will be pleased to learn, Miss Veeldrop, that my nephew has taken reprisals.'

'Reprisals?'

The old buck's look was sombre. 'These dreadful kidnappings have terrorized us for long enough. For some time I – that is, my nephew – has thought those heathen Vagas are certain to be implicated. I remember in Irion – that is, in my youth . . .'

'Irion?' Cata's brow furrowed.

But the noble gentleman did not pause.

'Suffice to say, my dear, that more than one dirty little caravan has been lapped in flames this afternoon. Alas, none of them were found to conceal your friend.'

'Vagas?' Cata said now. 'You don't mean the Silver Masks?'

Lord Foxbane smiled.

'But you are an innocent, Miss Veeldrop. One speaks of the lowlier forms of Vaga-life, who inhabit a squalid camp some distance – mercifully, some distance – from the city walls.'

The old buck led Cata to the window, standing a little behind her as she looked out wonderingly. All the pools of rain had dried and a gentle afternoon sun now bathed the familiar scene – the *too* familiar scene. With a lurch of excitement it came to Cata that she would be in Agondon soon.

The old buck's arm circled her waist. 'You are young, my dear,' he whispered. 'You look from this window and I suspect you see – what do you see? This abbey, this Pump Room, these people of fashion?'

'There's nothing else. I mean, you can't see beyond them.'

'Oh, raise your eyes a little higher, Miss Veeldrop.' Cata raised her eyes and saw a glimpse of green – the countryside, glistening beyond the city walls. 'There is always something behind, behind . . .'

The words trailed away. Cata turned, alarmed and fascinated.

'Miss Veeldrop, I have been commissioned to say that my nephew admires you, admires you more deeply than he can say. He seeks your hand, Miss Veeldrop. And tomorrow at dawn, when the Last Reel has ended, when sunbeams pour over the scene of the ball and you slump, exhausted, into his arms, it is my certain knowledge that he shall declare himself, as is the custom of the Equinox.'

'My lord! You mean he shall ask for—'

'Your hand, Miss Veeldrop!' Hungrily the old man covered it with kisses. 'And should the merest flicker of doubt cross your mind, let me assure you that I have no child of my own – that is, none but Vexings! (Don't blush, my dear, it is the way of the world!) Captain Foxbane is sole heir of all my titles, my estates, my revenues. And I am a *very* old man, Miss Veeldrop. . .'

A vision of the captain – so smooth, so handsome – rose before Cata like a phantom of delight. 'My lord, but I can't! I can't go to the ball!'

'Miss Veeldrop! Your fat guardian slumbers in a stupor of sleepy-treacle. Believe me, I have seen its effects before. Who is to watch you? The butler? The maid? My nephew shall be waiting in a carriage below. Remember, Miss Veeldrop, you are a woman now, and a woman, I venture to say, of remarkable talents.'

'My lord! Do you think so?'

'There can be no doubt of it.'

The old man clattered off noisily, rapidly down the stairs, leaving the door open behind him.

'No! It can't be! No, please!'

The raid had been a warning, that was all. There had been no shooting. No one had been killed. After much garnishing of Bluejacket palms, only a few carts had been set ablaze, only a few horses set free, or stolen, or maliciously lamed. In cursory fashion, several vans had been searched and looted. Beads, joss-sticks, lengths of spangle-cloth and ripped clothes lay scattered in the mud.

But there was something else, one other thing.

'No,' Rajal said again, 'no!'

Skidding back through the screening elms, the frightened boy had far outpaced his sister and his friend. Quickly he took in the scene before him. The Great Mother's van lurched dangerously sideways. The door hung off its hinges; from within came the glimmer of smashed glass.

But what appalled Rajal was Zady. Like an ungainly child the big man slumped by the extinguished camp-fire. Other fires blazed around him; Vagas tried to damp them down. But Zady only sat in the mud, hunched and shaking, cradling the shattered fragments of the triple-gittern.

'Zady! Oh, Zady!'

This time it was Rajal who comforted him, wrapping his arms helplessly, desperately about the sobbing dark head. But what could he say?

What comfort could there be? A corrosive anger burnt through Rajal's frame. Someone must pay. Someone must pay for this.

Only after long moments did he turn, looking for his great-mother, his sister, his friend.

Where were they?

Cata slumped, confused, into a chair. Her heart pounded heavily and she closed her eyes, thinking that life had become suddenly exciting. By now, she had forgotten all about Pelli, and thought only of her own romantic adventures. Could she go to the ball? Could she really?

She leapt up, gave a little twirl – or would have done, but her foot struck something, some obstruction in her way.

It span across the floor towards the door.

'Miss Veeldrop, you are a perverse girl.'

It was Aunt Vlada, stooping, capturing the spinning thing – the nobleman's cane.

'My poor niece has been – who knows? – murdered or worse, and here you are engaging in . . . I don't quite know what.'

The jewelled cane flashed in the afternoon sun as Pelli's strange aunt made her way into the room, perching gracefully on the edge of the sofa. On the table before her she laid the cane; beside her, on a soft cushion, a black kitten, with a green ribbon tied round its neck. Attached to the ribbon was a tinkling bell.

'There, Ring. Make yourself comfortable.'

'Ring?' said Cata. 'But Ring—'

She checked herself.

'Rheen,' said Aunt Vlada.

'Pardon?'

The fine lady dabbed her eyes. 'You forgive me, Miss Veeldrop, if I am confused? Grief, mere grief. Ring and I were companions of many years.'

'I'm sorry.' Cata hung her head.

'But' – Aunt Vlada sighed – 'life must go on. This is Rheen.'

Cata gazed at Rheen, then turned away. With the kitten, the strangeness that she had felt coursing, as if in waves, from the lapdog in the Pump Room now returned in force. The confused girl put a hand to her temple. For a moment it seemed that a subtle music was floating on the air, and that borne on the music was a snatch of song.

> *Everything is lemon and nothing is lime,*
> *But even the truth shall be revealed in time:*

Then we shall drink from the mocking-tree gourds,
And sup with the King and Queen of—

What could it mean?

The kitten shook his little head, tinkling the bell. It was over. Umbecca stirred; Aunt Vlada ignored her. Nirry appeared and the imperious figure snapped her fingers, demanding tea.

She turned back to Cata. 'And pray, my dear, who was that gentleman?'

'Gentleman?'

The lady toyed with the jewelled cane. 'The gentleman, my dear, who was *clattering* down the stairs.'

'Lord Foxbane. From the Pump Room, remember? He only came to offer his—'

'I know what he calls himself. I asked you, *who* was he?'

'I don't—'

'Miss Veeldrop, go to that bookshelf. Yes, beside the fire. No, don't disturb my niece's Duenna. But do you see that red book there, that large red book? It is a book you will find in every establishment of quality.'

'An El-Orokon?'

'Pah! I speak of Vork's Peerage. Now, my dear – no, don't disturb the Duenna – but at some point, at some time in the future, when you have a free fifteenth or so, might I ask you to study the history of the family of *Foxbane*, late of the province of Vantage?'

'He mentioned Irion—'

'I'm sure he did. He comes from there, or Upper Harion – not Vantage, I'll be bound. My dear, if you learn one thing about Varby, you must learn that it is a place of illusion. The "great world"? Pasteboard and tinsel! Here, you meet a man who says he owns half a province. He's plausible enough, wears fine clothes . . . in truth, he couldn't pay for a loaf of bread. Here, we see a prince – but he's somebody's tailor; there, a great lady – really, a whore . . .'

Umbecca stirred dangerously; Aunt Vlada rushed on, 'Did you know that even the Prince of Chayn – the man who appears here under that name – is in fact the Prince's youngest brother, with no more right to the title than I?'

'But Lord Foxbane—'

Aunt Vlada rolled her eyes. 'There is a type, my dear, who thinks it bad form – positively bad form – not to present himself as the incumbent of some remote or extinct peerage. Your guest' – her fingers slid over the cane – 'may indeed have been a charming fellow, but I do not think he has come to you in his true guise.'

'Aunt Vlada, but why?'

'Oh, my poor innocent! I can see that I must take you in hand. Come to me. Yes, closer.'

Somehow, strangely, Cata could only do as she was told. Cross-legged, she sat on the carpet like a child. Aunt Vlada's eyes glowed like gemstones and the girl looked up, with sudden trust, into the soft, young-old face. The lady leaned forward and kissed her on the lips. The kiss was tender, lingering, and when Aunt Vlada drew back, Cata saw tears in the gem-like eyes.

'Dear Miss Veeldrop. I knew at once you were the one I sought.'

'Aunt Vlada?'

But the soft face hardened as she muttered urgently, 'Toy with the man. Toy with him, but keep yourself aloof. That way lies power. Forget my insipid niece. She is dead or ravished – what of it? You and I have a future together, my darling. A great future.'

'Great Mother!'

Breathless from running, Jem and Myla were flailing through the elms when suddenly Xal appeared before them. The old woman's hands were raised as if in warning and the jewel in her turban flashed sharply, painfully.

Quickly she drew them back into the trees.

Myla breathed, 'Great Mother, the camp, the van—'

'Forget these fripperies! My children, can you not feel the evil in the air?'

A stitch ached in Jem's side. He gasped, 'The Varby—'

'The Varby, yes, and a hundred, a thousand, a million Creatures of Evil, stirring from their slumbers as the anti-god calls! This is but the first stirring – there shall be more, more. Before another cycle of seasons has passed, the anti-god shall be among us, bursting through the barrier that divides this dimension from the Realm of Unbeing!'

The old woman reached forward, grabbing Jem's tunic. She wrenched open the fabric. Jem cried out. The strange burning he had felt at his chest, all through the scene in the mysterious cave, had returned now in force. He looked down. The crystal was glowing, blazing through the leather bag!

'Mighty Koros!' Myla sank to her knees. Eo, fluttering above her, screeched in alarm. The Great Mother only gazed into Jem's eyes, her claw-like hands still twisting at his tunic.

'Great Mother,' he whispered, 'how can this be? The harlequin said the crystal would shield its power, remaining only an inert, dull stone until the time when it joined its fellows. What can it mean, this sudden burning?'

The old face loomed closer to Jem's and the voice through the wizened lips came, harsh and terrifying, 'TOTH!'

'The enchanter?'

'The anti-god! The Rejected of Orok seeks the crystal too – it glows in warning that his minions are near. We had thought there would be time for you to prosecute your quest before the danger lay so heavily upon us. Pray, pray, we have not been wrong!'

'But what are we to do?'

'Key to the Orokon, soon you shall be gone from me, beyond my power to aid you. But there is one thing, one last thing I can do for you now.' A terrible weariness passed across the withered face. 'I had hoped I need not cast the Allaying Spell, for it is a sore test, even for my powers – but cast it I must, to protect the crystal.'

The Great Mother reached almost brutally to Myla, dragging the child up from her muddy abasement.

'Child, you must assist. You are young yet, too young – but the danger is great. Link your mind with mine, focus your powers. Quickly now, quickly – join hands, all of us. Myla, say along with me the words of the spell.'

The strange trio turned in a clumsy circle, their feet slithering in the undergrowth. Eo fluttered over them, circling first slowly, then faster and faster. Through dripping trees the light was purplish, like a dim reflection of the glowing crystal. Sobbings, keenings, sounded from the camp, and sometimes a defiant snatch of song.

A stench of burning hovered on the air.

Xal closed her eyes, her face screwed up in pain. Like a third eye, the stone at her forehead burnt on, empurpled, coloured like the crystal. Through cracked lips, her powers taxed to the limit, the old woman forced out the spell.

Wide-eyed, Myla mouthed the words too, repeating each line like a high, strange echo.

> *Light from the crystal shines anew!*
> *Creatures of Evil must be breaking through!*
> *Spirits of the gods – shine through me!*
> *Channel my love to the one called the Key!*
>
> *Flames of purple burn at his breast!*
> *Gods grant him strength to go on with his quest!*
> *Grant him strength to find once again*
> *A crystal hidden from the eyes of men!*

Crystal of green – then red! blue! gold!
Then the powers of the gods take hold!
Never never broken, ever and yon,
Burning bright in the Orokon!

As the chant went on, Xal cried the words out louder, desperate to transmit the protecting power. Sharp bands of pain tightened round her skull. Tears ran down the furrows of her face. Whether she would be strong enough, she did not know. She clutched Myla's hand, tighter, tighter, drinking in the waves of the child's raw strength.

Yes, yes!

Burn out the power of evil and wrath!
Save this dimension from the power of TOTH!
Bow to the saviour! Bow down and kneel
To the child with the spirit of Nova-Riel!

Purple light fizzed from Xal's forehead, striking the crystal, crackling round the glowing leather bag. Astonished, Jem was blank-faced, his jaw hanging open. Myla was writhing, her eyes white, her tongue drivelling in a terrible ecstasy. Round and round went the slithering, clumsy feet. Round and round fluttered the terrified Eo.

On and on Xal willed forth the rays.

Child of the spirit! Child called the Key!
Drink in the light that shines through me!
O Gods keep you safely, ever and yon,
Praised be the Key to the Orokon!
Praised be the Key to the Orokon!

It was too much, too much. Myla cried out, breaking from the circle.

Eo flopped, stricken, to the ground.

'Myla!' It was Rajal. Alarmed, he had rushed back through the trees. 'What foolery is this?'

The Great Mother doubled over, gasping. 'Child, speak not of what you do not understand—'

'Don't understand? The Ejlanders attack us, and you cast spells? Old woman, what use have your spells ever been?' It was cruel talk, but Rajal was enraged – as much, perhaps, by his exclusion from the ritual as by what had happened in the camp that day.

He went to his sobbing, terrified sister. She was cupping Eo in her hands. Was he dead? Poor Eo! Poor Myla! Rajal would have comforted her, but she turned on him viciously, shouting that he was a fool, shouting that she hated him, shouting at him to leave them, leave them.

Rajal blundered away, his eyes hot with tears.

Alarmed, Jem looked between the exhausted Great Mother, slumped

133

against a tree, and his friend's retreating back. He stepped towards Xal, but she waved him away.

'Go after him,' she breathed. 'He may do something foolish – go after him, please.'

Jem hesitated for a moment, then was gone.

'Goodbye, Prince Jemany. Goodbye, Child Rajal.' Xal's words were only whispered, only the faintest stirrings of breath. It was no goodbye, no goodbye at all, but the old woman knew that neither Jem nor Rajal would return that night to the Vaga-camp.

Perhaps she would never see them again.

She doubled over, clutching her heart. How old she was, how weak! Her powers were fading, dying within her. With a shuddering agony the knowledge came to her that soon she would be dead. The old woman's head lolled back. Soon, too soon, her great burden must be passed on to Myla. She reached again for the child, felt for the tiny hand.

'Myla? Myla-child?'

But where Myla had been was only the fading, stiffening corpse of Eo.

Chapter 18

LURID

'My dear, you look ravishing!'

It was true.

Cata swayed lightly, this way and that. She could not stop smiling. Candles glimmered in the waning light, mingling with the soft hues of dusk to lend all the air a curious enchantment. Enraptured, she stared into the looking-glass.

'But no, the effect is not quite—'

What else could there be? A fifteenth earlier, the glass had shown only a shy academy-girl, crushed and cowed in Agonist black. Now Cata beheld the image of a woman, a beautiful woman in a trailing golden gown.

In Pelli's gown.

'Aunt Vlada, do you think Pelli will come back?'

'Perhaps to live in shame, as a fallen woman. Hold still. That's right—'

Pelli's aunt stood behind Cata, pulling and tugging at the girl's dark hair, pinning it in place with efficient fingers. Cata closed her eyes. There were moments of pain, but she did not protest; the pain flowed at once into a welling pleasure.

Still Umbecca and the Widow slumbered.

Aunt Vlada stepped back. 'But the rubies . . . Damn the girl, she's taken them.' Quickly the old woman unfastened her emeralds. 'These will do – they'll have to . . . Now, your lover will meet you by the Abbey?'

Cata nodded; Aunt Vlada laughed.

'Hardly the behaviour of a respectable man! Honourable marriage? Pah! Mark my words, my dear – he wants to ravish you, that's all.'

'But Lord Foxbane—'

'That old fraud!'

There was a rumbling at the window. Spots of rain pattered at the glass. They had not drawn the curtains and the sky outside was the colour of a deep, dark bruise.

'Oh, but how can it be raining again?'

'The sky is heavy. It must cast down its burden—'

'But the Equinox Ball—'

Aunt Vlada laughed again, a laugh of warm affection. 'My dear, you will learn in time that this world is not made for our happiness.'

'Then what is it made for?'

Aunt Vlada answered a different question. 'Look in the glass. You are a woman now, my child. You see your beauty – but do you not see in this very beauty a tragedy, crouched hungrily, waiting to claim you? What do men care for the finery we wear?'

Cool dry fingers touched the girl's lips, then drew down slowly over her chin, her throat, over her soft breasts.

Cata shivered.

'A woman's finery, my dear, is for herself – herself, and other women. For what do men care but to rip it from us, taking their pleasure like grunting beasts? Tonight, my dear, you shall encounter a test. Pass it, and you are destined for greatness. Fail, and you are nothing but a harlot from the gutter, for all the gewgaws of fashion you may wear.

'Look at these crones, slumbering at the hearth like broken old bitch-dogs. Were they to flounder back to consciousness now, how they would rage at us, howl and whine! They are fools, for in their very ardour to cow, to curb, what do they do but exalt what they condemn?

'But ah, my dear, there are other pleasures, other and finer. What does a fat old fool in black know of the deepest secrets of the heart? With me, child – but pass my test! – you shall enter every hidden chamber.'

Aunt Vlada leaned closer and Cata shivered again, violently this time, as the old woman murmured in a voice like a caress, 'Pass, and you are mine. Fail, and I wash my hands of you, like the dirt you shall be.'

An explosion shook the sky. The fireworks!

Eagerly Cata ran to the window, but Aunt Vlada grabbed her, spinning her back.

'No, my dear. Go! Go, and meet your lover.'

A quick embrace, then Aunt Vlada almost flung Cata from the room, slamming shut the door behind the lovely woman – the lovely child – just in the moment when Umbecca, shaken awake by the explosions in the sky, burbled suddenly, 'What? What?' and started up from her chair.

Umbecca saw Aunt Vlada – and screamed.

'Raj, look,' Jem shouted, 'I don't think this is a good idea. You're tired, I'm tired, we're leaving in the morning—'

'Then go back. Go back to camp. What's left of it—'

'Raj, don't be silly! I'm not going without you—'

'Oh? Very concerned all of a sudden—'

'I've always been concerned about you—'

'Not enough to tell me who you are—'

It was raining again and the boys were trudging up the muddy hillside towards the city walls.

Jem cried, 'Forget who I am! Raj, give up this plan—'

'It's the Equinox Ball. They'll all be in the Assembly, won't they? Well, let's see how they like an indoor rain.'

'What are you talking about?'

But it was only too clear. As he strode forward, Rajal's hand swept down, then down again, gathering stones from the path beneath his feet. Some he shoved haphazardly into his pockets, others he flung far away into the air.

His violence frightened Jem.

'Come on, Prince—'

'Don't call me that—'

'Wouldn't you like to see those tall windows, showering glass over happy dancers?'

'Well, no—'

'Oh, of course. Sorry. It's that thing you've got about boot-polish, Prince. I keep forgetting what you are. You'd like to be in there with them—'

'That's not true . . . Look, Raj, you're no Silver Mask. How will you even get back into the city?'

Rajal flung back, 'What a poor memory!'

'What?'

'It's an exciting night in Varby – I think a boot-polish boy might slip through the cargo gate, wouldn't you say? Look, it's up ahead! No one's there, they're all off, watching the fun—'

'Raj, it's not worth it. If they catch you . . . Oh, you're a pig-headed, spiteful fool!'

Rajal hurled a stone.

Jem ducked. 'Think of Myla, if you won't think of yourself!'

'Leave Myla out of this!'

'I can't, she's in it! You're in it, I'm in it . . . Raj, don't you know what's going to *happen*? Soon? Don't you understand what happened in the cave? This doesn't mean anything, it's *nothing*, it's—'

They blundered through the cargo gate. Rajal was right – no one challenged them. The streets were dark and all around them was only a clutter of empty carts.

Suddenly an explosion shook the air.

They started, almost cried out. In the darkness above them, the sky exploded into a million stars.

'Oh Raj, the fireworks! Let's watch, just watch—'

Jem caught up with his friend now, grabbing his arm. Rajal went limp. All at once his anger was gone, and a sharp sobbing racked his frame.

They slumped against a cart as the wild display roared defiantly in the wetness and wind. Bolts of light shot through the rain, purple, green, red, blue, gold. There were Elabeth reels, Eldric spirals, weird twisting Sosenica-rockets.

They spoke in the spaces between explosions.

Rajal said, 'Did you know I saw my father hanged?'

'What?' Jem's heart gave a sickening lurch.

'They said he tried to kidnap some boy – this cripple-boy, who lived in Irion.'

'Cripple-boy?'

'They said he was a Simple – I suppose he was. But oh, how I remember that boy! I was far away and could barely see, but they made him stand on the scaffold that day, while they read out the lies about my father—'

'Raj, that was . . . but I—'

Boom, boom.

'Nova, I saw this boy just standing there *looking*, even when the trapdoor fell. I thought then, that's what all you Ejlanders are like – like that Simple. There they are in front of you, the most cruel and awful things, and there you are acting as if *nothing's happening . . .*'

'Come on, Raj, we're not all like that—'

There was no time to say more. At that moment a fine coach came thundering suddenly towards the cargo gate, and from the coach came a woman's piercing cries.

'Leave me alone! Get off me! Coachman, coachman, stop!'

'Oh, my darling—'

'Captain—'

'Come—'

The night sky tumbled with water and fire. Brightly the rain fell through the darkness, lurid in the radiance of exploding rockets.

Recklessly the carriage plunged through the streets.

Recklessly the captain forced himself on Cata.

'The ball!' she cried. 'But this is not the way—'

Hot kisses smothered her lips. 'Ball? A nursery for bored children! Come, my darling, let me kiss you again—'

But the captain's ardour was for more than kissing. Urgently he rucked up Cata's skirts, tearing her petticoats with rough, impatient hands.

Oh, but he was such a handsome man!

'Where are you taking me?'

'Where else, my darling, but to love's bower?'

'You're hurting me—'

'Never! Sweet innocence, have you thrilled to no previous lover? Just one stab of pain and a spurt of blood – then you shall know the ecstasies of the gods!'

It's true then, everything Aunt Vlada said.

This is your trial. Fail, and you are a harlot.

Cata struggled. She scratched, kicked, screamed. In moments she would have flung herself from the coach, leaving the captain bloodied, gasping.

Instead there was a sound of shattering glass.

'Curse it, the lamp!' the coachman cried.

A heavy thump and a struggle came next. Dangerously the carriage skewed from its path.

New hands grabbed the reins. *'Whoa!'*

'What, what?' Roughly the captain flung Cata from him. He tore down the window-sash.

A fist smashed his face.

Now it was the captain's turn to swoon. Cata cried out again, then cried out louder as a Vaga-boy with a face like boot-black ripped open the door, dragging her out.

What new assault was this? She struggled harder, harder.

'You silly girl, I'm saving you!'

The Vaga-boy was trying to stop the girl's cries, but all he could do was spin her in his arms and kiss her suddenly, full on the lips.

Cata was so shocked that she ceased her struggle. She gave herself to the moment, and the moment was long.

So sweet a kiss!

Not at all like the captain's!

But what was she doing? To be ravished by a man of fashion was one thing; by an anonymous street-boy, quite another.

She pushed him away. She slapped his face.

'How dare you! You dirty, common ruffian!'

'Cata, don't you know me? Do you really not know me?'

But the Vaga-boy had no time to wait for an answer. The girl's screams had brought a Bluejacket patrol. They were drunk, but angry, with their muskets primed.

'Vagas! Get them!'

The boy had time for only a last, seized kiss before he spirited himself away, as if by magic, into the dark and rainy night.

A moment later Cata, wet and almost fainting, was enfolded into a Bluejacket's warm cape, and a soldier with stubble like a Harion corn-field was urging her to say just what had happened, precisely what had happened.

Cata could barely think what to say.

Cata, don't you know me?

But what was the answer?

A low moan came from inside the coach, and a face with a nose like a blood pudding bobbed up in the window like a monstrous, ugly puppet.

'*Vaga-attack,*' came a thick lisp. 'This good lady – this virtuous young maiden and I . . . have been the victims of a *Vaga-attack.*'

Jem lay panting in the rain again.

What had he done? What could he do?

When he had seen Cata by the Abbey steps, he had known it was over, all over. They had changed her, moulded her into a different girl. Oh, it was hopeless! He would always love her, but what could he do when she did not even know him? What could he do when his quest lay before him?

Still his face smarted where Cata had slapped him.

'Oh, Raj—' he moaned.

But Jem was alone.

He would have tried to find his friend, but just then he heard the shouts of approaching Bluejackets. A cluster of traders' carts stood close by.

Quickly, Jem bundled himself into the nearest one.

140

Chapter 19

THREE NOSES

'Now really, young gentleman—'

'What?'

Morning light streamed through the lodging-house window, disclosing a scene of squalor. Squalid was the carpet, strewn as it was with discarded playing-cards, playbills and papers, snot-filled handkerchiefs and an upended chamber-pot; squalid was the table and the several sofas, with their sticky glasses and spattered stains; squalid was the bed on which the young gentleman lay, his armpits reeking and his breeches undone, in sheets stiff with dandruff, sweat and ... who knew what else?

The apothecary eyed his patient with distaste. How much more pleasant to treat the ladies! Why it was that young gentlemen of fashion – from good families, too! – should live like this was beyond him. This particular fellow he had not seen before, but the type he knew well enough. Handsome, of course – or would be, when not disfigured, as now, by a nose swollen to a monstrous size! The type who sported the sleek dark wig and lacquered moustaches of the unconscionable *cad* – though one of the moustaches was missing now, and the wig had slipped, revealing fiery curls beneath. Why, a professional man might consider it an affront to be asked – to be commanded! – to squander his skills on such riff-raff. Just when one was ready to go to bed, too! After all, the ball was barely over, and it had been an exhausting evening – if a splendid one, not least for the occasions upon which the apothecary was obliged to turn his hand, so to speak, to the needs of certain ladies, who had the misfortune to faint in the heat.

He began again, 'Young gentleman, I said you can hardly expect to recover yourself if you partake of that *particular* breakfast—'

'Bollocks of Agonis, what's wrong with it?' demanded the young gentleman, perhaps a little more loudly than intended. He slumped back, groaning, holding his head, before struggling back up on his elbows again and swigging irritably at a tankard of ale.

But he could do nothing right. Slops spluttered down his chin and shirt-front and he cursed loudly, flinging away the tankard, smashing it against the wall.

The wig had slipped off completely now. Polty's red hair flamed in the light.

With a wince, he ripped off his remaining moustache.

'Bollocks of Koros, what the—' came a second voice, and another young gentleman floundered out of oblivion, his face emerging blearily over the back of a sofa. Now *that* one the apothecary knew well enough. Mr 'Jac' Burgrove. Well, it looked as if *he* was out of action for a while . . .

'Apothecary,' cried the captain, 'you're useless! Where's my cold compress? Bean! Bean!'

The apothecary pursed his lips. Fortunately the young man addressed as Bean, a lanky side-officer, emerged at that moment from behind a screen in the corner, where for some time he had been attempting, with noisy sloshings, to wash the dried blood from his superior's handkerchiefs.

It occurred to the apothecary that really, this was rather a droll scene. Three young men, all sporting the same injury – all with bashed-in noses. But only the sufferings of the captain, it seemed, were to be considered of account . . .

Evidently a forceful fellow.

'Coming, Polty—'

'Foxbane!' called the captain reprovingly.

Foxbane? A pained look passed across the apothecary's face.

'Bollocks of Theron,' said the young man called Bean, dropping a sopping handkerchief to the floor. 'Good apothecary, will he be all right?' he added, as he squelched his dripping burden over Foxbane's – over Polty's – ruined nose.

The apothecary recovered himself again and stroked his chin. 'Your friend' – he gestured to the bed – 'your captain . . .'

'Foxbane,' Bean offered helpfully, brightly.

The apothecary winced. A son, a nephew, of that dreadful old buck? Yes, he had known there was something *familiar* . . . That was when he noticed the wig-stand in the corner, and the wig that teetered on top of it, threatening to slump to the floor at any moment.

And were they not the bright garments of the buck, winking mischievously from that open cupboard door?

The apothecary might have risen with the remnants of his dignity and retreated, there and then – but did not. Distaste fought in him with greed, and swiftly lost. With a smile he forced himself to open his bag, putting his neatly ordered wares on display.

On the bed, Polty moaned – growled, even. Frustration churned inside him like bile. What a miserable night he had passed! At first, it was the Vaga-scum that made him curse and rail. To be smashed in the face by a dirty black fist! If the pain in his nose had not been so great that even to

142

stand was to risk passing out, Polty would have ridden down to the Vaga-camp himself and taken out his fury. How he ground his teeth, how he screwed shut his eyes, imagining orgies of beating and bludgeoning! Now – so little time later – he barely cared. Vagas? A man would be an imbecile to waste his hatred on so lowly a life-form. There was no need for passion. He had made his report; already, he knew, it had fizzed through the chain of command like a fuse. Baral, Supreme Commander of Varby and Holluch, had ordered fresh reprisals. Yesterday's Vaga-raid had been but the prelude; by now the camp would be a smoking ruin, and those who were not dead or injured would be scattered, fleeing, who knows where.

No, it was not the Vagas that troubled Polty now.

'Of course,' the apothecary was saying, 'some kind of recovery is expected, indeed inevitable, without the aid of art; nonetheless one might suggest that – the humours after all are in precarious balance – a course of twelve nose-leechings to draw the radical heat, with accompanying – *hem!* – enemas for radical moisture, a sachet or so of Wenaya-cream and a large order of unic pills would be not so much advisable as *imperative . . .'*

Polty removed the compress from his nose and looked at the apothecary with a peculiar intentness. He might have been about to rise from his bed, march the interloper from the room and fling him down the stairs; instead he attempted a wry smile, and said softly, 'Apothecary, I like you.'

The apothecary smiled nervously. 'Your friends,' he endeavoured, his voice shaking a little, 'are suffering, Captain, as you do. Perhaps' – he raised his voice, calling towards the sofa, where Mr Burgrove appeared, once again, to have slumped back senselessly – 'perhaps just some unic pills . . . or *one* leeching . . .'

'Apothecary, I like you!' Polty boomed this time, 'oh yes, I like you! Bean, a bumper for our new friend! Was ever there such a display of insight? Such acumen, such integrity?'

The apothecary patted his perfumed periwig. 'One comes from a long line of medical men.'

'One can tell. Friend, what is your name?'

'Waxwell. Franz Waxwell.'

'You don't say?' Polty looked as if he might have been about to make some observation, but checked himself and instead, rising from his bed, began, 'Tell me, good apothecary, what would you prescribe for an ailment of the heart?'

'Your heart ails you?'

'Sore, sore.'

'You speak of the strength? The rhythm? The *thud-thud-thud*?'

Polty thrust his swollen nose close against the apothecary's face. 'I speak, dear apothecary, of a crack, like a flaw in china, that has opened and is widening – oh, painfully! – in that most tender and delicate part. I speak of a dream, a vision, that danced before me, only to be snatched violently away. You see me now, reduced and smarting; who could believe that, but a night before, the pleasures of the gods were within my grasp? You understand, dear apothecary, I speak of . . . the ladies.'

'Ah.'

'You have, no doubt, an interest in ladies?'

'I like to call it an inside knowledge.'

'I'm sure you do. Bean, that bumper! Apothecary, I have a little proposition for you.'

With that, Polty circled a friendly hand round the apothecary's neck and, speaking low and rapidly, engaged him in a long, intent discussion. From time to time the apothecary nodded, and Polty smiled, and when Bean at last scurried forward with the bumper, Polty only flicked him irritably away.

Bean looked on miserably. What could Polty be up to now? Another devious plan, no doubt. As usual, Bean would know nothing about it until its dire consequences, whatever they were, became clear at last.

Lieutenant Aron Throsh – that is to say, Bean – had seen much in the service of his senior officer. In the Valleys of the Tarn, had he not shared the field (why, shoulder to shoulder) with the great man at the celebrated battles of Cat-Under-Van, of Catayane, of Hayloft Heights, of Killing Rock, not to mention innumerable skirmishes at the Lazy Tiger? The hero, of course, was Polty – Bean claimed, desired, to be a subordinate, no more – but ah, the bliss to have played his part, even his small part, in those Famous Victories!

That Theron-season, Bean had seen action in the glorious campaigns of Bichley, Rextel and Heva-Harion, exulting dutifully (but genuinely, too) at these latest conquests – no, not so much of Polty, but rather of that secret god known to Polty as 'Penge'.

Bean – apart from Polty, of course – was the only person who knew about Penge (knew him, that is, by name). Sometimes, indeed, the lanky side-officer felt himself to be almost as intimate with Penge as Polty himself. Impossible, yes; but a monarch needs a man to watch and serve him, and were there not times – it had to be admitted – when Polty had treated his great charge laxly? How many times – why, Bean had lost count! – had Polty slumped insensibly on his bed, leaving it to his humble side-officer to ensure that Penge was comfortably quartered for the night? How many times had Bean cupped the poor, spent victor – softened after battle – in his bony palm, dabbing and wiping at the reddened flesh, the tender glistenings, that a swordsman brings home from the fields of praise?

Ah, but what a sweet task to serve so fine a master! Yes, many a moment had Bean shared with Penge, while Polty lay all inert and unawares; and oh! the gratitude that flooded him when Penge (his owner all unknowing) would stir himself again to his battlefield glory!

Then Bean would feel his own paltry equivalent of Penge – there could be no name for a part he held in such contempt – stirring in sympathy, aching once again to cast its bitter, lonely seed.

The side-officer turned to the window, looking out on the bleak morning. Varby after the Equinox. Already the town looked dead, dead. Bean would have taken a swig from the bumper, but Mr Burgrove, stirring again, claimed it eagerly, downing it with noisy gluggings. A wave of self-pity swept over the side-officer. Their season here in Varby had promised much – promised, not least of all, many moments with Penge. Even in that respect it had proved disappointing – could there ever be moments enough with Penge? – but in other ways, too, Bean had found it a desolate time.

Since their transfer to The Inner, Polty and his side-officer had been seconded to Intelligence, under the command of a certain Lord E——. It had seemed a splendid promotion, but Polty had treated their missions almost with contempt. Sent to report on the 'Varby Vanishings', how far had they got? In various guises, they had mingled among the revellers – in search, said Polty, of information – but what had it been, in the end, but a debauch?

Bean looked sourly at 'Jac' Burgrove. If only they had kept to themselves, at least, and not taken up with this shabby rake!

The gluggings turned into anguished writhings and Mr Burgrove let the bumper fall.

'Bean, help – I'm going to throw up—'

Swiftly Bean looked about for a vessel, but could find only a chamberpot, which Polty had filled plentifully during the night. It did the trick. A thick stream of orange-brown muck spattered from Mr Burgrove's lips.

'Captain's busy,' he observed when he had recovered himself, wiping his mouth on a cravat already stained liberally with blood.

Sighing, Bean fell into the required banter. 'Says his heart is broken.'

'Don't believe it, it's only his nose. Now my heart . . . only yesterday, too! Ah, Bean, I was on the brink of bliss!'

'Only the brink?'

'Virgin scruples. Hers, I mean.'

'Of course.'

'And you? In the service of which lady did *your* nose suffer?'

'No lady. Only Polty. I mean, the captain.'

'The captain?'

'I was his coachman.'

'Ha! But Bean, you must lower your sights.'

'As low as yours?'

'In your case? Lower.'

The banter would have continued; Mr Burgrove, indeed, as his nausea subsided, might have proceeded to the most elegant drolleries; from his lips, instead of the churned, stinking evidence of his evening's debauch, there might have flowed epigrams that would not have disgraced the works of Mr Coppergate – that might, indeed, have *come* from the works of Mr Coppergate – but at that moment there was a knock on the door.

Bean opened it.

Standing there, stiff and imperious in the distinctive sash of the military police, was a senior officer from the Holluch barracks, flanked by a small but determined-looking corps. It could mean only one thing.

The girl, last night.

Bean blanched. He had always known Polty would go too far!

'Mr "Jac" Burgrove?'

Bean pointed, confused.

The senior officer, in a tone of polite apology, said, 'Mr Burgrove, I'm afraid you must come with us.'

Polty demanded, 'Major, what is this about?'

The major ignored him. With strutting little steps, his chest puffed out, he picked his way across the cluttered floor towards Mr Burgrove. The gentleman had been disporting himself in languorous abandon; suddenly he was on his feet and quivering, his face white, his cloth-of-gold cravat twisting anxiously in his hands.

The major's eyes were sad. 'Jac, it's no good. Your reign is out.'

'What?'

'We found the cabin. By the Lord Agonis, there was evidence enough there! But oh, Jac, then we found her necklace in the pinewood, her little ruby necklace ripped from her neck. Had the girl been only a whore, a waiting-maid . . . But Jac, you leave us no choice—'

Mr Burgrove's face was ashen. 'But she ran away—'

'I'm sure she did. And Jac, we found her. Were you so drunk, so driven with lust? That poor little neck, twisted and bruised—'

Mr Burgrove wailed, 'I don't understand—'

'Come, Jac, you must see. You silly man, didn't you know it was a hanging offence? You're under arrest, Jac—'

'But what? Why—?'

'Jac, for the murder! Of Miss Pellicent Pelligrew!'

This time, Bean was too late with the chamber-pot. Vomit gushed afresh from Mr Burgrove's lips.

END OF PART ONE

PART TWO

The Metamorphosis

Chapter 20

FOUR LETTERS

Darling Catty,
What ever can I say about your funny letter? Why, I laughed until my sides would burst! I felt a split, I really did! But now I'm sad, for how can my reply be half as good? But then, I'm not half as clever as you, Catty! (I think you'd better keep Mr Coppergate's book! I'm sure I'd never understand a line, let alone have time to read one!)
But my dear, you'll never guess who's coming to Agondon, to make her Entrance? That's right, your dear cousin Jeli Vance!! You'll believe I was angry (Ju-Ju said I was a positive terror, & you know what a terror Ju-Ju can be!) to be left out of Varby, but after all, Ju-Ju does say Varby-girls (but she calls them worse) are SOILED BEFORE THEIR ENTRANCE, & who am I, now answer me that, to say she's wrong? Oh, but what a tease dear Ju-Ju's been! Here was I, thinking I was going back to Orandy for good! But it was all a lark!! Ju-Ju says, now they've kept me off the scene so long, my Entrance shall be STUNNING. Mark my words, she says, NO OTHER GIRL of her year shall make so SPECTACULAR an Entrance as Miss Jeli Vance – or so SPECTACULAR a match!
Oh dear, dear Catty! To think, I'll soon be back in Agondon – hugging you tight again, my dear, dear cousin!!
Love J. xxxxxxxxx

P.S. So funny, what you said about the Prince-Elect! Do you know, I had a letter from Huskia Bichley, & she says, would you believe, there's rumours in Varby that I've married him!! What cat put that about, I wonder? You didn't hear anything, did you, Catty?
But no, you would have said.

O Eay!
The throbbings of my heart are stilled! My fears, my womanish fears, are beaten, banished, buried! Would you believe, the most splendid news? Like me – like all who thrill to every motion of the great world – you have been troubled by these 'Varby Vanishings'. The mystery is no more! Why did we not see the truth at once? In

the Tarn, I tell myself, we would have been wiser, for in our dear Valleys have we not sounded Vaga-depravity to its fullest depths? Yet how, even in Varby, a hint of mystery could inhere in these late tragedies is itself a source of wonderment, is it not, when all through the Season a filthy Vaga-camp has nudged, nay nestled, at the city's very gates? More, that its dusky denizens have been empowered – welcomed, at the mere flash of a licence! – to swarm and slither through those gates? (I tremble at the thought of so many Ejland-maidens, bared to the gaze of Koros-lust!)

The Inner has paid a price for its liberal ways. The Vaga-camp is destroyed, its dangers passed, but alas – oh alas! – that never again shall the beauty of Miss Vyella Rextel, of Miss Mercia Teasle, of young Lady Vantage – not to mention MISS PELLI PELLIGREW – beguile the great world! (O foolish Widow, to believe that one hand could accomplish what is hard work even for two!)

But my theme is more than this, for Eay, who should have been the last *victim of this Vaga-evil but – no, not Miss Pelligrew – but OUR OWN DEAR CATAYANE? (But do not start!) A victim, yes – but the one, the only one to be SAVED! I had been ill (Eay, do not fret – it is but infirmities of womanly nature), and in my illness, struggle as I would, my vigilance, for the briefest of moments, was lost! (So precarious is virtue's tenure in the world, when easily, so easily, its sentinels are laid low.) Bless our intrepid Bluejackets, who charged so boldly to the rescue (I shall write to the Dragoons-Commander, urging promotion for young Captain Foxbane) – but O! curses that the Vaga-filth, who would rend the veil of our dear girl's innocence, could vanish, with their dusky faces, into the night!*

But Eay, do you not see what this means? Such celebrity as our CATAYANE now enjoys may last the full length of a moonlife, or more! (And with Miss Rextel, &c., now absent from the stage, shall not the great world be celebrity-hungry – nay, more than hungry? Ravenous!)

I am still a little low from my late illness, but soon we must pack to leave for Agondon, where my brother-by-marriage shall receive us – if grudgingly – as we make the preparations for our dear child's Entrance. If only there were not so long, so long still to wait until the First Moonlife Ball, when at last she must take her place on the stage!

For am I not convinced now that her triumph is assured?

> *Enraptured,*
> *I remain*
> *Your*
> *U.V.*

(Received before the above was sent)

Dearest dear,

Again a gentleman settles at his escritoire, his pen at the ready to serve a lady's pleasure. Her pleasure, yes, for in what else could he delight – he, whom it pleases to call himself her long-serving counsellor? Yet, does it not seem that days – too many – have passed since last his heart could throb in tune with hers, in that sweet imagined consort of the EPISTOLARY? – In short, my dear, the gentleman fears the lady has neglected him of late. Yet why, after all, should one caught up in the Varby Round (and have we not reached the Time of Equinox?) find her thoughts turning, for the merest moment, to the stricken and – has not the taint caught him, by now? – provincial figure whose joy it once was to join with her in ardent devotion? Yet think not – no, not for a moment, dearest dear! – that the gentleman upbraids, that the gentleman chides. For what can be these tears (coursing down his cheeks) but tears of joy, that the lady should be what she should always *have been?*

Yet not quite; for in the world in which she finds herself, are there not many – too many – who boast of titles, degrees, far in excess of any she *may claim? Of course, the gentleman has said many times that all* mere *worldly distinctions must pall before the* one, *the* only, *that matters in truth. In the Empire of the Heart, what Empress can reign but – ah, but dear lady, you know my mission is to* translate *(as I may say) this distinction of yours, so that soon, very soon, UMBECCA THE GREAT shall prevail not only in the heart, but in the world!*

But I sink to banter, forgetting the respect which is due to your person. Dearest, forgive me, but my heart is sore! I am worried for your husband, more worried than I have been at any time since he descended into this trough of sickness. For long, too long, we have known that never again shall we see in him the uprightness of his glory days; a rigidity has gone from him that can never be resumed. And yet his mind, his noble mind, did not seem wholly *vanquished! Alas, I fear now even that last and most vital bastion has been stormed—*

> *Storm'd, storm'd and sack'd, by Time, exulting Time –*
> *His cruel and cunning Siege at last is o'er!*

Secreted in the fastness of his enjungl'd chamber, does Olivan Tharley Veeldrop ponder any longer the affairs of the province that is governed in his name? Dear lady, he thinks only of the past, of regrets and sorrows – often, of regrets I barely understand. Then, too, his ramblings will turn to the girl, and sometimes it seems he has forgotten that we have taken her from his side. Instead – O, chilling it is to hear! – he believes himself again in those early moonlives, when still Miss Catayane was a Beauty of the Valleys, an innocent without memory, dream or desire, whom he took to sit by him during his long days of suffering. Many a time, my dear, I have had to tell him anew (O, the poor gentleman!) that his 'little reader' (for so he calls her) is gone from us, gone far away! I had hoped to reconcile him to her absence, but – poor gentleman – should some crisis come to pass, I fear this absence may yet bode ill. Pray that he is saved from fresh shocks and torments, for (dear lady) it may be that a time is coming when only the girl might pull him back from that threshold that now seems edging ever nearer, nearer, insisting through the susurrus of the foliage round his bed!

We must arrange for proper and more constant care.

Excuse this sad subject.

> *Dear lady,*
> > *I remain,*
> > > *As ever,*
> > > > *E.F.*

Postscript.

Dear lady, the time of crisis has come! In the very moment that I was heating the sealing-wax, a footman entered, bearing a silver tray. A letter! Ah (but as always) my heart leapt with hope, for might it not be franked with the Seal of Varby? Yet alas, the satisfied sigh that was welling in my throat issued forth, instead, as a groan of pain. For what was this? No missive snatched from the fires of virtuous love, but instead the cold pages of formal command!

> *And yet, and yet!*

Read, dear lady, read, and think what this means!

(Enclosed)

S.H.I.A.M.
SERVICE OF HIS IMPERIAL AGONIST MAJESTY

To His Excellency General Olivan Tharley Veeldrop, District Governor, 'Valleys of the Tarn' (Kingdom of Ejland, 9th Province) from (office of) Lord Elion S. Margrave, Under-Secretary (17th) to His Imperial Agonist Majesty, King Ejard of the Blue Cloth, His First Minister & Ascendancy, &c., &c.

Honoured sir:

I am instructed by His Imperial Agonist Majesty through his First Minister & Ascendancy to inform you that it has been seen fit over these coming moonlives to conduct a wide-ranging & penetrative inspection of certain matters pertaining to present arrangements vis-à-vis *that is* in respect of *as well as* for the continuance & furtherance of *the Governance of the Provinces as established under*

154

the GOVERNANCE OF THE PROVINCES COLONIES &
PROTECTORATES DECREE 996e; that the said inspection to be
known as the P.G.A.E. (Provincial Governance Assessment Exercise)
shall include as part of its remit the making of certain
recommendations as to the status powers &c. of those presently
responsible for the said Provincial Governance; that accordingly a
representative of His Imperial Agonist Majesty shall be empowered to
visit & inspect the 9th Province ('Valleys of the Tarn') forthwith with
a view to putting forward said recommendations.
I expect to be with you by Year's Turn.
May the Lord Agonis Protect the King.

I am, sir,
&c., &c.,
(Lord) Elion S. Margrave

(Addendum in the hand of Lector Feval)

This Margrave sounds a pompous fool, of that there can be no doubt –
but dear lady, 'recommendations as to the status'! Of course this is
couched in vilest flannel – O, for that sweet LANGUAGE OF THE
HEART which is yours and mine – but what can this mean but that
my long campaign, my endless epistles to the Under-Secretary, have
borne fruit? Is not our dear commander at last to receive his reward?
Dear lady, I have to believe it! Did I not say a PEERAGE was always
the best, the most certain way? (Would my lady bask only in the mere
reflected glory of a niece's – how ever spectacular – marriage? Fie on
the world, that UMBECCA THE GREAT should be in its eyes but a
Dowager Aunt!) I say again, dear lady, the crisis has come! Bring
back the girl, bring her back at once – that we may keep the old man
alive!

Chapter 21

FIVE COME TO AGONDON

Agondon.

Magnificent and squalid, hideous and glorious, the great city crouches in the heart of the empire like a vast spider at the centre of its web. Here, where the Gulf of Ejland relents at last, after insisting its way between the smooth curves of Lexion and the Tiralon Peninsula; here, where the rolling downs of The Inner cushion the coast from the sweeping plains of Harion, from the rocky plateaux of Chayn and Vantage and the darker, wilder outlands of the Zenzan realms; here, long ago, when the Vagabondage of the women and men of earth was barely over and even the Juvescence still memory, not dream, the peoples of Agonis made their first city.

Agondon was only a crude fortress then, raised on a rocky island in the Riel Delta. But from the first, The Island had in it a forbidding power. All around, ready to swallow any enemy, lay the green marsh-lands of the spreading river. Thus do all our glories, as all our miseries, have their origins in military might.

Since those earliest days there have been many Agondons: Agondons of wood, Agondons of stone, Agondons heaped upon ruins of Agon-dons. Successively the cities have been burnt, battered, ripped down time and again, only to spring back into fecund life. And each new city has been bigger, bolder, sprawling further, ever more firmly, over marshlands that once barely supported a footstep. But in each new Agondon has been something of the old, some vestige of creaking timbers, of spidery corners, some sagging gable, some smooth-stoned unyielding wall. Now, as the thousandth Cycle of Atonement draws near, the city is an immense indecipherable palimpsest, its traces of the past like some secret confirmation that yes, in truth, it has endured for ever, and yes, in truth, it shall always endure.

Yet even now a time without Agondon may be glimpsed – by the traveller, say, one misty morning, whose tired eyes blur as he drags his torn feet over the last rise of the Pale Highway. Looking down towards the Delta then, he sees the flatlands stretched around the city only as a rich, brown-grey murk. This, it seems, is a place of mud and mosquitoes, of half-seen mysterious scaly things, swishing swiftly through dank reeds. Rising from this, the great central island is only a jagged, forbidding heap. The heights are empty save for cawing seabirds.

The traveller rubs his eyes.

A chill pallid sun is piercing the mist; down, down he stumbles into this last of valleys before the greener deeps of the Gulf begin. Now the murk becomes something more, a mean huddle of houses. Here, at these very edges of Agondon, it is as if we are privy to some dark metamorphosis, the primaeval ooze just beginning to shape itself into some semblance of human life. The stench is overwhelming. This is a place of sackcloth and mud, of diseased creatures in human shape slithering, scurrying like beetles over mounds of filth and rottenness. At such sights, the traveller's eyes grow wide. He hurries on, glad only that his raggedness attracts no eager eye, not here, not in this place. Can this be Agondon, City of Aeons?

In his provincial fastness, he had imagined that everything in the great capital would be splendid. In time, he will come to know these splendours: the ballrooms and parks and pleasure-gardens, the pungent glittering shops, the plush boxes at the Wrax Opera. But he will know too this other Agondon, a place of pungent alleys and scurrying rats, of suppurating docks and the dank Embankment, of the Erdon Tree, out on the Wrax Road, where miscreants are taken in carts and hanged while drunken, brawling hordes gather to cheer. By then, perhaps, he will understand that a great metropolis is a place not merely more splendid than any other, but more extreme, as if its very heights – of breeding, wealth, learning, art – must call forth complementary, degraded depths. A city is like a body with a bejewelled heart, but a heart that must lodge within a putrescent carcass.

The Shambles slip behind him. Now the mist and the sun and the traveller's eyes, too, are rising. Now in the gathering pale gold of the morning the great mound of The Island begins to reveal itself. No longer is it the bleak rock, the mournful presiding deity of the land of mud. Heaped high with chimneys and windows and walls, pale with sandstone, dark with terracotta, instead The Island is a tangle of winding streets, weaving their way upwards to the vast tapering spire that soars above an enormous many-columned temple. Soon the chill winds will sweep down from the north, but now, as the traveller looks on, the last glories of the Equinox break through. Gold flashes from the temple spire and at once, as if in answer, the clouds give way to the sun's insistence, bathing the high city in a molten radiance. The traveller gasps. He sinks to his knees there in the road and tears, unbidden, burst from his eyes. Never has he seen a place of such beauty.

There is more. Channelled through the walls of the high Embankment sweeps the Riel, new-swollen with shimmering life. Across the river, over fine bridges, Agondon New Town, with its great boulevards, its magnificent terraces and lush parks, sweeps like a vaster Varby over the rich reclaimed plains. Soon the traveller will make his way through these streets, gasping now not with awe but exhaustion, as he searches, not daring to ask assistance, for the house where a man in a silver mask told him, long ago, that he would be received.

Thus does the rightful heir enter his city, a shabby stranger, dragging his feet, frightened at the passing of each fine carriage. Perhaps this is what Jem will remember; but I think he will remember, most of all, the sudden splendour when the sun broke through, and for a moment, his vision blurred again, he saw only the magnificence of this ancient, evil city, and was able to think, absurdly, *I have come into my kingdom.*

'Ju-Ju, I'm frightened!'

'Nonsense girl, whatever is there to fear?'

Miss Jelica Vance was not quite sure. Wide-eyed, she peeped beneath the edges of the gauze. Below, the gradient of the cobbled streets was sharp; above, far above even the high houses, the immense spire of the temple loomed through clearing mist. The carriage juddered as it made its way upwards. Cries, oaths, chaos of all kinds sounded from the surrounding streets. Jeli winced as the coachman whipped the horses; they seemed to be making their way through a market. Perhaps it was all a bit much for the girl. She had been to Agondon before, it was true, but only in rapid ferryings to and from the gates of Mistress Quick's. The Island, and her uncle's mansion, were things quite new to her.

But oh, the excitements that lay ahead!

The coach drew up before a dark narrow house, barely a street away from the crowded market. A steep flight of stone stairs led to a shabby door. Jeli's brow furrowed. Could this be the place? Footmen in the livery of the Archduke of Irion sprang forward, ready to assist them from the coach.

Climbing the steep stairs, Jeli whispered, 'But Ju-Ju, what of Agondon New Town? Why doesn't Uncle Jorvel have his house there?'

'Hush, girl!' returned her Duenna. 'Your uncle is old nobility. This house has been in the family for generations. Besides, would you not be close to Temple? Stray not far from Lord Agonis, my girl, if you would not be lured into a life of turpitude!'

And Jeli had to giggle, in spite of herself. Ju-Ju's sayings were always so lurid! On impulse, halfway up the stairs, the girl hugged her old companion. Dear Ju-Ju! How Jeli loved her! Time and again she had strained at the leash, as an Unentered girl was wont to do, but always she had known her Duenna was there, eager to smooth her forehead, to kiss away her tears.

'Dear girl!' Exhausted from the stairs, Ju-Ju gasped. At that moment a cawing seabird flew overhead, for after all, the Gulf was close by. Delighted, Jeli looked up. But it was then that a wince of pain came suddenly to her Duenna's face. The old woman clutched her breast and tottered, then tumbled like a sack down the steep stone stairs.

Jeli screamed. She would have rushed down, pushing aside the footmen. But somehow she could not. Somehow she was rooted in place, white-faced with shock halfway up the stairs.

The door at the top of the stairs clicked open. Turning, Jeli saw a fine lady, dressed in luxurious emerald satin. In the crook of an arm, the lady held a magnificent black cat.

'My poor child! Fear not, I shall look after you now.'

Aunt Vlada smiled and Jeli stared wonderingly from the top to the bottom, from the bottom to the top, of the steep stone stairs.

Days passed.

Loneliness, like an ache, throbbed in Jem's heart. What had he expected when he came, a ragged stranger, to the house with golden scrolls above the windows and doors? It was a question he could not answer; all he knew was that the world had become strange, stranger than he had ever known it before.

There had been no question that he was awaited. He walked up the steps and the doors opened. Servants, unbidden, led him silently into the hall. No need to say, *I am Jem*; no need to say a thing. The cool gloom of the house gleamed with marble and mahogany. Awed, Jem ascended the immense stairs. Through golden glass in the landing windows shimmered a wild garden.

Up, up. Vast candelabra branch like trees, in avenues receding down long vistas of corridor.

Up. In the long gallery at the top of the house they have filled a steaming bath. The servants act in concert, without need for words. Dressed in the simplest of lemon-yellow tunics, they are ciphers without voices. Some are men, some are women; it does not matter.

Surrendering the rags he wears, Jem feels no shame. Long supple fingers lave his hair, golden in the glow of the Javander-light. Jem sinks deeply, as if into sleep. Only when a hand brushes at the crystal, concealed in the leather bag at his neck, does he start awake. He pushes away the hand and his eyes flash. Then from somewhere – somewhere far away – comes an echo of laughter.

Jem turns his head and the voice comes: *Key to the Orokon, you are with me now. Key to the Orokon, you have arrived.*

But the man called Lord Empster is nowhere to be seen.

'I wish, Bean—'

Polty did not say what he wished, because the corporal on the desk looked up sharply. Polty shifted irritably on the hard bench. Half the afternoon ago, when they began their waiting, the stiff-backed fellow had commanded them to silence. He might have been a steward in an exclusive gentlemen's club, giving orders to the tradespeople. Not that Polty had ever been into an exclusive gentlemen's club; but he could imagine, and liked what he imagined.

He did not wish to be one of the tradespeople, that was all.

An olton-clock ticked loudly somewhere behind his head, marking off the mechs with a stiff precision like the polished boots that from time to time click-clicked mechanically over the tiles. Long chill rectangles of light fell through the windows, at an angle which might have been laid down in regulations and measured carefully.

It was their third day in the Ollon Barracks. Yesterday, and the day before, they had waited in this hall in just this way, only to be informed at last by that cold fish of a corporal that Colonel Heva-Harion could not see them yet. Really, it was intolerable! In Irion, Polty would have made a scene; but now, he knew, he was a long way from Irion, and the power he enjoyed there, as the governor's son, carried little weight in Agondon.

In fact, none at all.

They were awaiting fresh orders. Polty knew nothing of this Heva-Harion – though of course he knew the name. It belonged to an old Ejland family; perhaps that was why it set Polty on edge. He had imagined that they would see Lord E——, who was in charge of the Special Agents. Why he thought this, Polty did not know. After all, they had never seen Lord E——, who seemed to communicate only through others. But Polty, by now, was becoming more and more sensitive to real or imagined slights. Last night in the officers' mess he had become alarmingly drunk, and only the timely intervention of Bean had saved him from approaching, and punching, an old fellow whom he took to be Colonel Heva-Harion.

Staggering out of the mess, Polty had hung heavily round Bean's neck, and told him slobberingly that he was much obliged to him. Bean was gratified, and only too glad to help Polty into bed. Dear Bean! Where he would be without his loyal side-officer, Polty did not know. He reached out, giving his friend's thigh a friendly squeeze. Bean flushed, and looked gratified again.

Very gratified.

Time passed. The clock ticked; the angle of light shifted slowly, as if according to a strictly-laid plan. *Scratch-scratch* went the corporal's pen. *Click-click* went another set of boots, then another, crossing the chequerboard tiles. From time to time the corporal looked up, engaging in murmurous consultations with this or that functionary, before the functionary clicked away and disappeared through one of many doors. All the doors were tall – at least twice the height of a man – and polished to a high sheen. When they were closed they echoed loudly, though always they were closed with the utmost care.

Poor Polty! The echoes hurt his head. He rubbed his eyes, then his temples. He was feeling more than a little sick, and was wondering if he might repair to the latrines when a voice came, 'Colonel Heva-Harion will see you now.'

Polty and Bean followed the functionary through one of the tall polished doors. The echo sounded again, behind them this time, and they found themselves in a plush office, as rich in ornamentation – stuffed heads of animals, regimental swords, native masks from the Jarvel Coast – as the hall outside was barren.

Behind the rampart of a huge desk sat a hard-faced elderly man in full dress uniform, topped by a neat steel-grey wig. Unsmiling, but with immaculate manners, he bade the two young officers be seated, offering tobarilloes from a golden case.

Polty relaxed. This Heva-Harion seemed not a bad sort. Perhaps the son of Commander Veeldrop was to be treated, after all, with the respect he deserved.

The colonel shuffled through the papers on his desk. Through the windows came the muted rituals of the parade-ground, the shoutings, the stampings, the clatterings of musket-drill. Idly Polty wondered what their next mission might be. His thoughts gave him no apprehension; after all, had they not been called to Agondon? Drawing back on his tobarillo, he imagined the plush drawing-rooms, the theatres, the pleasure-parks, the glittering balls. What fun they would have! And what fun for Penge!

The colonel eyed his interviewees with a smile. They were handsome young men, or would be, when their noses returned to normal size. Captain Veeldrop in particular. Yes, he would be a very handsome fellow.

Perhaps that was why, in what followed, the colonel addressed himself wholly to Polty, ignoring the side-officer almost entirely.

'Your career, Captain Veeldrop, appears to have been an unusual one.'

'Sir?'

'Throughout, you have enjoyed particular privileges. Now why do you think that might be?'

'Sir, I am sensible of my position. As a Veeldrop, much has been given to me; but I know, too, that I must give much.' At this point, Polty might have launched into a long disquisition upon the responsibilities of power; had he done so, it would have been filled with fine phrases, but alas, his head was aching too much, and in any case, the colonel was impatient to continue.

'I would say, Captain, that you have given remarkably *little.*' Here, another man would have raised his voice, even shouted. Colonel Heva-Harion remained calm, even icy, but his words were devastating nonetheless. 'Young man, do you think we are fools?'

'Sir?'

'Do you imagine, even for a moment, that your utter disregard of your duties has gone unobserved through the long length of a Varby Season? The Special Agents are, by definition, an élite. You had just joined our ranks, and were on probation. Did you think no other agent was abroad, ready to report upon your fitness for your task?'

The colonel's mouth twisted into a wry grimace. 'Lieutenant-Colonel Burgrove has put in his report—'

'Burgrove?' Polty gasped. 'But Burgrove—'

The colonel waved him aside. 'Burgrove has had difficulties of his own, it is true – nothing not to be expected in the career of a Special Agent. But we are speaking of *you,* Captain Veeldrop. And I am empowered to tell you that we are not impressed.'

The colonel waved a crumpled letter.

'As to this latest cynical exercise – really, contriving that your own mother-by-marriage should beg promotion for "Captain Foxbane" – why, I am flabbergasted!'

'But sir, she didn't know! You don't think—'

The colonel leaned forward. 'Captain, it hardly matters what *I* think. I am, let me assure you, the merest conduit for the commands of Lord E——. Lord E—— is a member of The Ascendancy, and his orders carry the authority that rôle confers upon him. They are not to be countermanded. They are not to be questioned.

'Had you acquitted yourself well in Varby, I should now be entrusting you with a greater mission – why, a mission that my best agents would fight each other for the honour of taking! Instead, I must tell you that you are recalled to normal duties. The Fifth Royal Fusiliers of the Tarn march to Zenzau tomorrow. You, Captain Veeldrop, shall be marching with them. Let us see how you find life as a common patrol-commander.'

'But sir,' Polty spluttered, 'my position! My – my name!'

At this, the colonel's façade cracked, and he permitted himself a snickering smile. 'Position? Name? Captain Veeldrop, had you been heir to a *noble title*, I admit we might have shown a little more leniency. To a *nobleman*, much is permitted. But my young fool, if you imagine that a fellow like you – the merest provincial, and a bastard to boot – is possessed, by right, of *any distinction at all*, then I am afraid you are sorely – nay, *ludicrously* mistaken.'

Polty's face was white, as white as the long cylinder of ash that was forming on the end of his tobarillo. Nervously, Bean studied his stricken friend. For a moment he feared that Polty might be moved to some violence, suddenly juddering back his chair and launching himself at the colonel. Bean braced himself, restraining arms at the ready; as it was, all he had to do was reach forward gently, removing the tobarillo from his friend's trembling hand.

In a moment, Polty would have burnt his fingers.

'So we join the Fifth immediately, sir?' Bean asked, if only to break the awkward silence.

Still the colonel did not speak to Bean, but he added, his eyes fixed bemusedly on Polty, 'Your side-officer might be a subject of some debate. Whether, that is, he is your partner in depravity, or the merest innocent you have drawn into your web. However, Lord E——'s orders are clear. Lieutenant Throsh is *not* to accompany you to Zenzau. He is to stay in Agondon, assigned to duties with another agent.'

And the colonel, once again, gave his snickering smile.

Days passed.

With a strange blankness Jem slept, woke, dressed, donning the pale tunics that were left for him each day. He ate alone and read randomly, remembering little, in a library pungent with oak and leather; he wandered through the secluded garden as it died whisperingly with the turning year. Everything was strange in Lord Empster's house, but nothing seemed stranger than this sense of time suspended.

Only in the changing of the season could Jem see that time indeed was running, running as it had always done.

Jem began to feel lost to himself, to the Vaga-boy of his long travels as much as to the cripple on sticks he had been, an aeon earlier. Had life in the House of Golden Scrolls drifted into a lonely, eternal dream? His past, it seemed to him, had slipped from him like a phantom on the day he had walked up the steep steps outside, his heart pounding hugely, slowly, his eyes fixed on the scrolls above the door.

Then came Pellam.

The first time they met, Jem was wandering once again in the garden that stretched, within high walls, behind Lord Empster's mansion.

Within days the snows would come, sweeping down too early as they always did now. But that day the Javander-time still lingered; wild roses and tangled vines draped over trees whose leaves detached themselves, fluttering down with each rustle of the stealthy, insidious wind. To walk was to crackle over a carpet of gold and red, orange, brown, purple. Elsewhere leaves had been raked into piles, and the smoke from the burning drifted on the air with a sad, tart fragrance.

With a troubled countenance Jem was thinking of the future, wondering what could lie before him now, when a braying young voice cried out suddenly:

'On guard!'

The plump figure burst through from the undergrowth, waving a snapped-off branch like a sword. Running towards Jem, he almost knocked him down.

Jem rallied. His assailant wore the richly patterned garb of a fop, but with his bulk and jagged stick, whipping back and forth, this fat dandy was a formidable opponent. In a matter of moments Jem lay, winded and humiliated, on the carpet of leaves, while the stranger sat astride him, waving his tree-sword in whooping triumph.

He released Jem suddenly and tossed the branch aside.

'I say, one does get a little carried away. Let me introduce myself more formally. I'll call you *Nova*, shall I? I'm . . .'

By now Jem had scrambled to his feet; the fop, with a smile, had extended his hand. Jem ignored it and punched this new acquaintance suddenly, deliberately, in his fat stomach. He doubled over, purple-faced.

A laugh rang from the trees and a voice came, 'Jemany, this is Pellam Pelligrew. Pellam is a young gentleman – which, as you have just demonstrated, *you* can hardly claim to be.'

Jem turned. The new voice belonged to a man in a cloak and a wide-brimmed hat, a man not quite old, not quite young. In one elegant hand he held a curving pipe. Smoke, like the smoke of the burning leaves, curled about his face. He was elegant, noble, gracious, but in his demeanour there was something strangely distant, as of one who has seen all the follies of the world, taken their measure and judged them truly.

Of course, Jem knew him at once.

He blundered, 'The quest! My lord, tell me—'

But Lord Empster only brushed his words aside. Reaching forward, he placed his splayed fingers lightly on Jem's chest, feeling the place where the Crystal of Koros lodged, dark and secret.

'Dear boy, you are hardly fit to embark upon such trials – not yet, not now! In the life that lies before you, many doors shall be opened to you

164

– and you must open many doors. You are green, and need a teacher – Pellam here shall be that teacher. I trust, too, he shall be your friend.'

Lord Empster smiled. So did Pellam.

Jem only looked from one to the other, confused and wondering.

Chapter 22

SPLENDOURS OF A COURT

Draped, almost sprawled across the shoulder of rock that slopes away from Agondon's Great Temple is the vast ramshackle edifice of the Koros-Palace. Not from the god but from the season does the palace take its name. Now, as it happens, the season is Javander's, the moonlife still only Ichios. But in Ejland, the seasons are not what they were. Already the palace lies deep in snow.

Come. It is dark; above, clouds muster ominously in the blackness and only a trickle of moon shines down. At the gates, on the battlements, the sentries shiver, even in their thick bearskin coats. In the courtyards, in the alleys, the few passing figures are huddled and rapid, eager to return to the crackling fires that send up smoke from a thousand chimneys. Light shines from the many and varied windows.

Come, look inside. Here, in the chink between velvet curtains, we see a gentleman adjusting his ruff. Behind him, a primped footman moves – almost glides – through an apartment rich in leather and gold. Here? A little low window, tiny square panes. No, don't tap: there is tapping enough inside. The royal cobbler, mending a shoe. Here? A lower window, little more than a vent. But ah, the stentorian sounds from within! This is the bustle of the palace kitchens.

There is so much we might see. A fellow with his breeches down, squatting over a jakes? Some wretched tax-defaulter – one of the King's less willing guests – scratching out a desperate plea? Fine ladies, parading in petticoats, before a bulging bay window, brilliantly lit?

Alas, there is no time, no time.

Higher we travel, higher but deeper, into the heart of the vast edifice. Come, let us alight on this snowy balcony, stepping into the throne-room of Ejard Blue.

Courtiers, mingling:

'Not Miss Laetitia?'

'Lord Empster, you flatter me.'

'I spoke not of *you*, Lady Cham-Charing.'

'You spoke of my daughter. And no, I think not.'

'You would not, then, be mother to the Queen?'

Lady Cham-Charing sighed. 'Would and will be are different things, Lord Empster. No, I fear it is not my little daughter who shall ascend in glory to the King's bed. Laetitia, square up those shoulders, do!'

Courtiers, mingling:

'What shocks one is the effrontery.'

'Effrontery? But is she not the widow of Sinjun Flay?'

'Why no, she was married to Lord Hartlock.'

'Hartlock? Some colonial administrator, wasn't he?'

'But still she calls herself by her maiden name.'

'Shocking!'

'There was an understanding, was there not, that she would keep to her colony? Now, bold as day, she returns among us. Do you know, there are already rumours?'

'Really? Of what?'

'What else? An affair!'

Courtiers, mingling:

'Sir Pellion?'

'Lord Empster!'

'Old friend, you have returned? Why, we thought you would be sequestered away all this season. But you are well? Alas, I fear not! There is white, fresh white, in your forky beard! Foolish fellow, need you torment yourself with the petty cares of Court?'

'Hardly so petty, Lord Empster. But no, my sorrow shall be undiminished, whether here, or in the fastness of my Harion estate – in lonely Harion, it might be greater. A fond foolishness, perhaps, but I think I should not like to miss the Round my poor Pellicent had so looked forward to!'

'The girl was to be Entered? What a fair flower the great world has lost!'

'Indeed.' A tear trembled in Sir Pellion's eye. 'Still, I have her brother, who is very much like her. Pellam, come. But have you met Lord Empster?'

'Sir Pellion, your great-son and I have indeed met. Why, Master Pellam has befriended my young ward, who arrived just recently from the remote wilds of Chayn.'

'Is that so? I see, great-son, you have not been idle.'

'Activity, great-father, is the killer of care.'

'Ah, that is well spoken, is it not, Lord Empster? I see in young Pellam the makings of a poet. Do you know, Coppergate himself began as a Court wit? Of all the young sparks in my day, he was the brightest. I declare, Pellam, you shall be his heir.'

The young man – a handsome enough blade, if a little plump,

resplendent in all the foppish finery of youth – blushed with a becoming modesty and said, turning to Lord Empster, 'Nova is not here tonight?'

'Master Nova must attend to his studies. As you know, Pellam, he has not had your advantages. With your help, he shall lose his rustic manners, but only with steady application to his books may he fill the gaps left by a provincial education.'

'You are a demanding teacher, my lord. But you will relax your leash on the evening of First Moonlife? I have told Nova all about that illustrious occasion, and since ... well, I declare, he talks of nothing else.'

Lord Empster smiled, 'Fear not, Pellam. Would I deny a young man the chance to appraise the fresh beauties on the occasion of their Entrance into the Court? This I should see not as a distraction from his education, but as a crucial part of it. By contrast, tonight is but a commonplace ritual.'

Pellam would have denied it; the young man was at the age when nothing of the Court could seem commonplace.

At that moment a polite little bell rang, and the company prepared to receive the King. Trumpets sounded in the hall outside and on Lord Empster's face there played a smile as the great doors opened and His Imperial Agonist Majesty, King Ejard of the Blue Cloth, flanked by a train of pages, made his stately progress towards the Throne of Empire.

Or not quite stately. Was that the hint of a little *trip*, just on the brink of ascending the steps? And dear me, there was quite a *waft* of rum-and-orandy! Empster at once felt the tension in the air. He looked up slowly and his smile faded. How long had it been, the Time of Retirement? A season, of course: no longer than last year. But what a change had that season wrought! While the courtiers had amused themselves in Varby or Kolkos-Cascos, or dozed in the sunshine on their country estates, the King's decline had accelerated rapidly.

Of course, none would speak of it. Only last year, had not the young Prince-Elect of Urgan-Orandy (a provincial, clodhopping fool) been ejected from the palace when the First Minister heard him making *certain remarks*? Rumour had it that the young fool was even now banished to his villa in Orandy, forbidden ever again to take his place at Court! Certainly, none had seen him since his sudden departure.

Oh, but there were *certain remarks* to be made! Could this, before them, be the form of a King? Pitilessly Empster surveyed the broken, wheezing creature that hunched, almost slumped, on the vast bejewelled throne. Ejard Blue's eyes were red-rimmed and watery, his cheeks bloated, his lips purple, fish-like and drooling. What finery – what ermine, what gold, what rich drapery of imperial blue – could disguise the hideous-ness that lay beneath? Where had they gone, the manly grace, the firm gaze, the proudly jutting jaw of a monarch? In the official portraits, distributed to the furthest reaches of the Empire, the King was possessed abundantly of these fair features. Once, had he not possessed them in truth? There was a time, before he was King, when Ejard Blue had appeared to all eyes to be an exact copy of his brother, Ejard Red. But he was only the most imperfect echo. Now, as if to show the folly of a people who had cast aside the red King for the blue, it was as if time, with merciless rapidity, were stripping away all veils of false seeming, manifesting for all to see the true nature of the usurper King.

But no: not for all. The common people would never know – *must* never know. Let them gaze adoringly on their official images, their slick paint-by-numbers portraits in oils, their busts squeezed rapidly from mould after mould in the palace studios below! But what, Empster wondered, would sit on the throne, when another cycle of the seasons had passed? An immense swollen toad, sweating poison from its slimy skin? To think, they were seeking a wife for this creature! Beside the throne, a second chair – less gaudily resplendent, but still glittering richly – lay vacant, awaiting its fair sacrifice.

In rapid review these thoughts crossed Empster's mind as he gazed on the dispiriting visage before him. But his gaze was not steady. Among the Sworn Injunctions of Court was the pledge that one would never, when His Majesty entered, left, spoke, bade silence, raised his hand, snapped his fingers and so forth, permit one's eyes to stray to any other. Really, it went without saying; still, Empster felt his attention turning surreptitiously – irresistibly – to the figure that had appeared behind the King, standing at his elbow like some strange familiar. Other eyes, he knew, had turned in the same direction. As always, silently and without ceremony, the First Minister had slipped from a narrow door at the back of the dais, just at the moment when the noble sire slumped himself down in his richly cushioned seat.

A greater contrast with the King could hardly be imagined. Throwing into relief the flabby, sated debauchee, swathed in velvet, fur and jewels, the First Minister was a lean ascetic figure in a monastic robe of the simplest, purest white – a White Friar. Not for him the gaudy Court-dress affected by his contemporaries, rich in fripperies unchanged since – oh, at the least – the time of the Regent Queen. He wore his own hair, cropped short against his skull. No jewellery, powder or paint. He was meticulously clean. But was he really a pleasant man to look upon? Coldness glittered in his icy eyes.

The First Minister's name was Ethan Archon Tranimel. Since the time of Jagenam the Just, father of the Twinned Ejards, it had been Tranimel whose task it was to issue King's Orders. The Friar's status, as laid down in Injunctions, was officially that of a servant, principal servant of the

King's Will. In truth, His Excellency The Right Honourable First Minister was no more a servant than the puppet-man, crouching inside his striped booth at the fair, is servant to the diverting little figures that bob and strut on the stage, with their fixed painted faces and paltry stumps of arms. Even in Jagenam's time, Empster knew, there had been those in whom the First Minister inspired greater loyalty than the King. In the brief – the too-brief – reign of Redjacket, there had been no question where the true power lay.

But hold: the King would speak!

In a voice at once mechanical, yet weak and wavering, the man whose many titles included Great Excellency of the Tarn, Blood Potentate of Varbyshire and Holluch, Sacred Emperor of Lexion, Imperial Grand High Master of Tiralos, Supreme High Commander of Zenzau, Ara-Zenzau, Ana-Zenzau and Derkold – in short, the Claim-Monarch of all the lands of the earth, Ur-Archmaximate and Defender of the Faith, and Orok's Representative in the Realm of Being – bade his courtiers a drunken welcome, and slumped back into something like insensibility.

The Court Round was open again!

As ever, The Round began with a ceremony that had stiffened during the Bluejacket reign into the drabbest of formalities. After a consort of viols had played a selection of traditional airs, one from each of the Nine Provinces and one from each of the colonies, after a juggler with the same number of coloured balls had tried, and failed, to capture the attention of the dozing King, and a conjuror had produced, to dutiful gasps, an equivalent number of coloured birds, the way was cleared for a troupe of actors, portraying various forms of poverty and distress. Here was Wounded Soldier, with his convincing bloody bandages; here, Crippled Orphan with her calipered legs; here, Bankrupt Farmer, Virtuous Widow, Leprous Beggar, Ruined Maiden. One by one they hobbled forward, beseeching the King with their impassioned entreaties; one by one they knelt to receive his blessing, sobbing in gratitude as the First Minister read, from a scroll, the prepared responses. A pension of a crown-a-moonlife. A charity-bed in Ollon Hospital. An under-gardener's place in the Theron-Palace. Such mercy! Such compassion! Politely the courtiers applauded each turn.

There had been a time – Empster recalled it well – when The Petitioning had been more than this mere sham. Until the present reign the petitioners were genuine, not actors; the King had listened intently and replied from his own lips.

That was hardly possible now. In the late wars it had been too dangerous to allow mere commoners into the Royal Presence. Redjacket

170

agents, Zenzan rebels: who knew what traitors might insinuate themselves into the palace? Besides – it had to be faced – His Imperial Agonist Majesty was hardly one to weigh and consider; he was hardly one to listen.

But now he need do no more than flop his right hand over the side of his throne, that the actors might bob their heads beneath it, just for an instant, in the pretence that they were receiving some scrap of benediction. Perhaps it was worth it. The Royal hand was reputed to have curative properties, most particularly for boils, hives and leprosy.

Did it matter that Blue King was missing his middle finger?

Empster shuddered.

No, I could not let the boy see this. Not just yet.

For the nobles it all made for a trying evening, being not only interminable, but offering, to boot, not a single chair to sit on and nothing in the way of refreshments. In the stifling heat of the underfloor steam-pipes the best quality-folk in the kingdom sweltered, shuffled and swayed. Constansia Cham-Charing felt her ankles swelling, and could only divert herself from time to time by pinching her plain daughter – Entered these four Rounds, and not a beau in sight! – whenever the poor girl showed signs of imminent fainting. Pellam Pelligrew admired the performances – if he were not a gentleman of quality, which of course he was glad to be, he should have liked nothing more than to be a Player – but had to admit it all went on a bit.

Idly Pellam gazed about him. Fancy, that the Throne Room should be so tatty! Tatty Tiralos carpet, like an old theatre in the provinces. Tatty old rep curtains, tatty old tapestries, tatty old wallpaper with big bright squares where pictures had been taken down and not replaced. If Pellam were King, he would have the whole place done out.

Stripped and done out, no expense spared!

Then the young man was suddenly sad, because he thought how much fun he could have had with his sister, planning the new decorations.

Poor Pelli!

❋ ❋

As Virtuous Widow moaned out the tale of her sufferings, Empster's gaze wandered back to the throne. Would the King, he wondered, leave his own Virtuous Widow? The need for a bride was clear enough. Or not so much a bride: an heir. There was a danger, after all – indeed, it seemed likely – that Bluejacket would soon guzzle his last beaker of rum-and-orandy. Well, let him. *But sire, just one thing, one thing more. Might you not (ahem) vent yourself, into this particular fleshly receptacle?*

Ah, what a field for the First Minister then! The throne empty but for a mewling infant, tied tight in swaddling-bands!

Unfortunately the King had shown a certain resistance, even to the fairest receptacles that had been presented to him thus far. He was – had been – a man of normal passions. By all accounts, there had been whores enough – titled ladies, too – in his early years. Perhaps the King had been too much, too long a voluptuary. Perhaps, as the jaded palate of an epicure is tempted only by the most pungent sauces, so the customary charms of the sex had palled for him long ago. Could only the depravity of the vilest harlot stir his lust from its rum-and-orandy torpor?

Alas, a harlot could not be Queen of Ejland!

By now Leprous Beggar had retired, concealing his artfully festering stumps, and Ruined Maiden had staggered forward, sinking imploringly on her knees before the throne. This particular member of the King's Company was a lusty-looking redhead, no longer quite so young, no doubt, as her rôle required her to be. She wore a peasant-girl's white gown, ripped about the bodice and stained liberally at the hem with – oh, chicken-blood, perhaps. Clattering from one hand was a milkmaid's pail, and from her apron spilt a burden of crushed daisies. Her thighs were parted and her large breasts heaved, almost rolling free, as she moaned piteously of her violation.

In the beginning the fine gentleman had been all vows, imprecations, promising honourable marriage; after he had conquered her innocence, he spurned her:

> *Alas! Fine words! Can words be more than vain*
> *When now, alone, I must endure this pain*
> *Of the Vexing's life that within me grows –*
> *Of a shame that time only swells and shows?*
> *Sire, what can life for me hold now but dread?*
> *At my betrayer's door to lay my head*
> *Is but to be spurned like a mongrel stray,*
> *With kicks and curses in the public way!*

The passionate words were the merest form, laid down in the prompt-book like instructions. How often had Empster witnessed this sad speech? He could not remember. But tonight there was something different, something strange; an intensity in the words he had not heard before. The redhead's cheeks were wet, her neck blotched. Her hands trembled, her breasts and thighs quivered in the throes of what might have been real distress.

Empster felt his attention quickening; he saw the King's quicken, too.

> *Should this poor girl, then, away to the town?*
> *Ah, what can that be but another way down?*

172

> *Am I to sink in the green-gartered masses*
> *Of hundreds, thousands of poor ruined lasses?*
> *Sire, let me die if I must be a whore!*
> *But whither a maiden when maiden no more?*

Why, this redhead must be an actress of genius! There were shufflings, snifflings amongst the courtiers. Empster looked to his left and right. That old rake, the Earl of Down Lexion, was flushed and trembling. The apple in Pellam Pelligrew's throat was bobbing up and down; his greatfather had resorted to his tear-cloth.

Even Constansia Cham-Charing was troubled, if only because her daughter was blubbing on her shoulder.

The King led the way. Roused from his stupor, he leaned forward ardently, eager for each new impassioned wave that crashed against his throne.

> *Say, what is left for this poor girl but tears*
> *Of sorrow, surceasing but with her years?*
> *Ah me! For the time when the memory dies*
> *Of the day when, his breath hot with sweet lies,*
> *In fields strewn with daisies bright as the sun*
> *The cruel man slipped my virgin knot – undone!*

Only the First Minister was unmoved, staring forward icy-eyed, scroll at the ready for the King's Reply. Inevitably his own Reading would be mechanical, registering not the merest flicker of feeling. In clunking couplets he would declare the King's compassion for the wretched girl, assuring her that no, she need not be a whore. Her Vexing deposited in the Ollon Orphanage, instead she would be transported to the Deliverance, there to labour in the cane-fields until the fatal beauty that had been her ruin should at last be burnt away, ensuring her future virtue. How the grateful girl would sob, blessing the King's goodness!

But Tranimel would never make the King's Reply. In a climax as shocking as it was unexpected, all at once the redhead abandoned her set words, rushing forward and flinging herself on the Royal Personage of the King!

'Sire, sire!' Desperately she clutches him, claws at him, bursting with all the emotion that she has invested, a moment earlier, into her set speech.

'Guards!' Tranimel starts forward, alarmed. But in the moment before the weeping form is ripped from the King's breast, the courtiers catch the following exchange:

'Sire, do you not remember me?'

'Maddy? I thought you were dead!'

173

'They tried to kill me! But I had to come back! Oh, take me back to your heart, sire, and never let me stray!'

There would be more, much more, but here come the guards; then Tranimel, his icy exterior shattered, is bawling out a command to clear the Throne Room. Everyone, everyone, must go, go. The evening is over; but there is a moment, as the redhead is dragged away, when one of her hands flails in the air.

Only then do the astonished courtiers register something they had not seen before: that this hand, like the King's, is missing the middle finger.

Chapter 23

QUEEN OF SWORDS

'Raise you?'

'Aunt Vlad?'

'I'm trying a bluff, my dear.'

'Bluff?'

'Didn't I explain?'

'I – I don't know!'

'Come, my dear, you must learn decision. In the great world, you shall play for more than buttons.'

'But Aunt, Ju-Ju said cards were—'

'My dear?'

Jeli faltered, 'She said they were fit only for idle brains who had turned away from the love of the Lord Agonis. Why, she said nothing could be more immoral.'

'Nothing? Indeed you are an innocent, my dear. Or would wish to appear as one – which, may, perhaps, be the same thing. I dare say *Uly* has much to say on the subject, hm?'

The girl looked wonderingly at her strange new guardian. Several times Aunt Vlada had mentioned this *Uly*, but who this might be Jeli still did not know. They sat at a green baize table. Beside them, a fire crackled cheerfully in the grate, warming the funny little sloping attic which Aunt Vlada had commandeered as her boudoir. On armchairs around them were scattered gowns, scarves, gloves; on a dressing-table, jewels glittered amongst the powder-puffs.

Jeli looked down at her hand of cards. 'Perhaps you'd better start again, Aunt Vlad. From the beginning, I mean.'

'From the *zenzals*?' Aunt Vlada smiled. One might not have expected so notorious a woman to display such patience with an ignorant girl. But sitting with Jeli in this cluttered room, The Remarkable seemed entirely content.

She swept up the cards and shuffled them again.

'First, my dear, the *zenzals five*. In Ejland, quality-folk call them *suits*; I dare say so should we. Here're the Quills. See the King of Quills, gripping tight to his feathery-topped pen? In each suit there is a King, Queen, and Prince, then five common-cards with the numbers four, five, six, seven, eight. Do you see? On each card is the quill-pen. That is how we know they belong to Quills.'

As she spoke, Aunt Vlada laid out the cards in question. To Jeli it did not even seem extraordinary that the correct cards came at once to hand. Rapidly – too rapidly – she had become accustomed to her aunt's subtle magic.

Earnestly she studied the cards.

'Next, the Wheels – see the spoky wheel, bright against the garments of the proud Queen? As the quill is the symbol of the scholar, so the wheel denotes the inventor. Wheels are cards of mechanism, of motive power. Now see the Spires, the Rings, the Swords? The spire for faith, the ring for love. And the sword – but of course, you know what the sword is for.'

'Aunt, I'm not sure I can remember it all!'

'Poor child, furrow not that pretty brow! You need only know there are five suits, that's all. Do you think the bored old dowagers in their drawing-rooms, or drunken Bluejackets in their taverns, know the meaning of the cards? They know their values, that's all. In a moment, I shall show you how to play. But first, the *God-cards* – you see the gods, my dear, Orok's five children? But you *do* know all this, don't you? What do we call the remaining cards?'

'Wild-cards, Aunt Vlad?'

'Very good, my dear. Warlock. Vaga. Harlot. Horseman. Harlequin. Together with the five suits or *zenzals*, these comprise the fifty cards of Orokon Destiny. Of course,' Aunt Vlada added, 'there are the two extra cards, which represent the Ur-God and the serpent Sassoroch. Never to be stored with the rest of the pack – so say the sticklers. But the Orok-rules are complex, and can wait another day. Let us begin with a simple hand . . .'

But before Aunt Vlada could deal the hand, there was an interruption. Through all this, her black cat had basked before the fire, stretched long like a furry accordion, purring contentedly in the warm glow. From time to time Aunt Vlada would reach down, stroking an idle finger over the cat's belly or behind his ears.

All at once the cat was alert, letting out a sharp *miaow!*

Aunt Vlada raised an eyebrow. 'Ring?'

The cat padded cautiously beneath the baize table.

'What's he looking at?' said Jeli. Then she drew in her breath, for flitting nervously amongst the debris of the floor was a tiny white mouse.

Such a dear, dear little thing!

Ring pounced. In an instant, the mouse was hanging from his jaws. He jerked his head, whipping his prey back and forth. Then he crunched.

Jeli screamed, 'Aunt Vlad, make him stop!'

But Aunt Vlada only laughed. Reaching down, she scooped up Ring in her arms. Easily she extracted the mouse from his jaws, cupping the bloodied form in her hand. Jeli's face was white and she could not speak. But when Aunt Vlada opened her hand, the mouse was unharmed. She set it scurrying over the green baize table.

'Really, my dear, you don't think Ring would hurt Rheen, do you? Not really?'

'Rheen?' echoed Jeli.

'Where Ring is, Rheen is never far behind. Oh, you'll see a lot of Ring and Rheen. Inseparable.' Aunt Vlada smiled. 'As I hope we shall be, my dear. Hm?'

The cat, in her arms, purred loudly again. Jeli looked down at the green baize, where the mouse nuzzled curiously at a single upturned card.

The Queen of Swords.

✻ ✻

'Aunt Vlad?'

'My dear?'

'When will Catty come?'

It was later that evening. Jeli lay in bed, in a room next door to Aunt Vlada's boudoir. There was a connecting door. Smiling, Aunt Vlada sat on the edge of the bed. Ring was in her arms and she stroked his sleek fur. 'My dear, didn't I tell you? I'm afraid your little cousin has been called away.'

'Aunt Vlad? What do you mean?' Jeli felt a stirring of alarm. All the way from Orandy, how she had looked forward to seeing Catty again! What fun they would have, as they prepared for the ball!

'I did mean to tell you, my dear. Your Uncle Jorvel had a letter.'

'From Catty?'

'From Aunt Umbecca. Called back to Irion urgently, I gather. Situation dire! Still, one should hardly be surprised. In the provinces, the situation is always dire. Believe me, my dear, I know of what I speak. Was I not bound in holy wedlock for eight cycles to the Collector of Derkold? But yes, it seems your cousin's Entrance must wait a little longer. Poor Umbecca, and it took her so long to persuade Jorvel to have her here in the house!' Aunt Vlada smiled. 'You don't really mind so much, my dear?'

'No, aunt. Oh no.'

But Jeli's look belied her words. Since climbing the steep stairs outside, her days had drifted into a strange dream. Now it seemed to her a lonely dream. First she had lost Ju-Ju. Now Catty was not coming. Wonderingly she looked at her green-garbed aunt. Until now, she had never known she had such an aunt.

'Aunt Vlad?'

'My dear?'

'Where's Uncle Jorvel?'

Aunt Vlada smiled, 'Now my dear, when did you ever see your uncle? He's a busy man. You know he has the ear of the First Minister.'

Jeli was not sure what this meant. She only knew that her uncle had not come to see her, not even after her long journey.

Not even after Ju-Ju died.

A servant appeared with a glass of hot milk, which Aunt Vlada had insisted on ordering for Jeli.

'Come, my dear. Drink your milk, then snuggle down. Ring shall sleep with you, and keep you warm.'

A fresh wave of loneliness swept through Jeli. With strange sadness she thought of the snow, falling implacably behind the drawn curtains. She imagined it slithering down the temple spire; she imagined it heaping first lightly, then heavily over the terracotta roofs of the town, or fluttering down, down, to the dirty streets below. She thought of it massing, white and ominous, on the eaves of the dormer windows. She thought of it sinking to the steep stairs, shrouding the place where Ju-Ju had fallen.

Poor Ju-Ju!

'Aunt Vlad?'

'My dear?'

'You wouldn't tell me a story? Before you put out the lamp? Ju-Ju always used to tell me a story.'

Aunt Vlada smiled. 'The story of Uly?'

Jeli's heart gave a hard thump. 'She never told me that one, Aunt Vlada.'

'Silly girl! I meant, shall I tell it to you now?'

And suddenly Jeli's loneliness was gone.

THE STORY OF ULY

'There were three of us,' Aunt Vlada began. 'Uly, Marly, and me. Often I think of us as we were then – in the schoolroom on long lemony mornings, yawning as the light slants over our copybooks. Imagine us, innocent in our white muslin, gauzy and dappled as we wander in the woods above Uncle Onty's house. Through the trees we look down at the house below, laughing at how small it seems. Only the lake never seems small. Far beyond our walls it stretches, flat and gleaming as a

178

great recumbent looking-glass. How I remember that lake! Round and round its edge we would row in Pell's boat, when Pell was with us and the weather was warm. In the Season of Koros our skates cut like scythes across the frozen waste.

'Poor Uly – she was so clumsy! She would fall again and again, and Marly would laugh. But when Marly built a snow-god, it was always lopsided. Then it was Uly's turn to laugh at Marly, pelting her with snow-balls . . .'

'Uly and Marly!' Jeli said dreamily. The words had lulled her into a pleasant doze, and she stretched beneath the blankets. 'How I should like to have a sister!'

'Sisters?' A harshness entered Aunt Vlada's voice.

'Aunt Vlada?'

'But I see I have tired you already, my dear.'

And Aunt Vlada leaned over, snuffing out the lamp.

Chapter 24

THE WHITE FRIAR

O mighty one, we await your coming!
Mighty one, consume this world in fire!
Mighty one, sink this world in flood!
Mighty one, swallow this world in mire!
Mighty one, bathe this world in blood!

It is happening again. Urgently, ardently, deep beneath the temple, Toth's Brotherhood mouth the mantras of evil. Again the white-garbed figure stands before them, stretching forth his arms, radiant with the strange light that glows all around him. Soon he shall turn again, tearing away the curtains from the magic mirror. Soon his dagger shall swoop through the air again, cutting and slashing through tender infant flesh, disgorging the steaming organs within.

But first, Tranimel – for, of course, it is he – must address the worshippers. Faces upturned beneath their cowls, the finest noblemen of Ejland look on, drinking in his words like a sweet, restoring ichor.

'Brothers, when first the mighty TOTH appeared before me, shimmering like a phantom in my looking-glass, I knew that I gazed upon the true god. At once, new knowledge flooded my heart, and all I had been taught was revealed to me as a lie. At once, the fair Agonis – *fair*? I call him *foul*! – became instead a vicious, canting hypocrite, dissembling virtue while thinking only of his lust for a lost, invisible lady. His brothers, his sisters likewise stood naked before my eyes, stripped of all the habiliments of goodness they had worn.

'Goodness? How could even a droplet of goodness flow in their veins, when each of them had knelt in submission, trembled and prayed before the father-god? How could they redeem the peoples of this world, when their father had suffered them to shelter in his palace, and they, with meek gratitude, had accepted that shelter?

'In a dazzle of insight, imprinted suddenly and for ever on my being, I saw that the Ur-God was the enemy of my country, my race and my world. Where did goodness lie but in the Rejected of Orok, in those the hateful father would cast from him like vermin, flinging them into the horror that is the Realm of Unbeing?

'Orok would call them Creatures of Evil, but what is evil? What is

180

good? Brothers, in that moment I knew that henceforth EVIL should be my good, that DARKNESS should be my light, that DEATH should be my life! In that moment I knew that it was TOTH – TOTH-VEXRAH, First of Rejected Creatures, who should be my true god!

'My Brothers, think how we shall rejoice – soon, soon – when the power of TOTH bursts forth freely, consuming this world in the mercy of his wrath! Then, those who have been TOTH's true servants shall have their reward – eternal life! eternal bliss! god-like power! – in the world that TOTH brings forth from the ashes! Brothers, weep with joy that this world shall be ours – not the old world of Orok, where we must scuttle like the vilest insects, fearful of stamping feet, but the new, empowering world of TOTH!

'We have waited long for this time of redemption. For too long, the crystals – the sacred crystals, which alone can give TOTH the power of all life, of all death – have been hidden, awaiting the one called the Key. But Brothers, soon we shall wait no more!'

The white-garbed figure turned sharply, pointing into the darkness as if in accusation.

Heads turned.

'Brother E——! In your daylight guise, you have directed the movements of the Special Agents – some more special than others. Have you new intelligence to impart? Can it be true, that the Key is close? Your Brothers are hungry for your knowledge, Brother E——! Tell us now, tell us what you have learnt.'

In reply came a voice strangely meek, eager to please. Those who knew its owner only in the world above would never have guessed that it belonged to the same urbane courtier.

'It is true, Master. All through the Varby Season, the Key has been close to us. Soon, indeed soon, he shall be within our grasp.'

'Do you promise, Brother E——? Do you swear by mighty TOTH?'

'Master, I swear! In this world there are many things that cannot be certain, but on this, I would stake my life itself! Before you now, I make this pledge: that ere this season is ended, the Key to the Orokon shall be among us, here in this crypt, bearing with him the first of the sacred crystals!'

'Yes!' shrieked Tranimel. 'Yes, it shall come to pass! And when we have wrested that crystal from his grasp, when his heart and lungs and liver are spilling across this altar, what limit shall there be to the might of TOTH? What power shall restrain him then? Brothers, the chant—'

Stamping feet beat out the rhythm.

A god we await! Beat the drums!
Locked in the glass till the crystal comes!

Locked from his love, we burn with wrath!
Only one god and the god is TOTH!

With the first crystal, TOTH *breaks through!*
Then he finds crystal Number Two!
When he has crystals Three, Four, Five,
Then the Orokon comes alive—

On and on it went, until the stamping was so heavy that the very stones might have crumbled and fallen, until the crypt was so rancid with crazed evil that bats and hideous birds seemed to screech about the vaults, that serpents seemed to slither and writhe across the floor. Sunken again into the cowled horde, Lord Empster chanted too, as ardently as the others. Once again he had played his part, and played it well. Tranimel must not guess his true allegiance.

Not yet, not now.

But the time was coming.

Oh Tranimel, Tranimel, what I have said is true, but it must come to pass differently than you can imagine!

The next day, in the world above, Lord Empster would meet the cult's leader again. In sleek, formal phrases they would discuss the business of government, but neither would allude to the secrets of the crypt. Not even the merest look would pass between them, to acknowledge what had happened the night before. It was always the way. One by one – long ago now – Tranimel had summoned Ejland's noblest lords, compelling them to look at a face in a glass; one by one, all had lost the allegiances they once had held so dear. Their identities fell from them like discarded shells. All were now slaves of the anti-god; but in the daylight world, they remained as they had been before.

Or so it seemed.

Only Lord Empster could resist the evil – or resist, at least, *this* evil. Secret hatred burned behind his eyes as he gazed upon the white-garbed First Minister.

Little was known about Ethan Archon Tranimel. Some went so far as to call him a *self-made man*. In Ejland, this description carried overtones of insult, and thus was ventured, *à propos* the First Minister, only between intimates and in private. Still, it was not strictly true; or was true, rather, in a limited sense only. One expected a man of the highest nobility to occupy Tranimel's great office – a Prince, an Archduke. Tranimel could hardly claim as much.

True, he was no commoner; he had come into this world with a title, but an unimportant one. The Lord Warden of Milander Lock (such was the title) was the only son of a baronet from Ara-Varby, downstream from Varby on the floodplains of the Riel. His childhood was said to have been deeply provincial, tethered to the tyranny of a boorish, miserly father. Ancient courtiers spoke of a skeletal boy who looked on enviously from the Lockhouse windows as the plush carriages rolled by, bound for Varby.

It was difficult to imagine this youthful Tranimel, without his white robes, his clipped colourless hair, his passionless gaze. When he came to Agondon after the death of his father, the young lordling had already passed his Fifth, and was bound not for Court but for Temple College. If he had ever been eager for the world of fashion, he had put this all behind him. He was an Agonist of the utmost piety.

Now his was a late vocation, he was ill-connected, and his father had left him nothing. Such a fellow could hardly hope to rise in the Order. No rich Lectorate beckoned, no princely household, no soft-cushioned sinecure in the Great Temple. In due course he joined the White Friars, oldest and most austere of the Brotherhoods of the Enclosed. Here only faith, not fortune, prevailed. It seemed the place for him. In the dying days of the Regency, Court was given over to luxury and excess. The pious Tranimel retired from the world, devoting himself to a life of simplicity, humility and prayer.

It was not to last.

It happened that the Advisors Royal had for some time resented the White Friars; the Queen herself saw them as possessed of great power, though in quite what this consisted neither she – nor anyone else – could say. Perhaps it was merely a *moral* power, and thus resented all the more. In their monastery opposite the Koros-Palace, the Friars stood like a rebuke to the Queen's decadent Court.

Naturally, the Queen considered abolishing the monastery. This was an attractive option, but risky. The commoners respected the Friars too much, speaking of them with an ignorant awe. The Enclosed, too, were exempt from taxes. Perhaps some other means could be found to break their power? Yes, the Queen would force them out of Agondon, drive them into the provincial wilds! In a decree dripping with concerned piety, invoking the poverty, &c., that blighted her fair city, Her Regent Majesty ruled that no religious house could remain within its walls unless its members devoted themselves to *labour for the public good*.

The courtiers chuckled and rubbed their hands. What did the Friars do but eat, snooze, mumble a few prayers, and ring their bells too early in the morning? In a moonlife or so – who could doubt it? – a white-robed procession would be winding downhill, taking their sorrowful leave of Agondon. Architects eagerly drew up plans to convert the monastery into luxury apartments.

What no one expected was that the White Friars would fall in dutifully with the Queen's decree. In a little time the white-robed figures, once only glimpsed over the monastery walls, were a sight familiar throughout the city. They collected alms. They relieved the sick. They distributed blankets to Rejects on the Embankment. In the Great Temple they served as ushers. Some became tutors at Temple College. One even entered the palace itself, offering his talents to the Royal Service.

This was Tranimel.

His place was a lowly one – of course it was a lowly one. But as Second Under-Secretary to the Lords of the Exchequer, the young Friar was soon to distinguish himself.

After a scandal linking her to the Zenzan Ambassador, the Regent Queen was prevailed upon – at long last – to retire to her estates. Her reign had been ruinous. Called to power during her son's minority, she found no desire to relinquish her status. Again and again, when it seemed the time had come, the Queen would insist that her son was not ready, that only a cruel and heartless mother could thrust responsibility so soon upon his shoulders. Her son reached his Fourth, his Fifth, his Sixth, and still the Queen reigned on. She was selfish, ignorant and improvident, but after all, she was loved by Court and commons alike. Now, three reigns later, in the time of Ejard Bluejacket, there were many who still looked back fondly – nay, more than fondly – to the 'roaring days', the 'great spree', the 'gilded age' of the Regency.[1]

When her son Jagenam came to the throne, he found the Royal coffers in a parlous state. Fresh revenue was vital, but in the absence of new colonial conquests – Mother had not much cared for the colonies – it could be raised only by taxes or loans. The Epicircle, the outer cabinet of Advisors Royal, were all for doubling the Harion corn-tax. The Circle, the inner cabinet, were having none of it. 'The Harion' had been doubled twice before, and in the space of a cycle; already there had been stirrings of rebellion. Would the new King shame himself before his subjects, appearing as little more than a robber baron? Certain discreet appeals – to the Earls of Orandy, to the Prince of Chayn – would ease the crisis, would they not? Perhaps. But would the new King live in thrall to his nobles, the merest mortgagee? His mother had left him with a burden of debt that already would take the entirety of his reign to pay, if he lived for – oh, an epicycle!

What to do? In the absence of any resolve, the Exchequer Lords were

[1] See Lord Venturon's *Gilded Days* for a full – if by no means impartial – account of the Ejland Regency.

sent off to prepare a report; and as it happened, the task devolved through the ranks of the Royal Service to Brother Tranimel of the White Friars. To explain in full what Tranimel did then, to detail the ingenious programme of reforms which would come to be known variously as The Golden Bounty, The Rout of the Earls and The Mulcting of the Inner, would be a task impossible without figures, tables, graphs, statistics, much of the higher mathematics and the higher philosophy, too; let us leave it to the professors at the University of Agondon, who by all accounts are puzzling over it to this day. Precisely how it worked, why it worked, no one quite knew. Suffice to say that within a short time The Bounty, The Rout, The Mulcting had not only saved the King from bankruptcy, ended his humiliating dependency on the nobles, and rapidly repaid his outstanding loans, but saved his face in Harion, too. Not for nothing would the father of the Twinned Ejards earn from the grateful commoners the name-of-honour, Jagenam the Just.

Within the palace, another name-of-honour was soon in currency: Tranimel the True. It was at the King's behest. Where he found his talents, this Varby Friar, was a moot point. Many revered him. Some reviled him. The Exchequer Lords burned with envy, and let us not speak of the Epicircle, the Circle. The Fool babbled of dark powers. No matter of it: where Tranimel came, others melted away. Soon the Friar was the King's most trusted advisor; soon, indeed, his *only* advisor. It was Tranimel who took the reins of finance, trade and war. A vigorous Zenzan campaign – the glorious Nine Eight-Nine – was all his doing. Triumph followed triumph.

What happened next is open to several interpretations.

One goes like this.

The King was of an impressionable nature. This had aspects both good and bad. In the beginning he trusted implicitly to his wise counsellor, and the kingdom prospered. With Tranimel to guide him, the King kept in check the powers of the Court, conquered and enslaved large numbers of Zenzans, married the beautiful Princess Margatane, and was much loved by his people.

Then the King turned from Tranimel, and the kingdom foundered.

Some said it was the birth of Jagenam's sons that marked the beginning of troubled times. In Ejland, the Coming of the Twinned was an omen. Twinned daughters were a sign of good luck. Boy-and-girl meant dissension in families. Twinned sons foretold a wider, deeper evil.

The Brothers Ejard were born on a stormy night in the depths of Koros-season. Many courtiers would remember that night, as they waited, eager for news, in the Queen's antechamber. There was fear in the air. The Queen was not strong, and her confinement had been a harsh one. When the Surgeon Royal emerged at last, his face was ashen. *The Queen is dead, but delivered of a son. A son – and his reflection.* Behind him emerged a train of the Queen's women, weeping. Thunder crashed round the palace walls and the Fool scurried about the chamber like a monkey, crazed, and jabbering of the fearsome times ahead.

Perhaps it was his sorrow at the Queen's death that now began to turn the King's head. With a mawkishness, some said, that was almost womanish, he devoted himself to his heir. This, of course, meant to his first-born, the child who had been swaddled in the Royal red. The blue cloth of the brother-infant denoted his inferior status – a latecomer, an interloper. There could be no question which of the infants was to reign; no question, either, that they would be raised, according to ancient practice, as 'looking-glass children'. Ejard of the Red Cloth was King-to-be, accorded all privileges and more or less worshipped; the Blue Prince was his brother's mere reflection, his familiar, his almost-servant, to fetch and carry for the King-to-be, to be whipped when the King-to-be required whipping, to be fed the nasty medicines the King-to-be refused.

So that he could not be mistaken for his brother, a finger was cut from his right hand.

All this was according to tradition.

Now as the princes grew older, entering their Third cycle, then their Fourth, Ejard of the Red Cloth began to be more than merely the object of his father's doting affection. A precocious lad, from the first he took a keen interest in policy. He saw the injustices that still racked the kingdom: the poverty, the cruelty, the overweening power of the Order of Agonis. Of the First Minister, Tranimel, he was deeply suspicious. Should so much fall into the hands of one man? What had happened, asked the King-to-be, to the time-honoured system of Advisors Royal? To the Epicircle, the Circle?

Soon the young Redjacket had impressed his views on his father's pliant nature. Once again, Jagenam the Just would earn his name. A new King's Council was formed. Consultants were appointed, and Correspondents to spread the news of policy openly, freely, amongst the quality-folk of the land. There was talk of a 'Review of Zenzan Policy', of an 'Enquiry into the "Vagas", or Children of Koros'. Ancient privileges were taken from the Order of Agonis.

Upstaged – usurped – by a mere stripling, Tranimel was doubly furious; for after all, had he not encouraged the King in his doting on the boy? Done all he could, for his own part, to win the boy's trust? Would Tranimel, Tranimel the True, be cast out like this?

This, one stresses, is but one interpretation. Others had it that Tranimel, as befitted a pious Friar, meekly accepted the wisdom of his superiors and worked on in the court, quietly, in a lower capacity, content only to serve.

It is true that he worked quietly, and when Jagenam the Just died suddenly in AC 994*d*, the Friar's quiet work bore fruit.

Imagine that you are Ejard Bluejacket, teetering at last on the cusp of manhood. What a miserable lot yours has been! Watching, reflecting like a looking-glass as your brother enjoys every privilege, every favour. That is bad enough; but to cap it all, his nature is sweet. Does he hate you? No, he loves you, and wishes you well! Passionate about justice, bent on doing good, why, of late he has even persuaded your foolish father that really, there is no call to be so harsh on Jardy (he calls you Jardy). *Poor Jardy*, he says, and will have you sit by him. *When I am King, Jardy, you shall serve on my Council.* You smile, you bow . . . *Brother, my humble thanks.* Ah, but what a swirl of feeling is inside you! And is all of it anger? Not at all! Don't we love our sufferings as much as our joys?

You have been trained to obedience like a dog. There is something in you that longs to be the looking-glass, to shimmer dully behind your bright brother. You believe in tradition. You believe in virtue. You are a pious follower of the Agonist faith. Crushed first by unkindness, then by kindness, you want nothing more – this is what you tell yourself – but to know your place and fill it. Sometimes in your chamber you sob in gratitude, weep, with heaving shoulders, for your brother's goodness.

But a dog, for all its training, has sharp teeth and claws, and in the sun the dullest glass can flash, dazzle and blind. Isn't there the smallest smouldering ember, under even the damp, ashy heaps of your fires?

For now, a breath comes to stir.

To blow.

Blue Prince (it whispers), *you have played your part well. Why, at the coronation of your brother-King, how stiffly you stood in your place at the side! Ah, but have you wondered why that is your place? Blue Prince, with what certainty can you know it was your lot to be the mere looking-glass – your brother's, to be the visage reflected within? For a foolish superstition, your body is mutilated, your nature crushed. By what right? To what end? Is this not evil?*

What's that? Treason, you say? Heresy? But Blue Prince, listen. Can you know that you were not the first? Was it truly your lot to be second, second? Deep inside your skin are there still not the scars where your brother kicked and clawed you in the darkness of the womb?

But I say more than this. Think of the confusion of the night of your birth. The crashing thunder, the flickering candles, the women hysterical at the death

187

of the Queen! Yes, Blue Prince, think hard! With what certainty can we know what is false, what is real? Which the reflected, which the reflection?

You turn from me? But you are a staunch Agonist! Blue Prince, think too of your faith! Your brother threatens dangerous innovations. Already he has stripped all dignity from the Order. Now, his reforming zeal seeks wider scope. Would he tolerate Vianu, the heathen faith of the Zenzans? Would he grant freedom to the Vagas, whose dark god polluted this world with his wickedness?

Blue Prince, there are those who look back to the night of your birth, and recall the wild babblings of the licensed Fool. A Fool, yes, but had there not always been wisdom in his words? A false King is coming, the Fool said. A false King is coming and shall eject the true! What could this mean but that your red brother should vilely impose himself upon an abused kingdom, casting the rightful heir from his place?

The Fool's words were prophecy! And the prophecy is fulfilled!

Blue Prince, there are those of us who oppose your usurping brother. There are those who wait for but a sign from you that we might go to war against him in your name. In your name, his red standard shall be trampled in the dust! In your name, his evil head shall be rent from his body! Your armies await. Your hour is at hand. Oh, Blue Prince, come – turn to us!

But why do I call you Prince?

Soon you shall be Prince no longer, but King!

Yes, imagine that you are Ejard Blue. Imagine the envy, the loathing, the shame. Then the exaltation. Then the guilt. Ask yourself, is it any wonder that Brother Tranimel should have returned so triumphantly to power?

But of course, this is only an interpretation.

Chapter 25

GENTLEMEN OF FASHION

'Swordplay?'

'But of course.'

'Riding?'

'Indeed.'

'Shooting?'

'Inevitable.'

'Let's see – skating?'

'Is not the Riel freezing as we speak?'

'A commission? The Guards, perhaps?'

'Not just yet. My cousin is young.'

'So I see. The legs a little wider, sir? That's right.'

'Emperor, you'll remember all this?'

'You trust my bills, Master Pelligrew?'

'Of course, Emperor!'

'Then you trust my memory.'

Through all this, Jem was silent. Bewildered, he could only gaze at his reflection in the glass. Stripped to his undershirt, he stood with his legs parted, his arms spread wide, while a funny little man with frizzy hair scuttled about him like a friendly spider, poking and prodding with a measuring-stick. From time to time the little man would mutter to himself, or sometimes count surreptitiously on his fingers, but never did he write anything down.

Close by, Pellam sat up on a counter, whistling and smoking, swinging his legs. He looked happy. Outside was bustling Lund Street, deep in the heart of the old city; there, the air was chill and grey, harsh with cries of cabmen and hawkers, with barking dogs, with carriage-wheels rumbling over slushy cobblestones. In here, a haven, a place of lamplight and shimmering glass, perfumed with the scent of luxurious cloth. Outside, the Great Temple teetered above, as if at any moment it would collapse, crushing the street; but in here, too, was a temple of sorts, a temple to the true religion of the Pelligrews.

These were the premises of Japier Quisto, Outfitter to the King, Agondon's most exclusive gentlemen's tailor.

'I was told in my youth, sir,' said Master Quisto, 'that there were two laws of business. At the time, alas, I was not told what they were; now, however, that I have risen above the ignominy of my birth to become, as it pleases my superiors to call me, "The Emperor of Lund Street", I might perhaps be presumptuous enough to state them. They are: (1) never spurn the custom of quality-folk; (2) forget nothing. And sir, I do not!'

'I know it, Emperor. But I have a list – in Lord Empster's hand!'

The Emperor waved away the offer. 'Were it in the hand of His Imperial Agonist Majesty, I should trample it underfoot! Come, my young sirs – Canonical black? Court blue? Opera-suit, Garden-suit? Equinox-suit, Festival-suit, God-suits for each of the Meditations? Linen, twenty sets? Think you, Master Pelligrew, that the Emperor of Lund Street is unacquainted with all that a gentleman might require?'

'The Opera?'

'We've said the Opera.'

'I beg your pardon, Emperor, so we have. Nova, you can put your clothes back on now, you know.'

'Clothes?' sniffed the Emperor. 'Mere rags!'

'Really, Emperor, they were mine. You made them yourself. Last year.'

'Precisely, Master Pelligrew.' The Emperor folded up his measuring-stick and gave an obsequious smile.

'Pell, can we go now?' said Jem.

His voice was sharp. It was the first time he had spoken since entering the shop, and his two companions turned to him wonderingly.

'I think you'd better put on your breeches first, Nova.'

Jem smiled, flushing, and quickly complied. In the last moments a strange alarm had come over him. Gazing at his own reflection in the glass, for a lingering moment he had felt transfixed. The Emperor enumerated the clothes of a gentleman, and the thought came to Jem: *This is me. These are mine.* But how could this be? Like pages in a flicker-book, a new life of fashion passed before his eyes. The Wrax Opera, the Volleys, the Ollon Pleasure Gardens . . . *Bang!* goes a gun, bringing down a bird . . . A skate's heel swoops across the frozen Riel . . . *Clip-clop, clip-clop*, horses in the park . . . Simpering faces, thick with paint; pursed lips descend on a glove. *Why, Lady ——, how delightful to meet you* . . . Tiralos and Jarvel in a padded booth. Someone dealing from a deck of cards . . .

But this is all wrong! Is this my mission, to be a gentleman of fashion, a pampered creature of silk and lace? Jem clutched the crystal at his chest. Something was wrong, it had to be. But when he had tried to talk to Lord Empster, somehow he could not. Somehow he could only give way, give way, like a sleepwalker, oblivious, to the hand that leads him. Where was his vision?

He turned quickly and made for the door, eager for the chill air of Lund Street again. But in the doorway, Pellam turned back.

'Oh, Emperor?'

'Sir?'

'Ah – I meant to ask, how is your daughter?'

'Heka is well. She is to be Entered this season.'

'Entered, now?'

'I know what you are thinking, sir. Trade, mere trade.'

'Not at all!'

The Emperor shrugged. 'I have been fortunate enough, sir, to rise high enough that I may tap, as it were, at the ceiling of the floor above me. My daughter, so I flatter myself, may walk upon that floor.'

'A noble sentiment, Emperor. But have you not forgotten your other daughter – have you not another?'

'I do believe you are mistaken, sir. Oh no, Heka is quite enough for me.'

'Funny, I could have sworn you had two,' Pellam smiled; then having established, as he thought, a mood of pleasantry, moved swiftly to his real theme. 'The Festival-suit.'

The Emperor tapped his forehead. 'I have it on my list.'

'I meant mine.'

'Yours, sir?'

Bored, Jem stared impatiently into the crowded street. Night was falling and the Temple spire loomed above Lund Street like a massing, evil mountain. Already the link-boys were readying their torches. Jem rubbed his arms. From an upstairs window a girl stuck out her tongue at him; weaving through the traffic, an old crone banged and barged her way, bearing two miserable chickens by the feet. Their squawking heads swung alarmingly back and forth.

'You have stretched your line a little far, Master Pelligrew,' the Emperor was murmuring with the utmost respect.

'True, Emperor. But I have expectations.'

'All young gentlemen have expectations. It is their defining character-istic. But if I am to fulfil them, I ask only that they be of sufficient capacity.'

'You are a hard man, Emperor.'

'A generous one, surely?'

'I meant generous.'

'So, an Opera-suit in "Ejard", too? A Sosenica-gown? But you'd agree with me, sir, that *one* season is quite enough for – well, *anything* a gentleman wears?'

'Emperor, of course!'

And a spark, despite himself, shone in Pellam's eye.

Now for an interlude at the Koros-Palace. But no, not in the noble state-apartments; remember we saw there was more, much more, than the parts that the people of fashion know. Let us descend to the darkest depths, to the dungeons, which have a new inhabitant. They have put her in a cell by herself, which is as well; otherwise by now she would have been raped repeatedly, by this or that gentleman with matted hair, grizzled beard, claw-like nails, &c. The ladies, too, would have torn and gouged her, for Maddy – big-breasted, blowsy Maddy – is a beauty, a veritable celestial wraith, among the filth and vileness of the dungeon-world; how eagerly its denizens extend grasping hands, ready to wrench, rend and ruin! (The degraded must degrade, it is a law of nature.)

But Maddy is luckier, at least for now. In her dark solitude of straw, stone and stench, she is able to think a little, even to dream, but what she dreams makes her moan and sob. Many – very many – might do the same, if they found themselves dreaming of Ejard Blue; but Maddy dreams not of the drunken sot who seems fated to turn (any day now) into a immense vile toad, oozing poisons through its stinking skin. Can it be that even the King – even *this* King – may inspire love?

Poor Maddy is growing old now; there are strands of grey in her red hair and her big breasts are unpleasantly mottled. Her latest part was an irony indeed. Ruined Maiden? Maddy Coda was ruined long ago, if 'ruin' is the parting of a curtain of flesh. But she is no harlot, though they treat her like one – men, that is. Men! She has sounded them to their depths and heard no return but a chill, dull echo, as of an empty drum.

But in her long progress through a sad and bitter world, there is one man Maddy has always remembered. No, not an ugly, bloated toad; for ever, her King is a young man in the playhouse, noble and fair, gazing up enraptured as she dances and sings. Did she not fall in love with him at once, this beautiful shy boy, long before she knew of the destiny before him? How she remembers their first delicious interview! In those days, 'Blueby' – it was her pet-name for him – was awkward indeed, and long moments passed before he could pay his compliments. How he blushed, how he stammered! She would have laughed at him – if sweetly, affectionately – but then when he went to kiss her hand, his sudden passion stopped her laughter in her throat. She would have stopped him, would have slapped him away. But somehow she could not; perhaps, in truth, she would not, as ardently, he peeled away her special glove.

That might have been the end; in that moment, another man might have seen the measure – so he would think – of a woman he had fleetingly believed to be a goddess. Repelled, he would turn away, muttering of deception; calculating, at best, if the demands of venery might allow him to overlook this unfortunate, this regrettable ... But Blueby first bathed her poor hand with tears, then – this was the moment she cherished – brought up to the gaze of her astonished eyes a matching hand, a hand just like it.

Oh Blueby, Blueby!

Now, in the foetid darkness, Maddy rubs and kneads at her poor ruined hand. So many cycles, so many cycles, and still the raw nerves throb with pain! But perhaps the pain is only in her memory ... Again and again she sees herself as a little girl, spilling her father's ale as she brings it to the table. How she cries! How she wails! She had tried to be so careful! But though she would sink to her knees in shame, piteously begging her father's forgiveness, at once the angry drunkard leaps up, seizing his little daughter by her puny wrist. Then, from his belt, he snatches a rabbit-knife; then off with her finger, like a length of sausage! 'That's the first one! The first, do you hear? Do it again, and you lose another!'

It was as well that Maddy's father had met his death in a street-accident some nights later. Maddy remembers pressing her way through the crowd; she sees again the bottle still clutched in his hand, and his rib-cage, her father's poor rib-cage, crushed like a shell beneath the gentleman's carriage. Before he died he kissed her face, then kissed her bandaged hand, and said – she understood, didn't she? – he only wanted to teach her to be a good girl.

Always, Papa, always.

Poor Maddy Coda! One could say much more about her. But in a little while, not long now, she will be dead.

'Avast, varlet!'
    'What?'
    'Nova, parry!'
    'I'm trying!'
    'I'll kill you—'
    'Hey—'
    'Die, Redjacket traitor!'
    'Ouch!'

Jem's rapier clattered to the floor. He fell heavily and the crash echoed along the gallery. Breathing deeply, he lay staring at the high beams above, his arms and legs twisted in the pose of death.

Killed again!

Light from the long windows draped him like a pall, chill with the pallor of the snowy street outside.

'Oh, I didn't scratch you!' laughed Pellam, peeling back his blue leather mask.

Jem sat up. Gingerly he inspected his padded jerkin. Very well, no scratch. But it was a close thing. He hauled himself back to his feet and sighed, 'I'll never get it, Pell. I don't think you'll make me a gentleman of fashion.'

'There's always pistols.'

'I don't think we'd better try *them*.'

'Well, the rapier *is* more a gentleman's weapon. Come on, then.' Once again Pellam fixed his blue mask over his pleasant, pink face. For all his worldly confidence he still had about him an element of the little boy. Ladies always wanted to protect him, or so he claimed.

His rapier glinted. 'Remember, it's only a matter of time before you're challenged, Nova. *On guard!*'

Imitating him, Jem bounced on the balls of his feet. Had he ever felt so ridiculous? Here he was in the full fencing-garb of a fine gentleman, complete with feathered cap, cod-piece and tights. And all blue, 'Ejard' blue! Curiously it did not even occur to him that Pellam looked, if anything, still more absurd.

Jem was still in awe of his plump new friend.

Zing! Zing!

'Have you been challenged, Pell?'

'Countless times! Did I tell you about the Prince-Elect of Urgan-Orandy?'

'Don't think so!'

'A clodhopping, provincial boor! Do you know, he had the temerity to insult—'

Zing! Zing!

'A lady?'

'Bother ladies – me! Called me fat. Now, if you'd seen "Binkie" Urgan-Orandy . . .'

With an expansiveness that seemed hardly suitable to the occasion, Pellam embarked upon a droll narrative, something to do with 'Binkie' and his lust for some fine Court-lady who wanted nothing of him. But the tale circled round the subject of Binkie's girth. There was the time when Binkie had been kicked downstairs at school and *bounced*, all the chaps swore to it; there was the time he had got stuck in the park-railings and the time when he had sat down at Lady Cham-Charing's tea-party and his breeches had ripped with an immense farting *zzzip!*

In comparison to such grossness, Pellam Pelligrew did not consider himself to be fat, not even a little plump.

But Jem was barely listening. Striving, straining, he felt the sweat beading hotly beneath his mask as he warded off blow after nonchalant blow – yes, *nonchalant*. How could this be so easy for Pell? Jem could only defend, barely attack. It was as much as he could do to repel his friend's thrusts, and Pell, he knew, was only toying with him, offering little more than the lightest playful flurries. It was infuriating. In Jem's Vaga-days, it had seemed so easy. But back then, he had only a wooden sword; and back then, his only opponent was Rajal.

Zing! Zing! How Jem would like to flame out suddenly, a hero, a master-swordsman!

Anger fought in him with a gathering despair.

Then came the voice. *You're hardly trying, Jem. You can't punch gentlemen in the stomach, you know.*

Lord Empster!

Jem rallies. His mysterious guardian stands against the fireplace, warming his back at the crackling flames. How is it that he appears like this, so suddenly? He is just back from the palace and wears riding-boots, but was there any sound of footsteps on the stairs? There is a strange evanescence in this noble courtier. Always he wears his dark cloak and sometimes – to Jem, at least – it seems he has only to turn, sweeping the cloak, and he is gone. Always he wears a wide-brimmed, plumed hat, and smokes tobarillo that burns in a bowl at the end of a long, carved ivory stalk.

Blue-grey smoke wafts before him like a screen.

Like a curtain.

With sardonic compassion he watches his ward as he thrusts and parries, thrusts and parries, with the laggardly confusion of a sleep-walker. Jem holds his rapier as if it were heavy, as if indeed it were made of wood.

His legs twist, he stumbles.

Come, you have conquered worse.

Again the swords clash, but when Lord Empster speaks he seems barely to raise his voice. Like a smoky tendril it slithers over the air, curling imperceptibly into Jem's awareness. Sometimes he has thought: *Perhaps Lord Empster is always here, looming somewhere near . . .*

Now his lordship speaks of the gentleman's weapon, of the virtue and wisdom and grace to be found in it. To shoot a fellow down in a fiery burst of powder, what art is there in that? The vilest barbarian of Ana-Zenzau could blast at another from a distance, like a dog! But to whip from its scabbard the gleaming stem of steel, dart and twist and turn in a deadly dance, spindly blades gleaming and flashing, ready to thrust thrillingly, suddenly, into flesh . . .

Zing! Zing! Jem's face is burning red. Very well, shall he be a swordsman? Now Pellam has him backed against a window. Jem's blade is upright, horizontal, resisting his friend's with a slow scraping squeal.

Right now I could kick him. But Jem is a gentleman. He leaps sideways. Through unexpected emptiness Pellam's rapier slashes down, the tip tearing screechingly at the window-glass.

Suddenly Jem is in control. Pellam pirouettes. Always his agility surprises Jem. Plump, but not heavy; a big gaudy balloon, whipping this way and that in the wind. But too late!

Zing! Zing! Perhaps Pellam had become too confident. With a succession of quick slashing strokes, Jem drives him back.

'Die, Bluejacket cur!'

The rapier clatters from Pellam's hand, skidding and spinning across the polished floor.

'Oh I say, Nova!'

'Better?'

'Ra-ther!'

Triumphant, Jem turns to his noble protector. He wants praise, he is aware, as if from the father he has never known. But Lord Empster is gone. There is only a cloud of smoke, hanging on the air.

'How does he do that?' Jem whispers.

'Hm?' Pellam wipes his pink, pleasant face.

'Lord Empster. Come and go like that.'

'Empy? Don't know what you mean, old fellow. I say, Nova, you were a little overwrought. Do you know, you even called me "Bluejacket cur"? I think you meant "Redjacket", didn't you?'

Jem smiles. 'Of course!'

But he is troubled. The triumph of moments earlier has ebbed away. His brow furrows and a strange loneliness tolls inside him, like a bell.

No, it is only the clock downstairs.

Chapter 26

CHILD OF THE OPERA

'Aunt Vlad, it's magnificent!'

'My dear, did I not say you should conquer all hearts?'

Jeli's pretty little mouth gaped wide. 'But Aunt, such a gown! Why, it's fit for a Queen!'

'Fiddle-faddle! In Orandy, I dare say, not even the finest lady would go garbed in cloth-of-gold. But are we not in the heart of the empire? Are you not soon to make your Entrance? Let me impart to you a piece of wisdom, my dear – perhaps the single most important thing I have learned in my long womanly career. It is this: that for a woman – provided, of course, she attains to a minimal beauty – nothing, nothing at all is so important as dress. And a woman must strive with every power at her disposal – why, if needs be she must sell her very virtue – to *dress for her destiny*. Do you know what I mean, my dear? Not for her actual place in the world, but for the *destiny* that lies before her. Now you are but a simple provincial girl, barely freed from the confines of Duenna-dom. But Jelica Vance, your *destiny* is a great one!'

Pride welled in Jeli's heart. A short time ago – but already, how long ago it seemed! – Aunt Vlada's words would have filled her with alarm. What destiny could a woman have, Jeli might have wondered, if in the pursuit of it she sold her virtue? But already the girl had grown accustomed to her aunt's sophisticated ways. Jeli, after all, had never been quite the innocent she liked to seem. Back home there were many who whispered behind their hands about that shabby business with young 'Binkie' Urgan-Orandy. Had they not been good as betrothed? Had Miss Jeli not been marked out for a *province-wedding*? Her mother, it was true, had put her name down for Quick's, but on his wife's death her father reversed that policy. Alarmed by tales of Varby Vanishings, alarmed still more by tales of the Court, the old man was determined that his girl should return to her provincial home, never straying. But when scandal threatened with the Prince-Elect, what was for it but to send the girl to Court?

Provincial tittle-tattle found no listeners amongst the capital's promiscuous fray.

Jeli hugged her aunt, gazing once again on the beautiful gown. In the bright pallor from the dormer windows, the gold glittered like stars.

Already the two women had filled their apartments with the most dazzling finery the capital had to provide; hat-boxes and wrapping-paper, jewellers'-cases and shoe-boxes covered every surface. But now this gown! Such a splendid surprise! Could anything ever excite Jeli more? Impatiently she bundled herself into the glittering fabric, parading up and down before her admiring aunt.

Then suddenly Aunt Vlada's brow furrowed. 'But my dear, something is missing!'

'Aunt?'

Aunt Vlada's eyes glittered and she held up her hands. First she wrung them together, then opened them again. Cupped in her palms was a magnificent ruby necklace. Jeli gasped. At once the cool stones circled her neck.

She sobbed with joy, collapsing into Aunt Vlada's arms.

That afternoon, as they sat at tea, Aunt Vlada resumed the story she had promised.

'But first, I must explain something about myself – oh, only incidentally of course, my dear, to further your understanding of *Uly*. Uly is the subject of the story I tell, however far from her I seem to stray.'

'Only Uly?'

'Most definitely Uly. Not I.'

'Not even Marly?'

'Marly is another matter. No, I am afraid this is the story of Uly, though Marly of course must play her part.'

THE STORY OF ULY

'Understand, first, that Uly was not my sister. Nor was Marly. Why, the very thought would have made them scream! You see, my dear, your Aunt Vlada was a Vexing – a bastard, as coarser tongues will put it. Though, as it happens, there was nothing in her parentage that need have *vexed* anyone. Her father's identity, like her mother's, was only too well known.

'That was the scandal of it.

'I remember sometimes, when the girls and I were old enough to eat with the family, my Uncle Onty would stare at me, suddenly stare at me as if his eyes would burn me away like a heated sun-glass. There I would sit, trembling, as an awkward silence descended, then the silence would grow and keep on growing until the footman, perhaps, stepped forward with a discreet *hem-hem*, when the meat was about to fall from Uncle Onty's fork.

'Then gravely my uncle would shake his head and say, *That child should never have been born.* That's all: *That child should never have been born.*

'Poor Uncle Onty, with his big grey head and wet, livery lips! I was terrified of him in the beginning. The first day I arrived, when they took me before him, he turned in disgust from my swarthy skin, thundering that they should take the *little Zenzan* away – that's what they all called me after that, the *little Zenzan*.

'And that, I suppose, is what I still am. Yes, my dear – paint has whitened my face and hands, but under this finery there is still the taint of Zenzau-blood.

'But is it a taint?' Aunt Vlada's voice, which had been melancholy, was dashed suddenly with bitterness. 'My uncle cast me from his presence like the Ur-God Orok, banishing his own children! Even then I knew this was wrong. Was I to be blamed for the fact of my existence? I was his flesh, his very own flesh.'

Aunt Vlada paused, lighting a Jarvel-roll. Thick smoke twined round her temples as she leaned gently back on the Regency sofa.

'My Uncle Onty was a merchant, grown rich in the Zenzan trades. By the time I came to his house he was retired; all thought of business had long been buried. Yet it had been his desire, I was to learn, not only to acquire personal riches, but to be the founder of a great trading dynasty. His life's work had been to *raise the family*: that was how he put it. He had made himself rich; in time, he hoped, he would be ennobled, too, and the life which he had begun as a barrow-boy he would end as a baronet. Or an earl: I suspect his ambition knew no bounds. Instead, it had all ended in bitterness.

'I was the symbol of that bitter defeat.

'You see, my dear, if there is one thing essential to this dynasty-building, it is heirs – male heirs. Now, as it happened, there *had* been a son – but my father had been a bitter disappointment. Alas, from the first his only interest in the trade had been, I'm afraid, in the rich, bejewelled Wrax-rarities my uncle imported from the Zenzan capital. Golden eggs within golden eggs – you know the sort of thing. Ornamental orbs, crosses and crowns. Mirrors and mantel-clocks and musical boxes. Valuable – oh, immensely. But my poor father cared only for their beauty – and beauty, of course, was to be his downfall.

'One might have predicted he would become an artist – a degenerate of some sort, at any rate. As it was, he grew into a raffish young man-about-town, one of the "New Agondon" set that so scandalized the court of the Regent Queen – yes, even the court of the Regent Queen!

'But of course, my dear, you would not remember.

'In those days, there was no Wrax Opera permanent in Agondon. The company came to Ejland only once in each cycle; so when they came in – 984? 985? – my father of course had never seen them before. Well, even today, the Opera can turn a young man's head. But my father – oh dear. He was smitten – with the costumes, the music, the cardboard castles. But most of all, with the charms of a certain Hartia Flay.

'You have not heard of Madame Flay, my dear? Well, such is fame. It blows away like chaff on the wind. But I wonder, is it true – as they say – that death levels us all? Can even a Hartia Flay exist for nothing? Does she leave nothing behind? How many times, I wonder, did my father sit enraptured as she sang, her voice pouring endlessly into his ears like liquid crystal? How many times, I wonder, did his eyes stare, entranced, as the Diva of Wrax descended on the clouds (the cloud-machine, really) to sing the Song of the Skies? After she sang, they say the roses would rain over the stage until it seemed that all the world would be buried in petals.

'Alas, I barely remember her – not really. I like to think I recall her face, but I only know it from the portrait in my locket – my father's locket.

'Look, my dear – have you seen a woman of more surpassing beauty?

'After I came to Uncle Onty's, they would tell me she was a harlot – a vicious, designing harlot who had ruined my father's life. Sometimes I would sob – it pleased them when I sobbed. But when I escaped at last to some secret corner, I would take the locket from my neck and gaze longingly on my mother's picture. Then she seemed to appear before me, holding out her arms to me, and I sank – oh, so very gently – into the perfume of her breasts.'

Here Aunt Vlada was obliged to pause, applying a handkerchief liberally to her eyes. Then gently, with a smile, she took back her locket from Jeli, snapped it briskly shut, and continued:

'Hartia Flay! There are some who maintain there has been no greater diva in all the history of the Wrax Opera – and that season, she was in her prime. When she sang Hofma's great Maidenhead Aria, they say the very whoremongers would break down and weep. Could my father resist? Hardly. He fell hopelessly in love with the ravished and dying heroine; but the true Hartia Flay, he was to find, was no languishing virgin.

'She was, one might say, a woman of remarkable capacities – oh, remarkable.

'But my dear, I shock your innocence! Suffice to say that many a rake, accustomed to breaking women's hearts, found instead that it was his

200

heart that was broken by Hartia Flay. But when that season ended and she returned to Wrax, it was my father she took with her.

'I was born a few moonlives later.'

Jeli stared admiringly – almost enviously – at her aunt. To be a Zenzan Vexing suddenly seemed the most desirable thing in the world. A child of the Opera! After her Entrance, her aunt had promised, they would regularly go to the Wrax Opera. Already the tall building by Aon's Gate seemed to Jeli a place of wonderment, and they had only driven past in the Archduke's carriage. Rapturously she imagined the boxes, the plush seats, the quality-folk in their finery, surveying each other through special lorgnettes.

Aunt Vlada's story only fuelled her impatience.

Fresh snow fell outside the dormer windows. Stroking Ring, petting Rheen, Jeli huddled close against her aunt. Her love for her was boundless. To think, that a little Zenzau-blood could become so fine a lady! What prospects, then, awaited Miss Jeli Vance, with the fair complexion of an 'Ejland Rose'?

'Then what happened?' her aunt went on. 'Oh, but you are a child, my dear! Were the years heavy upon your heart, as they are on mine, there would be no question for you to ask. I was born in Cycle 985. In 986 came Ender's Hornlight, an event for ever indelible in the bitter annals of Zenzau. Ender's Hornlight! As if time itself would end and start again, when the Ejlanders were driven from our lands.

'Driven, as it happened, for but a brief span.

'But I was only a little child, swooning on the incense of the Wrax Opera. How could my innocence be sweetened yet more by the victory my parents were determined to secure? In the event, it was only made sour.

'Later, my dear, when I lived in my uncle's house, I often had the oddest dream – it was many years before it went away. Afterwards I would wake up afraid and trembling. In my dream I was somewhere on high, like a hovering bird, looking down dizzily; below I saw a column of men dressed in red, an endless column, marching, marching, as if to the crack of doom. *Thud! Thud!* went the beating drums.

'Years later, when I went back to Wrax, I found Elpetta, my mother's old handmaid. Poor Elpetta was a wrinkled crone by then, but my mother still filled her memory, and her love for her was strong. Sadly Elpetta told me of that last day, when the rebellion lay in ruins. We had cowered together on the balcony of mother's apartment, when mother was missing and father was gone. Down we looked to the street below as Ejlanders paraded through the devastated city. Of course, my dear, in those days your King's soldiers wore red.

'Oh, I dare say it all had to come to grief – the rebellion, and my

201

childhood. My mother had been killed. Foolish woman, to take to the barricades! Only in Vassini's *Wars of the Vast* should Hartia Flay have been a goddess of battle.

'My father? I never saw him again. But I learnt later they had sent him to Xorgos Island. Poor father! He survived in filth and chains for less than a cycle, and my uncle – my wicked, foolish uncle – never even tried to have him released.

'I was rounded up with the other strays, and I too might have ended my life soon enough. Oh, I have imagined my fate. A child-harlot if they thought me pretty; a pigswill-girl if they did not. Which would you choose, my dear? Hm? Death in a filthy alley in the Quarter, rotted inside from a soldier's syphilis? Or death on the bleak steppes of Derkold, when you fell in the snow and could work no more?

'Elpetta's five sisters all died on the Royal Farms.

'As it was, I was lucky. Everybody knew the Child of the Opera; and if the shame of her birth deserved only execration, nonetheless she had about her a certain charm that was to save her – a lingering remnant, perhaps, of her mother's special magic.

'They sent me to Agondon, to live with my father's family.'

There was a pause. Aunt Vlada, it seemed, had slipped into reverie. By now it was dark outside the dormer windows. A maid appeared, lighting the lamps.

Jeli attempted, 'And that's when you met Uly, Aunt?'

'Hm?' Aunt Vlada roused herself briskly. 'Oh my dear, I haven't said much about Uly, have I? But Uly must wait. Come, let us get ready for dinner.'

Aunt Vlada would tell no more that day.

Chapter 27

FIRST MOONLIFE BALL

'A highwayman? Oh, abominable!' Constansia Cham-Charing cried.

But distractedly.

'Abominable,' agreed Sir Pellion, waving his jewelled stick with a vague air. The old man was unsteady on his feet, and quickly lowered the stick again; this was fortunate, or he would have tripped a passing footman bearing a tray of rum-and-orandy.

Eagerly Lady Cham-Charing seized a glass.

Lady Margrave ploughed on obliviously, 'My daughters were stripped, entirely stripped—'

'You don't say?' giggled the Prince of Chayn, who always got drunk quickly at the First Moonlife Ball.

'Freddie, that is not quite what I meant! Do you know, the fiend demanded every last ring from poor Bindy's hands? And Jammy – why, Jammy was in fits for weeks!'

'More, then, was demanded of *her*?'

'Perhaps less,' said Lord Empster. 'But come, Freddie, does it not appal you that a virtuous woman is unsafe even on the Wrax Road? If the vital thoroughfares of the empire are prey to these brigands, what dangers must lurk upon the lesser roads?'

'My lord, I have heard there is no danger greater than the notorious Bob Scarlet.'

'Bob Scarlet? What?' murmured Lady Cham-Charing. Fluttering her fan against her powdered breasts, she was gazing anxiously at the dance-floor. Round, round, went the Holluch Reelers.

Now where was that wretched girl?

Lord Empster leaned towards Freddie Chayn. 'Constansia,' he murmured, 'thinks we are speaking of a little bird. Come, Constansia' – he hummed a few bars, clashing with the Reel – 'would you take Bob Scarlet to your breast?'

It was an old song, 'Bob Scarlet, Come Nest in My Breast'. Cycles ago, had it not been the favoured piece of every young quality-lady when, in company, she was required to take her place at the harpsichord? Generations had learnt it at Mistress Quick's knee.

Alas, the joke was a poor one. Lady Cham-Charing mumbled assent; the company dutifully laughed. But there was little profit in it. Craning her neck for sight of her daughter, the lady did not realize that she had agreed to nurse, like an infant, the notorious outlaw who had plagued the Wrax Road these late moonlives.

Simply everyone was talking about him.

But the lady was looking elsewhere for embarrassment. Now where was she, her clodhopping daughter? Clumping on young Pelligrew's feet? Worse still, tripping and falling, exposing her petticoats for all to see? Oh, Tishy! Every year the wretched girl found some new way to render herself unmarriageable. What a burden a mother's lot could be!

The Holluch Reel ended to a round of polite applause and much fan-fluttering from Lady Cham-Charing. The Palace Ballroom was hotter than an inferno. Outside, all the world, even the river, was frozen to ice, but how one longed to fling open every window, every door! Overhead, in immense chandeliers, ten thousand candles blazed and dripped. From below rose the steaming fumes of – it may as well have been – the same number of bodies, bewigged, corseted, stuffed into layer upon layer of elaborate quilted costumes.

Make-up ran like sticky icing down the faces of women and men alike.

'I say,' said Freddie Chayn, as the orchestra re-tuned their slithering strings, 'it's the Tiralon Two-Step next, isn't it?' Swaying a little, he leaned annoyingly over Lady Cham-Charing's shoulder, consulting her programme. He giggled, 'You'll never guess who I'm booked with.'

'Freddie, you promised it to Tishy!'

Freddie coloured. 'Shouldn't a gentleman help the Entering girls? Miss Jelica Vance is quite a rip, you know. Say, she must have been at Quick's with . . . Ouch! Empster, you kicked me!'

Lady Margrave came to the rescue. 'And how's your young ward getting along, Lord Empster?'

'Nova? With Master Pell to guide him, I should think quite well.'

'I hear he's frightfully provincial,' said Freddie.

'He's from Chayn, isn't he?'

'Ooh!' Freddie laughed and excused himself.

'Pellam has nothing but good to say of the lad,' Sir Pellion was musing. 'Poor Pell, I think he needed something to keep his mind off . . .'

The old gentleman trailed off, fumbling for his tear-cloth.

'Oh dear,' said Lady Margrave.

'Freddie!' Flushed, Lady Cham-Charing turned back to the company. 'What if I were to offer—'

'He's gone, Constansia.'

'Looking for his Entering girl, I suppose? Hmph! What of those girls who are Entered already, and after four years have yet to find a beau?'

'Poor Constansia,' Lord Empster said kindly, 'you're overwrought. Come, let us take some air. Leave the girl to shift for herself, she's old enough. You'll join us, Sir Pellam? You, too, are feeling the heat, I can tell.'

'Aye, let us leave the young folk to their pleasures. But I do want to see the King's Chosen this year. Always so droll.'

And Lady Cham-Charing flushed again, for the climax of this interminable ball would come with the Entrance Walk, when the King inspected, like a line of troops, the ladies who were at Court for the first time. Of these, His Highness selected one particular young lady, with whom he would lead off the Last Waltz. To be Chosen, in olden times, had been the making of a girl's fortune. By now the custom was in sad disrepair, and everyone knew that the Choice was made, in any case, not even by the First Minister but by Mistress Quick's redoubtable deputy, Goody Garvice. Rumour had it that the woman was open to bribery. How else to explain that the Chosen, in the year of Tishy Cham-Charing's Entrance, had been none other than flat-footed, round-shouldered Tishy herself?

Still, it had not been good for her career in society. That was the year when she had fallen over, exposing her intimate garments, and the King – far gone on rum-and-orandy – had collapsed on top of her, making rutting motions.

The courtiers had pretended to an urbane amusement.

'You're not tired, my dear?'

Miss Jelica Vance cried, 'Oh no!'

'Do you know, more gentlemen than I can say have exclaimed upon that golden gown? I declare, I could have filled your programme four times over – five!'

'Oh, Aunt Vlad!' The girl hugged her new protectress. 'Has there ever been so wonderful an evening? So wonderful an aunt?'

Aunt Vlada laughed, kissed the girl quickly and said, 'Come, my dear, your charms are not to be wasted on an old woman! Here comes the Prince of Chayn!'

Jeli turned, enraptured, as the vision of manly splendour swayed glitteringly towards her, crooking his arm in sophisticated invitation. The orchestra struck up the Tiralon Two-Step.

'Why, Lady Flay,' the Prince attempted gallantly, 'how can this fine creature have been kept from us for so long? I declare, if she is not King's Chosen then – well, I shall demand to know why!'

'Fear not, she will be,' breathed Aunt Vlada, herself a magnificent confection of green feathers and emeralds. From a distance, she too might have been a pampered young belle, freshly embarked upon a woman's greatest adventure.

She smiled indulgently as the young folk took to the floor.

By the wall behind her, two decrepit old creatures, sex indeterminate, sat side by side in wheeled chairs. One was almost blind, the other deaf; pox had eaten away the noses of both. Incapable of partaking of other pleasures, eagerly they turned over the Court gossip, at such a volume that it reached the ears even of their intended victim.

'I call it disgraceful. That tender young girl, thrust into the jaws of that viper.'

'Hardly the jaws?'

'One can't be too sure. Do you know, if it hadn't been for her, that Pelligrew girl would be alive today? Poor Sir Pellion can't even bring himself to speak to the woman.'

'Indeed. But really, what a fool he must have been – to trust his daughter to a common prostitute!'

'Hardly a common one?'

'Worse. She's a Zenzan!'

'Dear me. The Zenzans rebel, and we send an army. Must we have an army for Vlada Flay?'

'One hears she's a demanding woman.'

'Indeed. This affair – with whom?'

'Why, the Archduke of Irion.'

'Irion? Then this is an old flame, burning bright again.'

'They didn't! Is that so?'

'Friend, when you are as old as I, you shall know that history only repeats itself, round and round again.'

'I wish my youth would come round again. Are they playing the Lexion Revels?'

'No, the Tiralon Two-Step.'

'Ah, but the colours have grown so dull!'

Vlada Flay only kept smiling. Then she caught a gaze from across the room, and her face suddenly hardened.

'Is it a big place?'

'Hm?'

'Chayn?'

'Massive.'

'Rich, I should imagine?'

'Groaning with brass. Well, gold. I say, that wasn't your foot, was it?'

'Not at all, Prince.'

'Call me Freddie. Why, a shindy like this would be the commonest little barn-dance in Chayn. These fine folk? Peasants! These costumes? Rags!'

'Really? Oh, Prince, you dance frightfully well.'

'Freddie. No, my girl, I'm a bare-faced liar. Piddling little hole, really. Provincial as – well, as you like.'

'No, really?'

'Really. Well, can't say I've spent much time there, these last cycles.'

'But you're the Prince.'

'Ancient title. Alas, empty. Power surrendered to the empire – oh, epicycles ago. Of course, between you and me, my dear, I am a Prince rather as your – ah – *Aunt Vlada* is a fine lady. Know what I mean?'

'Prince, I'm not sure I do!'

'Freddie, call me Freddie. And I haven't got a bean to my name. But I think you're a smashing girl, you know.'

'Ouch, my foot! Freddie, what's the King like?'

Now *that* was a question without a glib answer – not one, at least, that Freddie would give. Ah, these girls, these Entering girls! In the beginning, everything they saw was magic. They were overwhelmed, their little brains whirling with wonder at the lights, the music, the crowd. Then came the lull, when they would look around, beginning to glimpse things as they really were. The ballroom, they would realize, was old-fashioned and ugly, unchanged since the time of the Regent Queen. The wallpaper was a dingy orange-brown, faded and filthy with time and smoke.

And the King? But let the girl find out about the King! Hitting the rum-and-orandy harder than ever, by all accounts, since his harlot of an old mistress had been carted off by the guards. But really, what else was the First Minister to do?

Poor, poor little Miss Vance! Freddie was rather dreading the Entrance Walk.

❋ ❋

Your scheme goes well.

Was that all it said, that long smoky look? Through gap after gap of the vast crowd the eyes burned into Priestess Hara's – or rather, Vlada Flay's. She held the look boldly.

My scheme goes well? The world knows it. Have you nothing else to say to me, old deceiver?

Then Lord Empster turned back to his party, as they made their way to the comforts of the ante-hall. The Priestess – but no, we must call her Vlada – could almost have laughed. His party! That bitch, Constansia Cham-Charing. Stupid Lady Margrave. Doddering old Sir Pellion.

And you, a respectable courtier. Trusted intimate of Tranimel, no less? And what else? What would they say if they knew who you were?

The thoughts burned across the crowded hall.

207

Then Vlada Flay's face softened, and the being who wore that face turned her attention back to her young charge. Up-down, up-down, twirl and twirl about, Jeli disported herself with womanly grace. Ah, but she was a child!

Vlada sighed. She was fond of the girl, she could not deny it. Perhaps she recognized in her something of herself, and felt tenderly towards her. But Jeli was an instrument, an instrument to be played.

Vlada Flay would not forget it.

Gaining the girl's trust had been easy enough. Little Miss Vance was innocent as the new day, for all her airs. Innocent and vain: innocent enough to see only the sophistication in a woman like Vlada Flay; vain enough to believe that, with a little practice, she too could have that sophistication.

Well, perhaps she could – she had little else.

Jeli seemed wholly unconscious of her own precarious position in the world. Motherless, shut away in that appalling school, had the girl ever realized that nobody cared for her? Vlada almost laughed. Only one visit to Jorvel – an old lover from oh, too many cycles ago – was all it took to have his niece delivered into her hands, like a present newly wrapped.

I'm so concerned about the girl, Jorvel. How will she make her Entrance on the great stage of society, with only the guidance of a provincial, tottering Duenna?

For a moment Jorvel had rallied, stirring himself from the slough of his massive selfishness. *You've changed, Vlada.* But had she? Always she had burned for the cause of justice. If Jorvel's girl was to be a tool of that justice, so be it.

Vlada had drawn forth her handkerchief. *I am a woman mellowed by years, Jorvel. And tears – too many. Will you not permit me an outlet for my – alas! – thwarted maternal longings, now that my poor Pellicent has been taken from me?*

Two young men, gorgeously bewigged. One, perhaps, a little too fat, one a little too skinny. But Fat is tightly corseted, and Skinny padded by the fine clothes he wears, it must be admitted, with an unaccustomed air. He has barely danced, and lingers near the walls, looking at the crowded brilliance all about him with a wonderment that is almost alarm. He is a mere boy, almost an innocent: could it be, a country cousin? All evening he has barely moved; Fat, for his part, has just returned from dancing with a young lady, to find his friend in the same place, same attitude, gulping too eagerly at a beaker of punch.

208

FAT: I say, go easy on that rum-and-orandy.

SKINNY: I'm hot.

FAT: I'm the one who's been dancing. Ugh, that Tishy Cham-Charing has trodden all over my feet. Still, your uncle insisted.

SKINNY: I get the feeling you do what my uncle wants, Pell. What do you make of him?

FAT: Empy? Ripping fellow.

SKINNY: Do you know, sometimes it's as if I – can't quite see him. Clearly. Do you know what I mean?

FAT (*taking his arm*): Don't follow you, Nova. Now come, don't linger in the shadows.

SKINNY: There're no shadows here.

FAT: There're walls. We must promenade, Nova! Shy fellow, aren't you? We'll have to beat that out of you, if you're to shine in Agondon society.

SKINNY: I'm not sure I want to.

FAT: Nonsense! We all do. You're just a bit provincial still, that's all. But didn't you go to balls in – Chayn, was it?

SKINNY: Oh, once.

FAT: Only once?

SKINNY: It was very provincial.

FAT: Don't let Freddie hear you say that! But didn't you dance the night away?

SKINNY: I sat in a corner.

FAT: Nova, I don't believe you! I'll bet you took a young lady's hand that night.

SKINNY (*flushing*): Well all right, I took a young lady's hand.

FAT: Or two?

SKINNY: There was only one for me. Pell, who's that girl?

FAT: Dancing with your Prince?

SKINNY: My Prince?

FAT: Freddie Chayn! Really, Nova. That's Miss Vance. Niece of the Archduke of Irion, don't you know?

SKINNY (*intent*): Irion?

FAT (*oblivious*): Hm. Some say she'll be King's Chosen for certain this year. Do you know, her programme was full from the first dance? Not like poor Tishy Cham-Charing's! Why, Nova, your eyes are goggling out of your head! Come, you're not in Chayn now.

SKINNY: What?

FAT: The provinces! This is the King's house!

SKINNY (*faltering*): When does he come? The King?

FAT: Not till the end. Great-father said in the old days he'd dance away the ball. I mean the King. I mean the King we had then.

SKINNY (*stopping, sinking back towards the walls*): Have you
    noticed the colour of this paper?
FAT: What?
SKINNY: The wallpaper.
FAT: Orange. Well, brown.
SKINNY: It's red, Pell. Faded by age, faded by smoke. Why is the
    Palace so tatty, do you think?
FAT: Tatty! It's magnificent! Really, that's rich for a boy from
    Chayn! Do you know, Nova, sometimes you stand in the
    funniest way?
SKINNY: What do you mean?
FAT: As if you were – I don't know, a cripple. Leaning on
    crutches. I suppose it's provincial. I say, that Miss Vance
    is the belle of the ball, isn't she? To think, and I have to
    dance with Tishy!

'Ugh, the chill!'

Constansia Cham-Charing rubbed her bare arms.

'Really, Constansia! If we take you back in there, you'll just be too hot
again.'

'Mathanias, you are irritatingly practical.'

Lord Empster smiled. But it was true, the ante-hall was as chilly as the
hall was hot. The ballroom was in one of the oldest parts of the palace.
Once – so it was said – the Great Hall of Aon the Ironhand, it was hardly
adapted for civilized use. This ante-hall had not even been decorated
since – why, since the time of Aon the Ironhand!

'I think it's these suits of armour round the walls,' said Lady Margrave. 'Hardly warming, are they?'

'More these unglazed slit-windows, I should think,' said Lord
Empster.

'This stone bench!' contributed Lady Cham-Charing.

Sir Pellion sneezed noisily into his capacious tear-cloth.

'I much prefer a nice hanging,' continued Lady Margrave, gazing
gloomily at the stony walls.

'Your husband, dear lady, might say the same.'

'Really, Lord Empster! You know full well I was thinking of a tapestry.
An arras. My husband is away on a dangerous mission, yet you speak
of him quite disrespectfully.'

'Quite, Mathanias,' said Lady Cham-Charing, swigging at the remnants of her rum-and-orandy. 'I doubt Lord Margrave hanged anybody
in his life. He is an inspector of dungeons, only an inspector – is that not
so, Elsan?'

Lady Margrave rose from the uncomfortable bench. 'Constansia, you make my husband sound positively lowly. I'll have you know he is charged with heavier responsibilities than you might imagine. They have sent him to the Tarn!'

'The Tarn?' Lady Cham-Charing considered this for a moment, her face colouring markedly.

'Warmer now, Constansia? Friend of yours was exiled to the Tarn, was he not?'

'Canon Feval—'

'Oh, Lector by now, surely! I wonder if he's still such a little tittle-tattle? I suppose there's rather less for him in the outer provinces! Or does he speculate on the amours of dairymaids?'

Lady Cham-Charing ignored all this.

'Canon Feval,' she continued pointedly, 'was not *exiled*, Mathanias. He was given an opportunity to advance his career. To do something useful.'

'For a change.'

'Very well, for a change.'

Lord Empster smiled. Everyone knew that Eay Feval had enraged Constansia with one of the many rumours he had spread so promiscuously abroad. Constansia, after all, was a woman of a certain position. A Temple lady. A pious servant of the Lord Agonis. She could hardly wish it to be thought that she, of all people, had been mother to a Vexing!

Whether this was true or not, no one quite knew; only that her wrath was such that the Archmaximate had no choice, it seemed, but to cast Feval into the outer darkness. Constansia had triumphed; still, it was an ignoble chapter in her social career. Some, it was true, were glad to see the last of Feval. Understandably: he was a fool and a snob as well as a gossip, skewering the characters and reputations of others while seeking desperately to elevate his own paltry status.

Who was he anyway? The son of some impoverished, sick old gentle-woman, wasn't he? Why, he was almost nobody! But if there were those who were glad to see him go, there were many more who mourned their handsome spiritual advisor, and swore lasting enmity to the author of his ruin.

Poor Constansia! What a fool she had been!

'What, what?' Sir Pellion had fallen into a light doze; the little party, had they been paying him attention, might indeed have feared that he was dead. Now he rose up, spluttering over Constansia, 'Your husband has been exiled?'

Lord Empster sighed, 'Constansia's husband is dead these four cycles, Sir Pellion, as well you know. It is Lady Margrave's husband who is in exile.'

'No! Why, poor poor lady!' The old gentleman seized the lady's hand, snuffling over it immoderately. Really, he had become quite unhinged

211

since the death of that useless girl. 'Oh, what injustices does this world rain upon us! Why, they say they are mustering for war again!'

'My husband is not in exile,' said Lady Margrave, snatching away her hand. She would have gone on to expatiate upon her husband's noble mission, but no one was interested. Instead, Lord Empster, swooping in close to the old gentleman, asked him if he were prey to treasonous thoughts.

'You would call the Zenzan campaign an injustice? Now why could that be, when the rebels have vowed never to rest until they have taken back Wrax itself?'

Sir Pellion was suddenly frightened. 'That is hardly what I meant. You – you misunderstand me.'

And the old gentleman drew out his tear-cloth again.

'Mathanias, you are cruel,' scolded Lady Cham-Charing.

'Cruel? Is not the loyalty of every Ejlander a matter for concern?'

Lady Cham-Charing looked at him levelly. She had known Mathanias Empster for – really, she had quite forgotten how long – and there were times when she was not quite sure how to take him. Not sure at all. She might have said something, but at that moment her wretched daughter came blundering from the ballroom.

'Mama, there you are! How could you leave me? Oh, Freddie, Freddie!' Sobbing, she flung herself upon her mother's breast.

'My goodness,' snuffled Sir Pellion, 'whatever is the matter with the poor child?'

'It's Freddie,' said Lady Margrave. 'He's not dancing with her.'

There was little that could be said, but Sir Pellion blew his nose again and said matter-of-factly, 'But my poor child, you're ugly. You really are the most frightfully *ugly* girl.'

❈ ❈

'Really, that gold gown!' came a hissing voice. 'What does she think it does for her?'

'I know what *she* thinks. But she's wrong. I always thought she was ugly.'

'She was always horrid to poor Pelli Pelligrew.'

'Wasn't she? And to poor Catty.'

'Catty? Where *is* Catty Veeldrop?'

'Haven't you heard? Married already!'

'A *province-wedding*? Oh no!'

'Some clodhopping boor from Orandy, Jeli says!'

'Silly Catty! But did you hear about Heka Quisto's little sister?'

'Jilda? Has she vanished, too?'

'They're trying to hush it up. But I heard she'd been *ruined*.'

'No!'

The girls giggled heartlessly. Glittering, gleaming in their gorgeous ball-dresses, the fine flowers of Mistress Quick's stood in two long parallel lines down the centre of the ballroom, awaiting the arrival of His Imperial Agonist Majesty. It had been a long evening, and if some of the flowers had become a little wilted, they were doing their best to conceal it. This was their test, their moment. All eyes were upon them. Earnest society-matrons fluttered about their darlings, wielding powder-puffs, smoothing skirts, scratching at gobs of fallen wax from the blazing chandeliers. On the stage behind, the orchestra had fallen silent and only the hubbub of expectant voices filled the immense high-beamed chamber.

'Aunt Vlad,' Jeli whispered, 'I'm so frightened!'

'My darling, let me kiss you one more time! You remember all your steps, don't you? And your curtsey? Of course you do. Don't look so worried! Tonight marks the beginning of a brilliant career!'

'Aunt, are you sure?'

'Sure? Look at these drabs, and look at you!'

'It's always exciting, isn't it?' came a voice from behind.

Constansia Cham-Charing could not help but stiffen. Elsan Margrave, rather to her surprise, had grabbed her by the arm. She squeezed tightly.

'Don't you remember our year, Constansia? King Jagenam was Prince-in-Waiting then, wasn't he? Can't you still see the Regent Queen, magnificent on her throne, as her son parades up and down before the line of beauties? Oh, who would have thought he would choose me?'

'He didn't, Elsan.'

'He stopped in front of me for long enough! Do you remember, he had the most dreamy eyes?'

'Poor Elsan! What a pity you had to settle for your husband.'

'Constansia, really! But who did the late King choose that year?'

'Come, Elsan, don't you remember? You were green with envy for long enough afterwards! It was Lolenda Mynes, wasn't it?'

'Lolenda! Still, she never came to much, did she?'

'She married the Archduke of Irion.'

'Jorvel Ixiter? Don't be absurd.'

'His father, Elsan. Died years ago – she did too, didn't she?'

'Oh, Constansia!' Lady Margrave wailed. 'How did we ever get so old?'

'Elsan, you're drunk. Now shut up, here comes His Majesty.'

Voices fell silent at the *thump! thump!* of a steward's staff, striking the floor. Horns rang out, then a stately scraping of viols as vast gilt-painted doors swung open.

The Royal Procession!

Down the line of fine flowers, hearts fluttered. On the King's arm was the steely grey figure of Mistress Quick, making her single Court appearance of the year. If colour rode high in many a cheek and many a thigh chafed tight, constraining sudden urgencies, it may have been more the schoolmistress than the King who inspired such terror. To the girls, His Imperial Agonist Majesty was the merest blur of ermine and blue velvet, too awesome even to look at squarely.

It was left to others in the assembly to remark upon the extraordinary alteration in the Royal Person.

'My goodness,' Lord Empster whispered, 'the fellow's not even staggering! Where's his flushed face? His slack jaw?'

'Mathanias, you don't think—?'

'I do, Constansia.'

'What is it?' hissed Lady Margrave.

'Elsan, can't you see? *The King's not drunk.*'

'Well, I never!'

With a gracious smile His Imperial Agonist Majesty relinquished the arm of Mistress Quick. The steely figure stationed herself at the head of the line, where she stood largely without expression except for a single, quickly averted glance at the harlot, Vlada Flay.

There had been a time when the Great Teacher had taken it upon herself to introduce her Fine Flowers in person to the monarch; for many cycles now the task had devolved upon her loyal assistant, Goody Garvice. As the viols scraped on, and to the amazement of many a courtier, the King now proceeded unswaying, unaided down the line of young beauties, nodding and smiling politely as Goody Garvice, with an air of solemn declamation, announced each name, and its flush-faced owner simpered and bobbed, her eyes downcast towards the wax-bespattered floor.

'Miss Huskia Bichley . . . Lady Berthen Beechwood-Bounce . . . Her Royal Highness Karellen, Princess of Down Lexion . . . Miss Alfredina Flonce . . . Miss Ethelreda Flonce . . . Miss Regina Hamhock . . . The Right Honourable Tristina Harion-Zaxos . . .'

In each young bosom lodged a terrified heart. To be King's Chosen! Could a woman know greater bliss? That the state had proved less than bliss to many a young lady in the past – not least of all to one snuffling, plain creature who watched now, resentfully, from the crush of the crowd – was neither here nor there.

Of the young ladies gathered there that evening, any one might have made a fine partner for a King. But when His Imperial Agonist Majesty arrived at a certain dazzling creature in gold, the signs of favour were unmistakable – especially when Goody Garvice bowed particularly low, and took particular care in announcing the name.

Vlada Flay smiled. Triumphantly her eyes swept along the line. First she sought Jeli's gaze, then Mistress Quick's. The stately viols modulated into a dancing rhythm as the King turned, turned, all according to custom, ready to make his choice. He held out his hands.

Jeli swooned. Enraptured, she closed her eyes, extending her own hands to receive, like a blessing, the Royal touch.

All at once there was a commotion. The music faltered, there were gasps.

Jeli opened her eyes.

What was happening, what could be happening? Sailing through the ballroom, parting the crowd like blades of grass, was a huge-breasted, dishevelled female creature, barefoot and dressed in a pauper's garb. The woman was filthy and stank abominably. Her red hair was a wild mass, sticking up at angles, and her dress, once white, was ripped and stained and stuck about with straw. Courtiers started forward, but the guards did not. The King held out his arms.

'Maddy!'

'Sire, sire!'

There was a shocked silence as the King embraced the prisoner from the dungeons. Lovingly he enfolded her into his velvet, into his ermine. When she stepped back at last, her enormous mottled breasts rolled, almost bursting, over her tight bodice. The King looked around him, blinking, then stamped his foot on the waxy floor.

'Orchestra! Play!' he barked, almost shouted, but only slowly, only raggedly did the lutes and the viols and the horns and the harpsichord lurch into the familiar strains of Schuvart's celebrated Waltz in J. By now, the neat line of Fine Flowers had broken up in confusion, some to sob, some to flee, some to stare in blank horror as the King and his reeking strumpet circled round and round the floor.

Then, one by one, others joined them.

Freddie Chayn grabbed the first Entrance-girl to hand. So did Pellam Pelligrew; so did his friend, the young man he called Nova. Sobbing, Miss Jelica Vance barely registered the gentle pressure that pulled her into the dance.

Freddie?

But it was not Freddie.

'You're crying. Don't cry.'

'What?'

'You're beautiful.'

'Who are you?' Jeli brushed the tears from her eyes. Her brow furrowed as she gazed into the limpid eyes. 'Lord Empster's ward? Let me go! Who said you could dance with me?'

215

'We have to dance, don't we? I think the King wants it.'

'The King! I've never been so humiliated in my life.'

'Who is that woman?'

'I've no idea. Nor do I have any idea about you.'

'You just said I was Lord Empster's ward.'

'A ward, precisely. You could be anyone. Haven't I seen you somewhere before?'

'Never. Call me Nova. Do you know, your eyes are flashing like jewels?'

'I think you're a most impertinent young man.'

'Not at all, I'm frightfully shy. You must bring it out in me.'

'Bring out what?'

'Everything you don't like about me.'

'I didn't say I didn't like you. I said I didn't know who you were.'

'So you do like me?'

'Are you sure we haven't met before?'

But of course, they had not. Later, Jem would barely understand the impulse that had driven him to his blonde, flouncy cousin. Perhaps it was the call of blood; but more than this, it was the call of desire. It was as if something inside him were free at last. For too long, it seemed to Jem now, he had loved uselessly, fruitlessly, a girl who barely existed any more. Of course, he had urged Pell to discover if a certain Miss Wolveron might be among the Entering girls – but Pell had turned up no intelligence of her at all. Even tonight, Jem had wondered if he might suddenly find himself, across the ballroom, gazing into Cata's mysterious dark eyes. But Cata had vanished, vanished as if she had never been, and when he thought back to their meeting in Varby, Jem found himself almost relieved. That girl had not been Cata, not his Cata. What could Jem do but forget the days that had gone? Cata was a memory he would always treasure, but the door that led to that memory was one he now must close behind him, gently but firmly.

Now a new door was opening in his heart.

But there would be no chance that night for it to open wider. Suddenly a high-pitched scream rang out. Then a desperate, guttural cry. The dance broke up in a flurry of running, shrieking, shouting.

Where Jeli went, Jem did not know. All he knew was that, a moment later, he was looking back wildly, transfixed in terror, to the vast cleared space in the centre of the ballroom where a lean figure, a stranger to his eyes, rose slowly above the slumped, still form of the King's harlot, and the hunched, shuddering form of the King. The lean figure wore robes of brilliant red.

But no, not red.

In his hand he held a dagger.

The robes were white, and drenched in blood.

Only later would Jem come to understand just what had happened. The King, it seemed, had arranged for his old mistress to be brought up from the dungeons. Had this been some public declaration of his love? In any case, the guards had seen fit to obey, but they reckoned without the wrath of the First Minister. Finding himself betrayed, Tranimel had determined on his vengeance at once, insinuating himself through the dancers, weapon at the ready.

Now, his icy eyes swept the company as he declared levelly, 'The King is distressed, realizing the perfidy that has almost claimed him.' With a contemptuous foot, the Friar turned over the bloody corpse, and all at once his voice rose to an unaccustomed thunder as he cried, 'An enemy agent! A deceiving harlot sent by the Zenzans, aflame with evil powers that would beguile even a King! Fear not, sire, you shall be avenged! And all the hosts of Zenzau shall fall, as this wicked harlot has fallen!'

Suddenly, wildly, the bloody Friar kicked the corpse, sending fresh gouts of blood spurting across the floor. The King only sobbed, insensible of this new outrage. Jem, like many others, almost sank to the floor in terror. There was a force in Tranimel, he saw at once, that would brook no opposition, that would settle for nothing but absolute power.

Then the storm was over, as suddenly as it had begun. The Friar dropped his dagger to the floor, turning away.

'Quick, some rum-and-orandy, to calm His Majesty's nerves.'

Chapter 28

SHADOW OF THE ERDON TREE

Jem was learning about chivalry. Lord Empster had set him to study many things, ponderous tomes of history, languages, philology, philosophy. Left in the library, the young ward hunched dutifully over the big books, wondering how the pages could be so thick and the type so small and faint. He would screw up his eyes in earnest effort, but all that seemed to induce in him was sleep. More often, when he felt himself alone, Jem would repair to a dusty corner of the library, away from the formidable ramparts of leather and gleaming gold. There, almost hidden on a shelf by the floor, was a shabby set of volumes bound only in cheap cloth, the titles faded by time.

Of all the books in Lord Empster's house, Jem would come to love these most. They were Silverby's Novels, those stalwarts of the circulating library in the time of the Regent Queen. Pell would laugh and call him absurd, but something in the romances of Sir Bartel Silverby stirred Jem quite as much as any excitements his real life, at that time, seemed to hold.

In Silverby's novels, dashing gentlemen with names like Reeves Roamer and Viscount Vyles Venture embarked on dangerous missions, clashing swords thrillingly with evil opponents in the service of justice, truth and love. In *Crime and a Quest*, a young lord, branded a Vexing by his evil half-brother, could prove the honour of his birth only by a journey to the furthest reaches of Ana-Zenzau, beyond the Vianan Ranges. In *Prince of Swords*, only one young member of a noble set dared to pursue the villainous Skyle Kelming-Skyle, who not only cheated at cards and spread slander but fought dirtily, killing his duelling partners with a poison-tipped rapier. Always the Silverby hero was a young man of the utmost honour, despised wrongly by an unthinking world; and always his honour was rewarded in the end with the love of a noble and virtuous young lady.

Sometimes these endings made Jem sad, and he would think of the young lady *he* had lost. Dear Cata! How he missed her! But then Jem would think of the adventures, and the future looked brighter.

In *From Cabin-Boy to King*, the disinherited scion of the throne was forced to go to sea, undergoing many perilous trials before at last he came into his kingdom. For a time Jem was passionate about the sea, and dreamed of the dangers he too would face in far-flung lands.

One day when he was driving with Pell, Jem looked down intently over the ramparts that ringed the upper reaches of The Island. The day was short and the air was dim, but the Gulf of Ejland glittered icily in the distance like glass. For the first time, Jem considered its strangeness.

Before he came to Agondon, he had seen the sea only in pictures, in the engravings in his mouldering books or in smoky paintings that hung askew against the panelling of the castle walls. Wonderingly he had stared at elaborate, arrested waves with their stiff curves of foam, at ships angled obliquely with artfully wind-whipped sails. In one story in The Mythologicon, a huge scaly Creature of Evil reared up from the waters beneath a rocky coast and destroyed a fishing-village; Jem could not remember why. In the accompanying picture, the sea – element of the serpent – tore and churned like a raging dark fire. Jem had still not seen the sea like that, and wondered if one day perhaps he would. The Gulf of Ejland, so it seemed, was only a dull unmoving glimmer, stretching away from the great reclaimed plains like a change in the texture of the land, that was all.

A man might have walked upon those hard, tensile fields.

'Pell, what is the sea?' Jem said suddenly.

'Nova?'

It was a foolish question, Jem knew; but then he wondered why it was foolish. What is the sea? What is the sky? Perhaps there were really no other questions. He thought of the cabin-boy who became a King and the knowledge came to him that one day, if he were to prosecute his quest, he too would have to cross that strange shifting medium that divided land from land. Then he knew that the sea was as much a highway, winding its way towards mystery and adventure, as the pale dusty road that undulated away over the green hills of his childhood.

After that day, Jem would often go down to the docklands, where he inspected creaking ships with their elaborate webs of rigging, their flags and furled sails, knocking and sloshing against suppurating wharves. His eyes lighted, almost in trepidation, on huge barnacled chains and nets and scaly snake-like coils of rope. He watched strange men with tattoos and pigtails unloading barrel after tarry barrel. Once, seeing the young man standing by, a gentleman – for he wore a wig as well as a wooden leg – stumped his way towards him and asked, in friendly tones, if the young fellow might be looking for a passage.

Jem, confused, said he was not sure.

'Then make up your mind, young fellow, make up your mind!' The gentleman had an enormous red nose and little twinkling eyes. Gently he reached up, tapping Jem's forehead. 'I be Captain Porlo, Faris Porlo, master of the *Catayane*—'

'The *Catayane*?'

'Now let me guess, you be a young trader, about to embark upon your first mission? Ah, I remember me own green days! See me ship before you' – Jem had been admiring the figurehead, a lady who, indeed, looked a little like Cata – 'in her, you may be borne to the furthest shores – to blazing lands where the sun flames high, to the far, scattered islands of the west. Why, for a price, you might journey on and on, far beyond these paltry Lands of El-Orok!'

Jem looked thoughtful. He had read something of geography, it was true, but when it came to the question of lands beyond the Four Lands, the books became circumspect, the maps sketchy; there were hints of places unformed and inchoate, refuges of the Creatures of Evil.

But the captain was plunging on, 'Look at the *Catayane*! Is there anywhere she might not go? In her, you may be transported as on a Sosenican carpet, to courts of caliphs and evil enchanters, of genies and eunuchs and luscious veiled maidens you have only read about in your books of stories. Come, young gentleman, lay down your fortune: would you not venture to the lands beyond the sea?'

'Good sir,' Jem said impulsively, 'had I a fortune to lay down, assuredly I should come with you. But I detect something strange in your manner, and suspect you are a foreigner. Tell me, what standard does your *Catayane* fly?'

'Standard? We are in Ejland, are we not? Why, then, me *Catayane* flies the Blue Ejard' – the gentleman dropped his voice to a whisper – 'but is not her true kingdom the one with no King?'

'There is such a kingdom?'

'Aye, and it be without a Queen, too, though there's many a wooden lady' – he gestured to the figurehead – 'who would think herself its mistress. Think herself, dream herself, till the salt spray lashes her, to teach her better.'

'Then the sea is your kingdom?'

'But I say, it has no King!' Still the captain's voice was low. 'What need have we of Kings, when we have the sea and sky?'

Wonderingly Jem looked to the horizon, a steely haze far across the waters of the Gulf. He would have prolonged this conversation, but the air was chill, and something in the captain's tone began to frighten him. To the last question, he only smiled tightly, and bade his new friend a hasty goodbye.

'Goodbye, young trader!' the captain called cheerfully. 'Remember me name: Porlo, Captain Faris Porlo! I'll see you on the *Catayane* soon, I'm sure!'

The *Catayane* ... As Jem hurried away, he seemed to hear the ship's name echoing behind him, bouncing against the slimy timbers of the ships, the wharves, the warehouses. The encounter left him shaken, but as he reached the carriage, where Pell – bored, alas – was waiting impatiently, something made Jem turn, pause. The question hung on his lips:

Captain, tell me – why is your ship called the Catayane?

But when he went back, the captain was gone. Jem came to the docks again the next day, searching with some ardour for his strange new friend; but he only learnt that the *Catayane* had sailed, bound for the rocky Zenzan coast, far round the furthest tip of Tiralos.

But the sea, for all that it would still divert him, might have evaporated like a puddle in the road after Jem finished *From Cabin-Boy to King*, and turned to *Shadow of the Erdon Tree*. In this novel – the darkest, perhaps, in the Silverby canon – the hero faces hanging for a murder which, of course, he has not committed. The novel begins and ends in a grim crowd-scene at the infamous Tree out on the Wrax Road, where the good folk of Agondon would gather for public executions. This was a long-established entertainment, but one perhaps lacking in variety or wit; in late generations, quality-folk would profess themselves weary of it, finding in the Tree a taint of the provincial. From time to time, it was true, the death of some quality-rogue would bring even the carriages of the nobility rumbling *en masse* along the Wrax Road. After Lord Varry Vignal had killed his wife's lover, he flung from the scaffold a shower of epigrams that (so the critics agreed) would have hushed even the chattering promenaders at the Theatre Royal, Juvy Lane. But alas, the criminals were seldom in this class, and after all there was a limit – so Pell would expatiate – to the diversion afforded by the sight of (say) some filthy Reject first cowering in chains as the list of his crimes was read to the crowd, then jerking his ragged legs in the air in a manner quite devoid of style or grace. No, Pell would conclude, the Tree, when all was said and done, was a diversion very much for the lower orders, and no, on no account would he permit Jem to go there.

So it was that Jem had to slip away alone, one afternoon when the hangings were scheduled. Why he had to go he was not quite sure; he supposed he wanted to see what Silverby had described. In the novel, the Erdon Tree seemed a place of sad nobility, of grand emotions and gestures; Jem had not quite wanted to believe Pell's dry ironies.

By the time he arrived on the outskirts of the city he was hungry, dusty and tired, and wishing he had not worn his fine clothes from Quisto's. But there had been no difficulty in finding the way. Many went

221

in the same direction. At the Erdon Tree, the crowd was huge and rowdy. Most, it seemed, were drunk. They jostled, laughed, sang bawdy songs; when the prison-carts rumbled into view they milled clamorously around them, jeering and throwing rotten apples and tomatoes.

How disappointing! In *Shadow of the Erdon Tree*, an unearthly hush possessed the crowd as Reeves Roamer came to face his death: hard to imagine this crowd hushed and reverent for anyone! Besides, the day's prisoners were entirely unexceptional: a few Rejects from the Riel Embankment, some Zenzans, a couple of harlots. Some Vagas.

A boy behind Jem moaned, 'And I heard they'd got Bob Scarlet!'

'Bob Scarlet?' A hand cuffed the boy's head. 'Don't be a fool, boy! Do you think they could ever take old Scarlet Bob?'

'Traitor-words!' called a drunkard, somewhere else.

'Traitor yourself!' came the angry response.

Another: 'Traitor? Bob's a hero!'

Jem struggled to force his way forward, distancing himself from the impending brawl. He found himself crushed between an old man and woman – peasant-folk, of the lowest class. Smelly, dirty and ugly, they bellowed at each other, their breath gusting foully into Jem's face. Dismayed, he looked between them but they barely noticed him – or his fine clothes.

'And to think, I remember when they killed the King!'

'The King? That was never the King they killed, crone!'

'Who you calling crone?' the woman spat, reaching over and tweaking the old man's whiskers.

There was pinching, slapping. The old man held a pot of ale unsteadily in his grasp, slopping much of it down the front of Jem's coat as he cried to the crone, 'There was a mask on his face the whole time, wasn't there?'

'What, do you think they'd show his face to the likes of you? That was respect, you fool! Respect to a King!'

'Respect? To bring him to the Erdon Tree? I tell you, crone, that was never the King!'

'Why did they say it was the King, then, if it were never?'

'Stupid crone! Don't you know the Red King has to be dead?'

'Dead, what do you mean?'

'Why, if the Red King were alive, would we have the Blue?'

'Old man, don't you know the Red King was a traitor?'

'Traitor? How can the King be a traitor?'

But the old woman was in no mood for logic. 'Redjacket! Redjacket!' she shrieked in glee, as if she would gladly have given up her husband to the clawing hands of an angry mob.

Jem writhed and wriggled, longing to be free. But there was no time for the altercation. By now the first cart had reached the Erdon Tree, and the eager crowd surged forward afresh. What had this filthy Reject done? Perhaps he had stolen from a muffin-stall; perhaps he had raped a quality-child. In any case, the crowd would shriek and bay until the Reject convulsed on the Tree.

The black-garbed canon, who was reading the charge – murder, but he had to draw a moral lesson – began to go on a trifle too long. Slow handclaps broke out among the crowd. 'Noose!' came the cries. 'Noose, noose!'

That was when Jem saw something extraordinary. The surge of the crowd had brought him close to the front, close to the carts with their miserable cargo. It was as he ducked a bombardment of tomatoes that he saw the face on the other side of the carts, straining eagerly for a view of the prisoners.

A face he knew.

A dark face.

'Raj!' Jem burst out. 'Raj!'

But if it was Rajal, he was too far away, and Jem could not push his way fast enough through the stifling press of bodies. There were angry cries.

'Here, watch out!'

'Thinks he's quality, this one do!'

'Hey, young fellow, why so fast?'

Rough hands tore at Jem's fine clothes; someone aimed a punch at his teeth; he felt a tomato splatter in his wig. Desperately he struggled to escape, gasping with relief when the crack of a whip sounded above the heads of the mob, and a voice he knew came: 'Nova!'

For a wild moment, Jem thought it was Rajal.

But it was not.

Again, 'Nova!'

'Pell!'

Chapter 29

THE EDDY

'Raise you.'

'You're bluffing.'

'Raise you.'

'Very well.'

'No!'

'Trumped!'

Jeli, with a gleeful laugh, swept up her aunt's cards. Now the green baize on her aunt's side was empty. Not for the first time, all the cards, all the buttons were Jeli's.

'You're learning, my girl!'

'Aunt, you're not just letting me win?'

Aunt Vlada's eyes glittered. 'Now child, how could I *let* you win? It's your way with the Queen of Swords. Did you know you had a way with her?'

Jeli did not.

A spinet had been brought up to their apartments that morning so that Jeli might practise. She had not yet done so, but now Aunt Vlada moved to the little velvet-seated stool. 'You don't know "Queen of Swords", my dear? Miss Sorretti's immortal lyric – addressed,' she added, 'to a girl with just your name. Now isn't *that* the oddest thing—'

And Aunt Vlada warbled in a voice which, if a little strident for the bagatelle melody, left no doubt that she was the daughter of Hartia Flay:

> *How comes it, Jeli, that whenever we*
> *Play cards together, you invariably*
> *As if with silken cords,*
> *Must draw the Queen of Swords?*
>
> *I've scanned you with a scrutinizing gaze,*
> *Resolved to fathom these your secret ways:*
> *But sift them as I will,*
> *Your ways are secret still.*
>
> *I cut and shuffle; shuffle, cut again;*
> *But all my cutting, shuffling proves in vain:*
> *Vain hope, vain forethought too;*
> *That Queen still falls to you!*

Charmed by the song, Jeli allowed her eyes to roam dreamily about the room. But it was then she noticed that Ring seemed somewhat out of sorts. His tail jerking, his whiskers quivering, the black cat paced round and round the carpet. Picking his way through the customary debris, from time to time he would halt suddenly, peering into a hat-box or beneath the sofa or into the little tunnels made by folds of fabric. He padded beneath the card-table, but when Jeli reached down to stroke him, he flicked his ears angrily.

What could be wrong?

> *I dropped her once, prepense; but ere the deal*
> *Was dealt, your instinct seemed her loss to feel:*
> *'There should be one card more,'*
> *You cried, and searched the floor!*

Her eyes closed, Aunt Vlada had invested the little song with rather more feeling than it might, perhaps, have merited. She had not noticed Ring.

It was left to Jeli to realize what was wrong.

'It's Rheen!' she cried. 'Poor Ring, you've lost him!'

At once Jeli was on her knees, crawling about the legs of the oblivious Aunt Vlada. The maid, entering at that moment, was somewhat taken aback.

> *I cheated once; I made a private notch*
> *In Sword-Queen's back, and kept a lynx-eyed watch;*
> *Yet such another back*
> *Deceived me in the pack!*

If, in Aunt Vlada's voice, the connoisseur might hear the ghost of Hartia Flay, this was, alas, a Hartia Flay quite without training, and one whose abilities had long been untried. The maid – in general, no enthusiast for her new mistress – would have stopped her ears. Instead she was obliged to participate in the following exchange:

MISS: Elpetta?
MAID: Miss?
MISS: Elpetta—
MAID: Miss, there's no Elpetta here.
MISS: Aunt Vlada says all maids should be called Elpetta.
MAID: Begging your pardon, miss, but I can't answer to no
      Zenzan name. Why, I'm a good Ejland-woman! Berthen
      Spratt my name is, and I answer to no other.
MISS: Never mind your silly name!
MAID: Silly? No sillier than some.

MISS: Never mind, I said! Elpetta – Berthen – have you seen a
mouse?
MAID: A mouse, miss?

> *The Queen of Spires assumed by arts unknown*
> *An imitative dint that seemed my own;*
> *This notch, not of my doing,*
> *Misled me to my ruin!*

MISS: A white mouse. Answers to the name of Rheen.
MAID: Answers? Well, I never heard the like. But pleasing you,
miss, I did put out a mouse of that description, only this
morning.
MISS: Put out? What do you mean *put out*, Berthen?
MAID: I mean, I found a white mouse in my trap. Neck broke
and all, from being too greedy with my Varby-cheese.
Flung him out the window I did, miss, like I do all no-
good vermins I finds in the Archduke's house. Well, the
small ones—
MISS: You wicked woman! You wicked, wicked woman! Out of
my sight! Out of my sight, do you hear? (*Exit* MAID,
slamming door.)
ALLEGEDLY LARGE VERMIN (*improvising rippling instrumental break,
she stretches towards precarious reaches of the keyboard*):
Berthen Spratt, indeed! Her name's Vanta Shessey.
Highest kicker in the Varlan Follies, when she was a girl.
Gone to pack now – those Varl-women always do. But
one of Chokey's finest in her day, believe you me. Why,
she had them queuing round the block!
JELI (*uncertainly*): Chokey's? Whatever is Chokey's?
HER MYSTERIOUS AUNT: Ah, but I go a little fast for you, my
dear. You shall understand, all in good time.

(*Aunt Vlada attempts a daring key-change. Why, having struggled in
commonplace V Major, she endeavours to scale the exacting heights of
J Flat, is one of those curious conundrums with which human
behaviour so frequently presents us. The modulation is not a success;
still, there is a class of musical performance in which fervour is felt to
atone for all; Aunt Vlada's belongs to that class.*)

> *It baffles me to puzzle out the clue,*
> *Which must be skill, or craft, or luck in you:*
> *Unless, indeed, it be*
> *Natural affinity!*

(*The song is over.* JELI *is sobbing.* THE REMARKABLE *seems
remarkably unconcerned about* RHEEN.)

226

BUT CONCERNED, OF COURSE FOR JELI: Come, my dear, let me comfort you. Come, come and sit with Aunt Vlada.

JELI: Aunt?

AUNT: My dear?

HER DEAR: Perhaps you could tell me a story.

AUNT: To cheer you up?

JELI: To cheer me up.

THE COMFORTER: Well, perhaps I *could* tell you a story.

THE COMFORTED: Dear Aunt Vlada! Can all aunts be so dear?

AUNT (*with a sly smile*): Had you considered, my dear, that *my* aunts were Uly and Marly? They were, after all, my father's sisters.

THE STORY OF ULY

'Of course, to call them *aunts* hardly gives the correct impression. They were mere girls, barely older than me. And they were beautiful. Why, they were the most beautiful girls of their generation. Even now, to think on them makes my heart exult – if, that is, I think only on their outward forms. They were tall and fair, while I was squat and brown – like a peasant, they said. I dare say they were right. They were proud, confident, fearless. And here was I, a jangling heap of nerves, frightened to walk down the nursery stairs in case I should make too loud a creak!

'It was Ulinda who was the eldest, and I venture to say the proudest, too. But that Marlia was the greatest beauty, there could be no doubt. Why, there were those who said it was rather as if Uly had been but a sketch, a first draft for Marly. Still, when two girls are so particularly radiant, what can comparisons be but odious? No, they were both exceptional beauties. In years to come, everyone said, they would conquer Agondon society. Do you know, when they were the merest girls, with still many seasons before their Entrances, gentlemen would connive to visit Uncle Onty just in hopes of glimpsing them? Regularly he received offers of betrothal; a lesser father would have given away his daughters at once, bundled them out of the very door for the settlements some would offer, could they but pluck those blooms before their time!

'But after the terrible disappointment of his son, Uncle Onty was determined that his daughters should deviate not one jot from the proper path. First, each would make a spectacular Entrance (Uly's, perhaps, the harbinger of Marly's greater glory), then would come a still more spectacular wedding (Uly's, again, would prepare the way), only to the highest and noblest of suitors. Why, Uncle Onty would muse fondly, who could say that Prince Jagenam himself might not choose a girl so fair as Marly! Imagine, his Marly – Queen of all Ejland!

'It was expected that I should be a governess or companion.'

'Poor Aunt Vlad! How bitter you must have been!'

'Bitter? No, my dear. You must understand that at this time I was wholly under the spell of my cousins. To feel inferior to Uly and Marly was simply a fact of the world, something clear as day – why, like seeing that the grass is green, that the sky is blue, that the sun goes round the earth. They were cruel to me, but could I question their cruelty? In my childish mind, it was wholly justified.

'But this is to digress.

'The prospects before the girls were fair – more than fair, they were radiant. But first must come the long shrouded cycles, the seasons of seclusion, before my uncle's dreams could be realized. Nothing must interfere with his plan, and he kept the girls carefully screened from the world. But for all that, I am afraid these fair ones were not quite ... innocent.'

'Aunt Vlad!' Jeli's eyes widened.

Her aunt laughed. 'No, Jeli, I speak not of that tender little curtain of which Mistress Quick, no doubt, has adjured you to be so careful. What is innocence? Is not true innocence a disposition of the soul? Is that not why – the true reason why – nothing in nature can be more fair than a girl in the glory of unfeigned virtue?'

'But Aunt Vlad, you wouldn't suggest...' Even after several moon-lives with her aunt, Jeli felt a lingering respect for tradition.

'My dear, what *you* have learnt to call virtue was lost to me soon enough after I left my uncle's house! I was cast upon my own resources, and had to make my own way in the world.' Aunt Vlada leaned back, lighting a stick of Jarvel. 'But I speak here, I say, of a different innocence. It is an innocence no man can violate, yet one which may melt imperceptibly as snow. It is warmed away from within. No effort to retain it is even made, for none know of its passing until it is gone. But I'm sure you know all this, my dear. Know it in your heart, if not in your head.' Aunt Vlada leaned forward, smoothing Jeli's curls. 'Such pretty ringlets. Do you know, Marly's were just like yours?'

Jeli only looked wonderingly at her aunt. But now her aunt, drawing back deeply on the Jarvel-weed, entered upon her story in earnest. Soon the deep rich voice and deep rich smoke had lulled Jeli into a dreamy fascination.

'My uncle lived in a big house on a lake, across the river from Agondon. Yes, it was possible to be "across the river from Agondon" then – this was before the New Town was built.'

Jeli tried to conceive of such a time, and failed.

'Did I tell you about the walks we would take by the lake? With Nurse, these would be stiff, formal affairs, except when the old woman would doze under a willow, leaving my cousins to tease and torment me. Sometimes they would chase me and make me hide. Their particular delight was to chase me so far that when at last it seemed safe to come out of hiding, I would realize I was lost. Of course, they would not tell Nurse where I was, only say I'd run off, they did not know where. How angry she would be! Other games were designed to make me dirty – for of course, Nurse hated dirt with a passion like that of the Ur-God himself, when he discovered that the Vaga-god had gone and created the earth. Once, I recall, the girls threw me into the reeds by the bank. My white shift was all wet and muddy! Oh, how Nurse punished me that day!

'But things were better when Pell came to stay.'

'Pell?'

'Oh, not the young man you know by that name *now*, of course! I refer to his – why, to his great-uncle.'

'Sir Pellion?'

'Hardly Pellion! His older brother – Pelleas.'

'Pelleas?' By now, Jeli was quite confused, but in the comforting dreamy state, she accepted her confusion. Idly she stroked poor Ring's ears. He had ceased his pacings now and was sitting on the sofa. Perhaps the warmth of the fire, hoped Jeli, perhaps even the softness of her lap, might help him feel just a little less miserable.

'Dear Cousin Pell!' Aunt Vlada was saying. 'For a time, he was much favoured by my Uncle Onty, who hoped, indeed, that Pell – his sister's son – might replace the heir he had lost. He trusted Pell and loved him. How I loved him, too! When Pell came, Uncle Onty let him take us out alone. Nurse grumbled, but she grumbled to herself. What freedom to leave her behind! Then how we gambolled! How we danced! Or rather, Uly and Marly did. Of course I was more reserved, but Cousin Pell would make sure I was not left out of the games. For a fond season, I even believed my cousins might come to love me. With our hat-bands loosened, our hands swinging, we played away the warm Theron-days.

'One day stands out. Nurse had never allowed us on the lake, though a row-boat had been moored – it seemed for ever – to a little jetty on the far side of the house. There was talk among the servants that the lake was dangerous, for long ago, when even Nurse was young, a footman had drowned when he tried to swim across. Powerful currents in the centre drew him down. But when we told Pell he only laughed, and rowed us out on to the still waters. How the breezes played through Marly's golden curls! Idly she twined them round her fingers, smiling. Even Uly was amiable, and sang an old ballad in a voice of charming sweetness. How happy we were! For long afterwards I would think of that afternoon as the happiest of my life.'

'It was only once, Aunt Vlad?'

'My dear?'

'Only once you rowed on the lake?'

'Oh yes. Never again.'

'Aunt, but why?'

'Ah, my dear, as we approached the centre, Pell's look grew stern. "Look!" he called, silencing Uly. "Can you see the eddy?" He pointed. Uly's brow furrowed; Marly gave off twining her hair. We all looked, and there in the very centre of the lake – otherwise so still – we saw a mysterious dark swirl. I cried out. It was a vortex, ready to draw us down, and yet for a wild moment – so entrancing was this eddy – I almost longed to vanish into its depths!

'Just in time, Pell heaved us out of range. We were frightened, shaken. But as he rowed us solemnly back to shore, he instructed us to reflect on what we had seen. Like giddy fools, we had allowed ourselves to be taken close to the eddy, disbelieving all we had been told. Then – at this I was abashed – had not something in us yearned for the eddy?

'That night I lay awake for many hours, thinking on the strange day we had passed. First, I imagined again the idyll Pell had shown us, the soft butter-yellow dazzle of the sun, the fragrant flowers of the retreating shore, the cool waters with their lilies and reeds and droning gossamer insects. Again I heard Uly's sweet song, lilting in time to the rhythm of the boat. Then I would stare, again and again, into the dark rushing chasm of the eddy; then at last I would tear my eyes away, and think on the lesson Pell had taught us. It was a lesson I did not quite understand, yet I knew it was profound.

'Later I would think of Cousin Pell as the greatest teacher I was ever to know.'

Troubled, Jeli tried to imagine the eddy. Then she tried to imagine the lesson.

'But Uly and Marly? What did they think?'

'Why, they were angry. That night they told Nurse what Pell had done. The next morning, she told their father. Uncle Onty burst into his Ur-God anger. To think, that his daughters – his dear, blessed daughters – had come so close to death itself! Pell was dismissed from the house at once, suffered never to come within its doors again.

'Poor Pell! To think, I dreamed that one day I should marry him. Of

230

course, it was only the fondest fantasy. He was drowned some moonlives later, on a walking-tour of the Deliverance with an old college-friend. His brother, Sir Pellion, quite lacks his wisdom. I am afraid *he* has never much liked me, believing me the harlot some said I became after I left my Uncle Onty's house.'

'Poor Pell! Poor, poor Pell!'

The story was over for that day, and Jeli was sobbing. Her aunt reached forward, ready to embrace her; but it was then, just as an ashy cylinder fell from Aunt Vlada's Jarvel-weed, that there came a strange rapping at the dormer window. Jeli started; then her face overspread with surprise and delight, for outside the window, pecking at the glass as if eager for entrance, was a rainbow-feathered Wenaya dove.

Swiftly Aunt Vlada opened the casement. At this, Jeli was certain, the bird would fly away; instead, it hopped happily forward, perching on Aunt Vlada's proffered wrist.

'Why, Aunt, he's tame!'

'Tame?' Her aunt laughed. 'But my dear, don't you know him?'

'Aunt Vlad?'

'It's Rheen, my dear! Can't you see it's Rheen?'

And the bird, as if in cheerful agreement, gave a pealing cry of *Ul-ul-ul-ul-ul!*

Chapter 30

JUMBLE'S JAUNTS AND JOLLITIES

'Pell?'

Now the young men are in Lord Empster's library. Experimentally Jem smokes a Jarvel-roll. Always Pell carries with him a little silver case, concealed in a pocket of his gaudy waistcoat. A secret catch makes the box spring open. *Zing!* Jem finds the action delightful. On one side, wrapped in white leaves, are sticks of tobarillo; on the other, the darker, more potent Jarvel. Smoking, says Pell, is a prime attribute of a gentleman – and must he not teach Jem a gentleman's pleasures?

Jem draws back deeply, restraining his cough. This is something he feels he must accomplish. There has been enough shame today. Jeers accompanied the two young gentlemen as they cleared a path back to Pell's carriage. *I thought I'd find you here*, Pell muttered wryly. *You see now, I trust, that Sir Bartel Silverby was the merest romancer?* At first Jem was bitter and taciturn; now he would say more, but it proves difficult.

'Pell?' he tries again.

His friend has not replied. Feet up on a little round table, Pell lolls in a deep chintz chair, chortling over a folio of sporting prints. His own roll has burnt far down; teetering over the Tiralos carpet is a long ashy cylinder. It is almost evening and the saffron servants have lit the lamps, drawn the curtains. Leather and mahogany exude a rich glow, a hint of goldenness concealed deep in darkness.

This Jarvel-weed is potent. Jem feels the room beginning to spin. He shuts his eyes, opens them again; the gold in the darkness leaps out like flame. Pell giggles and holds out his book. *Look.* Goodman Jumble going over a stile! The wily fox, in the bottom of the picture, slips away through a thicket of gorse.

Jem giggles, too. His fat friend looks just like Goodman Jumble.

But beneath Jem's mirth is a rumbling unease. He rubs his eyes. What has happened to him? He thought of Agondon as the place where his life would at last take focus, form. Moonlives have passed since a ragged boy stumbled up the steps outside this house. In his braided jacket, his tight silken breeches, the boy is Nova Empster now, Lord Empster's young ward. He has gained much; but what has he lost?

Jem, went the beguiling, *you're here with me now*. Safe, safe. But something is wrong. At night, as he lies between his slithery sheets, Jem feels a longing for the quest before him, the quest his guardian would seem to deny him. Fervently he clutches the secret burden he has carried for so long, rasping at his skin. Only a dull stone, dug from the mud . . . But Jem has seen it when it flames out, filling the world with its dark purple power!

One night, stirring from a troubled dream, Jem had thought his guardian was hovering over him, his hand reaching for the bag that held the crystal. But when Jem started awake, his guardian was gone.

Who is Lord Empster? Who is he, really?

A spasm shudders through Jem. Then a stab of fear. Somewhere, somehow, has there been a mistake? *I have come to the wrong house. Somewhere, the real Empster awaits me urgently. But here they hold me, a prisoner, tethered by silken cords, but a prisoner all the same.*

It is only an illusion of the Jarvel, of course, but for a wild moment Jem is sure it is true. What does Lord Empster really know of the quest? He has said nothing, nothing! What have they been, these words curling into Jem's ears, but a long smoky trail of sweet beguilings? Blank-eyed, untrembling, Jem had surrendered to the saffron servants. Luxuriating, he had descended into the steaming, scalding bath.

Since then? The candelabra in the corridors, the golden glass on the landings, the marble and mahogany and the wild garden and Pell, with his own beguiling, *Come, Nova! My tailor has sent you another suit*, or *Nova, shall we take another Jarvel-roll?* They have been out riding and have skated on the river that has frozen hard with the Koros-chill. Round and round they have driven in Pell's smart carriage, Pell doffing his hat to the ladies, shouting his *hulloos!* to the other young fops. Side by side on Canonday they have stood in the Great Temple, Pell booming out the Songs of Prevailing with a lustiness Jem has never quite managed. Yes, they have done much, and there is much to do. The Ollon Pleasure Gardens! The Wrax Opera!

It is all a trap, it has to be. But each evening when Pell drives away, Jem looks miserably after him, down the long vista of Davalon Street. His friend is a foolish, vain fop, who says *Redjacket traitor* and really means it, but each time he goes, Jem longs for him to return.

'Pell,' Jem struggles to say now, 'what do you know about Lord Empster?'

'I say, Nova, that's a dashed funny question.'

And Jem can almost hear the laughter on the air.

Now it is later and Jem can hear bells, tolling from the temples over the Riel.

Bong, bong.

He looks up. Pell is sleeping in the chintz chair; *Jumble's Jaunts and Jollities* has fallen to the floor.

Bong, bong.

Jem goes to a window. Quickly, fearing he is about to be sick, he pushes his way through the velvet curtains, turning the handle of the long Wrax-casement.

He steps on to the balcony. The air is so cold! He looks up at the sky – a Hornlight moon.

Jem looks away. Didn't he hear – somewhere, but where? – that you shouldn't look up into the face of the Hornlight? Now why should that be? Jem doesn't know. He counts the tolling of the midnight bells.

Five. Six. Seven. Eight.

A deep and terrible oppression is upon him. He thinks of the scene at the Erdon Tree. He thinks of Captain Porlo. He thinks of the boy who looked like Rajal and the ship's figurehead that looked like Cata.

The bells strike nine, ten, eleven, and Jem fears he has slipped into a shadow-world, where nothing real will ever happen again.

Oh, he feels sick! His stomach churns. He leans over the balcony, but the expected, relieving tide does not come. Blearily he looks down at the world below. Snow has fallen since the time of curfew, and Davalon Street is chalky white.

The clock strikes twelve, thirteen, fourteen.

Had he not been hanging so far over the balcony, Jem might never have seen the figure below, slipping silently, carefully along the wall.

A figure in a cape and a wide-brimmed hat . . .

Now why should Lord Empster venture out – alone, with no carriage, on so cold a night! – so long after the passing of the curfew?

Jem's brow furrows.

The clock strikes fifteen.

For a moment he thinks he shall follow his guardian, slipping after him through the darkened streets. Then – but this, perhaps, is some Jarvel-illusion – Jem hears a song, drifting on the air, lingering in the wake of the echoing bells. He strains to hear and it seems to him that this is a song he has heard before, long, long ago, he does not know where.

How does it go?

> *Everything is lemon and nothing is lime,*
> *But even the truth shall be revealed in time:*
> *Then we shall drink from the mocking-tree gourds,*
> *And sup with the King and Queen of—*

What can it mean?

Suddenly Jem's face is pale as the snow. He doubles over. Long strings of vomit swing from his lips.

Chapter 31

LIZARD-MAN

'Marked cards!'

The young lieutenant started up from the table, almost overturning it. A mug of ale sloshed across the green baize. There were jeers, whistles, slow handclaps as the befuddled fellow twisted himself this way and that, tugging unsuccessfully at the hilt of his sword. The chap who had prompted his fury, a down-at-heel dandy, stared at him blearily for a moment across the baize, then jerked suddenly to his own feet, seizing his accuser's throat.

'Boys, boys!' came a placatory wail, cawing through the noxious air. Its source was an ugly old man in a long quilted smoking-jacket. Between his lizard-lips burnt a fat Jarvel-roll; rings of gold and silver circled every finger of the claw-like hands that quickly swept away the impugned set of cards.

'Now settle down, boys, really! Marked cards at Chokey's? I never heard the like!'

The old man wore no wig and his bare head was a mottled, hairless dome; the face below was a mask of crumpled parchment. With the faintest blow either of the young men might have struck him aside, but like a charm his slithery voice at once soothed their passions.

They slumped down, abashed.

The old man flashed a brown grin and snapped his fingers, calling to a servant for 'Ale! Ale for all!' as a round of applause filled the crowded room.

This was the scene that greeted Jem late one evening in the last moonlife of the year. It was Canonday, and it had been a long one, all of it spent in the company of Pell. After Morning Canonical, exchanging the pious garb of the faith for their best dandy-clothes, the friends had paid polite calls on several young ladies of Pell's acquaintance before spending the afternoon at the Ollon Pavilion, where they ate chops, drank punch and ale, played at quoits, shot clay-ducks and swaggered, rather less politely than before, in front of other young ladies, let off the leash for the afternoon by lazy, liberal Duennas.

As darkness fell, they drove back up to town, stopping at Lund Street while Master Quisto opened specially, though it was Canonday, to give Pell another fitting for his Festival suit; then Professor Mercol, Pell's old tutor, treated them to a glass of Tiralos in his cosy college-rooms before accompanying them to a reception at Lady Cham-Charing's, where the vixen-in-Varl-sauce was a little underdone. After more chops and ale at the Pig and Garter, the friends had looked in on the Volleys, just in time to see Miss Tilsy Fash, the Zaxon Nightingale, perform her celebrated rendition of *The King's Old Jester*.

A stirring performance; perhaps that was why, as they made their way back to Pell's 'Lasher', Jem's friend was moved to say, 'I'm not ready for bed yet, are you, Nova? How about Chokey's?'

'Chokey's?'

They proceeded on foot, winding between the imposing mansions that jammed and jostled in the heart of the Old Town. Curfew was long past, and only quality-folk still braved the streets.

Chokey's, Pell explained, was a club of sorts, frequented by the finest young men of Agondon. Jem pictured a temple-like portico, a massive flight of steps, perhaps vast doors encrusted with jewels and ancient symbols.

His face fell a little as Pell veered instead into a dark backstreet, where a single lamp burned over a low, narrow doorway. Could this be the place? Pell tapped out a sharp tattoo and a tiny panel in the door slid back. There were cold appraising eyes, then a grudging grunt. The door opened and they were ushered inside.

'Chokey's,' murmured Pell, 'is a vital part of the education of a young gentleman. But it might be an idea, Nova, if you didn't mention this to Empy. Promise?'

Jem promised.

❋ ❋

'Master Pelligrew!' came Chokey's wailing voice as the two friends descended the steep steps into the cellars.

Eagerly the old lizard seized Pell's hands, calling for a servant to take their coats, their gloves. Quite as drunk as the young men at the tables, a footman in shabby livery reeled forward.

The braid on his jacket was unravelling like rope.

'And who is your young friend?' Chokey said caressingly, swooping towards Jem. 'Master Empster? I never knew old Empy to have a relative in the world. From Chayn? Ah, that explains it. My late wife used to say that provincial life was tantamount – she used words like that – *tantamount* to a living death, and do you know, I'm quite sure she was right? In that, at least. Welcome, young sir, to *life!*'

And the lizard-man gestured proudly at his domain.

Looking round uncertainly, for a moment Jem was prey to a curious illusion. The lighting was dim and the thick smoke churned about on the air like fog, obscuring any clear view of the further reaches of Chokey's establishment. But to Jem, the cellars seemed strangely endless; again and again, repeated to infinity, he saw these gaming-tables, these young officers, these courtiers, even the occasional man of the cloth, poised broodingly or leaning back, laughing, with their Jarvel-rolls, their mugs of ale, their hands of cards.

For a disturbing moment the thought came to Jem that this place really did go on for ever, under the ground. Only later, looking though a lattice of clearing smoke, did he see the sudden startling image of himself, growing shabby in his fine clothes, and see that looking-glasses lined Chokey's walls.

Much of what followed passed as in a dream, the sort of restless, dispiriting dream from which one wakes, time after time, only to sink again unwillingly into its embrace.

So at least it seemed to Jem; Pell, by contrast, was in his element.

The friends found themselves sitting with the two young men who had been causing the disturbance a little earlier. Jarvel, and an ever-replenishing tankard, had soothed the lieutenant; his companion, for his part, remained morose, hunched sullenly over the table since Chokey had confiscated his original set of cards. On the baize before him glinted a pile of coins; from time to time he would cup his hands about it possessively and scowl.

A golden cravat burgeoned at this moody fellow's throat.

'Be kind to Master Burgrove,' Chokey hissed. 'He's been in a bit of a scrape. Didn't really enjoy himself in Varby this year.'

'Oh?'

No details were to follow, but 'Jac' Burgrove stirred himself at least to say, 'Dreadful about your little sis, Pelligrew. Of course, I'd left by then.'

Pell – he was tired of sympathy – only gulped his ale.

'Come, Jac. Deal. Jac's been up to no good again,' he murmured to Jem. 'A lady, I'll warrant you! Chokey's always bailing out his boys,' he added. 'Do you know, they say he has the ear of the First Minister himself?'

Wonderingly Jem gazed after their host. For one whose mission was to entertain the fashionable, Chokey's neglect of his own appearance was absolute. The smoking-jacket he wore would once have been magnificent, an ornate dazzle of gold thread and pearls, but now it was filthy with sweat and slops and Jarvel-burns. The pyjamas he wore beneath seemed equally squalid, stiff with sweat and dribbled piss. As the old man shuffled eagerly back to the door, welcoming new guests, Jem saw the ankles above the flapping slippers. They were swollen horribly, ringed with festering sores.

Revolted, he looked away. 'Why is he called Chokey?'

'You'd have to ask the girls.'

'Girls?'

Pell said no more. 'Come, play. Remember the rules, Nova?'

Cards flicked, face-down, across the green baize, but try as Jem might, he could understand little. He picked up his hand. A Five of Quills, a Four of Swords, an Eight of Rings . . . what did they mean?

They were playing a game called Orokon Destiny. Pell had explained the rules before, but Jem was poor at games like this, and seemed unlikely ever to master the complex system of bluffs and trade-offs by which a player sought to build up a full set of 'God-cards'. Something about the pictures on his cards disturbed him. One of them even showed a harlequin.

Experimentally, Jem laid the card face-up.

'Vaga-scum,' Jac Burgrove murmured – why, Jem did not know.

'Nova, no!' laughed Pell, leaning over to inspect his ignorant friend's hand. 'You don't just throw out Wild Cards any old how!'

'Wild Cards?'

'Give me a light, someone,' slurred the lieutenant. A lanky, beanpole sort of fellow, he had in his manner a certain nervousness, for all that it was overlaid with drink and drugs.

His eyes were sad.

'Vaga-scum,' Jac Burgrove repeated, gazing on the particoloured figure of the harlequin. He took a long swig from his tankard. Ale slopped over his cravat, and he cursed, 'When are they all going to be wiped out, that's what I want to know!'

'When we've wiped out the Zenzans,' the lieutenant said wearily, as if this were a question he had answered often before. 'Priorities are priorities. Jac, give me a light, will you?'

Jac Burgrove ignored him. 'If I had my way,' he thundered suddenly, 'every last piece of Vaga-filth in this empire would be rooted out and hacked to bits like a noxious weed!'

'Fine fighting talk,' said the lieutenant, waving to a servant for a tinder-stick. 'Jac had a commission once – in the Blue Ejards, too! Bought his way out, would you believe? Yes, fine talk, talk, talk.' He laughed mirthlessly and leaned back, puffing at his fresh roll. 'Your play, Jac.'

'I tell you—' Master Burgrove turned suddenly to Pell '—it was Vaga-scum who did for your little sis, you know!'

'That's not true!' Jem burst out. He stood, flushed and trembling. For long moments he had lingered on the cusp of a realization.

Jac.

Jem had known there was something familiar about the fellow.

'Boys, boys!' came Chokey, eager to put out another little brushfire. 'Come now, young Empster, don't go upsetting yourself. Master Burgrove's a little sour these days, that's all. Seems they gave him rather a nasty time before he could get word to me. You'd think he'd show a bit of common gratitude, wouldn't you? But I expect no virtue of my young men – only vice!'

With that, Chokey erupted into a wheezing laugh, and Jem felt obliged to laugh, too.

Pell was shaken. He had tried to steel himself, but sometimes he would still be overcome by the thought of poor Pelli. If only he'd been there, been there in Varby!

He shook himself, squeezing back tears.

'I say,' drawled the lieutenant – his urbanity began to look ever more false – 'your pal's not a Vaga-lover, I hope? I leave that to the chaps in the ranks, and the ugly ones at that.'

'Come,' Chokey was saying, 'the evening is but beginning. Won't you sing for us, Master Pelligrew? Get us in the mood. You know we all like to hear you sing.'

The card-game broke up as Pell, giving way to this solicitation, moved to a battered harpsichord in the corner. From somewhere, beneath the laughter and oaths, the fidgety scrapings of a consort of viols had accompanied all the proceedings of the evening; now Pell joined them with his own more vigorous entertainment. Among his gifts was a stentorian baritone; at Temple that morning it had boomed impressively, investing the Songs of Prevailing with a martial certitude that was, perhaps, appropriate. Applying itself to more sentimental fare, somehow it made even the moving ballad they had heard at the Volleys – it had brought tears to Jem's eyes – into something resembling a soldiers' march. Tankards swung back and forth all over Chokey's at each swaggering chorus of

> *Burble, babble, went the King's jester*
> *In the days of yore!*
> *Now the poor little chap's*
> *Had a mishap*
> *And he'll burble, babble no more!*

Propelled by an unctuous Chokey, Jem now found himself sprawled on a sofa, his head resting on soft cushions. Someone was loosening the laces of his boots; someone put a Jarvel-roll in his hand. Slowly, cautiously, Jem drew back the smoke. The lamps, always dim, had been turned down further and Chokey's now became less a gambling-den than a dark enchanted cave where a hundred young men – drugged, drunken, or both – lolled in languorous abandon.

Then Jem noticed another change, too.

Filing in slowly among the lolling young men was a succession of

239

young women. Where had they come from? Dressed only in flimsy nightgowns, they sashayed forward invitingly. To Jem, they were like visions, wraiths; others, it seemed, had no doubt they were real. There were whistles, whoops, clutchings and clawings.

A sudden, sick fear thudded at Jem's heart.

By now, Pell had ceased to play; there were only the viols again, swooning and moaning, and Jem looked over to see his friend, swung round on the harpsichord-stool, abandoning himself to a wraith's embrace. All over the dim cellars the scene was repeated, multiplied with murky endlessness in the mirrors. Again, again, the white-garbed forms descended like spectres on the figures lolling in armchairs, sprawled across sofas, slumped almost insensibly over green baize, slopped ale, scattered cards.

But if these were spectres, they swiftly became flesh. Human swooning, human moaning mingled on the air with the sighing of the viols; white gowns slithered up smooth thighs; there were gasps, tuggings, tearings, and somewhere in all this, looming first here, then there, licking his lizard-lips eagerly, was Chokey. The ruined face loomed over Jem; old hands fondled, caressed. Jem started, confused. He would have struggled up from the sofa, but Jarvel had taken all power from his limbs.

'Master Empster, you are, perhaps, a stranger to pleasure? Fear not. What is Chokey's, if not an academy for youth?'

The whisper was kind; now the old man reached behind him and produced, as if by magic, a very young, slender girl. Blonde hair hung about her face like a curtain.

'My newest. The fresh, for the fresh. Chin up, Jilda, let the gentleman see. Pretty little thing, isn't she? I had long admired her – a pert little piece, don't be fooled by her airs – and told her that if ever she might happen to misplace her virgin-purity, she was assured of a career at Chokey's. Ah, how I bless the young Bluejacket who broke her in! See that quality, Master Empster? Yes, there's none of your common tarts at Chokey's. Quality for quality, that's my motto . . .'

There might have been more, but already the old man was fading into the background; already the girl, with an experienced air, was unfastening the buttons of Jem's fashionable breeches. *That's right, that's right,* came Chokey's whisper, ethereal now.

The girl loomed forward, kissing Jem on the lips. Her long hair brushed his face, his neck.

A tide of lust crashed inside him. How long had it been since his wild days with Cata? He had vowed always to keep himself for her, but what use was that? Would he ever see her again? She, in any case, had not kept herself for him!

For a moment the vision of Cata hovered before him, her face and the sweet remembered contours of her body; then the tide crashed again, washing the vision away.

This, happening now, was too much, too real.

Now the girl, with all the arts Chokey had shown her, was rousing his lust to newer, more desperate heights. *That's right, that's right.* In moments, Jem knew, he would push the girl beneath him, pinning her down as he took his pleasure, riding high on wave after crashing wave.

Wildly Jem's gaze zigzagged through the darkness. The last thing he saw, before he abandoned himself wholly, was the plump form of his foppish friend, humped over the harpsichord, thrusting ardently, urgently between the thighs of his partner.

Crazed discords sounded on the air.

Later, Jem would regret what he did that night; he would think of it and feel a terrible ache of loss.

But only sometimes, and not for long.

He would go back to Chokey's again.

Chapter 32

ICE QUEEN

'Such grace!'

'Such precision!'

'How smoothly they glide!'

'Even Freddie has a certain elegance, does he not?'

'Freddie is always elegant. It is his principal task in life.'

'I always knew he was shallow.'

The speakers were Lady Cham-Charing, Lady Margrave, Lord Empster and Tishy. Sir Pellion sat with them too, but had nothing to say. It was the day of Lady Cham-Charing's Festival Levee. From the celebrated Glass Terrace of Cham-Charing House, the party was able to look down over the Riel, where certain of the younger guests were skating on the ice.

'I worry about Freddie,' said Lady Margrave. 'Should he be seen so much with that girl?'

'I don't know why Mama asks her. She's nobody at all, really, is she?'

'That's not quite true, my dear. But it's not the girl I worry about. Did you have to invite "Aunt Vlada", Constansia?'

'One can hardly have one without the other. And one does so want to keep Freddie happy.'

'I thought you wanted to keep him miserable.'

'Mathanias, that was uncalled for. If I appear to have forced certain attentions upon Freddie, I'm sorry.'

Poor Tishy cast down her eyes.

'But the Prince of Chayn is an ornament to any gathering.'

'A trophy you must keep?'

'I can hide nothing from you, Mathanias. How glad I am to be no longer young! Society is not what it was.'

And Lady Cham-Charing, not for the first time, glanced back into the drawing-room behind them. In a corner by the fire, The Remarkable Vlada Flay was deep in conversation with the Archmaximate.

The great man's eyes twinkled. Replete after his Festival-dinner, he had crossed his hands over his roly-poly stomach and every so often it would shake appreciatively, wobbling like a jelly in time to some hearty chortle. To think, thought Lady Cham-Charing, I have lived to see this! Still, there were all manner of riff-raff in society these days. What could one expect, when even quality-folk – the true quality – behaved with such an alarming absence of standards?

Lady Margrave ventured, 'Your young ward has become quite the gentleman, Lord Empster.'

'Hasn't he?' offered Lady Cham-Charing, glad of the fresh subject. 'One hardly recognizes him as the lad from the ball. Why, he seems to be shorter, fatter, and altogether redder in the face.'

'That's Pellam Pelligrew, Mama. I think you need your spectacles?'

'Tishy, you know full well that my spectacles are merely decorative.' But the lady brought them to her eyes nonetheless; they gave her an unexpected resemblance to her daughter. Since First Moonlife, Tishy had affected a pair of horn-rims and wore her hair tied back severely.

'Ah yes,' her Mama went on. 'Those boys have become inseparable, haven't they? I always find it pleasant to see young people of good moral character enjoying themselves, don't you, Sir Pellion? The young, the insensible young, are the fortunate ones.'

Sir Pellion looked up, dazed. All afternoon, attempts to draw the old gentleman out of himself had failed. Really, he was not in the Festival spirit! The five days to come were the Meditations, or 'God-days', when the pious devoted themselves to fasting and prayer. Should not one attempt a little good cheer while it was possible? From Tishy, it was true, one could expect little. One's guests, thought Lady Cham-Charing, were a different matter. To accept an invitation that – so she told herself – half Agondon would kill for, only to sit about morosely all day, was tedious in the extreme. How many times, how many times had one made the effort of sympathy? It was becoming harder. One thought of little Pellicent, but all one could think of was an oily nose. Still, it had been a shapely nose in its way, and might in time have responded to powder. The girl's death was tragic, of course it was. But must it be lamented until the end of the world?

'Alas, I know of *one* who will never enjoy herself again,' sighed Sir Pellion, and wrung his dripping tear-cloth in his hands.

'I know of *one* who has never enjoyed herself at all,' murmured Lady Cham-Charing, with a glance at her daughter.

Tishy's face flushed and she returned her attention to the heavy book that lay open on her knees.

Noisily, she turned a page.

'Such precision!'

'Such grace!'

'I'll say! Ripping girl, what?'

'I saw her first!'

Pell laughed, 'Have her, Nova, if you can! Chokey's ladies will do me, until the time comes for a son and heir. But I think perhaps Miss Vance is destined for Freddie Chayn?'

'That fat fop! What can she see in him?'

'He *is* a Prince. Besides, fat fops may be not without charm, Nova.'

Jem flushed, 'Of course. But!'

'But!' Pell laughed again and recited:

> *Woman cannot know the mind of a Man;*
> *Man, for his part, can no more Woman scan:*
> *Strange as the stars and as certain to vex,*
> *Such are the ways of the contrary sex.*

'Pell, I'm impressed!'

'Coppergate, actually. But you'd know that, Nova, if you'd been studying.'

'But!'

Now they both laughed. The two friends were resting, sitting side by side on Lady Cham-Charing's wharf. Above them, a zigzagging flight of steps led down steeply from Cham-Charing House. Before them, whizzing and arcing on the ice, were the cream of Young Ejland: here, the Duchess of Vantage and the Marquis of Heva-Harion; there, Lord Xorgos, heir to the Earl of Cascos; here, the Princess of Down Lexion, the Duchess of Fargold, young Erina Aldermyle; there, the Brothers Venturon and the Sisters Flonce, Miss Huskia Bichley, Lady Berthen Beechwood-Bounce.

Yes, the cream of Young Ejland, but wheeling through them all, dazzling like a comet in furs the colour of frost, was Miss Jelica Vance. She might have been a Queen, Queen of them all, and Freddie Chayn, pursuing her, her merest consort.

Jem gazed after her, fascinated and enthralled. What was it about his cousin? Was she the prettiest girl of her year? Not at all. The most personable? She was not. To look at her closely, to look levelly, was to see something insipid in her fair features. By now, many another Entered girl had given 'Nova Empster' an encouraging smile. Miss Alfredina Flonce blushed and simpered whenever 'Nova' walked into the room, and Miss Alfredina, Pell agreed, was the equal of Miss Vance – at least.

Sometimes Jem had thought Jeli had a secret power. Last Canonday in the Great Temple he had known for certain. With Pell, he had arrived late. Respectfully, with copious apologies, the young men took their place in the row behind her. Their hearts pounded. They were exhausted; they had come directly from Chokey's, where all night the finest harlots had taken them repeatedly to the heights of pleasure. Then, in the tinted light of the Temple-windows, Jeli turned her blonde head just a little, catching Jem's eye. That was all; it was a look which could have meant anything, or nothing. She turned away at once, but for Jem, it was enough. All through the service, he thudded with desire.

With the memory, desire came again.

'Not one of Chokey's.'

'What's that, Pell?'

'You do know, Nova—' Pell dropped his voice '—that the quality-lady is a wholly different prospect from the girls at Chokey's? Chokey does us a great service, bless him, but his ways are no guide for gentlemen in society. Just thought I ought to mention it, Nova. In case you get mixed up.'

Sudden anger overcame Jem. 'Pell! Do you think I'm stupid?'

'I think you've got a cock-stand.' Pell laughed and slapped Jem's thigh.

Jem laughed too.

'And in this cold, that says something.' With the surprising grace he always displayed, Pell launched himself on the ice again. 'One more turn,' he called back. 'Then it should be time for the Vaga-show.'

'Vaga-show?'

'Didn't I say? Old custom at Ma Cham's. Always has the Silver Masks, specially for us.'

Then Pell was off, swinging far out into the middle of the ice. Jem floundered after him. Newer to this art, it took him a moment to find his stride, but he was a good skater once he got started. How he loved the gathering speed, the smooth scything motion of the blades beneath his feet! When he thought back to his old life, his life as a cripple, Jem could laugh out loud. Joyously he took his place in the great ice-dance, a dance more elegant, he suspected, than any to be found in the stuffy ballroom of the Koros-Palace.

Round and round swept the frozen world: Cham-Charing House and its fine neighbours, massive and rambling at the bottom of The Island; Agondon New Town, rising elegantly over the Riel Embankment; the bridges – old Agondon Bridge to the north, heaped high with teetering houses; to the south, the spare arc of Regent's Bridge, marking a boundary between the fashionable city and the sinister labyrinth of the docklands beyond.

Whirling, Jem saw it all, clear as an etching in the brittle cold, but more than this, he saw his pretty cousin, circling in an orbit always beyond his reach.

Oh Jeli, Jeli!

Could she really be in love with Freddie Chayn?

Now the Prince has caught her arm and they almost slip, laughing; now she is breaking from him, whizzing ahead, a silver comet, fast as fast can be. The Prince might have pursued her, but now bold Miss Bichley comes forward, replacing Jeli in his crooked elbow; now, on the Glass Terrace above, the bell is tolling.

Children, it says, *time to come inside!*

On and on sweeps the silver comet; on and on gazes Jem, marvelling. *Oh, Jeli.*

'Time, Nova!' Pell comes circling round him.

'She's gone!'

'Hm?'

But in the next moment Pell is pushed aside, thudding heavily on the ice as Jem careers away from him, swooping over the scored surface towards the arc of Regent's Bridge.

'She's gone too far!' he shouts back. 'She's in danger!'

Pell only sighs, rubbing his rump as one of the Brothers Venturon helps him back to his feet.

'I don't think Miss Vance is in any danger, do you, Ulgar?'

'I'm Ruddy.'

'What?'

'The other one.'

'Sorry. Never could tell you chaps apart. What it must be, hm, to have a sibling so very . . . similar.'

Pell swings round. Already the sun is setting. He shields his eyes against the glare. Soon the silver river will be gold, burning gold. His blades at angles, he stands still, gazing down towards Regent's Bridge. His glance flickers to the Embankment: its traffic, its streetlamps, its leafless trees. On the Island side, the others are clambering dutifully up the zigzag steps, silver blades jangling from mittened hands.

'Come on, Pell!' someone calls, but Pell does not move.

Silence envelops him, a sudden aloneness. A chill wind gusts up from the Gulf; whistling beneath the bridge, it seems to bear with it a foreboding. *I am not what I seem*, Pell thinks, and the thought startles him. What can it mean? Since his sister's death, he knows, he has been only going through the motions of life. But hasn't it been longer? When did it start?

But of course, it began when he found his master. *Empy*, Pell will call the noble lord, and joke about him, laugh about him; but from the first, his employer has filled him with alarm.

This is how it began. With wavering vision Pell looked, deeply, deeply, into the smoky eyes. Slowly Empy – Empster – drew back on the ivory pipe; slowly he exhaled. *I know you, Pellam Pelligrew. Come to me, and your shyness shall melt away like snow. Come to me, and your graceless form shall*

246

acquire a new grace. Come to me, and you shall know the love of women. All you must do is serve me, Pelligrew, all you must do is serve me.

But had he become a servant of good, or evil? To most, Empster was a loyal courtier, a reliable fixture on the social round. But to those who could see it, he was something else. Something more. Nova saw it too, Pell knew that much. But the one time Nova had tried to talk about it, Pell could not. It was as if something prevented him, as if a veil descended.

Besides, who was Nova?

My young ward is coming, Pelligrew. You shall take care of him. See yourself, if you will, as a sort of male Duenna. (Empy laughed at this.) *But mark you, my ward shall never think of you as such. You are his friend, Pelligrew, his loyal friend.*

His loyal friend ... But it was true! And all at once Pell shuddered in the cold and gazed more ardently into the gathering haze.

'Nova!' he cried, and was about to take off, careering after him.

But there was no need. Emerging through the haze as through a parting curtain, all at once two figures came forward, hand in hand, shushing smoothly beneath the arc of the bridge. The setting sun tinged them with gold; they might have been gods. Absurdly Pell was startled, so startled that he fell down on the ice again.

'One more time and it'll crack, Pell,' laughed Jem, sweeping past. Oh, there was triumph in his eyes! The Vance girl laughed too, a girlish giggle.

Resentment surged through Pell.

'And may I call on you?' he heard his friend say, in tones of utmost gallantry, as he assisted the young lady back up on to the wharf.

Pell was left behind, slumped on the ice. The sky took a little lurch closer to dusk. Traffic clip-clopped and jingled on the Embankment, and from closer came a sound Pell had not heard, or registered, for many years.

To-whit! To-whoo!

A little bird, a Bob Scarlet, gazed up at him curiously.

'*To-whit to-whoo* yourself,' Pell said sourly.

Chapter 33

GOLD AND GREEN

'Such grace!'

'Such precision!'

'There are none better than the Masks, are there not?'

'None.'

Wrapped warmly in their furs, the party had assembled along three sides of the Great Gallery that hung above the courtyard of Cham-Charing House. On the fourth side, a Vaga-orchestra, the only one of its kind – tabors and herd-horns, gitterns and 'Harions', Pipes of Orandy and Pipes of Koros – unleashed their strange melody.

Below, tapers flamed around the walls, loaded with rare slow-burning weeds that cast up a coarse, potent incense. In the centre of the court-yard, passing over the flagstones with the ease of wraiths, dancers in masks and purple capes slid forward, back, sideways, forward, their arms waving to this side, to that, in perfect formation. Only arduous training could have produced such harmony, yet the troupe contrived to make it all seem effortless, as if they could think as well as move in unison. Their capes billowed behind them, giving the effect of a rippling purple sea.

Then in the next moments the Purple Players had gone, to be replaced by figures in green; but at quite what point the purple ones had vanished, none could say.

Jem was not watching. Pursuing Jeli, he weaved through the tight-packed crowd. 'You haven't answered my question,' he urged.

'Question?'

Jeli did not turn. Suddenly cold, she seemed to regret the familiarities she had permitted him on the ice. On the zigzag steps she had declined his arm; inside the house, she was pulling away at once, eager to return to her eccentric companion.

Could she really have held his hand?

Madly, Jem reached out, seizing her arm. 'I asked if I could call on you.'

Jeli's eyes flamed. 'We're never at home.'

'I know where you live. I'll stand outside and watch.'

'That would make you a remarkably persistent young man. It would also make you a fool.'

This last comment was not Jeli's, but Aunt Vlada's. Flushing, Jem surrendered his cousin's arm. The crowd closed around her and she was gone.

In the courtyard, the capes were now red, now blue, now gold; now the Black Guard, with his long segmented body and huge burning eyes, was lolloping this way, lurching that, in maddened pursuit of the Jumping Jongleur. Monkeys, at their feet, swarmed in and out of geometric patterns, but never did the Jongleur lose a single one of his many-coloured orbs. Gold rained down from the gallery. All through the performance came a cascade of coins, flung by the quality-folk at each impressive turn. By the end, the flagstones would be a glittering sea, flashing in the taper-light.

Lady Cham-Charing flung down a crown.

'How they take one back to one's girlhood!' she sighed.

'You spent your girlhood among Vagas? Why, Constansia, I had not known you were a caravan-child. Did they daub your face with boot-black?'

'Mathanias, that is not what I meant, as well you know. Don't you recall the huge Vaga-fair they used to have every year on Ollon Fields? The Masks were a new troupe then, and smaller, but oh, what a sight they were! Remember when they brought the first lion back from Unang Lia? How frightened we were, until we heard they had drawn its teeth and claws!'

The old woman sighed.

'The Fields are all bricked over now. But ah, how happily we used to set off in our straw bonnets, those warm Theron-days! That was before they built Regent's Bridge, of course. We used to go over on the barge.'

'We?'

'You remember, don't you, Elsan? Why, there was Mazy Tarfoot and Ary Heva-Harion and Dahlia Flonce and – who else, Elsan? What's that? Vlada Flay? Well, indeed.'

Constansia could not restrain a disapproving glance. Across the gallery, The Remarkable towered imperiously between her young charge and the pink-faced Archmaximate. *Remarkable*, indeed! Even her coat, a gaudy amalgam of fox, bear and tiger, was of a flamboyance seldom seen in Cham-Charing House.

'What sort of society is it,' Constansia was moved to ask, 'where a harlot, a Zenzau-blood at that, can push herself into the finest quality-circles, with no more than notoriety to smooth her way?'

'You did invite her, Constansia.'

'Mathanias, one has to keep up one's place.'

Lord Empster only smiled. Poor Constansia! Once she would never have deferred to the world; there had been a time when she reigned over society like an unofficial Queen, her rambling mansion a second, rival palace. In those days, only those of the most exquisite breeding could expect to cross her threshold; her invitations, penned in a girlish hand on little gilt-edged cards, had been prized more than jewels.

Now, the Round was busy as ever; the splendour remained, but there was something hollow, something brittle at its heart. Across the river in Agondon New Town, splendid new dwellings made Cham-Charing House seem shabby, old-fashioned; its hostess, too, had lost her old lustre. Once, her very name had been spoken with hushed awe; had this been replaced now by a hushed contempt? At Lady Venturon's, parties were consecrated to art, music, letters; at Baroness Bolbarr's, all was youth, beauty, love. What had Lady Cham-Charing ever valued, endorsed, but birth and a superficial observance of the proprieties?

> On Lady C——, sir, do not waste your wit,
> For this I know: the shaft will never hit.

So said Coppergate; Contansia had been delighted at the compliment, until she realized it was no compliment at all.

Canon Feval, with a superior smirk, had been fond of quoting those lines. A callow gossip, he had never quite belonged in Cham-Charing House, with its stately traditions, its decent reticence. If Constansia's friends were relieved that he was gone, they knew, too, that the threat he posed was by no means over. Had it been such a good idea to have him sent away? Increasingly, Feval's ladies were coming out against Constansia; increasingly, Constansia's long reign looked as if it might be about to end.

'The Cham tries hard, doesn't she?' murmured a Court fop at the back.

'Does she? The Silver Masks, I ask you! Hasn't simply *everyone* seen them a hundred times?'

But *everyone* had not.

At first, Jem barely attended to the spectacle below. His eyes were only for Jeli, dear Jeli, smiling demurely on the other side of the gallery. The girl was perverse, but could he blame her? Perhaps, Jem thought, she could sense something vile in him. How many times, in Chokey's dim cave, had he closed his eyes, pretending that this or that little minx, moaning beneath him, was Jeli?

Fear and a sudden welling shame filled him.

'There you are, Nova.'

There was, perhaps, a hint of reproach in Pell's manner. Puffing, he squeezed himself into a space beside his friend.

'I see the Vance Affair was short-lived. Or do I misconstrue?'

'What?'

'You dog, Nova! Let me guess – had her under the bridge, eh? Must have been chilly! Still, I dare say parts of her were – hey, steady on, I was only joking!'

Below, tall figures in garb of gold and silver, the Imperials, were striding with twirling sceptres through the ragged, scurrying Beholders; the many human forms made a five-pointed star, and at each point was a leaping-lion, vaulting back and forth through a flaming hoop. A fresh cascade of coins rained down; in the excitement, no one noticed that young Nova Empster had seized his friend by the throat.

'How dare you speak of Miss Vance like that? Have you no respect for a virtuous woman?'

'Virtue!' Pell blanched. 'Nova, hasn't Chokey's taught you anything?'

'You disgust me.'

'What?'

'You think you're so fine, so fashionable. You're nothing but a dirty, pox-ridden whoremonger.'

Shocked, poor Pell did not even think to say that if this were true, then it must also be true of his friend.

He staggered back, gasping, as Jem cast him aside.

Longingly Jem gazed across the gallery at Jeli. On the impulse of a moment he renounced his depravities. Like Silverby's heroes, from now on he would be worthy of his beloved. He would serve her, suffer for her. But could Jeli ever accept his love? The girl was looking down, intent on the spectacle. Quickly Jem looked down, too, as Aunt Vlada offered him a wry little smile.

Pell was saying, 'Nova, I do respect a virtuous woman, I do. One day I hope to marry one. I was only joking, Nova.'

It was no good.

Jem stared fixedly at the star in the courtyard, shimmering before him like an idle, bright vision. Now, immense figures on stilts surged forward, filling the spaces where the star pointed inwards. The stilt-men wore huge grotesque heads of papier-mâché, coloured like the capes the first dancers had worn: purple, green, red, blue, gold.

There was more, much more: in a moment would come the Routing of the Horn-Horse, and the Vision Dance, and the celebrated Circle of Destiny routine, all of it leading up to the climactic conflict of Destiny Blue and the Scarlet Endeavour. It was the Blue and Red Play, the same play Jem had performed in Varby, but embellished so richly as to be wholly different. Below, from beneath the dancing feet, a flight of bright birds came wheeling suddenly upwards.

Jem gasped, delighted. All at once he forgot himself, intent on the brilliant exhibition before him. There were none better than the Masks! It was true. On and on beat the tabors, blew the horns, and the gold rained down. Upwards, ever upwards, curled the potent incense, brash in the cold of the courtyard air.

It ended quickly all the same. For all the splendid elaboration of their play, the Masks left the audience wanting more. When Destiny Blue, on the horn-horse, had slain his rival with a golden lance, the full company swarmed suddenly into the courtyard, up the gallery steps, and danced through the audience in a bright, bewildering chain.

Then they were gone. All around the courtyard the tapers fizzed out, leaving just their lingering, acrid perfume.

Darkness. It was over.

But not quite. There was a brief, subdued encore. This was a special privilege, granted to few. Lady Cham-Charing's heart swelled. First came a single lamp, glowing in the centre of the courtyard. In a moment there would be two elderly figures, standing on either side of it, the first lean and wizened, dressed in a tight particoloured costume that only emphasized his stooped and shrivelled frame. His mask flashed mysteriously in the lamplight.

Jem had been enraptured; all at once his rapture turned to alarm.

'I almost forgot,' he said aloud.

'Nova?' Pell was lingering, hoping his friend's mood might change.

To great applause, Harlequin had been joined by Clown. Lady Cham-Charing wiped her eyes. These were the oldest members of the company, sole survivors of the days on Ollon Fields. Retired almost wholly from performance now, they deployed their talents mainly behind the scenes. All the great routines had been of their devising.

'I was frightened of them,' Jem murmured. 'But do you think they can really be evil?'

'Nova, what are you talking about?'

The two old performers exchanged stately greetings, bowing with the measured grace of age; then a succession of younger figures converged on them, swaying as if in a breeze. These figures wore costumes of rich green, fluttering and rustling in frond-like leaves.

In moments these new figures surrounded the old men. Round and round in a circle they turned, and when they drew back there was a third figure, standing between Harlequin and Clown. Concealed before, this was a gorgeous youth, garbed not just in green but green and gold. Even his mask was green and gold, with long curling horns, one of each colour.

Through all this, the Vaga-music had been writhing, ethereal; now heavy chords rang out on the gitterns, the Koros-pipes skirled up a stirring melody, and the youth, standing straight and tall, began to sing. His voice was at once high and grave, sweet but possessed of an ineffable sadness. As he sang, he slipped slowly into the background, while Harlequin mimed his words with all the expansive gestures, the gesticu-

252

lations, the twistings and turnings that the youth withheld. The youth might have been Harlequin's disembodied voice.

The song began:

> *Everything is lemon and nothing is lime,*
> *But even the truth shall be revealed in time:*
> *Then we shall drink from the mocking-tree gourds,*
> *And sup with the King and Queen of Swords!*

It was a song Jem had heard before, though only in part. The part had seemed like nonsense; soon he realized that the whole was nonsense, too. But a strange enchantment crept over him as the foolish rhymes unfolded. After a while he barely glanced at gesticulating Harlequin, his eyes straining after the singer instead, hidden away in the shadows.

> *Everything is hidden and nothing is known,*
> *For even the truth is like a cur's old bone:*
> *Come, let us kneel at the mocking-tree boards,*
> *And pray for the King and Queen of Swords!*

Nonsense, yes, but idly Jem wondered about the strange words. The King and Queen of Swords? Who could they be?

But the answer was soon supplied. Looming out from the arches, gliding across the courtyard, there now came a succession of figures garbed in thin rectangular boards, strapped to them back and front. The boards were painted to look like playing-cards.

Of course. The Suit of Swords.

Lady Margrave, a great one for gaming, was most diverted, and flung down a tiral.

Down, down the coin spiralled, flashing.

> *Everything is water but nothing is wet,*
> *And even the truth is like an unpaid debt:*
> *What, you would anger the mocking-tree lords?*
> *Still, you may lie with the Queen of Swords!*

What did it mean?

Slowly, but very surely, the conviction crept over Jem that the song was not nonsense at all, but meaningful, if obscurely; more than this, that it was meaningful to him.

But how?

For a moment the crowded gallery faded away, and it seemed to Jem that he was alone, alone with the Green-and-Gold singing just for him.

> *Everything's a pebble and nothing's a stone,*
> *When even the truth is left to lie alone:*
> *Fool, you would plunder the mocking-tree hoards?*
> *Then die with the King and Queen of Swords!*

253

While the song lasted, Clown stood off to the side, playing as if randomly with a small bird. It was a rainbow-dove, like Myla's Eo. A string was wrapped round one of its legs and the other end of the string was attached to a small baton. As the melody sounded, with one hand Clown would twist and twirl the baton, while with the other he juggled a succession of hoops. Again, again that fluttering bird would pass through this circle, then that, and that, the size diminishing as the song neared its end. On the final chord, as Harlequin took his bow, the bird would slip free, soaring up, up past the gallery and out of sight.

> *Everything is falling but nothing will fall,*
> *Though even the truth will vanish when you call:*
> *Come, let us take all that mocking affords—*
> *Come, let us live in the Land of Swords!*
> *Come, let us dream in the Land of Swords!*

'Nova?' Pell nudged his friend.

The song was over, the bird had flown, applause and gold showered the courtyard. Still Jem only stared down, dazed, to the shadowy wall where the Green-and-Gold stood. Harlequin and Clown took all the applause, while the youth who had sang so sweetly remained impassive.

Then it happened.

In the moment before he slipped away, the youth suddenly moved the arms that had hung motionless beside him throughout. Away went the cape, away the horned mask, revealing the garb he wore beneath. The youth was dressed like Harlequin – exactly like Harlequin.

Jem's jaw fell. He cried out.

Pell laughed, 'I think you've snuffled too much of that incense! Steady on, Nova, Miss Vance is looking.'

But Jem, for the moment, had forgotten the girl. All that filled his mind was his thwarted quest, and the strange powers that seemed to hold him in their grip. Mired deep in mystery, suddenly he knew he had been seeking a key, and that when he turned that key his confusions would all be gone.

Who but the harlequin could give him this key?

He turned suddenly. 'I've got to see him!'

'What?' Pell caught his arm, but Jem wrenched himself away. Roughly he pushed through the departing crowd, flinging himself down the gallery stairs. At the bottom, Jem nearly slipped and fell.

He stumbled into the courtyard, breathing deeply.

There was a strange, sudden silence. Jem looked around him. All the gold still lay on the cobblestones and in the middle the lamp still burned. He looked up. Above, the gallery was deserted now; higher still, the sky was dark, laden heavy with the snow that soon would fall.

There was a sound of crunching.

Jem turned around. A team of little Vaga-boys came into the court-yard, sweeping up the coins with long-headed brooms. Others milled around them, collecting the spoils in little leather bags. *Clink! Clink!* They scooped them up gravely.

They did not see Jem.

He cleared his throat. 'I'm looking for Harlequin.'

'You mean me?' came a familiar voice.

Jem started. He had thought the youth was gone, vanished with the others; he had only hung back. Now the gaudy figure stepped forward from the shadows, his silver mask gleaming in the lamplight.

Jem whispered, 'You're not the one I seek.'

'You're so sure?'

Jem was. This was not his harlequin: of course not. This harlequin was younger, shorter, darker of skin; the thought came to him that this was, in truth, the elderly harlequin, made miraculously younger. Could there be two versions of the same man, both present at the same time?

Clink! Clink! went the coins into the bags.

The youth came closer, and his voice, when he spoke again, was familiar, teasing. 'I saw you watching. You know who I am, don't you?'

A pause.

'You don't?'

He skipped forward, dancing round Jem in a circle. Jem reached out, grabbed his arm.

'No need to be rough, Nova!'

'Raj!'

The youth lowered his mask.

Chapter 34

QUICK, SAID THE BIRD

'Aunt Vlad?'

'My dear?'

'That boy.'

'Which boy, dear?'

'Aunt, you know the one!'

'You refer, I take it, to Lord Empster's ward?'

'He *is* persistent, isn't he?'

'So I told him.'

'You said he was a fool, too.'

'I did.' Aunt Vlada smiled. The Festival Levee was over. In ornate shawls, their arms wrapped round each other's waists, the two women sat in the Archduke's carriage, trundling back up the steep streets of The Island. Curfew had long passed and the streets were clear of commoners, silent but for the tolling, from time to time, of the meditation-bells.

'Aunt, why?'

'Why is he a fool? Might I say, for presuming to touch the hem of your garment?'

Jeli did not recall that he had done so, but let it pass and said, 'He's a respectable young man, isn't he?'

'My dear, the world is full of respectable young men! But is not my darling designed for something more?'

'More?'

'A young ward from the provinces? Who is he? Nobody! My dear, you made a brilliant impression at Cham's. Think on it. Constansia Cham-Charing loathes the very sight of me, yet she had to invite me to her little soirée. Politeness? Not a bit of it! That class of people is devoid of politeness. She invited me so she could have *you*. Already, Miss Jelica Vance is gaining a reputation.'

Jeli looked a little disconcerted.

Aunt Vlada laughed. 'My dear, I don't mean what Mistress Quick meant by the word! No, it is my mission to make Miss Jelica Vance the most desired young beauty of her generation. And she shall be. Fear not, she shall be!'

'Oh Aunt, why are you so good to me?'

256

'Good to you? My dear, in being good to you, am I not being good to myself?'

Jeli did not quite understand the answer, but it seemed a good one nonetheless. Resting dreamily in her aunt's arms, she gave herself up to visions of glory. Quite what that glory might be she did not know, but its very imprecision seemed part of its magic, like the haze that surrounds, say, a crown of gold, shining in the dazzling rays of the sun.

Lord Empster's ward was soon forgotten. He had been amusing for the moment, that was all.

In bed that night, as she drank her hot milk, Jeli could not imagine going to sleep. She was too excited. Smiling, Aunt Vlada sat with her, stroking her wrists and hair. Ring lay curled on the counterpane. Rheen perched on the bedstead, burbling contentedly.

'Dear Aunt Vlad!' Jeli sighed. 'If only Father had given me to you, right from the beginning! What years we wasted! To think, for a whole cycle I languished at Quick's!'

'Not quite wasted, my dear. I dare say Mistress Quick had some useful things to teach. Are you not confident in the use of a fish-knife? Can you not walk up a flight of stairs with a copy of Coppergate balanced on your head? No, let us not be too harsh on your old teacher.'

Jeli had to laugh. How long ago, already, those girlhood days seemed! 'Did you go to Quick's, Aunt Vlada?' she asked now, for it seemed her aunt knew the regime well.

'Quick's? Really, my dear! Mistress Quick is old now, it is true, but do you think her so ancient as that? In the days when I lived with Uly and Marly, there was no thought that girls should be sent away to school. We were taught at home, if we were taught at all.

'But as it happened, my Uncle Onty was a little more enlightened. One might say, indeed, that his enlightenment was to have far-reaching consequences.'

'Aunt Vlad?'

THE STORY OF ULY
(CONCLUDED)

'You know that Uncle Onty wanted the best for his girls. As Uly approached the time of her Entrance, he became concerned that she should not be one of those mere, ignorant society misses. Why, said Uncle Onty, banging the dining-table, the average Entered girl – vividly he recalled his courting days – was such a fool that she could not even point out Agondon on a map!

'Uly coloured. So did Marly.

257

'So it was that Uncle Onty decided to engage a tutor. A young gentleman of the cloth seemed the best option, and in a matter of days such a gentleman was found within the walls of Temple College. The Archmaximate provided him with copious references. Clearly the young gentleman was a serious, studious type, for whom the mere thought of impurity was abhorrent. Why – so the Archmaximate assured Uncle Onty – it was not to be credited that this fellow would even register the sex of his pupils. His name was Silas Wolveron.'

'That's a funny name, Aunt.'

'Isn't it, my dear? But such names are often found among pious provincials. Where this Silas Wolveron came from, I dare say every young boy was burdened with some such appellation as "Ebenezer" or "Nathanian" – why, even "Poltiss"! Still, we were not to call him by his Agonist-name, but rather "Candidate", or "Candidate Wolveron". That was his title. Not yet a Received man, he was still looking forward to the time of his Immersion.

'Rapidly our old nursery was fitted out as a schoolroom, complete with copybooks and chalk-boards, ink-wells and sloping desks. Uncle Onty would brook no opposition. All three of us were to take lessons every morning except Canonday.

'I remember Uly's and Marly's moans that first morning, as we sat in our schoolroom awaiting Candidate Wolveron. What would he be like? Uly and Marly vied with each other in ever more grotesque and absurd imaginings. Candidate Wolveron, if they were to be believed, was at best – worst did not bear contemplating – a hugely obese fellow with brick-red cheeks and a shining bald head, reeking of snuff. The reality – a creamy-cheeked, slender boy with limpid eyes and curly dark hair – rather took them aback.

'Now, my dear, I would not wish to suggest that Candidate Wolveron was a young fellow of unusual beauty – I seek to inspire no girlish dreams! No, he was pleasant enough, but in many ways quite a commonplace young man. You must understand that Uly and Marly had seen almost nothing of the male sex – that is, of the eligible part of it.'

'But Aunt Vlad, this Candidate could hardly be eligible!'

'Indeed, my dear, he was shortly to pledge himself to a life of celibacy. Of course, I speak loosely.'

Jeli's brow furrowed. 'And what of Cousin Pell?'

'True, but they thought of Pell as a brother, and besides, they did not like him any more. No, I dare say it was inevitable that Candidate Wolveron should become the focus of their ardour. At night when they ceased tormenting me – for alas, the three of us shared a room! – Uly and Marly would lie awake, speaking excitedly of the glories of the tutor.

258

'Of course, it began as the merest game. But ah, my dear, what begins as a game may proceed, soon enough, to deadly earnest! Candidate Wolveron was so delicate, so sensitive. How quick, observed Uly, were his creamy cheeks to overspread with a beetroot blush! What, said Marly, of the apple in his neck, and the fascinating way it bobbed up and down? Often they would picture the young man shaving – for was it not extraordinary, that men should shave? The mere thought made them giggle. How they longed to see the razor in his hand, poised to begin its journey down his neck! How could he not cut that bobbing apple? But then, when they looked close enough, they saw there were nicks. Little bloody nicks.

'Yes, it was too good a game, the young man too good a quarry. Soon the stakes were sure to be raised, and raised they were one Koros-afternoon – how I recall the cold glare of snow, falling across our inky desks! – when Candidate Wolveron, endeavouring to demonstrate some point of geometry, laid down his hand beside Uly's slate. That was all, a hand beside a slate; but then idly, as if it were an accident, Uly placed her hand over his. He flushed scarlet, drawing away. So small an incident! Between the time it began and the time it ended, there was barely the tick of an olton-clock. The warm fire in the schoolroom that day may have crackled just once, or not at all.

'But that was the beginning, the true beginning.

'After that, the girls were determined to draw forth the attentions, the favours of Candidate Wolveron. If Uly would dandle her hand against his, Marly would brush her skirt against his calves. Soon the fellow's life became a round of torment – perhaps, one might surmise, of temptation, too. His creamy cheeks were perpetually flushed.

'Of course, if Uncle Onty had imagined for a moment that the tutor inspired such passions in his girls, Candidate Wolveron would have been ejected with the same dispatch that had seen off Cousin Pell. But Uncle Onty – he was, I realize now, a simple man – only remembered the Archmaximate's reference. Did he not say that Candidate Wolveron would not even register the sex of his pupils? Sometimes, hailing the tutor in the hall, Uncle Onty would chuckle gleefully, "Tell me, Candidate, how are your *boys*?" The query gave Uncle Onty inordinate pleasure; Candidate Wolveron must have thought he was mad.

'Yes, it was a game, a delightful game to ease the boredom of Unentered girls, in a big lonely house when the lake was frozen and the Koros-snows lay thick upon the ground. But as the snows gave way to long hot days – what blissful Theron-days we had then, my dear! – the game took on a darker, more sinister colouring.

'I used to think it was Uly who led the campaign. Marly, I thought, followed in her wake – but would be sure to stop if things went too far. I was wrong.

'Now I ought to have explained that Candidate Wolveron was a young man of the highest moral character – I mean, my dear, that he *really* was, not merely that he appeared as such. No, he was no callous seducer, cloaked in a false garb of piety. That he would have made his vow of chastity in the full sincerity of his heart has always seemed to me undeniable. Alas, he reckoned without Uly and Marly. For now, the wicked thought came to the girls that our poor tutor should never make that vow. Uly and Marly made their own vow, and vowed that he should fall.

'The temptations became ever more ardent. I told you, my dear, that Uly and Marly were never what could be called *innocent* girls. But now, what had once been girlish folly was prosecuted with a real urgency. The girls vied to find opportunities to be alone with Candidate Wolveron. As the days grew warm, Uly begged her father that they should be permitted to take their lessons out of doors. Uncle Onty, all unawares, could only encourage nature-study. Why (he boomed), in his courting days there were girls who could barely tell the difference between a root of ragwort and a long purple!

'I dare say our Theron-rambles must have been a torture for Candidate Wolveron. Sometimes we walked round the circumference of the lake, pausing to gaze with spurious intentness upon the reeds and fragrant flowers and draping branches of willow. A red and gold glimpse of darting fish threw Uly into a wildness of delight. Seizing Candidate Wolveron's arm, she would march him off ahead, demanding that he satisfy her scholarly questions.

'Then there were the woods. In those days, forests rolled almost uninterrupted from the Valley of Varby to the Ollon Marshes. From Uncle Onty's windows, we could look out not only upon the silvery sheet of the lake but to a rambling range of thickly wooded hills. At first I thought it hardly likely that Uncle Onty would let us stray so far beyond his estate. But the hills, in Uncle Onty's eyes, were part of his estate – as good as such – and after all, were not *his boys* (how he chuckled!) safe with Candidate Wolveron?

'The walks in the woods were my particular torment. Only the thought of our tutor's disapproval stopped the girls from chasing me off, as they had done many years earlier. After all, neither would run the risk of shouting, or breaking into a gawky run. Each sought to be attractive, even demure – or so they absurdly imagined. In truth, far from any prospect of observation, Uly and Marly now became ever more outrageous in their attacks – the word, my dear, seems scarcely exaggerated – upon poor Candidate Wolveron. Flagrantly, they would lower their eyes as he addressed them! Staggering on uneven paths, they clutched his hand, his arm! Once, after a shower of rain, only the discovery of an alternate way saved the poor young man from carrying the girls, one by one, across a deep puddle!'

Aunt Vlada smiled, almost laughed. But Jeli was angry. 'Really, Aunt, I am impatient with the man! Was he a fool? Could he not see what those girls were doing?'

Her aunt's smile grew sad. 'Ah, my dear, we must recall that Candidate Wolveron was a young man of the most exquisite innocence. Nowadays, I dare say such a fellow could hardly be found – nay, not even within the walls of Temple College. Could our tutor imagine such depravity, lurking in the hearts of Unentered girls? I dare say he thought them the merest innocents, their indelicacies all unintended and unknown.

'How I longed to comfort him! But Candidate Wolveron, too, was a most obedient young man, and Uncle Onty had instructed him to squander only the most minimal of attentions upon *the Zenzan*. Too often, I was left to skulk behind alone in the sunny dapples of the woods while the girls plunged on ahead with our tutor, each one aching for him to take her hand. Sadly I looked down on the white walls of Uncle Onty's house, dazzling on the flatlands far below. What exquisite sorrow I knew in those days! But how far-off now! How long, long ago!

'The season burnt on, but still the campaign produced no more than blushes and stammerings in Candidate Wolveron. Soon the girls – contriving opportunities to go on ahead – were taking it in turns to walk with him ever deeper into the forest. Had they been too much together? Would he respond more freely to *one* girl, not two? All that mattered, Uly said, was to force the tutor to declare himself, making a mockery of his impending vows. What she did not consider was how she might feel if Candidate Wolveron declared himself to Marly. The torments they would mete out so eagerly upon others had been a source of unity for the two girls. But envy, like a serpent in their path, had always lain in wait for them.

'One evening in bed, Uly hatched a delicious plan. The time of our tutor's Immersion drew near. New and more urgent methods were needed. As Marly distracted him – "Take him on ahead a little, talk about ragwort," her sister sniffed with a wave of her hand – Uly would contrive to sprain her ankle. Whether she really intended to sprain it, or simply to pretend, I was not quite sure. In any case, I was to rush forward, bringing the tutor back – this, said Uly, would create a greater sense of crisis. That her injury would stir new feeling in Candidate

261

Wolveron's breast, Uly had no doubt; nor did she doubt that he would have no choice but to carry her back down the hillside to the house.

'Of course, I wanted no part in this plan. But how could I resist, when if I disobeyed any command of theirs, Uly and Marly would hold me down in bed, whipping me with the knotted cords of their dressing-gowns?

'It began as planned. Next day we repaired once again to the woods. In due course, at a signal from Uly, Marly began to question Candidate Wolveron about a species of plant she had observed the day before. Guilelessly (it seemed) she took his arm, drawing him away. Soon they had vanished deep into the woods.

'I waited with Uly. So happy was she that day that she almost smiled at me. Dreamily she cast herself down on a log, looking down to the gleam of her father's house below. One day, she mused, she would be mistress of that house. It would be hers, all hers. She could wish for nothing more.

'I asked, "But heart-sister, what about Candidate Wolveron? Should you not like him to be its master?"

'You must understand, my dear, that in those days I, too, was the merest innocent. Uly only looked at me, bewildered and a little annoyed.

'After some moments she told me to seek out the tutor.

'"Heart-sister, you have not yet sprained your ankle."

'Uly's annoyance grew. "Stupid little Zenzan! Go, go."

'I went. Pretending to alarm, I called out the tutor's name. But no reply rang back through the trees. Soon Uly was far behind, and where the others were I did not know. Soon, even the comforting sight of the house below was lost to me. Still I plunged ahead. The woods were thick and deep, and I was frightened.

'I found myself in a strange part of the wood. Brambles and bracken choked the way. I had to go very slowly.

'Then I saw them. As I approached I heard a curious snuffling sound, like the sound of an animal whimpering in distress. My heart had always been much engaged by animals, as you will appreciate, my dear—' Aunt Vlada paused, stroking Ring's neck '—and as you may imagine I was somewhat alarmed. Could it be some dear little stoat or fox-cub, caught in some cruel hunter's trap?

'At first I did not believe what I saw. Candidate Wolveron was on his knees, clutching Marly round the waist and sobbing. I knew at once that he had made some declaration. "My dearest," he whimpered, "my darling Marly!" At that moment – my heart pounding, my hand up to my mouth – I would have crept away, quiet as could be. I vowed that Uly should not know what I had seen – no, not on any account!

'What I did not know was that Uly, meanwhile, had become impatient.

She had been alone for a long time, and had come to look for us. Of course, she had made no attempt to sprain her ankle. The plan would have to wait for another day.

'It was as I was turning, about to go, that I saw her. She opened her mouth, about to ask me angrily what I thought I was playing at. But the words never left her lips. In their place came a long wailing cry, as suddenly through the branches she saw what I had seen. Sobbing, she would have flailed away; instead, her ankle turned and she fell into the bracken.

'Poor Uly! Her dream came true: Candidate Wolveron carried her home. Alas, he was hardly the dashing rescuer she had imagined. Trembling with shame – and then, I dare say he was not very strong – the young man could barely support his burden. Painfully Uly's ankle thudded against branches, and on the way downhill it began to rain. Once Candidate Wolveron nearly slipped in the mud.

'I hung back with Marly. She did not speak.

'From that time on I watched the sisters intently. Uly was laid up for only a few days. Ointment soon soothed her scratches, and the sprain was not a bad one. But those few days were enough to cement the ardour between her sister and the tutor.

'What a terrible, consuming thing is envy! I trust that you, my dear, feel no such emotions?'

Jeli shook her head. 'Oh no, Aunt Vlad!'

Aunt Vlada only smiled and carried on:

'The game was over. Or rather, it was a game no longer. Uly confronted her sister. How I remember the scene! It was morning in the schoolroom, and as the sun's rays slanted through the long windows I found myself remembering that this room was once our nursery. Screwing up my eyes, in place of the chalk-boards and desks and ink-wells for a moment I saw instead Uly's old rocking-horse and Marly's big doll with the smiling stitched face. I was deeply sad.

'Uly had called her sister there specially. Just risen from her sick-bed, she could walk only with difficulty. Red scratches still covered her face, and Nurse had daubed them liberally with a purple lotion. Never had poor Uly looked so ugly. That Marly was the prettier of the two sisters could hardly be made more cruelly clear.

'"Sister," said Uly, "you have betrayed the game."

'"Sister, how so?" Marly raised an eyebrow. "Did you not say the man should declare himself?"

'"But have you not fuelled his passions in secret?"

'Now Marly drew herself erect. "I have no need to *fuel* his passions. He loves me, and we are to be married!"

'Uly gasped. "Sister, tell me you jest!"

'But it was no jest. As her ugly sister looked on, incredulous, Marly now revealed the astonishing truth. Like her *foolish sister* – these were her words – she had begun by merely tormenting poor Silas.'

'She called him by that name?'

'Indeed, my dear. As you see, things had gone far. Silas loved her, she said, and his intentions were honourable. Uly tried to reason with her sister. What would their father say? Was a girl who might have ascended to the bed of a King to throw herself away on a poor Temple-Candidate, fresh from the provinces? Father would never allow it!

' "Father may allow or disallow as he pleases. But I shall marry Silas with or without his blessing. In a phase, Silas was to have made his Immersion. That Immersion now will never be made. Tomorrow Silas is to go to the Archmaximate, and beg his release. We shall marry swiftly, and go away."

' "But what are you to do? How are you to live?"

' "Silas shall devote himself to a life of scholarship. In the far province from which he came, he shall set up a little school. I shall be his helpmate. What care I for the fripperies of society, when I have the love of such a man? Oh sister, what a fine spirit it was that you, in your vanity and cruelty, sought only to vex!"

' "Sister, this is madness!" Uly cried, but Marly would listen to no more. Candidate Wolveron was waiting in the garden, ready to begin the day's ramble.

'But only Marly would accompany him that day.

'Left alone, Uly fretted herself to a passion. She cursed. She sobbed. She moaned. But after all, the solution was clear. Foolish Marly, to reveal her plans so frankly! "I shall go to Father," Uly cried. "Shall he not put a stop to this madness? Why, he would lock Marly in a room and starve her, rather than that she should squander her virtue on some worthless young provincial! As for the man – why, Father shall fling him into the mud of the street!"

'Alas for Uly, Uncle Onty was away that day, visiting an old business-crony. It was to be a fatal absence. In rage, then in sorrow, then in pain, then in fear, Uly stumped her way about her father's grounds. When she grew tired, she called to Nurse for a wheeled chair, then demanded that I – I! – should push her about the lake. Nurse demurred, but Uly attacked her so angrily that the poor old woman burst into tears.

'We started off round the lake. What a burden is an angry, ugly girl! Theron-season was almost over. Ripples disturbed the glassy waters, and a chill breeze played through the willows and reeds. Where was Marly – Marly and her lover? Spitefully Uly imagined them in the woods, secreted deep in some ferny cavern, indulging themselves in the vilest impurities.

'Quite what these impurities may have been, neither Uly nor I was then quite aware. Still, the mere thought was sufficiently alarming.

'As it happened, we came across them suddenly. Remember our old boat, my dear, moored at its little jetty on the far side of the lake? This was the place they had chosen to conceal themselves. Enfolded in each other's arms, Marly and her lover lay in the bottom of the boat. They were sleeping.

'How happy they looked!

'The passion this sight raised in Uly was so great – so I have assumed – that no expression could do it justice. Stiffly she rose from the chair, inspecting the scene. But there were no tears, no cries. At once she turned away, and her face was white, deathly white, beneath the scratches. She lowered herself back into the chair again, quietly commanding me to push her on.

'We made the round of the lake again. By this time I was exhausted, and dark clouds were gathering in the sky. Yes, Theron-season was almost over; spots of rain began to fall, and I pleaded with Uly to let us go inside. She hushed me impatiently. As we came close to the little jetty again, I began to be afraid. Uly had gone so quiet! I prayed that the lovers would have moved by now.

'When we reached the place, Uly raised her hand and commanded me to stop. I almost collapsed into the chair myself. Instead, I only looked on, breathing deeply, as Uly made her way on to the jetty. Swiftly, careful not to disturb the lovers, she removed the oars from the bottom of the boat. Then she slipped the painter from side of the jetty and gave the boat just a little, just the lightest push. She returned to the chair, commanding me again to push her on.

'Why, my dear, did I obey that command? After all these years, I do not know. Yet even as I say this – even as I profess this ignorance, as if I hope that ignorance and innocence are the same – do I not find myself recalling, perhaps even dimly understanding at last, the mysterious lesson of Cousin Pell? Have I not known, deep in my heart, that something in me yearns for the eddy? Once I thought I wanted to disappear myself, into the horror of that swirling vortex! I see now that there are other ways in which we may know the eddy, know it too well.

'We were already halfway round the lake by the time we heard the shouts, the screams, drifting over the water. Candidate Wolveron leapt from the boat. I suppose he had some confused notion of going for help. Alas, he hardly acquitted himself as a hero. Desperately his thin arms cleaved the water, struggling to escape the hungry eddy. Meanwhile, he had left Marly in the boat, as it whirled ever closer to the dark vortex. She could not swim. Jerking like some fool puppet, she jumped up and down in the rocking boat. At last, too late, I flung myself into the lake, but what could I do? In mere moments the boat had capsized, and Marly, screaming piteously, had vanished into the eddy.

'Through all this, Uly sat in her chair, rigid, corpse-like, white beneath her scratches.

'It was a matter of moments, mere moments. By the time the servants rushed from the house, there was nothing they could do. Nothing they could do for Marly, at least. Candidate Wolveron they dragged from the lake, spluttering and sobbing. He was dismissed in disgrace. Only the mercy of the Archmaximate, I gather, dissuaded my uncle from criminal proceedings. Of course, Uncle Onty never knew the truth. Devastated by his loss, he died soon afterwards.

'Now Uly was indeed mistress, sole mistress of her father's house. What went through her mind as she took up her inheritance? It is hard to imagine. After Uncle Onty's funeral, I never spoke to her again. I had a legacy from *my* father – small, of course, but I would harbour it well – and no need of her assistance. Of course, I would see her across crowded rooms – oh, many times, many times.'

'But Aunt, what happened to her? Did she marry?'

Aunt Vlada laughed. 'You know well enough what happened to her, my dear! Perhaps – was it guilt, I wonder? – Uly thought of her sister's dream of starting a little school with her lover. Perhaps her thoughts lingered sadly in the schoolroom – once the nursery! – where she had been so happy, tormenting our tutor. In any case, she turned her father's house into an academy for the education of girls.

'The lake, alas, she did not maintain, and her high whitewashed walls now look out only on marshes.'

Jeli leaned forward, her mouth gaping.

'Then Uly is—'

'But of course, my dear! Why, don't tell me I neglected to mention my uncle's name? It was Quick, my dear. Quick. Quick.'

At this, Rheen skittered on to Aunt Vlada's shoulder, squawking like a parrot, *Quick! Quick!* Then Aunt Vlada was laughing, flinging back her head, as if the terrible story had been, in truth, only some strange but uproarious joke.

Chapter 35

A CHALLENGE FOR NOVA

'... Coppergate? Why, sir, you have not the beginnings of criticism in you! My old friend Farley Cham-Charing would say of Coppergate, that he is to wit as a swinging door, creaking on its hinges, is to Schuvart's sublime Quintet in J!'

'... Marrick? Marrick! I tell you, his King of Swords was all bluster and bombast, not a shred of feeling! As I said to Reny Bolbarr, if I wanted to be battered, abused and spat upon for the length of an evening, I should repair to Chokey's, not the Theatre Royal, Juvy Lane!'

'... My good doctor, I can barely believe you! You would take Vytoni's *Discourse on Freedom* as your model? Pshaw, it is a theoretical work, referring to conditions never to be expected in this Time of Atonement! Blasphemer, would you doubt the El-Orokon, which declares that all must live in sorrow?'

'They're on form tonight,' Rajal grinned.

The coffee-house was crowded. Outside, snow heaped high in the lane that wound away from the University gates, but in Webster's – so the place was known – quite as much heat was generated by the furious disputes as by the roaring fires and Zaxos Black.

'Tonight?' said Jem. It was later that evening. 'Then you haven't just arrived in Agondon, then? And it was you, at the Erdon Tree? Raj, our paths have been criss-crossing like a spider's web!'

'I knew you'd find me eventually. I've been waiting to see how long it would take.'

'You knew I was in Agondon?'

'I've seen you! Why, just the other day I looked down from my window in the Royal, and there you were.'

Jem looked puzzled and Rajal added, 'Agondon's finest lodging-house, Nova. We can't own property, but we rent the best.'

By 'we', Jem knew, his friend meant the Masks. He shook his head, marvelling. 'But Raj, what happened to you? You still haven't told me a thing.'

Rajal grinned again and looked down, toying with his coffee-dish. For a moment, just a moment, he seemed almost shy. Then he looked up and his eyes, it seemed to Jem, flashed defiantly.

Jem studied his friend's face. Rajal had changed. He looked older, wiser, or at least more knowing. Boyish fat had vanished from his cheeks, giving his dark face a gamin handsomeness that had not been there before. The eyes had acquired a certain heavy-lidded quality. Even his mouth seemed somehow different, fuller perhaps, more defined; it was some moments before Jem realized that his friend was wearing paint.

He joked uncertainly, 'You're quite the fop.'

'That's you, Nova. I'm a Vaga, don't forget.' Rajal had a readier grin but a new smile, too, an arch, twisty way of pursing his lips.

Jem said, 'But such a Vaga!'

'Oh, still a Vaga.'

Jem had to laugh.

Rajal had changed out of his harlequin costume into a splendid purple suit with lacy ruffs at the wrist and neck and the royal seal embroidered at the chest. On a coat-stand in the corner hung his matching cape, lined in rainbow colours, and his fashionable wide-brimmed hat. He even sported an ornamental scabbard, richly bejewelled.

His confidence matched his new attire. It had been Rajal, not Jem, who said they should repair to the coffee-house; Rajal, not Jem, who snapped his fingers as they stood in the doorway, calling *'Boy!'* and demanding a booth.

Jem was almost envious. Then he reflected that this was mean of him. Webster's, after all, was one of the few places where a Vaga-boy could play the young lord. In the great world, what were the Masks more than servants, mere servants? Lady Cham-Charing might exclaim over the Blue and Red Play, but not even Harlequin, not even Clown would be invited to her house as a guest.

Rajal sipped his coffee. 'Remember that night we went back to Varby?'

'Equinox-night?'

'Well, I could just as easily ask what happened to you.'

Jem laughed, 'Would you believe, I dived into a trader's cart? Head first – *thunk!* When I woke up, I was halfway to Agondon. Not very smart.'

'I don't know. You got where you were going. I ran the other way. Into the city.'

'Now *that* wasn't smart!'

'Wasn't it? Well, let me tell you: I turned a corner and what should I see but a huge golden serpent, slithering towards me! I dare say I screamed, but I laughed an instant later. It was a paper dragon, soon to be hacked in half with wooden swords.'

'Sassoroch?' said Jem. The image of the flying serpent passed across his mind, and he shivered.

'Yes, yes,' said Rajal knowledgeably, 'the Masks do Sassoroch every year at Varby. Big finish to the Equinox Parade. Well, I walked right into it, you see.'

'That must have been something.'

'Something? It was everything! Oh, Nova, there they were, Vaga-boys like me, milling this way, milling that, all down the length of Eldric's Parade. Tabors beat, pipes rang out. Fireworks exploded in the rainy sky. Harlequin says there's nothing like Varby Equinox. You must see it one day, Nova. This little shindy at Her Ladyship's tonight – pish-pash!'

'Pish-pash?'

'Let's just say I made some new friends that night.' Rajal gave his new, arch smile. 'You'll take some Jarvel? *Boy!*'

'I suppose we both got where we were going,' Jem murmured.

He looked down. He thought of his old life on the road with Rajal and a wave of sorrow coursed through him, a terrible regret. He was not sure he liked this new Rajal.

But then, he was not sure he liked this new Jem.

'Raj,' he said, 'what about Myla? Or the Great Mother?'

Rajal shrugged his shoulders. He flipped a tiral at the servant-boy, stretched, yawned, smiled.

Jem grabbed his friend's arm, suddenly earnest.

'Raj! Don't you even know where they are?'

Jem would have said more, but at that moment there was a disturbance. The door burst open, letting in an icy blast, and an imperious voice demanded service. Its owner, it was clear, was more than a little drunk.

'The wits!' he slurred contemptuously. 'I should have known! Every other place in town shut for Meditations – even Chokey's turfed us out tonight! But the wits never shut up, eh? *Shut up*, get it? *Boy!* Come here, boy!'

Angry protests rang round the coffee-house.

'Damn you, sir, shut the door!'

'Impertinent fellow, does he think this is a common tavern?'

'What, what?' blustered an old scholar. Deep in argument on the subject of prosody, he was most annoyed to have lost his thread. 'Sir, have you no feeling for the Agonist hexameter?'

'Pox on your hexameters!' returned the drunkard, and seizing a coffee-dish from the startled old man, he flung it to the floor. 'Filthy muck! For the sake of the Lord Agonis, somebody bring me a drink, a proper drink!'

Fascinated and appalled, Jem and his friend were peering round the corner of their booth.

'Haven't we seen this fellow before?' said Rajal.

Jem nodded. 'Oh yes, we've seen him before.'

It was Mr Burgrove, but so dishevelled that only his golden cravat, half-pulled from his neck, made his identity certain. His fine clothes were filthy, his eyes were bloodshot and his cheeks were flaming red. Accompanying him, hovering nervously behind, was the lean young Bluejacket from Chokey's. By now, the serving-boys were milling around, alarmed and ineffectual, and a little weedy fellow in an apron – evidently this was Webster – had burst forward from the back of the shop, eyes glowering, arms akimbo.

Rajal could not help but smile, enthralled, perhaps, to be entertained by Ejlanders for a change.

But the violence he might have hoped for was forestalled.

'Please,' stammered the Bluejacket, 'don't mind him. He's very drunk, but he means no harm, really.' Quickly he put an arm round Mr Burgrove's shoulder, to prevent him falling and smashing more crockery. 'Don't worry, we'll pay for any damage. He doesn't really want another drink. Couldn't we just have some coffee, to sober him up? Coffee, good and strong?'

Webster pursed his lips. 'All my coffee is good and strong. Very well, gentlemen, won't you take a booth? Up the back, I think,' he added tartly.

Mr Burgrove was almost passing out as the young Bluejacket bundled him into his seat. Rajal, looking on eagerly, could not help but laugh as the drunkard's heavy head fell forward with a thud.

Conversation resumed. 'So what's the future, Raj? Are you are the new Harlequin?'

Rajal laughed. 'You mean the costume? No, that's just Clown's little joke. There's only one Harlequin of the Silver Masks. There *was* another, Clown said, many years ago. Poor Harlequin never got over it after he left.'

Jem's heart throbbed. 'Another?'

'Harlequin taught him everything he knew. Then he left. This boy, I mean. I don't think he was really of the Vaga-blood, that was the trouble. A runaway Ejlander. Like you, Nova. This boy, I mean.'

Jem looked down thoughtfully. 'I wish I could find him.'

'Who?'

'I've met him. The other harlequin.'

Rajal laughed, 'There are many harlequins! I was just talking about the Silver Masks. Oh, Nova, I'm so happy! Who would have thought, back in Varby, that Rajal of Xal-Blood could ever be part of something so fine, so noble?'

Jem's look was sour.

'What about Myla?' he attempted again. 'Do you think she'll ever join the Masks?'

Rajal grinned, 'You're not very observant, are you, Nova? Haven't you noticed, we're all *boys*? No, I've found something Myla can't have.'

'Raj, that's spiteful!'

'But true, Nova. Don't you see, I've found myself? I mean, I've found what I *am*.'

Then Rajal paused, and added with a wry twist of his mouth, 'Nova, do you think every new boy in the company sleeps in sheets of finest silk?'

Rajal did not go on; Jem did not quite follow. Reflectively he sipped his coffee. Then he remembered things the old Harlequin had said, just before he escaped from the coach in Varby. *You shall be our friend, our special friend. Clown and I have had many such friends, haven't we, Clown?*

Then Jem understood.

He slammed down his coffee-dish and burst out, 'Raj, you're a harlot! A boy-harlot!'

'Shh! That's unkind, Nova.'

'But true!'

'It's what I am. It's what I'm good for, don't you understand?'

Jem did not.

'Raj, how could you? What would the Great Mother say?'

Rajal only sighed, 'Doesn't she know everything? Before it happens?' His elbows were on the bench and he leaned close, his chin resting on his laced knuckles. Helplessly Jem gazed into the dark eyes.

'Don't judge me too harshly, Nova,' Rajal said. 'Let me tell you something. As soon as we got to Agondon, I went to the Vaga Quarter. Oh, not dressed like this, of course. I've kept my old rags, just in case – well, I don't know. Suffice to say I wandered downhill from the Royal, towards that cluster of dirty streets around Old Agondon Bridge. Where did you say you live, Nova? Agondon New Town? Well, I dare say you've never bothered with the Vaga Quarter. Remember the camp in Irion, up by the old barn? At least it was on a hill. And spread out. Imagine fifty times as many people – a hundred, for all I know – squashed into filthy tenements, row upon row, floor upon floor heaped so high that the sun never strikes the street below.'

The Jarvel, ordered long ago, had arrived at last. They inhaled deeply.

'I came through the Shambles when I arrived here.'

'The Shambles! Well, pardon me, Nova, but there's hardly any comparison. The Shambles are for Ejlanders with no money, no hope. They aren't there just because they're Ejlanders, are they?'

Jem gestured to his friend's rich costume. 'Not all Vagas are in the Quarter.'

271

Rajal twisted his mouth. 'Precisely. You haven't even been there, have you? It's a maze. Like the biggest Vaga-fair you've ever seen. How many curtains spangled with stars? How many stalls piled high with trinkets? How many robes, how many paste-jewels? How many harlots sitting in windows? Hawkers hawking, singers singing, rumbling carts and angry shouts, gitterns and whistles and hurdy-gurdies mixing up a jumble of a hundred different tunes.

'Think of it. No space, no sun, no silence. And it never stops. Oh, we'd rather be out on the road, believe me, if they hadn't banned us here, there, everywhere. I've heard even Varby is off-limits now to the common troupes. Why should they want to herd us all together? But then, I can answer that. There'll be a fire in the Quarter one night. Or a bomb. Fairly soon, I should think. Fairly soon.'

Jem said bitterly, 'But you're not one of them, Raj.'

'They're my people.'

'Not any more.'

'Don't say that.' Rajal had lost his confident air. Tears sprang suddenly to the dark eyes and he burst out, 'Nova, I've looked for them, I've looked for them, I tell you! Night after night I searched that filthy warren. Then I've checked every execution, too! Why do you think I was at the Erdon Tree that day? The Great Mother's a Vaga-legend. Do you think she could arrive in Agondon, and everyone not know it? They're gone. They never reached here. That's all I know, Nova, I swear.'

He slumped forward, his face in his hands.

Jem leaned across, wanting to comfort him, but could think of nothing to say. This latest news struck him with a terrible foreboding. For a moment the bright warm chamber around them seemed suddenly dark and cold, as if the walls had been blasted open to the wind and snow.

That was when a shout rang through the coffee-house, 'Vaga-scum!'

Jem's head swivelled. In his booth by the far wall, Jac Burgrove had rallied, but the reviving coffee had revived only his belligerence.

'Who let this dirty scum in here?'

The young Bluejacket attempted to silence him, but it was hopeless. Already the drunkard had staggered from his seat, pointing in outrage at the dark figure of Rajal.

'I said, who let this dirty scum in here?'

Rajal's face froze. Aghast, all the customers had turned to look. Webster burst back into the shop, but before the little man could intervene, Jem was on his feet.

'Leave off, Burgrove,' he said levelly.

Burgrove rounded on him. 'Nova Empster! Well, well, life is full of surprises, isn't it? So he's yours, then, the painted little darky?'

'I said, leave off,' Jem repeated.

The drunkard's lip curled. He did not leave off; instead he expanded, in a spluttering slur, 'What would Empster say, I wonder? But you know, the one I feel sorry for is Chokey . . . No, listen, there he is, the old fellow, working his poor twisted fingers to the bone to provide the likes of you with – oh, the most *exquisite* pleasures nature has designed. Quality for the quality, that's his motto. But there's no telling, is there? Do what you will, there are those among us who would *actually prefer* to wallow in a sty of filth, disease, and unnatural vice . . .'

There would have been more in this vein, no doubt, but Jem stepped forward and struck the flaccid spluttering face, once, twice, quickly, hard.

Burgrove fell back, crumpling to the floor.

Jem looked over to the young Bluejacket, who was twisting his hands in ineffectual shame. 'Take him home, can't you? Let him sleep it off.'

'Don't touch me!' Angrily Burgrove shook off his companion. Staggering upright, he took one shaky step forward, then another, pointing contemptuously at Jem as he had pointed, moments earlier, at Rajal. Jem shrank back as the drunkard came close, whispering hotly on reeking breath, 'You, sir, have insulted me.'

Jem turned away, but Burgrove grabbed his shoulder, wrenching Jem back to face him as he roared, 'I said, sir, you have insulted me! I demand satisfaction!'

There were gasps all over Webster's. Jem blanched and span around again as a new voice intruded, 'He's right, Nova. It's the code of a gentleman. I've taught you that much at least, haven't I?'

'Pell!'

Pellam Pelligrew stepped forward, shaking the snow from the shoulder of his greatcoat.

'I would have said, Nova, I was glad to have found you, before you'd got yourself into any trouble. As it is, I don't see how you could have got yourself into more.'

END OF PART TWO

273

PART THREE

Face in a Glass

Chapter 36

THREE LETTERS

Dearest Constansia,

It is with a heavy heart that I reply to your last. After so many years (need I say?) there can be no affirming of my love for you, for we have passed beyond affirmation. Our love is a cord that none can sever, running from your fine Riel-side house to this shabby palace within the walls of Wrax. No, it is safe, this tie-that-twines,

> *This sacred bond around my heart,*
> *Not time, nor plague, nor death can part*

– but do not be alarmed, my dear, if yet I say you are cruel – say, indeed, that you are my tormentor.

How can this be? For so long – locked, like a prisoner, in this colonial fastness – have I not looked to the letters of my Constansia as to an especial joy? In these despatches from the far centre of the empire, have I not revelled in the imagining that I, too, was with you in the Great Temple, in the imperial throne-room, at the First Moonlife Ball, at the Festival Levee? Indeed, my dear, there have been times (such are the burdens of a governor's lady) when I have seen in these epistles my only happiness. Alas, it seems even this happiness is over for your poor Mazy (that was). For now my Constansia grows melancholy, and if happiness has fled from her heart, how (pray) can she prompt it in another?

Yet even at your last I knew, for a time, something other than pain. Like a welling tide, sweet memory lapped around me, and the tears that came to me were tears of joy. Again, my dear, I saw us in our virgin-days – punting across the Riel before they built the Regent's Bridge, running and laughing through the daffodils and daisies where now sprawl the villas of Ollon-Quintal. Yes, my dear, there were moments (so potent to recall, I must believe them real) when again we were girls, and our lives were all before us! But how soon my happiness turned to sorrow, when I knew that all I had seen was illusion, that in truth never again could I return to that place – drenched for ever now in the golden sun, its air for ever sweet – where I was Mazy Tarfoot, and you were Consy Grace!

This is a sadness we must share, but I say again, my dear, that you have been cruel. Our lives draw to a close; yet though you (unlike your Mazy-that-was) have lost the best of husbands, have you not lived the finest life that can be vouchsafed to a woman? When the history of our times is written, shall any woman (that is not a Queen) take in it a more central and striking position? As a governor's wife, my dear, you may believe that I have received many dignitaries; believe, too, that I have hung on their words, eager for all that I may hear of Agondon; and have I not heard, again and again, of the triumphs and glories of Constansia Cham-Charing? And may your old friend not put to you – but delicately – that what you see now as the passing of your glory is but the passing (sad but inevitable) of time?

We are old, Constansia, but your life has been a great one. Can you not think of your Mazy-that-was, consigned to the distant reaches of Wrax? That my home is a palace should not beguile you. If once the dwelling-place of monarchs, this Government House is but a mean abode, I assure you, when put in the balance with Lady Cham-Charing's! Think of the provincial – nay, colonial – life I endure, in which the vulgarity of the colonists is exceeded only by the stupidity of the natives, and visitors from the far centre of the empire constitute the only tolerable society. Alas, I fear such privations may be too far even from the imaginings of the one I have heard called the Great Cham!

Perhaps, then, there is no hope of explaining to you the new and additional sorrow which assails me here in this benighted colony. Will the placid surface of an Agondon drawing-room tremble even for a moment, I wonder, at the knowledge that, in far Zenzau, war descends again? Pray, dear Constansia, that your heart remains open, sufficiently at least to pity your Mazy-that-was, as she looks to the Fields of Ajl that lie below this city, and thinks that soon they may be stained with blood!

There have been times (to you, my dear, I may admit it) when indeed I have wished that my Michan had been a man less brave. Would that I, too (but pardon this bitterness!) had married the merest fop, a dandy-fellow of silk and lace, and not one whose fate it was to be recorded in the annals of war! But yet – mistake me not, my dear! – I love my dear Michan, and in the battle that shall come I have the glad knowledge, too – for is not Michan, like us, growing old? – that now he need only look from behind the lines, as the heroism of the day is left to others.

My dear husband tells me that no army of Zenzans could succeed, in these times, in shaking the walls of Wrax. Why then, does fear chill my womanly heart as I hear that, in the far reaches of the colony – on the steppes of Derkold, in the hills of Ana-Zenzau, on the rocky coasts of Antios – they rally round the standard of the Green Pretender?

Pray for me, my dear, in the times that lie ahead. Ah (but mistake not my meaning!) how I wish that sweet dream had been real, that

278

again we ran in white through those fields of daisies and daffodils, in
the days when my Constansia was yet my little Consy, and your
Mazy T. had not yet to sign herself
 Her Excellency,
  Lady Michan

Postscript.
One thing in your last leaves me puzzled. You say that Vlada Flay
has returned to Agondon. You refer, I take it, to the present Lady
Hartlock, widow of the former Collector of Derkold. But how can this
be? I am sure, my dear, that even in Agondon you have heard of the
notorious Bob Scarlet. Can you not know that Lady Vlada's coach was
waylaid on the Wrax Road, early last Theron-season? Other travellers
were merely robbed, but Lady Vlada was taken prisoner, and has never
been found.
 But perhaps you made some slip of the pen, and meant some
other lady.

To: Capt. P. Veeldrop,
5th R. Fusil. Tarn,
c/ Ollon Barracks

Honoured Sir,
 It had been my intention to write to you at this time with
apologies of the most earnest and copious character. A man of my
profession is a servant of sorts, tending to his betters with the utmost
of respect. (This, at least, is my intention: I speak not for others, for —
such is the world — even in a profession such as mine there is, alas, a
disreputable element.) But what sort of servant would you think me, I
feared, when it reached you that my part of our little bargain had
been, thus far, wholly unfulfilled? I can only plead the times, for alas,
this year I delayed a little long in prosecuting my intention to return
to Agondon. Now, as perhaps you have heard, a certain distemper has
broken out in Varby, and (such is the need for our skills) all
gentlemen of my profession have been charged to remain in the town.
(How shocking to relate that some were tempted to flee! Fortunately,
the guards now keep them within the walls. You see, sir, the need to
choose wisely when you engage the services of a man of my
profession.)
 Yet it seems that my apologies would not be wholly appropriate.
In your concern for the health of a certain young lady, you urged that
I should attend upon her regularly, ensuring that certain potions
should not fail to pass her lips. Yet now I understand from my

correspondents in Agondon that the young lady has not, after all, arrived in the city; I gather, sir, that you, too, have also left the capital. It seems that our arrangement must (for the time, at least) be void. O pray for the health of the dear young lady, too far (alas) now from the reach of my art!

Nonetheless, sir, I should like to ensure you that my services shall always be at your disposal. You will appreciate that during my time in Varby I have gained a somewhat intimate knowledge of your affairs. Perhaps, too, you shall understand me when I add that my plans for the coming year were much dependent upon the arrangement we had made.

I am, honoured sir,
Delighted to be your servant,
F. Waxwell
(Licensed apothecary)

S.H.I.A.M.
SERVICE OF HIS IMPERIAL AGONIST MAJESTY

To Mjr. M. M. Heva-Harion, Secretary-General ASA, c/ Ascen. Mil. Cmd. Cent., Ollon Barracks, Agondon, from Lt. V. Vance, Under-Secretary to His Excellency Lord Michan, Governor-General & Supreme Commander of His Imperial Agonist Majesty's Forces in Zenzau.

Sir,

His Excellency the Governor-General has bade me convey his thanks for your intelligence of 1Wa/Vend., 999d. inst., pertaining to the secondment of Capt. Veeldrop. His Excellency wishes to state that he considers this idea an excellent one, & during the term of this secondment shall receive regular reports from Capt. Veeldrop's immediate commander. His Excellency remarks that voices, thought to be for ever silenced, have been raised again in support of the elder Veeldrop, whose reported success in governance of the Tarn has been thought by some to reflect poorly upon the present Zenzan administration. In view of this, His Excellency expects Capt. Veeldrop's inevitable disgrace & demotion, which he trusts shall be sufficient to warrant court-martial, to be of considerable use in putting the name of Veeldrop into correct perspective.

His Excellency further wishes to ascertain, before taking up the matter with higher authorities, the truth of a rumour which has now reached Wrax. It is said that the 17th Under-Secretary has been dispatched to the Tarn, with a view to recommending the ennoblement of its governor. His Excellency considers this prospect objectionable in strongest terms, wondering if the authorities have considered at all the impact such a move might have on the present Zenzan situation. In making this remark, His Excellency wishes to stress, however, that the support enjoyed in Zenzau by the Green Pretender is in no way attributable to the present administration, adding that the assumption that this might be the case is, in his view, a calumny of the first order. His Excellency wishes to remind those in Agondon of the difficulties of governing so intractable a colony, castigating those who sit in comfort in Agondon as mere parasites on the wealth of the empire, with no right to judge colonial affairs.

I am, sir,
With compliments,
V. Vance (Lt.)

(Govt, House, Wrax, B/Aros, 999d.)

Chapter 37

A RED BIRD

'Nirry!'

The bell jangled.

'Nirry!'

And again.

'Drat the girl, where can she have got to now?'

Umbecca Veeldrop sat up in her immense bed, propped against cushions of many colours. By her side, on the ornate counterpane, was a tray bearing the remnants of a greasy repast; on a little marble-topped cabinet by the bed, a further clutter of plates bore testimony to the hunger that had gnawed at her during the night.

And to the slovenly ways of her maid.

'Nirry!'

'Pray, dear lady, do not distress yourself,' came an urbane voice. Its owner was a slender fellow of indeterminate age, dressed in the black garb of the Order of Agonis. Perched beside the bed on a spindly Regency chair, he had crossed one long leg over the other and on his hands wore dainty white gloves. At his temples was a hint of grey. He was handsome, yet there was something a little cold, too cold, in his demeanour.

Eay Feval rose, making his way to the window. Outside, the Lectory garden lay frozen under a pall of snow. 'Perhaps you will allow me to relieve you of the annoyance?'

The annoyance in question was a small bobbing bird with a bright red breast and a ready song.

To-whit! To-whoo!

For some days the bird had kept returning. Happily it hopped on a high branch outside the window, a lone dash of colour against the barren garden. *Ugh! That jabbering*, Umbecca would say, or *Nirry! Your broomhandle!*

Sternly, Feval rapped his knuckles on the glass.

To-whit! To-whoo!

No good.

'Ma'am?' Nirry stood in the doorway, bearing a hastily brewed pot of tea. Her face was flushed and strands of lank hair escaped from the lacy frills of her cap. Tightly she clutched the heavy teapot as her mistress informed her – it happened every day – that she was an ungrateful, stupid girl, whose laxity could be tolerated no longer.

'Nirry, I hope you have not been entertaining a lover?'

The maid flushed.

'Too many girls in this village have gone to the bad since the soldiers came. Girls of precisely your class and type. Be warned, Nirry: should rumour of any sluttish dalliance come to my ears, you shall be dismissed at once without references.'

Nirry was moved to exclaim, 'Ma'am, I've been making the tea!'

'Really, girl! And why couldn't you bring in the tea with my tray?'

As it happened, Nirry had done so. This was the second pot; evidently Umbecca had forgotten the first. But Nirry attempted no further protest. The exchange was over for another morning. Umbecca's jowls swelled like a frog's and she gestured impatiently to the annoyance at the window. Nirry's lip trembled as she bobbed and withdrew. The bird was too high to reach from the ground, even with the prodding handle of the broom; a little later Nirry would appear outside the window, splay-footed on a branch halfway up the tree.

'Really, Chaplain, I don't know why one keeps that girl on. A sterner mistress would have thrown her out on the streets – oh, long ago.'

'But dear lady, you are all compassion. Here, allow me.' Eay Feval took up the teapot, pouring the liquid into the lady's cup. Umbecca smiled winsomely at her companion. It was his wont – or rather hers, to which he acceded – that they should meet like this each morning, before the household – the *family*, as Umbecca liked to say – had assembled for breakfast.

To Umbecca, breakfast was a meal in at least three stages. If the seed-cakes, the bread and cheese, the salt pork and Tarnfish and jars of pickle and chutney that she kept by her bed were for nocturnal emergencies, it must be admitted that no night, for Umbecca, was without emergency. The lady slept poorly, and invariably the early dawn found her awake, tucking into the first of what might be called her *unofficial* meals. To Umbecca this constituted not so much a breakfast as its preliminary, standing in relation to that meal as an artist's first sketch stands to a finished portrait in oils. After the cold collation came a steaming fry-up, brought by Nirry – and woe betide if it were not! – promptly upon the lady's official time of rising. There was not much to this tray-in-the-bed affair – a few meagre eggs, sausages, chops, fried tomatoes and onions, rashers of bacon, that sort of thing, just to take the edge off any gnawing hunger which might disrupt the lady's composure before at last, after the elaborate ritual of dressing, she descended to the dining-room – the *informal* dining-room – with its groaning sideboards of porridge and cream, apricots and prunes, more eggs, sausages, bacon, devilled kidneys and jellied eels, pressed ham and tongue, cold roast chicken, grouse, partridge, pheasant, venison, more dried fruit and fruit-in-orandy, scones and toast and honey and marmalade and jam, more pots of tea and rich Zaxos coffee.

There were some who fasted during the Time of Meditation, but as the practice, it seemed, had no scriptural warrant, Umbecca had decided it was hardly necessary. The servants of the Lord Agonis must keep up their strength.

'You slept well, dear lady?'

'Alas, not well. But Chaplain, as you know, I am a martyr to my digestion.'

'Ah, that one so dear should be so afflicted!'

'Chaplain, you are kind, but is it not a small burden the Lord Agonis has laid upon me? Am I to bemoan my own paltry ailments, when my dear husband' – Umbecca's eyes at once seemed to mist – 'languishes close to death in a room filled with foliage?'

'Speak not of it, dear lady!'

Umbecca blinked her tears away, reaching fondly for the chaplain's hand. Often she thought their sessions together were her favourite part of the day, the recompense – the *one* recompense – for her return to Irion. Of course, for a governor's wife there were things to look forward to – the fine clothes, the openings, the parades, the receptions, the Very Important Persons to amuse (Lord Margrave, their current visitor, being a case in point). But a woman in her position must be always on display. Only with the chaplain could Umbecca be herself. Yet there was nothing improper in their intimacy; theirs was a relationship of the spirit. Quietly, calmly, they would review their affairs. There was much to discuss – after all, with her husband so unwell, the lady was running not so much a household as a province!

The chaplain sifted through the morning's post. A tradesman's bill. Latest despatches. A top-secret report on the Zenzan crisis, marked for the eyes of the governor only. Umbecca sighed, brightening only at the prospect of *The Ladies' Gazette*.

'There is an account of Lady Cham-Charing's Festival Levee, I trust?'

'I'm sure there is,' said the chaplain glumly.

The last thing was a letter.

Honoured FATHER,

Alas, my return to my dear HOME is delayed again. Zenzau beckons, and every SOLDIER OF THE KING must play his part. The talk is of reprisals on a scale never seen, now that the Pretender's forces threaten Wrax itself.

'Oh my poor Poltiss!' Umbecca's voice trembled; Feval's, for its part, took on a certain sourness as he went on:

> FATHER, I curse anything that keeps me from you. How I long to bask again in your love! Yet this time, this one time – how, I ask myself, can I regret the cause? For though there is no bliss I could desire more than to cast myself at the feet of my FATHER, first – how I know it! – I must avenge his dear HONOUR on the fields of the hated enemy kingdom. FATHER, if I should die, weep not for me, I pray you. For know, whether I live, whether I die, it is in glory – for I live, I die, as a MAN, an EJLANDER, but more, more – as a VEELDROP!
>
> My great love to my honoured MOTHER UMBECCA, and CATAYANE, the dear SISTER of my heart.

'Hm.' Respectfully the chaplain waited for Umbecca's tears to subside. 'I barely think the father should survive the son's loss.'

'We should none of us,' sniffed Umbecca.

'But Catayane? Your husband is determined she should marry the boy.'

'Speak not of the girl! Her behaviour makes me ever more impatient.'

'Then you have put it to her, dear lady?'

'Put it, Chaplain?'

'Your husband's wishes? You do not think she would resist, were it necessary – shall we say – to *enforce* those wishes?'

Umbecca sighed, 'The girl is as ever – *as ever*, that is, since returning home. I knew it was a mistake to bring her here. Every day, the same faraway look in her eyes. Every day, the profits of an expensive education whittled away a little bit more.' Umbecca dabbed her eyes, and bitterness entered her voice. 'And where shall we be, I wonder, if this Margrave proves ungenerous, and we are left with the girl still Unentered, her hour already past?'

'Lord Margrave likes her,' observed the chaplain.

'Chaplain! Lord Margrave is a married man!'

The chaplain only smiled and cleared his throat. After a moment he said brightly, pouring more tea, 'Trouble in the Dale of Rodek again.'

The Vaga-camp had been shifted there, to remove it from the eyes of respectable folk.

'Another riot?' Umbecca's voice was distant.

'Stolen pitchfork. Hedgerows trampled. Flock of sheep released and running wild. Goody Orly's barn burnt again. All the winter feed—'

'Feed? Oh, abominable!' That did the trick. 'Chaplain, should we – should my dear husband – order another *round of hangings*?'

'My thoughts exactly.'

To-whit! To-whoo! came the bird at the window. A flicker of annoyance crossed Umbecca's face, but she rose above it and continued, with a pleasant smile, 'Perhaps, after Lord Margrave has departed—'

'Or while he is here, dear lady?'

'Chaplain, you surprise me. Lord Margrave enjoys such sport? He seems so refined a man.'

'He is a politician, dear lady!'

It was almost as if there was no more to be said.

But there was.

'Think of it: we have exercised restraint, these late moonlives. Since the Fifth Royal were ordered south, one has felt, it cannot be denied, a little ... vulnerable, with fewer men than we had before. Now the Blue Irions, too, are off to Zenzau. But restraint, for all that, is no policy. What can it seem but weakness to the lower orders, the Tarn-trash, the Vaga-scum—'

'And to Lord Margrave?'

'Quite. When the Koros-season thaws, that gentleman will leave us. Before then, might we not reveal to him the rod of iron beneath the soft garb of our justice, our mercy, our compassion and clemency? I mean, our dear governor's.'

'His ... rod?'

'His firmness.'

'Hm. Indeed.' Umbecca cast down her eyes.

The poor lady! Before her marriage to Commander Veeldrop, she had known many, too many, disappointments; but there were, too, certain disappointments she had known *since* her marriage.

She enquired delicately, 'You have not, then, managed to speak to Lord Margrave?'

There was a scuffling at the window. Nirry, at last, was carrying out her orders. Shivering in the lower branches of the elm, the maid prodded her broom-handle at the oblivious bird.

To-whit! To-whoo!

'Dear lady' – the chaplain chose to ignore the interruption – 'one speaks to His Lordship daily. The weather, the Zenzan crisis, the merits of Coppergate's early work and late ... But alas, he is a gentleman of great reserve. Of formality—'

'Oh, formality!' cried Umbecca, a little too loudly, riding over the muted crashings that sounded from the vicinity of the window.

Nirry, it seemed, was climbing higher in the branches.

'What is formality,' her mistress plunged on, 'but an encouragement to the *cold* nature, such as seems to have afflicted this noble lord? I would do away with it forthwith, and have only natural intercourse!'

The chaplain smiled his assent. Leaning forward, he may have been imparting a confidence to the lady.

'His Lordship is calculating as well as cold. To another, his mission would be the merest sinecure, just so much amusement for an old gentleman on the brink of retirement from the King's service. Another, entertained so fulsomely at our expense, would recommend the peerage without demur. But this lord, I am afraid, will weigh and consider, weigh and consider.'

'I begin to think this lord is a monster!'

'He is scrupulously fair.'

'But could it be that his report will not be favourable?'

Thwack! Thwack! went the broom-handle, crashing through the barren branches outside.

The bird ignored it; the chaplain did the same. 'This lord, as I say, is scrupulously fair. Like a goldsmith's scales, he will hold in the balance: on one side, the offence – the *presumed* offence; on the other, all that has been done to redeem it. Alas, dear lady, we cannot forget that your husband was sent here as a punishment of sorts, after his humiliation at the hands of The Red Avenger . . .'

Thwack! came the broom-handle, and *To-whit! To-whoo!*, but this time Umbecca's abstractedness was real. Her bulk shuddered suddenly as she recalled her dear Torvester, swinging from the gallows on the village green. *Oh, Tor!* she had sobbed on the day he died. *Why, why did you do these things to me?* Afterwards something inside her had hardened, hardened and kept hardening, but still, from time to time, would come this wash of emotion.

Umbecca lowered her eyes; the chaplain, understanding his error, altered his course with typical finesse, speaking not of the commander's humiliations – it was a large topic – but rather of the immense good, the *peerage-earning* good, he had done here in the Tarn.

His words were buoyant, but inside he was troubled. If he prayed – though he did not, not for himself – his prayer would have been a desperate plea, *Liege of Light, give the old man the peerage, please – and keep him alive just long enough to accept it!*

Umbecca had her own private thoughts. To think, that all the children of her care had gone to the bad, then forfeited their lives for wickedness. It was just, but oh, how cruel! Tor . . . Ela . . . even poor little Jem, sizzled to cinders in a lightning-flash . . . The boy had been depraved, corrupted by Vaga-evil. And yet, when he died he was about to be saved. Had he been wholly abandoned, even in the end? Fondly Umbecca had prayed it was not so. Tor, Ela, she must cast to the winds, but Jem – dear little Jem . . .

And what would become of Catayane?

The reverie ended suddenly.

Thwack! came the broom-handle at the window again, but this time the sounds – familiar by now – were followed at once by a crash and a scream.

'What?' The chaplain leapt up.

But it was simple, of course: climbing too high, the maid had lost her balance; the broom-handle had crashed through a window-pane, the bird had started and flown away, and Nirry had fallen out of the tree.

'Oh,' Umbecca burst out, 'that stupid girl! That stupid, stupid girl!'

Chapter 38

VOICE FROM THE FOG

'This is the place?'

'It is.'

'The fog! I can hardly see a thing.'

'I dare say it will clear by dusk.'

'If not?'

Pellam gave a curt laugh. 'Postponement, Nova, is up to the defender. Like everything else, really, when a gentleman issues a challenge. If you refuse this duel, Burgrove can seek you out and kill you in the street. Go ahead, and you play by his rules. Still, the fog may be to our advantage. The fewer people who know about this, the better!'

Jem looked out into the churning whiteness. Sober in their Meditation-suits, they had driven out early to inspect the scene of the impending duel. The Verge, a slushy strip of land to the west of New Town, was the last remnant of the old Ollon Fields. On the Town side, behind high hedges and a spiky fence, were the Pleasure Gardens. Dimly Jem made out the great wheel of the circle-ride, rising silent and ghostly in the morning. To the east, invisible through the haze, were the neat roads and gardens of the merchant precincts, Ollon-Quintal, Elabetha, Ejland Park.

Yes, perhaps it was good that the fog had fallen. On a clear day only a line of larches, barren now in the cold, protected the Verge from sight.

Pellam flicked the horses and they drove round the rim, looking despairingly at the mud and slush. In the centre, Pell explained, was Marmy's Stump, formerly Marmy's Tree, where Marmy Heva-Harion had bested Sir Rentby Dravil, Agondon's great dandy in the time of the Regent Queen. Now the stump was the place where all duels began.

Jem looked at it curiously.

'Of course, Marmy himself died of his wounds, a phase later,' said Pell. 'Internal bleeding. Very nasty. No, Nova,' he added, 'I don't think you know what you've got yourself into!'

'Do you have to keep saying that?' Jem shifted irritably. He was cold and had developed a sharp desire to relieve himself. 'You've made it abundantly clear that no gentleman would lower himself to challenge a cad like Burgrove, so it's bad enough I did that. Then of course I went and did it in Meditations, when anyone caught duelling will be carted off to the dungeons, flayed, then drawn and quartered.'

Pell laughed, 'Hardly! But Nova, you do realize what happens if the Watch find you? As challenger, you're liable.'

'For what?'

'Everything! Oh, as Lord Empster's ward, you'll be let off with a caution, of course you will. But the scandal, Nova! Do you want to end up like Burgrove, outlawed from decent society?'

'He spends a lot of time at Chokey's.'

'Droll, Nova. But I don't think you saw him at Lady Cham's, did you? Well, you won't – ever. Really, Nova, I ought to check under your wig. I fear there's a hole in the back of your head, and all the knowledge I've put in there is leaking out again. Drip, drip, out it comes.'

Jem squirmed. 'Would you mind stopping for a moment, Pell?' He leapt down, retreating modestly into the fog, his gloved hands fumbling awkwardly at the front of his breeches.

Steam rose acridly from the gurgling current.

'Hello, Nova,' came a voice.

Jem turned, buttoning. A shivering figure in purple loomed through the fog. 'Raj? What are you doing here?'

'Same as you. I wanted to see the place.'

'Raj, go home! I thought you'd gone back to the Royal. Don't you know what they'd do to a Vaga, if they thought you were caught up in this?'

'You might be killed.' Suddenly Rajal seemed much younger, much more vulnerable.

'Raj, it's Burgrove!' Jem said kindly. 'It'll be a miracle if the sot can hold his rapier straight.'

'He's angry and stupid and doesn't play fair. Your fine friend talks about the code of a gentleman. The Children of Koros have their own code, Nova.'

'Nova!' came a call from the carriage. 'Nova?'

Jem ignored it. 'What code?'

'I was a coward last night. You defended me. Now I must defend you. I shall fight for you.'

'Raj, you're mad!'

'I'm not.' Rajal's voice came levelly now and a proud determination flashed in his eyes. 'You're too important, Jem. If you die, what happens then?'

Understanding came only slowly to Jem. He stumbled forward, gripping his friend's hands. 'Raj, what did you call me – just then?'

'Jem – Jemany. It's your name, isn't it? And one day you'll be Jemany the First.'

'You knew all along? But I thought—'

'Nova!' called Pell. 'Really, Nova, have you frozen in the cold?'

They ignored him again and Rajal muttered quickly, 'I didn't know, I didn't know for a long time. It was after I broke from you, that last day. The knowledge came to me – just came to me, as if with a fluttering of bright wings. I like to think it was a parting gift.'

'Myla?'

'And I thought she didn't love me. Oh, what a fool I've been – such a fool. But not any more. That's why I know I have to fight for you, Jem.'

'No!' Wonderment, alarm churned in Jem's mind. 'Raj, I don't care who I am, but you're not fighting for me or anyone! How can a Vaga win a duel?'

Rajal broke away, insulted.

'You think I can't use a sword, is that it? I was always better at the Swords Play than you, and I've learnt a lot with the Masks, Jem.'

'Raj, it doesn't matter! I tell you, you can't win. If he kills you, you're dead. But you kill him and you're dead, too. Burgrove's an Ejlander. He can get away with murder. He's done it before and he'll do it again.'

Flustered, Jem grabbed his friend again, ripping the glove from the end of his arm.

'Raj, look at this skin! Get it into your head, you're a Vaga!'

'I know that, Jem!'

'Do you? Then you know what happens if you kill an Ejlander? Your own father was hanged for less. Raj, you're my friend – I begin to think you're my best friend. But if you don't give up this mad idea, you're no friend of mine.'

'Jem, please!'

'Promise me, Raj. Just promise me this.'

Rajal bit his lip. He nodded.

'Nova!' Pell, his patience worn thin, trudged towards them. 'You're not going to spend all morning talking to that Vaga-boy, are you? Wasn't it enough, gadding about with him last night?'

'We weren't gadding about.'

'I'll be the judge of that. Or rather, the great world shall – and frankly, Nova, at this rate I fear your career in society is over before it's begun. I hope you weren't thinking seriously about Miss Vance, is all I can say. I'd think she's pretty much off-limits to a Vaga-lover, wouldn't you? Now come on, First Canonical starts soon.'

During this speech, Pell did not look once into Rajal's face; he did not even bother to lower his voice. Indignation churned inside Jem, but all he could think to say as he was bundled back to the carriage was, 'Pell, you don't understand.'

They drove off in silence.

Rajal slumped down on Marmy's Stump. He wept.

Chapter 39

PORCELAIN OF THE FINEST

'Dungeons? Well I never!'

The chaplain intervened, 'Dear lady, there are those in Agondon who look on a dungeon rather as we might regard a theatre. Is that not so, Lord Margrave?'

Deftly Lord Margrave extracted a strip of bacon-rind from his porcelain teeth. So deftly was it done, indeed, that Umbecca could not help admiring the gentleman. A cold fellow, yes, but was not there a hint of suppressed fires? She felt the corner of her little mouth twitch, as if about to form her *enigmatic smile*.

Instead she offered with a sigh, 'The theatre! Alas, our little province is barren of such amusements. What must you think of us, Lord Margrave?'

'Madam, I am not one given to the theatre.'

'Ah.'

'Lector Feval, I gather that you, in your Agondon days, were perhaps more familiar with such establishments?'

'Hardly, my lord! Yet it may be that a man of the cloth must explore life in all its diversity. And when he serves in a great metropolis, is this not, perhaps, doubly so?'

'Dungeons?' came another voice, like a slow echo.

Lord Margrave turned, and would at that point have explained his interest in Irion's dungeons. Since arriving in the province, he would have said, he had seen much: the spiky new railings round the village green; the new 'Varby' layout of the Lectory gardens; the splendid new temple that was rising so rapidly above the ruins of the old.

In the castle, he had seen the new towers on the keep; he had seen the Blue Irions in their dress uniforms and the boys' band performing the Canticle of the Flag; but it was vital to his report, too, to explore the less *pleasant* aspects of the province. What were the stories that had reached his ears about the establishment called the Lazy Tiger? Why had the Children of Koros, he wondered, been hidden from his view? And how many miserable folk would he find, languishing in the cells deep beneath the castle?

Lord Margrave was a gentleman of the old school; he sought not merely appearances, but what lay beneath them.

But before he could begin, the questioner went on, in a faraway voice, 'A dungeon is a place beneath the ground. Beneath the ground there may be many secrets. Beautiful secrets. Terrible secrets . . .'

'Ignore the girl, Lord Margrave,' Umbecca burst out. 'Catayane, had you not better be eating your breakfast, instead of troubling Lord Margrave? Widow Waxwell, help the girl to a little more pressed venison.' Umbecca dropped her voice. 'See, my lord, the compassion of my husband, in taking in such waifs and strays?'

'Extraordinary.' The noble lord looked frankly at the two figures who sat at the far end of the table. Admiringly his gaze lingered on the dark-eyed, faun-like girl, in her little-girl costume of crisp white satin. With her long black hair scraped severely back, her expression had in it something disconcertingly startled, as if there had been some secret she had once known, but forgotten, she knew not how or where. Last season, he gathered, she had been in Varby, but it was difficult to imagine this girl before him now as a young lady of fashion. Several times Madam Veeldrop had hinted that the girl had been unwell.

The figure opposite Miss Catayane was different as could be, a withered crone dressed piously in black, white-haired and thin as a stick. Often Lord Margrave had been disturbed by her demeanour. The Widow Waxwell spoke seldom; few expressions passed across her parchment face; if there were a pattern in her slow movements, it concerned the careful folding and concealing of her arms – in her lap, behind her back, beneath the table – to mask the fact that she was missing a hand.

The old woman's deformity was cruelly exposed as blunderingly she endeavoured to help her young companion to further, and unwanted, slices of meat. For some moments Umbecca watched the inept perform-ance; at last, with a compassionate smile, she waved the Widow away and rang the little bell she kept beside her plate.

'Ma'am?'

Umbecca drew in her breath, ready to issue a stream of instructions; instead, she looked at her maid in astonishment. 'Girl, what are you playing at?'

But the answer was obvious. On Nirry's last appearance, she had been limping; in the interim, from some dusty cupboard or other, she had acquired a pair of crutches.

'Ooh, ma'am, my ankle's swelled up something shocking!'

Loudly the crutches clumped on the floorboards as Nirry dragged herself slowly round the room. Annoying, it was true; but Lord Mar-grave found himself puzzled nonetheless by the ashen tinge which had come to Umbecca's face, and the stranger look – as if some memory had flashed through her mind – that came over the face of Miss Catayane.

The girl intrigued him.

'And you say she was a wild creature, living in the woods with no human language?' he whispered, turning back to Umbecca. 'Yet now she seems – why, almost genteel!'

The chaplain laughed politely, 'The girl *is* a product of Mistress Quick's. Your wit does you credit, Lord Margrave!'

'I intended none.'

'Ah, but does not a gentleman often accomplish more than he intends?' Umbecca had collected herself; her little mouth twitched at the corners again. 'But come, Lord Margrave, if your wit does you credit, your appetite does you none. Can you claim to have made a good breakfast? So vital, would you not say, for the energies a gentleman might be called upon to expend?'

'Madam, your generosity knows no bounds. But you will join me, then, in a little more jellied eel?'

'Lord Margrave, you are a tempter! A lady must peck at her food, like a dear little bird, peck and no more. How else she is to keep that *sand-timer shape* you gentlemen insist upon, I don't know.' Umbecca essayed her enigmatic smile. 'Why, often it is as much as I can do to *keep down* the merest morsel—'

The chaplain cleared his throat. 'The girl Catayane,' he murmured, 'is a bird who has been tamed. And might not her taming stand as a symbol for what our glorious commander has achieved, here in these wild and mysterious valleys?'

Lord Margrave eyed the girl with a chaste admiration.

'Of course, it was our old friend Goodman Waxwell who *cured* her,' burbled Umbecca, a little too loudly, heaping her plate high with eel, onion rings, partridge and prunes. 'Our family physician. The child was the last case he treated before his tragic death, was she not, Chaplain? Ah, but we must not distress Widow Waxwell . . .'

'As I was saying,' Eay Feval said tightly, 'the commander—'

'There is no prospect, I gather, that the distinguished gentleman may join us?'

Lord Margrave looked pointedly to the head of the table, where once again the commander's throne-like chair stood empty. Since arriving in Irion, the noble lord had been granted only the briefest of interviews with the commander. Shocking; but the interview itself had shocked him, too – he, who recalled the Grand Victory March through Agondon, when Veeldrop had returned from the Siege of Irion! How could it be that they were one and the same, the steely victor of those glory days and the stricken old man who bore the same name, a monstrous inert doll in his epaulettes and sashes, who kept his eyes shaded with a visor and permitted his chaplain to make his replies?

'Alas, my poor husband must be conspicuous by his absence – a *little* longer, just a little longer.'

Umbecca smiled again; Lord Margrave's look was stern. 'But he does, in the regular course—'

'Does! Good my lord, what does he not?' Eay Feval gestured expansively, 'Why, even now, Lord Margrave, might we not ask if the governor is really absent? Like the Ur-God's, his works lie all around us.'

'Hm.' This bordered on blasphemy, but Lord Margrave let it pass. In truth, he had been distracted, and was making another attempt, less successfully this time, to remove some obstruction – some little eel-bone? – from his porcelain teeth.

He gave up and plunged on, 'Since arriving here in Irion I have seen much—'

'Explored life in all its diversity?' said the chaplain.

Not all, the noble lord would have continued, but the chaplain's intervention had been unfortunate. Tripping over his words, suddenly Lord Margrave was seized with a fit of coughing. He slumped forward, his teeth swinging loose.

'Oh dear me! Water!' cried Umbecca, leaping up, jangling for Nirry again. 'Chaplain, beat Lord Margrave on the back!'

A hollow *thump!* echoed round the room as the chaplain, with a surprising heartiness, complied with the instruction. Lord Margrave barked out a last loud cough and his teeth fell, clattering, into his plate.

'Oh dear, oh dear.' Umbecca seized his hand. 'Lord Margrave, you are not well. Come, you must lie down—'

'Madam, please . . .'

It was over in an instant; really, it was nothing. With the deftness Umbecca had admired before, Lord Margrave sat erect again and pushed his teeth back in place.

'No damage done . . . One must be careful, it is true. I am an old man, and my heart has not the strength it once had. But this is nothing, nothing.'

Chapter 40

GIRL READING

'I'll have you, Becca!' the vile man cried.

'Have me, then!' I ripped open my night-dress.

He lingered before me, licking his lips, gazing on my heaving, exposed breasts. When he stepped forward, I steeled myself for his rough embrace, but none came.

'Ah no, Becca! Offer yourself to me, will you, in superior contempt? In self-sacrifice, to protect your foolish brother against the wrath of my bailiffs? No, my haughty beauty! When you ascend to my bed, it shall not be as a martyr.'

He ran his hot fingers down my cheek. I shuddered.

'Becca, don't you understand? Is it only your body I seek? You are a weak woman, and I am a man. We are alone in a remote moorland mansion, leagues from help. Why, you might call all you would, and no one would come. Now, at this very moment, I could fling you to the bed and take my pleasure.'

His voice was soft, hot against my ear.

'No, Becca, it is not only your body I want. Don't you understand? I want your heart.'

'Poor Becca! What shall become of her?'

But reading-time was over for another afternoon. Cata slipped the marker in place and closed the book. Sighing, the old man pushed back his visor, wiping at the tears that had gathered in his eyes. How many times had he heard the story? He had lost count. But never had it been so moving before.

Oh, the child's reading left much to be desired. With his wife, or the chaplain, there had been a colour, a fire, far beyond the range of so novice a performer. But what did it matter? Behind the child's words was a welling love; there had been no love, he knew, in the other voices. Fondly the old man looked back on the days when the child had first come to him, confused and barely knowing her own name. But he, too, had lost himself, he saw that now. Perhaps each had called to the other out of a mutual loneliness. She had taught him to love, freely, selflessly; and slowly, laboriously, he had taught her to read.

He should never have let them take her away.

The fire crackled through a clearing in the foliage. Snow pattered lightly on the glass above, and on the marquetry table by the commander's bed an ornate lantern gave an insistent, snake-like *hiss.*

'Dear child.'

The old man pressed Cata's hand to his lips; she smiled shyly. Could it be, he wondered, that this was truly Wolveron's daughter? Often the old man felt an impulse rising within him, immense but obscure. One day, he saw dimly, he would heave forward his stricken bulk, clutching the child to him; *Becca's First Ball* would slip from her hands and thud to the floor. Perhaps then his faded eyes would flame, burning into hers as he sobbed, 'Child, how can you love me? You pity me, but do you not know why these eyes have failed? Why the body in which they lodge – once the body of a hero – has been reduced to a diseased hulk? It is fate's punishment, the punishment of my evil! Child, I am the one who blinded your father, tortured him and blinded him in the dungeons beneath the castle.'

And then?

It was unimaginable; but the old man, more dimly still, fancied that the child might reach forward fondly, running her hands over his ruined face, his hair. Together they would sob, and her tears of forgiveness would fall upon his head like a soothing balm.

But no. What use could it be to speak aloud? Waxwell's potions had done their work; the child remembered nothing of her Wildwood days, and besides, her father could not be restored to her now. For a time, the blind man had languished in the dungeons; but he had died – oh, long ago, died in filth and darkness.

Now the commander felt his own death looming near, and in his last days had come to feel a pained kinship with the man he had wronged so grievously. In agony he saw himself, again and again, his mailed fist taking up the rod, his thin lips creasing into a cruel smile as he quenched the searing tip – once, then again – in the implacable dark pools of the hermit's eyes.

Hiss! went the eye-flesh; then again, *Hiss!*

The commander shivered at the memory of his evil, and shame, like the death that would soon claim him, descended over his stricken being like a pall. There was nothing he could do for Old Wolveron now.

But oh, but if he could make it up to the dear, oblivious daughter!

He kept her hand in his and pressed it, long and hard; Cata gazed back wonderingly. How drawn she felt, how strangely drawn, to this old man with the faded eyes! But though she loved him, still she felt troubled. Once, he had asked her to call him *Papa,* but she could not.

Why was that? Sometimes she seemed to sense a voice on the air, whispering words she could not quite catch.

But now it was the commander who was whispering, drawing her close as he murmured, like a lover, 'Do you know what a notary is, child?'

'A notary? Miss Cata, why?'

'Oh, something the commander said. I wondered.'

'There's a gentleman in the village. It's all to do with – oh, quality-folk, isn't it? Things they want to write down.'

'Hm. Yes.'

It was later that afternoon. Huddled in furs, the maid and Miss Cata were taking their daily walk – or rather, Miss Cata was taking her walk, while Nirry stumped miserably behind her on crutches.

Nirry was not sure where the crutches had come from. She had not seen them in her broom-cupboard before, but there they were, waiting, just when she needed them. Odd, what you saw. Odd what you didn't. But oh, they were wretched things, these sticks! Again and again they stuck in the snow, or slithered on the grass-clumps and tree-roots underneath. More than once the maid had swayed and almost fallen.

She hung back, panting. They would go home soon, wouldn't they? Already the sun was descending sharply, bathing the frosty tombyard in a rich haze of gold.

'Nirry?' Cata turned back. 'Tell me about my husband.'

'Miss Cata, what can you mean?'

But Nirry knew. It was a demand Miss Cata had made before, though as the days passed, it seemed, her curiosity was greater. The commander had put the idea in her head that one day she would marry – of all fellows! – Master Poltiss. Nirry would have thought Miss Cata would be hardly pleased by this idea; Nirry herself by no means approved. But Miss Cata did not quite remember Master Poltiss, or much else from the days before they sent her to Quick's.

Nirry began, 'Your husband-to-be—'

'My husband-to-be!'

Miss Cata hugged herself and did a little twirl, spinning with strange lightness in her Koros-season clothes. Whatever did she imagine? What had become of her Varby-dreams? Oh, she was a strange girl, right enough!

Nirry's eyes flickered over the tomb-slabs, the wall, the clean, spare lines of the new Temple of Agonis. Now Miss Cata sprang up on a tomb-slab, kicking powdery snow in all directions.

'Miss Cata, really!'

Was there ever such a girl? For a moment Nirry wished she could haul herself away, just haul herself away and leave the girl. But of course, she would not – could not. She loved Miss Cata, loved her as much as she hated the mistress.

Of course, the girl was wilful, perverse. Since coming back to Irion, she had been worse than ever. She needed to be watched all the time. *Where is Miss Catayane?* It was a question Nirry must be able to answer. Once, the girl had gone wandering in the Wildwood, all by herself when night was falling. More than once, when they had thought she was sleeping, she had left her fine apartment and all its silk and lace, only to be found huddled on the pile of old clothes that Nirry kept for rag in a room behind the scullery.

Sometimes it was hard to believe Miss Cata was a quality-lady. But then, wasn't she a feral, and a Vaga-blood, too? There were times, thought Nirry, when it was only too clear. The time when she had climbed up on the gable-end, moaning and chanting at the Hornlight moon. The time when she had burst into Nirry's kitchen, shrieking and upending a cauldron of stew. Poor Nirry had almost been scalded to death!

They should never have brought her back to Irion.

Twirl, twirl, went Miss Cata on the tomb-slab. Above her spread the branches of an ancient yew-tree.

'And my husband will be a fine gentleman, Nirry?'

Fine gentleman? Nirry remembered Polty when he was a fat drunkard, lying in his own filth in a room at the Lazy Tiger. But she called back tightly, 'Master Poltiss is the governor's son. A finer gentleman you could not hope to find.'

Twirl, twirl. 'You knew him, Nirry?'

'Of course. So did you.'

'Before I was sick? I knew there was a gentleman, before I was sick!'

Nirry blanched. 'You'll be sick again, if you're not careful. Now come on, Miss Cata!'

Nirry only wanted to be home. Would a bluff work? Her arms and back were aching, not to mention her ankle. She turned sharply, swung herself away. It was no good. Pain coursed through her and she wailed, 'Oh, I don't know how Master Jem coped!'

'What's that?'

Mid-twirl, Miss Cata stopped. She did not even stagger.

Nirry faltered, 'I said, I don't know how I cope.'

What else could she say? Hadn't the mistress warned her – on pain of instant dismissal – never, never to mention Master Jem? *Not to me, not to the chaplain. And never – do you understand me, girl? – never to Miss Catayane.* Tears welled in the maid's eyes as the image of the young master rose before her. Oh, how could he be dead? How could her dear little boy be dead? And to think, he had loved this strange, wild girl!

Nirry sagged on the arm-holds of the crutches.

'Poor Nirry!' At once Miss Cata was beside her, circling her arm tightly round the maid's shoulders. For a hopeful moment Nirry thought they might go back. Instead, Miss Cata plumped herself down on the tomb-slab.

'Come Nirry, sit by me. Will you tell me a story?'

Awkwardly the maid lowered herself to the slab, her crutches clattering as they slipped from beneath her arms. Tell a story, out here in the snow? They'd catch their deaths. But oh, the relief, to sit just for a moment!

'Will you tell me of the castle, Nirry? Or the times before the soldiers came? It must have been lonely, wasn't it, Nirry? Just you and the mistress? Poor Nirry, did you have no one else to care for?'

Nirry snuffled, eyeing glumly a certain small bird that hopped about nonchalantly on a neighbouring slab, its bright breast almost purple in the waning light.

What could Nirry say? Much, too much; but nothing that wouldn't break her promise to the mistress. The bird trilled a soft *To-whit! To-whoo!* and fluttered up to the yew-branch above. That was when Nirry had an idea, and turned to her companion with a guarded eagerness.

'Perhaps *you* could tell me a story, Miss Cata. I mean, a sort of story—'

'Nirry! You know I have no memory.'

'No, but you can read.'

'I have no book.'

She needed none. Carefully the maid reached into her moth-eaten coat, drawing forth a crumpled letter. 'It's for me, isn't it?'

Proudly she pointed to the back, where a squiggle of ink formed the shape of an ear. 'Wiggler said he'd ... Then I'd know it was him, you see. Oh, you'll read it to me, Miss Cata, won't you?'

Nirry was ashamed as much as excited, flushing scarlet as Miss Cata broke the seal. The first impression was of swathes of Sosenican ink, applied in thick brushstrokes, obscuring many lines. What was left was written in a sharply sloping, intelligent script, not the blotted, wobbling characters of a member of the lower orders.

The phrasing was often of the most convoluted kind.

Miss Cata's brow furrowed, but the explanation was clear: sender and scribe were not the same, and references to *the Professor* and *good old Morvy* soon indicated who the latter might be.

'Good old Morvy,' Nirry echoed, but his sharp, small writing was hard to read; only laboriously did Miss Cata make out that Wiggler had been back in, of all places, Holluch-on-the-Hill – 'Holluch!' Nirry wailed. 'Why, we just missed him!' – and would you believe his old Dad could still wiggle his ears with the best of them? Miss Cata stumbled, but Nirry's eyes shone.

Dear Miss Cata! Was there ever a more wonderful young lady? Alternately the poor maid smiled and frowned, then laughed and cried as she learnt that her young man was a corporal now – 'Ooh, he'll be strutting like a turkey-cock!' – and Sergeant Bunch **BLANK** and those rotten Zenzans **BLANK BLANK** and one day, one day when **BLANK BLANK BLANK** that little tavern they'd . . .

Understanding dawned only slowly on Miss Cata.

'Nirry! You have a husband-to-be? Just like me?'

'Oh no, miss! Not like you! Why, you shall be a quality-lady, and I shall . . . I mean, it would only be if . . . Oh, Miss Cata, you won't tell the mistress, will you?'

Laughing, Miss Cata swore that she would not.

'Why, Nirry, perhaps one day you shall be *my* maid! You and your husband, perhaps, shall tend my husband and me?'

The girl, it seemed, had not quite understood Wiggler's reference to the little tavern. Nirry thought it best not to mention it now. She only smiled gratefully and blinked away her tears as she returned the precious letter to her coat.

Next to her heart!

Oh, how could she ever thank Miss Cata?

※　※　※

'Nirry,' the young mistress said, as they made their way back towards the Lectory. Fondly, supportively, she gripped the maid's arm. 'You'd like to send a letter back to Wiggler, wouldn't you?'

Nirry gasped, 'Miss Cata, would you?'

'Of course! But Nirry, as you know, I'm only a simple girl. I can't write as well as the Professor, now, can I? I wonder if . . .'

Behind them, the solitary bird in the yew-branch trilled a desultory *To-whit! To-whoo!*

Miss Cata paused, considering. She turned to her companion, her eyes wide. 'Nirry, the notary! Do you think he would see us?'

Chapter 41

THE CLASH

'Draw, villain!'

'What, against a whelp like you?'

'No whelp, villain, but your nemesis, facing you at last!'

Gazing with contempt on the flaxen-haired young Ejlander, Skyle Kelming-Skyle only sneered. The villain was the very embodiment of depravity. The nose was long and hooked, the lips thick and sensual. A mongrel of a man, his hot veins sloshed with the degenerate blood of Zenzan, Sosenican, even Vaga-kind. He sported golden earrings and an oiled black beard, after the fashion of Kal-Theron. 'What, ho!' cried Kelming-Skyle, 'Debauch my young ward, whelp, then call me villain?'

Reeves Roamer could barely contain his contempt. All around them the stones of the great castle pressed evilly, suppurating and dank. 'I have offered my hand,' Roamer breathed, his teeth gritted, 'in honourable marriage to the Lady Olwena!'

'Your hand? Yes, and she shall have it, whelp, when I hack it from your arm!' Skyle drew. 'Let her clutch it to her breast tonight as I take my ancestral rights at last, rending the frail membrane of her virtue!'

Their swords clashed.

'Jemany?'

Jem sat glumly in Lord Empster's library. For some time he had been barely attending to the pages of *Prince of Swords*. Once it had enthralled him; now it seemed merely flat, stale. It was late afternoon. Outside the windows, the fog still churned; on the mantelpiece, the clock ticked loudly, thudding away the mechs, oltons, fives. Dusk would come early at this time of year. Soon, very soon, Pell would return. Then they would drive back to the Verge.

Lord Empster said again, 'Jemany?'

Jem started. His guardian stood before the fire, warming his hands. Beneath one arm were his gloves and stick, and he still wore his hat, as if he had returned just moments earlier from some expedition. There were spatters of mud on his boots. He turned, his cloak swishing. Suddenly Jem was frightened.

'I hear, Jemany, that you have insulted Mr Burgrove.'

'My lord?' Blunderingly Jem pushed back his chair, rising. Above the mantelpiece was a large gold mirror. The room swam in its sepia haze; Jem snapped his eyes from it. 'My lord, you are mistaken.'

Lord Empster smiled wryly, 'It is untrue, then, that you and Mr Burgrove are to meet at dusk? I am glad to hear it. A sad comment on the age, is it not, that such tales flutter from ear to ear even in this most hallowed of times? Why, the very pews in the Great Temple ripple with gossip of Nova, Nova!'

Jem said softly, 'I meant, my lord, that I have not insulted Mr Burgrove.'

'You did *not* strike him in Webster's Coffee House? I may comfort myself, then, with the old saying, *The mills of rumour grind small, but theirs is a grain without flavour of fact?* But of course, my young ward could not be such a fool.'

Jem said softly, 'You may be right, my lord, that I am a fool. But am I not *your* fool? Have you not instructed me in the code of a gentleman? Now, when I would live by that code, you condemn me. Burgrove has grievously insulted my friend.'

'Your friend? A Vaga-boy! Jemany, I call you a fool, and mean it.'

'Save your breath. Pell said as much.'

'Pellam is as bad! He was to be your second in this folly, was he not?'

'Was? What do you mean, *was*?'

Lord Empster stepped forward, lighting his pipe. Blue smoke curled round the brim of his hat. 'There will be no duel, Jemany. Moments ago, I returned from Mr Burgrove's lodgings. The code of a gentleman has little meaning, I am afraid, with one who barely deserves the name. Ask yourself, which would our gold-cravatted friend prefer: a duel at dusk, or a purse of gold tirals in the afternoon? I did not even have to ask him twice.'

For a moment Jem did not understand. 'You can't do it. I won't let you.'

'I've done it. It's over, Jemany.'

'You bribed him? You sold my honour?'

'Jemany, Mr Burgrove has no honour. Surely you have learnt that much about him?'

'I'm not talking about Burgrove! I'm talking about me!' Jem was trembling. Rage flooded suddenly, scaldingly through his veins, rousing him to an unaccustomed eloquence. 'You call me fool, but am I any more a fool than you? My lord, it is *you* who have insulted me! Am I not the heir to this kingdom? I am your ward, you say, but how have you been my fit and proper guardian? What have you done but keep me here, frittering away the days of my youth? I put myself in your hands, but you have betrayed me! It is at your behest, is it not, that I have lived as if the time before me were endless, an endlessness only of frippery and fal-de-lal? If I quarrelled with Burgrove, I was right to do so. Pell calls me a Vaga-lover. Very well, I *am* a Vaga-lover. How can I not love the Children of Koros, when I wear their crystal, concealed against my heart? My lord, the harlequin told me to come to you. I only wish I could understand why, for I fear he was mistaken.'

Jem broke off. His cheeks burnt and he was close to tears. Already he was astonished at the things he had said, as if he had merely mouthed the words of another. Lord Empster, for his part, was not astonished at all, only pacing before the fire, drawing back dispassionately on his ivory pipe. He might have been the manager of a theatrical troupe, contemplating the latest of many auditions. Jem almost cried out. It was true what he had said: Lord Empster had insulted him, was insulting him now. There was something maddening in this calm, this impassivity.

'Jemany, there are many things you do not understand yet.' The voice was cool, level. 'But the time is drawing near when you shall ... when you shall know more.'

'No!' This was too much. 'Tell me everything. Tell me now.' Jem clenched his fists, screwed up his eyes. What was to become of him? Helplessness possessed him. Was Empster his friend, his enemy? A wild idea came to him. It had come before; now it returned with gathering force. *This has all been a test.* Lord Empster had sought to seduce him from the way. What was this lord, in truth, but a false guardian, beguiling him with trinkets of fashion and fame?

Jem sprang up.

'Yes,' he cried accusingly, 'this is a test, a game!'

But Lord Empster only smiled. Jem groaned. He clenched his fists. Wildly he gazed around him, at the glimmering spines of a thousand books, at the murk of the looking-glass, at the blue twists of smoke dispersing on the air. On the little round table by his reading chair, the pages of Silverby still lay open. *Draw, villain!* It was like a taunt. Jem seized the book, flinging it into the fire. He slumped back into his chair, his face in his hands. It was true, he was helpless, useless. If he could not even fight Burgrove, what else could he do? The quest before him seemed unreal, impossible. He thought of the night when he found the crystal, and longed to know again that exaltation, that power.

And still his guardian only smiled!

'Master Nova?'

Jem started. A footman stood before him, bearing a silver tray. On the tray was a small, neatly folded square of paper. A letter. Blankly, Jem took it. For a long moment he did not even unfold it, only gazing incuriously at the hasty, scrawled inscription: *Nova Empster*.

A dark flame burnt in his guardian's eyes.

That was when a sudden excitement surged through Jem, and he had no doubt who had written the note. Jeli! Dear Jeli! His guardian had said that all Agondon knew of the duel. That meant Jeli must know. She was concerned for him, she must be – desperately worried. How could he leave without thinking of her? Jem crumpled the note, unread, into his pocket. He pushed past the footman, sending his silver tray clattering to the floor.

Left behind, Lord Empster permitted himself a wry, sad laugh. The child was hot-headed, but easy enough to fool. Alas, many moonlives still must pass before he would be ready for the quest before him.

After all, they must not risk failure.

They had waited for so long – so interminably long!

Outside, Jem saw the lantern above a sedan-chair, casting its hazy glow through the fog. He hailed the chair and made his way, with maddening slowness, to his uncle's house.

Reverently, thinking how he would comfort his cousin, Jem ascended the steep stairs. Tapers burned in brackets along the ancient stone banisters. A footman in the livery of the Archduke of Irion opened the shabby door, just a crack. Jem gave his name and the door closed. He waited for long moments, only to be told at last that Miss Vance was not at home. Jem did not believe it. It was the Time of Meditation; of course she was there, and longing to see him.

He gave his name again, pleaded his case, but the answer was the same.

This time Jem's fist lashed out.

'Jeli! Jeli!' He rushed into the hall.

It was the action of a fool. The footman, a burly fellow, reeled only for a moment. In the next, Jem was caught, kicking and struggling in a strong grip. But his vision veered up sharply through the gloom, and there on the stairs, looking down at him, was his cousin.

From the window above she had seen him at the door, glowing strangely in the taper-lit fog. Now her pale face was a mask of astonishment.

'Wait!' she cried, as the footman was about to throw Jem from the doors.

She swished downstairs. Swiftly she looked from side to side. Some impulse made her ardent for this confrontation, but still there was uncertainty, even fear in her eyes. Her blonde hair shone like gold and her beauty, even in the gloom, was dazzling.

Jem breathed, 'I had to see you.'

'See me? Why?'

'Because you had to see me.'

'I don't know what you're talking about.'

'Your letter.' Jem struggled to reach into his pocket, but the footman's grip was too tight. For a second time the servant asked if he should put the intruder out of doors.

Jeli raised a hand. 'I wrote no letter,' she hissed, but Jem could barely take in the denial.

He wailed, absurdly, 'You held my hand!'

Now Jeli's eyes flashed. All her astonishment was anger now. Seeing the boy struggling in the footman's grip, an impulse of cruelty had been gathering inside her. Now it welled forth. She stepped close to Jem and muttered through clenched teeth, 'You stupid, coarse boy! I was amusing myself, that was all. Don't you understand, I have a destiny – and you're not part of it!'

'Jeli, I love you!'

'How dare you!' She flung back her arm and would have slapped Jem's face. Instead she turned, bursting into tears, and ran back up the stairs.

The last thing Jem saw, before the door slammed in his face, was the green, imperious form of Aunt Vlada, illuminated beneath the iron ring of candles that flickered and shimmered above the half-landing.

Weeping, Jeli flung herself into the woman's arms.

Below, the fog still swirled, viscous and grey. Jem rubbed his leg beneath his Koros-season coat. Lucky not to have tumbled all the way down the stairs, he was breathless now, and ashamed. Miserably he paced before the house. He slumped at the foot of the stairs. Something was wrong, it had to be. That Jeli wanted to see him, he had no doubt. That wretched old aunt must be keeping the girl from him – yes, that was it.

But what to do? He must think, think. He would walk around the house, from back to front. He trailed his fingers along the brick walls. He pushed his hands deep into the pockets of his coat, feeling the crumpled ball of the letter – Jeli's letter. He would not leave until he had seen her again. Fondly he imagined her falling into his arms, revealing her true feelings to him at last. Tenderly, reverently, he would kiss away her tears . . .

He passed down an alley, then into a backstreet. No light burned there and it was almost dark. Jem heard the clanging of the Temple bells – just above him, echoing down the spire that was close, very close, but invisible through the fog.

That was when he felt a backwash of doubt. *You stupid, coarse boy.* What cruelty had flashed in his cousin's eyes! What was he doing? Who was he fooling? For a moment the accumulated miseries of the day were too much for Jem. Tears sprang to his eyes. How he longed for his old life again, when he had loved Cata and Cata had loved him! Everything – Jem thought now – had been so simple then, everything so fine. The thought came to him that his passion for Jeli, that his indulgences at Chokey's, that his fine costumes and this foolish duel were all of a piece, all part of the corruptions of this great fogbound city that pressed evilly, insistently all around him.

Slumping against a low, narrow doorway in the backstreet, Jem sobbed for the innocence he had lost.

A little panel slid back in the door.

'Be off with you!' cried a voice.

Jem started. Brushing away his tears, he found himself looking into a pair of mean eyes. Their owner must think him some Reject, sheltering in the doorway. Jem stepped back. That was when he recognized this low, narrow entry, and the lantern above, cold now, that would burn at night with a fiery red glow.

Could it be? Jem stumbled back to the front of the house. Astonishment and horror churned through his mind. He had thought he had never met his mysterious Uncle Jorvel, betrayer of Ejland's rightful king. Now he saw that he knew his uncle well – very well indeed.

Straining his eyes, Jem gazed up at the house.

'Chokey's,' he breathed.

Again he slumped down on the stone stairs. For a moment it was as much as he could do not to curl up there like a dog, aching for comfort. But there would be no comfort inside this house. Wildly the thought came to Jem that Jeli was a prisoner, trapped in the clutches of her evil uncle and aunt.

Then he thought again of the cruelty in her eyes.

Then he shuddered.

That was when, almost idly, Jem pulled from his pocket the letter he had assumed – wrongly, absurdly – to be from his cousin. What a fool he had been!

But then Jem recalled the strange dark glow that had shone, just for a moment, in Lord Empster's eyes, after the footman had appeared with the letter. Jem's mouth hardened. Once again, his guardian had betrayed him.

He read, tremblingly, in the taper-light:

Jem,

I have lied to you. Try and understand that I could do no more. I promised I would give up my plan, but I cannot. You have your code and I have mine. This moment, I have returned from Burgrove's lodgings. I have laid down my challenge and he accepts me – you, he

exempts from all tax upon his honour. I ask only that you be my
second – I can ask no other.
    The Verge at dusk, just as before.
    Your friend, Rajal

Jem flung down the letter. 'I've got to stop him!'

Chapter 42

DOLLY, DOLLY

'A virtuous young woman might well feel alarm.'

'Of course.'

'A certain trepidation?'

'Oh yes.'

'Feel, perhaps, that she is on the brink? Feel an abyss, opening before her?'

'Mm.' Down, down a flight of stone steps they went. Cata was distracted, gazing about her at the dark walls. From the chill brightness of the bailey they had descended to the lower reaches of the castle. Tapers lined the passageways, leaping red and gold. Sentries stood to attention, their uniforms a bruised purple in the fractured light.

Lord Margrave was compelled to use a stick. 'To wed, Miss Catayane, is after all a momentous step,' he continued. 'For a young lady especially. How does Coppergate put it?

> *While marriage, for* master, *takes but a part,*
> *For* miss *it consumes the whole of her heart.*

Aptly put, would you not say, Chaplain? Aptly put, Miss Catayane?'

Exasperatedly the noble lord smiled at the young woman. Was she listening at all? Fascinated, she stared at the heavy grilled doors, wide-eyed at the moans and cries that issued from behind them. In Agondon, cell-descending was the commonest of amusements; any quality-lady, by Miss Catayane's age, would have affected the merest indifference. But Miss Catayane, Lord Margrave had to remind himself, was no ordinary lady. She did not look frightened. But she looked strangely troubled. Had it been a good idea to invite her here? Oh, but he was glad of the girl's company!

The chaplain offered urbanely, 'Lord Margrave, you would not have the young lady tremble in fear? Dark abysses open, it is true, for those light-of-head creatures who rush, thoughtless and excited, into hasty matches. "Varby-weddings"? Speak not of them! But good my lord, Miss Catayane's union is to be with—' the chaplain steeled himself '—the dear friend and companion of her tender years.'

'Indeed.'

And for a moment Lord Margrave fell silent, assuming the mask of the public man as their guide slid back the grille of a cell. Blandly the two gentlemen took turns to gaze in, noting the straw, the bench, the chamber-pot, the irons. Their noses wrinkled. A hot reek of excrement wafted through the grille and the prisoner, with matted hair and beard, claw-like nails, and oozing sores up his legs and arms, was drivelling and rocking on his haunches. Rats scurried around him.

'And this fellow's crime, Turnkey?'

'Theft, m'lord. Sucking-pig from Goody Orly's barn.'

Lord Margrave tut-tutted.

The chaplain said, 'Before the fire, then?'

'Oh, well before the fire, sir. Coming up for trial next season, this one. Then the gallows.'

'Hm.'

Lord Margrave moved on. Everything seemed to be in order, well up to standard. But the delicate girl was lingering back, gazing on the prisoner with an air of alarm, turning away only when the chaplain took her arm with a tight *Come, child. Come.*

'And you say it was young Veeldrop,' Lord Margrave murmured, 'who lured the innocent child from the woods?'

Eay Feval cleared his throat. He must be careful.

'My lord, a more tender concern could never have been displayed by any young gentleman. But those who know him could hardly be surprised. Captain Veeldrop – is he not a Veeldrop? – is a remarkable young man, as Miss Catayane, you will agree, is a remarkable young lady.'

'Remarkable! I would call her exquisite.'

A guard slipped silently down the side of the corridor, bearing a bowl of lumpy gruel; Eay Feval drew Cata gently forward, tilting her jaw upwards in the taper-light.

'Might she not stand with the finest of our Ejlander beauties, my lord? Were such a creature one of the ladies of the Court! But the poor child . . . my lord, if there is but one impediment to her happiness, is it not that Captain Veeldrop may not bring her the *title* which is her due? Now, if only his poor father were ennobled! *Lord Veeldrop*, yes. But in time . . . *Lady Catayane!*'

The chaplain smiled again for their noble guest, displaying the utmost courtesy and respect. Had he gone too far? But this, surely, was his angle . . .

There was the clunk of a lock, echoing down the corridor. A door swung open; the guard with the gruel stepped inside. An instant later, he cried out. His tray flew through the air, clattering tinnily on the hard stones, and a high-pitched scream came, 'Give me your sicked-up vomit, would you? What do you think I am, one of your common-as-muck trollops? By the Lord Agonis, don't you know I'm a woman of means?'

Cata started forward, intrigued.

The dazed guard staggered out, but before he could slam the door again, the girl stared full into the open cell. Its inhabitant was a hideous, witch-like old woman, dressed in the tatters of a fine gown. On her face were the remnants of a thick glaze of paint. Red, like raw scars, lined her toothless mouth and a fuzz of wild white hair formed a wispy corona round her scabious, bald skull.

Cata gasped; then a moment later gasped again as the crone hobbled forward, gripping the girl's hand and spitting, 'Dolly! My pretty, is it you? Why, Dolly, you've come back to me, your old mother, have you?' Her eyes glinted as she gazed first at Cata, then the gentlemen behind her. 'Why, good sirs, there was no finer lass in all my service than Dolly – oh, all the gentlemen were *very* satisfied! We used to have a little song about you, didn't we, Dolly dear? How did it go?'

And the crone, still gripping Cata's hand, forced the girl to shuffle round with her in a circle as she sang:

> *Dol-ly, Dol-ly! Gentlemen agree –*
> *There's no finer you shall ever see!*
>   *Hair like a raven,*
>   *Moist of lip and eye,*
>   *Desires, however craven,*
>   *Sure to satisfy!*
> *Dol-ly, Dol-ly! Hang it, let's be blunt!*
> *In all Ej-land, there's no finer—*

Indeed, it might have been a witch's spell. For a moment the gentlemen stood transfixed until the chaplain blustered suddenly, 'She is mad, mad!' and the Turnkey strode forward, flinging the crone back into the cell and slamming the door. Roughly he turned on his inept guard. 'Stupid boy, haven't you got to grips with old Wynda yet?' he cried, and the crone rattled at her grille and cackled leeringly, 'Aye, there's a-many's got to grips with Wynda! Come in here, lad, I'll give you lessons!'

Lord Margrave comforted Cata.

'Poor child, how unpleasant for you ... I'm so sorry! Turnkey, this is not a common occurrence, I hope?'

'Every dungeon has its difficult ones, my lord,' sighed the Turnkey as the guard scuttled away. 'But you remember old Wynda, your reverence,' he added, turning to the chaplain. 'I recall you signed the order, sir.'

'Turnkey, I'm sure you know such orders come only from the governor.' *Yes, it was a few moonlives back, wasn't it? When we first knew*

His Lordship was coming. 'You see, Lord Margrave, our dear governor permits no deviation from the strictest Agonist virtue,' the chaplain added smoothly.

But his smile was tight. He was shaken. *Dolly?* Yes, the old bawd was crazed! And yet, just for a moment, he had believed that she knew the girl – and that the girl knew her. Who knew what the girl's history may have been, in the days before she came into Umbecca's family? Master Polty had said she was the merest innocent, a child of nature living in the trees, until the wicked boy Jemany had endeavoured to ravish her. But did the chaplain believe Master Polty? Hardly! There was a mystery here, a mystery he would do well to investigate.

When the noble lord had declared that Miss Catayane should come with them to the dungeons, the chaplain had done his best – taken, as it were, a *certain step* – to ensure that the girl would not be upset. It seemed his best was not enough. Now the girl was sobbing in His Lordship's arms, and the chaplain was troubled, deeply troubled.

'Turnkey,' he murmured as they were about to leave, 'I think we have been a little harsh on Goody Throsh.'

'Sir?'

They lingered back.

'She has strayed from the path of virtue, it is true, but has she not indeed been – as she says – a woman of means? Give her what she wants, hm? No more gruel. A pot of ale, now and again. And perhaps you could arrange a little clothing for the lady? Even a little . . . *fresh paint?*'

He pressed a purse into the Turnkey's hand. 'Wynda Throsh is not without a degree of quality. I shall speak to the woman. Perhaps she may still be claimed for the Lord Agonis.'

❋   ❋   ❋

The Turnkey stroked his chin as he pocketed the purse. Really, he didn't understand quality-folk! Today the chaplain was all compassion, all Mercy-of-the-Lord-Agonis. Yet hadn't he, only a day or so ago, sent an order of a quite different kind? Urgent, too. Another prisoner, that old blind fellow, was to be put out in the snow – governor's express orders, he said, and would you mind.

Out in the snow?

Really, it was cruel!

But after all, it was hardly the Turnkey's place to say so; besides, along with *that* order had come an even bigger purse . . . Good old chaplain, he was a fine one and no doubt about it!

Chapter 43

BLUE VELVET

'Ooh, Miss Cata, what have they done to you?'

The afternoon sun declined sharply through the stained glass of the landing windows. Poor Nirry was only just off the crutches, and her ankle still ached. Wincing, she gripped the young mistress hard, hauling her up the stairs like a sack.

'Just a step or two more, miss. Come on.'

Miss Cata's eyes were glazed and she could not speak; she only moaned and shuddered. What could be wrong? The chaplain had snapped, *She's over-tired, that's all*, as he shifted his burden into the astonished Nirry's arms. *Over-tired?* Nirry didn't believe it. Miss Cata had the strength of an ox. Why, only a few nights ago, hadn't she gone all the way across the green in the snow, to fetch the notary for the poor commander? Not that you could tell *that* to the chaplain, of course: the young mistress had been cautious as a cat, bringing the fellow back here when the others had gone to bed. Nirry didn't pretend to understand what Miss Cata had been playing at; she didn't understand Miss Cata much at all. But something had happened in the castle today, she knew that much. That Lord Margrave, him with the cups-and-saucers choppers, he'd had a rum look on his face when they got back ... A rum look indeed.

'Now, miss! There we are.'

Leaden but unresisting, Miss Cata only lolled and moaned in Nirry's arms as the maid pulled off her shoes, loosened her stays, slipped her between the crisp clean sheets. Why, anyone would think old Waxwell was back, up to his evil tricks again! There was no sleepy-treacle on Miss Cata's breath, but Nirry almost wished there were. That, at least, would make sense.

Shyly she kissed the girl's cheek, gazing on her with troubled eyes.

'There, Miss Cata. Sleep.'

But as Nirry drew the bed-curtains, a voice came suddenly: '*Dolly.*'

'Miss?'

The voice was high, strained, not like Miss Cata's at all. It might have been the voice of an old witch, about to burst into a leering cackle. Nirry looked back carefully at the young mistress, but she seemed to be sleeping after all. In the hall below, the big clock sounded the fifteenth.

313

'I'll wake you for your dinner, Miss Cata, hm?' Nirry muttered nervously. 'You wouldn't want to miss your dinner.'

There was no reply, but just as Nirry had reached the doorway, the voice came again: '*Dolly.*'

Nirry shuddered. What could it mean?

❄ ❄ ❄

Cata lay trembling, suspended uneasily between sleeping and waking.

Dolly. The name beat at her temples like a mantra, boomed about emptily in the curtained darkness. *Dolly.* It was the song the crone had sung; had it been a charm, an evil charm? Something was stirring in Cata's brain. Oh, there had been glimpses enough, sparks of memory. On her name-day – the day they said was her name-day – Uncle Olivan had given her a miniature, a little painted oval of porcelain in a locket. *Open it, child. Here, like this. Child?* The locket showed the image of a young man, a handsome young man with hair of flaming red. *Child, don't you know your husband-to-be?* But Cata, instead of the joy she should feel, had felt at that moment a sudden, sharp horror. She cried out and flung the locket to the floor. *Child! Child!*

The fit had soon been over, but then there were the stirrings, subtler but still strong, that sometimes overcame her as she sat in the Glass Room. Among the thousand ferns and fronds and flowers it would seem to her that some mysterious presence lingered, and sometimes behind the commander's ruined eyes she imagined the eyes of another old man, eyes that were only seared and blackened pits.

Now Cata dreamed. How long since she had dreamed? Her mind had been in chains; now it broke free. At first there were only colours, bright and sharp, dull and dark, shifting as in a kaleidoscope. Sounds like voices overheard from afar. Then they resolved themselves into – what? The Glass Room? No, it was more. A forest, hissing and cackling with life. Fish bobbed and leapt in a glittering stream, birds swooped and skittered through the green laden branches.

Who'll ride? But no, it was a fair, a fair blazing with bright tents and booths. Children, milling, milling. Squeals. Delight. Here come the puppet-men; here come the clowns. Oh, but look at this beautiful silk! Pull at it, pull at it, skein after skein. And this, what is it? A rock, a stone?

Cata shifted, twisted in her bed. Now she dreamed of the rock rising before her, glowing purple-black with unearthly light; she dreamed of a boy who fell from the sky, buckling his legs against the hard ground. She took his hand, then together they flew upwards into the light, the purple-black light that shone like the sun and would burn up all the world.

Oh, how they longed for the light to consume them!

Impossibly their limbs tangled, twined. They rolled and tumbled through the blazing air.

❈ ❈ ❈

Cata woke, bewildered. She was sodden with sweat. Her sheets and counterpane were a crumpled mass. Lying at the wrong end of the bed, she clutched hard to a velvet cushion. Somewhere, ahead of her, was a purple light.

It was the firelight, glowing through the fabric of the bed-curtains. Slowly Cata crawled from the end of the bed, huddling by the hearth like a little frightened animal. Still she clutched the cushion tight in her arms. Such a lovely cushion! So rich the fabric! The same blue velvet as the curtains of the bed, the same blue velvet that was everywhere in the Lectory. And the stuffing, so soft! But wait, wasn't there something hard inside the cushion, too? Something jabbing into Cata's cheek? She wondered what it could be. Hadn't she watched Nirry sew this very cushion, stuffing the inside from her pile of rag? Obscurely she recalled that she had liked that rag. Cross-legged, her hair tumbling about her face, the confused girl ripped at a seam of the cushion.

Easily, almost too easily, the stitches came apart.

Cata's heart pounded.

No light surrounded her but the red-gold firelight, soft and flickering, as she extracted first – what? – a little black jacket, made for a child. Then came a torn scrap of – could it be? – a boy's breeches, and a handkerchief, mysteriously stained and stiffened . . .

Cata moaned. Her breath came hot and fast as she extracted next a strip of – was it? – a woman's white night-dress and a scrap – so it seemed – of a harlequin's motley. Then came a crumpled, dirty little shift, a shift such as, oh, some poor girl might wear . . .

Cata held it up, watched as the firelight played through the sackcloth. Unbidden, tears sprang to her eyes. And yes, there was some mysterious weight in the shift . . . Convulsively she clutched, clutched and tore at the hard metallic circle that was sewn into the hem – sewn, she knew suddenly, by her own childish hands. She ripped it free and the coin flashed suddenly, blindingly in the firelight . . .

The harlequin's gold!

Cata cried out, a primitive ululation like an animal's.

In the hall below, the clock was sounding. Cata slipped the coin into her mouth, sucking and licking.

She sobbed like a child. She remembered everything.

Chapter 44

A CUP OF MILKY TEA

What was that sound?

It sounded like a keening, an animal's keening, and it seemed to be coming from the other side of the wall. The girl's room? Lord Margrave stirred and rose painfully in his bed. The trip to the castle had quite knocked him up. He felt he had needed his nap this afternoon. He was, after all, an old man, too old really for government work.

Too old for anything, he thought grimly.

But he had not slept. For a time he had lain with his lamp unlit, looking out through a chink in the curtains at the chill white world that made him think now not of skating and sledding and crackling pine-logs and merriment over mulled wine – all those things were gone for him now – but only of the cold approach of death.

After a time he lit the lamp and read through again the report he had written, some days before. His recommendations, already made ... Devious? But no, he would change nothing, there was no need. He would send it ahead of him, send it off tomorrow. Cast it, as it were, away on the winds. Then it would be over – his career, his life. Already he seemed to feel his last days, closing in on him like a melancholy twilight. Only the long journey back to Agondon to come. This time he would close the curtains in the coach ...

But had there been a keening? No, it could not be. Lord Margrave sighed, gathering up the scattered pages of his report that lay about him on the big bed. Hadn't he just been drifting into sleep? Below, from the hall, came a sonorous *bong*. Now that was a real sound, a definite sound. Dinner-time soon? Lord Margrave barely looked forward to it. What pleasure could he have in eating now, with these cup-and-saucer teeth and the pain in his mouth? The quack in Agondon had said he had some disease, some disease that was eating away his jaw. Well, he would be dead soon, jaw or no jaw. There were times when he would see in his rotting mouth – opened a million times in patriotic fervour – some allegory of the decay of the state that he served. They called him a lord, but after all he was a servant – a servant of the King, as all true lords should be. He served the new King as he had served the old, as he had served, indeed, the King before that ... He was loyal; he had done his duty, and throughout he had believed his duty to be right. But now, as he lay awake with the pain in his jaw, the dreadful thought came to him that perhaps his duty had been, in the end, no duty at all, no duty at all to the things that mattered . . . Sorrowing, he gazed at the glass by his bed, where his porcelain teeth lay glinting in water.

Then he heard the sobbing from the room next door.

Oh, but it was real . . . there *had* been a cry! A sharper anguish filled the old man's heart and he hauled himself from the bed, reaching for his robe. In the moment before he blundered out on the landing he paused and turned back to his lamplit room.

First, an impulse of vanity: he champed down painfully on his porcelain teeth.

Second, secrecy: he gathered up the folded pages of his report, stuffing them swiftly into the pocket of his robe.

Then came the sound of a slamming door and Lord Margrave, flinging open his own door, was startled to see a ghost-like figure in white, sweeping rapidly past him.

'Miss Catayane!'

But the child did not hear him, only hurtled down the stairs.

'But the child. Where is the child?'

'Olivan, have you forgotten? Catayane was going to the castle today.' Umbecca, with a pleasant smile, arranged her husband's tray. Broth, bread, weak tea. Poor old gentleman, it was all he could stomach!

'The castle? It is an evil place.'

'Husband, you speak of my former home.'

'The scene, sir, of your greatest triumph,' added the chaplain, who sat on the other side of the bed. Legs crossed, he flexed his fingers in his white gloves, yawned and stared distractedly into the surrounding foliage. Really, these consultations could hardly be necessary any more! The chaplain was bored, bored. By the bed, the lamp gave out its customary *hiss* and through the glass above the sky was an ugly purple, like the old man's cheeks.

Like Umbecca's, for that matter, when she had applied insufficient paint.

'The home of my maiden years,' Umbecca expatiated, looking down demurely, as if the fact that she had once lived in the castle were after all more important than the Siege that had changed the course of Ejland's history.

'Sir, perhaps you could sign these death-warrants?' Eay Feval shuffled the papers on his lap.

'Yes, dear, then you can have some nice broth.' Umbecca scooped up a tempting spoonful, wafting the aroma before her husband's nose.

'Death-warrants?' The commander's face was stony.

Dear me, he was in one of his moods again!

'The Vagas, sir.'

'Yes, Olivan, you know you've always hated those dreadful Vagas.' Umbecca smiled and swallowed the spoonful of broth. Mm, it really was remarkably good.

'I know of some more dreadful,' the commander murmured.

'What's that, dear?' Didn't he even want his broth? *Waft* again, *waft*, *waft*. 'Nirry's best broth. You know you always like her chicken broth.' Umbecca spooned a little more, as if in encouragement, into her own mouth.

Mm, delicious. Absent-mindedly she tore off a chunk of bread.

The commander turned to her. His visor was up and his faded eyes struggled to gaze into her bloated face.

'How could I have believed you were "Miss R——"?' he whispered. 'To think, that even for a moment I ascribed to you the sensibility of that divine creature!'

Umbecca only laughed. But it was a bitter laugh. She had heard this before, too many times. First her husband had worshipped her, believing her to be the mysterious authoress. When she had broken down at last, sick of the pretence, he had turned from her, loathing her, accusing her of lies.

It was a calumny. Had Umbecca encouraged his absurd belief? Besides, who was her husband to accuse her of failings? In the Siege he had been a hero, a lion among men. What woman of Ejland would not have been proud to be united in wedlock to Olivan Tharley Veeldrop? But he had decayed, grotesquely decayed. If she had failed as a wife, had he not failed more grievously as a husband? Umbecca's face reddened as she stuffed herself with bread, muttering between mouthfuls, 'It seems my poor husband is in an irritable mood. You know the poor dear gets annoyed if he doesn't get his chapters of "Miss R——"!'

On the little table, beside the lamp, there glinted the tooled spines of the 'Agondon Edition'. Sometimes Umbecca would like to have seized the little books, seized them and flung them through her husband's glass walls!

Eay Feval cleared his throat. 'The papers—'

'Oh, Chaplain, sign the wretched things yourself, why don't you? The old fellow's hand is so shaky, who will know?'

The outburst was a spur to further emotion. Bewildered, the old man could only look from the chaplain, to his wife, then back again, as all at once, like lovers rushing together in a comic opera, they came together, clutching hands, across his stricken form. Their voices came hotly, like whispers of love.

318

'Dear lady, do not distress yourself, I pray! How it tears at my heart to see you sorrowing! For now, your love lies spurned, crushed and bleeding. Oh, what a torment to have thrown yourself away! But think of the future, the glorious future that rushes towards us like a coach-and-six, with the horses whipped to frenzy and the road downhill! I've worked on old porcelain-chops. The peerage is secure, I'm sure of it. Dear lady, don't you see? The commander must live just long enough, that's all, just long enough to accept his honour!'

Umbecca moaned, kissing the chaplain's gloves. 'Oh, Eay!'

'Think of it! A peerage, and the old man dead! *Lady Umbecca*, as you have always deserved to be!'

'And you my loyal companion, Eay!'

'A pension from the Royal List! An apartment in Agondon! What price provincial servitude then?'

'Oh, Eay!'

They were rising to a frenzy, but the frenzy halted suddenly as the commander cried, 'Child!'

They had not heard the crashings that had come through the foliage. Umbecca turned; so did the chaplain. Standing before them, dressed only in petticoats, was Cata. Her hair was dishevelled and her breasts were heaving, but if there was a strange, blazing look in her eyes it seemed to be directed only to the commander. The awkward figures who had sprawled across him might barely, at that moment, have existed at all. Slowly the chaplain, then Umbecca, rose to stand on either side of the bed. *Oh dear.* Umbecca saw the mess they had made. They had upset the tray and the cup of milky tea was soaking into the bedclothes. As if the old fellow had disgraced himself. Again.

'Child, you've come. Oh, how I've missed you!' Smiling, the commander seemed to have forgotten the drama that had enacted itself only moments before. Was that all they were to him, Umbecca would think later, only so much chaff on the wind? With blundering hands the old man reached beside his bed, taking up the volume of *Becca's Last Ball*. 'Come child, let us find out what happens to poor Becca, shall we?' He held out the book, but Cata took it only reluctantly, shuffling forward like a mechanical doll.

'What's wrong with the girl?' Umbecca hissed.

'Miss Cata?' attempted the chaplain. What could he say?

'Come, child. Child? Why do you not sit by me?'

The girl could only whisper, 'You burnt Papa's eyes.'

'Child?' The commander's face turned pale.

'You're an evil man. You burnt Papa's eyes.'

'Pretty child, what nonsense is this? Come, read to me about poor Becca. Oh, what can have become of her now?'

There was silence. In pained wonderment the girl stood staring at the old man, the little book clutched tight in her hand. Then suddenly the book was hurtling through the air, smashing into the lamp beside the commander's bed. The lamp exploded, plunging the room into darkness, as Cata shrieked, 'Murderer! You lying murderer!'

She plunged away, crashing back through the foliage.

At once, all was confusion.

The commander cried out.

Umbecca shrieked.

The chaplain stamped desperately at the flames on the floor before they took hold of the trailing counterpane. But almost in the moment that the flames went out, another light came juddering greenly through the leaves.

Umbecca shrieked again.

'Ma'am?'

'Nirry!'

The maid stepped into the clearing, holding her lamp aloft. 'Oh, she gave me such a turn, she did! I went to look in on her, I did, and she was gone! Well, I was just on my way to tell you, ma'am, when she ran past me like nobody's business. I tried to follow her, ma'am, but . . .' Nirry's chatter trailed off. She pointed at the bed. Suddenly pale, she added in a whisper, 'But ma'am, what's happened? Wh-what's happened?'

Umbecca laughed, 'No, girl, it's only a cup of tea! Just a cup of tea, not what you think!'

But then she saw the look on the maid's face.

She glanced at the chaplain. His look was the same. Understanding flickered in Umbecca's mind and she turned slowly, slowly back to the bed.

She screamed again.

'Olivan!'

In an instant, oblivious of the soaking tea, Umbecca was sprawled grotesquely across the bed, abandoning all dignity in her efforts to revive her dead husband. But her kisses and caresses, like her slappings, were useless.

'Oh Olivan, Olivan,' Umbecca sobbed.

Could he be dead, and not yet a peer?

❋ ❋ ❋

The chaplain cleared his throat. 'Dear lady, perhaps—'

It had taken Umbecca some moments to notice that her husband was dead; likewise it was some moments until she became aware that another had joined their little party.

'An affecting scene,' said Lord Margrave.

The chaplain gave an awkward laugh and smiled, 'Yes, the lady is a little overwrought – as the fair sex must be, after all, when their menfolk are indisposed. But, but. As you suggest, Lord Margrave, what could be more affecting than a virtuous woman, venting the excess of her sensibility?'

The noble lord stepped forward; the chaplain blocked his path.

'Lector Feval, may I see your commander?'

'The commander?' The chaplain smiled fondly, and in an aside exhorted the maid to hold the light higher, just a little higher. 'Don't get it in the commander's eyes, there's a good girl. No, Lord Margrave, I think perhaps we must take our leave, just at this moment. The commander is . . . unwell.'

'Lector Feval, the commander is dead.'

'Dead! Droll, Lord Margrave. Alas, there are conditions which look like death, but in time, nursed by a virtuous woman – there, there, Madam Umbecca, dry your tears – the most amazing recoveries are positively commonplace.'

'You don't say?'

'Lord Margrave, I do!'

'Feval, you are a viper.'

'Well really, Lord Margrave . . . Give me that lamp, girl! And back to your duties!'

Reluctantly Nirry surrendered her lamp. What followed was punctuated by the sounds of the maid, blundering back in darkness through the commander's little jungle.

'Lord Margrave—' the chaplain leaned forward confidentially '—quite how *long* have you been skulking amongst the foliage?'

The noble lord reared up.

'Skulking, sir? I deny it! I saw the young lady leave her room in distress. I followed her. And here – I must say, before I quite knew what was happening – I witnessed things quite as remarkable as this . . . *remarkable* room.'

'Yes, it is extraordinary, isn't it? As I always say, my lord, one doesn't expect – out here in the provinces – to come across a truly *innovative* decorating idea, but I must say the Glass Room leaves me stunned. Why, I'm sure it's only a matter of time before simply everyone has one just like it. I can quite see Constansia Cham-Charing amongst the ferns, can't you? Well, cacti. But do you know Constansia . . .?'

The chaplain would have gone on, but Lord Margrave grabbed him by the throat. The lamp juddered in the chaplain's hand and his eyes bulged as the noble lord stepped close, his words gusting on diseased breath, 'I saw you and that evil woman on the bed, romping in ecstasy at the prospect of the peerage. I saw the girl – that beautiful, abused girl – denouncing your late commander for the villain I knew him to be. Then I saw your commander die. Oh, a revealing scene, Lector Feval, a revealing scene and a tragic one. To think, I had written my report already.'

'Report?' the chaplain gasped as the grip was released. Flung back, he almost lost his balance. Shadows swept hugely over the bed, over the corpse, over Umbecca, still weeping.

'Give me the lamp, Lector, I have something to burn.' From the pocket of his robe, the noble lord produced a sheaf of folded papers. 'Ironic, isn't it? I knew what you were, all of you. Did you think you fooled me, even for a moment? As if Veeldrop were not disgrace enough to the nobility of this land—'

'Disgrace?' croaked the chaplain. 'Foolish old man, have you ever really *looked* at the nobility of this land?'

'Lector, you forget yourself. I am part of that nobility.'

'And an unworthy part, spitefully to deny—'

'Deny? No, Lector, that's where you're wrong. You see, my report is full of lies. I recommend unreservedly that Commander Veeldrop be restored to his place as a hero of Ejland, receiving at last the highest honours that he may. Oh yes, Lector, you knew my weakness – the girl, the lovely girl. Only to see her ennobled in time, I would have let you succeed in all your schemes. But now, alas, your schemes are no more. There can be no peerage for a man who is dead. I say again, Lector, give me the lamp.'

'Wait!' Eay Feval's voice came hoarsely. 'You say you would have let us succeed. Why not still? Good my lord, look at the commander, he is not yet cold! A little sleight-of-hand, who will know?'

'Never! What has been my long career in public life, if not one of the strictest probity? You would have me connive at the foulest calumny, in defiance of all the laws of Ejland?'

Eay Feval laughed. 'You fool, Margrave – you senile old fool! What are the laws of Ejland that they are not swept aside at the merest promptings of the First Minister's whim? What are they, too, that your own pathetic lusts would not fling them contemptuously away? Didn't you just *say* that your report was full of lies?'

'Oh, you are a monster, Feval!' The noble lord endeavoured an ungainly lunge, snatching unsuccessfully at the flickering lamp.

'Wait!' It was Umbecca this time. 'You are in love with the girl? But she is mine to dispose! Come, come. Good my lord, what would you not give, could you be the man to break her virgin-knot?'

Umbecca had risen from the bed by now. Her fat arms circled Lord

Margrave from behind and her voice was a desperate, hideous caress, rising only to shout suddenly, stridently, 'Nirry! Nirry! Find that girl!'

The response was a screech and a confusion of crashings, adding to the evil echoings in the Glass Room as, with a cry of horror, Lord Margrave broke from Umbecca's grip and lunged again for the lamp. His fingers brushed the hot glass. Then he fell.

That was when something snapped in Eay Feval. Who was this noble lord, this old fool, to deny them everything they had wanted for so long?

The chaplain kicked him. Lord Margrave moaned. He staggered up, racked with coughing, his porcelain teeth hanging askew.

The chaplain kicked him again, then punched him hard on the back, several times. The teeth clattered from the old man's mouth and Umbecca watched, appalled and fascinated, as the chaplain stamped on them, crunching them to powder. Only when it was too late did she cry out, 'No! Eay—'

But it was over.

Umbecca fell back, sobbing again. Shadows leapt massively across her heaving form as the chaplain bent swiftly, efficiently, extracting the papers from Lord Margrave's hand.

'What a pity this good lord shall die, before he returns to our fair capital. Still, his excellent report shall precede him. To the last, he did his work well.'

Through the foliage, Nirry looked on, appalled.

Chapter 45

SCARLET LETTER

Clang!

All over Agondon, meditation-bells were ringing out again as Jem ran through the empty, cold streets. Twice he darted into doorways, once down an alley when the soldiers of the Watch came trudging by, muskets over their shoulders, looking mechanically from left to right, right to left, in the thick abrasive air.

Dusk was falling already when he arrived at the Verge.

'Jem. You came.'

'Of course I came. You can't go through with it.'

'I've got to. I'm not a coward, Jem.'

But there was no bravery in the dark face, only a sick fear. Huddled against the cold, Rajal hung back in the line of larches. Still he wore his finery from the night before, but the plush purple had something shabby about it now, something pathetic.

Jem's heart hammered painfully. He peered into the centre of the slushy field. A lantern burnt on Marly's Stump and in its diffused light, dark in their thick coats, stood Mr Burgrove and his second, the young Bluejacket. A carriage lay close by, ready for the getaway. Perhaps there was even a surgeon, waiting in the carriage; if Mr Burgrove was no gentleman, he had taken, nonetheless, all a gentleman's precautions. Absurdly Jem thought of Skyle Kelming-Skyle, Silverby's villain, with his poison-tipped rapiers. As Rajal's second, he must examine the weapons.

The Bluejacket trudged towards them.

'It's time,' Jem said.

'A moment. Just one moment.' Rajal retired behind a tree-trunk. There were sounds of retching.

'You'll join us, gentlemen?' The Bluejacket affected a wry, urbane manner.

'Wait. My friend is unwell.'

'Your friend is a coward.'

'No. He – he has been betrayed. This duel is being carried out under false pretences!'

'What?'

Jem thought quickly.

'We are here, are we not, to satisfy Mr Burgrove's honour? Has not that honour already been satisfied? I know that he received a visit this afternoon; I also know that he received a purse of gold tirals. He has sold his honour – he has none left to defend!'

As he spoke, Jem looked levelly into the Bluejacket's face. The young man's composure was soon disturbed, but then it had never been very convincing. His brow furrowed and he trudged back to his companion. For some moments they murmured together, dark against the lamplight.

'Jem, what are you doing?' Rajal blundered out from behind the tree, a string of vomit swinging from his lips.

'Trust me, Raj, just trust me.'

Later, Jem would regret these words. A shout erupted from Mr Burgrove. Pushing his second angrily aside, he made his own way over to Jem, his step remarkably brisk and firm. For once, Jem realized, Mr Burgrove was not drunk, not drunk at all. The cravat glowed strangely in the scarlet evening fog.

'Mr Burgrove.' Jem bowed.

But Mr Burgrove attempted no politeness. His lip curled. 'It is true, my cowardly young friend, your guardian came to plead for you; very prettily he pleaded too. But you must see that this is a different matter.' He jerked a thumb towards Rajal. 'This is between the Vaga and me.'

'And you call me a coward? Burgrove, no gentleman would fight a Vaga! What contest is it, with one party assured of death whether he loses, whether he wins?'

'Impudent little Vaga-lover! You dare to instruct me in what becomes a gentleman? Come, Vaga, and meet your death! Or are you as snivelling a coward as your friend?'

'Wait! Burgrove, I don't care if I must strike you again, but I tell you it is I who shall duel with you now! Forget Rajal. He was fighting for me. Now I am here and I shall fight for myself.'

Burgrove's eyes glittered. 'What, Vaga-lover, you would take up your challenge after all?'

'No!' Rajal burst out.

'Yes,' said Jem.

'Very well.' Burgrove's eyes glittered. 'As defender, I have prepared the weapons. Come, you will inspect them, and make your choice?'

And he turned on his heel, making his way back to the middle of the Verge with the same admirable, unaccustomed poise.

Rajal grabbed Jem's arm. 'Jem, please, don't take this away from me! You think this is all about your honour, or Burgrove's. Can't you understand it's about *mine*? Or you don't think a Vaga can have honour, is that it?'

'You didn't think about that when you joined the Masks!'

325

'That's not fair!'

'Raj, I don't care. You know who I am, you know what I must do. How can I be fit for my quest if I won't even fight a dog like Burgrove? Now come on. Raj, you're my second.'

Jem's words were decisive, but only his words. His heart hammered hugely. For a moment before they joined Burgrove, he closed his eyes, willing himself not to fail in this challenge. Absurdly, images from Silverby filled his mind: he saw himself on the battlements of Wrax Castle, clashing swords with the evil Count Malevol; he saw himself swinging down suddenly from a rope, confronting the villain's henchmen on the greenwood path. *Zing! Zing!*

'The weapons, Master Empster.'

Burgrove smiled and gestured to his second. Then, if not before, Jem knew the emptiness of all his bravado. The Bluejacket held out a plush velvet box. He opened the lid.

Inside, on a cushion, lay two flintlock pistols.

Jem swallowed hard; sensing his discomfort, Mr Burgrove laughed pleasantly, 'Remember, my friend, you are fighting in the place of a Vaga. The rapier, I would agree, is the gentleman's weapon. But you have made it clear to me by now, I think, that you do not consider me a gentleman? Yes, you have made that abundantly clear. Your second, perhaps, will examine the weapons?'

Jem cleared his throat. 'Raj, you will choose for me?'

Trembling, Rajal stepped forward. Beautiful in the lamplight's soft glow, the pistols lay curled against each other like lovers in a silken bed. One was decorated in ivory and silver, one in inlaid pearl and gold. Rajal picked up one, then the other. The choice was meaningless; or rather, it was a choice only of ivory or pearl.

Rajal chose first pearl, then ivory. Gingerly he turned the pistol over in his hands.

'Careful, Vaga-boy,' said Mr Burgrove. 'They're primed, of course. And very delicate.'

Rajal caressed the dangerous trigger. Suddenly he raised the pistol, pointing directly at Mr Burgrove's face.

'Raj!' Jem stepped forward, terrified. But somehow he could not bring himself to intervene.

'I'm sorry, Jem. I can't let you die! This is mine to do, and I've got to do it!'

There was a dull click.

Mr Burgrove, who had made no move to defend himself, only laughed again pleasantly; those who had known him before his recent troubles might indeed have thought he had recovered, in this present crisis, much of the old charm that had made him so dreaded by all the Duennas of Varby.

'But of course,' he said, 'there is a safety-mechanism.'

Rajal sobbed suddenly, sharply, as Jem grabbed the pistol from his hands.

'You fool! Is this your honour?'

'I'm sorry. I'm sorry.'

'Keep away from me!'

But even as he pushed Rajal in the chest, and Rajal staggered backwards, Jem knew there was little honour in his own righteous anger. It was not that Rajal had tried to shoot Mr Burgrove: it was the fact that he had failed.

'I think we're ready now, then?' smiled Mr Burgrove.

Night was approaching rapidly. Already sunset, like a scarlet stain, seeped through the churning whiteness of the air. Jem swallowed again, aware of the painful drumbeats of his heart, aware of the heaviness of the pistol in his grip. Rajal lay sobbing, somewhere off to the side; through the fog came the jingling of Mr Burgrove's horses, harnessed and ready for his rapid escape.

Beyond there was only emptiness, silence, but for distant meditation-bells. At another time, fine carriages might have lined the Verge, with ladies eager for a contest of arms, hiding their faces behind fluttering fans.

None dared stir at this forbidden time.

Solemnly, attempting no urbanity now, the Bluejacket gave Jem a few murmured instructions.

'Remember, the barrel always drops *down* when you fire. Aim a little *above*, if you see what I mean. But of course, the defender fires first.'

'What?'

'He fires, then you fire. That is the way.'

'That's not fair!'

'It's the way.' Then unexpectedly, the Bluejacket added, 'Haven't I seen you before?'

Jem could barely take in the question. All he could see was his opponent, smiling pleasantly above his golden cravat.

'I've seen you somewhere before, I know it.'

'Chokey's,' Jem murmured.

'Before that.'

'What does it matter?' What did anything matter? For Jem, there was nothing, nothing at all now but the boomings of his heart. The Bluejacket turned away, abashed; it was up to Mr Burgrove to hear the carriage, approaching rapidly from the direction of New Town. His lips pursing, he signalled for his second to hurry, hurry. It might be something; then again, it might be nothing.

The Watch, at least, did not travel in carriages.

The Bluejacket had explained the ritual. Now, numbly Jem followed the steps. By Marmy's Stump, he stood with Mr Burgrove, back-to-back. They paced forward. The Bluejacket counted.

One. Two. Three.

The carriage was coming closer.

Four. Five. Six.

Jem felt his legs almost giving way beneath him. The apple in his throat was swollen hugely; a sickening, sharp urgency burnt inside his bowels. Distantly, as from another world, he heard the sound of the carriage.

Closer. Closer.

Seven. Eight. Nine.

Rajal screwed up his courage tight. His eyes were dry now, dry and hot, focused intently on Jem's pacing form. In the next moment, if he did not act, Jem would die: he was sure of it. From somewhere came the sound of a whinnying horse, then the sound of a voice calling urgently through the fog.

Ten.

Jem stood sideways. He closed his eyes. His finger trembled on the trigger. But what was the use?

He fires first.

What happened next was the work of an instant.

'Fire!'

A *boom!* of powder slashed redly through the fog.

'No!' In the same instant, Rajal lunged forward, grappling Jem. Whether he intended to take the shot himself, or merely to save his friend, he did not know. He only knew Jem's raw cry as the ball crashed shatteringly into his shoulder, then the second deafening *boom!*, close to his ear, as Jem, in his astonishment and pain, squeezed his own trigger and fired wildly.

'Raj!' Jem crumpled to the ground. 'What have you done?'

'Jem, forgive me. I had to save you.'

'No, Raj. What have you done?'

White-faced, Jem pointed. Only then did Rajal take in the third appalling detail, almost cloaked from view in the fog. Had there not been a voice, a new voice, calling urgently, calling a name? That voice was silent now, its owner lying still, some lengths away.

'No, it can't be. No, please.'

Pain seared through Jem's shoulder. He clutched it hard, blood spilling through his fingers, dragging himself in spasms across the slush. 'Help me, Raj.' In a moment he would pass out, but before he did, Jem saw that the worst of his fears was true. From behind them came a whipcrack, a whinny, an oath: Mr Burgrove, making his getaway.

Meanwhile, Pellam Pelligrew lay before them, a hole blown clean through the back of his head.

'Raj, no.'

'Jem, I'm sorry.'

But already Jem had sunk deep, deep, and Rajal was left holding his inert form, looking up in terror as a dark, caped figure loomed towards him out of the fog.

Coolly Lord Empster took in the scene.

'I take it, young man, you are the author of this?' A scrap of paper hung from his hand and he let it fall, fluttering down into the snow beside the corpse. It was Rajal's letter.

In a moment it would be soaked in blood.

Chapter 46

INTERLUDE IN SUNLIGHT

The first thing Jem saw, when he came round, was the butterfly. Bright-winged, almost invisible in the sunlight, it fluttered nonchalantly about his head, lighted for a moment on a branch above, then was gone. The bird, the little red-breasted bird, stayed longer.

'It's a Bob Scarlet,' Rajal said.

Jem turned, but only briefly. At once he was aware of the pain in his shoulder. How much time had passed? He was lying on a grassy hillside. Over his head, spreading branches cast their sweet shade; below, the hillside was bathed in golden light. What was this place? Jem had never been here before, but from the first it seemed strangely familiar. Strangely right. Yet he wondered, with a troubled awareness, how it could be that they were here at all. Again the feeling came to him that he had slipped into illusion. He sighed. Dimly he remembered a foggy carriage-journey, the blood soaking his jacket, his guardian's face taut with anger. Dazed, he had passed in and out of consciousness. Yes, he must be unconscious now.

He felt the crystal around his neck.

'Raj, tell me: how long have we been sleeping?'

But Rajal was not listening. Dressed in the brightly-coloured costume of a page-boy, he stared dreamily at the bird in the branches. In his hand he held an ornate lute. 'I learnt a song about him,' he said.

'Him?'

'Bob Scarlet. A Green-and-Gold, just back from Wrax, said they all sing it there. Shall I play it for you, Jem?' And taking his friend's silence for assent, Rajal picked out the following ditty. His voice was soft, breathy, sad.

> *Scarlet, scarlet, his coat was of scarlet,*
> *With a hey-zown zerry,*
> *Zerry-zown;*
> *In Viana's kingdom he was often seen,*
> *In the years after they had killed the Queen.*
> *With a hey-zown zerry,*
> *Zerry-zerry zown,*
> *With a hey-zown zerry,*
> *Zerry-zown!*

330

'That's nice, Raj. Do you know any more?' By now Jem had turned carefully on to his side. With no particular surprise he saw that he was wearing a black robe, like the garb of a friar. Why was that? His hand reached up to the pain in his shoulder. He felt wetness. Blood, soaking through the coarse fabric. But more than this, he was aware of the crystal, glimmering, burning as he had felt it burn before. Jem sighed again. On the bright slopes below, he saw sheep. Or perhaps they were goats.

> *Evil, evil, he fought against evil,*
> *With a hey-zown zerry,*
> *Zerry-zown;*
> *Though scarlet may be the colour that's true,*
> *There's too many who say that it's blue!*
> *With a hey-zown zerry,*
> *Zerry-zerry zown,*
> *With a hey-zown zerry,*
> *Zerry-zown!*

Rajal recalled more verses – but no, they were other, similar songs – devoted to the exploits of the highwayman. Invariably the songs were long and much the same, differing only in the patterns of 'zerry-zowns'. It could become very complicated, remembering which was which. But then, perhaps it was easy for Zenzans. There was the story of Bob and the Brown Friar. There was Bob's Derring-do at Oltby Reach, whatever – wherever – that might be. Bob and the Fine Lady. Bob and the Escape of the Zenzan Prince. Repeatedly Bob was outwitting the Bluejackets; repeatedly he saved some innocent or other; again and again the Governor was fuming, reduced to impotent fury.

Whether these stories were true was, perhaps, beside the point. Bob was a symbol of Zenzan resistance, as much as he may or may not have been real. There were many references to his black stallion, his silver pistol, his brilliant scarlet jacket; of the fear the highwayman inspired in Ejlanders, there could be no doubt. Rajal smiled. There was hardly a call for these crude ballads at the balls and plush theatres where the Masks would play! Besides, to be caught singing them was treason. Softly he strummed through the chords again.

'Raj, this tree,' said Jem. 'What sort of tree is this?'

'It's an apple tree, Jem,'

'Are you sure, Raj?'

'I'm sure, Jem.'

'But Raj, the fruit is funny.'

'What do you mean, funny?'

'I mean it's made of gold.'

'No, it's not! They're apples, Jem.'

'Apples? You're sure?'

'Green apples, Jem.'

'Raj, is this real?'

Jem's blood was real, wasn't it? Carefully Rajal set aside his lute. In bright dapples of sunlight he studied the glistening, spreading dark pool, soaking through the fabric of the friar's robe. Jem slumped back. Rajal pushed the fabric aside. For a moment his fingers played over the wound, as if his hands alone might staunch the flow. Sorrow, deep and terrible, shuddered through his frame. Dimly he knew that what was happening – this, now – was indeed unreal, somehow and crucially; but in another way he knew it was more real, more profound, than any moments he had passed before.

Memories possessed him of these late moonlives. Already his days with the Silver Masks seemed to have retreated far into the past. He saw himself in the agonies of training, twisting his body this way and that; he saw himself primping and preening at his *toilette*, dusting white powder over his wig; he saw himself sweeping his rainbow-lined cloak proudly behind him as he stepped down from a coach. What a fool he had been! One afternoon he stole Clown's paint and smeared it liberally over his face, neck and hands. When he was finished, his dark skin was white, whiter by far than Jem's had ever been. Fascinated, Rajal gazed upon himself, stared and stared at his image in the glass. Then the gathering dusk made his whiteness fade and Clown discovered him and called him – yes – *fool*.

They often called him that, Harlequin and Clown. Sometimes they called him a base ingrate, too, who might best be thrown back into the mud where they had found him. But then, they had not found him in the mud; they must have been thinking of another boy. Still, there was something about Rajal they liked. There had to be, hadn't there, to make him the favourite of the masters' chamber? With a shy, proud reverence Rajal had played his part in the dark devotions of Harlequin and Clown. If at first he had been shocked, alarmed, he soon learnt there was nothing to fear, not really – only, perhaps, the envy of other boys. But though he knew himself an object of resentment, none had dared to challenge him openly. What Vaga-boy, chosen for the Masks, would risk it all for a point of honour?

That was what Rajal told himself, too.

To call him a harlot was not quite accurate. His body was undefiled, unless merely to touch was to defile. Many a time the two old men had made the boy strip off his clothes; many a time they had him lie with them, pressing his young body against their own withered flesh; they kissed him; they licked him, moist tongues straining from tortoise-necks.

But they attempted nothing more and, after a time, Rajal realized they were capable of nothing more. Only once, just once, at the moist workings of Clown's mouth, did Rajal feel a shivery tension burst from him unawares; afterwards, for some days, Clown treated him with a particular tenderness. But for the most part the old men required – indeed, expected – no response, and the boy gave none. He began to see that, in a sense, he may as well not have been there; he was wanted not for himself, it seemed, but as a reminder of past loves, from the days before the two old friends had sunken into decrepitude. What was he, really, but a species of ghost?

Then it came to him that the old men, too, were ghosts of a sort, phantoms of a love he had not yet come to know. Poor Harlequin! Poor Clown! Rajal would not go back. Not now. Quietly, carefully, he would close the door that led to the room where he imagined them waiting, waiting for ever, nursing their pathetic memories of lust. He did not hate them. He did not resent them. They were a dream he had once, that was all, a dank and troubled dream.

But they had taught him things he would remember.

Still the blood flowed from Jem's shoulder. Still Rajal, wondering and troubled, touched the wound. Then he knew what he must do. He knelt down, drinking the blood; and when he had finished he saw that the wound had knitted over. Later, he would wonder how this could be so, for he had always known that he possessed no magic. No, Myla was the one with the magic; and what Rajal learnt in the Masks was not magic, but a method of love.

Could that be enough?

Jem's eyes opened. That was when the knowledge came to Rajal that would taunt him, torment him for long years to come, perhaps until the end of his days: *I love him*. And it seemed to Rajal that in the same moment – but of course, it was inevitable – he heard again, too, a voice behind him, echoing as it echoed on that afternoon when he had lingered too long, into the evening, watching his painted face in a glass.

Fool, said the sad Clown. *Fool, fool*.

❉   ❉   ❉

The bird, the Bob Scarlet, is twittering in the branches. A warm breeze hums through the strings of Rajal's lute. Clouds float like dreams across the pallor of the sky. And now, from below, a figure hails them, striding up the hillside with a crooked staff. At first – it must be the staff – there is a sense of the pastoral; but no, the robes the figure wears are black, like Jem's, and he smokes, too, an ivory pipe. Cross-legged, the noble lord sits beneath the tree. (The staff disappears.) Blue-grey smoke curls up into the leaves as he looks first to Jem, then to Rajal. For a moment they are alarmed, for after all, when they last saw Lord Empster, was not his face twisted in fury?

Now he is calm.

Too calm.

He begins to speak. That is when something strange – or stranger still – begins to happen. The friends had known – of course they had known – that this tree, this hillside, this bright sunny day could not be real. Now slowly, the deception fades. Slowly, walls of brick close around them. Instead of the sky there is a dark vaulted roof; tapers burn in brackets, fixed to thick columns. From somewhere, from some opening in the roof, a chill ray of moonlight shimmers down. It is intensely bright.

But all this happens slowly, only slowly.

Now Lord Empster is talking about Pell – poor foolish Pell, who shall never again tie his cravat with aplomb and gaze at himself in Quisto's mirror, never again raise his stentorian voice in the Great Temple on Canonday, never again know the delights of Chokey's – for of course, His Lordship knew all about *that*. As well for the fashion of wearing wigs, or poor Pell's brains would have scattered so far there would have been no hope of scooping them back. Not quite the conventional duelling end; still, perhaps the boy would be glad to have it said that he had met his death on Marly's Field.

His Lordship's eyes are sad as he looks at Jem. Pell, poor Pell, was a faithful friend, was he not? A good companion? Then repeating this last phrase, His Lordship looks at Rajal – for now Rajal must be that companion. There is no other. There can be no other.

Reverently, Rajal bows his head.

His Lordship stands. Now he is pacing, pacing back and forth; mysteriously, the staff appears again. He says, and there is urgency in his tone now, 'Tomorrow, very early, I am leaving Agondon. Important business takes me abroad; all my servants have been dismissed, and I am shutting down the house in Davalon Street. You boys, too, must leave. Sir Pellion Pelligrew is distraught enough at his daughter's tragic death; when he learns what has happened to his son, you may be certain he shall prosecute to the full measure of the law.'

Jem hung his head. He was sorry for Pell, and for Pell's father; still, some contrary impulse made him say, 'My lord, Burgrove is a murdering swine, yet is not obliged to flee. I had thought gentlemen of fashion were immune to the laws that constrain common folk.'

'The thought, young Prince, is an ignoble one – for all that it is often true. But Burgrove, you must remember, is a favourite of that gentleman best known to you, perhaps, as "Chokey". *That* you have divined; less likely is it that you know the reason why. It is put about that Burgrove's is a trade-fortune – but what, one might ask, was the nature of the trade? As it happens, the senior Burgrove was – so the phrase goes – *made* not through dint of his ill-advised investments, but rather as a result of selling his unusually beautiful young wife to Chokey – or perhaps I should say, to *Chokey's*, for no doubt it is the same in the end. Young "Jac" is the favoured of many bastards.'

Jem took this in. At once an important piece of knowledge came to him. 'Then Mr Burgrove – he is my uncle?'

'Very good, young Prince. I see, then, that you have divined the identity of "Chokey". Indeed, he is your great-father, the Archduke of Irion. More than this, he is one of the few among the nobles who retains the ear of Tranimel. The betrayer of Ejard Red, no doubt, may be considered a trusted ally. So you see, young Prince, we must permit Mr Burgrove his – ah – *little indiscretions*. Alas, I fear that a ward of mine would meet with less favour from the First Minister.'

Rajal said, 'My lord, you say we are to leave tomorrow. Should we not leave at once – tonight?'

Lord Empster brushes the question aside. 'Fear not, boy, you shall leave soon – soon.'

Jem says, 'With you, my lord?'

His Lordship considers, or appears to consider. But the reply is oblique. 'No, Jem, not with me. The time is hardly right, is it?'

'My lord?'

'Jem, I had hoped that when we reached this point, your training would have been completed. I put my poor Pellam to quite a task, did I not, to turn you from a green Tarn-lad, a runner after Vagas, into one who could prosecute the quest before him? For yes, Jem, that was my scheme, though it seems you never had the wit to see it. Now, in your impatience, you have cut this scheme short. I shall watch over you, for your mission is vital; but you – and your Vaga-page, of course – must travel into the depths of Zenzau alone. Perhaps, if this adventure ends in success, it may constitute an atonement of sorts for the folly that has ended so precipitately your high life in Agondon.'

'Then we are to go to Zenzau?' Jem breathes.

By now, the brick walls and the vaulted ceiling, the tapers and the chilling rays of the moon have long since replaced the hill, the tree, the sun. The bird, the Bob Scarlet, has flown away; instead of the grass, Jem and Rajal find themselves sitting on hard wooden benches. Pews, as in a temple? What is this place? This cannot be Lord Empster's mansion! But Jem barely notices the scene around them. It is Rajal who is troubled. Now he remembers a carriage climbing, climbing the high streets of The Island. In his mind he sees a street, a door – a great oaken door? – illuminated only by the harsh moonbeams that insist their way through the swirling fog. Desperate, tearful, he sees himself following, as Jem's stricken form is bundled from the carriage. Then winding steps going down, down. Then a hand on his forehead, and Jem's. Lord Empster's hand?

Now the taper-light is flickering, flaring; the moonbeam in the centre of the floor glares gold. But darkness presses enviously all around the light; Rajal struggles to see the noble lord, pacing, pacing, in his friar-like robes. A slow, spreading fear is consuming Rajal; but still Jem thinks only of Lord Empster's words.

Suddenly His Lordship seems to be angry. His face swoops close to Jem's. 'Fool, boy, fool! You ask where you are to go? Where *else* but to Zenzau, where even now Viana's crystal aches to join its dark companion! Why, have you forgotten The Burning Verses, that flamed out at you in the days of your ignorance, calling you upon your sacred quest?'

Lord Empster's hand is tight on Jem's shoulder, and all at once it is Jem who is consumed with fear. For the first time, it seems to him, he sees the dark vault that has closed around them; for the first time he sees clearly his guardian's clouded face. The face shocks him. Yet why can that be? It is an ordinary face of a man in middle life – wrinkled a little, shaven smooth – a man who would have been handsome in youth, and now is handsome no more. But in the texture of the flesh (so it seems to Jem now) is there not something dead, something waxen? In the eyes there is a chill flame that flashes like the glare of a gold tiral, spinning, spinning down to lie in the snow. And crouched on the cold pew in the darkness, rocking back and forth, Jem recites:

THE CHILD WHO IS THE KEY TO THE OROKON
SHALL BEAR THE MARK OF RIEL
& HAVE IN HIM THE SPIRIT OF NOVA-RIEL:
BUT HIS TASK IS GREATER AS THE EVIL ONE IS GREATER
WHEN THE END OF ATONEMENT COMES

Rajal almost cries out. Is this Jem's voice? It cannot be – not unless his beloved, too, has partaken all at once of Empster's waxy death. Yet still His Lordship grips Jem's shoulder, the shoulder where the shot had entered. Could it be that he is transmitting the words, forcing them through the conduit of Jem's lungs, his larynx? But no, it cannot be. These are words that are burned in Jem's brain. His heart.

FOR SASSOROCH SHALL COME AGAIN FROM UNBEING
& HIS POWER SHALL BE A HUNDREDFOLD:
BUTNOW HE SHALL BEAR THIS TRUE NAME & TRUE VISAGE
THAT WERE HIDDEN FROM THE WORLD
WHEN HE WAS—

There is more, of course, but suddenly Empster is dragging Jem from the pew, hauling him over the floor into the harsh ray of moonbeam.

'Look up, boy!'

In that moment a bell – it is the Temple bell – begins to toll from somewhere far, far above. Never has it seemed so deep, so sonorous; to Rajal it seems the very pillars around them are vibrating in time with the mournful clangings. Jem barely hears; Jem only sees, and what he sees is so bright that he cries out, almost in pain. He is looking up into the face of the moon, focused down the length of a long, long shaft.

'Leave him!' Rajal tries to intervene, terrified at the light that blanks his friend's face. To no avail; brutally the noble lord brushes Rajal aside, forcing Jem to stare up at the dazzling moon. Would he burn Jem's eyes away? Rajal's lute, struck as he falls, echoes out a shivery note.

Now the voice comes muttering, close at Jem's ear: 'Hornlight! Boy, did you even know that tonight a full moon would burn in the darkness above the fog? Yet, on the calendar, the day is not right! How can that be? Have you ever wondered? Prince Jemany, Key to the Orokon, have you ever looked upon the ruins of time?'

Sprawled on the floor, Rajal cries: 'Stop! It is forbidden to look into the Hornlight!'

Lord Empster flings back his head and laughs, 'Vaga-boy, save your fool superstitions! What can you know of my old friend, the sweet mistress of my midnight ramblings? On and on she has stared, sorrowing, at the follies that drive this world deeper into decay – and yet, as the Atonement ends at last, may she not dream that her beauty shall return? There is a rhyme I heard long ago. Peasants recited it – oh, in another country. Shall I tell it to you, Jemany?

> *Moon-lady, moon-lady,*
> *Come back alive:*
> *But through the power*
> *Of the Crystals Five!*

Come, sweet Prince, it is time for your quest!'

Chapter 47

VISION IN THE WILDWOOD

'Papa! Papa!'

It was mad.

But she was mad.

Cata's white petticoats flapped around her like sails as she plunged on blindly through the frozen world. Snow lay everywhere, thick and hard. Shards of cold stabbed up like glass through the naked flesh of her feet, her legs. Wildwood trees stood pitiless and barren in the cold silver of a Hornlight moon.

'Papa! Papa!'

Had she died already? She was a desperate ghost, a wailing spirit, skittering through the darkness to the place of lamentation. But no fire awaited her in Papa's cave. No caress, no kiss to warm her.

Only icicles, only emptiness.

Cata collapsed before the cave, moaning, sobbing. But now her tears froze on her feelingless cheeks and her tormented lungs could barely gulp in the air.

It was no good, no good. They had killed Papa, long ago. They had killed the boy Jem and they had killed Papa, too. Like some wounded Wildwood creature, ready to die, the frozen girl doubled over in the snow. Cold roared in her ears like the sea. She was drowning, and she didn't care.

That was when something extraordinary happened.

In the beginning it could have been nothing, just some illusion of her tormented brain. She was dying, after all. So it was true, then, that just before death time would peel backwards, as if it were a picture-scroll read in reverse? At first it was only a twittering in her ear, the meaningless burbling of some frail bird. *To-whit! To-whoo!* Bob Scarlet, out here in the night? Shouldn't his little head be huddled in his breast, safe in some barn, under some eave? Cata's eyes had closed and her face was pressed hard into a pillow of snow. *To-whit! To-whoo!* But what did he want? No, Cata could not open her eyes. The lids were frozen shut. But then – so delicious this illusion, so sweet! – it seemed to her that a warm breeze was playing at her temples. And the snow beneath her, had it changed to grass? If her lips had not been fixed shut, Cata would have smiled. Then, in the illusion-world, it seemed that she could. It seemed, too, that she could open her eyes.

Cata did, and gasped. Before her startled vision fluttered brightly coloured butterflies, purple, green, red . . . She scrambled up.

This is her vision:

Sunshine streams down brilliantly into the clearing. Grass (it was true!) is growing beneath her. Soft draping leaves hang caressingly from the trees and curling about the branches are luxurious vines. Perfume from a thousand brilliant flowers fills the air, mingling on the senses with the warm wind and the buzz of bees, drunk on pollen, and the birds – bluebirds, nightingales, gorgeous rainbow-doves – piping out their fanfare as all around, like sentinels, the animals gather . . .

Here comes the hare with his long twitching ears. Here comes the mole, popping out of his mound. Here comes the squirrel, skittering shyly, clutching a nut in his nimble little paws. And who is this? The otter, glistening wet? The fox, his tail a blazing fire?

The brown bear, stirred from his Koros-season sleep, comes rearing on his hind-legs, stretching and yawning.

Yes, they are all here, Cata's friends; even the wise damask-owl is here, mingling his hootings in the golden daylight with all the sweet music of his brother-birds.

And then, through the trees, comes a flash of stripes. In proud, shy reverence Cata sinks to her knees.

'Wood-tiger?'

Would he come to her? Would even he come to her? But Cata never knows if he joins the circle, for now, swooning in the perfumed air, she feels herself lifted on a cloud of vision and suddenly, in a spasm of ecstasy, she is aware once again of all the mystic power that for so long has lain dormant inside her. In rapturous communion Cata's senses flow with the senses of the birds, the beasts, the flowers. She moans, shudders; but even now something is wrong, even now the chill has not left her.

'But why?' she whispers. 'Why this rapture, when sorrow can never leave my heart?'

'You are hasty, Queen of Ejland.' A voice? Sweet, kind. But whose is it? Why does it call her Queen? 'Look, Queen of Ejland. Look at the picture.'

And Cata, forgetting that the voice has called her Queen, sees before her now the image of her Papa, as clear as if he were real. She cries out his name, but of course he does not hear. Pain tears at her heart. The old man is wandering blindly through the woods, and in the picture the woods are chill and white again. Directionless, bewildered, he plants his staff before him, his cowl flapping coldly about his ruined face. Poor Papa! He cannot go on; he collapses in the snow. Yes, he is dying as

Cata almost died, moments before in the dimension she has left. Cata screams, cries out. Why can't she save him? But there is nothing she can do. What she sees is just a picture, a cruel remembrance of something that has already happened.

But then there is the hand. Dying in the snow, the old blind man does not realize, until the hand grips his, that his terrible loneliness is over at last. *Papa*, Cata sobs, as she hears him speak, speak to the stranger who has come to him in his dying-time. *But I can see you*, Old Wolveron is saying. Has his vision returned? The figure that stands over him is robed as he is robed, and, like him, carries a staff; but the staff is made of silver, and the robes are gold. *You see me*, says the figure, *because it is my will. Come, old man, you have done your work. You are safe now. Come with me.*

And now Old Wolveron is rising to his feet, standing with a steadiness he thinks he has lost; now, more than this, he is rising from the ground, rising up above the icy trees, enveloped in the aura of his golden protector.

Tears stream down Cata's face. Is this her Papa's death? The question is only a thought in her mind, but the presence that stands behind her has heard it, heard it as if it were spoken.

'Queen of Ejland, can your Papa be dead? He is a Guardian. It is ordained that he shall be there at the end. *It is ordained that you shall meet him again.*'

'I don't understand. Tell me what you mean.'

'Queen, I speak of the end. The end that is not an end, but a beginning.'

'You speak in riddles. And why do you call me Queen?'

'I speak of a time when what is foretold in The Burning Verses shall come to pass.'

'The Burning Verses? Papa spoke of them.'

'And did he not speak of the Key to the Orokon?'

'But that is Jem. My love, my life.' Sobs choked in Cata's throat. 'And he is dead.'

'Dead?' There was laughter, gentle laughter. 'Child, I thought you had remembered everything! How can it be ordained that you are to be Queen, if the King who is to raise you up is already dead?'

'Jem and I are to be King and Queen?'

Only laughter, the laughter again.

Cata tried to turn to the stranger, but could not. Dimly she sensed the presence of the figure, a tall man, strangely garbed, but all her powers could not bring him into focus. A bony hand rested on her shoulder and a fresh wave of sadness swept shudderingly through her. It could not be true, could it, that Papa was alive? That Jem would be with her again one day?

She whispered, 'No, all this is unreal. This Theron-season, deep in the Koros-time. These beasts and birds that gather to welcome me. And you who speak to me. You do not exist. I am dying in the snow.'

The stranger's lips bent close to her ear, whispering in return, 'Oh my precious child, believe in your vision! What is real, what is illusion? We stand at this moment in a special place, but what if this place were more real, more true than the one you see around you in the ordinary world? Dear child, there was a time when you would have known this in your heart. For too long, you have been a stranger to yourself. For a full passage of the seasons – longer – you have lived in a world without vision, dream, or memory, chained to the lingering evil of the depraved Waxwell. Was that your real life? No, child, that is now. Here. It was ordained that you should know this blindness, so that vision when it came back should be yet more precious. And vision is back! Turn to me, child, and know your destiny.'

The hand gripped Cata tighter by the shoulder, spinning her round, and unresisting, she turned to face the stranger at last. Cata looked up into a silver mask.

'Harlequin! But they killed you on the village green!'

'Child, remember! What is real, what is not? Know only this: that as the boy embarks on the next stage of his quest, so you begin your own quest to find him. I have said that you are to be Queen. But only if the crystals are saved from Toth-Vexrah—'

'Toth-Vexrah? I don't—'

'You shall know, you shall know. Child, I must speak fast. This reality is unstable. Only for a few moments more shall we sustain it, then I shall be lost from your sight again. Listen: in time, the boy must travel to the furthest reaches of the Lands of El-Orok. On his quest depends the future of this world. But he shall never complete his quest without you. For as he is the Key to the Orokon, so you are the Lock. Seek him.'

'What? But how? Where?'

'The time is fast approaching when you shall make your escape, following the path that leads to your destiny.'

'But now? At this moment? What shall I do?' Cata was desperate now, breathless and gasping. She believed everything with an absolute faith. Believed everything, yet knew nothing, and already, around them, the animals had gone and the sweet bower where she had returned from death was sinking back into the Season of Koros. Petals fell. Leaves shrivelled. Greenness was fading into the white of snow and an icy wind was on the air again. In a moment it would all be gone; Cata would collapse in the snow again, just at the moment when the anguished Nirry came floundering through the darkness, calling her name.

But there was one moment more. Cata shuddered as the harlequin clutched her tight, like a lover, but instead of endearments his whispered words were only, 'In days, the Blue Irions depart for Zenzau. They need more men, and seek them actively. You are a bold and fearless girl. Do you understand what you must do?'

Chapter 48

THE SHATTERING

'I don't understand you! Why are you hurting me?'

Jem breaks suddenly, violently from his guardian. Wildly his eyes swivel this way and that. How the scene flares out, the columns, the pews, and somewhere, hidden in shadows, an altar. It comes to him now that this place is a chapel; comes to him, too, that they are far underground. And still the clangings of the bells go on, echoing as in the depths of a well. Again, again. How many more? Could this be midnight, tolling over the city?

But at that moment there is a sound of footsteps, echoing hollowly down a flight of stone stairs. Jem staggers in the radiance of the moon; coldly, Lord Empster laughs again. 'Is it not ingenious, the Hornlight Focus? Down comes the light from the pinnacle of the spire, burning through the great central column of the temple. The bells, too, burn in their own strange way—'

Jem says blankly, 'Temple?'

'But of course! Far, far beneath. Come, my young friends, there is a scene we must witness. But Vaga-boy—' His Lordship's look is wry '—I have neglected to dress you properly. Your page's costume flares like a jester's motley. Hide yourself, hide yourself, deep in the shadows. And keep the strings of your lute still, hm?'

And Rajal can only retreat to the shadows as first one, then another black-garbed figure comes filing into the crypt. How swiftly the Brothers take their places! His Lordship assumes a position at the back, clamping Jem's shoulder tightly with his hand.

'Draw close your cowl, Prince. Draw it round your face.'

In moments the scene is ready. Terrified, Jem peers from behind his cowl. No one speaks. No one looks right, no one looks left. Here, he sees a glittering eye; there, a curve of cheek. But is not this eye, this cheek familiar? Of course, what are these black-garbed forms but the silhouettes of figures Jem knows? Who are they, these Brothers, but noble lords who parade in finery at the First Moonlife Ball, at the Canonday service, at Lady Cham-Charing's Festival Levee? Yes, the greatest in the land are here, defiling this most sacred Time of Meditation.

A hunched form takes its place near the front, apart just a little from the column of moonlight. This one Jem recognizes at once. Chokey.

Raising his hands, the treacherous Archduke bids his brothers be seated. The Black Canonical is about to begin!

'Watch, young Prince. Watch and learn.'

The ceremony proceeds with chanting, prayers. Dutifully Jem opens and shuts his mouth. He thinks of litanies his aunt made him learn; but here, there is no reference to the Lord Agonis. Here, there is no reference to peace, mercy, love.

> *O mighty one, we await your coming!*
> *Mighty one, consume this world in fire!*
> *Mighty one, sink this world in flood!*
> *Mighty one, swallow this world in mire!*
> *Mighty one, bathe this world in blood!*
> *One who came as Sassoroch,*
> *Come to us as* TOTH—

Again and again Jem hears the sinister name; then, as the prayers draw to a close, the long litany-lines wither away and there is nothing but this single, repeated word. TOTH, TOTH, the Brothers chant, until it seems to Jem that the mantra is an acid, burning, searing through the tissues of his brain. If it were not for his guardian, gripping him tightly, Jem would rush forward with his hands over his ears, screaming at them all to *stop, stop*. He bites his tongue hard, digs his nails into his palm, gazes into the glare of the Hornlight Focus.

Then all at once the mantra is over; Jem's dazzled eyes make out the lean, ascetic figure, standing in the very glare of the Focus. It is a figure that he has seen before.

But of course.

The First Minister!

Now the Archduke retires into the shadows, as one who has merely prepared the way. Tranimel's face is a dazzling glare. He spreads his arms wide, crying his words into the column of light. In an ecstasy of loathing he denounces Orok, false Orok and his five vile children. Fervently he praises the power of TOTH, who soon shall break free to wreak his just revenge.

But now, something strange is happening to the light. Now, as Tranimel's words spill out, a thunderous rumbling begins overhead. Jem looks up, terrified. Is the anti-god coming – coming already? But this is the sound of the stone vaulting, shifting as if at the prompting of some mechanism. Slowly the angle of the Focus changes. The First Minister steps back, keeping in the light, as it falls now on a curtain at the back of the altar. Still he speaks, but as he speaks, Jem becomes aware of the mysterious form that is throbbing, pulsing behind the dark fabric.

'Come to us, GREAT ENCHANTER! Come to us, BANISHED OF

OROK! Come to us, FIRST OF REJECTED CREATURES, O greatest, O mighty, O magnificent TOTH-VEXRAH!'

Now, as he shrieks the name of the anti-god, Tranimel steps from the glare of the Focus. In the same moment he tears away the curtain.

It is as much as Jem can do not to cry out.

Protuberant eyes, more red than white, burst from beneath the lumps of a misshapen brow. One ear has been torn away; there is no nose to speak of, only a suppurating hole; the lips are torn and bloody, pushed back by long twisted fang-like teeth. Sores, dripping with pus, gape open in the cheeks; worms thread through the lattices of corruption. Moments pass before Jem sees that the face is but a reflection, magnified horribly, shimmering in a vast sheet of glass.

'Fools, vile fools!'

Viciously the anti-god shrieks out his contempt, his hatred, his abomination of his worshippers. Hastily Tranimel gestures to the Brothers. At once a chant rises from their ranks, louder than before, urgent, desperate.

The Brothers stamp their feet, cry themselves hoarse.

> *A god we await! Beat the drums!*
> *Locked in the glass till the crystal comes!*
> *Locked from his love, we burn with wrath!*
> *Only one god and the god is TOTH!*
>
> *With the first crystal, TOTH breaks through!*
> *Then he finds crystal Number Two!*
> *When he has crystals Three, Four, Five,*
> *Then the Orokon comes alive!*
>
> *TOTH for the power to destroy and create!*
> *TOTH for the power to love and to hate!*
> *Never never broken, ever and yon,*
> *Burning bright in the Orokon!*
>
> *Burn up the world in fires of wrath!*
> *All shall bow to the power of TOTH!*
> *Bow to his lash! Kneel to his rod!*
> *Kill all the creatures of the father-god!*
>
> *Only one god! The god is TOTH!*
> *Burn up the world in fires of wrath!*
> *Never never broken, ever and yon,*
> *TOTH's is the power of the Orokon!*
> *TOTH's is the power of the Orokon!*

The chant, as it goes on, is ever more frenetic. In a kind of ecstasy, laving in the worship, the face in the glass bulges and lolls. Bloody tears wash across lidless eyes; fresh pus oozes from the sores. Drivelling, the hideous mouth opens wider, exposing a rotted stump of tongue. Worms wave out from the corrupted flesh, dancing in time to the depraved rhythm. Disgusted, Jem turns away; yet almost as horrible is the sight of his guardian, stamping beside him in a passion that seems quite as real as that of all the others.

Why, why has his guardian brought him here? Distraught, Jem clutches the crystal at his chest. That is when a new horror overcomes him. What is this heat, this burning dark power, that seems to be pulsing through the fabric of his robes? Then he looks down and sees a purple-black light, glowing through the fabric – glowing through his hand! Jem starts. How can this be? Alarmed, he looks to his guardian, but still his guardian is stamping, chanting. Jem bunches his robes tighter around him, trying to conceal the strange glow. In moments, he is sobbing. What can it mean, this aching in the crystal, as it comes before the image of the anti-god?

Suddenly, from the glass, comes a high, grotesque shriek. It is a shriek of joy. Still the god is lolling, drivelling, but his pleasure, it seems, has reached new heights. The chant breaks off. Ecstatic, the First Minister turns to his god.

'Ah, mighty one, drink in our devotion! Yes, mighty one, lave in our love! But now, let us prove our love to you afresh!' His hand rises into the blazing Focus as he signals urgently to an inferior Brother. The next part of the ceremony must begin at once. A gift, an offering. For the first time Jem sees the stone slab, jutting up from the floor before the magic glass. The inferior Brother produces a wriggling burden, shrouded in a sheet of white. A sheep? A goat?

'O mighty Toth,' cries Tranimel, 'accept this our offering! With eyes of love, burning in devotion to your great cause, once again your Brothers have scoured the empire, searching for only the finest offerings. Once again, I have personally inspected the succulent dish we lay before you now!' As he speaks, Tranimel draws a huge knife from underneath the folds of his robes. Now, in the glass, Toth is leering forward, the bloodshot eyes bursting, the rotted tongue dripping hungrily with slime. Again Tranimel signals to the Brother, this time telling him to peel away the shroud. Jem's eyes widen. Suddenly a terrible sick fear, worse than any he has felt before, is thudding, almost tearing, at the fibres of his heart. Suddenly his guardian's hand is tighter on his shoulder, so tight now that Jem could cry out. And still he feels the crystal burning bright. He hunches forward tightly, arms across his chest.

'O mighty Toth, let this be balm to your sores!'

Then comes the moment Jem will always remember, seared into his heart and brain like a scar. At once, everything happens quickly, too quickly. Tranimel raises the knife, ready to plunge. The shroud falls away. The child, gagged and bound, struggles on the slab.

It might have been Jem who cried out first. Instead, there is a crash at the back of the crypt, a crash and an echo, as of a lute smashing to the floor, and in the same moment the agonized cry:

'Myla!'

Then Rajal is rushing forward, desperate, his bright costume lurid in the taper-light. A commotion breaks out. Brothers turn, cry. In the glass, Toth shrieks, and his shriek, it seems, is Tranimel's too:

'Treachery!'

It is Jem's guardian who springs up first. Whether he acts for Tranimel, whether he acts for Myla, Jem will never know. But now Lord Empster is grabbing Rajal, wrestling him to the floor. Rajal's limbs flail in all directions, he is screaming, punching, kicking. But the terrible shriek of the god in the glass rings out higher, wilder:

'My blood! Give me my blood!'

Tranimel's eyes flash in the Hornlight. The dagger arcs down. Myla writhes, twists. In the next instant, she will die. But Jem rushes forward. Purple-black light burns from his chest. He seizes the crystal, tears it free. Tranimel cries out. What is this light, this terrible light, blinding even the rays of the Focus? But at once he knows. The prophecy! It is true! From the glass, the shrieking grows wilder, wilder. On the floor, Rajal thrashes, writhes. Then suddenly he is limp. Suddenly all his strength has channelled from him, coursing into the shoulder his love has cured. Jem flings back his arm.

He hurls the crystal with all his might.

✵ ✵ ✵

What happens to Myla in that moment will remain a mystery for long seasons to come. The knife falls from Tranimel's hand. But where is Myla? Where has she gone? At one moment she lies on the slab, about to die. In the next, she is nowhere to be seen. Is it some power of the Crystal of Koros, snatching her away in the moment of danger? Has she merely been crushed in the affray? In moments, the walls of the crypt will shudder. In moments, ancient columns will totter. Great stones will crash to the floor.

But there are no eyes for Myla now. Not even Rajal's, not even Jem's. Now, the crystal shatters the glass. Tranimel swoops forward. He snatches the crystal, raises it up. Purple-black light shoots from his hands.

'The Key! Mighty one, it is as was foretold!'

Ecstasy radiates from his juddering form. But even as he cries out, gouts of flame, billowing clouds of noxious gas come leaping, swirling from the shattered glass. The Brothers scatter. All thought of worship over now, they are desperate only to escape, escape.

In instants, Tranimel's ecstasy is agony. His robes catch alight. He screams, staggers. The crystal falls from his hands. Crazily it spins on the floor, its light spiralling wildly into the dazzle of the Focus. Jem just has time to grab it again. It burns his hands afresh. In an instant all his resolve is gone. Suddenly Lord Empster grabs him, dragging him brutally back from the altar.

'This way, this way, quick—'

'No! Myla—' Rajal gasps, but still his body is limp; he, too, can only be dragged away.

In the last moment, as the crypt rumbles, as gas and dust and flame consume the scene, Jem turns back just in time to see what happens to the crazed First Minister. Tranimel is burning. His body bucks and writhes in the flames. Then, as if a dagger has ripped his torso open, all at once his heart, his lungs, his guts burst from him, spilling over the sacrificial slab like offal.

Then it happens.

Before the body even staggers and falls, a wraith, some blazing serpent of flame, comes swirling out from the glass behind, entering, filling the emptied shell.

The body reunites.

Tranimel – but it is no longer Tranimel – stands tall and proud, impassive in the midst of leaping flames.

Chapter 49

A BLACK AND WHITE CAT

What was that sound? It might have been claws, skittering over a floor; it might have been a branch, tapping at a window.

As a diver, on the far coasts of Tiralos, edges up from the ocean depths with a slow spiralling motion, so Miss Jelica Vance roused herself from sleep. Had she been dreaming? But if she had, her dream had vanished, leaving her puzzled in the warm darkness. Jeli raised her head from her pillow. In the grate, the embers made glowing red caverns; at the dormer window, through a crack in the curtains, there shimmered the disc of the Hornlight moon.

Then she heard the sound again. The skittering.

'Ring? Rheen?'

But Ring's warm flank was not beside her, and Rheen was no longer perched upon her bedstead. Jeli felt suddenly troubled, bereft. She screwed up her brow, as if in the forgotten dream – for, to be certain, there had been a dream – she would find some clue as to why, all at once, the moonlight seemed so sinister, the red caverns of the fire so ominous.

Then the sound came again, more a restless tapping this time, and with it Jeli heard the murmur of a voice. She stiffened. It was coming from Aunt Vlada's boudoir. Reaching up, Jeli clutched the curtain, drawing it back from the window just a little. The sliver of moonlight widened and she saw that the door between the two rooms was ajar. Swiftly, careful to be quiet as she could, Jeli padded across her little room, putting her eye to the crack in the door.

A strange envy gnawed at Jeli's heart.

Many times the temple bells had tolled that night since Aunt Vlada tucked her young charge in bed. That her aunt should still be in the adjoining room was no surprise to Jeli. Aunt Vlada had a bedchamber elsewhere in the house – so Jeli assumed – but often of late Jeli would find her in the mornings, dozing fitfully on the sofa next door. It might have troubled Jeli, might have alarmed her; in truth, she was gratified that her aunt – so it seemed – could never leave her. It was good. It was right. Only the day before, Jeli had gazed for long moments on her sleeping aunt. Pulling back the curtains – more fervently then – Jeli studied dispassionately the cracking paint, the lines, the sagging jowls.

With a strange rapture she bent down, putting her face close to Aunt Vlada's, sniffing the hot reek of the exhaling breath. Strange, she had not considered it before: Aunt Vlada sweetened her mouth with mint, and whitened her old teeth in the front with paint. But as she slept, the rottenness inside her mouth crept back, overwhelming all efforts of disguise.

Then Jeli had smiled, and her smile grew broader as the light penetrated Aunt Vlada's thin eyelids and the old woman – for indeed, she was an old, old woman – shook herself awake. At once relief overspread the old face, relief to see Jeli standing there, Jeli smiling. It was as if she feared the girl had been only a dream, and that when she opened her eyelids the dream would be gone.

But Aunt Vlada was not sleeping tonight.

Now, through the crack in the door, Jeli looked into the glow of a single candle. Illuminated in the flame was her aunt's hunched figure, staring into a looking-glass. What could the old woman be doing, gazing on her reflection in the candlelight? Perhaps, thought Jeli with sudden spite, her aunt would look on the remnants of her beauty only in the mercy of this dimmest light.

But there was more to it, Jeli was sure.

Something had happened between Jeli and her aunt; when it had happened, neither could say, but the foolish child was a child no longer.

It was only to be expected. Assured again and again that she was a great beauty, promised that her destiny was even greater, Jeli's vanity had grown rapidly. Now, if she found it in herself to patronize her aunt, did this not testify to her aunt's success? For what, after all, had Aunt Vlada wanted, but to turn the silly academy-girl into a haughty woman of fashion?

The tapping came again, and the murmurous words. The first, Jeli saw, was easily explained: Aunt Vlada's fingers – her wrinkled old talons! – beating out a rhythm on the edge of the glass. But if at first it seemed the old woman was merely muttering pathetically to herself, soon it was clear to Jeli that this was not the case.

There were two voices, not one.

Jeli's eyes darted about the boudoir, but if a second figure loomed in the darkness, it had concealed itself well. Then her hunched aunt turned just a little. Jeli was about to shrink back, fearful that the glass might catch her reflection; then, instead, she saw the face in the glass.

It was not Aunt Vlada's face.

That was when, quite unexpectedly, Jeli remembered what she had been dreaming. The dream was about Ring and Rheen. Often Jeli had thought of her aunt's notion – her senile insistence – that Rheen the mouse had returned to them as a bird. That the bird fulfilled the role of Rheen, there could be no doubt. Equally there could be no doubt – could there? – that a mouse could not suddenly turn into a bird. Yet in Jeli's dream she had seen Rheen and Ring, too, cavorting wildly about Aunt Vlada's boudoir, transforming themselves into an infinite variety of creatures. There was Ring the hound and Rheen the fox, Ring the horse and Rheen the bear, Ring the goat and Rheen the lamb, charging round and round, trampling the furniture and the dresses and the boxes, filling the air with their ever-changing barking, bleating, roaring. And though each incarnation was over in an instant, each time Jeli was certain – what doubt could there be? – that these were the animals, the very same, that she had lived with all along since meeting Aunt Vlada.

So strange a dream. What could it mean?

But there was no time to wonder now. Pressing her ear hard to the crack, Jeli struggled to hear the murmured words exchanged between the gazer and the glass.

GAZER: But old friend, how can this be? Oh it is soon, too soon!

GLASS: It was ordained. How could I prevent it?

GAZER: Yet you go away? You would leave me here in Agondon, when the Evil One is afoot?

GLASS (*scornful*): You think I flee him? Why, if he is present in any part of this Realm, is he not present in *every* part? You know I must further the work of the boy, for if he fails, we all fail.

GAZER: But if he succeeds, do not I fail?

GLASS: Fail? Do you not fulfil yourself? Weak woman, has your long tenure of existence made you arrogant? What greed is this, a lust to live on in one who has lived already too long, too long?

GAZER: Old deceiver! Who are you to say my life has been too long? (*Sobbing*) Oh, that my reign shall be out – so soon! Yet there is so much I still must do! It is all too soon, I tell you, too soon!

GLASS: But can you not work quickly now? The wedding has been mooted these five seasons or longer. The First Minister – if still we may call him so – shall be eager to cement patriotic fervour, preparatory to the trying times ahead. Indeed, these late events have made your task lighter!

GAZER: Old friend, how little you know of the feminine heart! I had hoped to work softly, softly – *after* the wedding, not just before! How else am I to secure the hold we need? Oh, I need time!

GLASS: Time! Always time, more time! Have we not had enough of time? I would have thought you would be glad, only too glad that your struggle soon is over. Would I not change places with you now, that soon I might be one with the dust and dirt?

GAZER: Heartless, cruel man! How can you speak of the dust and dirt? Oh, I spit on your masculine arrogance! There is something in you I despise as much as – why, as I despised the King of Swords!

GLASS: (*laughing*): Come, I am no King of Swords!

GAZER: No, he was precipitate to possess a lady.

There was more in this vein, but little that Jeli could understand. Of only one thing was she certain: that this talk of a wedding was talk of *her* wedding, and that it was a matter of supreme importance. Troubled, fascinated, Jeli crept back to bed.

A warm purring form came nuzzling beside her.

'Oh, Ring!' Jeli whispered, reaching out to pet him; but that was when she noticed an extraordinary thing. Jeli had not drawn the curtain that she had parted earlier to let in the Hornlight moon. Now, in the chill pallid light, she saw that something about Ring had changed.

'Ring?' she whispered again.

That it was Ring she was certain; equally, she was certain that his fur was now white.

❋ ❋ ❋

Next morning, Jem woke to find himself in a carriage, rattling through snowbound countryside. He was alone. Opening his thick coat, he looked curiously at the clothes he wore. Hardly the finery to which he had grown accustomed, it was the garb, perhaps, of a shopkeeper's son. The carriage, too, was modest, with unpadded benches and walls.

On the bench opposite was a letter, sealed with green wax. Jem picked it up cautiously. It was addressed to him. With a stab of fear he broke the seal and read:

Jemany,
The time of our ordeal has come, perhaps too soon. Destiny is upon us and we can delay no further. When you read this you shall be on your way to Zenzau. At the first staging-post across the frontier, the coachman shall set you down. Then you must find your way to the Zenzan capital. It is ordained that there you shall find the second crystal, but if this is to come to pass you must bear with you a message.
The message is this: THE TIME HAS COME. *To whom you are to take this message, I cannot tell you: only that there shall be a sign when the time, indeed, has come.*

*For now, I can do no more. It is vital that you succeed in this
mission, but vital too that you complete it without my assistance. The
events of yesterday have meant you must leave Agondon before,
perhaps, you are ready for the quest that lies ahead. Yet I am sure that
if you complete this stage, you shall make up in experience what you
miss in education. The evil enchanter is but newly reborn, and we
have time, if but a little, before his powers grow to fullness. Pray that
within this time we may secure the second crystal.*

*You shall not see me now until the crystal is in your possession.
Know, however, that I shall be looking out for you, and when the time
comes I shall appear before you again. You are suspicious of me, but in
time your suspicions shall fade. Think not ill of me, until you discover
who I am, and why I have acted as I have done.*

Remember: THE TIME HAS COME.

Your guardian, E.

Later, Jem would often read this letter again. Throughout his time in
Zenzau, he would keep it by him. When he took it from his pocket he
would smooth the page, then study it intently, as if puzzling over a
meaning he could not quite catch. Perhaps it was the part about THE
TIME HAS COME. Perhaps it was the part about *who I am, and why I
have acted as I have done.*

That first day Jem merely let the page fall, and looked out at the
monotony of the colourless landscape. Already his life in Agondon
seemed unreal to him. He tried to think of Pell, of Mr Burgrove and
Chokey and Jeli, but all of them fused and blurred in the horror of the
last things he had seen, deep beneath the temple. Sadly Jem remembered
Pell lying dead, but then it seemed to him they were all dead now, all
the people he had known in Agondon.

Except his guardian. But who was his guardian? And where was
Rajal?

Suddenly Jem felt terribly alone.

The coach halted by a mean inn, isolated in the world of whiteness. In
the pocket of his coat Jem found a few coins. He paid the coachman. The
coachman did not alight from his box. He looked at the sky, and Jem
did, too. It was late afternoon, and there would be more snow. But the
coachman drove on. Uncertainly Jem made his way towards the inn. The
thought came to him that he had crossed a border. He was in another
country. How strange it seemed!

Jem entered a parlour, empty but for a fellow in the garb of a servant,
warming himself by a roaring fire. His back was to Jem, and at first he
did not turn. Jem looked at the fire, leaping red, then out through the
window at the blank, white fields. At his chest he felt the Crystal of
Koros, digging its jagged edges into his flesh.

353

Jem coughed. But the fellow at the fire was not a tavern-boy.

'I'm your page. I'm waiting for my man.'

And suddenly, though the memory would shame him, Jem flung himself into Rajal's arms, sobbing freely.

END OF PART THREE

PART FOUR

Stand and Deliver!

Chapter 50

TWO LETTERS

My dear heart-son,
    It is with a sad heaviness (O too, too heavily!) that your loving heart-mother now takes up her pen. To think! – in the simplicity of my womanly nature I had hoped to write of fripperies and follies, of innocent joys of home and hearth, that my noble POLTISS, braving in defence of this our kingdom what torments no mere light-headed woman can imagine, might smile and think fondly on those feminine souls who without the stiffening of your masculinity would wilt like vines untethered to a rod. But now (O cruel fate!) what must be your emotions, when I tell of you of the tragedy which has befallen our little family? For O, alas (dear POLTISS, be firm!) it is my mournful and melancholy duty to inform you that a great and noble heart, a heart which once boomed like thunderous drums in a cause so great as to save this very kingdom (yet a heart, too, which fluttered with the fondest domestic affections) is still! For yes (dear, dear POLTISS), the wife who pens these words is a wife without a HUSBAND, and the son who reads them with (for how can it be otherwise?) brimming eyes, must endure the long years ahead without a loving FATHER.
    O my SON! – for yes, this I must call you, for do I not love you as if (O pray it had been so!) you had in your coming bruised my tender loins? – how are we to support ourselves? How can we not totter under this grievous affliction? And yet, though my womanly affections burst from me in copious floods, I am without fears for you, for you are a man, grown to full size, and I know the faith we share shall keep you upright.
    In the love of the Lord Agonis,
      For ever & assuredly,
        I am & remain,
          Your mother,
            UMBECCA

Postscript.
My dear son (though of course it can be but as chaff, blown away on the winds of our sorrow) there is one comfort of which I may inform you. It is this: that mere days before our beloved one was taken from us, His Imperial Agonist Majesty, through his Under-Secretary Lord Margrave, saw fit at last to grant to the best of men the reward which

357

*for so long had been his due. Of course, mere worldly titles can mean
but little (why, nothing!) to faithful and humble Agonists such as we
are; still, dear son, perhaps there is some small joy for you (as for me)
in knowing that the noblest of Ejland's heroes entered the Portals of
the Vast with the title which (so some, more worldly than I, had
hoped) should have been his in his long and virtuous life: LORD
VEELDROP (a Viscount, no less!).*

S.H.I.A.M.
SERVICE OF HIS IMPERIAL AGONIST MAJESTY

From: His Excellency the Honourable *OLIVAN THARLEY
VEELDROP*, Provincial Supreme Commander & Governor by
Appt. to His Imperial Agonist Majesty *EJARD OF THE BLUE
CLOTH*, Kingdom of Ejland, 9th Province ('Valleys of the
Tarn'): *To: POLTISS VEELDROP*, Capt., 5th R. Fusil. Tarn (Zenz.
Miss.); as dictated this day, 1Wa/(ARC) Ichios, AC 999d, to
EBENEZER SULGWYN WORMWOOD, Esq., Notary by
Appointment & Licence.

Honoured & beloved son:
*In the pain of what I am certain are my last & final days in this the
Realm of Being I your father dictate to you these words: & now my
son that you read these words you know my fears have not proved
vain & your loving father at last has passed whether into The Vast or
into the Realm of Unbeing only the all-merciful LORD AGONIS god
of our people can say: yet my son I say to you as I face my end that
were I consigned with Sassoroch & His Creatures to the Eternal Pain
that is the Realm of Unbeing I could not question so heavy a
judgement: though it is my hope that the repentance which floods my
heart may yet now lead to the LORD AGONIS affording me some
measure of mercy however undeserved: for yes my son in these my last
days I have come to see the errors of my past life: this hard heart has
softened & I look back now on my wickedness with execration &
shame: FIVE MERCIES led to my reformation: ONE the virtue &
goodness with which I communed in the pages of the greatest genius
this our kingdom has yet produced: & yet by paradox designed to
humble our proud sex a genius in petticoats: the incomparable MISS
R——: ONE the religious teaching I imbibed as if it were mother's
milk in this my late reduced & sickly state from my faithful
CHAPLAIN: ONE the love which led me at last in this twilight of my
life to honourable marriage with your heart-mother UMBECCA: for
there was a time when she seemed a good wife to me: then wonder not
my child what may be the two remaining: ONE the discovery of my
long-lost son: ONE the blessed heart-daughter who came to me in the*

shape of the beautiful CATAYANE: these then are the things which have changed me & my son believe me these last two I cite have been by far the most decisive of all: & know that in this my reformed state my fatherly earnestness for your moral & spiritual fealty burns now as the brightest ember in this my dying breast: for my son I am not so blind as to be insensible to the wicked impulses which possess you now in your hot youth: nor may you deceive me as others are deceived by the hypocrisy you adopt as a mode habitual: for have I not as if by contagion passed to you the contaminated blood of a VEELDROP: & is there not in your veins too a contamination still worse: for O my son though I had planned never to tell you of your shame it is my duty now as a faithful follower of LORD AGONIS to reveal to you that you were born in sin of the blackest dye: for who was your mother but a foul strumpet your sinful father took to his bed: supplied to me during the Siege of Irion by the wicked keeper of the LAZY TIGER: a man so steeped in wickedness that he wd. prostitute his very wife: my son you are the fruit of that sinful union: O pray that one day you may forgive your erring father: but my son this I know: that in ordering now my affairs before my death I must as your father do all I can that your ways be redeemed: to this end I have determined & lay down in my Last Will & Testament this the following: that as only VIRTUOUS LOVE may reclaim the wildness to which so sin-born a young man may sink so it is that other than provision &c. for my wife & dependants I leave to my son POLTISS VEELDROP all my worldly goods titles &c. as appropriate CONDITIONAL UPON HIS MARRIAGE TO MY WARD MISS CATAYANE WOLVERON with subsequent cohabitation intercourse &c. subject to inspection by my executors: I know my son you are wildish & wd. stray but trust too that in time the sweet influence of this virtuous maiden may soften your manly pride as it has that of the loving father who now takes his leave of you in fondest & yet alas not unfearful hope that one day he may salute you again in The Vast: with manly tears & deepest love my son I leave you:

FATHER

Chapter 51

SALT-PIG

'Tighter!'

'Ooh, miss, this fair takes me back, it does!'

'Takes you back?'

'Lacing the mistress. Tighter, tighter, she used to call, but there's some lumps you can't go hiding. Miss, I declare you'll be doing yourself some damage!'

'Got to be done, Nirry – I felt them getting loose.'

'Miss Cata, really! You won't find me squishing and squashing what the Lord Agonis gave me. Not much, I know, but I shouldn't like to meet my Wiggler, accidental-like, and him not know me for my proper self. Come, Miss Cata, we're a long way from Irion. Why don't you give up this soldiering lark and turn back into a lady good and proper?'

It was early morning, somewhere in the Zenzan woods. The two women, up before the bugle sounded, had crept away from camp for a secret meeting. The leaves all around them were green and new in the bright dawn of the burgeoning season.

Cata smoothed the strapping round her breasts, and put her shirt back over her head. 'But Nirry, how can I be a lady again?'

'Take off them britches for a start, Miss Cata!'

Cata laughed. 'Silly Nirry! A lady's more than petticoats, as well you know. What is a lady but her silk and lace? Her fine house? Her quality-friends, to shield and protect her? No, Nirry, I can't be a lady any more!'

'But Miss Cata, really! What will Master Jem think, seeing you like that? If it's true what you say, and he's alive after all—'

'Oh, he's alive, Nirry – and I'm doing this for him.'

Nirry sighed, 'You're too deep for me, miss. All I know is, you were a lovely lady.' Emotion cracked in the maid's voice. 'You were the best lady I ever served, you were!'

'The best, Nirry?' Cata smiled. 'I thought I drove you mad with my wild ways.'

'Well, it's true Lady Ela was less of a handful. But I shouldn't like it if you were quiet like her. There's such a thing as being too quiet, Miss Cata, and they could never keep you quiet for long. I won't say you don't worry me, though, because you do.'

Fondly she looked on the young mistress. Cata had resumed her blue jacket now, and her three-cornered hat. Really, it was uncanny – why, even Nirry thought she would be fooled! Reluctantly they bent their steps back to camp. Soon the bugle would split the air; soon Cata – or rather, Recruit Wolveron – would be packing up his kit for another day's march, and Nirry the Cook, sweating over her cauldrons, would be stirring up stew for five hundred men. She hoped those wretched girls had got the fire started this morning, that was all. And done the taters!

Sometimes – now was a case in point – Nirry wanted to put an idea to Miss Cata. Very well, she would say, you can't be a lady. But couldn't you at least be your own sex? You need not starve. There's a job on the cook-house side of things, make no mistake, if only you'll wear a dress again. All the stew and dumplings you can eat, and none of this nonsense of guns and fighting.

The plan was sensible, of course it was, but somehow Nirry could not bring herself to propose it. It seemed disrespectful – a lady like Miss Cata scrubbing pans, chopping scrag-mutton into little bits? Besides, Nirry thought glumly, Miss Cata would hardly agree. Oh, she was a wayward girl, this one!

'Poor Nirry! I do upset you, don't I?'

Nirry sighed, 'Well, Miss Cata, as my old mother used to say, it's not for me to question my betters. But I'd have thought if there was one advantage to being one of our sex, miss, it was having no truck with all that fighting. Lot of nonsense, noisy and dirty and dangerous to boot. You could stay behind the lines with me – and what do you do? Dress up like a man, and go and join them. It's not natural, miss, it's just not natural!'

'I suppose not!' Cata laughed. But then her face furrowed and she added, 'But a lot of things aren't natural now, Nirry.'

'You're telling me!' Nirry lowered her voice. 'Why, in the castle we was Redjackets, we was, through and through. To think, and it's all come to this. Poor father driving Bluejacket coaches. My own young man dressed all in blue – and now my young lady, too! Oh, how can you fight for them, Miss Cata, how?'

Cata smiled, 'Nirry, how can you cook for them?'

'It's my job, Miss Cata, and I've got no other. Didn't I cook for the mistress all these years? And would have been fair chuffed if I choked her, let me tell you. Why, if it hadn't been for Her Ladyship – and Master Jem . . .' Nirry shuddered. 'Ooh, I'm never going back to that old cow, never!'

But Cata was barely listening any more. A strange coldness had crept through her bones. All through their long march from Irion, she had felt her old powers strengthening within her. In the birds that fluttered in the sky above them, in the foxes and squirrels that skittered from their path, even in the horses that drew their carts, Cata had sensed a strange agitation. Now she could feel it all around her. Something was wrong in the world, she knew. Something was very wrong.

The bugle sounded on the chill morning air.

'Salt-pig!'

'Your Reverence?'

'Salt-pig!' cried the canon again. 'Did I ask for salt-pig, boy? I asked for beef, fresh-killed.'

'That be roast beef, your Reverence.'

'What?' The canon banged his fist on the table-top. 'You call this roast beef, when patently it is the rotten flesh of a pig, pickled in brine? What folly is this? Do words have no meaning in this Kingdom of Zenzau?'

'Words have meaning here, sir, much as anywhere. That be beef-gravy on your meat, made with beef-bones. You ask for mutton, I gives you mutton-gravy, made with mutton-bones. Venison, partridge, we do you them too, if the price is right.'

The canon would not be beguiled. 'You serve nothing but salt-pig, with a choice of gravy?'

'Aye!' The pot-boy seemed astonished that anyone could object to something which, to him, was a point of honour. 'It not be every tavern that gives you beef-gravy or mutton-gravy on your briny-pig. There's some that's no gravy, and some that's only pig-fat. We aims to give a good luncheon to all our gentlemen and ladies. And we serves with onion-and-taters, too.'

'"Onion-and-taters"!' The canon rolled his eyes, then jumped as the pot-boy banged down on the table, at last, the tankard he had been carrying throughout this exchange. Fresh slops frothed over the stained surface.

'Our friend,' murmured a gentleman close by, 'seems determined not to accustom himself to the ways of this land. But what shall we expect of a Zenzau-canon, hm?' He winked through wiry spectacles at the nearest of his companions, a young fellow who had joined the coach only at Evion. Obliged to sit on the back box with his Vaga-servant, the youth had thus far exchanged few words with the other travellers. He seemed a shy youth, rather than a surly one, so the gentleman went on, 'I came among this party just a little before you. I surmise, however, that our friend has been making the same complaints all the way from Agondon. In a moment, mark my words, he shall taste his watery ale and remonstrate with the pot-boy again. *Am I a child, to sup on small-beer?*'

It happened just as the gentleman predicted. The young fellow, who had been keeping his eyes down, looked up at his companion, interested. Behind the spectacles he saw a scholarly countenance, care-worn but kindly; the gentleman, for his part, saw a fair youth who was not, on inspection, quite as nondescript as he seemed at first. Both of them, it was clear, were persons of quality – in reduced circumstances, perhaps.

'Your judgement is acute, sir,' said the youth.

'Hardly judgement,' smiled the gentleman. 'Only a little experience. See that florid face, those popping eyes? That air of outrage at the merest irritant? Our friend imagines himself, no doubt, to be a person of particular distinction. A glittering fob-chain hangs across his girth and he walks with an incongruously dandyish stick, topped with the silver head of a lion. Only too typical, I'm afraid, of the Zenzau-canon. Overfed, idle, a braggart and a fool.'

'Sir, have you no shame?' hissed an old lady who sat close by with her companion, a dour creature with one eye. 'Such disrespect, to a man of the cloth!'

'Good lady, I beg your pardon. But I speak only what is widely known. Could such a fellow secure a fine Agondon lectorate, should we see him in the colonies, do you think? Sent here to preach the true religion, he shall have little compassion for his flock, I fear. Even now he shakes his head and says, *The Zenzans, the Zenzans*. Does he not know that swine is the only flesh permitted to these people, small-beer the only libation? All else is taken for the fine houses of their masters.'

He raised his voice. 'Fear not, Zenzau-canon, when you are installed in your comfortable lectory, there shall be good beef and wine enough for you. Then you may reflect with satisfaction that these things are denied to our Zenzan cousins.'

'Zenzan cousins?' The canon, with rather more gusto than might have been expected, was chewing a mouthful of swine-flesh. Swallowing, he peered suspiciously at his interlocutor. 'You are not speaking *politics*, sir, I hope?'

'Canon, I was anticipating your splendid future. You are headed for a living, are you not? Let me guess – in some ancient temple, where the Icons of Viana have been stripped from the altar, and the golden vines from the pillars, to be replaced with the trappings of the one true faith? I imagine,' he added quickly, 'it shall look magnificent.'

'My appointment,' sniffed the canon, 'is to a town called Derkold-Vend.'

'Derkold-Vend?' The scholarly gentleman bowed his head. 'Why, sir, if you have found me guilty of any impertinence, I humbly beg your pardon. I did not realize we were travelling with a gentleman of such distinction.'

Innocently the canon puffed himself up, observing that in the depravity of the present age, proper degrees and distinctions were often overlooked.

'My thoughts exactly,' returned the scholar, but to the youth he muttered beneath his breath, 'What sort of embarrassment to the Order of Agonis must one be, do you think, to be banished to the depths of Ana-Zenzau?'

The old lady heard this and pursed her lips, but her disapproval turned to alarm as the scholar went on, 'Canon, you have a long way to go. Wrax will be only another stage upon your way; make sure, though, that you inspect the fine Temple, which surely must uplift you for the task ahead. You'll see none like it where you're going. Why, I've heard it said the Ana-Zenzans – but I'm sure you've studied these matters intently – still worship the goddess Viana amongst the trees!'

'Barbaric!' tutted the old lady. 'Canon, you must forbid it at once.'

Her companion, as if in assent, blinked her single eye; her employer shot her a warning glance, as if telling her not to speak, it was not necessary.

The scholar said, 'To forbid is one thing, to be heeded another. I am not without my correspondents in the east. Do you know, there are those who say Derkold-Vend will be the mustering-place of the rebels – you are aware, canon, that a rebellion is afoot?'

'Of course I am, sir! But that is far, far to the east! What concern can it be to those of us in the west?'

'We are in the west, but travelling east. Those in the east may travel west, may they not? Especially if they are bent on taking Wrax.'

The canon spluttered, 'Taking Wrax? Preposterous!'

'W-Wrax?' The old lady's companion spoke for the first time, her eye widening with fear.

'Hush, Baines!' said her employer; the eye moistened. Like the canon, both ladies were thoroughly discomfited, rising from the table with evident relief when, at that moment, the coachman appeared, asking his passengers to resume their places. The road that led up through the Hills of Wrax was notoriously narrow and winding. They must reach Wrax by dusk, and had a hard ride ahead.

The youth, who had been quiet through all this, sat gazing for a moment at the scholarly gentleman. The gentleman arched an eyebrow. 'I seem to have upset our friends,' he observed dryly. 'You, young sir, are of a different temperament, or so I sense.'

The youth looked thoughtful as they made their way out into the tavern-yard, a shabby place of rubble, peeling whitewash and drains. In Theron-season it would stink abominably. 'Is it true what you said,' he enquired cautiously, 'about taking Wrax?'

The scholar laughed, 'Now, young sir, how should I know that? A

364

mischievous speculation, to prick the self-righteousness of our clerical friend! Still, what fonder dream may a Zenzan have, than to take back his ancient imperial city?' He paused, his spectacles glittering. 'Lord Agonis forbid that such a calamity were to occur!'

'Oh, indeed. Lord Agonis forbid!'

The scholar swung his foot on to the carriage steps. 'Eldric Hulverside is my name. A poor scholar, on his way to the Wrax Library.' He extended his hand. 'I sense, young sir, that you are a friend.'

'Jem. Jemany.'

A cloud passed across the scholar's face. 'I once knew one who – who spoke of a boy called Jemany.' He smiled. 'But I dare say it is a common enough name where you come from?'

'Oh, there are hundreds of us.'

'Come, good sirs, Wrax by dusk! If we leaves it too late, why, who knows what risks we run!' The coachman was in place, whip at the ready. His line-boy sat up in front beside him, from time to time spitting with a preoccupied air; Jem jumped up on the back again, where a glum Rajal was waiting.

'A splendid luncheon, no doubt? It was mouldy bread and cheese for the lower orders, let me tell you – and that boy hawking up phlegm all the time. Still, never mind. We were out the back by the swine-trough, appropriately enough.'

'We had quite enough swine where we were, Raj.'

They were about to drive off when the scholarly gentleman's head appeared through the window. 'Young sir, our numbers are fewer this time. You need not ride on the back-box with your Vaga. Come—' he smiled, and dropped his voice '—you will not abandon me to our clerical friend?'

Disapproving sniffs greeted Jem as he squeezed into the musty interior of the coach.

Chapter 52

MY ONE-EYED BEAUTY

The white world had retreated now, but still it was early in the Season of Viana. Already the sun was sinking lower in the sky and a chill breeze fluttered at the fledgling leaves. The coach jogged, sometimes violently, over deep ruts and potholes. Green woods pressed thickly on either side of the road.

'To think,' the pop-eyed canon glowered, 'that this road is a major thoroughfare! I think we can take our measure of these Zenzans easily enough.'

The scholar said, 'May I remind you, canon, how long this realm has been occupied?'

'Occupied? What are you saying, sir?'

'Only that Ejlander warmaking has contributed to the condition of this road. And Ejlander policy to its present disrepair.'

'By the Lord Agonis, sir, I declare you speak like one of these rebel fellows yourself. It is well known, is it not, that the Zenzans would grovel in barbarism, but for the beneficent sway of His Imperial Agonist Majesty?'

'But of course.'

The canon looked mollified. Reaching into his waistcoat for a silver snuffbox, for a moment he seemed almost tempted to offer it to the scholar. His brow furrowed, and he adopted a different tone. 'Sir, I am a new arrival in this land. You, it is clear, know it well. You don't mean what you said about Derkold-Vend – the rebels, mustering?'

In counterpoint to this exchange ran a stream of mumbling. Straining her eye in the waning light, the old lady's companion read blandly, expressionlessly, from a tattered old novel. From time to time she would leave off, thinking her mistress asleep, but each time, with an irritable snort or grunt, the old lady bade her continue.

The scholar turned to Jem. 'Young friend, I take it your business is in the fair city of Wrax? What may that business be, I wonder? No, let me guess: you are a rebel agent, taking a secret message to the Resistance?'

Jem looked alarmed. The scholar burst into a hearty laugh.

'Hmph!' said the canon, and drew forth his fob-watch with an impatient air. Jem caught a glimpse of it: ornate, golden, with inset jewels in the face.

'I'm going to see my father,' he said absently. Why he had said the words, Jem did not quite know; it was something to say, that was all. He hoped the scholar would not ask him more questions; fortunately he did not, and only smiled, almost knowingly.

But what could he know?

For three moonlives or more, Jem and Rajal had been making their way towards the heart of Zenzau. It had been a precarious journey. Only now, with their destination close, were they riding in coaches and dining in inns. For much of the time they had travelled on foot. Progress was slow until the snows began to thaw. Finding a warm place to spend the night was often the main concern of each day. They had little money, and sometimes had been tempted to steal. For much of a moonlife they had worked on a farm, and several times Rajal had been a singer in taverns. Everywhere the wretchedness of Zenzau was clear to them; everywhere, equally, was Bluejacket tyranny. More than once they had seen the blue regiments, marching indomitably towards the capital.

The two friends had hidden, taking no chances.

Baines droned on, reading from the tattered book. Once, when she let it slip down a little, Jem saw the title: *A Lady's Maid? A Lady!*

※　※　※　※

The sky was darkening; rain drizzled down; the old lady wrapped her travelling-rug tighter around her. Rings of silver and gold glittered on her fingers and at her neck was a flashing emerald brooch. As she jogged up and down, Jem was aware of the muffled *clink! clink!* of the coins she kept in pouches under her skirts. The effect was hypnotic.

But soon they would all be jolted awake.

The road, at this point, was narrowing, beginning its climb through the Hills of Wrax. They came to a sharp bend. The ladies gave a cry as the coach lurched suddenly, too suddenly. Everyone lurched with it; Baines, for a moment, found her face jammed in the scholar's lap. The horses whinnied; the coach swayed, shuddering, to a halt.

To call it an accident would be going too far. It was an interruption, an annoyance – but too much for the canon. Indignant, he thumped the ceiling with his silver-topped stick. 'Coachman!'

'Aye, coachman,' echoed the scholar, 'would you deprive the benighted folk of Derkold-Vend of the light and love of the Lord Agonis?'

Jem would have laughed, but he was distracted. 'Raj!' he called guiltily from the window. 'Raj, are you all right?'

There was no answer. Worried, Jem jumped down from the coach. His friend was just around the bend in the road, sitting miserably in a ditch. He looked so bedraggled that Jem had to laugh.

'Very well for you! I could have been killed.'

'I'm sorry, Raj.' Jem extended his hand. 'Come on, I'll tell them you have to sit inside with us.'

'A muddy Vaga? Some chance.'

But there was no chance to test whether Rajal was right. At that moment there was a crash of branches, a flurry of hoofbeats, a wild neighing. Cries rang out, and one cry, louder than the others:

'Stand and deliver!'

'Quick!' Jem grabbed Rajal's arm, drawing him into the trees. Already the rain was falling harder, but through a screen of leaves the friends saw clearly what happened next. Rearing up before the stricken carriage, magnificent on an enormous black stallion, was a man dressed in scarlet, wielding a glittering pistol. On his head he wore a three-cornered hat; a dark mask concealed his eyes. Two henchmen rode behind him, also armed and masked.

'Into the road,' demanded the first.

'Hands in the air,' chimed the second.

Reluctantly the passengers lined the muddy roadway. Their luggage was jammed into the back-box or strapped to the roof or underside of the coach. While the henchmen ripped open trunks and cases, stuffing their saddle-bags with valuables, their leader dismounted only after some moments. Parading in leisurely fashion before the trembling party, he shifted his pistol idly from hand to hand.

'Well, well, what have we here?' The voice was precise, aristocratic; wry rather than cruel. 'A fine Zenzau-canon – gorged on salt-pig, I dare say? Let's hope his purse is as full as his belly. Then a respectable dowager lady, visiting her colonial relatives, perhaps? And you, sir, a dried-up pedant? I thought as much. But what's this, what's this? After the brains, the beauty.'

Baines simpered.

'Shut up, Baines!'

'But alas, we must turn from beauty to . . . *booty*. Coachman, I must of course relieve you of your fares.'

The coachman obliged. Lingering on the edge of the party, he twisted his face into an unctuous smile, as if eager to deliver up all that his passengers possessed. The highwayman inspected a jingling bag, then tossed it nonchalantly to a henchman. 'Your boy, I need hardly add, shall be taxed with nothing.' He fluffed the boy's hair. 'The lot of a line-boy is hard enough. Treat him well, coachman, treat him well.'

The line-boy furiously snuffled back snot. 'Thank you, Bob Scarlet!'

'Stupid boy,' blustered the canon, 'don't you realize we have been captured by a vicious villain? A traitor and murderer?'

The highwayman's mouth, beneath the black mask, twitched. 'Zenzau-canon! Yes, you're another matter, aren't you? Quite another matter. Now, let's see what one mired in gluttony and sloth, dedicated to the unyielding exploitation of this benighted kingdom and profanation of its true faith, may contribute to the relief of its sufferings.'

'Relief of its sufferings? Pray, how do you propose to relieve the sufferings of this kingdom, when you make it your business to assault innocent travellers?'

'Bob gives everything to the poor of Zenzau,' said the line-boy, lost in admiration.

'Indeed, boy, I do. Look, this is a fine stick our friend leans upon, is it not? Quite the dandy, hm? And the head of a lion, fashioned in silver.' The coach-boy giggled. 'Dear me, and what's this? A fob-chain? Your hand, boy, your hand: follow where it leads, hm? Not tickling, are we, canon?'

At this, Baines could not help laughing. The old lady shot her companion a warning look. 'Need I remind you,' she hissed, 'that I have my silver knitting-needles in my carpet-bag? Oh, I could put out your other eye, you exasperate me so!'

'Silver knitting-needles?' said the highwayman, overhearing. 'Now, there's an idea. Could you pass me that carpet-bag, my pretty?'

Baines complied radiantly.

'You unconscionable blackguard! You coward!' burst out the old lady.

'Coward? Have *you* ever held up a coach, dear lady? Why, a coach I held up last moonlife had a fat canon in it just like this one. *He* dared to call me a coward, too, then produced his rod from his breeches.'

Baines drew in her breath.

'Fear not, my one-eyed beauty, I intend no lewdness. No, this fellow dared draw upon me, quite unexpectedly – all the time taxing me, Robin Scarlet, with cowardice! Of course, I had no choice but to blow out his brains, there and then.' The highwayman smirked and blew the end of his gun-barrel, as if he had just fired it.

In the trees, Rajal whispered, 'When they're not looking, we'll rush them. Ready, Jem?'

Jem said, 'Don't be silly.'

'What? I thought that's what you'd want.'

'He's a Redjacket, can't you see? He's on our side, Raj.'

'Are you sure?'

Jem was not, but watched intently as the masked man, with many further levities, relieved the reluctant travellers of their valuables. Even Baines had a plenteous purse, which she disgorged coyly from beneath her capacious skirts.

Only one thing was odd. The highwayman had taken nothing from Eldric Hulverside. A scholar, it was true, might be expected to be poor.

But as he watched, Jem saw that Bob Scarlet, from time to time, would look to Hulverside, and Hulverside would look to Bob Scarlet. Then, to Jem's astonishment, the scholar moved forward, whispering something in the highwayman's ear.

The highwayman laughed. 'What's that, a snuffbox? A fine silver snuffbox? Canon, it seems you have not been entirely honest with me. I am shocked at such behaviour in a man of the cloth.'

'Snuffbox? What are you talking about?' Indignantly the canon's gaze swivelled between the highwayman and the scholar; but in the next instant the scholar, with a smile, had stepped forward, patting his hands over the canon's coat-pockets. With a flourish he produced the missing treasure.

'You villain!' The canon tried to snatch it back, but instantly the scholar, too, had whipped forth a pistol, jabbing it against the canon's temple. The ladies screamed; the line-boy capered joyously; the canon collapsed at once to his knees, squelching into the mud of the road. 'Lord Agonis, spare me!'

'Shoot, Hul!'

'Shouldn't we rush them now?' whispered Rajal, among the trees.

But events, in an instant, were to overtake them.

Chapter 53

A RIDERLESS HORSE

'Out!'

'Cook, have mercy!'

'Out of it, I say! Sergeant or no sergeant, I'll not have you putting your hands on my dumplings.'

'Plenty of fellows'll be at them soon enough.'

'Never mind your *insinnuendoes*, Sergeant Floss. You can do what you like with my dumplings when they're served, but before then, out of my kitchen, I say!'

The sergeant took a swig from his hip-flask and looked around him, grinning. Behind them was a ramshackle cluster of tents. Nirry's cauldrons bubbled under an open sky. 'Funny sort of kitchen, Cook.'

Nirry sniffed, 'It's my kitchen, whether it's in a castle or out on a dunghill like this. And I'll have you know, Sergeant Floss, I've served in a castle in my time.'

'Why, so have I – served in the King's best dungeons, I did!'

'And a pity they didn't keep you there,' Nirry muttered, then raised her voice, shouting at the girls who bustled, but not fast enough, about the cauldrons.

She turned away miserably. 'Oh, what a life! Riding all day in a rickety cart – my poor bones fair ground up to soup-stock . . . I thought the Blue Irions was a good class of regiment, and here I am with only dirty trollops for help, and dirty sergeants pawing at the food before it's served! To think, and I've cooked for the finest quality, I have!'

'The finest?' said the sergeant. 'Why, I was a footman in the grandest house in Agondon, I was. One of Lady Cham-Charing's very own.'

'You were?' Nirry said suspiciously.

'Until they caught me pawning the silver. So, what did *you* do, eh my girl?'

Nirry's suspicion changed at once to scorn. 'Don't you "my girl" me, Carney Floss! What do you think I am, one of your dirty camp-followers? I'm a good woman, I tell you – and I didn't *do* a thing!' Her face hot, Nirry pushed back her sleeves, returning vigorously to her dumpling-dough.

'Poor Cook!' Sergeant Floss laughed. 'You've not been on the road much, have you? Never mind, we'll be in Wrax Barracks soon enough.

No more tents, no more sky. They'll treat you right then, just you wait! Proper quarters – soft bed to sleep on – big stone kitchen, all your own.'

Nirry brightened. 'Really?'

'Would I lie to you?' With a grin, the sergeant slipped an arm round Nirry's waist and proffered his battered hip-flask. Nirry wrinkled her nose at the flask, but let the sergeant's arm remain where it was – just for the moment, of course. It was a comfort, if not the one she wanted.

'Sergeant?'

'Cook?'

'This place we're going – this Wrax. Will all the regiments be there, then?'

'Well, a lot of them.'

'The Fifth Royal?'

'Now that I couldn't say. What do you know about the Fifth then, Cook?'

'Not much. Only . . . I heard they was a good sort of regiment, that's all.'

The sergeant spluttered, 'The Fifth! Whoremongers the lot of them! Why, a lass like you – you wouldn't be safe five ticks of an olton-clock with a man from the Fifth! Give you the pox, get you with child, then run off and you'd never see him again!'

Nirry's eyes grew wide. 'No! Why, I knew a fellow from the Fifth and he . . . he wasn't like that at all.'

'That's what you think.' Again the sergeant grinned, and swigged from his flask. 'Known a few army-chaps then, eh Cook?'

'Ooh, you . . . not the way you mean! I'll have you know I'm – I'm a respectable married woman, I am!'

'Ho! Married, now? First we've heard about it.'

'Well – engaged, then!'

The sergeant guffawed, 'I've heard that one before!'

Nirry bridled, 'It's true, I tell you – I've got a lovely young man, I have. Wiggles his ears,' she added proudly, '*without* moving the rest of his head. Which is a lot more than you can do, Carney Floss, so put that in your pipe and smoke it.'

The sergeant tightened his grip on Nirry's waist. 'And what might he say, this wiggly-eared fellow, if he'd heard what I heard, just this morning?'

'Heard? What do you mean?'

'Oh, nothing. At least, I'm sure it's nothing. Only' – the man's look was sly – 'there's talk you were coming out of the woods just this morning – with a fellow, like. Know what I mean?' The grin returned, all black-toothed and crooked. 'Know what I mean?' the man said again, and winked.

'Ooh, you wicked man!' Nirry flounced out of the sergeant's grip. 'How dare you? I told you I'm a respectable woman, and I am! A pox on you, and your *insinnuendoes*! Out of my kitchen I say! Out! Out!'

And seizing a ladle, Nirry would cheerfully have beaten the bold man, but he skipped out of reach, swigging at his flask. The kitchen-girls shrieked with laughter, but their laughter ceased at once when Nirry turned on them. 'What are you looking at, you dirty trollops? Back to your work – though the Lord Agonis knows, flat on your backs is the only place you lot ever work!'

Delighted, Sergeant Floss guffawed again, but cursed a moment later when Nirry threw a dumpling, knocking his hip-flask out of his hand.

※　※　※　※

'Hear about Wiggler?'

'What?'

'Wiggler. He's got a girl.'

'His powers of concealment must be remarkable. Or is she very small?'

'What?'

'I was wondering where he kept her.'

'Morvy, you're being silly again.'

Side by side in a drizzle of rain, Soldier Morven and Soldier Crum rode along a dreary stretch of highway. Its ruts, its holes, its bumps were becoming tiresomely familiar. Up and down, up and down, they had patrolled all day, and a dull day it had been. They had seen three coaches go by, one or two pedlars, and a cart of turnips going to market. Crum remembered the turnips with a particular fondness. His stomach rumbled. They had eaten their sandwiches long ago. Oh, it must be time to go back soon! Their backs ached and their muskets hung heavily from their shoulders, clinking in time to the rhythm of their horses.

'Actually, Crum, I know all about it.' Morven's spectacles flashed in the setting sun. 'Who do you think has penned the epistles of love? Why, I have contrived the most eloquent tributes to the fair Nirrian – her beauty, charm, grace.'

'You know her?'

'Not at all. There are techniques,' Morven explained airily, 'where women are concerned.'

Crum's eyes widened. 'Morvy?'

But Morven fell silent. To think, he had been reduced to this! Patrols, parades, marches – and in between, what was he? A scribe for illiterate soldiers! Sometimes he longed to return to the University of Agondon, resuming the studies the army had interrupted. There was so much he did not understand, so much he wanted to know. Then sometimes he longed for something else: not the old life, but a new and different one. But of quite what sort, he could not say.

Inevitably Crum interrupted his musings. 'You haven't seen her, then?'

'Hm?'

'Wiggler's girl. The one in Irion.'

'He has more?'

'One's enough! Morvy?' Crum, directing his horse away from a rut in the road, seemed to be sidling purposefully nearer to his companion. Trees hung heavily above their heads, shushing and plunking with droplets of rain. 'How do you get a girl, do you think?'

Morven sighed, 'Turn out your breeches.'

Crum reddened. 'What?'

'Turn out your pockets and count your coins.'

'Oh, very funny. You know I've been docked again.'

'Then I don't think you're going to get a girl, are you?'

Pause.

'Morvy?'

'Oh, what now?'

'Have you had one?'

'Crum, shut up!'

Crum was miserable. To be sore, cold and hungry was bad enough; to envy Wiggler was worse. Wiggler not only had a girl, but everyone said he'd soon be promoted again. Corporal Olch was one thing, but Sergeant? Rottsy said Nirry would come down from Irion then, and Wiggler would marry her, sure as hamhocks. At the very thought, Crum felt awe. To be married was an extraordinary thing, wasn't it? It must be the most tremendous piece of luck. If he could wiggle his ears too, would he have the same luck? Sometimes at night, when no one could see, Crum would sit up in bed and try. It was very difficult; in fact impossible, at least for Crum.

'Life's really not fair, is it?' he said aloud.

A moment later, he wished he had not.

'Life? Fair? Now *that*, Crum, is a question.' Morven adjusted his spectacles with a scholarly air. Poor Crum understood little of what followed. It was all about human nature and the body politic and something Morvy called the *common wheel*. Crum thought of the big wheel on his uncle's mill in Varl. But that was rather a special wheel. He thought of a cart, being drawn along by a cart-horse. Was that a *common wheel*? That made him think of his father's old cart-horse. His name was Drover.

'Poor old Drover!' Crum spoke aloud again.

'What?' Morven broke off.

'He fell down and died in the hop-field, just fell down and died he did, the day before I went off for a soldier.'

'Crum, what are you talking about?'

'Same as you. The *common wheel*.'

'I was speaking, Crum, about Vytoni's *Discourse on Freedom*.'

'I know – I know it well.'

'You do?'

It was hardly possible. Morven knew full well that Crum could read only a little. He could read what was painted on posts in the road or on inn-signs, underneath the pictures; when he was a boy, back in Varl, he had learnt the letters on his great-father's tomb-slab, or so Morven had been told, often enough. But Vytoni?

'Of course I know it! It's got a brown leather cover with scratch-marks all over it, and the pages are all pulpy where it got wet, that time you had to wade through the river with your pack. It doesn't half smell, Morvy. And there's a worm that lives in the back, did you know? He popped out his head just the other night, when you were sitting by the fire. I saw him – a little yellow fellow. I tried to tell you, but you were all grumpy. So I thought I'd better not.'

Crum paused. The rain was falling harder, plunking steadily on the brim of his hat. Ahead the road narrowed and there was a sharp bend, leading away darkly through thick walls of foliage. The setting sun cast a reddish glow.

'Have you quite finished?' said Morven sourly.

'Is it a big wheel, or a little wheel?'

'What?'

'The *common wheel*?'

'Crum, really! What do you know about it? You're nothing but a peasant – an ignorant Varlan peasant! I was trying to tell you, if you'd only listen, that Vytoni explains how government must represent all in the *commonweal*, and maximize the freedom of each member. We're all equal! Crum, can't you understand the implications? We are the servants of a corrupt regime! As a boy, I was a keen patriot – even at university, I believed Ejland's way was best, and was eager for its hegemony to spread over all the Lands of El-Orok like – like the glutinous, liquefying unguent of uncongealing lard!'

Lard? Crum thought fondly about the turnips again. He imagined them baked in his mother's oven, then smeared with butter – cream, too! If only! Oh, it must be time to go back. Rations here weren't much, but after all, rations were rations. Their sandwiches had been rather good, really – if only there had been more! He leaned forward, patting his tired mare. 'And you're ready for your oats, too, aren't you, Myrtle? I'll bet you are.'

Morven ignored him; gesturing expansively, he was no longer looking at his companion at all. 'Then I read Vytoni's *Discourse on Freedom*,' he was saying. 'Garolus Vytoni, the martyred genius of Zenzau! Denounced by the Archmaximate! Imprisoned by the Holy Empress! Reviled to this day by Professor Mercol, and other loyalist lickspittles! Don't you see how he opened my eyes? Why, Crum, I could tear this uniform from my back, tear it from my back and stamp on it!'

Morven flung out his arms. Unfortunately his horse, disturbed by a depression in the road, chose this moment to shy. Morven's musket clattered from his shoulder. He overbalanced, falling to his back in the mud.

'Morvy, you silly thing!'

Crum had to laugh. He was about to dismount and go to his friend's aid when the evening was rent suddenly by a scream, coming from just around the bend in the road.

'That's a lady!'

Crum started, cantering ahead.

'Crum!' Morven scrambled up muddily. He fumbled for his musket. But where was his horse? Mud spattered his spectacles and he could not see. Staggering forward, trying to smear the dirt away, he would be too late to see what happened round the corner.

❊ ❊ ❊ ❊

'Bluejackets!'

It was the man called Hul who gave the cry, but Bob Scarlet who whipped his pistol from the head of the sobbing canon, blasting it instead at the oncoming soldier. Crum's horse reared up, flinging down its rider. Baines shrieked again, more piercingly now. The passengers scattered, scurrying for cover.

But it was over already. In the next moment, highwayman, henchmen, and Hul too, swinging up behind his scarlet leader, had crashed back through the undergrowth and galloped away.

'Go, Bob!' The line-boy danced ecstatically in the mud.

Jem burst forward. 'Raj, come on! Let's see which way they go!'

'Jem, no! They're killers!'

'They're on our side, Raj!

'You're crazy!'

'Come on!'

'How?'

Jem pointed. 'Horses!'

'I've got him, mister!' The line-boy rushed forward, grabbing at the reins of a riderless horse. It was Morven's; but Morven, at that moment, neither knew nor cared.

'Crum!' The body lay face down in the mud. Morven collapsed over it, stricken. 'Oh Crum, Crum!'

Chapter 54

A CREATURE MADE OF MUD

'Jem! Wait!'

Rajal was no horseman. At first he thought he would not be able to control his mount at all. Frightened, protesting against the new rider, it crashed here and there through the undergrowth, lurching over stony hillocks, gullies of ferns, mires of mud. Only because the horse was tired was Rajal able to still its tossing head. By that time he had been dragged under several low-lying branches, and several times almost fallen to the ground. He sat askew on the saddle, straining to right himself.

'Jem!' he called again.

But Jem had stopped already, gazing this way and that. 'We've lost them!'

'What?' gasped Rajal, drawing beside him.

'I said, I don't know which way they went.'

'Good! Then perhaps we can find our coach again?'

'Coach? We've got horses now, Raj!'

'Oh yes. Stolen horses,' Rajal said glumly.

Jem had to laugh. 'You should see yourself, Raj!' His friend was not only muddy, but had leaves, twigs and burs stuck all over him. He had lost his hat and his hair spiked up at angles. Blood oozed from a scratch on one cheek.

'Oh, marvellous!' Rajal burst out. 'It's not enough that I've clung to a back-box all day and eaten slops by a pig-trough – *from* a pig-trough, more like it. It's not enough that I'm bruised, battered and bloody. No, I have to entertain Prince Jemany as well. I didn't come all this way to be your jester, did I?'

Jem was contrite. 'Raj, I'm sorry. But we had to come after them.'

'I don't see why. Do you want to be shot, too?'

'They wouldn't shoot us! That fellow, the scholar, was talking to me. There were things he said ... oh, I don't know.' Jem looked down thoughtfully. Red glimmerings of sunset splashed around him, plunking doggedly downwards like the raindrops from the leaves. 'He said there'd be a sign.'

'The scholar?'

'Lord Empster. He said I'd know when to give my message. Raj, something happened back at that inn. I told the scholar my name and . . . he seemed to know it already. He looked at me . . . it was as if he could see through me.'

'You don't say?' Rajal's voice was wry.

'But there was more. It was the strangest feeling – as if I knew him. As if he were someone I'd met before. Raj, don't you see? What if that was the sign? What if I've missed it? Oh, I should have been looking out for it!'

'You're forgetting something, aren't you?' Rajal gestured around them. 'Doesn't the sign come when we get to Wrax?'

'So?'

'I don't like to remind you, but we're leagues from anywhere, lost in the woods!'

'We're nearly there, aren't we? We just have to find the road again, that's all.'

'Hm.'

The friends rode on in the gathering evening. For a time they thought they were going back the way they had come. Then it became difficult to know which way they were going. The Hills of Wrax did not ascend in any neat, unbroken progression. There were hillocks here, hollows there, as if long ago the land had been crumpled up by some vast being and flung back, willy-nilly. By now the evening light was fading rapidly. Soon they had dismounted, leading their horses carefully over the rugged forest floor.

Only once did they meet anyone. Dragging a bundle of sticks along an overgrown trail were two ragged children, swarthy little Zenzans, skinny as the sticks they laboriously hauled.

'Speak to them, Raj.'

'Why me?'

'You look more like a Zenzan.'

Rajal stepped out from behind a tree. 'Excuse me—'

The first child screamed.

'The Vichy!' cried the second.

They took to their heels, vanishing into the trees. In the merest moment the woods were silent again. But for the abandoned sticks on the path, the children might never have existed at all.

'I don't think I adopted quite the right tone.'

Jem was puzzled. 'What's the Vichy?'

'I don't know.' Rajal picked twigs from his spiky hair. 'Well, all right. The servants talk about him – an evil monster who lives in the woods. He's made out of river-mud and covered in leaves.'

'Oh, Raj!' Jem had to laugh.

'It's not funny. We're lost, remember!'

'Well? Let's follow this path.'

But the path, like the children, soon vanished amongst the trees.

'The city's near, it's got to be.'

'I wouldn't be so sure.'

Jem licked his finger and held it in the air. 'This way. Just over the next rise, mark my words.'

※ ※ ※ ※

Over the next rise were only more trees.

'Wrax *is* east, isn't it?' Jem mused.

'Are you going to lick your finger again? What is that, some Agonist magic?'

'Wind direction.'

'There's no wind, you idiot! Only rain and mud and scratchy branches and a thousand trees that all look the same. And soon it will be dark and we'll wander round in these woods until we drop dead of cold and hunger or a murderer comes and kills us! Oh, why didn't we stay with the coach? We can't even find the road, let alone the city!'

Jem rolled his eyes. 'You're such a misery, Raj. Why is it, I ask you, that you have to put the worst face on everything? Why can't you have a bit of pluck, answer me that! I've lost count of the number of times you've moaned about this, moaned about that. It gives you some sort of satisfaction, doesn't it? Why, if I'd been like you, I'd still be a cripple in Irion, being pushed around in a chair like a useless sack of—'

'Jem! Listen!'

They stood in a purple hollow, with branches criss-crossed above them like the web of a huge spider. From somewhere close by came a sound of singing. It was a girl's voice, humming wordlessly. But the melody was familiar. Accompanied by the taut high pluckings of a Wrax-harp, it drifted over the evening with an air of strange enchantment.

They left their horses tied to a branch and picked their way uphill. Lying on their stomachs, they peered over a leafy ridge. Screened by thick trees was a tumbledown tower, the last remnant, perhaps, of some fine ancestral home. No door was visible, but in a high window was the warm glow of candles. It was from here, curling down towards them like a smoky tendril, that there came the pure, high music.

'That song,' Jem whispered. 'Is it what I think it is?'

Rajal's reply was to rise to his feet.

'Raj! What are you doing?'

Rajal strode towards the tower. A tiny, burbling rivulet ran between the stones that clustered round its base. Standing beside it, murmurously at first, then in the clear carillon of his days with the Masks, Rajal supplied the words the song was wanting.

Everything is lemon and nothing is lime,
And even the truth shall be revealed in time:
Then we shall drink from the mocking-tree gourds,
And sup with the King and Queen of Swords!

Jem's heart hammered hard. Could this, perhaps, be the sign he awaited?

From the tower came a startled cry. The music broke off. Lit from behind by the candles, the girl appeared in the window. She opened the casement, peering into the gloom. Jem made out a slender arm, a white bodice, tawny hair fashioned into long braids.

It was enough: the girl was beautiful.

'Oh, who is it?' she whispered. 'Orvik, is it you?'

Rajal began another verse. The girl looked down. Then she screamed. 'The Vichy!'

Jem sprang forward.

'Fair maiden, please!' He grabbed at Rajal, locking his muddy head under his arm. 'He's not the Vichy, I promise.' Eagerly, as if to demonstrate this, Jem pushed Rajal down, swishing his face in the burbling rivulet. Rajal spluttered, struggling.

Looking on, the girl had to giggle.

Jem called, 'See? He's fallen in the mud, that's all. We're poor travellers who have lost our way. Could you not give us shelter for the night?'

'Oh!' The girl, as if alarmed, brought her hand up to her mouth. Quickly she vanished, closing the casement.

'There's your answer.' Rajal wiped his face with his sleeve. 'I suppose she still thinks I'm the Vichy. Or you're something worse.'

Jem laughed again, but his laughter trailed away. Rajal had slumped down miserably by the rivulet. Jem sat beside him, looking down into the chill water. Rapidly it ran over jewel-like, hard stones.

'Raj, the song. Why did you sing it?'

The tower loomed behind them, purplish in the sunset. 'I wanted to,' said Rajal.

'Wanted to?'

'Had to.' Rajal turned, looking in his friend's eyes. 'I had to, Jem.'

'What is this place?'

A voice came, 'Welcome, young sirs.'

Jem jumped. Standing behind them was an old man, bent and wizened, in garb which might have been the tattered remnants of livery. It was not a livery Jem had seen before. With one hand the old man leaned on an ashplant; in the other, he held aloft a lantern. 'Come. At Oltby Castle, shall we turn away a wayfarer?'

The question evidently required no answer. Exchanging glances, the friends followed the old man. His lamp shone like gold in the purple evening as he led them round to the other side of the tower.

Jem looked about him. Stretching away into the woods beyond were jagged remains of other walls, long overgrown with vines and moss. Ramshackle outbuildings leaned here and there, clinging forlornly to the castle's remains.

The old man turned back, beckoning through an ancient, low-lintelled doorway. He held the door ajar. A spiral staircase was visible within.

The sign, Jem thought. *It's close now, I know it.* But why that should be, he could not say. All at once he felt intensely aware of the light, the dripping branches, the mossy stones.

So strange was the moment, so enchanting, that only with a start did he recall the horses. The old man chuckled as he led them to a tumble-down stable, some distance from the tower. 'At Oltby Castle, we accommodate all. All our friends,' he added, after a pause, and smoothed the brown flank of Jem's horse.

With a stab of alarm Jem noticed the horse's saddlebag. Stamped on the coarse fabric was the Bluejacket coat of arms. He exchanged a second glance with Rajal. Did the old man realize? It must be obvious that their horses were stolen.

'My daughter will tend to your horses in a moment. But my pardon, young sirs, I have not introduced myself. I am Dolm, steward of this castle – as my father was steward before me. And his father before.'

Jem thought it best to be cautious. He thought quickly. 'Mej is my name. And this is my friend – ah – Jaral. We're poor travellers, bound for Wrax.'

'Why, then, you have missed your way. But come, you are cold and hungry. We must get you out of your wet things, and fill your empty bellies.'

The old man smiled, revealing the yellow remnants of his teeth.

Chapter 55

MOPPING UP GRAVY

Time had passed. By now, the darkness outside was deep. Rain fell steadily. Jem and Rajal were wrapped in thick blankets while their clothes dried before the fire.

Warm and welcoming, the chamber at the top of the spiral stairs was filled with a superfluity of rich furnishings, sofas and cushions, carpets and hangings, vases and lamps, decorated in the distinctive Zenzan patterns of vines, leaves and flowers. They sat down to supper at a table covered in rich brocaded cloth. Silver plate had been set before them, glinting mellowly in the candlelight, and their goblets brimmed with rich purple wine.

The impression, at first glance, was one of splendour. But the cloth was moth-eaten and fraying, the goblets battered and tarnished, and the food they ate was simple peasant fare, a thick hot ragoût with chunks of bread, served without ceremony by a hobbling crone. There was a melancholy sense of the remnants of riches, of things salvaged from wreckage. Jem felt a stab of strange familiarity. Dust and mould hung heavily on the air. He thought of Irion, of the castle as it had been when he was a boy.

'After the Siege,' he mused aloud.

'But you know our history, young sir?'

'Father, all must know our history!'

'All, child?' The old man turned to his daughter. 'But I think our friends have come from afar, have they not?'

'Their horses were tired. Very tired.'

The girl cast down her eyes. Her hand toyed idly with her long braided hair and she sipped delicately, briefly, from a silver goblet. Jem watched her. Her name, they had learnt, was Landa. Her shift was coarse and she wore no ornament, but her beauty, quite unaided by art, was dazzling. In spite of himself he found that he was eager to address her, gazing into her eyes as she answered shyly in her soft, musical voice.

'My man and I have travelled far,' Jem improvised. 'I seek my father, who lives in Wrax.'

'Your father? And who is your father, sir?'

'A scholar, fair maiden. Alas, his researches have kept him here, long

382

after he should have returned to my mother. Now my mother is declining, and I have come to bring him home.'

'Agondon?'

'Orandy,' Rajal offered. Jem shot him an irritated glance.

'Orandy!' said Dolm. 'Why, young sirs, you have travelled the length of the empire! But eat, eat – drink, too. Here at Oltby Castle, we have lost much, but I managed to keep my cellars secret.' Chuckling, the old man clapped his hands. 'Mother Rea! Wine, more wine for our young guests!'

Jem coloured, embarrassed that this command should be issued, it might seem, on his behalf. Whether Mother Rea was a servant or the steward's wife was unclear; in any case, Dolm treated her with scant respect. From behind a screen in the corner the crone emerged again, bearing a capacious silver jug. It was a heavy burden, unsteady in her hands; a dark gout of wine sloshed across the carpet.

Dolm cursed.

Jem sprang up, offering to take the jug, but the crone turned, shunning his gesture. She wore the 'curtain-snood' of a Zenzan peasant-woman and her face was barely visible; Jem was aware only of a scowling mouth, of eyelids turned down. Not once had the crone spoken, or looked at the guests directly. Gracelessly she banged down the jug and retreated into the shadows again. From time to time, as the evening wore on, sullen grunts and snufflings would come from behind the screen, even the occasional burst of humming. But Dolm never allowed the humming to continue, calling to the crone to *shut up*, or *put her thumb in it*, or *eat her snood*. Jem was shocked. But the wine was rich and flowed freely; he could not quite bring himself to protest.

'I say, that was remarkably good,' he said, spooning up the last of his meal. 'We've had nothing but salt-pig for days, have we – ah – Jaral?'

'Mouldy bread and cheese for some – Mej.'

Landa wrinkled her nose. 'Mother Rea cooks only vegetables, don't you, Mother Rea?'

No reply came from behind the partition.

'But she knows how. To cook them, I mean. It's like magic, isn't it, Father?'

Dolm grunted.

'Magic!' Jem smiled eagerly at the girl. Rajal rolled his eyes. He was still hungry. Tearing off another chunk of bread, he mopped up the gravy, tracing round the silver circle of his plate. Wiping it clean, he saw the pattern the ragoût had concealed: a tall, many-branched tree, flanked on either side by the stylized figures of a man and woman. In their hands were swords, and on their heads they wore five-pointed crowns.

Rajal's brow furrowed.

'More? Mother Rea!' Dolm clapped his hands again.

'Oh no!' Jem said quickly. 'We're full, aren't we, Jaral?' He nudged his friend. 'Aren't we, Jaral?'

'Yes, Mej. Full as can be,' Rajal said distractedly. He wanted Jem to look at the design on his plate, and wondered if Jem's plate might be the same. Then he realized he was still hungry, not full at all. He need not have worried; Dolm insisted that they were starving travellers, and could hardly be satisfied with such meagre portions. Jem thanked the crone fulsomely when she brought back the plates, heaped high and steaming; she only grunted.

Dolm winked merrily, filling their goblets again.

'This must have been a fine castle once,' said Jem. He swigged deeply. All around, the gloom pressed richly. He was intensely aware of the hangings on the walls, of the stones behind them, of the wormy wood beneath the tablecloth and the curving, scratchy arms of their overstuffed chairs. On the wall above the fireplace, almost beyond the reach of the candlelight, hovered a portrait in a golden frame. Jem could see little of it; only that it was a man, a man in uniform.

'Fine castle?' said the steward, after a pause. 'It was the finest in Zenzau!'

'The finest,' echoed the girl. Bitterness entered her voice. 'So it had to be destroyed.'

There was a pause; then Dolm, to Jem's surprise, laughed. 'But of course. For had this castle not met its fate, would our kingdom know the joy of Deliverance?' He turned to Jem. 'Sir, you are an Ejlander, are you not? You know, of course, that this realm once languished in the thrall of the Vianan Queen? We are sad for our castle, of course we are. But can we be sad for what we have in its stead – the wisdom and mercy of His Imperial Agonist Majesty?'

The old man's eyes glittered. Not for the first time that evening, Jem had the feeling that he was involved in some kind of game. Quite what sort of game it was, and where it would end, he was not sure. Could the old steward really be loyal to the conquerors?

It seemed so. Sipping his wine, Dolm began to expatiate on the benefits Ejland had brought to his realm. Shufflings came from behind the screen. Bellowing to Mother Rea to *stuff her worry-beads up her nostrils*, Dolm spoke of rebels who would defy their new masters, execrating their folly and lack of vision; eagerly he anticipated the day when all El-Orok would be Ejland's empire, united as one under the Agonist Deliverance. He raised his goblet, pushed back his chair.

'The Deliverance!'

Reluctantly, but pretending otherwise, Jem and Rajal joined the toast.

This was too much for Landa. As her father spoke, her face had become flushed; at this last excess she dashed down her goblet, bursting out, 'Deliver us from Deliverance!' It was a rebel cry. Tears sprang from her eyes, and she cried out what might have been the name of a god. But it was not the name of Agonis, or of Viana. Blundering from the table, she sank to her knees, gazing up imploringly at the portrait above the fire.

Dolm's response was a cackling laugh. Jem was stricken with shame; he was also more than a little drunk. Pursuing the girl, he almost tripped over the blanket that was wrapped round and round him, and plunged, more forcefully than he had intended, to the floor beside her.

Awkwardly he reached for her. 'Fair maiden, please. No one could have meant to upset you, I'm certain.'

'Oh Orvik, Orvik,' the girl was sobbing.

Orvik? Jem recalled the girl's words as she stood in the window, while Rajal sang the song about the King and Queen of Swords. *Orvik, is that you?* It was clear to him at once: Orvik was her lover, a rebel, at odds with her father. He raised his eyes to the portrait above the fire: it showed the image of a handsome, dark-eyed young man, stiff-backed in military uniform, but a uniform such as Jem had never seen before. Everything about it was unfamiliar, the epaulettes, the collar, the cut of the jacket, the little square hat on the young man's head. But strangest of all was its colour.

It was green.

Fascinated, and not a little envious of this Orvik, Jem gazed intently from girl to portrait, from portrait to girl. Then he became aware of something else, something more. His drying breeches, his tunic, his cape, hung across a sofa-back just beside the hearth. Under his blanket, he was naked. He felt a certain unmistakable, troublesome swelling. Oh, he was drunk! Swiftly he rearranged the folds of his blanket. Did the girl know? Could the girl tell?

She sprang up suddenly, wiping her eyes. 'Father, I'm sorry.'

'Come here, daughter, and kiss me. My daughter,' Dolm explained to the guests, 'is a little highly-strung – a little simple, too, as young girls are. It is regrettable, but what am I to do? Girls are girls,' he laughed. 'I think of reality, she thinks of romance. I should burn that old portrait if it were not for my child. At the very least, I should curse the day I salvaged it. But, but – I have not the heart. Since Landa was little, she has loved it so.'

'Old portrait?' said Jem, more loudly than he had intended. He resumed his seat, still fussing with his blanket.

'Old!' laughed Dolm. 'Why, Landa was not even born when that portrait hung in the Great Gallery, that now lies in ruins in these woody depths! It is Orvik, Prince of Wrax – Orvik the First that once was, whose castle this used to be. Dead, dead these many cycles. That is so, isn't it, daughter?'

The girl nodded numbly.

'And a tyrant he was, too, wasn't he? See, she knows. But a girl's fantasies – ah, a girl's fantasies! There shall be no more Orviks on the throne of Zenzau. And a good thing too!' The old man chuckled. 'But come, daughter, this is no entertainment for our guests. Will you not sing for us, hm? Sirs, you should like it if Landa were to sing?'

The guests agreed at once, but Landa protested. 'Father, don't expose me so! Will you not tell a story instead? You tell them so well. Tell . . . tell "The Shopkeeper of Wrax". You know how much I love it when you tell that story.'

The old man eyed the girl. 'Daughter, I thought we were to entertain our guests. It seems you care only for your own pleasures. Will these young men enjoy such foolish old tales? Very well, I shall bargain with you: I shall tell the tale, if *then* you shall sing.'

The girl hugged her father's neck. 'Oh Father, thank you!'

The old man cleared his throat. At first, Jem barely listened to the tale that followed. His eyes were only for Landa. Then slowly, beneath the surface of Dolm's words, Jem sensed a meaning, beating insistently. But quite what it was, he could not have said.

This was the tale.

THE SHOPKEEPER OF WRAX

Once below a time in the city of Wrax, close within the sound of the Temple bells, there lived a shopkeeper. He was a poor man, for his shop was a hole-in-corner place that sold only oddments and unnecessaries. Folk that lived hard by were poor too, and could give him little custom. Yet the shopkeeper dreamed of riches that one day might be his, for though he was not a covetous man, he loved his wife and son. His wife, who was fair, he would dress in silk and lace; his son, who was quick of wit, he would send to college, that the boy might become a man of learning.

Now it happened one day, as the shopkeeper was dusting his oddments and unnecessaries, that the shop-bell rang and the door opened, revealing a fine gentleman. The shopkeeper's eyes widened in surprise, for a fine gentleman in this hole-in-corner place was rare indeed. The gentleman wore a black cape and on his hands were many rings, glittering richly with inlaid stones.

'Shopkeeper,' said the fine gentleman, 'I would purchase your odd-ments and unnecessaries.'

'Sir,' smiled the shopkeeper, 'all I have are oddments and unnecessaries. Which of my goods would you buy?'

Now it was the fine gentleman's turn to smile. 'Shopkeeper, I would purchase them all, and I would pay you with this bag of silver.'

'Sir, such wealth would buy my goods many times over. Are you certain of this offer?'

The fine gentleman nodded. 'The offer is firm. There is just one condition I would make.'

At this, the shopkeeper's joy clouded, and he asked what the condition might be. But the fine gentleman said, 'Only if you accept my offer may I tell you of the condition.'

Longingly the shopkeeper looked on the silver. Then sadly he shook his head. 'Sir, my wife is beautiful. How do I know you might not take her from me? How do I know you might not do her harm? Then, what should this wealth avail me? No, sir, I must refuse your offer.'

'Shopkeeper, in my heart your honour does you credit. But alas, you shall have little credit in the world.' And the fine gentleman bowed and withdrew.

Now the shopkeeper was proud of what he had done, but when he told his wife, her eyes grew red with tears. 'But husband, have you forgotten how poor we are? How can you refuse this gentleman's condition? Why, it may not be what you fear. Why, it may be light as air! Think of the chance you have let slip by! Ah, husband, I fear you are a fool!'

And the shopkeeper feared his wife might be right.

Seasons passed and a time of famine came upon the kingdom. The small custom of the shop dwindled away. What place was there for oddments and unnecessaries in a city where few had food to fill their bellies? The shopkeeper saw ruin looming near. His heart sank in his breast, and the shelves of the shop grew dusty. Often he thought of the fine gentleman, and the offer he had been so quick to spurn. But much as he agreed that he had been a fool, still he was plagued by an ache of doubt. 'What could riches have availed me,' said the shopkeeper, 'if in gaining them I had lost my wife?'

Then one day, as he sat behind the counter, the rusty shop-bell rang. The shopkeeper looked up in surprise, for once again the fine gentleman stood before him, with his black cape and many-ringed hands.

'Shopkeeper,' the gentleman said, 'my offer stands, except that now I would increase its value.' And on to the counter, the gentleman spilt first a bag of silver, then a bag of gold; adding only, 'You are concerned

387

about the condition I would lay upon you? This I may say, and this alone: that I seek not your wife, and would bring no harm to her.'

Longingly the shopkeeper looked on the riches; then once again, sadly, he shook his head. 'Sir, my son is quick of parts. How do I know you might not take him from me? Then, what should this wealth avail me? Alas, sir, still I must refuse your offer.'

'Shopkeeper,' the fine gentleman said again, 'in my heart your honour does you credit. But alas, you shall have no credit in the world.'

And again the fine gentleman bowed and withdrew.

What had passed left the shopkeeper troubled. Still, he thought he had acted well, but when he told his son, the boy looked down thoughtfully. 'Father, have you forgotten that we are poor and hungry? Why did you judge the gentleman's condition, when still you do not know what it may be? Why, it may be soft as down! Poor, fond father, I fear you are a fool!'

And the shopkeeper feared his son might be right.

Now a time of pestilence descended upon the city, and all around him in that hole-in-corner place the shopkeeper saw his old customers dying. Dead-carts trundled past the shop-door each day. The poor man feared for his wife and son. Many times he cursed himself for a knave and fool, for spurning once again the fine gentleman's offer. In times such as these, he told himself, what condition could be anything but light? Soon they might all be snatched by death, after lives of nothing but poverty and despair! Whatever the strange condition might be, at least his wife might have dressed in silk and lace.

Yet still, in his heart, the shopkeeper wondered if perhaps he had been right. For had the fine gentleman taken his son, how could he ever have supported his pain? What should he have done? Many times in his dark and boarded shop, the poor, foolish man would give way to tears.

Then one day the dead-cart stopped outside his door, and springing down from the box was a figure he knew. It was the fine gentleman, and this time he emptied on the counter first a bag of silver, then a bag of gold, then a bag of the finest gemstones. Spreading the wealth over the counter, the gentleman leaned forward and whispered, 'Shopkeeper, all this shall be yours, if you but accept my condition. And though I cannot tell you the condition, this I may: that I seek not your son, and would bring no harm to him.'

At this, all doubt left the shopkeeper's heart, and he leapt up and cried, 'Then I accept! Fine gentleman, I accept your offer!' He rushed into the back of the shop to tell his wife and son. There, in the midst of this time of pestilence, the little family was the picture of happiness. They hugged each other, they laughed and cried. Long moments passed before they remembered the condition.

A little anxious, they crowded behind the counter, where the fine gentleman still waited patiently. With a smile he sorted through the gemstones, and picking up one particular stone, an odd-looking green one, placed it carefully in the shopkeeper's hand.

'The condition is this. All this wealth you may use as you will. All, that is, but for this one stone, which you must keep by you until a seeker comes, claiming it for his own.'

Now the joy of the little family was boundless, for what was the condition, after all, but light as air, soft as down? The fine gentleman only bowed and withdrew, failing even to take the goods he had once proposed to buy.

Now the little family realized all their dreams. The shopkeeper became a great man in the city. He lived in a fine mansion and kept a coach-and-six. His wife he dressed in silk and lace, his son he sent to college to became a man of learning. Years passed. The shopkeeper became Lord Mayor of Wrax. He founded schools and hospitals. Often he wondered how it could be that a man who had been so miserable could become so happy.

Never again did he see the fine gentleman, but often he mused upon the condition that had been laid so mysteriously upon him. Sometimes he would revolve the green stone in his hand, and wonder when the seeker would come. Then he would laugh, thinking of the long years he had wasted in foolish fears. How light, how easy the condition had been!

At last the shopkeeper grew great in years, and still the seeker had yet to come. He began to think of the condition as a joke, a joke he had yet to understand.

In due course it happened that his wife died. The shopkeeper was saddened, for he had loved her much, but he did not repine unduly. She had lived to her allotted span, and would he not join her soon, beneath the earth? Besides, the shopkeeper had his son to comfort him.

But now the shopkeeper grew older and older, passing far beyond the common span of men. Plagues ravaged the city, and never did he succumb. The son died, and still the father lived. In time, there were mutterings that so old a man must surely be in league with dark forces. The shopkeeper had enjoyed an active life in the world, but now he was forced into lonely seclusion. Citizens who once admired him now shunned his house. Stones rained through his windows. In due course, he was driven from his fine home, and all his wealth was lost.

He was left with only the strange green stone. By now, the shopkeeper would have sold the stone, but none would buy. Once, in anger, he would have thrown it from him, but the stone would not leave his hand. Only then, too late, did the shopkeeper realize the bargain he had made:

he had given himself to guard this stone until the seeker came. But for how long would he await the seeker?

Epicycles passed, and still the shopkeeper lived. He is living still, alone and sad, back where he began in some hole-in-corner place, within the sound of the Temple bells.

This then is the legend of THE SHOPKEEPER OF WRAX. The shop-keeper made a bargain which brought him first much joy, then eternal sorrow. Was he right to make this bargain, not knowing the condition?

My friends, I leave this question with you.

❋ ❋ ❋ ❋

It was the traditional ending of a Zenzan folk-tale. For long moments Jem looked down thoughtfully, and so did Rajal. Then suddenly they jumped as Dolm clapped his hands, calling once again for Landa's song.

This time the girl did not protest. With a shy smile, she took up her Wrax-harp. 'Father, what shall I play?' Nestling the instrument beneath her chin, she assumed an air of peculiar intentness.

Rajal cleared his throat. 'Maiden – if may I be so bold – there was a beautiful song you were singing when we arrived.'

'"The King and Queen of Swords?"'

'Pish!' said her father. 'A nursery catch! Will you not have *The Battle of Gelzin*, or *My Love, She's A-Gone with the Derkold Chief*?' Parched after his story, he gulped back his wine. 'But listen to me, how rude I become. Sing, Landa-child, sing your sweet lullaby.'

Landa swept her fingers over the strings. Frail and wraith-like in her pale peasant shift, she was standing by the fire beneath the portrait she loved. Goldenly the flames crackled behind her, leaping and glowing as if in time with the compelling, slow rhythm she plucked and strummed. Dolm looked on fondly; even the crone emerged from behind the screen, hovering in the shadows as the song unfolded. At first the girl's voice matched her frailness; it was reedy and hollow. But as she sang, she acquired confidence, filling the words with a grave, haunting beauty.

> *Everything is hidden and nothing is known,*
> *For even the truth is like a cur's old bone:*
> *Come, let us kneel at the mocking-tree boards,*
> *And pray for the King and Queen of Swords!*

Rajal could not help himself. First he felt compelled to hum along; in a moment he had pushed back his chair from the table, his voice blending with Landa's in full-throated accord. The girl tossed her head, beckoning him forward. In Agondon, it would have been a forward gesture; here, it was artless, expressive only of joy. His blanket wrapped

390

round him like a robe, Rajal stood beside the girl at the fire. The exquisite purity of their voices filled the room.

> *Everything is water but nothing is wet,*
> *And even the truth is like an unpaid debt:*
> *What, you would anger the mocking-tree lords?*
> *Still, you may lie with the Queen of Swords!*

Jem at first felt a stab of envy. Then this was replaced by a different emotion. A knowledge of Landa's purity suddenly filled him, humbling him. Her beauty was dazzling, but it was the beauty of innocence. With shame he thought of the lust that had overcome him, even in the moment when he had sought to comfort the girl. This song she sang now, this moment with Rajal, was a better, finer thing. Jem thought back to his life in Agondon and felt himself coarsened, spoiled, by the nights he had spent in Chokey's. He closed his eyes, and in place of the beautiful Landa, two images instead filled his mind – Cata, his first love, and Jeli, his second. He had lost them both. Had he deserved them, either of them? Jem blinked rapidly, his eyes filled with tears. He did not dare look up in case Dolm should see.

> *Everything's a pebble and nothing's a stone,*
> *When even the truth is left to lie alone:*
> *Fool, you would plunder the mocking-tree hoards?*
> *Then die with the King and Queen of Swords!*

Idly Jem smeared his bread around his plate. That was when he registered, as Rajal had before, the curious design etched into the silver surface. Jem was drunk, his senses hazy, but later he would feel that it was almost as if the song had come to life, taking on a meaning it had never had before. The singers sang of some strange King and Queen and here they were, scored into silver, the same King and Queen he had seen on the cards that flicked back and forth across Chokey's tables. The singers sang of a tree, and here between the King and Queen was a tree, drooping heavily with many plump fruits. What sort of tree was a mocking-tree? Why did the singers sing of lemon and lime? The fruits shown here were apples, were they not? But then, Jem had never seen a lemon or a lime, fruits of the warm provinces of the south . . .

There were many things he did not understand. In the grassy foreground, at the feet of the King and Queen, was a series of objects. At first, Jem could not make them out. Then he thought of the words of the song. Here, by a gorgeous flower, lay two horn-shaped vessels. The mocking-tree gourds? Here, by a rock, were two jagged planks – furred, perhaps, with moss. The mocking-tree boards? There were other things, but what most arrested Jem's attention was a row of little chests, like jewel-cases, each with a golden key in a lock. *Fool, you would plunder the mocking-tree hoards?* Jem looked again at the King and Queen, at the tree, at the heavy-hanging fruit. Apples, golden apples. And there, in the middle of the tree, attached to no branch but embedded, it seemed, within the trunk, a larger, different apple.

The harp and the voices – beautifully, painfully – twined round Jem's heart. Yes, there was much he did not understand. He carried his message THE TIME HAS COME, waiting only for the moment when he must give it. Still he did not know when that moment would be. But all at once he knew the real thing, the main thing. What a fool he had been! How many signs had he seen, all this time? Somehow, here in the vastness of Zenzau, he must find the Crystal of Viana. This song was not the nonsense, the nursery-catch he had always assumed. This song was the guide, the key to his quest.

The King and Queen of Swords!

They were the keepers of the crystal!

> *Everything is falling but nothing will fall,*
> *Though even the truth will vanish when you call—*

Jem was not listening to the song any more.

'I know everything,' he whispered. 'But I know nothing – at the same time, I know nothing.'

He staggered up from the table, the blanket falling from him, exposing his nakedness.

'The King and Queen!' he burst out. 'Who are they? Where are they?'

It was a foolish thing to do. But the others barely noticed. In the same moment, a thunderous thumping came at the door below. The song broke off. Landa flung down her harp.

'The Bluejackets!'

Chapter 56

A RED AND BLUE PLAY

'Bluejackets?'

Jem dived for his steaming breeches. Rajal did the same.

'Young sirs!' Dolm flung up his hands. 'Calm yourselves, now calm yourselves – you are our guests. The patrols come – oh, often, often. We have nothing to fear, have we? We are all loyal subjects of His Imperial Agonist Majesty, are we not?'

But Jem did not believe Dolm's beguiling words. The scene was transformed. While Landa's song had hovered on the air, the cluttered chamber might have been an enchanted cave, a place rich with mystery and impending revelation. Now it was only a place of fear.

The thumping from below came again, then again.

'Daughter, what are you thinking of? Go, go – quickly now, open the door.'

As his daughter rushed out, her hand cupping a candle, Dolm lurched across to the black-garbed crone. Like a slatternly housewife, stirred into sudden activity by visitors at the door, she was clearing the table, rapidly hiding away the greasy plates, the spoons, the goblets, the bread. She brushed the crumbs to the carpet and turned to face the steward. His manner towards her was altered. Suddenly he treated her with a new respect. He had seemed to despise her; suddenly it looked as if this had been an act. But why? What did it mean?

Urgently the two old people whispered together.

Quickly Jem and Rajal finished dressing.

'I don't like it,' Jem hissed. 'There's something wrong.'

'But what? Why?'

'The old man's a loyalist.' Jem thought quickly. 'The horses – he knows we stole them. He's going to give us up, Raj.'

'There's no other way out?'

It was hopeless. Heavy-booted feet came thumping up the stairs.

They dived behind a sofa.

From the footsteps, Jem surmised that three, maybe four Bluejackets had entered the room. He heard the shiftings of their heels, their heavy breathing, the clinking of the muskets they carried over their shoulders. They were still wearing their waterproof capes; rain dripped steadily, steadily to the floor.

'Greetings, good Master Dolm,' came a voice.

'My dear Captain! A poor night to be on patrol, is it not?' Dolm's voice was unctuous; Jem imagined the gnarled hands, twisting together. But no, he was leaning on his stick; as he spoke, the end of the stick tapped on a barren patch of floor, tapped then scraped, sounding out a nervous tattoo. 'Your visit is merely routine, I hope?'

The captain sighed. 'Ah, Master Dolm, a *routine* visit to your little remnant of castle would be a fine thing, and make no mistake – especially in view of a certain delight which always awaits one here.'

Tap. Scrape. 'Thank the captain, Landa.'

There was an awkward pause, in which Jem had the suspicion that this Bluejacket dog might be fondling the girl – pinching her on the cheek, perhaps, chucking her under the chin. Would her father stand by, accepting such an outrage? For a wild moment Jem would have burst out of hiding.

Rajal reached out a restraining hand.

'But my visit,' the captain was saying, 'is not as routine as I might wish. Pleasure, alas, cannot be its only purpose.'

Tap. Scrape. 'No! No trouble?'

'Two of our men have gone missing.'

'Deserters? Deplorable!'

Rajal relaxed his restraining hand. 'Jem?' he whispered. 'Why are we even bothering to hide?'

'Shh!'

'I mean, it might go against us.'

'Raj, don't be silly! Are we deserters?'

Rajal was confused. But so was Jem. Once before with Dolm, he had had the feeling that they were playing a game. Now the feeling returned in force. Dolm was a loyalist: how long before he gave them up?

'Deserters?' the captain was saying now. 'You have a low opinion of my men, Master Dolm?'

Scrape. 'Oh no, Captain, no!'

The captain laughed; peering over the back of the sofa, Jem could see little of the tall form in blue, only the bright jacket, only the pale hand that held the three-cornered hat. But he saw Dolm clearly enough, squirming, almost writhing; at any moment he expected to see the old man abase himself, cringing and salaaming. 'What indignity!' he muttered, outraged. 'I'd rather be a rebel a thousand times over, before I'd be a lickspittle like that!'

'Jem! Come down!' Rajal tugged his friend's shirt-tail.

'Make up your mind!'

The captain said, 'Our men were on the Wrax Road this afternoon. A routine patrol, but they did not return. I have also had reports that the "sunset stage" has yet to reach the city. Rather late, would you not say?'

Dolm, with a scrape, agreed that it was.

'Quite. And the stage also travels the Wrax Road.'

'There have been many accidents on that road, Captain.'

'You feel the stage may have met with an accident?'

Tap. 'No, no, Captain. I was speaking generally, generally.'

'Not from any particular knowledge?'

Scrape. 'Oh no, not at all.'

'As well for you, Dolm – less well for me. You understand, do you not, what suspicions these two events, side by side, have roused in my commanding officer?'

'Suspicions?'

Jem heard the captain's feet shuffle closer to the old man. 'Bob Scarlet!' came the whisper.

'No!' Dolm staggered back. 'But surely he is dead?'

'Dead, Master Dolm? Why should you think him dead?'

Dolm's voice was wheedling, whining. 'Captain, I know the might and splendour of your army, do I not? I know the forces that have been massed against the traitor, do I not? I know of your own determination to root out treachery wherever it may be found. Do I not?'

Tap. Scrape.

There was a pause. The captain's tone, when he spoke again, was cold. 'Do you know what is meant by *irony*, Master Dolm?'

Tap.

'Because if I thought you were attempting it, I should be displeased. Most displeased.'

Dolm said nothing, but there was a flurry of tappings, scrapings. The captain turned swiftly, efficiently, on his heels. 'You know where we stand, Master Dolm. We have reason to believe that rebels have returned to this area. If you see anything, if you hear anything, I want to know. *Never trust a Zenzan*, my brother-officers say. But *you*, I like to believe, are a good man, Dolm. In time, perhaps, this castle may be restored. It would make a fine Theron-season residence for the governor, would you not say?'

Tap. Tap.

'And the governor would need a steward, would he not?'

Scrape.

'Very well. Remember, Dolm, anything suspicious – strangers in the area, anything – I want to know. I shall be back tomorrow. And the day after. And the day after that.'

Jem looked at Rajal. Rajal looked at Jem. Moments earlier, both had been convinced that Dolm was about to reveal their presence, denouncing his guests with a sudden flourish calculated to win, perhaps, the captain's appreciative, cynical applause. Now they were not sure. But why should Dolm save them?

He had every reason to give them up.

There was a pause before the Bluejackets withdrew. In the pause, Jem suspected that the captain was eyeing – maybe even fondling – the girl again. Useless anger churned in him, and he could not resist peering over the sofa, one last time. He was right. The captain was toying with a braid of Landa's hair, smiling knowingly as her father looked on, tapping and scraping with a strained indulgence.

But it was not this that made Jem's heart lurch. All the time, as he heard the captain speaking, a strange, dim awareness had been stirring in his mind. Something about that voice: that cool, superior tone. Something about that manner: so amiable, so ominous. Something about those fondling hands. Now, for the first time, he saw the captain's hair.

Red as flame.

Then the face.

Jem slumped back behind the sofa, breathing hard. Now it was his turn to clutch Rajal's arm. 'It can't be!'

'Jem! What is it?'

The Bluejackets were tramping down the stairs again. 'Raj, do you remember Poltiss Veeldrop?'

'Veeldrop? It is a name cursed among all Children of Koros!'

'That was him!'

'The commander?'

'Worse! His son – Polty. My sworn enemy. Raj, he thinks I'm dead. He mustn't know I'm here. I tried to kill him once. But I tell you this much – if I get a chance to do it again, I will.'

But there was no more time to talk. Silence fell in the chamber like a curtain. There was only the crackle of the fire, dying now, and the endless running of the rain outside.

'Young sirs?' came Dolm's voice.

Jem bit his lip, rising up. 'Master Dolm, it seems we must thank you.'

Dolm's eyes were downcast. He shuffled about, this way and that, leaning heavily on his twisted stick. Behind him, the crone hovered darkly in the shadows. Only Landa looked directly at the guests, her eyes wide with a strange, sad wonderment.

Rajal nudged Jem. 'What is it? What's wrong with them?'

'Come here, young sirs. Closer, that's right.'

Awkwardly they obeyed Dolm's command, weaving their way through the cluttered gloom. The old man looked up. He flung down his stick, standing four-square, suddenly formidable in his tattered livery. All at once a pistol gleamed in his hand.

'Hands up! You think we're fools, don't you?'

'What?' Jem started back, but the crone had moved behind them. From the table she seized a heavy candelabra.

Appealingly, imploringly, Jem looked to Landa. She held something in her hands. Slowly she raised up the saddle-bags, stamped with the Bluejacket seal. 'Their papers are inside,' the girl said bitterly. 'Even the names they gave us were false. One of them's called Morven. The other's Crum. Soldiers of His Imperial Agonist Majesty.'

'I told you!' Rajal hissed. 'They think we're deserters!'

Jem attempted an urbane laugh. 'No, no! Good Master Dolm, you've got it wrong—'

'Shut your mouth, Bluejacket pig!'

'*Pig?* I thought—'

'Shut up, I said!' Menacingly Dolm waved his pistol. 'Deserters? You're spies! The old "travellers lost in the woods" routine, indeed! Who do you think you are dealing with, ignorant peasants? You pretend to be frightened of the Bluejackets. A patrol comes, we protect you. Then you wheedle out all our secrets, and denounce us!'

'No! You've got it wrong!'

But Dolm would not listen. He called to the crone, 'Mother!'

There was a sudden sharp *crack!*

Jem gasped. Beside him, Rajal had rumpled to the floor, knocked out by a blow from the candelabra. Jem turned, about to remonstrate, but before he could do so the *crack!* came again, this time on his own head.

That was the last thing Jem knew that night.

※　※　※　※

'Father! I thought you were going to kill them!' Landa sobbed.

'What am I, a Bluejacket thug? No, daughter. Help me now – let's drag them to the storeroom. Our leader shall decide what to do with these two.'

'What a pity!' Landa sighed. 'The dark one sings so beautifully. And the fair one is so – fair.' She shook herself, and was motioning for help with the unconscious boys when a cry erupted suddenly from Mother Rea. The crone's hand went to her mouth and she staggered back, collapsing into a chair.

'Dolm, you fool, you old fool! These are no spies!' moaned the old woman. 'Oh, why did I listen to you? How terribly, how grievously my powers have failed me!'

Dolm burst out, 'What are you talking about, crone? Quick, help us!'

But Mother Rea only moaned, 'Oh, what have I done?'

In the next moment, she fainted away.

Bewildered, Landa would have gone to the old woman, but her father snapped impatiently, 'Spies or no spies, these boys are a danger to us. Daughter, help me hide them in the storeroom – quickly now, quickly. The Bluejackets are wily, and may yet return tonight.'

Chapter 57

TRUDGE

Some way into the woods, Poltiss Veeldrop looked back on Oltby Castle, or rather its remains. Webbed through branches, refracted through the rain, came the glow of lamplight in a high window. Fondly he thought of the girl within. Was she lying down now on her narrow cot, her sweet mouth yawning, her eyes drifting shut? How he should like to lie there with her, arousing – first with kisses, then something more – the ardour that lay within her, unknown and secret!

Behind him, his patrol-men exchanged murmurous words.

'Cap's off again.'

'Deep thinker, like.'

'Like Morvy?'

'Not like Morvy. It's the red hair, like.'

'Red hair?'

'Deep, like.'

'Red, you say? But what about Morvy?'

'And Crummy?'

'Crummy, too.'

'Bob Scarlet?'

'No! Poor Crummy!'

'And Morvy?'

'Morvy, too.'

They trudged on. Above them the woods formed a dripping web, juddering in the pale glow of their lantern. But Polty's thoughts lingered behind. Sighing, he imagined the girl's body, the pert, uplifted breasts beneath the peasant shift. That the girl was a stranger to love was certain; why, she was innocent as the new day! In the barracks, lying on his own narrow cot, Polty had dreamed of her many times. Many times – too many – Penge had ached for her. It was not to be wondered at: Zenzau had been a trial for him. Though his master had sought only the freshest treats, the search was no easy one in this ruinous land, or necessitated the plucking of fruits so little ripened that Penge was sore tried to test their succulence. In happier days, after the taking of his delights, Penge had lolled across Polty's thigh like a satisfied Sultan, plump and warm. Too often now, after this or that pleasure – which, once passed, seemed no pleasure at all – poor Penge instead would retreat forthwith, becoming pale and cold, as if already he cowered, forlorn and weeping, before the regimental surgeon.

'What's that?'

'A branch!'

'A branch?'

'It's broken.'

'I thought it was a man.'

'Don't be silly.'

'A man in a cape.'

'A scarlet cape?'

They trudged on. Yes, Penge yearned for the beautiful Landa, and to gratify him, Polty knew, would be the merest play. What defence could the old fool Dolm mount, when a word – the merest word – from Captain Veeldrop meant irons, the dungeons, the firing-squad?

'They say he's a killer.'

'I don't believe he's real.'

'Who's real?'

'Bob Scarlet.'

'Oh aye, he's real.'

'I mean, he's not. I mean, I think.'

'Don't be silly.'

But Penge must give way to a greater need. Polty had determined on a policy of restraint. On finding himself consigned to Zenzau, it was true, he had yielded at first to the utmost licence. No day had passed on which his brain had not whirled on an eddy of Jarvel and rum-and-orandy. Wenching and cards filled every idle hour. Several times, games of Orokon Destiny had ended in blows. Barely had Polty's poor nose healed than his eyes had been blackened and he had cracked a rib. More than once he was called before his commander; for a time, only a knife-edge separated Polty from demotion to the ranks. It was a close-run thing. Without Bean to restrain him, Polty's recklessness knew no bounds; why, even the demands of Penge seemed ever more imperious.

'What about the Zens, then?'

'What about them?'

'The battle!'

'The Zens?'

'There'll be a battle, all the fellows say.'

'Don't go thinking about battles.'

'We're in the army!'

They trudged on. To say that Polty was chastened by his father's dying message would be, perhaps, not strictly true. Polty was shocked; then came anger. That his father should question his conduct at all was to Polty an unforgivable humiliation; sufficient, certainly, to smother any grief he might otherwise have felt for his father's death. That his father, too, should reveal to him the identity of his natural mother – and such a mother! – was to aggravate the offence more than Polty could bear. Of course Polty had an affection for Wynda Throsh; had not she procured for him his beloved heart-sister? Still, one may value the services of a butcher, yet not wish him for one's near relation; so Polty was appalled to think he sprang from the loins of so degraded a creature. Why, this meant that Bean – gangling, imbecilic Bean – was Polty's brother!

At once Polty determined that Bean must never know.

'What about the lightning?'

'What lightning?'

'Don't you know?'

'No.'

'In the Siege of Wrax.'

'What, then?'

'There was this lightning.'

Yet Polty's anger burnt swiftly away. Ignominy and shame cleared like smoke and he thought only of the future before him. How he longed to return at once to Irion, casting himself at his heart-sister's feet! What mattered it if he obeyed his father's will? That the girl would marry him he had no doubt: if she demurred, would not his heart-mother intercede? Polty exulted. Yes, it was good! Yes, it was destiny! Title, wealth, and his sister's body, all his to enjoy by right!

They trudged on. 'Was it lightning?'

'No, a flash. Like a bomb.'

'A bomb?'

'The Zens made it.'

'A flash, you say?'

'Well?'

'Well what?'

'What if they make it again?'

'Don't be silly.'

Polty had written to his regimental commander. His tone was gracious, even respectful. In treacly words Captain Veeldrop informed his superior of his impending marriage, begging leave that he might at once relinquish Zenzan duties, returning to his dear native land. Delicately he hinted at the ennoblement that would be made public in course of due process – Viscount, no less!

They trudged on. 'Why is it silly?'

'They lost, didn't they?'

'Yes, but.'

'Fellows went blind.'

'Shh! What's that?'

'A squirrel! And no, it's not.'

'Not what?'

'A scarlet squirrel!'

Polty sent his letter almost a moonlife ago. Since then he had carried out his duties as if in a daze. Time seemed suspended. He was waiting, that was all, but his mood was buoyant. The wheels of authority, after all, grind slowly, and Polty had no doubt that soon he would be rattling back along the Wrax Road, leaving this benighted colony behind.

Still, beneath his optimism, Polty was aware of a certain apprehension, drawn tight like a tensile wire. He found himself treading carefully, even meekly, where once he had bashed and blundered. No more Jarvel, no rum-and-orandy. To gaming, Captain Veeldrop had become a stranger; for the first time since receiving the gift of Penge, Polty had found himself reining him in. It was not easy. But necessary. Nothing must sully Polty's new virtue. Nothing must judder the tensile wire.

No, little Landa was safe enough!

'Are they cowards, like?'

'Who?'

'Morvy. And Crummy.'

'Morvy? Crummy? I suppose so.'

'I mean, did they run off?'

'Don't be silly.'

Polty had no fears of the impending battle. True, he had never taken part in a battle, and had little desire to do so. Mindless violence, in his view, was much better practised on an intimate scale. In the course of late duties he had shot several peasants and, on one occasion, gored a woman with his bayonet. That the actions had been pleasurable could hardly be denied; but the pleasure would be muted and the impact lost if similar atrocities were occurring all around him, and if, besides, the like might be directed towards his own person. But what need Polty fear? The enemies were only Zenzans, shabby peasants with pitchforks and clubs. What chance had they against the Bluejacket army? Moonlives would pass, besides, until it all came to a head; by then, Polty would be long gone!

They trudged on. 'Why is it silly?'

'Where would you run?'

'Wouldn't you run?'

'From what?'

'The lightning?'

'Oh, shut up!'

Polty's thoughts drifted back to the future. Where would he live, as a noble lord? Irion? Hardly! He pictured a mansion in Agondon, stuffed with gaudy riches, where the finest quality would come from all around to marvel and pay homage. To imagine this household more precisely was difficult; difficult at least for Polty, who had grown up with the Waxwells. He decided he would make Bean his manservant. Yes, Bean would be grateful to serve him. His heart-mother, too, would find her place; undoubtedly she would be a fine housekeeper, and watch over his wife for him when he was abroad. Why – Polty began to see – even his *natural* mother might be taken into the fold. What title he would give her, he was not quite sure; still, she would be an upper servant of sorts, making certain discreet arrangements for those times when the mistress must be treated with delicacy. Polty smiled. What a fond family he would gather around him, united in devotion to their master's happiness!

All this played pleasantly through his mind as the patrol regained the security of Wrax Barracks. It was as he flopped on to his mean cot, tugging at a tight boot and missing Bean – if only Bean were there, to pull at it for him – that an adjutant rapped imperiously on his partition and handed Polty two letters.

The first was from Colonel Heva-Harion.

S.H.I.A.M.
SERVICE OF HIS IMPERIAL AGONIST MAJESTY

Captain Veeldrop—
    As officially you remain attached to Lord E——'s division, yours of 4Wan/Evos has been referred to me. You will pardon my delay in response, but must understand that the affairs of the kingdom have reached a desperate pass. Accordingly I would have thought it clear that, with war imminent, no officer can be spared from Zenzan duties.
    I must add that reports of your conduct throughout this expedition have been of great concern to me. Further, that I regard this request you have made as an impertinence tantamount to insubordination. It is the last you shall be permitted. Any more and I strip you of your commission. You may consider that you have received a final warning.
    I am, &c.,
        (Col.) M. Heva-Harion

The second letter was franked with the Seal of Irion.

Dearest heart-son,
    O that I were with you, & could steel your firmness! Poor, poor child, grip yourself tight! O tribulation! O trial! See how the page is blotted with my tears! Still I am moist, struggle as I may – & how can your moistness not mingle with mine as I tell you (so hard upon her husband's loss) that your heart-mother now is bereft of a

403

DAUGHTER? *O suffering! O sorrow! For Catayane – Catayane,
comfort of my declining years! – has flown this house, & is nowhere to
be found!*
O pray she may return to us!
In deepest affliction I remain—
Your mother,
UMBECCA

Polty sat on his cot for some moments, trembling and pale. Then he
screwed the two letters into a ball, threw the ball into the barrack-room
stove and repaired with some speed to the officers' mess.

In a short time he would be drunk, very drunk indeed.

Chapter 58

WRAITH IN THE SMOKE

'Elpetta!'

Jeli rolled her eyes.

'Elpetta!'

This time she stamped her foot. Really, was there ever such a useless baggage? She called again; at last there came a clumping of coarse boots and the maid, flushed and gasping, stumbled into the room.

Jeli stood with her arms akimbo. 'Elpetta, what is the meaning of this?'

'The (*puff, puff*) meaning, Miss?'

Jeli took a deep breath. 'The olton-clock had barely struck twelve when you pulled my laces tight. By thirteen I had straightened my stomacher and arranged my hoop. Now, fourteen has come and gone, and where is my carriage? Where is my aunt? Is Lady Bolbarr's reception, for which I have worked to prepare myself this last moonphase – *worked*, Elpetta, like a Tiralon in the cane-fields – to come and go without its most desired guest? Can you not see that I wear my finest finery? Look at this satin, this intricate beading! All afternoon I've had Master Carrousel up here, dressing my hair! Now I pace and pace, I ring, I shout – I am reduced, Elpetta, to *shouting like a fishwife* – and still I am left alone and abandoned! Does no one appreciate that I am a woman of destiny? Why, and Miss Tilsy Fash is to sing tonight, too! Shall I arrive in the midst of her performance, muting the impression I have fought so hard to make?'

Something broke in Jeli's voice and she cast herself on to the sofa – carefully, nonetheless, and restraining any but the driest of sobs. The maid stood breathing. She might have been forgiven for assuming that Miss Jeli did not require her to speak – until, that is, the young lady looked up suddenly and shouted, 'Have you nothing to say, you stupid woman?'

Elpetta – or Berthen Spratt – drew herself upright. There were many things she might have said, after three seasons of tending the inhabitants of these apartments; instead, she remarked only that she was sorry, very sorry that miss had been incommoded, but that something – *something* – was afoot downstairs. Having divined the nature of that *something*, Berthen – or Vanta Shessey – had resolved on respect.

Jeli said suspiciously, 'What *something*?'

'Begging your pardon, miss, but there's a visitor.' The maid attempted a coy smile. 'Why, if you look from that dormer right now, you might see something to your . . . advantage, miss.' The maid held the coy smile as her young mistress rustled over to the window. Jeli looked down to the steep stairs, where Ju-Ju, long ago, had collapsed and died.

Jeli never even thought of her now.

'Elpetta, what's going on?'

So late at night, Jeli had expected to look out upon darkness, leavened perhaps only by the moon or the occasional passing link-boy's lamp. Instead she saw that tapers leapt and danced in rusting brackets beside the stairs. The night was a haze of flame, and there at the foot of the stairs was a magnificent coach-and-six – why, the finest she had ever seen!

And who was this? Descending the steps, leaning heavily on a servant's arm, was a hunched old man in a flowing wig; emerging from the coach was a man in white – thin, tall, erect – followed by a plump, red-faced figure swathed in ermine and blue velvet.

Jeli gasped. At once the maid was beside her, squeezing her arm in excited intimacy. 'Come, miss, there's no mystery here, is there? There's your uncle, and there're his guests. Look how graciously he bids them welcome! The First Minister – and the King!'

Jeli's face was pale. Now it was as much as she could do not to slump to the floor, rumpling her fine gown, jarring askew the elaborate, heaped-high coiffure that Agondon's finest hairdresser had worked so long to create. Instead, there was the sudden pressure of hands behind her, grabbing her round the waist.

Jeli turned, startled. It was her aunt.

Often now, Aunt Vlada seemed much faded, much reduced, not at all the formidable figure with whom Jeli had at first been so entranced. Sometimes, much to Jeli's irritation, the old woman lay on the sofa all day, grey-faced and haggard, sipping weak tea, sprawled unappealingly beneath an eiderdown. Now she was restored to her former glory, resplendent in an emerald gown, her eyes bright and flashing and her long tresses, freshly reddened with henna, wound elaborately round her head and stuck through with gorgeous feathers.

With a smile she led her trembling young charge to the door.

'Come, my dear. I'm afraid we have deceived you, just a little – but it was vital, that your little heart might not burst with excitement. No, there's no reception at Lady Bolbarr's tonight! Your finery is for a private meeting – ah, but *such* a meeting. Come, your destiny is about to unfold!'

The Archduke of Irion led his guests into a shabby drawing-room. Swiftly fitted out with fresh hangings and carpets – Vlada had organized everything, of course – the room yet had about it a decidedly dilapidated air. Incense burned discreetly in assorted corners, in an effort to disguise the reek of damp. The Archduke had little use for these apartments, and having to use them left him out of sorts. He leaned heavily on his servant's arm.

Formal meetings were anathema to him. Long ago the old man had given up attendance at Court, and seldom now did he even dress in the finery of his station. His wig itched; his shoes pinched; his stays and stockings chafed him sorely. How he longed to descend once again into the dark chambers beneath the house! Cycles earlier – why, by now it seemed a lifetime ago – Jorvel Ixiter had determined that a man, were he to support the ignominy and boredom of living, must fix upon a particular interest, prosecuting it to the exclusion of all else. The choice was arbitrary, or may as well have been; what mattered was that the interest should take on so potent a fascination, seem so inevitable, so vital, that it invested life itself with a sense of purpose.

Jorvel Ixiter had decided on depravity. To nurse it, to feed it, to prosecute its ends had become for him a mission so fervent that his empty life burnt bright with meaning. He was a taciturn man, confiding in nobody; but if any man – if any woman – had come close enough to see the wheels inside his brain, it might have seemed that guilt was the motor that set them whirring. Had the betrayer of Ejard Red determined to damn himself again and again, sinking ever deeper into an abyss of his own devising? The Archduke would have claimed that he felt no guilt. The Siege of Irion was long ago. So steeped in evil was he by now, indeed, that the giving-up of Ejland's rightful King seemed but a minor incident in the course of a long career. Yet perhaps sometimes, deep in the night, as he slept on his filthy couch in the brothel downstairs, the noble lord who had turned himself into 'Chokey' found his thoughts drifting in this direction, and called out violently for Jarvel or rum, or the attentions of one of his ruined young ladies.

Sourly the Archduke swept his eyes round the drawing-room. Vlada's furnishings filled him with disgust. So feminine, so fussy! For the merest moment he thought of his dead wife, then buried the thought again. How wretched he felt! The lamps were too bright for him and his eyes watered; fighting back a strong desire to adjust his crotch, he contented himself with a violent scratching beneath his wig. When he withdrew his hand, a bloody scab hung from one of his fingernails. Discreetly he flicked it to the fine carpet.

With infinite refinement and grace, showing proper deference to the primacy of the monarch, the party arranged themselves in a circle by the fire. Servants were at once to hand with tumblers of rum-and-orandy. The King and the Archduke guzzled theirs quickly, looking about impatiently for the replacements that soon came; the First Minister's sat by him, untouched, through the scene that followed.

'How great a privilege to see His Imperial Agonist Majesty within these walls,' the Archduke attempted, wringing his hands together unctuously. 'A privilege, but also a pleasure. Why—' he struggled '—were I now to be struck by a falling cornice that gashed open my brains, leaving me to bleed to death on the floor before Your Majesty, I should die happy.'

'His Majesty is as much privileged to be here,' the First Minister responded dryly, 'knowing that the meeting is to be so advantageous.'

The King was already very drunk. Discreetly he permitted himself a trumpeting fart. 'The girl,' he slurred, 'where's the – g-girl?'

'Patience, sire,' returned the First Minister. 'I doubt not that she shall soon be with us – hm, noble Archduke?'

'Soon, soon. My – ah, heart-sister is preparing her. But then, His Imperial Agonist Majesty perhaps recalls his previous meeting with this radiant young beauty? I am told she was almost King's Chosen.'

The First Minister shot a warning look.

'Maddy,' moaned the King, in the brief moment before the First Minister stamped on his foot.

The Archduke shifted in his stiff-backed chair. Really, he would be in pain, severe pain by the end of all this! How many times that day had he cursed Vladdy for putting him through this foolish charade? And yet, she had insisted, it was all worthwhile, and the Archduke had to admit this was true. To be sure, the sale would afford him no particular pleasure. Leasehold was much to be preferred to freehold, in his view, and the bargain, besides, was heavily in the girl's favour. A Royal Wedding? There could hardly be any humiliation in it, whatever the nature of the husband-to-be. Now, had Vladdy permitted him to take the girl below – might it not be desirable to *break her in*? – her uncle would have been more wholehearted. Several times he had licked his lips, picturing a team of Bluejackets, a regimental goat . . . The old man sighed. He must remind himself that after this he could buy the house next door, as long planned, doubling the size of his subterranean domain.

Vlada came forward, leading the girl. The women bowed low to the Royal Personage, but it was the First Minister who responded. 'Such beauty, sire!' he hissed. 'Would you not have her sit by you?' The King lurched dangerously sideways in his chair, drivelling a little, gripping tight to the tumbler in his mutilated hand.

Trembling, Jeli assumed her place. An awkward silence would have followed, but Vlada – with that art which women seem to possess – was quick to make good the gaps. Conversation turned to the affairs of the kingdom – the frivolous ones, of course, saving the presence of the virtuous girl. There was talk of the Opera's new programme, and Lady Cham-Charing's sad decline; talk of the murders on Regent's Bridge and the serious floodings in Agondon New Town. This year, when the ice thawed, muddy water had rushed into all the cellars in Ollon-Quintal.

'The cellars?' said the Archduke, a little alarmed.

'Indeed, heart-brother, have you not heard? I dare say you are glad to live upon The Island. First Minister, must not there always be some doubt as to the stability of *claimed* land?'

'You allude to something, lady?' came the First Minister.

Vlada looked squarely into the lean ascetic face. 'I hear, too, that a bout of plague has broken out in Varby. Some doubt that a Varby Season shall be possible this year! First Minister, should that not be a crisis of the first magnitude?'

'The first! Why, lady, it would be a crisis beyond magnitude.'

'Your people shall be restless, First Minister.'

'If they are not distracted.'

Vlada plucked a tumbler from the footman's tray and downed it quickly, like a man. With surprising force she banged it down on the little inlaid table between them. Such a woman! One almost expected her to reach into her dress and slap down a deck of cards and a purse of gold tirals!

Instead she said sweetly, 'Shall we, perhaps, leave the young people alone?'

Good old Vladdy! The Archduke had to rub his hands again, unaffectedly this time. Vladdy, he sometimes thought, was the one woman whose intelligence he respected. Had she really been a man, what might she have become? But then, he would hardly have wanted her to be a man! Fondly he remembered them in the days of their youth, rolling and tumbling on an unmade bed. What pleasures they had known! *You think I've ruined myself, don't you?* Vladdy had laughed one day. *Well, I tell you I haven't, Jorvel Ixiter. Men are fools, and I shall make the most spectacular marriage I can. Not for love, but for power, power!*

Poor Vladdy! Her ambition had been taken down a peg or two. Zenzau-blood and scandal was a potent mix, then as now; besides, had she not earned – Jorvel was never quite sure why – the undying enmity of Uly Quick? Quick – sour-faced protectress of the virtues Jorvel delighted in despoiling – had always been too powerful in Agondon. Vlada Flay was condemned to the colonies. And yet, thought Jorvel, I might have saved her. What constrained me? A foolish respectability.

In Ruanna, the woman he had married at last, he had hoped to find something of Vladdy's fire. He had found none of it. How he wished he had married the Zenzau-blood, and be damned to what the world – and Uly Quick – would say! But there was no repairing that mistake now. Marriage was a thing of the past to Jorvel Ixiter. Still, perhaps when the girl was gone, he might ask Vladdy if she would come downstairs, to help with the management of his growing team.

But no. She would want to stay with the girl, moving into chambers in the Koros-Palace. What was Vladdy doing, after all, but making – through the girl – the spectacular marriage she had once planned for herself?

So Jorvel thought.

Graciously, elegantly, Vlada led the Archduke and the First Minister to an area a little away from the fire. 'Perhaps, gentlemen, we might repair behind this screen, where I have arranged – things must, after all, be protected from the light – some of the most priceless prints in my heart-brother's collection?'

They were barely behind the screen before the First Minister slipped a bag of gemstones – more priceless than any prints – into the Archduke's eager, claw-like hand.

'And the *balance*, First Minister—?'

'The day of the wedding, Archduke. On the day of the Royal Wedding.'

✳ ✳ ✳ ✳

Left alone with His Imperial Agonist Majesty, Jeli found herself prey to contrary emotions. For so long – why, for a full three seasons – the girl had been assured that hers was a great destiny. To realize, at last, the nature of that destiny, was a little disconcerting. She was enthralled: it was more, much more than she had imagined.

And yet.

Bleary-eyed, loose-lipped, the Claim-Monarch of all the lands of the earth juddered his chair closer towards hers, clutching her arm. Jeli looked down. She drew in her breath sharply, seeing the mutilated hand.

'So they tell me I must take a wife,' slurred the Ur-Archmaximate and Defender of the Faith. 'You are a pretty thing, it cannot be denied. Still, do not think I shall love you, my dear! I have known love only once, and that is over – dead! I dare say I shall be cruel to you. I dare say I shall beat you. In our intercourse I shall take no pleasure. For your society, your wit, your accomplishments, I have no desire. Your beauty, your finery beguiles me not in the least. Your vanities, your expenses shall be resented sorely. In time, I have no doubt, I shall hate the sight of you. Yet I am a man, and must vent my lust; then, too, I am a King, and must have an heir.'

410

At this, leaning a little too precariously in his chair, Orok's Represent-ative in the Realm of Being slumped to the floor with a thud, but rallying – sensible, after all, of the delicacy of the occasion – he clutched at the girl's dress, and clawing himself upright on the thick folds of fabric, asked her, on a gust of drunken breath, if she would be his wife.

Aunt Vlada's party, alerted by the thud, had emerged discreetly from behind the screen, eager to view this climactic moment in the womanly career of Miss Jelica Vance; alas, that instead of the melting sigh, the maidenly blush, they should be affronted instead by a piercing scream! Why, the girl must be crazed! Suddenly rising, she threw her lolling suitor to the floor and rushed, sobbing, from the room.

The First Minister darted to the King, fearful that His Majesty had cracked his head. Aunt Vlada went in pursuit of Jeli. Only the Archduke lingered by the screen. Worriedly he weighed the gemstones in his hand.

✵ ✵ ✵ ✵

Jeli ran and ran. Pushing past the footmen, she blundered into the hall. What she intended, what she wanted, she could not say. She could barely think at all. All she could see was the ruined hand, clutching first her arm, then her gown, grabbing and crushing.

'My dear! My dear!' Aunt Vlada's footsteps tap-tapped behind her. Had she been thinking, had she been conscious, Jeli would have run to her room and slammed the door; now, desperate only to flee, she darted down an unfamiliar passage.

How shabby, how ugly were the walls! She was somewhere at the back of the house, somewhere she had never been before. This must be part of the servants' quarters. Underfoot there were only bare boards; paint peeled down in strips from the cracking plaster. Then somewhere behind her, a door swung shut. Jeli was in darkness.

Trembling, wiping her tears, she felt her way forward. In the excite-ments of the day, Uncle Jorvel had neglected his usual precautions. Jeli did not know it, but she was in a part of the house that was normally kept locked. She descended a flight of stone steps.

What happened next was inevitable, of course it was.

From somewhere ahead came a glow of greenish light, a sound of coarse music and voices raised in mirth, or anger, or desire. The fug of stale air was almost overwhelming.

By now Jeli had quite forgotten the distressing scene which had taken place upstairs. Fascinated, astonished, she stared at her uncle's basement: at the looking-glass walls, at the churning smoke, at the green baize tables, at the flick-flicking cards; and moving between it all, the figure of a girl.

But such a girl!

411

Jeli was shocked. Dressed only in a diaphanous shift, with free-flowing hair and rolling breasts, the girl disported herself in the most brazen manner, rubbing her hands freely over this or that drunken young blade, laughing delightedly as coarse hands reached, in turn, to fondle her breasts and thighs. In the thick smoke the girl was a dream-like wraith; but then, as she turned beneath a swinging lantern, Jeli suddenly saw the face clearly.

Could it be?

But her cry died away before it could be uttered, falling from her lips as the merest whisper. Memories flooded her of her days at Quick's, of a giggling girl who had dreamed of the husband, the home, the children that one day would be hers.

Jilda. Jilda Quisto.

Someone called for a song; then the girl was standing in the centre of the floor, swaying as she intoned a breathy melody. Still the men leered and pawed at her as she sang; only Jeli listened to the words.

JILDA'S SONG

> *This is my life,*
> *Slipped away,*
> *Blown and billowed on a windy day:*
> *All in all the promises men make shall soon be broken,*
> *All in all you're lucky if they leave behind a token.*
>
> *This is my love,*
> *Torn from me,*
> *Turning, tossing on a stormy sea:*
> *All in all a woman's hopes are sure to be mistaken,*
> *All in all she's lucky if she's not sad and forsaken.*
>
> *This is my heart,*
> *Bleeding red,*
> *Bruised and battered on a dirty bed:*
> *All in all my life, my love was barely worth a token.*
> *Ah, I wonder why my heart was made just to be broken!*

Tears came to Jeli's eyes. Trembling, she would have sunk back into the shadows, far as far could be, wanting only to forget that she had ever seen this place, this girl; then all at once, came a pressure of hands around her waist. It was something that had happened already that night. This time Jeli cried out, almost screamed.

At once, the comforting voice sounded in her ear, 'No, my dear, fear not. I thought you had come this way. It was as well, perhaps, that you should know the truth at last.'

'The truth?'

'Look,' said Aunt Vlada.

Jeli turned back. No longer could she see the girl who looked like Jilda; but now, she made out five, ten, fifteen girls moving through the smoke like the same wanton wraith. For a moment – it would be the last one she was to know – Jeli, leaning back in her aunt's arms, felt a surge of the old love. For suddenly Aunt Vlada was giving her, as she had given her in the beginning, the most profound and beautiful reassurance the girl was ever to know.

'Look on them well, my dear,' Aunt Vlada whispered. 'Look on them once, and this once only, and always remember that they are like you. All women are harlots. What else is our destiny? But my dear, think of the fate of these degraded creatures, then think of the fate that lies before *you*. For if we are harlots, is it not our greatest triumph to sell ourselves to the highest bidder?'

Jeli swooned; but perhaps, even in that moment, another awareness stirred within her. That what Aunt Vlada said was true she had no doubt. She must sell herself, she must. But then Jeli remembered a young man – a lean, boyish, blond young man – who had come to her one foggy day and told her that he loved her. That boy had vanished now, and who he had been – who he had really been – Jeli did not know. Didn't they say he had been involved in that dreadful business with Pellam Pelligrew? Why, he was probably a murderer! But often, in the days to come, the image of that boy's sweet face would return, troublingly, to Jeli's mind, haunting her like a ghost. Like a wraith in the smoke. Then she would curse, and bid the wraith be gone.

She must harden herself.

And she would.

Chapter 59

BIDDY-BIDDY-BOBBLE

There was not much time.

Gasping, Cata flung herself deeper into the woods. Before the bugle sounded, she must meet Nirry, but first there was something else she must do.

She stopped, looked around, made certain she was alone. The chill of darkness lingered in the air and the woods still dripped from last night's rain. The dawn light was a purple refulgence, glimmering through the rustling caverns of leaves. Cata shrugged off her blue jacket, flinging it contemptuously over a branch. Sinking to her haunches she cried out, calling to the creatures of these alien woods. Her cry was soft but ardent, wordless, but imbued with a meaning deeper than words. Leaving her lips, it seemed to twist on the purple-green air like smoke, as if it were not only more than words, but more than sound too.

Softly a robin alighted on her hand. Then came a squirrel, skittering forward shyly, then a badger and a feral cat. A slothful bear peeped through the branches and an owl, stirring from the brink of sleep, blinked the strange dark-brightness of its eyes. Humming, Cata reached out her hands to the creatures, linking them together in wordless communion. She tilted back her head and closed her eyes, letting her breath come slowly, slowly.

In the past, a great comfort would have flooded her being. Now it was different; Cata was aware of a curious unease, welling beneath the surface of the loved, familiar rite. The animals were frightened, and when she asked them why, they could not say. Cata screwed up her forehead, willing herself to see deeper into their minds. But all that came to her was a mysterious dark pulsing, a tom-tom thudding, colliding with the rhythm of her own gentle mantra.

Then Cata was frightened too. It was a pulsing she had sensed before, and she knew that something evil was stirring in the world.

'Bacon?'

A red nose protruded from a waterproof sheet.

'I say, that couldn't be bacon I smell?'

414

Laughter rang from beside the campfire. 'I think our fat Friar is stirring at last!'

'I say, it *is* bacon!' The red nose was followed by a tonsured head, with glinting little eyes and a moist, expectant mouth. The Friar kicked his waterproof impatiently away, scuttling over to join the feast. 'Have we bread and onions, pickles and cheese? Oh, I do like it when we come back to Oltby!'

The laughter came again. It was a beautiful morning. The woods were warm, basking in the burgeoning Season of Viana. In dappled green and gold the sun shone through the leaves of a secluded clearing, some distance from Dolm's tower. Bright beams danced in the pallor of the woodsmoke, on the toasting-fork that turned in a swarthy hand, on the spectacles that nestled on a scholarly nose.

The Friar, as usual, was the last to awake. In the glimmering dawn, Hul and Bando had been down at the river, cleaving exhilaratingly through the chill waters. Breakfast was their reward. Raggle and Taggle, Bando's little sons, had breakfasted long ago and played close by. Blackjaw, the scout, was patrolling for Bluejackets, while the Priestess, by now, must almost have finished her prayers, watched over protectively by their leader himself. Though the masked man could not share in these devotions, he always went with her into the forest depths. These hills, he would say, were no place for a woman, even one who called herself a Daughter of Viana. If the Priestess demurred, she seemed glad nonetheless that she did not have to go into the woods alone. In each new camp, she claimed, her powers protected them from harm.

It was true that they had never been caught. But they never stayed in one place for long.

There could be no rest for Redjacket rebels.

'Friar, you're in good form this morning,' said Hul. 'Last night, it was nothing but grizzle and groan.'

'Last night it was raining,' the Friar protested, through a mouth stuffed with pickles and rye-bread. 'Oh, and I was ever so hungry.' Longingly he watched the dripping bacon, curling on the end of Bando's fork.

The spectacles flashed. 'See, Friar, the goddess heard you. She protects us all, not just her own.'

Mushy bread fell from the overstuffed mouth. 'Master Hulveron, you are an Agonist like me! Would you blaspheme against the one true faith?'

'Friar, if it were *true*, would you be gorging yourself here with us now? Compare Priestess Ajl.' From deeper in the woods they could just hear the high, mournful sound of Vianan prayer.

'Heathen mumbo-jumbo!'

The scholar smiled. He had lost his faith long ago and was unlikely to acquire another. But he enjoyed baiting the Friar. Ejected from his Order for gluttony and sloth, the fat little monk liked to pretend, it seemed, that he was a man of the strictest principles.

'Careful, Friar! Would you offend poor Bando here? Remember he is a Zenzan, born and bred!'

'Pah!' Bando spat into the fire. A plump, swarthy fellow, he had a black moustache and wore a red bandanna tied around his head. 'Here, Capon! Or should I say *Here, boy*?' He flung a sizzling strip across the fire. With a little shriek the monk caught it, tossing it in panic from hand to burning hand until he stuffed it, at last, into his greedy mouth. His cheeks flamed and his little eyes were wide as the scalding meat slithered thrillingly, painfully down his gullet.

Hul laughed. 'Poor Friar! A pot of ale for your labours!'

Bando spat again and opened a leather pouch. Rolling a tobarillo, he recited laconically:

> *'Feed me! Feed me!'*
> *Glutton-Greedy*
> *Took the bread from Poor-and-Needy:*
> *Poor-and-Needy,*
> *Thin and weedy,*
> *Drove a dirk through Glutton-Greedy.*

'One you learnt at your mother's knee, Bando?' smiled Hul.

'Hmph! There's no Poor-and-Needy here, is there?' blustered the Friar, in between gluggings of the much-needed ale.

Bando blew out a long stream of smoke. 'Capon, you are such a fool! Tell him, Hul. Poor-and-Needy is all the people of Zenzau, under the yoke of the Bluejacket oppressors.'

'You, Master Bando? You are so fat!'

'Fat? He calls me fat? Capon, you're talking to a veteran of the Resistance!'

'But a fat one,' laughed Hul, slapping the Zenzan's paunch. 'See, Friar, the goddess has blessed those who serve her!'

'Master Hulveron, you will spare me this heathen talk!' Affronted, the Friar retired to the edge of the clearing. He hitched up his cassock.

A thick stream of urine gurgled into the grass.

Bando grunted, 'Capon finds *some* use for his pizzle, at least.'

'Master Bando, I wish you wouldn't call me that. I have all that you have.'

Hul laughed, 'Few can boast as much! Why, Friar, you must have had the wenches queuing. Exhaustion, perhaps, forced you into your Enclosed life?'

The banter ended suddenly. A crackling came from the woods, then a high, anxious whistle. *To-whit! To-whoo!* In the next moment a white-garbed form burst into the clearing.

Hul was on his feet. 'Landa! What's wrong?'

Rising, Cata donned her jacket again, grateful at least for the warmth it gave her. Sometimes she wondered what she was doing, following this hated army into battle. Trudging along the muddy Zenzan roads, often she longed only to fling down her pack, careering blindly into the woods.

Many a young Bluejacket felt the same. For five gold tirals, Nirry had learnt, a man could buy his way out of this army. But that was more money than most recruits would ever see in their lives. Desertion was their only means of escape. What held them back was fear. If they were caught, the punishment was death; and then, too, what common soldier could survive in these woods? To her fellow-recruits, Cata sensed, this was a prospect far more daunting than day after day of brutal marches, or even the bloody battle at the end.

Cata had no such fears. For the Bluejackets she had nothing but contempt, and when the time came would leave their ranks with a blitheness no man was able to display. What kept her with them now was the harlequin's promise. He had said she would see a sign, and more and more now, as they neared the heart of Zenzau, Cata knew where this sign would come. It would come to her before the gates of Wrax, as the Bluejackets clashed at last with the rebel forces.

It would come to her on the battlefield.

Landa's face was flushed and she was breathing hard. 'The Bluejackets! Oh, Hul, Bando – I'm so worried! They came to the castle again last night. They'll be back. The red-haired captain—'

'Landa, he hasn't hurt you?'

'No, no. It's the camp. It's not safe—'

The Friar groaned, 'As soon as we're back here! And after that splendid hamper from Mother Rea, too!'

'Shut up, Capon,' Bando scowled. Instinctively the Zenzan reached for the rifle he always kept beside him. Like the Friar, he may have been a pudgy, sensual fellow, but Bando's senses were sharp, his feelings true. Even now he seemed on the alert, as if at any moment the enemy would be upon them.

'But there's more,' said Landa. 'Last night . . .' A little breathlessly, she ran through the story of the strange visitors to the castle. 'I thought they were loyalists. Then I thought they weren't. But they were riding Bluejacket horses . . .'

'Spies!' Bando spat.

'We've locked them in the storeroom. Their names are Morven and Crum.'

Hul's spectacles flashed. 'What do they look like?'

An interruption came before the girl could say more.

'Biddy-biddy-bobble!'

'Diddy-on-the-double!'

Rolling, tumbling, bouncing like balls, two little boys came crashing into the clearing.

'Raggle!' Landa cried, delighted. 'Taggle!'

Laughing, dusting down their breeches, the Twinned boys sprang to their feet, eager-eyed. With their podgy bellies, springy curls and their own little red bandannas round their necks, the urchins looked like identical, junior versions of Bando. There had been a time when they had proper names; there had been a time when one wore a green, one a yellow bandanna, but it had been useless. They answered to the wrong names and swapped bandannas. Now the boys were always just 'Raggle' and 'Taggle', and which was which no one, perhaps not even their father, was sure.

'We know a secret!' they piped together.

'A secret!' Landa knelt down. 'What could it be?'

The girl was expecting some innocent prank. Her face was open, smiling, but her hand came up to her mouth in alarm as the boys cried together:

'Blackjaw's got prisoners!'

'What sort of prisoners?'

'Blackjaw's got their hands tied and they're running after his horse! Oh, they look so funny!'

'Their faces are red!'

'But their jackets are blue!'

Hul and Landa exchanged worried glances. Bando burst out, 'Oh, the fool! What has he done now?'

'I say,' the Friar said nervously, 'prisoners wouldn't need to be fed much, would they? Bread and water?'

'We'll torture them!' Bando flung back angrily. 'But first, we'll practise on you!'

'Torture!' The twins squealed with delight. 'Oh Papa, can I chop off their fingers?'

'Papa, can I chop off their toes?'

'Boys, hush!'
'Here they come!'

Nirry looked about her uncertainly. She was standing on a rise at the brink of the woods. Below her lay the sleeping regiment, with its tents, its wagons, its tethered horses; behind her, the glimmering dimness of the trees.

She wandered between them, just a little way.

'Miss Cata? Miss Cata, where are you?'

Nirry was worried. Usually Miss Cata would be waiting by now, and besides, these meetings were becoming foolhardy. As they neared the assigned battlefield, the atmosphere in the camp was ever more intense. Every morning Nirry was more nervous. For herself she had little fear, but she was worried for the young mistress. The sentries were growing sharper. How easily Miss Cata might fall under suspicion!

'Miss Cata?' Nirry was whispering, but her whisper was sharp. Already she was surrounded by trees on all sides. Round and round she turned in the greenwood light. Softly at first, then harder, harder, she heard the pounding of her heart in her chest.

A rustling sounded, somewhere through the trees.

Nirry gasped. That was when a new fear assailed her. It was something Sergeant Floss had said a few nights ago, leering at her over his tilted hip-flask. Of course he wanted to frighten her, but Nirry was sure there was truth in what he said.

Scarlet's patch, was the phrase he had used.

'Scarlet's patch?' Nirry had repeated.

'Aye, we're deep in it already, I'd say.'

'But what,' said Nirry, 'is Scarlet's patch?'

'Cook, can it be? Haven't you heard of the notorious Bob?'

'Notorious? The bird?'

And Carney Floss had laughed. With relish he told of the highwayman who lurked in these woods, a ruthless brigand who dressed in a jacket reddened by the blood of all his victims. At any moment, on the way to Wrax, a coach, a rider, a lone traveller might suddenly be set upon, robbed and murdered.

'M-murdered?' said Nirry.

'Indeed,' said the sergeant. 'There's few who meet Bob and live to tell the tale.'

Then drunkenly he had caterwauled a song about the highwayman, larded with many a doleful *zerry-zown*.

Now, in the purple-green morning woods, Nirry brought up a hand

419

to her mouth. This time, when she called Miss Cata's name, she called aloud.

Two things happened quickly.

First came the hand, grabbing Nirry's shoulder; in the same moment, as she turned, her foot struck something – something in the undergrowth, heavy, soft and still.

Nirry screamed.

'Shh! Nirry, Nirry!'

'Ooh, Miss Cata, you frightened me, you did! Don't you know we're on Scarlet's patch? Why, we could both be murdered, we could, wandering away from the camp like this!'

At another time Cata would have laughed; this time, she drew in her breath sharply, pointing to the ground at Nirry's feet.

'Miss Cata?' Uncertainly, Nirry followed the pointing finger. Then she saw it: lying between them, deep in the grass and ferns, was a corpse. She blundered back, gagging. 'Oh, that highwayman! That wicked, wicked highwayman!'

But Cata, for a moment, stood transfixed. If this, as Nirry thought, was a victim of the highwayman, clearly it was no recent victim. A fur of moss grew over the face; grasses twined about the limbs and torso. At first, even the sex was indeterminate; then, through the swathing vegetation, Cata made out the decomposing garments.

The corpse was a woman's, and wore a green gown.

Nirry called, 'Miss Cata, come away!' What else could they do? There could be no thought of reporting what they had seen. Causing trouble? Prompting questions? No, they must forget it, that was all.

But Cata, as she was about to turn, saw something else. Something still worse. Through the trees above, the early sunlight shone more brightly. Then the corpse's face was brighter too and it came to Cata that she knew this face.

No. It could not be.

It had to be a trick of the light, of course, but just for a moment, Cata was certain. Her eyes, in that moment, were wide with fear.

'Aunt Vlada!' Cata whispered.

※　※　※　※

Blackjaw tethered his horse to a sturdy pine-trunk. Landa's heart pounded. The big man frightened her. Perhaps it was just his immense limbs, his bushy black beard. He was a simple fellow, his loyalty fierce as Bando's. But there was a violence in him, an anger that filled her with dread.

'Prisoners?' came a voice.

Another: 'It bodes ill.'

Landa turned, relieved. It was the commander, with Priestess Ajl beside him. Instinctively she drew to the Priestess's side. The commander strode forward, resplendent in scarlet. He cocked his pistol, staring grimly through his mask as Blackjaw, with grunts and proddings, drove the Bluejackets forward.

In a moment his expression had relaxed.

A moment more, and he was laughing.

'Why, Blackjaw, this is your catch? But these are minnows!'

The prisoners were muddy and bedraggled. Their hands were tied behind their backs and they were tethered to each other. One was a squat, pop-eyed little fellow, the other lanky and bespectacled. They were mere boys, very young and very frightened. Within a few steps they had fallen to the ground, their limbs a hopeless tangle.

Raggle and Taggle squealed with glee. At once they were prancing about the prisoners like savages, chanting:

Off with their neckerchiefs!
Off with their coats!
Sharpen the carving-knife!
Slit their throats!

Burn out an eye!
Ooh, how it sizzles!
Down with their breeches!
Chop off their—

'Raggle! Taggle! Enough!' Bando clapped his hands.

The boys fell into the grass, tumbling one over the other, tickling, giggling, squealing.

The prisoners pleaded for mercy.

'Please s-sir, we were only g-going for h-help, there was a c-coaching accident—'

'S-somebody stole our horses—'

'We got l-lost in the w-woods—'

'W-we were just taking a sh-short cut—'

'Please s-sir, my friend's w-wounded—'

'D-dying! Oh, set us f-free, please—'

'Minnows?' boomed the highwayman, silencing the babble. 'I should have said stuck pigs! What do you think of the enemy now, Landa? If only they were all like this, hm? I declare, we've seen you fellows before, haven't we?'

'N-no, sir! Oh no—'

'N-never!'

Almost with benevolence, Bob Scarlet looked down on the unexpected

421

guests. With a contemplative air he tapped the muzzle of his pistol against his chin. Then he smiled.

'Fear not, my friends, we shan't let Raggle and Taggle loose on you – not yet. Blackjaw has subjected you to indignities enough. A well-meaning fellow, Blackjaw – but excitable, just a little.' He dropped his voice, 'And a bit simple. You will accept my apologies? But I'm afraid we can't let you go. You might be useful, in some curious way. What are your names?'

'M-Morven, s-sir!'

'C-Crum! Sir!'

'Stand up when you talk to the commander!' Bando was on his feet, brandishing his rifle.

'But my f-friend—' protested Morven.

'Stand up!'

The prisoners struggled upright, disentangling their bonds. For a moment Morven drew himself to an awkward attention, but staggered back as Crum lurched, pulling him down. Only now did the onlookers see the purple stain that discoloured Crum's jacket, spread wide across the left shoulder. His eyes were shut, his face pale.

'Is he dead?' Landa breathed. Her brain was reeling. Could this really be Morven and Crum? Then who were the other Morven and Crum, locked up in the tower?

Raggle and Taggle leapt up and down. 'Blood! Blood!'

'I tried to tell you, my friend's wounded! Oh, please don't let him die, please!' A shower of tears sprang from Morven's eyes.

Landa cried out, 'Cruel Blackjaw! And you dragged him through the woods!'

'He's a Bluejacket!' spat Bando.

The Priestess rounded on him. 'He's a boy!'

She knelt beside the soldier, peeling back an eyelid, wrenching back the jacket.

'He's passed out. Bob, he's badly hurt.'

The highwayman looked down. 'And I fear the shot is mine. In my rebel life I have had cause to be a killer, but only when the need is dire. Dread, not death, is my stock-in-trade.' He knelt down, putting a hand on Morven's trembling neck. 'I thought I fired at the air, but I was precipitate. My shot went low. But Robin Scarlet is a man of honour. Bluejacket this boy may be, but his blood is red as mine. Shall I permit it to stain my hands? Landa, fetch Mother Rea. Blackjaw, go with her. Swiftly now, swiftly.'

Chapter 60

EVERY DAY A LITTLE DEATH

'Oh, my head!'

Jem's eyes opened to a glimmering greenness. For long moments he was aware of nothing else, then he felt an ache that travelled, like languid arrows, from his skull to the base of his spine. Only slowly did he focus on the scene. Slumped awkwardly against a bank of sacks, he was lying on the floor of a small, cluttered room. Hovering on the air was a heady pungency of dust, coffee-beans, candle-wax, figs, apples, a hundred other scents. Around him, many shelves were piled with jars, boxes, bags; the green glow was the light of the forest, creeping through the panes of a high, narrow window.

A heavy weight lay across his legs.

'Raj, wake up!'

'Wh-what? Wh-where? Oh, my head!'

'Shh!'

'Shh why?'

'They've locked us in the pantry.'

'Huh! At least we won't starve.'

Awkwardly Jem extricated himself from underneath his friend. Holding his head, standing carefully, he crept across the dusty floor. The door was bolted fast. He looked for a crack, a hole, a way to see through.

Nothing.

'I don't understand,' Rajal said blearily. 'First I thought they were loyalists, then I thought they weren't. Now I'm not sure.'

'Look at these sacks.' The sacks were stamped with Bluejacket crests. 'Contraband?'

'Payment?'

'Whatever they are, they think we're the enemy.'

'You don't say?' Rajal rubbed his head.

'We've got two choices. Either we escape, or we convince them we're friends.'

'I don't want to be friends with people who hit my head.'

'Escape, then.'

'And how do you propose to do that?'

Jem looked up towards the green glow. 'Raj, give me a leg up.'

'What? Oh, I see. You're going to bring all this stuff crashing down on us. Just to see if our friends are awake?'

The shelves groaned as Jem clambered gracelessly towards the light. Rajal groaned, too; one of Jem's boots had grazed his ear. Miserably he imagined the impending crash, the crushed bones, the angry clamourings outside the door. If he flattened himself against the wall, he wondered, could he avoid injury? Could Jem? Half-heartedly Rajal pulled a sack away from the wall, thinking it might serve to break his friend's fall. He left off as a big rat, then another, scurried across the floor.

Jem clung precariously to the top shelf, peering over cobwebbed jars of preserves. He gasped, 'We're high up.'

'Not too high for rats. Jem, what are you doing?'

'There's a tree scraping against the wall outside. Thick one, too. If I can just get this window open . . . I think it's big enough. Come on, Raj.'

'Come where?'

'Follow me. Climb!'

'Oh, marvellous. Who's going to give *me* a leg up?'

Rajal would have protested more, but by now there were five rats scurrying about his feet. To think, they might have bitten him in the night! He shuddered and reached up, grabbing the splintery edge of a shelf. 'Oh well, falling will be quick and clean. How long does it take to die of plague, I wonder?'

By the time he had clambered up to the window, Rajal had twice almost crashed to the floor. He was filthy, covered in dust and cobwebs, and wanted to sneeze.

He breathed carefully. 'Jem, are you sure this is a good idea?'

'You have a better one? You've got your head through. Here, grab my arm.' Jem was already on the other side of the window, clinging to a high branch.

'I hope that bough is sturdy—'

'It's an oak! Come on, Raj—'

'I just need a foothold—'

Rajal was swinging an exploratory foot when a heavy, metallic *clunk!* came from below. The door opened. The rats scurried for cover.

'What? Treachery?' Dolm was standing in the pantry, puzzled. Where were the prisoners?

Rajal sneezed.

Dolm grabbed his pistol. In the same moment, Rajal's foot struck something. It may as well have been a secret switch. Dolm cried out. With a mighty crash, the heaped shelves descended upon him, bearing down an avalanche of apples, salt-pig, sacks of flour, jars of pickles, honey, jam.

'Just in time.'

Silence.

'Do you think we've killed him?'

Silence.

'Jem, you just about ripped off my arm!'

'Shh! Raj, look!'

The two friends perched on a high branch. Rajal was peering back through the window; greenly, dust rose from the debris below. Jem had turned away from the tower, looking out through the lattice of leaves. The bright morning disclosed a vista of greenwood, giving way to pasturelands and winding roads, leading up to a magnificent city.

'Raj, it's Wrax! I knew we were close!'

Rajal rubbed his shoulder. 'Close? That's leagues off!'

'Raj! Just look.'

In their long eastward journey, they had seen only the squalors and miseries of Zenzau. True, there were always the woods, the fields, the flowers, but where humans dwelt there were only hovels, shabby cottages and mean inns stinking of salt-pig, sweat, boiled cabbage.

Wrax was different. Flashing across the distance were gold and jewels, coloured glass, the gleam of polished tiles. Where had they come from, these ramparts of wall, these spires, these domes? All at once Jem saw the splendour, the brilliance, burning beneath the damped fires of a conquered people. How rotten, how ugly Agondon suddenly seemed! Even the river that ran through Wrax was beautiful, sparkling, clean. It was hard to believe they were still in Zenzau.

Perhaps, in truth, they had reached it at last.

Of course there was something deceptive in this beauty. Later, when Jem drew close to the city walls, he would see the pock-marks and crumbling stones that bore the bitter testimony of war; inside, everything would be shabbier than it looked from afar. Beneath the domes, beneath the spires, lay the inevitable dark alleys and dirty little shops with their noise, their clutter, their filth. There were backstreets where sewage ran down the gutters, there were beggars with limbs wrapped in pus-stained bandages. What Jem saw now was something finer.

It is said that everything looks better from a distance, but things seen from a distance are not just lies. Jem saw Wrax, and Wrax was a vision.

The vision was real.

That was when Jem saw a curious flashing, as of a glass tilted to the

425

sun. His brow furrowed. There was something regular, deliberate in the flashings. Could it be a signal, sent across the distance?

A signal, yes. A sign.

'Jem?'

'Hm?'

'Don't you think we should be getting down now?'

'Hm? Oh yes. Yes!' Jem turned excitedly. 'Raj, let's run to Wrax!'

'What?'

Jem gripped his friend's arm. 'The crystal is close, I know it. Last night I had the strangest dream. All the things in the song, I saw them. The King and Queen, the mocking-tree . . .'

'That wasn't a dream, that was a dinner-plate.'

But Jem was not listening. He pointed to the city. 'Can't you see the sign? Let's run and not stop until we're at the gates!'

There were several good objections to this proposal, but Rajal did not get the chance to make them. For some moments the branch had been creaking ominously.

Now it made a loud *crack!*

'Climb!' Jem commanded.

Rajal clambered quickly, clumsily after his friend. His hands were soon raw and his limbs aching. Leaves and twigs rasped against his cheeks and once a bird, an irritating little red-breasted thing, cawed in his face and pecked at his hair before fluttering noisily to a higher branch.

But something else was troubling Rajal.

'Jem,' he gasped, 'I don't like it. Dolm might be dead. Shouldn't we do something?'

'Do you think I like it, Raj? We're on an adventure. It's going to be dangerous.'

'Dangerous for Dolm!'

'He might have killed us.'

Rajal was not appeased; but now, Jem could think only of the crystal, the quest. Would they become cruel, Rajal wondered – as cruel, perhaps, as the red-headed captain? He thought of what lay before them with dread.

They were halfway down. Mercifully, the boughs were getting bigger. Intent on the climb, Jem carried on, his tongue stuck decisively in the corner of his mouth. Rajal paused, breathing hard. He spat on his hands, rubbing them together. 'Jem?'

'Hm?'

'That crash. The others must have heard it, mustn't they?'

'So? They'll think we're buried under that lot, too.'

'Jem?'

'What now?'

'I wouldn't be so sure.'

Jem looked up. His friend was looking down; then he pointed. Slowly Jem followed the path of Rajal's finger. Standing at the bottom of the tree was the crone, Mother Rea. First her head turned, this way and that. Then she raised her eyes towards them.

'Raj!'

'Jem!'

It was not the crone's mere presence that astonished them. Had she threatened them, they could easily have pushed her aside; it was something else that made them gasp. Last night the old woman had avoided the guests, hanging back mysteriously in the shadows. Last night, the snood had concealed her face. Now the capacious head-dress fell back.

In sudden joy Rajal scrambled down past Jem, swinging swiftly, boldly to the ground.

The old woman cried out, 'Child Rajal!'

'Great Mother!'

Enraptured, Xal enfolded Rajal, then Jem, into her arms. 'My children! Oh, but how my powers are failing! To think, you deceived me! To think, I should have listened to that fool Dolm! Yet I knew you would come, I knew it – I was only frightened you had gone again, before I had a chance to reveal myself!'

'Great Mother, how, why—? Where's Zady?'

It was no time for questions. But the last question, at least, was answered in an instant.

A cry came, 'Mother Rea! Come quickly, quickly!'

They turned. It was Landa, breathless, staggering. For a moment the girl was startled by the scene she had interrupted. Jem and Rajal were startled too, but not by Landa. Crashing behind her came her black-bearded companion.

'Zady!'

The big man's eyes were suddenly wide. His mouth hung open; puzzled, he looked to the Great Mother. She smiled, nodded. With a cry the big man rushed forward, crushing the two boys in his burly arms.

What could be happening? Bewildered, Landa gazed between the four people who embraced, sobbed and laughed beneath the sturdy oak.

'Blackjaw? Mother Rea? Mej? Jaral?'

Her amazement was matched only by Dolm's, who hobbled forth at that moment round the corner of the tower.

'Father! You're bleeding!'

'Oh, my head!'

427

Chapter 61

PRESENCE IN THE WOODS

'Amazing!'

It was late afternoon. Jem lay in the long grass. Lingeringly, caressingly, watery beads rolled from his naked flesh. In the pond, Hul and Bando still cleaved the deep, clear water. Somewhere close by were Raggle and Taggle, splashing in the marshy shallows, hiding in the reeds, rolling and tumbling through caverns of green. Their high childish voices rang about the branches like joyous animal cries.

'Amazing!'

Jem looked up through the green of the leaves. Could it be true that these woods were enchanted? The Season of Viana had taken hold rapidly. Only a day before the sky had been bleak, grey and drizzling; now it was a dazzling, cloudless blue. But it was the day's strange series of meetings that left Jem wondering if, in truth, he had entered an enchanted world. Gazing on Hul and Bando, he remembered a story his uncle Tor had told him, long, long ago.[1]

'Amazing?'

Hul's pale body flopped beside Jem's. Grey hairs grew wispily over the scholar's narrow chest. Ribs stuck sharply through his sides, but his arms were taut and wiry. He fumbled among his bundled clothing, retrieving a little tortoiseshell case. Carefully he hooked his spectacles about his ears.

Jem said, 'Things are amazing when you don't expect them.'

'Sometimes when you expect them, too.' Hul blinked kindly at Jem. 'When I saw you on the Wrax stage, I had an idea who you might be. Not a certainty, but an idea.'

'But how did you know?'

'Why, Mother Rea! She said you would come.'

Jem raised himself up on his elbow. 'Hul, why do you call her Mother Rea?'

Hul smiled. 'Habit, by now. It was the name of Dolm's wife. She was dying when Xal found her way to the tower, and all Xal's skill was powerless to save her. But her death provided Xal with the ideal cover – she assumed the garb of Mother Rea. Bluejacket patrols would take no

[1] See *The Harlequin's Dance*, Chap. 11: 'Hul, Bando and Me . . .'

notice of a downtrodden peasant-woman – a Vaga-seer might be another matter. Xal's powers are a danger to her, I fear. Many times we've worried that Zady might betray her.'

'Betray her? He loves her!'

'I don't mean deliberately. But Zady gets angry—'

'That's true!'

'I shudder when I think of the risks they took to get here. Do you know, they stowed away in a Bluejacket convoy? How Xal kept him docile, I don't know.'

'She has power.'

'Not that sort of power. We decided he must stay in the camp, with us – not in the tower, where the Bluejackets come. I'm afraid it hasn't made him very happy.'

Jem looked down thoughtfully. The cries of the children sounded far off now, pealing through the woods with a strangely mournful air. 'There's been no sign of Myla?' he asked.

Hul shook his head.

With a shudder, Jem thought of the scene beneath the temple. 'But surely Xal must know if she survived?'

'The power of prophecy is a funny thing, Jem. Xal saw where your quest was leading, and came here. But think of what that means. To see someone's future is to have power over them. To cure someone is to have power over them. Can you have power over someone who's as strong as you are? Myla was – *is* young yet, but her powers are great as Xal's – greater, Xal says. She cannot see the child and cannot help her.'

'So we don't know if Myla's alive or dead?'

Again, Hul could only shake his head. Poor Raj! Jem had left his friend with Xal and Zady, back at the camp. But much as Rajal loved them, Jem knew that he loved Myla more. The child had powers, but they were powers of vision. How could she survive in the world on her own? How could she escape from the clutch of evil?

Yet Jem sensed that one day they would see her again.

Bando joined them on the bank. 'Now where are those brats of mine? Raggle! Taggle!'

'They've gone quiet,' said Jem.

Bando sat up, shaking the water from his dripping hair. An anxious cloud passed across his face. He called again.

Silence.

Then suddenly the boys burst from the undergrowth, twin naked sprites, leaping, stomping, screaming.

'Biddy-biddy-bobble!'

'Diddy-on-the-double!'

Bando cried out. There was a tussle and in the next moment all his clothes, bandanna and all, were flying into the water.

'Little wretches!' Now it was Bando's turn to leap and stomp and scream, pursuing the boys round the pond, then off into the woods, weaving in and out of the trees, his fat belly – and other parts – bouncing up and down.

In the middle of the pond the red bandanna floated like a twisted, viscous stain. A frog looked on from among the reeds, unblinking, bemused.

'Poor Bando!' Hul laughed.

'Poor boys! Will he beat them?'

'Bando? He's soft as down! Except where Bluejackets are concerned, of course.'

Jem asked, 'The boys have no mother?'

Hul sighed. 'Her name was Iloisa. She was one of our band, and lived amongst us – a warrior-woman from the steppes of Derkold. She was brave, perhaps the bravest of us all. When Iloisa shot an arrow, it always reached its target.'

'Always?'

'Until the end. As I said, she was the bravest of us all.'

'Poor boys! At least they have Bando.'

'They have us all.'

The pursuit came to an end at last. Triumphantly Bando tossed the boys into the pond, then waded in after them to retrieve his clothes.

The fat frog leapt nimbly away.

❊   ❊   ❊   ❊

Watching, Jem thought of his own childhood. Like a cloud, a sadness passed over him. If only he had been able to run and leap! He envied the boys, but like him they had known the pain of loss, and known it early. The memory of his own mother welled up before him. In the end, she too had been a dead heroine, but how he wished she were still alive!

A bright bird fluttered down from the branches. Hul was saying something about the season, about the wood, but Jem was barely listening. He lay back, looking up through the leaves, and thought of another wood, another season. That had been an enchanted wood too, but all its enchantments were long gone; the season could never come again.

Jem was young, but was aware of time passing. He thought of Cata's hand reaching out to him, of the power of their love surging through his limbs. He closed his eyes. Could he really have lost her? Inside him welled an immense darkness of pain, clouding out the warmth of the bright afternoon.

He sat up, rubbing his arms. A breeze was stirring the leaves, bearing with it the memory of the chill bleakness that until so recently held the world in its grip.

Hul said, 'Cold, isn't it, all of a sudden? I think we'd better be getting back, hm?' Sensing Jem's sadness, the scholar had no need to ask its cause.

There was enough cause, too much.

Jem dressed solemnly. It was as he was putting on his shoes again that he sensed, just for a moment, the presence in the woods. Hul was distracted, helping the boys back into their little jackets; Bando bemoaned his sopping breeches. Jem's eyes flashed – rapidly, sharply – from tree to tree. It was not a sound, not a stirring that had come to his awareness, but a sharp animal sense of something there, something watching.

A bird, an animal: nothing more.

But for a moment, Jem had fancied it was something evil.

The boys and Bando, moments earlier, had run in a circle all round the pond, crashing and crying through the dense undergrowth. Jem shook his head. It was almost as if the memories that had washed through him so painfully had called up some echo, some ghostly trace, of Cata's strange powers.

Chapter 62

WOMAN'S WORK

'He's asleep.'

'Do you think so?'

'His eyes are closed. He's snoring.'

'Bluebottle used to lie like that.'

'Who?'

'Bluebottle. Our puss-cat. Back home in Varl.'

Morven rolled his eyes. 'Like what? Used to lie like what?'

'As if he were asleep. Then Jardy Red would come close, and Bluebottle would pounce. He tried over and over again, Bluebottle did, but good old Jardy was always too quick!'

Morven struggled against his bonds.

Useless.

He sighed, 'This "Jardy" was another puss-cat, I suppose?'

'Of course not!' Crum sounded affronted at the idea. 'He was a rat. I found him in Farmer Ryle's barn one day, at the back near the bran-tubs. His fur was ever so red, Morvy! Jardy's, I mean, not Farmer Ryle's!'

Crum laughed at the very idea; Morven laughed too, hollowly.

'Do you know, I never knew where he came from?'

'Where a rat came from?'

To Crum, the idea seemed perfectly sensible. After all, you didn't see a red rat every day, did you? 'Poor Jardy! Oh, he was so playful, Morvy!' A choke came to Crum's throat. 'Then he met Big Bulb.'

Pause.

'Farmer Ryle's basset-hound,' Crum added helpfully.

Morven burst out, 'Oh shut up, Crum!'

'Shh! You don't want to wake him, do you?'

Morven's face, not for the first time, contorted into a silent scream. They were tied back to back, and as Crum spoke, his companion performed to himself this dumb-show of exasperation. It may have been for the benefit of the Friar, if the Friar, like 'Bluebottle', were really awake, looking at them through half-closed eyes.

It seemed unlikely. Curled on a log beside the smoky campfire, the fat little man seemed sublimely oblivious of the Bluejacket prisoners. Chicken-bones lay in the long grass around him, picked scrupulously

432

clean. What contempt the brigands must have for them, to leave them with only a guard like this!

'Crum?' sighed Morven, after a moment.

'Morvy?'

'Your puss-cat. Why was it called "Bluebottle"?'

Crum laughed. 'Oh Morvy, didn't I tell you that story? The time he ate the bluebottle!'

'The what?'

'The bluebottle fly. That must be why they call him "Capon".' Crum jerked his head towards the chicken-bones.

'I don't think so, Crum.'

A fly – could it be a bluebottle? – buzzed round Morven's ear. Oh, for the talents of Wiggler! He strained at his bonds again.

'Steady on, Morvy! You're wriggling something shocking. I say, you don't want to *go*, do you?'

'I'm trying to loosen our bonds,' Morven whispered harshly. 'I would have thought, Crum, you might join me in the effort. Or have your *dreadful injuries* rendered you incapable?'

The sarcasm was devastating, so Morven liked to think. But of course Crum only thanked his friend for his concern, and assured that there was nothing to worry about any more, really nothing at all. Morvy shouldn't concern himself.

'Don't worry. I shan't!' Shame burned in Morven's cheeks. How he had humiliated himself, and for what? A flesh wound, the merest flesh wound! *I'm dying, Morvy. Morvy, hold my hand.* Morven's dumb-show became a silent cacophony. The Friar, if he had really been looking at the captives, would have seen a face leaping and jumping as if in the grip of some unfortunate convulsion.

Crum laughed, 'Jardy used to wriggle something shocking too. In my hand, when I was feeding him. I always saved a bit of my cheese for him – well, most of it, really. But I'd leave it under my pillow first, until it went mouldy. Do you know, he liked it better that way? A phase old, even! You're smart, Morvy. Why do you think that would be?'

Morven stiffened. 'Crum!' he whispered, suddenly urgent. 'My hand's free!'

'What?'

'I've got my hand free. That knot just slipped! Do you realize what this means, Crum? All it needs is a bit of working, that's all.'

'I know.'

'What?'

'Oh, my hands have been free for ages, Morvy. Back home in Varl, me and Zohnny Ryle used to play "slip-the-knot" all the time. I was good at

433

it, but Zohnny was better. Poor Zohnny, did I ever tell you what happened to him?'

Morven did not reply.

❈ ❈ ❈ ❈

'Hul,' said Jem, 'tell me about my uncle.'

They followed a narrow path through the undergrowth, making their way back to camp. Bando squelched miserably in the rear; Raggle and Taggle ran on ahead.

'Tor? He was almost as much a mystery to us as he must have been to you. He spoke of you often, and the destiny that lay before you.'

'He knew everything? Even when I was a child?'

'He was a great rebel, but he was more than that. There were things he knew, things he'd learnt.' Hul's voice was solemn as he recalled their lost leader. 'From the first he was a man of the highest integrity. His father's treachery in the Siege of Irion was the wound from which Tor would never recover. After that, he wanted no part of his inheritance. *What can it profit me*, he would say, *to be the heir of a corrupted dukedom?* He turned his back on it, taking to the road. How it was that he fetched up with a Vaga-troupe, I've never been quite sure. I only know he was apprentice, for a time, to a powerful mage.'

'Harlequin of the Silver Masks?' said Jem.

'You know him?'

'I've seen him. Raj was a Mask too, for a while. The Harlequin is old now, old and sick. I didn't know if he was good or evil. At first I thought ... but I don't know.'

'Jem?'

'Hul, the harlequin ... you haven't seen him since, have you? I mean, since my uncle died?'

Now Hul was confused. 'I've never seen the Masks.'

'No, I meant—' Jem did not go on. Of course he should have known: Hul could not see the harlequin. Could anyone but himself? Only at the moment of his destiny, Jem recalled, only when his mission was first revealed to him had the mysterious figure appeared to him. Tor's ghost? Or some other strange projection of Tor, surviving beyond the death of the body? Could the old Harlequin, Tor's mentor, explain the mystery?

Jem's brow furrowed. 'I think my uncle did have powers,' he said. 'Powers he'd learnt from the Harlequin.'

'But were they dark powers?'

'Hul?'

Hul would not go on to explain, not yet. Just then a strange, high music echoed about the trees. It was a human voice, raised in what sounded like supplication, or pain. Alarmed, Jem looked sharply, quiz-

434

zically at his companions. Hul smiled. Bando, suddenly grinning, caught them up. The Zenzan laid a finger across his lips.

'Woman's work,' he whispered. 'But we men may look, hm?'

They were standing by a thick screen of branches. Carefully, quietly, Bando parted the foliage, low down, opening a window on to the scene within. The little party squatted in the undergrowth, gazing into the centre of a tight circle of trees; even Raggle and Taggle, unexpectedly silent, huddled close against their father's fat thighs.

But who was there? Jem could see no one. Nor, for some moments, was there any repetition of the strange music; they heard only their own breathing, the tickerings of insects, the *plunk! plunk!* of Bando's sodden garments, dripping steadily into the bracken below.

'I don't understand,' Jem hissed.

Then he saw. In her green robes, almost concealed amongst the fronds of ferns, Priestess Ajl lay full-length against the earth. Around her head, her long hair was spread like auburn vines, tenacious, tangled, webbing her back and the thick roots that ran like sinews into the fecund soil. Above her spread the branches of an ancient oak.

Ul-ul-ul-ul-ul!

Jem started; it was a sound he had heard before, but this time it came from the lips of the Priestess. Like some strange creature, half-bird, half-animal, she raised her auburn head, gazing entranced at the bark of the oak. For a moment her hands clutched, convulsing, at the roots; then she drew herself slowly upright, her long nails clawing sensually, painfully, up the rutted surface of the bark. She flung back her head, gazing up into the branches. She swayed, her hair swinging back and forth. What she said next began in a whisper, but rose as she proceeded to a wild declamation.

'Daughter of Orok, see your supplicant. Sister of Koros, hear her cry. Most sacred Viana, soft as leaves, visit your unworthy, erring daughter. Viana, come to me in this woodland place, to one who dwells with you in sweet harmony, pledged not to violate your element of earth. Wrap the mantle of your greenness around me, enfold me, protect me, and those I cherish; but goddess, I beg you, withdraw your blessings from those who would strike at you, gouging and hacking. To them, let this land be a land of thorns!

'Sacred Viana, in your enveloping mercy, forget not the evil of those who torment you, of the blue-men who come to you with hearts of hatred! As you cursed the men-priests who built temples to your name, drinking to you in goblets of gold, curse now those blue-men who prate the name of Agonis, yet offer not mercy but a reign of terror! Daughter of Orok, see your supplicant. Sister of Koros, hear her cry.'

The Priestess left off, sobbing, moaning, embracing the tree-trunk with passionate abandon. At last she stumbled back, composing herself. Crossing her green-sleeved arms over her breasts, she bowed and said, 'Let no axe fall in the Hills of Wrax.'

It was the beginning of a mantra.

Jem glanced at his four companions. The transformation in the boys was extraordinary. One sucked his thumb, the other chafed his knees; both had shyly cast down their eyes, as if ashamed to be looking on this ritual. Even Bando, his irony forgotten, had assumed an attitude of awed respect. His eyes were tearful and his hands were on his heart, as if the ancestral call of his faith had driven out, at least for now, his customary character.

'The true faith of Zenzau,' Hul whispered.

'The true faith?' said Jem. 'I've heard talk of temples, of icons, of altars wreathed in golden vines.'

'It is the idolatry of men-priests. In ancient times, it was the Daughters of Viana who led the worship. Then indeed it was women's work, for only women-folk could look upon it. But as towns and cities grew in these lands of Zenzau, the men of power grew jealous of the Daughters. With rites of the temple they beguiled the people, women and men alike. The Daughters were reduced to a cult, haunting the greenwoods and the Hills of Wrax.'

'They were banished?'

'Ridiculed. Reviled. Oh, simple rustic folk would still come to them, believing that theirs was the true worship. Peasant-women would join them in prayer. But in the city, all was given over to priestcraft. Jewels, gold, silver flowed into the coffers of the men-priests; blessings were showered upon those who gave them. For a time the city flourished, and the kingdom grew strong. But as the men-priests had envied the Daughters of Viana, so the envious neighbour to the west cast its eyes upon the wealth of Wrax.'

Jem looked back curiously into the grove where the Priestess still stood, reciting the lonely mantra. 'What became of the Sisterhood?'

Hul looked down sadly. 'Jem, think of the words of these prayers. Viana, let us recall, is the sister-wife of Koros, the rich earth and leaves that shroud and make fecund his immemorial, stony darkness. As he is death, so she is life; and so they are one.

'But there lies the danger. Our race has driven the Koros-children almost to extinction. So the oppressions which are seen fit for the Vaga-kind are visited, too, upon those followers of Viana whose lives give no profit to the Bluejacket oppressors. Once, Ajl led a large Circle of Sisters; now, without us, she would be always alone.'

'She has *no* followers?'

Hul smiled, 'Oh no – she has *one*.'

436

Jem's brow furrowed. He had thought the ritual was over; in truth, it had barely begun.

'But Morvy, why?'

'Why?'

'Yes. Why?'

Pause.

'Crum, you're asking *why*?'

In the many moonlives he had spent in Crum's company, Plaise Morven had become accustomed, perhaps too accustomed, to the imbecilities that fell from the Varlan's lips. That Crum had an incapacity for abstract thought had been clear from the first; from the first, too, it had been clear to Morven just why it was that he – a man of intellect and refinement, after all – should be paired for guard-duty with so cretinous a companion. It was humiliation, ritual humiliation. In the forces of His Imperial Agonist Majesty, every man must be broken and bowed, permitted no pride but the pride of loyalty, unthinking and unquestioning. Sergeant Bunch was a wily one, that was for certain! He might have forced Morven to slop out latrines; but he had found something to distress him more, and that something was Crum.

Poor Morven! Had it really been only the Koros-season before last that his essay, *Issues of Prosody in The Jelandros, With Special Reference to the Provenance and Propriety of the Great Caesura*, had won the Jagenam Plaque? Had so little time passed since he sat in Webster's, a pint-pot barely regarded on the bench before him, disputing eagerly with this or that scholar on the inadequacies of the enjambments in Coppergate's satires, or the validity of Vytoni? So little time since he had slumped back, marvelling, as some white-collared fellow from Temple College held forth on the doctrines of Perpetual Sundering, or Korosan Creation, or the finitude or infinitude of the Time of Atonement? By now, even the gentle boredom of Professor Mercol's tutorials had assumed for Morven the aspect of a paradise lost. Sometimes he thought he could feel his brain rotting; sometimes he thought he had learnt as much – more! – about Peasant Life in Varl as he knew about even the Great Caesura. Nothing would shut Crum up, and worse than this was Crum's unconsciousness of his own stupidity. Had he considered, even considered, that there might be finer things, nobler things than life on a farm in Varl? Not a bit of it! To Crum, every detail of his vulgar boyhood seemed to glow with fascination. It drove Morven to despair. How any sentient being above the rank of a beast, even a Varlan, could be so deficient in imagination was beyond his understanding.

But, but. When all was said and done, Morven was used to it. Where Crum was concerned, nothing surprised him.

Except now. Morven was astonished.

'Crum, I can't believe you! Don't you know what Vytoni says? *No crime is worse than to deprive a man of freedom; no aspiration nobler than to wish to recover it.* You have no brain, of course not, but have you no instincts? Here we are, held captive in wild woodlands by a vicious and depraved band of brigands. Here we are, we've been trapped, terrorized, tied up – with who knows what else in store for us – and at last, when we manage to slip our bonds, when our captor lies insensibly before us, when I urge you triumphantly *Crum, we're free! Crum, let's go!*, what can you do but plump yourself down on the nearest vacant log, gnaw at a left-over chicken-bone, and ask me *why!*'

'Morvy, shh! The Friar!'

The fat fellow was snoring now, his swinish grunts forming a rumbling bass beneath Morven's shrill protests. Crum spat out a piece of gristle and looked resentfully at the brown-robed paunch, rising and falling. These brigands ate well, it seemed! Crum looked around. Satchels, saddle-bags, a basket or two lay about in the clearing. He began to investigate, rifling first here, then there.

'Crum, what are you doing?'

It was an easy question. Morven's plan was amorphous, enormous. Avoiding every peril, escaping every danger, they would hie them away into the woods, and something called freedom. Quite where their blue uniforms figured in this, Morven had not considered.

Crum's scheme was simple: a quick scout around the camp while the Friar was sleeping, raid the available foodstuffs, then back in position, rope and all, before the others returned.

The Varlan did not want to escape at all.

Chapter 63

MAN-CHILD

Ul-ul-ul-ul-ul!

The cry rang out again and a second figure, hitherto unseen, now rose from the undergrowth beside the Priestess. It was Landa. She wore the same green robes as the older woman, but her manner was very different. It was clear at once that she was a mere novice. As the Priestess stepped back, her hands held high as if in benediction, the girl went uncertainly through a series of prostrations, from time to time looking to the older woman as if to confirm that she was following the correct forms. In due course, Landa too would fall upon the oak, offering up her own impassioned prayer to the goddess.

'I have seen her,' Jem whispered, 'in a different worship.'

'A Prince in green? But Jem, is there really any contradiction? I see why Landa offers herself to the goddess. She fears she shall never see Orvik again.'

Jem was puzzled. 'But he's just a picture.'

Hul smiled. 'Jem, there are lies that it is wise to tell, if you think you may be speaking to a Bluejacket! The picture is of an ancestor, but Orvik resembles him exactly. As you are heir to the throne of Ejland, so Orvik is heir to Zenzau. Orvik's parents were killed long ago. Dolm smuggled him out of Wrax and brought him back to the ruined castle, pretending the boy was his own son. Orvik and Landa were brought up together, and since they were children they have been betrothed. By now they would have been married, but Orvik has gone to fight with the rebels, in the great battle that soon must come.'

With a new, special tenderness Jem looked on the girl, and thought again of the feelings that had coursed through him, last night in the tower.

'I am ashamed,' he began, 'of . . . of the torments our realm has heaped upon these people.'

'Your heart is good, Jem,' said Hul. 'But there are those – the Priestess is one such – who blame this kingdom's miseries not only on the "blue-men". What are they but a symptom? What could be expected, after all, in a realm that has abandoned its true faith?'

Jem reflected on this. He thought of the faith he had known as a child, of his Aunt Umbecca, of Chaplain Feval. He thought of poor Pellam

Pelligrew, who sang lustily in the Great Temple before venting his lust at Chokey's.

'Hul, I have stood in Temple on Canonday, as Hosannas of the Lady have rung around me. I have opened and shut my mouth in Canticles, I have let the chain-prayer fall from my lips. Ours is a race of victors, of conquerors. But can we believe ours is a true religion?'

Hul's look was wry. 'Remember the Zenzau-canon? Jem, there is no subject more ill-omened than faith. In my youth, I studied at Temple College. I was filled with reforming zeal. Poring over the El-Orokon in my candlelit cell, fondly I dreamed of the great treatise I would write, reconciling the five faiths of El-Orok. Vanity, mere vanity!'

'Must it always be so?'

'When even each single faith is divided among itself?' Hul sighed. 'In our fight against the Bluejackets, we have joined forces with the Zenzan rebels. But are the rebels at one? The rich temples have long been given over to Agonism. There are some who wish only to return them to Viana, resuming the priestcraft of days gone by. Others say the Daughters must be restored to their place. Within the walls of Wrax, I fear, such a view would find little favour.'

'And without?'

Hul smiled. 'Bando, I see you are *with* the Priestess today? Or have you changed your mind again?'

But Bando was not listening. Landa's devotions were rising in intensity. Embracing the great tree-trunk, now clawing, now caressing, the girl flung back her long braided hair, calling to the goddess to hear her, to see her. Her diffidence had gone and she was possessed now of a passion which made even that of the Priestess seem tepid.

Jem was startled. Where had she gone, the shy girl of the night before? Wave after wave of fervour poured from her as she entreated the goddess to protect her dear Orvik, make him fiery in battle, rain down destruction on all his enemies.

At last the Priestess had to reach forward, propelling the girl gently away from the tree. Landa was sobbing, but she brushed her tears aside, her face setting hard in steely resolve. The ritual must continue, she must be strong. All the time, as Landa cried out, Priestess Ajl had continued her mantra: *Let no axe fall in the Hills of Wrax.* Now, at a signal from the Priestess, Landa began a mantra of her own:

> *In the greenwood let me lie,*
> *Let me live and let me die.*

The mantras made no regular, simple chant. As the women intoned, their lines crossed each other, the end of one coming in the middle of another. Sometimes the words seemed hopelessly tangled; sometimes first one, then the other, seemed dominant. To Jem, the effect was at once moving and absurd: moving, as religious rituals often may be, even to those who understand them little; absurd, because he was aware of the meaning of the words. Had not many axes fallen in these hills? Would Orvik, if he won the freedom of his land, take his bride to live with him in the woods, not in a palace? But meaning, soon enough, was carried away on the surge of sound. The two women linked hands, moving slowly in a circle, then faster, faster. The chant grew louder, wilder. Round and round they went.

It was then that something extraordinary happened. Only later would Jem realize that he, and only he, could see the vision that the chant had summoned forth. Whether it descended through the leaves from the sky, whether it came from the ground beneath their feet, Jem did not know. He knew only that a mysterious green radiance was taking shape in the air around the two women. At first, like the chant, it was a diffuse, scattered glow, a green aurora glimmering first here, first there, amidst the leafy glade. It might have been an illusion, some knave's trick of the sun. But soon Jem recognized it as something more. The aurora became first a glowing cloud, filling the air with its emerald refulgence; then, as the chant of the women reached its height, the cloud took on a shape. First came an immense, green face; then, towering above the chanting women, suspended in the air above the circle they made, the form of a third woman, clad all in leaves.

'The goddess,' Jem breathed.

Astonished, he gazed upon the green vision. By now, the glow was dazzling, almost blinding, but Viana's beauty was more dazzling still. Slowly, slowly, she turned in the air, her leafy garb rustling, glittering like jewels. Her long wavy hair was made of vines, fluttering and swirling about her head. Wildly, madly, the grove beneath her seemed to be suddenly teeming with new life – vines, flowers, ferns, grasses, shooting up here, bursting out there, alive with the same strange radiance as the vision. On and on went the rising mantra, but the goddess seemed barely to regard it. At first her gaze was only for the ground, as if she were looking into the earth itself; then slowly she lifted her grave, sorrowing eyes. Flashing like emeralds, they stared through the leaves – stared directly into Jem's eyes. He struggled forward, clawing through the curtaining branches.

'Jem!'

Hul, then Bando, tried to hold him back. It was no good. Jem burst through the barrier, crashing into the radiant new growth. The women cried out, springing apart. Oblivious, Jem flung himself between them, abasing himself before the vision of the goddess. He cried out her name;

but when he looked up, the vision was gone, and the new life had vanished as if it had never been.

Illusion. All illusion.

Slowly he focused on the faces of the women. Landa looked upon him in bewilderment; the Priestess was first astonished, then alarmed.

Deeply alarmed.

Shamefaced, Jem's friends blundered forward.

'Jem, Jem! What do you think you're doing?' Bando was angry.

Hul said, 'Priestess, I'm sorry. Really, we didn't mean—'

Bob Scarlet stepped forward from the trees. 'Fear not, Hul. You're not the only man to see the ceremony.' The highwayman twirled his pistol with an ironic air. In the declining afternoon, the green of the grove was rich, almost too rich, and his scarlet costume shone sharply, painfully. His eyes, too, were bright behind the mask he never removed. 'The Priestess is not pleased with you, Hul, but I suspect she would be less pleased with a band of Bluejackets. Priestess?'

But the Priestess was breathing hard, her eyes fixed upon Jem's prostrated form.

'The man-child,' she whispered, 'has seen the goddess!'

'Viana,' Jem murmured, 'Viana, Viana.'

The Priestess crossed her arms over her chest. 'It was foretold that a man-child would come, to whom would be vouchsafed our most sacred vision. Then, it is said, would come the End of Atonement. Sacred Viana, what is to become of us?'

Jem rose to his feet; he bowed deeply. When he spoke again, the words issued from him in a deep, strange voice. They seemed to well from somewhere far within him, beneath the surface of day-to-day thought.

'Priestess, I stand before you in the grip of prophecy. The End of Atonement has come at last. At last, what was foretold in The Burning Verses must come to pass, or we shall perish.' He clutched the bag that swung from his neck. 'I carry with me the Crystal of Koros. I come for the Crystal of Viana.'

'No. No!'

'The thing I seek resides in a tree called the mocking-tree, guarded by the King and Queen of Swords; but which is that tree, I cannot say. Where is that King? Where is that Queen? Priestess, guide me: give me, at long last, the sign I have sought.'

Trembling, the Priestess sank to her knees. It was an extraordinary tableau. Bando and the boys were bewildered, silent. Landa's face was twisted in terror; Hul's was a study in troubled fascination. He had known, even believed, that these things would happen.

Nothing had prepared him for the reality.

Only the highwayman, it seemed, was unmoved. His jaw set; the eyes beneath his mask were hard as steel. He turned angrily. 'What is this madness? This boy is a poor traveller, nothing more! Is he in the grip of some foolish dream? Let him join with us and fight, or be on his way!'

Hul remonstrated. Calling to the commander, clutching at his arm, he could have been reaching across an implacable distance. But it was the Priestess who snapped at the commander's words. The change in her was astonishing. She scrambled up. Her face, which had been stricken, almost terrified, was transformed. For a moment it seemed she might turn upon the commander; instead, almost with relief, she rounded on Jem.

She grabbed him roughly.

'No!' said Landa.

The Priestess ignored her. At once her long-nailed hands were like claws, old and ugly, digging cruelly into her victim's arms. The face beneath her auburn hair was haggard, hideous. A thick cord pulsed in her neck and she spoke rapidly, spitting out her bitter words like bile.

'Man-child, what kind of fool can you be? You dare disrupt our most sacred rites? You dare pretend to the visionary gleam? What care I for some useless stone round your neck? What care I for words, mere beguiling words – I, who have devoted myself to the deepest communion?

'In times gone by there have been many like you, men-children ardent for power and wealth, seeking after the riddle of the mocking-tree. But, man-child, what greater mockery is there than this: the tree has vanished, and cannot be found! When our Sisterhood was formed, it was our mission to guard the tree. For epicycles we fulfilled our sacred task, until the men-children, in their greed and spite, drove us to wander despised and alone! Today, when the Sisterhood lies in ruins, who is there that knows the wisdom of the ancients? Which is the mocking-tree? Here? There? Man-child, you shall never find it, but if you did—' the Priestess flung back her head and cackled '—could you ever pass the Test of the Tree? Fool, fool! Your quest shall drive you mad!'

The cackle came again, and she pushed Jem to the ground. Still he clutched at the stone around his neck.

Chapter 64

DISCOURSE ON FREEDOM

There is this difference between the man of action – also known as the man of courage – and the man of learning. It is the role of the man of action to *do*; but to *think* is the task of the man of learning. The difference is obvious, but nonetheless profound. There are times when to think – so one might believe – is hardly to be enjoined. There are times – even the thinker will agree – when to *do* is all. When such times come, the man of action has no hesitation. His course is clear to him at once, and he will *do*; while the man of learning, for his part, will *think* about doing. While one weighs in, the other weighs and considers.

Of course, he thinks deeply, and his thinking occupies him for some considerable time; moreover, as he plumbs its abyssal depths, he thinks not just of doing, say, *(a)*, but *(a)*, *(b)*, or *(c)*. He deliberates. Agonizes. Ponders. Broods. The tendency is fatal. Soon he stands at a crossing of many forking paths, and why one is more desirable than another, he cannot say. *One might look at it this way*, he begins, *but then on the other hand* . . . and before he knows it he is lost in a labyrinth of *On one level* or *It might be considered* or *From another angle* or *For argument's sake*.

And so he does nothing.

'You're sure you don't want any of this Varl-bread, Morvy?' said Crum, tearing ravenously at a large loaf. How the Friar could have missed it was beyond him. But then, it had been concealed in some-body's saddle-bag.

'Varl-bread?' Morven's voice was distant. Miserably he hunched before the dying fire. In the last moments he had thought of *(a)* running off and leaving Crum, *(b)* running off and dragging Crum with him, *(c)* staying with Crum but – for all the world as if he were a hero – surprising the brigands when they were least expecting it, and . . . but he hadn't worked out all the details yet. 'Varl-bread? Must be stale, I should think!' was all he said.

'Oh Morvy, it's not really from Varl! They just call it Varl-bread, that's all. That's what Wiggler said, anyway. Do you know, once I didn't know any better than you? Mm, mm.' Crum stuffed the last of the bread into his mouth and delved deeper into the saddle-bag. There were no more delights.

At least, not for Crum.

'I say, this is your book, Morvy, isn't it?' Crum held up a battered volume.

'Show me that.'

For the first time that afternoon, Morven was grateful that his hands were free. Curiously he turned over the little volume, running his fingers across its cracked calf binding, its pulpy pages. Could it be?

He opened the frail boards and gazed upon the title.

Liberty OR *Licence?*
BEING A DISCOURSE
or investigation by
MR. VYTONI
into the NATURE,
desirability & attainment
of the STATE
or condition of
FREEDOM,
POLITICAL, SOCIAL
& MORAL:

Printed in the City of *Agondon*:
For the Free Philosophical Society:
AC 994*a*

Morven felt his heart beating deeply, slowly. Yes, this was his book. But not his copy. Scrawled across the top of the page was a faded signature in a scholarly hand: *Eldric Hulverside.*

Of course.

For the first time that day Morven felt his confused mind resolving itself into clarity.

'I know who he is,' he said aloud.

'Who?'

'Hul. The one they call Hul.'

There was no time to explain. A crash of feet came through the undergrowth. Quickly the prisoners arranged themselves again, feigning sleep, just as a breathless Rajal burst into the clearing.

'Where are they?'

The question was for the Friar. Rajal shook him. The fat little man started awake.

'Hm? Oh, Vaga-boy. I thought you were a chicken – I was dreaming about a chicken. Would you believe, a big fat chicken strutting round the campfire? Plucked already! And there was I, trying to push it into the fire.' He chortled with pleasure. 'And I did.'

The Vaga-boy did not even smile. 'The others – where are they?' was all he said, and the Friar, seeing that there was urgency in the lean brown face, waved a plump hand in the appropriate direction. Rajal crashed back into the woods again.

The Friar sat blinking glumly through the woodsmoke.

'Something's up,' he said to himself. 'Oh dear me, something's up.'

Just when they'd come back to Oltby, too!

❋ ❋ ❋ ❋

There was a rustle of foliage. Jem turned.

'Priestess, you are wrong,' came a new voice. 'You call the child a false seeker, but he is true. Are your powers so withered, so buckled and twisted under your burden of sorrow that you cannot see the Key to the Orokon, even when he manifests himself before you? I am old and my powers are declining, yet what I see, when I can see, is true. Do you give no credit to all I have told you, all I have predicted? Hold your hands to the air around you, feel the doom that impends even now! Without this child, that doom shall descend upon us. Vain, foolish Sister Ajl!

'As for you, Highwayman, your deceptions are beyond belief. But you must make your own destiny.'

It was Xal. The garb of Mother Rea discarded, she appeared before them now in her true form. Perhaps there was no longer any profit in pretence, or she had become weary of it and wanted only the truth. Hobbling into the centre of the circle, the old woman looked at once imperious and dangerously frail; looking up at her, Jem knew that she was nearing the end of her time. A terrible sense of her sorrows washed over him. Soon, with her people scattered, her successor lost, and evil about to engulf the world, she would die. Jem's eyes filled with tears.

He breathed, 'Great Mother, tell me – which is the way?'

The old woman looked up at him kindly, taking one hand in hers. A dark stone glimmered in the centre of her forehead, sunk into the purplish fabric of her turban. No one spoke, but in the silence Jem knew the question he had asked would soon be answered. Xal held his hand and his gaze alike as a crashing came now in the undergrowth behind them. It was as if she knew what was about to happen.

Of course, she did.

Rajal burst into the grove. He had run all the way from the camp, and was breathless. Doubling over, he caught at a stitch in his side as he gasped, 'Dolm says . . .'

'Dolm? What about Dolm?' The highwayman stepped forward urgently. 'Speak, Vaga-boy! '

'Dolm says they've sent the signal . . . from our agents in . . . in Wrax . . . he says . . . he says THE TIME HAS COME!'

There were gasps, cries.

'Then it has happened,' Hul breathed.

'At last,' said Bando.

Raggle and Taggle capered, danced. Landa looked this way and that, stricken, caught between joy and terror. The highwayman turned away, concealing his troubled eyes. Only Jem remained fixed as he had been, gazing into the face of the Woman of Wisdom. It might have been thought that he did not understand, could not understand what was happening around him. On the contrary, he understood at once. The stone flashed in Xal's forehead and Jem felt a sudden sharp pressure from her hand. He thought of the flashing glass he had seen that morning, coming from the woods on the other side of the hills.

THE TIME HAS COME.

Now the highwayman commanded the scene. 'Orvik's armies are assembling before the city. Ready to burst forth from the womb of time is the battle we have dreaded and desired for so long; again the Fields of Ajl shall flow red with blood. Oh, but it is too soon, too soon!'

'Commander,' said Bando, 'how can that be? After all these cycles?'

'It's too soon, I tell you! Prince Orvik is a fool, a precipitate fool!'

'No,' moaned Landa.

The highwayman's reply was harsh, almost cruel. 'Foolish girl, what can you understand? We dedicated ourselves to work secretly, furtively. What would Orvik do, sacrifice his people for his overweening pride? His "pitchfork-army" wins a skirmish here, a scuffle there, in the wastes of Ana-Zenzau – but to take on Wrax, to take it on now! What outcome can there be but a vicious massacre of hundreds, thousands of ill-trained, ignorant Zenzans? Can't the fool see, so catastrophic a defeat would destroy the Resistance, perhaps for ever?'

Landa cried, 'Cruel Highwayman, how can you doubt Orvik so – oh, how can you be so unkind?'

The highwayman did not even answer the question. Anger welled in Jem's heart, anger and a burning pity for the girl. But his attention remained fixed on Bob Scarlet as the masked man turned urgently, decisively to Hul, then Bando. 'We *cannot* lose this battle. Hul, there is only one thing we can do. Bando, you would agree?'

Hul's face was suddenly pale. 'The Shopkeeper . . .'

Bando breathed, '. . . of Wrax?'

Jem's heart pounded. THE TIME HAS COME. The sign, he knew, that he had awaited and feared was the same sign, the very same, that had come at last to this band of rebels, deep within the conquered kingdom of Zenzau. Everything was falling into place.

Or almost everything. What the King and Queen of Swords had to do with all this Jem still did not know.

'It's Tor's legacy,' the highwayman was saying.

'A legacy that killed him!' Hul cried.

'It's evil,' said Bando.

'More evil than the enemy?' There was contempt in the highwayman's voice. He turned to Rajal. 'Vaga-boy, go back to the steward. My horse must be ready. When darkness falls, I ride to Wrax.'

'Bob, please!' said the priestess. 'The guards! The patrols! Oh, it's so dangerous, and for—'

'For what?' said the highwayman. 'Priestess, surely you – you of us all – see that we must win this battle, or be ruined? Argue with me no more, my mind is made up. The Shopkeeper must be told: THE TIME HAS COME.'

With that, the highwayman would have stridden away, but Jem rose to his feet, his hand slipping from the Great Mother's, his eyes blazing.

Swiftly he placed himself in the highwayman's path and would not move, not even when the highwayman tried to push past him. With a surge of pride the thought came to him that he was almost as tall as this strange, cruel man. Fearlessly he looked into the eyes behind the mask.

'What is it, boy? More of your lies, your foolish fantasies? Out of my way, I have no time for you. I go tonight.'

'No – I'll go.'

'You, boy? You?'

For a moment Jem did not speak; when he did, his voice was filled with an authority that even the highwayman seemed suddenly unable, unwilling to challenge.

Jem only said, 'I must go. It's *my* message.'

Chapter 65

CRY BEHIND THE DOOR

'Raise you.'

'You're bluffing.'

'Come on, raise you!'

'Very well, my dear!'

'Ha-ha!' Jeli, with a laugh that was almost a jeer, swept all the cards to her side again. Really, it was too easy! 'Aunt, you're not trying.'

'I'm trying, my dear. I just can't try as hard any more, that's all.'

Aunt Vlada smiled wanly. The restoration of her glory had been brief. Again she lay supine on a sofa by the fire, a green blanket drawn close about her. Ring lay on her lap, looking at his mistress with big concerned eyes. Jeli, alas, showed no such concern. Another girl might have wondered, at least, how it could be that her aunt had fallen back – so soon, so suddenly – into the sickness she seemed to have conquered. Another girl might have been alarmed. But Jeli's only thought was for her coming glory.

She was restless. Letting her cards fall back to the table, the girl paced about the little boudoir.

'Careful of Rheen,' Aunt Vlada spluttered, and coughed painfully. 'He's on the floor, I think.'

Rheen, indeed! Some days ago the bird had flown away, but a little later Aunt Vlada had found a small lizard in the back of a cupboard. At once she insisted that *this* now was Rheen, and expected Jeli to share her excitement. Disgusted, Jeli would have flung the thing into the fire, or rather, called for Elpetta to do so; but at once her aunt had burst into a flurry of protest. It was too absurd.

Jeli went to the window, pushing the curtains roughly aside. Straining her eyes into the darkness, the girl was eager for each sheen of moonlight, each glow of a lamp, each flicker of flame. To think, it was evening, and she was pent up here! How she longed to be in the great world, with people, music, laughter and gaiety! But no, now she must be kept close like a child again, pending the time when her destiny was announced. *No one must know*, said the First Minister, *no one must know until the time is right*.

A coach passed in the street outside. Following it, Jeli's gaze fell once again on the steep stairs where her Duenna had fallen. Why, Ju-Ju would approve this present confinement! And for a moment the curious thought came to Jeli that the old woman, instead of dying that day, had merely changed herself into Aunt Vlada. She turned, looking at the invalid on the sofa. She hoped that Aunt Vlada would be well again soon. After all, there were preparations to make – more than ever before!

A girl in her position *needed* an aunt.

And just for a moment Jeli forgot her miseries, and thought with exaltation of the future that lay before her. Oh yes, she had been sold to the highest bidder!

There was a rustling on the window-sill. Jeli looked down. It was the lizard, nuzzling at a screwed-up ball of paper. Ugh! Jeli brushed the nasty creature to the floor. In an instant, the supposed Rheen had scampered beneath a chair-leg, but the ball of paper – Jeli saw now that it was edged in black – remained on the wide window-sill.

A letter.

Where had it come from?

Then Jeli remembered. Several times, since her aunt had declined, her uncle had climbed the stairs to the boudoir. He seemed to want to sit with her, to talk with her, to fondle her. Disgusted, Jeli had retired to her bedchamber; but she could not help overhear her uncle's ugly voice, droning through the door. Really, Jeli did not like him at all! How she longed to escape his vile house!

Earlier that day he had been reading out a letter. What it was about Jeli did not know; locked in her chamber, she heard only a murmur. But in the end her uncle had laughed, screwing the letter into a ball. Jeli assumed he had flung it into the fire; it seems he had endeavoured to toss it from the window.

Idly Jeli uncrumpled the black-edged page.

> *My dear brother,*
> *It is with much sorrow that I write to inform you of the death of my husband, Lord Veeldrop. I know you were once close to the dear man – shared with him, indeed, certain vital intimacies – in the time of the Siege which so convulsed our kingdom. That you will grieve for him as much as I do I can have no doubt; and believe me, Jorvel, I feel for you in your suffering. How tragic – you will agree – that this best of gentlemen (fondest of husbands, bravest of heroes) should breathe his last so soon after the ennoblement which for so long had been his due! How tragic, too, that this province – your province – should be bereft of so wise, so just, so merciful a steward!*
> *The Valleys must fall into other hands now. In my husband's time I had hoped that I – weak woman as I am – might have served the ends of government, influencing the moral and spiritual sphere. Alas, to stay here would be insupportable for me now, when in every*

cottage, every tree, every lane, I see inscribed the beloved name of my husband. You will see, then, that I now must return to Agondon, eking out the days that remain to me in a life of humble piety.

Jorvel, I shall soon be with you again, bringing your dear niece Catayane. (Pray that she may soon be safely married!) Perhaps – dear brother, say it can be so! – when we meet again we may hold each other close and weep, long and loud, remembering the days when the best of wives (my dear, dear Ruanna!) was living and yours, and the best of husbands was mine! Such happiness we have lost!

But humbly we must submit to the will of the Lord Agonis.

I am, most loving and loved *brother,*

> *Your sister, Becca*
> *(Lady Veeldrop)*

Postscript

Alas, my preparations are all but complete, but my dear niece Catayane is unfit to travel! Grief at her uncle's death has laid her low, yet she insists (so concerned is the sweet girl for me) that I must not lose my passage to Agondon while the weather is good and my health is able to support so long a journey. It grieves me sore to leave the girl, yet after all I know she shall be safe in the hands of my wise and faithful servant, Nirrian. (Dear Nirry! Such a blessing! In these last years I should have been lost without her!) My spiritual advisor, Chaplain Feval, shall accompany me to town, so have no fear for me, brother, in the journey that lies before me.

I trust little Jelica is well. Catayane sends her love, sorrowing much that she is too indisposed to write. How I wish we were all together! I long to devote myself to my remaining family.

Jeli's brow furrowed, and she let the letter fall. For a moment she had felt her heart leap, thinking that Catty might soon be with her; then her heart had sunk again on learning that this was not to be so. Yet when she thought how Catty had crowed last year – *crowed*, over a few paltry triumphs in Varby! – Jeli had to admit to a certain satisfaction. If Catty were now lying sick in the provinces, tended only by some slatternly maidservant, was it not the just punishment of her arrogance?

Jeli laughed and attempted a few chords on the spinet, hoping thus to express her joy; but she played poorly, and was soon bored. She cast herself down in a chair opposite her aunt, picking up the stick of Jarvel that still lay half-smoked in her aunt's ash-tray. Several times of late, Jeli had succeeded in taking a few puffs. She sniffed the pungent weed, then looked about for a tinder-strip. Her aunt made no protest.

'Aunt,' said Jeli, as she puffed on the weed, 'tell me a story. You always used to tell such fine stories.'

Her aunt's eyes had drifted closed. Her voice was weak. 'Alas, my dear, I cannot comply. When one's own story shall soon be ending, other stories have little appeal.'

At this, Ring miaowed piteously, and nuzzled closer to Aunt Vlada's face. But Jeli was annoyed. Too often, lately, her aunt had talked like this. What was wrong with her? Why was she doing this?

'Tell me a story, damn you!' Jeli burst out.

She had not intended this anger; the words shocked her, even as she said them. She slumped back, trembling. Was it the Jarvel?

Aunt Vlada only watched her niece sadly. Softly, distractedly, she stroked Ring's fur. What a fool she had been, what a blundering fool! Her eyes roved to the green baize table. Reaching out, she took a handful of cards. Eight of Wheels. Four of Spires. King of Swords . . . ah, King of Swords. It was all too late. Time had been distended, it seemed for ever, but suddenly it had rushed on too fast, too fast. Aunt Vlada shuffled the cards in her hands and thought of the girls she had shuffled like cards. Pelli . . . Cata . . . Jeli . . . cards for play, no more. So she had thought. And she would control the destiny of a kingdom. Perhaps with Cata it might have been better. Yes, Cata had something fine in her, something noble. Pelli was too weak, and so was Jeli in a different way. *Cata*. Yes, she had got it all wrong. And now time was running out, swiftly – too swiftly – running through her hands.

Aunt Vlada looked at the cards again and found herself staring at the King of Swords. Then she told Jeli her last story. As she spoke, she rose up on the sofa, and her voice, at first weak, acquired a new gravity. Had Jeli been listening – but she barely was – she might have thought that some other voice, some voice from afar, was speaking through the fretted, dying frame of Aunt Vlada.

THE KING AND QUEEN OF SWORDS

'In ancient days, when my people first came to the lands of Zenzau, they bore with them the Crystal of Viana. High Priestess Hara was the anointed of the goddess. She wore the crystal against her heart, where none could remove it without her consent. With her Sisterhood, she commanded the Hills of Wrax, and there was order and harmony in those heights. But as time went on, other powers grew up in the land. Jealous of the priestess, sects of men-folk known as *zenzals* would wrest authority away from her, casting her down in ignominy and shame.

'Five *zenzals* ranged against her. There were the *Quills*, who sought through the power of learning to prove themselves her superiors. In dank and cloistered brotherhoods they revolved their tortuous sophistries, until at last their outer senses were so befogged that they saw not

452

the trees nor the woods, nor smelt the perfumes that drifted on the air. The *Wheels* – but their symbol, in truth, represented a coin – were those in thrall to the power of gold. All arts that gold could supply were theirs, and they could purchase any satisfaction – except those whose source is only the truest, deepest wells. A coin, dropped in such a well, would fall for ever, plunging impotently through dark, empty space. Their hearts grew hard and cold.

'The *Spires* were a clan of blaspheming men-priests, who would worship in a way unsanctioned by the goddess. They combined the sophistries of the Quills with the avarice of the Wheels. The *Rings*, for their part, were men of love, who would enslave womankind in the bonds of their lust, permitting them no arts but the arts of passion. Last came the *Swords*, who devoted themselves to arms – whose powers were neither of the mind nor of the heart, but of brute strength alone.

'Now each of these *zenzals* grew great and strong, and drew to itself many disciples. Not just men, but many of our own sex were numbered among them, prostrating themselves like fools before empty, beguiling powers; so it was that as each sect had a King, so in time he took to him a Queen.

'The Five Kings corrupted the life of my people. By the Quills they were given laws, wills, learned disputes. By the Wheels they were taught covetousness, greed and avarice. The Spires instructed them in a grovelling, false humility; by the Rings, the equality between woman and man was upset for ever, never to be restored.

'The Swords encouraged the arts of war. My people had been dwellers in the woods; now the Five Kings built great castles, raising up ramparts of brick and stone where once the greenwood had grown wild and free.

'Finally, the Five Kings decided each would tolerate no longer the power of any other. Each King was jealous of his Brother-Kings; but above all, they resented Priestess Hara. So it was that each King laid plans to destroy her, seizing the Crystal of Viana from her keeping; for in such a theft, each King believed, he would destroy not only Hara's womanly power but prove his hegemony too over his four Brother-Kings.

'The Kings resolved that first they would take Hara's women from her, leaving her alone and defenceless before them. First came the emissaries of the King of Quills. With powers of false argument they would bedazzle and bamboozle, convincing Hara's women of the wrongness of their ways. Few were swayed by their sophistical reasonings. Then came the Wheels, with their promises of gold. The Sisters were strong, but not all were strong enough. Some gave way to these dazzling allurements; more gave way to the Spires. With elaborate rituals, with incense and goblets and rich robes, the men of priestcraft lured away many, too many of Hara's most devoted women, who falsely believed that in their defection they were, in truth, serving the cause of the goddess. Little did they know that the robes, the goblets, the incense that seemed to them so sacred were never to be touched by womanly hands; that as women, they were destined only to be passive spectators at the priestly displays of men.

'But it was the Rings who devastated the Sisterhood. There is no power more beguiling than the carnal power, and those who did not succumb willingly to its blandishments were soon reduced to compliance though force or fraud. Only Hara remained steadfast, clear-eyed and untrembling.

'So it was that she was alone, wholly alone, when called upon to face her most powerful challenge. The King of Swords sent no men. Instead, he came to the Priestess in person, bringing with him only his evil Queen. The Queen spoke kindly to Hara, but the Priestess declared that she should never give in.

'"Foolish Priestess," the Queen replied, "what use can there be in resistance now? Come, we have no wish to harm you. Only give us what is rightfully ours."

Hara looked contemptuously at the fair visitor, for once she had been the finest of her women. "Evil Queen, it is you who are the fool! Have you forgotten your days in this greenwood, when together we prostrated ourselves before the Presence of Viana? Think not that the crystal can ever be yours, when you have betrayed your goddess so grievously."

'Then the hasty King would have slain the Priestess, but his Queen bade him stay. She reasoned with her, but Hara stopped her ears. She offered her wine, she offered rich meats. The Priestess spilt the wine, she flung the meats away; the Queen offered her gold, but she trampled it on the ground. Then the Queen said she would build a rich new temple, where Hara should be worshipped as a living icon. Contemptuously the Priestess rejected the blasphemous thought.

'"She is a haughty beauty," intervened the King, "but where would she be without her purity? Let us see how proud she may be, when she is humbled to the level of her sisters!" With that, he seized the Priestess and, much as she struggled, she was powerless in his grasp. With glowing eyes the Queen looked on as her husband violated Hara's flesh.

'When he had vented his lust, he sprang up eagerly, convinced that her powers would now be vanquished, running away with the blood that flowed from her ruined body. Again the depraved man demanded the crystal; again Hara refused him, declaring that she would die rather than surrender this last and most precious prize. Now King and Queen alike were driven to fury. The Priestess, they knew, must give her prize willingly, but what woman had a right to such pride, such defiance, after the violation of her virgin purity? Again the Queen called the Priestess a fool; the King declared her an arrogant harlot.

' "Die, would you?" He drew his sword. "Then die you shall!"

'With that, the Priestess was slain; but her slaying marked no victory for the King and Queen of Swords. For they did not know that even after death the Priestess could not give up her crystal, not until the true claimant came at last. So it was that in the moment of her death the Priestess was transformed into an apple-tree, which kept the crystal as its most precious fruit. This tree would be called the mocking-tree, for neither fire nor axe, neither flood nor time could damage the tree, or force it ever to give up its secret. Yet still the King and Queen could not retire from the fray, for the longings that burned in them could never be assuaged. Their fate it was to stand guard for ever, repelling all others who came to the tree, protecting with their jealous fury the prize that still – in their corruption and blindness – they believed was theirs, rightfully theirs.'

❋　❋　❋　❋

Aunt Vlada slumped back, her story over. Dribble was running from the old woman's lips and her face had gone peculiarly white. Jeli eyed her aunt with distaste. What sort of story was that? Once her aunt told her about real people, living in the world they knew. What was this foolish fantasy, this nursery-tale? There was something unhealthy about it, something disgusting.

Jeli's head reeled in a haze of Jarvel, and she feared she might be sick. She staggered up, intending to lie on her bed; then she saw that her Uncle Jorvel was standing in the door. Each time she saw him he bothered less and less with the finery he had assumed for the King's visit; by now, he looked like a disgusting old Reject.

Ignoring the girl, he blundered towards the sofa.

The old man was drunk, Jeli could see at once. Oh, he was horrible! She rushed into her room, slamming the door. It was then – as she cast herself down on her bed, fearful not of her uncle but of the revulsion he inspired in her, that Jeli thought again of the letter she had read. *Poor Catty*. But no, this time Jeli was not thinking of Catty. She was thinking of Aunt Umbecca. Umbecca Veeldrop – Jeli had no doubt – was a fat, sentimental old fool, no more. She was hardly a fine lady. Why, she was little more than a servant.

A devoted servant.

A smile came to Jeli's face, and she thought again of her future.

Drifting through the door came her uncle's drunken words.

'Vladdy!' he was slurring. 'Vladdy, I meant what I said, I did. You don't believe me, do you? But I've always loved you, I have! Oh Vladdy, say it's not too late . . . Vladdy? *Vladdy!'*

Then all at once the Archduke was screaming, screaming and crying like a man who had been damned.

END OF PART FOUR

PART FIVE

Three Dragons

Chapter 66

DAZZLED

Where was the light?

Polty's vision was blurred, but he should have seen the light. All through the long Koros-season, when branches were barren and the snow was thick, Polty's patrol had trudged through these woods. Always, through webbing branches, there had been the golden glow; for Polty it had been a beacon, a promise, easing the ache of his loneliness and desire. It was Landa's light, shimmering its welcome in the high window. But now the light was gone. What had happened?

Polty spurred his reluctant horse.

He was very drunk. The debauch which had begun the night before was still not over. Whirling downwards in an eddying spiral, Polty had still not reached the bottom. His resolutions, all his good behaviour, lay far behind him, smashed beyond repair. Some time after midnight, on threatening to become violent, he had been ejected from the officers' mess. This was bad enough; in the morning he would have been on report, but Polty had never gone back to his quarters. Instead, he had staggered out into the city.

If the barracks were quiet, Wrax was not. First he went to a brothel, then an ale-house, then a gin-shop, then a Jarvel-den . . . Polty could not remember the rest. By now, his uniform was ripped and filthy, he stank abominably, his eyes were black, his cheek cut, and dried blood and vomit caked his lips and chin. All day he had been absent without leave. As darkness fell, he had stolen a horse, riding out recklessly through the massing lines of battle. Some had tried to stop him. Some had pursued him. But Polty, by a miracle, had escaped them all. Now, in the woods, they would never find him. Not tonight. Tonight he was free, free of them all, and would take at last the prize he had denied himself for so long.

Landa.

'It's my message,' Jem said again.

'I know. But I'm going with you.'

'Raj, think of the Great Mother! She's old, she's nearing her end. She's lost Myla – shall she lose you, too?'

Rajal's eyes were sad. Night had fallen and they were in the camp. Through the flames of the fire he saw the Great Mother, hugging Raggle and Taggle, squeezing Landa's hand, smiling encouragingly at Zady as he toyed with a shabby viol. The viol had lost its bow and the big man plucked the strings with his fingers; nonetheless he coaxed forth music of a sort. First came a string of arpeggios; soon they had wound their way into a tune. Rajal screwed up his eyes. He tried to focus on the Great Mother's face, looming close to Landa's, but it shimmered and danced through the curtains of flame. Rajal sighed. He loved the old woman and knew that she loved him: this day, at least, had convinced him of that. She would die soon, and it made him sorrowful. But he would not stay with her, could not.

He loved Jem too much to leave him now.

'Then you think you'll die, Jem?' was all he said.

Jem shook his head slowly.

'You think I'll die?'

'It's dangerous, Raj.'

'Then I'm going with you, Jem.'

Jem said no more. How many times, he wondered, had his friend infuriated him? Now he saw only loyalty in Rajal's dark eyes, loyalty and a grim, steady determination. They would wait until midnight, then be on their way.

Earnestly Jem imagined the mission before them. Hul had explained, Bando had explained, even the highwayman had come and sat by him, checking that he knew just what he must do. It was simple: in the heart of Wrax, just outside Temple Close, was a dilapidated little shop, sealed, almost barricaded, behind a lattice of iron. There lived the Shopkeeper of Wrax. Whether this was really the man in the story, none would say. *Go to him*, was all they said. *Go to him and tell him this:* THE TIME HAS COME.

The time had come.

By the great oak doors of Dolm's tower Polty slithered, almost fell, off his horse. At once the poor beast, its flanks slashed raw from its rider's spurs, whinnied in relief and cantered away. Polty barely noticed or cared. Slurring Landa's name, he pounded at the doors. Oh, how he needed the lovely girl! Oh, how he wanted her! His head ached. Dimly he recalled the night he had passed. Once, as he reeled from one tavern to another, he had taken a dirty old Zenzau-whore against an alley wall. The alley stank of piss and vomit, but in Polty's disgusted recollection the stench had all been the harlot's, rearing up like the foulest effluvia as he rucked up her coarse, damp skirts.

460

'Landa! Landa!' came his slurring cry. The lovely girl would purify him, redeem all his vileness.

❊ ❊ ❊ ❊ ❊

But how to get there?

All around the city, even now, the Fields of Ajl would be crawling with Bluejackets, readying themselves for the battle that must come. Their only plan was to travel under cover of darkness, but what difference would darkness make tonight when Zenzau's crisis had come at last?

'We've got into a city before,' said Rajal. 'Remember Varby?'

'Raj, this is Wrax.'

Hul came to sit by them again. He gestured towards Zady. 'It's hardly the triple-gittern,' he said.

'You know about that?' With an ache of longing Rajal thought back to the days when he had travelled in the Vaga-vans.

'The Great Mother has told us much,' said Hul. 'She lost everything to come and join us here, Rajal. Risked everything, too.'

They fell silent. Jem looked at Hul. The scholar had told him much about the world, about the past. To Jem, it was as if pieces of a puzzle had clicked into place, one by one. The puzzle was still far from complete, but there was one more piece to come that day. Dazzled by the sign he had been seeking for so long, Jem had barely considered the nature of his new and dangerous mission. He gazed up from the fire and saw the highwayman, hanging back in the shadows of the camp. Sensing the scrutiny of the eyes behind the mask, for an instant he felt a sharp stab of fear. He thought of other masks, other eyes.

'Hul,' said Jem, 'what did you mean about the harlequin? You asked whether his powers were dark or light.'

'I've often wondered, Jem, if there wasn't something in your uncle that longed for the dark.'

'I don't understand. He was a hero!'

'You know why he died, don't you?'

Jem bridled. 'He was betrayed!'

'Yes, but remember: he was sick. Dying. Had he not been hanged on the village green, he would have descended soon enough beneath the tombyard earth. It was the Siege of Wrax that destroyed him, when Veeldrop mustered his troops on the Fields of Ajl, determined to crush the power of Zenzau at last.'

'Just like tonight,' Jem murmured.

'But in reverse,' said Rajal.

'Hul, why must I go to the Shopkeeper?'

461

Hul, it seemed, had not heard the question. He said, 'You have heard, perhaps, of the explosion? The Red Avenger's secret weapon?'

Jem nodded. 'It was what made Veeldrop so sick, so decayed. But it ruined my uncle, too.' He thought of Tor, eking out those last desperate moonlives, hidden behind the wainscot in his mother's chamber. Would he have died, if the Bluejackets had never found him? Jem liked to think that, somehow or other, Tor would have survived. Even in those last days his uncle had spoken of the adventures before them, as if they would soon both be well, well and whole, setting out together on the Pale Highway.

Jem hugged himself. The fire roared in the centre of the camp, but he was cold. Through the flames he saw Landa, elfin and wan, and knew that she too, for all the warmth around her, was shuddering and afraid. Poor Landa! He should have liked to comfort her, but her thoughts, he knew, were all with her lover. Would Orvik meet his death in tomorrow's battle?

Jem turned back to Tor. 'Tell me about the weapon.'

'The Siege had grown desperate. Already the Bluejackets had battered us to bits. Veeldrop was the great victor of Irion. When they sent him in, we thought it was all over. By any reckoning, it would have been – if you reckoned without The Red Avenger. Your uncle had been working on a secret weapon. What elements went to make it, we never knew. In Wrax there is an alchemist, rumoured to have great powers, who assisted in the work. It was an effort, I believe, to harness powers that should never have been summoned into this dimension. But what do I know? Only this: that when Veeldrop attacked, there was a blinding flash, and the Fields of Ajl were littered with corpses.'

'What sort of flash?' said Rajal.

'I did not witness it. But a peasant once told me it was green – a sudden green refulgence, engulfing earth and sky. The poor peasant was blinded. It was the last thing he saw.'

'This alchemist,' said Jem. 'Who is he?'

Hul looked down. He might have smiled, but matters were too grave. 'Well, Jem, that's where it all links up.'

'Links up?'

'Another piece of the puzzle. You see, they call him the Shopkeeper. The Shopkeeper of Wrax.'

Jem was confused. Shopkeeper? The real one, the one in the story? Or was this some code-name? He murmured, 'But Dolm said nothing about . . . I mean, the story . . . it's different . . .'

Now Hul did permit himself to smile. 'In stories, as in dreams, there are many confusions. Stories shift and change like the light through the trees, or the leaves when they lie, scattered, on the ground. Inevitably it must be so. Stories, even the simplest, are paradoxical. It is in their nature – for what is a story, after all, but a lie which tells the truth?'

Jem looked down. Now it was Rajal's turn to speak.

'The blinding flash?' he breathed. 'That's the plan? It's going to happen again?'

'It's the only way,' said Hul.

'No,' Jem murmured slowly, 'no.'

'Jem, remember the sign!'

Jem clutched his face in his hands.

✵ ✵ ✵ ✵ ✵

The tower was deserted. Polty had bashed and bashed at the door. In the end he had kicked it and hurt his foot. Limping, cursing, he made a circuit of the ancient edifice, as if in hopes of some other entrance, as if in hopes that the fair innocent might be waiting for him there, her heart pit-a-pattering.

A terrible despair possessed Polty. He could have cried out, he could have beat the ground. How he wished he had another drink! Fondly, lovingly, all the way to the castle, he had imagined the scene he would find within, warm in the haze of the golden lamplight. First would come the finest wines from Dolm's cellars; then music, laughter, innocent games. Shyly, Landa would cast down her eyes, flushing as he chucked her under the chin; but in those moments when he caught her unawares, he would see her gaze upon him with the bold spark of love. Idly he would let fall that he was now a noble, and gasps of awed respect would escape the lips of Dolm, even of the crone. Bowing low, they would bless this day, bless it as if their castle were suddenly whole again and a new master had come to them, trailing clouds of glory. Eagerly the crone would scuttle away, to turn down the sheets of the best bed. When the time came for the fair sacrifice, the old parents would stand fondly by, weeping in gratitude to the fine gentleman, wishing only that were they blessed with a hundred daughters, that each might offer up the tribute of her virtue.

Bitter tears burned in Polty's eyes. How he had longed for this tender scene! How he had longed for this loving family! Yes, longed for them, and now they had betrayed him! His fists clenched, he blundered into the woods. If he found the girl now, there would be no mercy. He would have given her all his love, undressing her slowly, kissing her, caressing her, but she had forfeited all right to that now. To Polty, it was as if she had taken his finest feelings, laughed at them and trampled them underfoot. If he found her now he would strike her to the ground, rip off her shift and take his pleasure hotly, brutally, heedless of her pain.

Reeling, Polty crashed against a tree-trunk. He clutched it, clawing at the bark. All around him, darkness pressed, silent but for the sinister thuddings and skirlings that sounded from the Fields of Ajl, far below. Dimly Polty knew the battle was impending; less dimly, he knew that he had ruined his career. For a moment he tried to think. But what could he think? There was no going back to barracks now. Somehow he must find his way back to Ejland. Somehow he must find the bitch Cata, find her and force her to marry him. Yes, that was it. Once he had Cata, his troubles were over. No one would touch a nobleman. The little matter of his military career, and its ignominious end, would be consigned to oblivion. Yes, all he needed was Cata, damn her!

Polty leaned back against the tree-trunk, breathing deeply. Still the thuddings, the skirlings sounded on the air. He reached up, wiping the tears from his eyes. That was when he heard another sound, a closer sound, winding through the dark labyrinths of the woods.

Polty tensed again. What could it be?

Chapter 67

CLASP OF THE VICHY

Zady's music had become a song now, and in the firelight Bando was singing softly. His voice was rough, hardly tuneful, but imbued with a shabby, comforting charm. On the choruses, Raggle and Taggle joined in, their high childish voices winding round their father's like stems round a sturdy trunk.

> *When I was a child all the world was bright,*
> *I saw what I saw in the clearest light:*
> *Thought never came to me that life could change,*
> *But if it had I would have thought it strange—*
> > *For the sun was bright and the sun was gay,*
> > *And the sun was dancing all da-a-ay.*

'How can he sing?' Morven whispered. 'Doesn't he know what this battle will mean?'

Crum whispered back, 'He's a Zenzan.'

'Exactly. They'll be slaughtered.'

> *Deep in the woods I met a man of green,*
> *Who lives for ever and is seldom seen:*
> *He offered me a life so deep and strange,*
> *If I would cleave to him and never change—*
> > *While the sun was bright and the sun was gay,*
> > *And the sun was dancing all da-a-ay.*

'Morvy?'

'Crum?'

'This battle. It's just as well we're captured, isn't it? I mean, otherwise we'd have to fight.'

'Crum?'

'Hm?'

'Are you a coward?'

'I don't want to die, Morvy. That'd be silly.'

> *Out on the road I met a man of gold*
> *Who only lived within the dreams he sold:*
> *He offered me a life full of rush and change—*
> *I clutched it, thinking it so rich and strange!*

465

> *Yet the sun was bright and the sun was gay,*
> *And the sun was dancing all da-a-ay.*

'Crum?'

'Morvy?'

'You're right. We're not Bluejackets at all, are we? Not in our hearts. I thought at first we'd fallen in with a band of common brigands; I see now it is their cause, not ours, that is the noble one.'

'I only said I don't want to die, Morvy.'

'Don't want to die? Why Crum, is anything more noble than to lay down one's life for . . . *freedom*?'

Crum gulped, 'You'd still be dead, Morvy.'

'Crum, really! I'm ashamed of you!'

> *Now I am withered in a world of change,*
> *My sleep is restless and my dreams are strange:*
> *I think of the day I met the man of gold,*
> *But only the green knows what it was I sold—*
> > *While the sun was bright and the sun was gay,*
> > *And the sun was dancing all da-a-ay!*

'The Shopkeeper,' Jem mused, when the song was done. 'Is he a man of green? Or gold?'

Hul smiled again. 'Ah, Jem! Perhaps he is both.'

A pall of melancholy had descended over the camp. For long moments there was silence. It was a silence no one wanted to break, but as it went on they realized it was not silence at all. There was the crackling of the fire, the rustling of the leaves, a hooting owl; through the distance, drifting up from the fields before the city, came the howl of a Zenzan piper.

Then, from somewhere else, the thudding of a drum.

By now, Zady's prisoners had been almost forgotten. The excitements of the evening had been too much. But now something extraordinary happened.

'Excuse me.' Morven struggled upright.

'Morvy, what are you doing?'

'They're free!'

All around the campfire, faces turned, startled. Bando grabbed his rifle, ramming back the bolt.

'N-no, please!' Morven's hands were in the air at once. 'N-no, you've got quite the wrong idea. We w-weren't trying to surprise you. Over-p-power you, I mean—'

Hul had to laugh. Bando relaxed.

466

'N-No, not at all. You see, Crum's rather good at "slip-the-knot", and anyway ... You see, we want to help you.'

✵ ✵ ✵ ✵ ✵

Landa swished rapidly through the darkness of the woods. Caught in the trance of Bando's song, none of the others had seen her slip away. She had to be alone. To sit there in the firelight, waiting for the boys to ride off to Wrax, was suddenly too much for her. All evening, since she had heard that battle was imminent, Landa had hovered close to tears. Oh, she had tried to be brave, she had tried! But Bando's song was more than she could bear. The words disturbed her, deeply and obscurely, but more than this, it was the melody, winding ever tighter, tighter round her heart. To the girl, it seemed to contain all the sadness of the world.

She collapsed against a tree-trunk. Now the tears burst from her, hot and implacable. It was in that moment, Landa thought later, that the knowledge came to her that her kingdom was doomed. Orvik was a fool, they all said, to take on the might of the Bluejacket army. Landa had denied it; now, in her heart, she knew it was true. She loved him, but he was a fool. Whether he would live, Landa did not know. Perhaps, in the world that lay beyond tomorrow, they might still be lovers; but Orvik would never be King, and she would never be Queen. The tide of time was against them and could not be turned back. Already their destiny was sealed, with even their capital – once a wonder of the world – now only the merest colonial outpost, where the natives shambled, cowed and degraded, beneath the monuments of a glory they no longer even valued, nor could ever replicate in any future time.

It was over, all over, the story of their kingdom.

✵ ✵ ✵ ✵ ✵

Morven turned to the highwayman. 'S-Sir, I don't know who you are, but I think your cause is a good one. And y-you, sir—' he turned to Hul '—I *do* know who you are, and I *know* you're good.'

'What's that, Bluejacket? You know who I am?'

'But Mr H-Hulverside, of c-course! Why, you're a legend at the University of Agondon!'

'Indeed?' The highwayman was curious.

'Oh yes.' Morven was gaining confidence. At first, nerves had made his words halting; now, they almost tumbled, one over the other, in his enthusiasm. He gabbled at the highwayman, 'Why, sir, in Webster's – that's the coffee-house, you know – the fellows talk about Mr Hulverside all the time. He was the greatest scholar of his generation! How I've envied him! Would you believe, he was only – oh, no older than me

467

when they elected him to the Aon Fellowship. His future was assured – then, because he cared more for learning than lies, he got himself into the most dreadful trouble!'

The highwayman's eyes flickered curiously between the two scholars. They were strangely alike. With his lean frame, his gaunt face, his glinting little spectacles, Morven might have been a younger version of Hul.

'Why, Hul, don't tell me: your long-lost son?' the highwayman said satirically. Bright spots of colour had come to Hul's cheeks. 'Go on, young fellow. This is new to us. In what "dreadful trouble" did our friend here find himself? Could it have been as bad as yours?'

'Oh sir, worse – much worse! That's why Mr Hulverside's a hero, you see. I mean, to those of us who care for the life of the mind.' Morven's brow furrowed. 'Let me explain. You see, Mr Hulverside here started the Free Philosophical Society. Now, that was bad enough – well, later they said it was bad enough – but it was Vytoni, you see, that was really the trouble. That's Garolus Vytoni, V-Y-T-O-N-I, the famous Zenzan philosopher, who lived in the time of—'

The highwayman laughed, 'We know all about Vytoni, my boy! We've heard Hul hold forth often enough.'

Morven was unabashed. 'But sir, don't you see? If it wasn't for Mr Hulverside here, *none* of us would know about Vytoni.'

'How so?'

'Why, he risked life and limb! Can you imagine, for night after night stealing into the Chamber of Forbidden Texts? *Discourse on Freedom* – why, they've had it on the Red List for epicycles! It was almost forgotten, a matter of whispers and rumours, no more. But Mr Hulverside, you see, he copied out the whole thing by hand. At night. In secret. Then he had it printed . . . Was there ever a more dangerous feat of scholarship? Do you know, if he hadn't escaped, they would have sent him to Xorgos Island? So you see, Mr Hulverside's my absolute hero – *our* absolute hero – and I – that is, Crum and I – if we could help you, well . . .'

'Help *us*?' said the highwayman.

'*Help* us?' said Hul.

❄ ❄ ❄ ❄ ❄

For some moments Landa sobbed freely, the tears plashing, hot and stinging, down her cheeks. But her sorrow was not to last. Her sorrow was soon to be replaced – by fear.

The tree-trunk she leaned against was thick, quite thick enough to conceal a figure, lurking in the darkness of the other side. In a moment, when the creature was upon her – reeking foully, its garb in tatters, with its oozing face and goggling, black-rimmed eyes – Landa would know all the terrors of childhood, for what could this monster be, after all, but the hideous thing the Zenzans called the Vichy?

But of course, it was not the Vichy.

First came the scuffling in the undergrowth. Then the hand, slithering round the woody curve. Landa, intent on her tears, did not hear the scuffling; nor, at first, did she see the hand. Then all at once the hand snaked out, sinking its fingers into the flesh of her shoulder.

Landa screamed.

❋ ❋ ❋ ❋ ❋

Crum quickly stifled a groan. Oh Morvy, Morvy! What was he getting them into now?

Then Jem spoke. He leapt up, his eyes suddenly bright. 'But of course! Why didn't we think of it before? The uniforms. Look at their uniforms!' He turned to Rajal. 'We want to get into Wrax, don't we? A Bluejacket stronghold?'

The highwayman laughed; Rajal looked doubtful. Crum clutched his jacket tightly around him. If his teeth were chattering, it was partly through fear; but it was also, after all, a chilly evening.

Would they want his breeches, too?

Only Morven caught the enthusiasm.

'You're right! How can you get into Wrax alone? You'd never get past the sentries tonight, and if you got in, would you know your way? Too great a risk! But Crum and I – we're garrisoned there ... We'll take you with us as our ... our prisoners!'

Jem looked at Rajal. Rajal looked at Jem. But before either had time to speak, the air was rent suddenly with a piercing cry.

'What's that?' said Rajal.

Jem looked round wildly. 'Landa!'

❋ ❋ ❋ ❋ ❋

It was Jem who found her first. Bounding through the darkness, guided only by the sound of screams, he came upon her almost by accident. Lurid in a shaft of moonlight, suddenly she was there, the girl flailing and crying in the clasp of brutal hands. Recklessly – grabbing, ripping, gouging – Jem launched himself on the attacker. The attacker turned, enraged. Now his fury was all for Jem. Landa scrambled away, looking back in terror as the crazed Bluejacket first flung Jem to the ground, then straddled him.

'I'll kill you,' the man cried, 'I'll kill you, I'll kill you!'

He was drunk, but stronger than Jem – then all of a sudden there was a pistol, too, glittering evilly in the harsh moonlight. Landa screamed again. Bucking, writhing, Jem struggled to free himself, then gasped as

469

the attacker gripped his head, holding his skull and squeezing tight. Blunderingly, the drunkard tried to jab his pistol into the opening of Jem's mouth. Jem clenched his jaw, but resistance only added to the attacker's rage. With a wild cry he swung back the barrel, ready to smash Jem's teeth into powder.

It would have happened, but in that moment, as if time were arrested, the attacker looked on the face beneath him, and Jem looked up into the face of his attacker. Through the black eyes, the cuts, the swellings, he might not have recognized his enemy again, but the hair that flamed above the ruined face could never be mistaken.

'Polty!'

'Jem!'

The moment of recognition was brief, but long enough to save Jem from Polty's rage. By now, Landa's screams had brought the others. It was Zady who would have proved himself a hero, swooping down on Polty, flinging him aside; Zady, perhaps, whom Polty might have turned and shot. But there was another fate in store for Polty, and another in store for Zady too.

All of a sudden there was a deafening cry, rending open the darkness of the woods. The cry was inhuman; it was a cry of a hideousness such as Jem had heard only in the terrible ceremony beneath the Great Temple, echoing from the thing that burst through the glass.

It was the cry of a Creature of Evil.

Polty swivelled, pistol at the ready, but already the horrifying presence was upon him, enveloping, dripping, ardent for its prey. If a man could be made from earth itself, sprouting leaves and branches from the mud of his flesh, and if this man were a huge and crazed giant, this would be the creature that assailed Polty now, clutching him in its vile embrace, dragging him away into the surrounding darkness.

Now it was Polty's turn to scream, and Landa, this time, could only whisper, white-faced with horror:

'The Vichy!'

Chapter 68

RHYMES OF GOODBYE

'Come,' said the highwayman. 'It's time.'

Crum tugged at his crotch. Really, this Vaga-boy's costume didn't fit at all! Resentfully he looked at the two chaps who had taken their clothes. If this wasn't a silly idea, he didn't know what was.

Trust Morvy to get them in this pickle. The rebels were pleased enough with his plan, but at the last minute – of course – there had to be a change. *Just one thing,* said the one they called Jem. *How can we trust you? We'll be the Bluejackets – you'll be the prisoners. When we're safely in the city, then we'll change back.*

Crum could have told them what he thought of this idea, but what was the point? Glumly he remembered his mother's story about Uncle Franta and Uncle Hans. They'd switched uniforms once, hadn't they, when Uncle Franta was in the coastguards and Uncle Hans a footman up at the Hall? One thing led to another, that was the trouble. It only started as a lark, and what happened? Transported to Xorgos Island, the pair of them! Crum's mother would purse her lips like – why, like *Bluebottle's whatsit* when she got to that part of the story. It was a legend all over Varl!

Yes, Crum could have told them a thing or two!

Hul put his hand on Morven's shoulder. 'And you say Professor Mercol's still with us? Well, I never! He was the one who supported me for the Aon Fellowship. Then he denounced me, when he found out what I'd done.'

'He's an old fool,' said Morven bitterly. 'Do you know, he still cites Seavil – Seavil, I ask you! – as an authority on the Great Caesura?'

'Shocking!'

Miserably Crum looked on as Morven proudly proclaimed his background, prize-winning essay and all, and disclaimed responsibility for the fact that he was a soldier. 'Why, sir, I had no choice! I was only a scholarship boy – Juvescials, too. Considered inessential by the present regime, would you believe? So, when the Troubles broke out in Zenzau again, they called me before the Seeker Squad – *wrenched* me away, why, every bit as roughly as they wrenched poor Crum here from his farm in Varl!'

Morven laughed at the comparison; Crum blinked sadly, then jumped

471

as the crone, the Woman of Wisdom, touched his arm. 'Poor boy, fear not. You shall be rewarded for your bravery this night. If not in this world, then in The Vast.'

'Th-the Vast?'

For some time, Crum's knees had been trembling. Now they almost gave way beneath him.

❉ ❉ ❉ ❉ ❉

'Holluch.'

'The barracks?'

'The town.'

'Didn't know it was a town.'

'Oh, it's a town. Well, it was. When I was a nipper, like. Not much like that now. Like it was then, I mean. Still, it's home. Well, it was.'

'Raise you?'

'Hah! We were back there for a bit. First we marches down from the Tarn. Then it's Holluch. Back home, I think. Well, what'd they make me go away for then? Doesn't make sense, like.'

'Nothing makes sense.'

'Then we come away again. Here.'

'See the world, you do. Raise you?'

'Some parts you'd rather not.'

'Not what?'

'Hah!'

The men fell silent. In a shabby back-room behind the gates of Wrax, they were waiting to go back on sentry-duty. Cards, coins and battered tankards littered the rickety table where they sat. The air was thick with a fug of tobarillo; through the grilled window shone the Hornlight moon.

'But then, I'm not sorry about the Tarn.'

'To see it?'

'Nah. Met my girl up there, I did.'

'What's that, Wiggler? You've got a girl?'

'Raise you?'

'Hah! King of Swords.'

'What about you, then, eh, Rottsy?'

'What about what?'

'Where'd you rather be, then? If you weren't here?'

'Agondon.'

'That hole! Why?'

Soldier Rotts leered. 'Heard about this place, I have. Where the officers go.'

'What place?'

472

'Queen of Swords.'

'Bugger.'

'They call it Chokey's. Quality-ladies. Know what I mean?'

'Dirty bugger!'

'What about you, then, eh, Wiggler? You and your girl?'

The corporal bridled. 'Don't you go saying nothing about my Nirry! She's a good girl, she is!'

'All right, Wiggler, keep your hair on!'

Sergeant Bunch appeared in the doorway. 'Olch. Rotts. Back on duty.'

'Ah,' sighed Wiggler as he shouldered his musket, 'I wish I was with my Nirry now!'

❋ ❋ ❋ ❋ ❋

'Come. We must go.'

The highwayman was impatient. The night was at its darkest, and the horses were ready. For the first stage the masked man would accompany the little party, leading them to the edge of the woods; then he would point out the way they must go.

Jem hugged Bando, then Hul. 'You were characters in a story to me once – a story Tor told me.'

Bando smiled, 'As you were to us, Jem, as you were to us.' One of the boys huddled in his arms. Tenderly he shifted the sleepy burden, smoothing a childish curl. 'How fiercely Tor loved you!' the Zenzan mused. 'He spoke of you always, Jem.'

'Strange, then, to meet and find each other real! Dear friends, shall I ever forget you? Like giants you strode across the fields of my mind, in the days when all the world was new to me. You were heroes to me then, and you're heroes to me now.'

'Ah, Jem, we are but the players of a prelude. You are the hero of the story before us now.'

Jem took Hul's hand. 'Hul, it's not true. Magic and prophecy have made me what I am. It's you, Bando, Bob Scarlet – you're the heroes. And Orvik. Not me.'

He turned to Landa.

'Queen-to-be, it may be that your beloved is precipitate. Perhaps he is wrong, perhaps he is right, to bring forth this battle as he has done. But I know he acts in a righteous cause. Otherwise, how could he be assured of your love?'

With shy reverence, Jem kissed the girl's hand.

'Far away, long ago, there was one that I loved, as you love Orvik. I see now I have not loved her as truly as I might, and the knowledge fills me with sorrow. But Queen-to-be, you have shown me the true path of love. For that, I shall ever hold you dear in my heart.'

Xal was listening, moved. She reached forward, embracing Jem. For a long time the old woman held him in her arms. Then she stepped back and lightly, just lightly, her gnarled fingers touched the place where he kept the Crystal of Koros. At the same moment, the stone at her forehead glowed.

'Koros shall go with you, blessed one. And soon – oh, pray it is soon – his sister soft as leaves shall travel with you, too.'

'Great Mother,' Jem had to ask, 'what of Polty? There was a time before when I thought he was dead. But . . . he can't survive the Vichy, can he?'

'Ask not the fate of the red-headed one. As you have your destiny, so he has his. What we have seen was part of his destiny; in time, you shall know if we have seen it all.'

The Great Mother's words were cryptic, and Jem would have asked her to explain, but she turned to Rajal.

'You're a brave boy, Rajal-child. But why do I call you child? In these late moonlives, you have become a man.'

Rajal fell on her neck. 'Oh, Great Mother! I fear you are deceived. If I am a man, why then do tears come so swiftly to my eyes?'

'You are yet a man, great-son, if they flow like rain.'

Then Rajal looked at Zady, and saw that it was true.

Xal's hand wiped her own flowing tears. 'How my poor son – your father, Rajal – would have been proud of you! I shall dream of a day when we are together again, my Rajal. You and me. Zady. Jem.'

'And Myla?'

'Oh yes. Myla.'

How Rajal wished that this day would come! But alas, he knew it could come only in The Vast. Rajal was no magic child; The Rapture was not strong in him, but that night, as he slipped from the Great Mother's embrace, he knew he had embraced her for the last time. She would die soon, and absurdly Rajal thought she would die far from home. But then, where was home? All her life, she had been driven from place to place, an outcast except among her own outcast kind. Yet now, as her long life ended, even her family would not be with her. That night, only with a pain so strong as to be agony did Rajal restrain the terrible, keening sorrow that might have burst from him, like blood from a wound.

Jem looked around them. 'Where's Priestess Ajl?'

But the highwayman interrupted. In the sad scene, no one had noticed the Priestess slipping away. There was no time to look for her now.

'My dumplings? At this time of night?'

'Come, Cook, the men have been marching all day!'

'And what fault is it of mine if they're given such silly orders? No, sergeant, my kitchen is closed.' Nirry's voice was hollow and there were shadows under her eyes.

'Cook, be reasonable. There's a battle in the morning. The Blue Irions had to be in place.'

'A poor place, if you ask me – crouched on the edge of this miserable hillside. Why, you promised me a nice warm barracks, and here I am stuck out in a leaky tent, sloping all sideways in the wind and cold—'

'If you're cold, Cook, I could warm you!'

Tonight Nirry did not even smile as she slapped away the sergeant's hand. 'Enough of your sauce.'

The sergeant sighed, 'But Cook, we need yours! Can't you hear the battle-drums, beating over the fields? My men want all their strength for the morning – and right now they want food! Now where are your girls?'

'Flat on their backs, the lot of them!'

'Nonsense, Cook. Come, I'll put them to lighting the fires.'

And the sergeant, seeing he would have to take matters in hand, ducked back out through the flaps of the tent where Nirry sat, hunched and trembling. Barked orders sounded through the canvas.

'Drink is what your men want, Carney Floss, drink and nothing else,' Nirry muttered. 'Let them drink, I say! Fancy, putting good food in a poor boy's stomach, then sending him to be shot! Let them drink, I say, until they can't hear or see!'

With that, Nirry burst into tears. It was hardly to be expected: in the long journey from Irion, she had grown and changed. The mistress, with her bellowings of *Girl! Girl!*, had kept poor Nirry down for too long. The girl had become a woman, and a formidable one. Only now, and briefly, did Nirry's strength fail her. The day had been too long, and she was tired; but more than this, it was the battlefield that overwhelmed her.

Memories of battle lay deep in Nirry's mind. In the Siege of Irion she had been a child, just at the beginning of her long career in service, but still she recalled the battering cannons, the screams, the falling stones. In those days, men had died before her eyes, their chests burst open, their stomachs gored. Once in the kitchen garden, walking out early into a sunny morning, she had found a young man – such a handsome young man – lying among the radishes, bent and broken like a discarded doll. He must have fallen from the battlements above, spiralled down through the air and snapped his spine. For long moonlives afterwards, Nirry had pictured his face, so strangely peaceful, so strangely cold.

Now, so many years later, so far away, the memory of this boy whose name she had never known returned to Nirry in all its old sorrow, all its terror. Again she saw the dead face. She thought of Miss Cata. She thought of Wiggler. She rocked and moaned on her blanket-roll.

'Poor Cook, what's this?' The sergeant's voice was tender as he slipped back into the tent. Sitting beside Nirry, he stole an arm about her shoulders. 'Why, I didn't think a girl like you would be frightened of a silly battle, hm?' He proffered his hip-flask. 'Come on, do you good.'

Nirry sniffed, 'Oh, all right.'

'There's my girl. Seen a hundred silly battles, I have – got the scars, too, in places I don't often have on show!' He showed his blackened grin. 'Come on – little smile? That's right. I knew my Nirry was a brave girl, eh?'

'Less of the "my Nirry"!' But Nirry smiled again. She turned to the sergeant. Only one candle burnt inside the tent, and in its glow the sergeant's face – broken veins, stubble and all – looked soft and warm. It was comforting, and Nirry said, 'Carney?'

'Nirry?'

'You know the five gold tirals?'

'Gold tirals? What's this, a dream?'

'What a fellow needs, you said. To buy his way out. Do you think a lot of fellows would? If they had them, I mean?'

'If! I think we wouldn't have an army!' The sergeant grinned, but then his grin faded.

He looked down sadly.

'Carney?' Nirry came again.

'Nirry?'

'If I wanted to find a soldier—'

'Well, love, I'd say you was in the right place.'

'Ooh, you! That's not what I mean.'

'Well, I'd say you'd have to know his regiment.'

Nirry said shyly, 'The Fifth?'

'Ho, the Fifth again?'

'I told you I was going to be married, Carney.'

The sergeant swigged from his flask. 'And I told you the fellows in the Fifth were no good.'

'Not my Wiggler.'

'Not your Wiggler? Well, I guess you've made up your mind about that, eh?' The sergeant looked down again, studying his boots. When he looked up, his eyes were misty, but he did his best to grin. He said softly, 'The Fifth are up at the barracks, love. Been here this last season, they have.'

'They have?' At once Nirry's face was overspread with joy. 'Oh,

476

Carney! Really?' And before she knew it, she had kissed him on the cheek.

The sergeant laughed, 'Steady on, girl! Here, I could take another one of those, I could!

'Ooh, you!'

'All right, one's enough. But I tell you, girl, if this wiggly-eared fellow don't treat you right, you come and tell old Carney Floss. You can always count on old Carney, you can.'

Tears filled Nirry's eyes again. 'Oh, Carney!'

'You're a good sort you are, Nirry Jubb. Best sort there is, and I should know.'

'Here, who said you could call me "Nirry"?'

'You've called me "Carney" often enough, haven't you?'

Nirry giggled, 'That's because it's such a silly name!'

'Silly? Whose name are you calling silly?'

'Yours!' And Nirry said it over several times, each time making it sound sillier still. 'Carney Floss, Carney Floss!'

'Ooh, you bad girl, you – I'll get you!'

Then all at once, the sergeant and Nirry were wrestling on the blanket-roll. Shrieking, Nirry beat her legs in the air. It was hardly the behaviour of a respectable woman, but for the moment Nirry didn't care. She was so happy, so happy!

A sharp *crack!* came from behind.

Inert, the sergeant slumped on Nirry's breast.

'Nirry, are you all right?'

'What?' Nirry looked up. In the haze of the candle stood a young Bluejacket, brandishing Nirry's best saucepan in his hand. For a moment Nirry was frightened, until she realized who it was. 'Miss Cata!' she whispered. 'Oh, Miss Cata, what have you done?'

The sergeant moaned.

'Don't worry, Nirry, I've put him out of action – for tonight, at least. Dirty man! I've been watching him for you, ever since you said he'd been giving you trouble.'

Cata aimed a kick at the sergeant's ribs.

'Miss Cata, no! It's not what you think, it's – oh, never mind!' With a gasp Nirry squeezed out from beneath the sergeant's bulk. 'Poor Carney! He's not a bad fellow – just a bit saucy, that's all.'

'He's a drunken pig,' said Cata, with a shudder.

There was no use arguing. Nirry brought the candle close to the sergeant's head. Poor Carney, he would have a lump there in the morning! 'Ooh, you've done it now, miss! Mark my words, he'll find out it was you, and you'll be on a charge.'

'I shan't, Nirry.'

'Ooh, really? He's a sharp one, this one, make no mistake.'

'Nirry, I mean I shan't be here.'

'What?' Nirry lowered the candle slowly.

'I came to say goodbye.'

'Miss Cata, what are you saying?'

'Remember, Nirry, you asked me how I could fight for the Bluejackets? Well, that's just it, you see. I'm not going to – I never meant to. I'm going over to the other side.'

At once Nirry's face was pale. She brought a hand up to her mouth. 'Miss Cata, no! The Zens will be slaughtered, everyone says so! Ooh, you silly girl! I thought you were looking for Master Jem, same as I've been looking for my Wiggler! What use will you be to him, answer me that, if you've gone and got yourself killed? And all for nothing?'

'It's not for nothing, Nirry. It's for freedom.'

Tears burst from poor Nirry's eyes again. 'Ooh keep your freedom! I've got a little bit put aside from service, I have, and if my Wiggler's spared tomorrow we're going off to open our little tavern together, and the rest of the world can all go hang! Bluejackets, Redjackets, Zenzans – you can keep the lot of them, and keep your freedom!'

Cata cried, 'It's not that simple, Nirry!'

'Simple? Yes, Miss Cata, I may be a simple woman, but I've lived in this world a bit longer than you, too long not to know that everything important *is* simple, only too simple – life, love and health! And here's these men with their silly quarrels, going and spoiling it all for everyone. I've got a good mind to march up to those barracks right now, I have, get my Wiggler and . . .'

Nirry would have gone on, but by now the tears were flowing freely down her face; tears glittered in Cata's eyes, too.

'Ooh, Miss Cata!' Nirry brushed her cheeks. 'You've got your own ways, and you'll do what you want . . . I know that. I'm . . . I'm just going to miss you, that's all.'

'Oh, Nirry!'

The two women hugged each other, long and hard.

Chapter 69

HORSEMAN ON THE RISE

There was one further farewell that night. It happened later, on the brink of the woods. As the party rode away from the camp, making their way carefully along dark woodland trails, no one spoke. The four young men were all excited . . . frightened . . . excited by turns. Perhaps they might have spoken of their fears, their hopes, their sorrows. But the highwayman acted as a constraint upon them. Only at the end, as they looked down from the woodland heights to the Fields of Ajl below, did the surly figure turn to his companions and speak. The moon glimmered around them like a mysterious silvery pool.

'It is as well this is a Hornlight night. But why do I say so? We barely need it. Look at the watchfires burning below. When darkness lifts I shall lead my men to these fields, joining Orvik's forces before the city. The battle he fights may be a foolish one, but let it not be said that . . . that Bob Scarlet shied from it. Now, young friends, your task is clear enough. Give your message, and the rest shall follow.'

He held out his hand to them, one by one. Jem was the last to take his leave. Intently he looked, perhaps for a final time, into the eyes behind the highwayman's mask.

'Think not ill of me, my young Prince. Perhaps I have puzzled you, but I wish you well – know that, in truth, *I wish you well*.'

The words were unexpected and spoken with sudden, surprising emotion. It was then that a strange feeling came to Jem. In the highwayman's presence he had felt it before, but not so intensely as he felt it now.

No. It could not be. No, it was absurd.

Jem's brow furrowed and he turned away, troubled. Only a moment later, when he turned back on the path, did the feeling assail him with an intensity so great that he almost cried out, almost rushed back.

But he did not. Instead he only stared through blurring eyes at the highwayman, tall on his dark horse, gazing down mysteriously on the world below.

So alone. So ghostly. So familiar.

'Harlequin!' Jem whispered. 'Harlequin, why?'

But Jem was wrong. It was not the harlequin.

❄ ❄ ❄ ❄ ❄

479

'You never told him, did you?'

The voice came only when Jem was out of earshot. The highwayman turned, unsurprised, to Hul. The scholar was concerned for him, and had followed at a distance.

'Tell him?' murmured the masked man. 'Hul, how could I? You are a man of uncommon percipience, and have penetrated my disguise. But shall I reveal myself freely, willingly, to one whom the truth can only pain? Would I burden the Key to the Orokon with knowledge that can only distract him from his quest? No, Hul, none but you must know my secret – none!'

Hul looked down, troubled. 'But sire, think of the morrow!'

'Call me not sire,' snapped the masked man. 'But the morrow, Hul? What of it?'

'This battle of Orvik's is senseless, unwinnable – you have said as much yourself.'

'Hul, are you forgetting young Jemany's mission?'

'Of course I'm not! His mission, if it succeeds, shall wrest victory from defeat. But before the sun sets upon this land again, still it may be, sire, that you breathe your last.'

The eyes behind the mask flashed in the moonlight. 'What is this? You would have me turn from the field of battle? Or is it that you wish not to accompany me there? I had thought you many things, old companion-in-arms, but never a coward!'

Hul pleaded, 'Sire, you don't understand. I say again that tomorrow you may die – yet still you would be guilty of such stubborn reticence? Let me ride after Prince Jemany now, and bring him back before you!'

Suddenly the highwayman grabbed his pistol. 'Go after him, Hul, and it is you who shall die – now!'

'Sire!'

'I mean it, Hul! If I die, I deserve to die! If I live, what then? It is my heir who matters, and now that I have seen him and know him to be a hero, I shall die without compunction, if die I must!'

Bitterly Hul looked into the dark mask and spat, 'Then sire, you are a fool! Have you concealed yourself for so long, only to succumb to this reckless martyrdom? Sire, think of Jemany! Think of your son!'

'Hul, I told you – call me not your sire! And call him not my son! Companion-in-arms, I trust you more than any man, but defy me in this and you are no man of mine. Listen to me, and listen well, for before you now I make this vow: that never shall I acknowledge Jemany as my son until liberty is restored at last to this empire – until my usurping brother is deposed from my throne and the world sees me again in my true guise, His Imperial Agonist Majesty, King Ejard of the Red Cloth!'

The masked man spurred his horse and rode away.

✻ ✻ ✻ ✻ ✻

Behind Zenzan lines the air itself is febrile. For long days and nights, as the troops marched on Wrax, hearts have thumped in time with the rhythm of Aran war-drums; hopes have soared, pitched and tossed on the high strange wailings of the Derkold pipes. Only now, deep in darkness on the night before battle, does silence descend on Orvik's troops. But this is not the silence of sleep. This is a silence of ardent waiting, for Orvik, Prince Sacred, heir of Zenzau, is about to address the fifty thousand men who have gathered under his standard. On a high stage, flaming tapers leap into the darkness; down through the darkness, plunging through clouds, come the golden rays of the Hornlight moon. Fifty thousand pairs of eyes look upwards as the rightful monarch appears before them, resplendent in the royal cloak of green that proclaims his bondage to his people, his land. On his head he wears a golden crown; in his hand he holds a golden sword, and the voice that issues forth is one of passion.

'My people,' cries the Prince, 'the time of our destiny is at last at hand. For long, for too long my kingdom has languished in the iron hold of the conqueror King. The Ejlander called Bluejacket has displaced his rightful brother. So too his evil reach has snatched my kingdom from me. Now, I return to seize back what is mine! My men, you are the mightiest army in all the annals of Zenzau – I say the mightiest, and shall brook no contradiction. Raised from the very corners of this my rightful realm – from the furthest steppes of Derkold, from the hills of Ana-Zenzau, from the rocky coasts of Antios and beyond, beyond – you have travelled far to be here this night. You have suffered. You have endured. Many of you are cold. Many of you are hungry. I would that you all wore uniforms of green. Alas, many of you dress only in rags. I would that you all had horses, rifles, muskets. Alas, there are those who carry only the pitchforks, scythes, sickles of the fields that now lie fallow, the hammers of the forges that now lie cold.

'But men, this I say – our cause is a righteous one, and the goddess Viana is on our side. And this I say, too – that if among you now there is a man who would not fight for me, though his life be the forfeit, I would that he would come to my tent forthwith, that I may give him a purse of gold, sufficient that he may leave my service. For the King who would extract a forced fealty, there can be no victory – nay, though every man of the enemy's be slain. Would I die beside those who disdain my cause?'

There is more. Prince Orvik says that tomorrow is Hara's Feast, most

481

sacred of days in the Old Zenzan Almanac, that now has been displaced by the calendar of the conquerors. After his victory, Orvik says, the Almanac shall be restored; then the man who outlives the morrow shall mark his glory by the Feast of Hara. As that day approaches, his heart shall always quicken; stripping back his sleeve he shall show his scars, declaring, *These wounds I had on Hara's day*. Never, says Orvik, shall this day go by – from the morrow until the end of time itself – but it shall be remembered as the day of his glory; never, says Orvik, shall he forget that each man who fights beside him is his brother.

Oh yes, there is more, much more, but only the men at the front can hear. For the rest, the wind blows away the words, but they look on in wonder at the golden crown, the sword, and now – here there are gasps, then cheers – the golden armour in which the Prince stands at the end, his green robe discarded on the stage behind him.

Magnificent in the moonlight and the tapers, Orvik raises his sword above his head. A moment later he swiftly leaves the stage, repairing back to his tent with his aides.

※　※　※　※　※

'Ouch!' said Crum.

'I say, steady on!' said Morven.

'Don't whine!' Jem rolled his eyes. 'You're supposed to be prisoners.'

'*Supposed* to be. You don't have to tie it quite so tight, do you?'

'I don't see why we can't keep our horses,' said Crum.

Now Morven rolled *his* eyes. 'Crum, really! We're prisoners.'

'Prisoners, always prisoners! Couldn't they just tie our hands?'

'That would hardly be convincing, would it now? We're the Bluejackets. We know how it's done.'

'Taken lots of prisoners, have you?' said Rajal.

'Well, actually—' Morven winced as Jem completed his bonds. First his hands were tied, then a rope was bound round his torso, tethering his arms to his side. A dangling end of this rope was attached to Jem's horse, fastened securely to the bridle-strap. The prisoner had no choice but to scurry helplessly behind his mounted guard, hoping that the guard did not decide to gallop.

'We've never taken a single prisoner,' sniffed Crum. 'But *we've* been prisoners twice in the last day!'

'Once as Bluejackets, once as rebels,' Rajal laughed. 'You'll be Vagas next, the rate you're going!'

'Come on.' Jem did not join in the laughter. 'The Bluejackets are close. The real ones, I mean.'

※　※　※　※　※

In his tent, Orvik has two unexpected visitors. The first is a young man – or so it seems – who waits earnestly to speak with the Prince. It is Cata, dressed in peasant clothes now, come to vow her allegiance. Already her speech is welling behind her lips, a speech quite as fine as the Prince has just delivered. Alas, he shall not hear it. His head is swimming with fine visions; before he even sees this first visitor, one of his aides intervenes, assuming – he has expected such trouble – that Cata must be some cowardly trooper who has heard the promise of the purse of gold. The aide draws his sword; Cata can only turn on her heels and run.

The second visitor rushes forward recklessly. It is a figure in a cowl, and seems at first to be another young man. Swords flash, but then the cowl falls away, and Orvik is looking into the eyes of Landa. Eagerly the girl flings herself upon her lover. She had to come, she sobs, she has slipped away from her father; this night, of all nights, she must spend with Orvik.

And the Prince holds her in his arms, but only loosely. She is a foolish girl – this is a night for stratagem, not for love.

✳ ✳ ✳ ✳ ✳

The Fields of Ajl, which sweep in a green sward around the city, are divided into two great shelving parts. Below lies the Rheen, or Lower Ajl, in the dip of land between the hills and the city. By now, following the trails the highwayman had shown them, Jem's party had reached the soft ridge which marked the edge of these lower fields. Behind them, massed and ready, were the forces of Orvik's army. By now, perhaps, some were sleeping, readying themselves for the day ahead. Many more, it seemed, were keeping a vigil, strung taut as wires before the challenge of the morrow. Songs, pipes, drums sounded again; fires, endless fires glowed in the darkness. If they were beacons of hope, it was a desperate hope. As the Bluejackets found in the Siege of Wrax, the Rheen offered only the most precarious stage from which to challenge the city. Every advantage lay with the enemy.

The Upper Fields, surrounding the walled city like a protective collar, are called the Ring. In the great siege of 996d, it was not until they took the Ring that the Bluejackets had been even within sight of victory. But that had needed a long war of attrition, with an army superior to any Orvik could muster. Now, with the position of the armies reversed, the Ring was firmly in Bluejacket possession. Their least aim in the battle to come must be to make certain it stayed that way. It was an aim that seemed sure to be fulfilled – sure, indeed, to be surpassed. Could the Zenzans do to the Bluejackets what the Bluejackets had done to them, holding the city to ransom for moonlife after moonlife?

483

It seemed barely thinkable.

'We've got to do it,' Jem murmured to himself.

'Jem?' said Rajal.

'Whatever it is we have to do – Raj, we've got to do it.'

'I fear it may be evil.'

'It's the only way,' said Jem.

His voice was still barely more than a whisper, but a whisper filled with harsh, almost cruel determination. Yet in his heart, Jem was uncertain, troubled.

Silently they followed the road up to the city. Below, they had kept their distance from Orvik's army. Now the Bluejackets were all around. Tents, carts, wagons littered the green fields. Songs and coarse laughter rang out in the night. Beer and wine sloshed freely round the campfires and little bands of harlots roamed back and forth. It was almost a festive scene; it almost had about it a rude innocence. But there were the sentries, too, stiff-backed and grim-faced, lining the road, and all along the ridges of the Ring, sturdy ranks of cannons had been wheeled into place, their great iron muzzles glowing dumbly in the moonlight. To Jem, it was as if a second city had grown – cancerously, promiscuously – around the first. It was a city without brick and without walls, but more forbidding, perhaps, than the city that possessed them.

Or perhaps not. Perhaps something was bound to go wrong, bound to destroy the smooth workings of the plan. It was when they reached the gates of the city that things went suddenly, dangerously awry.

Their horses clattered over a heavy drawbridge.

'Halt!' called a sentry.

'Salute!' hissed Morven.

Jem saluted; so did Rajal. Until now, the guards had barely looked at them. Why should they? Riders with foot-prisoners were common enough. Peasants were always being rounded up, hauled in on charges of this or that.

But the guards at the gates were taking no chances.

'Papers!' called the sentry.

'Pocket!' hissed Morven.

Jem produced his papers – or rather, Morven's. Stiff-backed, expressionless, he handed them to the guard. It was not then, only later, that Jem thought there was something familiar about the fellow.

But what?

He was ordinary enough, a little, commonplace chap with an open, freckly face and big, rather flexible-looking ears. Hadn't Jem seen him somewhere before? The very uniform Jem was wearing at that moment should have given him a clue. On the pocket, on the hat, was the regimental crest, the same one worn by the guard before him. With all that had happened that day, that night, the thought had never occurred to Jem that their prisoners were from the Fifth Royal Fusiliers of the Tarn.

Hanging back behind the horses, Morven and Crum were quaking with fear.

'Morvy?'

'Crum?'

'We're done for, aren't we?'

A second guard demanded Rajal's papers – or rather, Crum's. Rajal fumbled for them awkwardly. For a moment he feared he would not find them; then he did. Handing them down from his horse, he was careful to keep his face low. Huge tapers burnt beside the city gates, lighting up the night with a refulgent, sickly yellow. Would they notice the darkness of his skin?

'Crum?'

'Morvy?'

'I think we're done for.'

They were right. It should have been a formality. It should have ended there. Instead, the sentry shouted suddenly, violently, 'Impostors!'

In the next moment the little party was surrounded by Bluejackets, bayonets at the ready.

Jem cursed. Wildly his gaze took in the bayonets, the soldiers, the cobbled street ahead. In the next instant they would be forced from their horses, marched away, flung into a cell. It could not happen, would not. Desperation seized him. Already his horse was rearing in fear. Like a warrior in a story, Jem cried out. He spurred his horse recklessly, breaking through the ranks.

'Raj! Quick!'

In the next moment they were careering through the cluttered, strange streets, the prisoners twisting, bucking, dragging behind them. Shots, cries, rang on the air. Behind them, all was chaos, before them only confusion, a whizzing, wheeling collage of strange windows and doors, onion domes, strewn rubbish, glimmering gold. The city was alive, febrile with the expectation of the day to come. Faces – angry, frightened – leapt out at them on all sides. Link-boys vaulted from their path, their torches guttering. A horse-trough upturned, sloshing across the street. They skidded through a market square, the paving slick with remnants of marrows, turnips, pumpkins.

'Stop! Stop!' The guards were hot in pursuit.

'Stop! Stop!' cried Morven and Crum.

There was no way out of the market square.

'Dead end!'

'Jem, no! Over there – an alley!'

'We can't get through!'

'Jump!'

They leapt from their horses. For a moment they clattered over trestle tables, boxes, slithering planks. By the time the Bluejackets came crashing through the debris, Jem and Rajal were gone, vanished into the labyrinth of dark cobbled alleys that wound between the market and the Temple Close.

'You men, split up! Find them!' barked Corporal Olch.

But it was useless. The chase was over.

Grimly, the corporal – that is to say, Wiggler – gazed about him. Moonlight glimmered, sinister and chill, in the high windows all around the square. He kicked at a squashed turnip; he sighed deeply. This was bad, bad. Sergeant Bunch would want a special report, and what could he say?

'H-help!' came a piteous cry.

'H-help!' came another.

'Morvy! Crum! We thought you were done for!'

'We are!' bleated Morven.

Bruised and battered, they lay on the cobblestones, still tethered to the abandoned horses. Wiggler sighed. He would have gone to help his stricken friends, but at that moment another voice sounded behind him, high-pitched and breathless.

Wiggler turned, startled.

Suddenly he had forgotten Morven, Crum and Sergeant Bunch too.

'Ooh, Wiggler, I'm puffed! I saw you and . . . I had to follow, I did. Couldn't wait a moment longer!'

'Nirry?' cried Wiggler. 'Nirry, is it you?'

Nirry gripped her side. 'I've left the mistress, Wiggler,' she gasped. 'Left the old cow, I have, and never going back I am, never . . . ooh, it's been such an adventure, I'll be telling you about it till we're old and grey! But now I'm never letting you out of my sight again, Wiggler Olch . . . and if you get yourself killed tomorrow, there'll be trouble, I'm telling you now!'

With that, Nirry burst into tears.

'Nirry! Oh Nirry, my dear, dear Nirry!'

A little later, the young couple were banging on the door of the company chaplain.

It was a hasty wedding, and a simple one.

But for Nirry, it was the happiest moment of her life.

Chapter 70

THE RING AND RHEEN OF SWORDS

'Jem, stop! I can't – oh, I'm puffed!'

'So am I!'

'We've given them the slip, haven't we?'

'Must have.'

'What a chase!'

Desperate, they had blundered here, there, forwards, backwards, through a warren of alleys in the darkest reaches of the city. There were places where the eaves of the mean houses teetered together so closely that not even the Hornlight moon could penetrate the tunnel-like depths below. Seldom were there tapers, let alone lamps to light the way; they scurried like rats through dark foundations. There were places where the stench – of garbage, of flowing sewage – was so overwhelming that it was this, the stench alone, that drove them on. Sometimes there were cries. Sometimes, footsteps slap-slapped behind them. Always they were aware of their own straining limbs, their pounding hearts, the breath tearing painfully from their lungs.

They collapsed against a vine-covered wall. The dark tunnels were behind them now, and the moon shone sharply, painfully.

'Jem?'

'Raj?'

'Only one problem.'

'What's that?'

'We've lost the Bluejackets. How can we find the place?'

'I think we might be close.' Jem laughed abruptly. 'In fact, Temple Close.'

A bell was tolling mournfully, somewhere over their heads. Jem stepped back from the vine-covered wall, drawing Rajal with him into the cobbled lane. Yes, it was as he thought. Sometimes the alleys had sloped up, sometimes down, but nonetheless it seemed to him that they had been climbing, always a little higher, higher into the city. He gestured downwards. Looking over the ramparts on the other side of the lane, they saw the dark city stretched below, and beyond, the watch-fires, orange and red and gold, glimmering like angry stars against the Fields of Ajl. They turned. Now Jem gestured upwards, and above the wall of vines they saw the entangled trees and weeds of an overgrown garden, pierced in the centre by a vast golden spire, wreathed in golden vines. The sight was astonishing, for the spire might have been some strange outgrowth of the garden.

'The Temple,' Jem breathed. 'We saw it from the hills.'

'Then somewhere round here—'

'The Shopkeeper!'

'But where?'

For a moment they peered curiously round the curve of the lane. They were about to begin their investigations in earnest when voices sounded suddenly from the archway behind them.

'Bluejackets!'

'Jem! There's a passage! Quick!'

Intent on the Temple, Jem had not seen the narrow gap in the vine-covered wall. They darted into the opening, their shoulders scraping against rustling leaves. The passage was a short one, emerging in the space of a few steps into a mean courtyard. On one side, the lane side, was a low-lintelled door. Beside the door was a shuttered window, and in the window a lantern was burning. On the other side hung a screen of trailing roots and weeds, hanging from the thickly wooded precincts above. A flight of stone steps, furred thickly with moss, led up towards the Temple grounds.

The voices came again, echoing now in the passage behind them. 'Damn them, damn them, where can they be?'

'They're following us!' said Jem. 'Did they see us?'

'I don't know.'

Swiftly they hid behind the screening foliage. Above, in the Temple, a bell was still tolling. It would toll all that night, deeply and slowly, keeping its lonely vigil until the painful dawn.

※　※　※　※　※

'They must be somewhere,' said the first Bluejacket.

'They won't hide for long,' said the second. He stepped forward, thumping at the door. A groan of protest came from within. The lantern shifted from the window-sill. Then came another long, tired groan, and the sounds of a bolt, drawing back.

'What is this place?' said the first Bluejacket.

'Caretaker's cottage.'

'Caretaker? Of what?'

'Why, the tombyard, of course!'

They laughed heartily.

'There he is,' Jem whispered.

An old man was standing in the doorway. In the cowled garb of a

Zenzan peasant, he held his lantern aloft in his hand, peering up irritably at the Bluejacket guards.

They were a shabby pair. One had neglected to shave; his chin was stubbled like a Harion cornfield. The other wore a jacket stained liberally with beer.

In answer to their questions, the old man only grunted. Had he seen two fellows? Fellows going past? Heard footfalls in the lane? Running? Fleeing? Emptily the phrases echoed round the courtyard.

Dangerous rebels.

Two young brigands.

Stolen uniforms.

'What's that?' The old man spoke for the first time. 'Dressed as Bluejackets, you say? Like you?'

The Bluejackets nodded.

'Why—' a wheezing laugh '—then how do I know they are *not* you?' And how—' the wheeze veered towards a cough '—how do *you* know you are not? Look towards yourselves, my fine young fellows, look towards yourselves before you search for another!'

The old man coughed in earnest, hacking and hawking.

It was during this exchange that Jem, then Rajal, became aware of an alarming fact. They were not alone in their place of concealment. Something – something breathing – was brushing about their legs. Jem felt the scratch of an experimental claw.

Please, he thought, clamping shut his mouth. *Please.*

'Why,' said Beerjacket, 'the old man is crazed!'

'Come,' said Harion Cornfield, 'we're wasting our time here. Shall we search the tombyard?'

'Do we have to? It's a Zenzan tombyard ... Those twisted trees! It's evil.'

'Oh, don't be so wet!'

Jem and Rajal exhaled slowly as the soldiers clattered up the mossy steps. But the old man did not close the cottage door. Instead he lingered for some moments until he was sure his visitors were gone.

'Ring!' he called in a whisper. 'Ring!'

A low, dissonant howl was the reply. Rajal gasped. Jem jumped. A sturdy tail whipped about their calves and a large, ugly tom-cat pushed his way from the screening foliage.

'Yes, my pretty. Ah, yes.' The old man shuffled out into the courtyard. His gnarled back bent further, his hand stretched forward; the flame of his lantern flickered and danced. 'My poor pretty. You're hungry, aren't you? Frightened? Don't worry, the bad men are gone now.'

As he said this the old man looked up, and for a moment Jem and Rajal were certain he was looking at them, staring directly into their hiding-place. Could it be? The caretaker was old, very old; his eyes must be dim, and the darkness was deep beyond the lantern-light.

'Dear Ring! Sweet Ring!' he was saying now. 'Did you catch many rats today? What's that? A tender little mother-mouse, and her six hairless babies?' The howl, by now, was a thunderous purr. The cat weaved in and out of the old man's legs, buffing its big head happily, excitedly. 'Lucky Ring, such sweet-meats! Why, in the time of Siege, that mouse wouldn't have been left for you, would it? Not even the babies! ... What's that? And a big succulent vole, too? Come, you have earned your dish of milk.'

The old man shuffled back inside the door, but as he was about to draw it shut behind him he turned back to the courtyard and added quietly, 'And I think you'd better join us, my young friends.'

Jem and Rajal exchanged glances.

Uncertainly, they stepped forward.

As they were entering the cottage, it occurred to them both that they could simply leave, pushing back through the passage into the lane. They could soon be far from the scene. Why, in straits as dire as this, should they obey the command of a weak old man?

But somehow they felt they could not go, not yet. The old man led them into an apartment as ignoble as its low-lintelled door.

A sour stench assailed them. They looked around in the lantern-light. The floor was made of dirt and there was no furniture besides a wormy table, a couple of rickety chairs and, underneath the window, a narrow, smelly couch. A little black stove burnt in one corner, but barely served to drive out the sepulchral cold. There were no books, no ornaments. Everything was squalid, ugly, mean. Only one feature of the room gave a different impression, not so much relieving the poverty as suggesting that once, at least, or elsewhere, things had been better. This was a heavy green curtain, like a theatre-curtain, covering the entirety of the wall opposite the window. Mildewed now, and moth-eaten, it could have been taken from the drawing-room of quality-folk – stolen perhaps, and cut down to fit this hovel.

With an unexpected graciousness – as if, indeed, he were showing them into that fine drawing-room – the old man bade them be seated. Repairing to the stove, he fussed with blackened pannikins, heating the dubious milk he poured from a still more dubious jug.

'How pleasant to have visitors,' he twittered. 'Hm, Ring? So seldom, so seldom, but tonight ... why, twice! But wait – am I wrong?' The old man turned, peering at the guests. He had set down the lantern on the table between them, circling Jem and Rajal in its fluttering haze. 'You're the same who just came to my door, are you not? I'm sure of it! Still not found what you're looking for? Well, well! Did I not say you must look to yourselves?'

The wheezing laugh rang out again. In the squalid little apartment it was louder, harsher, taking on a strangely sinister aspect.

In a moment the milk was ready and the old man set down three dishes on the table. One was for Jem. One was for Rajal. The third was for Ring. Tenderly the old man lifted the cat from the floor. Jem and Rajal exchanged glances. Not only was Ring an extraordinarily ugly creature, with torn ears, dripping eyes and scabious patches of mange; he also stank abominably. Jem shrank back as the cat stuck his hairless tail in the air, revealing a warty pucker of anus and a single, swollen testicle.

The old man hovered about the table, rubbing his hands. 'Ring drinks eagerly, does he not? See, he remembers the time of Siege. His poor ribs were sticking out of his sides – weren't they, my pretty? But come, friends, why do you not drink, like Ring?'

The answer was easy. Jem looked down at the steaming dish before him.

The milk was green.

'But good sir, we are denying you – please . . .' Jem pushed his dish towards the old man, but a hand waved the offer impatiently away. Jem shifted uncertainly. Had he offended their host? The voice that issued from beneath the cowl took on a suddenly sharp tone.

'You don't appreciate my hospitality? Well, hoity-toity—' then the laugh again '—there's some who do!'

The old man swung towards the green curtain. To Rajal, who faced the curtain, it seemed as if their host were about to throw himself into the wall. But in the next moment the curtain billowed back and Rajal realized that it was a partition, concealing some further part of the room beyond. There was a clattering from within, as if this further part of the room were as cluttered as the other was sparse. Something fell to the floor and smashed.

The old man emerged with a little cage.

'Ring?' he began in a wheedling voice. 'I've something for you, my pretty. Something special.'

Rajal brought a hand up to his face. Jem gripped the rim of his dish. Both wanted to protest, but somehow they could not. Ring looked up, his whiskers dripping milk, and gave a rattling purr.

Inside the cage was a white hamster.

With a click the cage was open, and the hamster was on the table. Shocked, Jem gripped his milk-dish tighter; then all at once, in a spasm of nerves, brought the dish to his lips.

He swigged.

491

He spluttered.

A foulness, like vomit, coursed through his throat.

But what happened next was not what should have happened. The hamster scurried towards the cat. The cat gave the hamster a light, friendly cuff. Then, side by side on the table-top, with all the ardour neither Jem nor Rajal could muster, the two animals lapped at the malignant milk as if it were the finest, freshest cream.

The old man chuckled. Leaning over the table, he fondled the tom-cat's ruined ears.

'Dear Ring, he loves Rheen so.'

'Rheen?' Rajal's brow furrowed.

'But I don't let him see Rheen every day, do I? Only when Ring's been a *very* good boy. But young sirs, would you like to see a game they play?'

The old man did not wait for the answer, vanishing through the curtain again; again came the clattering before something else fell to the floor and shattered.

Jem pushed back his chair. He said loudly, 'Well, Raj, I really think—'

But before he could continue, the old man was back. If he had been offended before, now he seemed to be possessed only by a febrile excitement. In his hands he held two little wooden crosses. Each was made of one long stick and a shorter cross-stick, forming a †-shape; on each, the longest end was sharpened, and attached to the shortest was a leather thong. They were swords – little wooden swords. With cackles of delight the old man fastened one to a front paw of Ring; then he did the same to Rheen. Quickly he moved the dishes out of the way as cat and hamster began their friendly duel. Like a Silverby hero, transformed mysteriously into a rodent, little Rheen reared up on his back paws, parrying boldly.

Jem groaned. This was too foolish. He juddered back his chair again, 'I really think—'

But for a third time the old man had disappeared. For a third time the curtain billowed, and there came a clattering; but this time, instead of a crash came a high, anguished wail.

Rajal started.

Jem jumped up; but then he was almost knocked out of the way as the old man blundered back through the curtain, his sleeves flapping as he squashed and dragged, squashed and dragged, coercing a tune from a battered old squeezebox. As the absurd duel continued, with a crazed merriment the old man capered round the table, his arms work-ing like bellows, his knees kicking up beneath his robes as he sang breathlessly:

Everything is . . . kitten and nothing is . . . twine,
And what? Is the hamster . . . pickled in brine?
Come, let us . . . strap on our weapons with . . . cords,
And clash like the . . . Ring and Rheen of . . .

'Stop it!' Jem burst out.

The song seemed to burn into his ears like acid. There was something vile about it, something diseased. What spell was this old man trying to cast, what dreadful beguiling? Jem swept his arm across the table. The little swords went flying. With a yowl, Ring leapt free; Rheen vanished, Jem was not sure where; the old man, coughing and laughing, collapsed across the smelly couch beneath the window.

Chapter 71

CARAPACE OF CLAY

First there was the dark. Not the dark of the night that had been, streaked with the golden rays of the moon. This was blackness, utter blackness. Then there was the stench, a terrible dank rottenness. Concentrated in this effluvia, it seemed, was the vileness of all the world. It was the stench of the torture-chamber when the floor is awash with entrails; the stench of corpses when the skin has rotted and the putrefied organs inside have burst.

Polty would have cried out, but something stopped his mouth. He winced, or would have done, but something seemed to press upon the muscles of his face. He would have raised his arm, pushing the burden away; then he realized that his limbs too were freighted with the same mysterious weight.

Only slowly did Polty recall what had happened, but it was not with horror, only a calm acceptance, that he saw again in his mind the thing they had called the Vichy, immense, dripping with mud, bearing down upon him. What happened after that he could not say. In that muddy embrace he thought his death had come. But he had been saved for this new and strange fate.

Polty wondered how it was that he could breathe. How could his lungs even swell out his chest? How could the merest particle of air find its way through the clods of earth – for yes, it was earth – that pressed all around him? But then a strange awareness came to him, and he did not wonder any more; for Polty saw that indeed he was dead, or that the life he knew now was no natural life. He was not breathing. The senses that gave him awareness were senses beyond the mortal.

At first Polty thought he was buried beneath the ground. Then he knew that this was not true. In the pressing earth, the earth itself, there was a presence, a being. It was the power that gave him this deathly awareness; the power, too, that held him.

He was inside the Vichy.

'Come on, Raj,' said Jem. 'We're going.'

But Rajal was still sitting at the table, gazing at the place where the duel had been, and if he raised his eyes from the table it was only to stare still more fixedly into the green of the billowing curtain.

'Raj, I said come on. Raj, THE TIME HAS COME.'

But all Rajal said was, 'The Ring and Rheen of Swords?'

'Why stop there?' the old man cackled.

Suddenly Rajal jumped up, vacant-eyed, jerking like a puppet. He capered about the room, stamping, babbling, 'Why stop there? Why stop there? The Sting and Steen of Swords! The Ting and Teen! The Ping and Peen! The Ving and Veen!'

With mad cacklings the old man joined in, 'The Ying and Yeen! The Bing and Been!'

'The Hing!'

'The Heen!'

'The Jing and Jeen!'

'Stop it!' cried Jem.

But they did not.

'The Ling and Leen!'

'The Drin and Dreen!'

The old man leapt up. *'The Grin!'* he cried.

There was a pause. For a moment it seemed it was over. Tears were streaming down Rajal's face as he raised his arm, pointing a trembling finger at the curtain.

'The Green,' he whispered. 'The Green.'

It was the colour, too, of Jem's face. He stepped forward and with one quick, sharp jerk would have torn at the curtain; instead he started, suddenly sickened, as his foot skidded in a slimy mess.

All that stamping.

All that capering.

It was Rheen, squashed flat, his guts smeared across the hard dirt floor.

Ring looked on, miaowing piteously.

Trembling, Jem looked to the old man; the old man rose up, beckoning him forward. A hand delved into the interior of his robes and he produced a dog-eared, dirty deck of cards. He shuffled them quickly, carelessly, then dealt a hand to Jem, slapping the cards down harshly on the tabletop. Jem sought the old man's gaze, but the cowled face turned away. He looked at Rajal, but Rajal still stared, unblinking, at the curtain. Slowly Jem uncovered his five cards. The first two were commonplace enough – an Eight of Rings, a Four of Quills.

The third was the harlequin.

The fourth, the fifth?

But of course. The King and Queen of Swords.

495

'Who are you?' There was violence in Jem's voice. He might have been about to grab the old man, shake him, beat him.

He did neither.

The old man had bent down, clawing at the smeared mess that had been the hamster. Coolly, passionlessly, while the cat miaowed, he gathered into his scooping hands the guts, the fur, the bloody dirt. Then, at the moment when Jem asked his question, the old man wrung his hands together. Blood squeezed through his clamping knuckles; then he released his grip and a brilliantly coloured bird fluttered upwards into the air.

It was a beckoning-bird, a Wenaya-dove.

'Who are you?' Jem cried, but the Wenaya-dove was beating madly, madly about the upper reaches of the room. It blundered into the green curtain. That was the moment when Rajal cried out. That was when the rotted fabric gave way, dropping to reveal the strange room beyond, mired in filth and immense draping cobwebs. Penetrating into the dusty depths, the lamplight disclosed walls lined with shelf after shelf, piled high with bottles, boxes, bags, books, bolts of fabric, and the rear of a long bench, divided into all manner of crammed compartments.

But of course, it was not a bench. It was a counter, and the Wenaya-dove came to rest on it, calling out its distinctive cry:

Ul-ul-ul-ul-ul!

Now Jem looked deeper into the shadows. He saw that the window and door of the shop were overgrown completely. In the lane, he recalled, they had leaned against a vine-covered wall; in truth, it had been the window – perhaps the door – of the Shopkeeper of Wrax.

Jem turned to the Shopkeeper. He might have asked him to explain himself; instead he only whispered, 'THE TIME HAS COME.'

❋ ❋ ❋ ❋ ❋

The time had come.

Lying in the grip of his dark paralysis, Polty knew that his life had reached a new and vital turning. For so long, for too long, he had lived only for himself. For Polty, there had been nothing but his own clamorous ego, bombinating at the walls of an empty sanctum. Now, slowly, his emptiness was filled. Now, slowly, his destiny was revealed to him.

Inside the Vichy, it was growing warmer. The dank mud was drying, baking like a vessel of clay in a fire. Soon the heat would be searing – searing, that is, to a man not held in the grip of strange powers. In this heat, Polty's skin might have reddened, then blackened; his lips might have shrivelled from his parched mouth and his eyeballs, the lids charred away, burst in twin ejaculations of jelly. Perhaps, in one dimension, these things really happened. But for Polty there was no pain, no terror

496

now. Instead, his awareness stretched far beyond his confinement, rippling out as if along the fibres of a web, a web so vast as to span the world.

He was at one with the Creatures of Evil. Spinning through his brain he saw huge hideous serpents, spiders, maggots; he saw women and men with animal faces – faces of wolves, apes, elephants – and birds, shrieking through the sky with flaming wings. In Agondon, he saw things like entrails, slithering through the filth beneath the surface of the Riel; in Varby, he saw the mad cavorting wraiths, bursting from their cave and prancing downhill, gleefully strewing infection through the valley. To the furthest corners of the world Polty's awareness stretched, vibrating along the tautened web, and everywhere he saw the same loathsome things, elated in the knowledge of their coming triumph.

'Yes,' he whispered to himself, 'THE TIME HAS COME.'

❄ ❄ ❄ ❄ ❄

Yet time, for a moment, seemed strangely suspended. For a moment, the Shopkeeper said nothing. He had turned away, reaching down to pet his mangy cat, but when he rose again his back had acquired an unexpected straightness and his voice, all at once, had unaccountably changed.

'The time? The time? Ah, but for such a long time I have kept my vigil. Strange, is it not, that for so long, so unconscionably long, the twine of time should play out as if the end will never come. Then all at once we tug sharply at – oh, this tangle, or that, and all we hold in our fingers is a fraying end. At that moment, infinity has shrunk to a pin-prick, and eternity turns on the tick of a clock. That moment lies before us now.'

Jem drew in his breath. The voice, he knew at once, was a familiar one, but before he could reveal his suspicion, a plaintive *miaow!* came from the floor. The curtain, when it had fallen, had covered Ring.

'My poor pretty!'

The Shopkeeper laughed, but made no move to set the cat free. Beneath the fabric, the writhings became wilder, then the *miaow!* became deeper, richer; it seemed that the creature was growing, changing. It was Rajal who stepped forward, twitching away the fallen curtain. He staggered back. The mangy cat had become huge and magnificent, striped black and gold.

'Wood-tiger!' said Jem.

The tiger padded round them, looking up mournfully through golden, flashing eyes.

'Not the true tiger,' the Shopkeeper explained, 'but a convincing version, would you not say? Ring and Rheen are metamorphs. Once, many such creatures roamed these lands, before they were banished to the Realm of Unbeing. My power protects Ring and Rheen and keeps them here, when all their fellows have been spirited away. With no fixed essence, they are able to take on the shape of any creatures they choose. Sometimes Ring takes his turn to be the rodent; sometimes, Rheen is a mighty, savage beast.'

Jem said quietly, 'I think, Shopkeeper, that you too are a shape-shifter of sorts.'

There was no need to say more. The Shopkeeper pushed back his cowl, shrugged away the robes he had worn. Underneath was a habit of green. Long auburn tresses sprang free.

'Priestess Ajl!' cried Rajal.

The Priestess laughed, 'But of course, my young friends! Who else would be guardian of the mocking-tree? The "Shopkeeper" is but a legend, that's all, twisted and contorted in the tangles of time.'

'But Priestess, you said I was a fool!' gasped Jem. 'You said my quest would fail—'

'How could I know you were the true one, the one I have awaited for so long, so interminably long? Even when you saw the goddess, could I know this was more than illusion? Could I know you were not deceiving me? Ah, across the aeons, there have been so many false seekers – so many . . .'

'Aeons?'

But the Priestess did not reply. For a moment there was a faraway look in her eyes. Then suddenly she seized the lantern from the table, darting to the door. 'But come – quick!'

'Priestess, where?'

'Where, Prince Jemany? Did you not say THE TIME HAD COME?'

She rushed into the night, her green habit billowing behind her as she clattered up the mossy steps towards the tombyard. Jem and Rajal had no choice but to follow. Cawing and crying, Rheen was flying above their heads; Ring, on his sturdy paws, bounded in their wake.

'Priestess!' Rajal was alarmed. 'The Bluejackets—'

'The fools! What would they do, halt destiny itself?'

❊ ❊ ❊ ❊ ❊

Could this be destiny?

Whether what he saw was prophecy, whether reality, Polty did not know; yet it seemed certain that even now, as he lay in this paralysis, the Creatures of Evil were rising, stirring as if from sleep. For epicycles, some had concealed themselves in this world, hiding in places that humans would shun; now they would come forward, brazen and bold. Others, long-banished to the Realm of Unbeing, were slithering, creeping, crawling through the million gaps and fissures in the walls of this

world. Sometimes they would slip through a grating in a street, sometimes through a crack in a vanity-glass; sometimes, they would heave
themselves up through graves, leaving the corpses exposed to the air.

These vilest of things were the Rejects of the Ur-God, his own botched
creations he had sought to destroy. Now these things would come forth
and multiply, for now their master, their King had come – but no, not
their King.

Their god, their new god.

TOTH, comes the mantra, TOTH, TOTH.

A new age was dawning, an age of pestilence, of wars and wild
catastrophes. Polty ached with longing. Round and round his brain
whizzed the images of horror; harder, harder his heart pounded, as if in
its excitement it would burst the baking clay. Now, the myriad vile
things were suddenly gone; now, in their stead, came a single face, a
face more terrible than any before. It was a god that once loomed in a
glass, in a chamber deep beneath the Great Temple. Now that god was
loose in the world. Released from his long confinement, he had slowly
gathered his strength. Now he was summoning his servants to him,
readying himself to begin his work.

TOTH, came the tom-tom in Polty's brain. Around him, the carapace
of clay began to crack.

Polty was hatching, as if from an egg.

❋ ❋ ❋ ❋ ❋

Above, in the Temple, the bell was still tolling as they hurried deeper,
deeper among the trees. Wildly the lantern-light veered through the
darkness, swaying, scooping, dipping across the foliage. This was the
Forest of the Dead, where for epicycles the great-folk of the realm had
been buried according to the Rites of Viana. Trees were planted above
the bodies of the dead, and these trees, it had been decreed, must never
be cut down. Long ago, all over Zenzau, Ejlanders had destroyed these
sacred places. Only this oldest tombyard, here on the highest of the Hills
of Wrax, was left, perhaps as a curiosity, perhaps because it made, with
the old Temple at its centre, a striking centrepiece to Ejland's finest
imperial jewel.

Or perhaps the power of the sacred, when it was strong enough, could
reach out and touch even Zenzau's conquerors.

'Priestess!' Jem called, urgently now. 'What did you mean, *aeons*?'

By now the bell was growing louder. They followed a winding path,
leading towards the Temple. A vast doorway loomed before them.
Decorated richly in gold and precious stones, it rose out of the Forest of
the Dead like an immense, forbidding sepulchre. Only now, in the
portico, did the Priestess turn back. Lamplight made her face a grotesque

499

play of shadows and sparkled against the rich doors like harsh, mocking stars. She spoke rapidly in a low voice, but the question she answered was not quite the one Jem had asked.

'Prince Jemany, for aeons there have been those who would possess the power of the crystal. Torvester of Irion was one such. He had studied the arts of the Koros-tribe, and knew much of magic; but he was endowed, too, with a shadow-power of his own.'

Jem said, 'Shadow-power? What shadow? Whose?'

'Why, Prince Jemany, whose shadow but yours? When a person is possessed of great power, we see in those close to him some reflection of that power. Torvester is your uncle, but when your father was lost to you, spiritually he became your father, too. Consequently his powers were great – as great, that is, as shadow-powers may be. But ah, alas, the use to which he put them!

'In the Siege of Irion, he convinced himself that only through some special, magical weapon could we triumph – and to triumph, he was convinced, would be worth any sacrifice. Sensing his powers, I was fool enough to believe that we could harness to our purposes the – the ... But no.' The Priestess waved a dismissive hand. 'You must know only so much, to carry out your mission. Only so much, and no more.' She touched a face made of carved gold and a hatch opened in the enormous doorway. 'Come!'

'Wait!' Jem grabbed her arm. Suddenly it seemed imperative to know everything, everything. 'The experiment – the explosion—'

'The mocking-tree, defending itself against violation.' The Priestess sighed; for a moment she looked old, terribly old, and made no effort to break from Jem's grip. 'Oh, what a fool Torvester was! What a fool I was, not to stop him!'

'But the highwayman—'

'The Scarlet One believes we can repeat the experiment. But he is mistaken – I have beguiled him. To one who has turned his back on truth, the truth cannot be told.'

There were more questions Jem would have asked, but the Priestess rallied. With a further barked command of 'Come!', she drew him after her into the dark interior of the doorway. He stepped forward; but when Rajal would have followed, too, the Priestess held up a hand.

'Koros-child, I am sorry. This is not for your eyes.'

Jem was about to protest when a shout rang out behind them. They reeled back towards the portico.

'The Bluejackets!' cried Rajal.

They burst from the undergrowth, jabbing with their bayonets. In the same moment there was a mighty roar. Ring pounced; Rheen swooped down; and all at once, instead of a rainbow-dove, the bird was a huge black vulture. In their terror the soldiers dropped their weapons, then shielded themselves ineffectually with their hands, first from the tiger's mauling claws, then the vulture's talons, then the harsh beak that pecked their eyes.

'No!' said Jem.

'Make them stop!' cried Rajal. He leapt forward; the Priestess gasped as he wrested the glowing lamp from her grip, flinging it into the fray. There was a crash of glass, a sizzle of flames.

Too late, too late.

Jem gasped; Rajal put a hand up to his mouth. The Priestess only laughed, and her laugh was harsh and cruel; it seemed that the cackle of the crazed old caretaker had not, after all, been entirely false.

Chapter 72

THE CARDS COME ALIVE

In the moonlight that shone through high leaded windows, Rajal made out a chamber of great riches. There were bejewelled pillars, a gleaming lectern. There were glimmerings of vines, leaves, branches, fashioned luxuriously from silver and gold. A strange, shivery feeling came over him, and it occurred to him that he had never, in all his life, been inside a temple. It would never have been allowed.

But the Priestess made no further efforts to stop him entering now. She seemed to have forgotten he was there at all.

He whispered, 'What's that glow?'

'Moonlight?' said Jem.

No, it was more than moonlight. Then Jem saw it too. It was the green glow he had witnessed earlier, playing about the clearing when the goddess had descended. Now it flickered up first one, then another, of the ornate pillars that supported the ceiling. Like strewn emeralds, spots of green sparkled on the richly inlaid slabs of the floor, then shimmered and danced on the golden leaves that loomed obscurely above the vast altar.

'They think it only an image, an artifice,' the Priestess was murmuring, moving slowly up the aisle. She seemed to be talking to herself, and her voice was old and weary. 'What is it, in truth, but the Tree of Faith, gilded over by the men-priests epicycles ago, after they drove my Sisterhood from these heights? The fools! In their pursuit of lies, even their own foul blasphemies have been forgotten to them. Around the tree they raised this palace of folly, and called it true religion. Pah! Where is their religion now? How can it help us?'

Jem was barely listening to her words. Following her, he was troubled. Shaken by the incident at the doors, he no longer knew whether to trust the Priestess, whether to believe she was a Priestess at all. Could she, too, be some mysterious shape-shifter, her form no more stable than Ring's or Rheen's? Once again her back was bent and her steps by now were almost a shuffle, as if unknowingly she were slipping back into the guise of the crazed old man.

Before the altar, she turned. Stiffly she mounted the lectern. Only then, when she looked down at him from on high, did Jem see her face again. He gasped, staggering back. Since entering the temple the Priestess had become rapidly, horribly wizened. She might have assumed some grotesque actor's mask; it might have been the face of a corpse. Only her eyes were still possessed of life, glowing with the same unearthly green that played in every corner of the vast sepulchral chamber.

Now the Priestess began to speak again. As she spoke the green glow around her became brighter too, and the altar emerged clearly from the gloom. Jem could not keep his eyes from it, nor could Rajal. The altar was lined with green baize, and rising from the baize was a vast tree. Its thick trunk, its many branches, its abundant leaves were all made of gold, and hanging from the boughs were many golden fruits. In awkward reverence, Jem sank to his knees. Rajal hung back, trembling, clinging to a pillar.

The Priestess spoke in a solemn, level voice, as if she were reciting a lesson she had delivered many times – too many times – before. It was the tale of the King and Queen of Swords, the tale she had told the girl in far-off Agondon, through the mouth of the projection she called 'Aunt Vlada'.

How it had tired her to sustain the illusion!

Entranced, Rajal heard the tale echo inside his skull. But still Jem barely listened, only gazing, intent and fascinated, at the golden tree. The spectral glow that emanated from its branches formed a kind of aura, a ghostly radiance that seemed to be beckoning him into its embrace. Tremblingly at first, then with a sudden boldness, Jem stepped forward.

It was then that a remarkable change came over the scene. The green glow grew and intensified in a slow, diffuse flash. For a moment Jem was blinded, but when the moment and the flash faded, he found himself standing in bright daylight, near the top of a grassy hill. Dandelions and daisies waved in the warm air. Gossamer insects wheeled lazily by.

Jem looked around him. It was a place he had been before, but now more vivid, now more real. Below lay two great semicircular plains. Five hills, thickly wooded, ranged in a ring around the hill on which he stood, for he was standing where he had been just a moment ago, but the Temple and the city and the armies were gone, the land returned to a primaeval innocence. Before him, dominating the summit of the hill, was the mocking-tree.

Now all the gilding was gone from the tree, and it was garbed only in bark and leaves of green.

A sigh rippled up Jem's body. Reverently he approached the tree. Behind him, looking on, was Priestess Ajl; she had returned again to the youth and beauty she had lost, but her form now was strangely insubstantial, fluttering and shimmering, as if perhaps it had become merely a mirage of the heat. Some distance from her, Rajal lay in the long grass, immobilized by the languor of the bright day. In the scene that was to come, he would struggle even to keep open his eyes, feeling himself lost in a strange and troubling dream.

Through all this, time was strangely distended.

❊ ❊ ❊ ❊ ❊

Hara's Feast dawns brightly over the Fields of Ajl. The thudding of drums begins again at first light. Then come the calls of imperative bugles, as troops – some in blue, some in green, some in red, some in rags – muster along the lines of the Ring and Rheen.

A hush of expectancy falls over the fields. First come the solitary riders, galloping with impunity uphill and down, bearing messages between the two commanders. Shots ring out just as the sun is spilling the first of its golden warmth into the greenness that lies below. That year, the Season of Viana has reached an early ripeness. Leaves burst and burgeon in the hills all around. In the fields, dandelions and daisies peer through the grasses that soon shall be crushed and stained with blood.

The infantry comes first, thousand upon thousand of wide-eyed young foot-soldiers, trudging forward with bayonets at the ready. Early skir-mishes are uncertain, almost shy. But soon there comes one, then another, leap of blood. The armies are like beasts, huge and fearsome, that rouse themselves only slowly from sleep, but then are possessed of a terrible power. Soon the golden air is a haze of smoke. Soon the neat battle-lines give way to chaos. Here, the charge of the Derkold pitchforks, there the clanging of steel upon steel; there the trundling of a Bluejacket gun-carriage, here a burning haystack, rolling downhill.

And somewhere in it all are faces we know. Somewhere is the rightful King of Ejland, bent on redeeming the honour he has lost. Somewhere is Orvik, the valiant fool, ready to go forth in his golden armour. Somewhere are Hul, Bando, Zady, Wiggler, Rotts, Sergeant Floss.

Somewhere in it all is Cata too.

❊ ❊ ❊ ❊ ❊

Slowly Jem circled the mocking-tree. It was then that he noticed, from the corner of his eye, the forms of Ring and Rheen – for he was sure it was they – altered again to a gorgeous panther, a fleecy-backed lamb. They hovered close by, circling and pacing, always not quite in the range of his vision.

Beneath the spreading branches, Jem sank to his knees. He looked up, gazing into the green of the leaves. In that moment it seemed that a meaning was impending, a meaning so profound that for the rest of his days it would fill him with wonderment and gratitude.

'Jemany,' came a voice.

Someone was holding out a parchment to him, a parchment scored over with a thousand strange hieroglyphs. First Jem looked wonderingly at the hieroglyphs, then up, up into the face of the one who held the parchment.

But he could not quite make out who it was.

'Harlequin?' said Jem. 'Harlequin, is that you?'

He looked around him, but it was a lazy, idle look. Yes, he was about to receive all the world's wisdom, and the harlequin was looking on, benevolent and smiling. The thought came to him that if only he slept here, slept here as it would be so pleasant to do, when he awoke he would know everything he had ever wanted to know.

Meanwhile Rajal screwed up his eyes. He could not see the figure that held the parchment, only Jem sinking down to sleep like a dog, curled round the trunk of the mocking-tree.

But no, there was something else. Something more. Appearing beneath the branches was a set of curious objects. There were silver goblets; there were golden boxes; there were gourds fashioned from long, curling horns; there were lutes, viols – for a moment, Rajal even thought he saw a band of minstrels, plucking and sawing at these instruments.

Illusion, to be certain; yet it seemed that a familiar tune was nonetheless floating, like the perfume of the grass and flowers, on the air around this magical hillside. Rajal felt a wash of deep, implacable sorrow. The song was one he had sung many times; why should it make him so sad, so sad?

He struggled to focus his eyes again, and among the many objects that lay about the tree his gaze came to rest on the golden boxes. On the lid of each box, a human form was carved; and slowly, blurrily through the waving grass, Rajal made them out. The knowledge came to him. Ah, yes. The *zenzals*. The first box bore the marking of the suit of Quills; there were boxes for Wheels, Spires, Rings.

There was no box, it seemed, for Swords.

Then Rajal saw the face, peering around the tree-trunk. The gimlet eyes, the forky beard! It was the King of Swords, exactly as he appeared on the sets of cards. The evil King rubbed his long hands, looking down with pleasure at Jem's curled body, falling into a stupor beneath the mocking-tree.

Suddenly Rajal was frightened; suddenly he understood, or thought he understood. This was a game, a game they must win. Still he could not raise himself from the grass where he lay. He called to the Priestess, but she could not help; she had become the merest spectre, transparent

and flickering. He looked to Ring and Rheen, but the shape-shifters –
one now a white goose, one a red fox – only chased happily here, there,
beneath the broad, spreading branches.

'Jem!' Rajal called, in the moment before his senses began to fail him
again. 'Jem! The boxes!'

It was all Rajal could do, but it was enough for now. Jem stirred,
raising his heavy head. What trick was this? Looming before his eyes
again was the parchment, but the hands that held it, he saw now, had
long and cruel talons, and hanging from the face that loomed above was
a flaming, forky beard.

'The King of Swords!'

※ ※ ※ ※ ※

It was a ragged battle, and unequal, but less unequal than some had
thought. Puffed up on power, the Bluejacket generals were lazy, barely
attentive. Too contemptuous of mere Zenzans to believe they posed any
but the flimsiest of threats, they found their first defences rapidly
breached. At once, urgent reprisals were in train.

Orvik's forces were desperate. All their hopes depended upon this
battle, and every man believed passionately in the cause. There could be
no surrender. They would batter through the gates of Wrax that day, or
die in the effort on the Fields of Ajl.

In hand-to-hand fighting, Orvik's men were supreme. But all their
ardour was as nothing against an army which made up what it lacked
in belief – many times over, far too many – in numbers, equipment,
training. Cannon after cannon blazed from the blues. The Blue Ejard
Cavalry thundered forth. Triumphantly the blue conquerors swept
down, battering back the shabby lines of green, of red, of rags.

And high above the battle, the Temple bells kept tolling in the golden
spire.

※ ※ ※ ※ ※

Jem seized the parchment, rending it. The King cursed, and vanished
again behind the broad trunk of the tree.

Jem turned, looking back down the hillside. Outside the range of the
broad branches everything was now a blur to him, but on the edge of
his vision he saw the golden boxes, and saw that the box marked with
the Suit of Quills had sprung open, disgorging a Jack-in-the-box. The
ugly figure swayed back and forth on its spring, grinning its imbecile
grin.

But now Jem too heard the melody that seemed to come from invisible
players, as if the wind, stirring at the instruments that lay close by, were
enough to coax forth such music on to the air. For a moment Jem thought

it was a merry song, then perhaps a sad one, and snatches came to him of the songs he remembered – *Hey, ho! The circle is round . . . Lady Fine, Lady Fair, ran her fingers through his hair . . . When the sun was bright and the sun was gay . . .* Then came the last, inevitable modulation. *Everything is lemon and nothing is lime . . .* Ah, but what did that mean, what could it mean? Dreamily Jem listened as Ring and Rheen nuzzled round him. Curiously, both were now timber-wolves. He stroked their backs; they licked his fingers. Cross-legged, Jem sat beneath the tree, and was drifting again into a mindless contentment when something hit him on the crown of his head.

Suddenly Ring and Rheen were gone.

Or were they?

Perhaps it was the blow on the head, but in what followed Jem would have the curious sensation that he – Rajal, too – had become strangely divided. It was as if they were in two places at once. Still the scene beneath the mocking-tree unfolded, but through it all Jem felt another existence, swirling like a river beneath, above, around the one he knew now.

In a corner of his mind he saw the timber-wolves sprouting wings and taking flight, soaring up above the sunny hillside. But now they were no longer wolves. Now they had grown into immense birds.

But birds with scales, like serpents.

They were dragons, and Jem knew that Ring and Rheen had reached their ultimate incarnations. Then he saw himself – himself and Rajal – riding on their backs.

But no . . .

No. Jem still sat beneath the mocking-tree. Was this part of its mockery, this foolish dream? He rubbed his head, looking round him, and then something else filled his attention. In the grass beside him he saw an apple. But this was a most remarkable apple. He brought it to his mouth, licked it experimentally. Could it be? He had thought the gilding was gone from the tree, but this was an apple that was made of gold.

Jem looked up into the branches above him. At first he thought it was only the sun, flashing through the gaps in the green canopy, but he screwed up his eyes and looked again. Yes. It was true! All the apples on the tree were gold.

Jem sprang up. Suddenly it seemed imperative to possess the golden fruit. He shook the boughs, but the fruit would not fall. He scrambled at the trunk, searching for footholds, but all the branches were too high. He looked around him wildly. By now, the Priestess was almost invisible, but that was when Jem saw Rajal, gazing at him again, gazing distraught. Locked on the brink of the hillside, as if in a special dimension of his own, Rajal struggled to stand, but all the time it was as if an angry wind were pushing him back, back, and he could barely fight against it. The wind played the tune of 'The King and Queen of Swords' and suddenly, instead of struggling, Rajal began to sing. He slumped to his knees, scrambling forward, but all the time the song spilled from him, the melody veering wildly with uncontrolled breath.

Everything is lemon and nothing is lime . . .

Again Jem looked at the apples above him. Yes, he understood! Over long epicycles the words, it was certain, had been corrupted, changed, as the "Shopkeeper" story had changed, as the Sign of Coins had become Wheels; but the meaning was clear enough, clear enough now.

Lemon, yellow.

Lime, green.

But there were no green apples on this tree; the fruit that manifested itself to him now, Jem saw, was not the fruit he sought. It was barren, dead. He laughed, triumphant. Drifting back from behind the tree he heard the curses of the King of Swords, and at his feet the box sprang open that bore on its lid the Sign of Wheels.

Dust and ash floated from the box, drifting up to form greenish, smoky clouds.

❊ ❊ ❊ ❊ ❊

Fast within the walls of Wrax, looking down from the guardhouse windows, Nirry sighs and wrings her hands. Below, she can see nothing but a rising cloud of smoke, slashed through here and there with a blaze of red. Even here, the cannons are deafening, crashing in the air around her like thunder. Behind her, the room is filled with other army wives. Some are slumped inert; some are pacing earnestly; some, in a corner, are playing cards.

By now, all the men have been ordered to the front.

'Oh, Wiggler!' Nirry mutters to herself. 'Oh Wiggler, keep your ears low!'

A girl beside her is sobbing. Moments earlier, word has come that the girl's young man is dead, dragged back on a stretcher with his heart burst open. Now it seems the girl's heart too will burst. She cannot bring herself to go to the body. All she can do is sob and sob; all Nirry can do is put her arms around her.

But now there are whoops and cries in the corridors. Somewhere a door slams; from somewhere comes the slap-slap of running feet. The cannons below have still not ceased, but the cry of victory is already on the air.

'Victory!' shrieks one fat lady, spinning round, spilling slops from a tankard of ale. 'Victory is certain, they say!'

The fat lady looks a little like Umbecca, and Nirry takes a dislike to her at once. Capering joyously about the mean room, the Umbecca-lady tries to grab Nirry's hand. She would draw her into the dance, but Nirry only shakes her head in anger, hugging the sobbing girl tighter to her breast. Victory? What victory? Yet Nirry, too, feels a moment's elation, hoping her Wiggler will soon be back safely.

But what of Miss Cata?

Nirry's elation swiftly fades.

Jem staggered, choking in the smoke. For a moment he was blinded, but when his vision cleared he was looking at a table, a long table spread with a white cloth, laid for a lavish banquet. Cautiously Jem seated himself, and Rajal did too. All at once they were ravenously hungry. They looked down at the plates before them. The plates were made of gold, but all they contained were dirty old bones, already picked clean. They doubled over, moaning. But was it hunger they felt? Now it seemed that the emptiness inside them was something deeper, something more terrible. Tears came to their eyes. On the air, Rajal's song still continued, though Rajal himself had ceased to sing out its words; from somewhere too, as if from the dimension they had left, they still heard the tolling of the Temple bells.

'Welcome, friends!'

They looked up. At the head of the table sat the King of Swords; at the foot was the Queen. But between them, Jem and Rajal saw many familiar faces. In their hearts they knew this was another cruel trick, but the faces before them were so real, so alive. There was the highwayman, there were Hul and Bando, there was the Priestess, there was Lord Empster; there was Tor and the Tor-harlequin, then there was the Harlequin of the Silver Masks. Rajal saw the Great Mother, Zady, Myla too; Jem saw the dwarf Barnabas, seated up on a special box; he saw Pellam and Lady Elabeth; he even saw his Aunt Umbecca, tucking greedily into a huge orandy-pudding. Cata, Jeli and Landa sat side by side, talking behind their hands, dissolved in girlish giggles.

With each moment that passed, there were more and more guests, and the table, it seemed, grew longer and longer – yet all the time, it was shaded by the branches of the mocking-tree. Tending to the banqueters were five stylish footmen, dressed like the common-cards in the pack, with swords and big numerals embroidered on their tunics. Laughter, conversation, the swish of pouring wine, the chinking of cutlery and goblets and plates made a merry counterpoint to the tolling, tolling bell.

'Drink,' came the King of Swords now. He had left his place, and was standing behind Jem, holding out a goblet.

'Drink,' said the Queen, coming behind Rajal.

They looked along the table. All down its length were huge juicy chickens, turkeys, geese, swans, sucking-pigs, haunches of venison, sides of beef, udders-in-cream, lungs stuffed with onions and stomachs stuffed with turnips, all dripping with gravy and oozing fat. There were massive cakes, tarts and pies; but none of these things were what they wanted, none of these things could allay their hunger. Jem and Rajal felt alone, terribly alone, for though everyone they had ever loved or esteemed sat round this table with them, it seemed that none of them, not a single one, could see them, know them, touch them.

'Drink,' came the King again.

'Drink,' said the Queen.

Chapter 73

DRAGONFLIGHT

'Morvy, come and look!'

'I don't want to look!'

'Oh come on!'

'Crum, get back into bed!'

'Spoil-sport!'

The two friends were in the Wrax Infirmary. All down the long ward, nurses, surgeons and wounded men alike were lined up at the windows, straining for a sight of the battle below.

'Spoil-sport?' Morven spluttered, and would have launched into a long disquisition on the evils of war, the march of folly, man's inhumanity to man, and so forth. Instead he only sighed, 'What boots it' – he liked this expression – 'what boots it to waste one's words on an imbecile?'

'It's not every day you see a battle, Morvy. Come on, up with you.'

Morven pouted, 'All very well for you, Crum. You've only got your arm in a sling. You forget, one of us has a leg in plaster.'

'Oh, poor Morvy. Here, I'll help you.'

'Crum, stop!'

It was no good. Crum was determined to help his friend. With his one good arm he swung Morven's cast from the bed; Morven had no choice but to swivel his body. His foot hit the floor and he cried out.

'Oh give over, Morvy. Chaps are in a lot more agony down there.'

'I'm glad you appreciate the cost of war, Crum. For a moment I thought you regarded it as a mere spectacle.'

'What's that? Oh, your spectacles! What a pity they're broken, Morvy. Can you see anything?'

'Not much,' Morven said glumly.

'Actually, there's not much to see. Only smoke.'

'Anything else?'

'More smoke.'

'Oh.'

'I say, I saw a little bookcase in the nurse's room. Perhaps I could get you a book, Morvy.'

'I just said I can't see.'

'I mean, I could read to you, Morvy.'

'Crum, you can't read.'

Crum bridled.

'All right, you can read big signs – I don't think you can manage a book, though. Besides, I'm sure they have only trash. All books are not the same, Crum. You'd know that if you knew anything at all. For example, trash – take the romances of Bartel Silverby, for example – would paint this battle below as a field of glory. Mere propaganda for guileless youth! Now on the other hand, an author such as Garolus Vytoni—'

Crum grinned, 'I'll say!'

'Say what?'

'I mean, I like that Vytoni.'

Morven sighed, 'The binding? The bookworm?'

Crum lowered his voice. 'I mean, it's because of him we had our adventure, isn't it, Morvy? I mean, if it wasn't for him, we would never have helped the rebels, would we?'

'Why, Crum!' Morven was delighted. 'I do believe you're beginning to see the light.'

Crum grinned again, 'I mean, Morvy, if it weren't for the rebels, we'd never be in this nice warm infirmary, would we? Why, we'd be down on the battlefield getting shot right now, I'll be bound. Good old Vytoni!'

'Oh, Crum!'

Morven might have said more, but at that moment there was a commotion among the watchers at the windows. Many gasped. Some screamed. Some fainted away. A terrible thunder tore apart the air, but this was not the thunder of drums, guns, cannons.

'Crum, what is it?'

It was some moments before Crum could speak. When he did, his voice was trembling. 'Morvy, you won't believe this! Two enormous . . . bird-things have flown over the fields.'

'Bird-things?'

'But big, Morvy.'

'Big?'

'I mean big. They're . . . dragons, Morvy!'

And poor Crum could say no more, only watch as the monsters swooped low over the fields. One was coloured green and one was red. With mighty wings they dispersed the smoke, revealing Bluejackets and rebels alike, scattering, scurrying in all directions.

❋ ❋ ❋ ❋ ❋

Solemnly Jem looked into the cup that had been proffered him, and saw that it contained the richest, reddest wine he had ever seen. A longing overcame him, and he touched it with his tongue. The sensation was

512

delightful. Wave after wave of pleasure coursed through him, for this was the sweetest nectar he had ever tasted; then suddenly he knew – knew, it seemed, with an entire certainty – that after he had drunk from this cup his loneliness would be gone, spirited away, and he would be present in reality at this banquet that was now nothing but image, illusion. In the next moment he would fling back his head, quaffing the wine; but it was at that moment that two hungry little sparrows – or were they Ring and Rheen? – chose to flutter down to the tabletop.

Jem looked up, and saw to his horror that the scene had altered. For how long had he stared into the red depths? Now, all down the table, the rich food was rotten and corrupt, fit prey only for cockroaches and worms; but there was something worse, something more terrible. Jem cried out, for all the banqueters were corpses, rotting corpses, flyblown and stinking in the heat of the day.

'Raj, no!' Jem reached over the table, smacking the goblet from Rajal's hand just as his dazzled friend was about to drink. Startled, Rajal fell from his chair, disappearing beneath the table. Jem closed his eyes. When he opened them again, he still sat at the table, but the table was clear, the food, the guests, the evil hosts vanished as if they had never been.

'Raj?'

Concerned for his friend, Jem was about to rise from the table, when all at once he was aware of a curious sensation, welling about his feet. Water? But how could that be? Then Jem saw that the Casket of Spires had sprung open and the red bloody liquid he had refused to drink was flooding from inside, bubbling up like a spring. It was then that he registered a second curious fact: that without his quite knowing when, or how, the hillside on which he sat had inverted its form, becoming instead a deep, well-like depression in the earth.

And the well was filling, filling.

Reverently, Cata gazed into the sky. All around her, soldiers were fleeing. Some, in their terror, discarded their weapons; some ran into the path of rearing horses. A gun-carriage, loosed from its moorings, careered downhill, crashing into a Greenjacket van. Suddenly, across the Fields of Ajl, all were convulsed in the same fear – blues, greens, reds, rags. Only Cata was still, oblivious even of the bloody figures that littered the ground at her feet. Now she did not see the stricken stallion, kicking ineffectually, a soldier's lance gored through his flank; at another time, she would have helped him die. Now she did not see the black-bearded man (so large a man!), cold already, with a broken lute strapped incongruously at his chest.

513

At another time, even on these fields of battle, the pathetic sight would have moved her.

Cata had fought valiantly that day, though who she had fought for she was not quite sure. Ranging herself with the men in rags, she had been among the first to brave the Bluejacket guns. With a savage cry, imitating the men all around her, Cata had thrust her bayonet into the belly of a Bluejacket. Later, in her dreams, Cata would feel again the weight on her musket, dragging it down as the boy collapsed; later, she would see again the boy's astonished face, his eyes popping absurdly as he realized he was dead.

How the blood spurted when she pulled out her blade!

In time, Cata had lost her ragged company and fallen in instead with a different one. Among this band was a man in red, who wore a black mask over his eyes. Cata did not know who he might be, but sensed at once that he was a commander, just as the golden-armoured Orvik was a commander. Valiantly, among the explosions, screams and cries, her eyes streaming from the smoke, Cata fought for the cause of Bob Scarlet. Beside her, all unknown to her, were Hul, Bando, Zady – poor Zady, dead now just a little away from her.

He had died beneath the Bluejacket horses, trying to save a gaggle of frightened peasants who had never left the steppes of Derkold before, and never even dreamed of a cavalry-charge.

But all these things were forgotten now. The dragons whirled thunderously in the smoky sky. Cata raised her arms, as if reaching out to them. She was not afraid. At once she knew they were forces for good. One coloured green, one coloured red, they had come to win the day for the rebel forces, just when it seemed that all was lost.

The dragons made a second mighty pass over the field, then turned and swooped towards the walls of Wrax.

'Raj! Raj!'

But Jem had no time to find his friend, for in a matter of moments he was floundering, struggling to keep his head above water in the rushing red tide. Wildly his eyes veered this way and that, to the grassy walls of the hole, to the bubbling redness, to the branches of the mocking-tree, high above him now, five, ten times higher above his head than they had been before.

Then came the hands, reaching out to him.

'Jem! Quick!' It was Cata. Desperately Jem struggled towards her.

'Nova! No, here!'

Suddenly Cata was gone. Now it was Jeli, calling to him from the other side of the bank.

Then she was gone, too.

'Mej! Let me help you – Mej, please!' It was Landa.

'Jem! Jem!' Cata again.

'Nova!' Jeli.

'Mej!' Landa.

The bloody hole was filled, and flooding over. Now appearing, now disappearing – separately, then together – the three girls slithered on the slimy brink, each one urgently reaching towards him. Exhausted, desperate, Jem would have grabbed any hand he had been able to clutch; but something told him this test was decisive, more than a matter of mere survival.

Cata was his love, his only love: he must choose her, or be lost.

Sometimes there were two hands reaching at once, sometimes one, sometimes none. At last, as Jem was about to sink beneath the redness, three hands – Cata's, Jeli's, Landa's – reached all at once towards the centre of the hole. He braced himself, ready to sink for ever; but the will to live was too strong. With his last effort he reached up, grabbing a hand; whose it was he did not know.

It was Cata's.

❋ ❋ ❋ ❋ ❋

Cata's upstretched arms were juddering like wires and tears flowed freely down her stunned face. Before, it had been smoke that made her eyes stream; now it was the sunshine, so golden, so brilliant, and the painful sharp flashings of scales and fangs and claws. Still her eyes strained after the dragons; still she yearned for them with every tautened nerve.

Even then, perhaps, Cata knew the creatures did not quite exist, not really, not in this dimension. In truth, she sensed, they were projections of another battle, a different one, but one that was vital to the outcome of this.

And she knew they carried a secret, a secret she must know.

Then it came to her. Through the dazzling air, through her blurring eyes, she caught only the merest glimpse of the riders, bucking and writhing on the scaly backs.

It was enough.

'Jem!' Cata cried.

Of course the Jem-phantom could not hear, nor see her tiny form, but at once, as she cried the beloved name, mystic knowledge flooded Cata's heart. At once, linking with the minds of the metamorphs, she knew their story, and knew Jem's too.

This was a revelation. This was a vision.

This was the sign the harlequin had promised.

Chapter 74

THE GREEN CRYSTAL

The ordeal was over, or so it seemed. Suddenly Jem was back on the grassy hillside. Behind him, the bloody hole shrivelled to nothingness, his clothes were dry, and all was as it had been before. But not quite. Someone lay beside him. It was Cata, Cata as she had been in the Wildwood. Tears came to Jem's eyes. He embraced her tenderly, then passionately, and his lips met hers.

But as they kissed, a voice was singing a slow, doleful tune.

> *A man might love a lady dressed*
> *In finest silk and lace,*
> *But if she did not love him, too,*
> *He'd run a fruitless chase—*
> *Ladies Fine, Ladies Fair*
> *Smooth his furrowed brow of care,*
> *But is he sure they really understand?*

Dressed again as a page-boy, Rajal sat beneath the mocking-tree, plucking at the lute that until now had merely lain, disregarded, under the boughs. Beside him, dozing fitfully, were a lion and an antelope.

Jem paid them no heed. Reverently he ran his hands over Cata's breasts, her thighs. The girl responded ardently. Sensation ran through every nerve of Jem's body as he felt her hands slithering across his back, between his thighs, then up, up over his belly, his chest.

His chest.

'Fool! You would plunder the mocking-tree hoards?'

Suddenly the tender hands were a fist, tearing at the bag that hung from his neck. Jem cried out, but it was too late. With a wrench that was agony to him the Crystal of Koros was ripped loose, and in the next moment the Queen of Swords – for it was she – had flung it contemptuously away.

'No!' It was Rajal. He grabbed for the crystal as it rolled downhill. It burnt his hands, but he clutched it hard, refusing to let go. The Queen cried out. She turned on him, attacking him like a ravening beast, but still Rajal would not yield.

Jem rushed to his friend's aid. Seizing one of the thick, heavy gourds that lay beneath the tree, he swung it wildly. The Queen cried out and

516

staggered as Jem hit her, then hit her again. He knocked the crown from her head and it rolled downhill. She grabbed for it, but Rajal was standing in her way, clutching the crystal tightly in his hands.

The Queen shrieked and the Casket of Rings sprang open. It was the Jack-in-the-box again and he was shrieking too, his little eyes flashing like meteors as he screamed out discordant, terrible songs that might have torn apart the very air itself. He was calling down chaos, but Rajal was steadfast. Rays of power leapt from his hands. The Queen looked round her, cursing and blaspheming. The trunk of the mocking-tree was bulging, rippling.

Jem swung the gourd again and a great hole, like a tear in paper, ripped open in the Queen's neck. The terrible wound only enraged her more. Her head swinging back too far, impossibly far, she sprang forward, knocking Rajal to the ground, but still he gripped the crystal.

Now Jem would have struck the Queen again, but all at once the King was in his path, brandishing an immense broadsword in a single hand. In his free hand he held another just like it, and flung it to Jem; Jem staggered, struggling even with both hands to lift the iron burden.

With a roar, the King was upon him.

❄ ❄ ❄ ❄ ❄

Now the dragons move in on the city. Now the greens, the reds, the rags are rallying round their standards again, cheering these astonishing magical champions. Across the fields, the mighty wings sound like a storm, the greatest ever known, rocking the ancient walls of Wrax. On the battlements, the conquerors lay down their arms. Some pummel the ground, some implore the skies.

It is over. The day is won.

But then a new horror erupts on the air, for suddenly, bursting from a cloud above the hills, comes a third dragon, mightier than the green and red!

This dragon is blue.

Cata cries out, for at once, with the power that courses through her being, she knows this dragon, and knows its rider. It is Polty, resurrected from the clasp of the Vichy. His skin is blue and his hair is in flames. In his hand he bears a burning brand, and his mouth is fixed open, filled with sharp fangs.

Screaming in time to the roaring of his dragon, Polty bears down on the fields below.

❄ ❄ ❄ ❄ ❄

As the *clang! clang!* of the duel rang out, somewhere in his mind Jem knew that it coincided with the sonorous clangings of the Temple bells, still ringing impossibly, invisibly on the air. Round and round the mocking-tree he struggled with the King; meanwhile the Queen would not relent, and nor would Rajal. She bit, clawed, kicked, but nothing would pull apart his hands. Rajal felt the flesh fuse searingly; his body bucked and twisted on waves of power. His teeth clashed, his eyes rolled. He was without thought, without memory, but never again after that day would Rajal feel shame to be a Child of Koros. It was his destiny, and a glorious one, for he knew now that he was chosen, chosen of his god.

The crystal worked through him, calling to its sister-crystal hidden in the tree.

Now the bulgings in the tree grew wilder. Now the branches were twisting, waving like fingers of a hundred crazed hands; green light fizzed and crackled from the leaves. Now a thousand rainbow-doves were fleeing from the branches, taking deafening flight; now the leaves were falling and the golden apples too, crashing to the ground like cannon-balls. Shrieking, roaring, Ring and Rheen raced round the tree, their shapes flickering with every circuit – pig, bear, eagle, elephant, then all manner of mutant horrors – wingèd tortoise, air-shark, two-headed monkey, camel with feathers and a chicken-beaked muzzle.

Clang! Clang! went the swords, but faster now, faster; now Jem felt himself growing stronger, ever stronger. He hacked and hewed at the evil King. Around the hill the sky was dark, then light; bright, then riven with a pelting storm. Suddenly Jem looked down and saw the clash of armies on the Fields of Ajl. Cannons blasted, muskets fired; there were screams and cries and stabbings of bayonets, and now all these were as vivid to Jem, as vivid and terrible as his own desperate battle.

Then it came to him that the battles were the same, for as he fought the King of Swords, so he was fighting the Bluejacket thrall.

❋   ❋   ❋   ❋   ❋

The dragons that have been were as nothing to this. Only through the spectacle of their presence, their power, did the green and the red dragon fill all hearts with fear. Now, swooping over the arc of the Rheen, the blue dragon breathes sheets of flame. Orvik's army is devastated in moments; in moments, Cata feels the lapping heat.

What follows is a fray more ghastly than any other that has been that day. Cries of burning men are like cries of the damned, cast into the horror of the Realm of Unbeing. Now, fleeing rebels – green, red, ragged – have abandoned all faith, all pride, all hope; now it seems the gods themselves would declare for Ejard Blue. For though the green dragon, then the red, come tearing to the defence, like Orvik's forces they are too weak.

They are doomed.

518

'No!' Cata cries, but her voice is lost. Then suddenly her power is lost to her too, and she too can only flee. But just for one moment, as the fields flame around her, she gazes up again at the green dragon. Desperately she clutches her hands to her heart, urging her love to shoot from her like a ray, exploding round Jem with all its power and longing. Never has she loved him more urgently, more ardently.

But it is no good. She has lost him again. Perhaps it is an illusion of the dazzling sun, but it seems now that Jem's dragon – Rajal's, too – is fading, fading back into its true dimension.

❋ ❋ ❋ ❋ ❋

It ended suddenly. Rajal reared up, screaming with the intensity of his crystal-power. He pushed the Queen from him and her head, that had been swinging dangerously, fell away from her neck. Swiftly Rajal stamped on it, crushing it like a beetle, and her body crumpled like a house of cards.

Inside, the Queen was filled with cockroaches, spiders, corrupting food – all the vileness that had lain on the banqueting-table, which at first had presented an appearance so fair.

In the moment of the Queen's death, the King cried out, as if a part of himself had died too. It was Jem's chance. He lunged, driving his great sword clean through the King's chest. The cry that came then was the most piteous Jem had heard, a cry filled with a sorrow so deep it might have destroyed the world itself.

Disbelievingly, the King lay down and died, side by side with his evil Queen.

❋ ❋ ❋ ❋ ❋

But the powers of evil are too great that day. Only one of the battles can be won.

Cata has no time to watch any more, for now Polty comes swooping again, eager to finish the work he has begun. Just one figure is steadfast against him; one figure only has not fled. It is Orvik, Prince Sacred, bursting on to the field with his golden sword. His hour come at last, he must slay the dragon; but Orvik, against the dragon, is the merest golden insect.

Orvik's horse rears.

The sword slashes the air.

But the merest flick of the dragon's wing destroys the hopes of Zenzau. Orvik is flung into a patch of briars. His spine snaps at once. Then the dragon sets the briars aflame. The Prince boils inside his golden armour.

The battle is over.

519

In the next moment the chaos in the air was gone. Again, it was a bright, still day, and Jem and Rajal stood beneath the mocking-tree. Jem looked at Rajal; his friend was dressed in his Bluejacket uniform again, but somehow, unaccountably, it seemed he had altered. Then Jem felt a sense of lack, a vacancy in his own heart. He reached up to touch the Crystal of Koros, but in the new peace that had come over the scene, the crystal had not been restored to its place.

An intimation came over Jem and he stepped towards Rajal, touching his chest, feeling what lay beneath the blue jacket. Around his neck, Rajal wore the Crystal of Koros. Troubled, Jem looked into Rajal's eyes.

But Rajal was staring at the mocking-tree.

'Jem,' he breathed, 'look!'

Now Jem turned, and in sudden joy he saw that a split, huge and gaping, had opened in the trunk of the tree, and that inside there lay the secret, green stone he had come to Zenzau to find. He reached forward, scooping the glimmering prize into his hands. He gasped, exulting. In that moment the old, old tree suddenly withered, collapsing into powder, and the powder, as it rose and dispersed on the air, formed an image he had seen before.

'Sacred Viana.' Jem sank to his knees, holding the crystal before him like an offering.

'Sister of my god.' Rajal sank down too.

For long moments they knelt in reverence, their heads bowed and their eyes shut tight, and when they opened them again they saw that the bright primaeval hillside had faded, vanished, and they were again in the Temple where the adventure had begun, before the altar of the golden tree.

Chapter 75

ONE LETTER

Dear, dearest Mazy,

How you wrong me! Do you suppose me insensible of your sufferings? Ah, I fear you have forgotten your old Consy, and send your words only to a name, a shadow! But how can my heart not throb in time with yours, as I think of you in those far regions, facing the wrath of barbarian hordes? Then, I am afraid, anger wells within me, and I find myself cursing the husband who would uproot so fine a flower, to plant it again in the colonial wastes! Forgive me, my dear – but if my own late lord was, as you imply, the merest fop, I thank the Lord Agonis that he died in silken sheets, his hand held in mine, and not in some bloody fray, far from home!

By the time you read this, I dare say Zenzau's destiny will be decided. All here in Agondon (for of course we speak of it) are certain of victory, and see no hope for the Green Pretender. Why, then, do I look to the future with alarm? Perhaps it is merely that I am growing old, and the dark shadow on the path before me is my own death, looming near. Yet often I feel it is more than this, and that something in the times themselves has turned. Only seasons separate us from the thousandth cycle (how far away it seemed when we were girls!). But should I see a portent in the calendar itself? Always I have scoffed at the primitives of our faith, who spoke of the end of this Time of Atonement. Now I find, like a primitive myself, that all around me I see omens of an ending.

As I write, I look from the windows of my house, at the waters of the river rippling below. It is evening, almost nightfall, and in the setting sun the river is gold. But seasons pass quickly: soon the city shall be hot beyond bearing, and the river shall peel its way back like a skin, exposing the reeking blackness below. In this, I fear – this black beneath the gold – I see an emblem of our empire and its fate.

But emblems are endless, for those who would see them. Only last moonlife, after the heavy rains, there were floods in Agondon New Town. One day, even Davalon Street was under water. Dreadful, many said, but a haphazard thing; yet as I looked across the river that day I found myself thinking that the New Town was built, after all, on a drained swamp, and that perhaps a time would come when the swamp would return, eager to take back what it had lost.

Then, too, there is the news from Varby. This year I would have taken Tishy there (forgive a fond mother, if she cannot forbear from effort after fruitless effort!). Yet now that is impossible, and we must go to Freddie Chayn's. To think, that plague should devastate this fairest of our cities! They say it came down from the Holluch Hills, though quite how and why I do not understand.

But what am I saying? Dear Mazy, I shall merely make you miserable again – poor payment for the happiness that filled my heart when I read of your dream that we were girls once more, running in muslin through the daffodils and daisies! Forgive an old woman, who sits alone, looking over a river at sunset. You imagine her at the centre of a round of pleasure, but this last season has been a sad one for her. She has suffered in the aftermath of that business with Feval (how I hope I need never see that man again!). Her dear friend Lord Empster has gone away. Her daughter has taken up a life of learning (I fear she is to become one of those 'Green-stockings'!). Then, too, there have been several tragic deaths, coming close enough to grieve her deeply. You have read, no doubt, about poor Lord Margrave? I have taken Elsan to live with me here, as I am afraid she is hardly fit to live on her own. In truth, I had not known how much she loved her husband, until the news came that he was dead. Then of course there is Sir Pellion – losing first his great-daughter, then her brother! I am afraid he shall never again be fit for society.

But enough: you see I am melancholy, and can stir myself to no other mood. I had meant to write more, and of happier things: dear Mazy, I shall make it up to you soon. All talk here is of the Royal Wedding, so you see there will soon be fresh excitements.

I puzzled much over your remarks on Vlada Flay. Indeed, my dear, it is you who must be mistaken, for assuredly the creature has moved amongst us, all through these last seasons in Agondon.

That is another of the burdens I have borne.

> I remain, my dear,
>> Now and always,
>>> Your loving heart-sister,
>>> Constansia

Postscript.
O my dear! Here I was, about to seal this letter, when Elsan burst in with the most startling news. 'The harlot is dead!' she cried. – 'Harlot?' said I. – 'Why, Constansia, you know who I mean! The harlot, Vlada Flay!' There was triumph in Elsan's voice, but I am

522

afraid (to her astonishment) that now it was my turn to dissolve into tears.

Often have I execrated Vlada Flay; now I find myself thinking only that (for all her flaws) she was one of us, and now she is gone.

Chapter 76

END AND A BEGINNING

It was evening, the evening after the battle. The sun was setting and greenish light refracted through the high windows of the Temple, flickering like chill flames over the mocking-tree that was now only a shell, the empty carapace of something that had died.

Outside, the world was returning to order, or rather, assuming a new order. Across the Fields of Ajl, stretcher-bearers were busy at their work. Dead-carts, trundling over muddy tracks, were soon heaped high with corpses. Later, huge pits would be dug on the edge of the woods, pit after pit until, some would say, it was rather as if the city were itself a monument, towering above a ring of graves.

The Battle of Ajl would swiftly become a legend – perhaps, indeed, was a legend even now, for few could quite recall just how it had ended. If they did, their memories would swiftly grow hazy. Next morning, waking from his victory debauch, many a Bluejacket would imagine himself to have had the strangest dream. The losers muttered darkly of Bluejacket trickery. Later, if there were still those who spoke of dragons, others would think of these dragons as a symbol, a metaphor for the fierceness of the battle that day.

Nirry, for example, shall remember little. But then, she has other things on her mind. Later that day, when she finds Wiggler again, Nirry opens up a purse of gold. It is her life's savings, carried beneath her skirts all the way from Irion: not much, given how long she has worked, but Wiggler's eyes goggle. Never has he seen so much money, and wonders if Nirry has robbed her mistress. He shall never dare ask, for then, to his astonishment, she is counting five tirals into his palm. And looking sternly at her new husband, Nirry delivers the first of a lifetime's orders.

'Now listen to me, Wiggler Olch. Corporal or no corporal, I don't care, you're not staying in this army one minute more. You're going to your commander now, and buying your way out. We're going back to Ejland tomorrow, we are, and opening our little tavern.'

'Tavern?' grins Carney Floss, who has decided he might just befriend the young couple.

Nirry turns on him. 'A respectable place, I'll have you know. Soft beds and my good cooking. And I tell the both of you—' she gestures towards the battlefield '—if any of you menfolk are ever brawling in my house, I'll take my best broom to you, I will, and beat you black and blue!'

❋ ❋ ❋ ❋ ❋

Of those who had been on the field that day, only five would recall the truth.

The first was a certain young rebel survivor, who ran from the blue dragon just in time. That day, the rebel had been vouchsafed a sign, but the sign was incomplete. Where – in all the world – was the young rebel to go? For now, what was important was to escape the Bluejackets. Returning to the fastness of the greenwood that night, Bob Scarlet's band would be missing one of their number, but in Zady's place would be the new friend they had made that day.

Wolveron, he said. *Call me Wolveron.*

Then there was Landa. Desperately at the end, when all hope was lost, she had struggled to prevent her dear Orvik from going into battle. That night, Landa was convulsed in sorrow. Yet even then, her way was clear to her. Though she would honour Orvik's memory and always love him, perhaps she would be a better, stronger woman without him. Orvik had promised to make her his Queen. Now, she would make *herself* into something – perhaps something more . . . Next morning, very early, she would repair deep into the woods, resuming the worship the Priestess had shown her. Her destiny, Landa knew, was to take Ajl's place, keeping alive the true faith of Viana's people.

Then there were the riders of the three dragons.

That night Polty found himself back in barracks. He also found that he had become an object of awe, even reverence. It was not because of his blue skin and flaming hair, for they had gone. Polty looked just as he had looked before, although perhaps his eyes were a little brighter – perhaps his hair was a little more red. Still, he barely had time to check himself in the glass. Every fellow wanted to shake his hand; officers' wives, even the primmest, rushed to fling themselves upon his neck. Raised high on the shoulders of the regiment, Polty was carried in triumph round the parade-ground. There were toasts, songs; urgently his company commander sought him out. Before the evening was over, young Captain Veeldrop, hero of the day, stood before Michan, Governor of Zenzau.

Now Lord Michan was one of Ejland's greatest heroes. In the last war it was Michan who had taken Wrax, after the abortive efforts of Polty's disgraced father. In this city, Michan would tell Polty, the very name 'Veeldrop' had been spoken only to be cursed: now that time was gone. He had heard that young Veeldrop had been a wildish fellow: if so, all was forgiven. Had ever a fellow vindicated himself more triumphantly?

Floridly the governor flung out his arms, eager to embrace this fine young man who had not only saved a city, but redeemed his family name.

❋ ❋ ❋ ❋ ❋

As for Jem and Rajal, let us leave them in the Temple. When the two friends rose from before the altar, the bells above them gave a last sonorous *clang!* It came to them then that the sound had never ceased, not in all the time of their fantastic adventure. That was when they gazed up the belfry stairs that wound in a tight spiral from the altar's side. Now the clanging was replaced by footsteps.

Jem and Rajal exchanged glances. Sunset light fell across the figure that appeared above them, midway up the stairs. Jem screwed up his eyes, but it was the voice he recognized first, echoing around him in the chill vastness.

'I suspect, Jemany, you are about to ask who I am. *Who are you, who are you?* It was the question you were doomed to ask, again and again in the course of this adventure. So many identities, shifting, changing. But in truth, Jemany, the question was the always the wrong one, was it not? Or the right one, but asked of the wrong person?'

Jem breathed, 'I don't understand.'

Slowly the figure descended the stairs. His long cloak billowed behind him and his wide-brimmed hat covered his eyes. As he spoke he lit his ivory pipe, and smoke billowed round him in the streaky light.

'Don't you see, Jemany?' said Lord Empster. 'Perhaps the question is not who am I, but who are *you*?'

Jem hesitated. 'I am the Key to the Orokon.'

'And sometimes, Jemany, have you not forgotten that fact?'

'It's true.' Jem looked down. Still the crystal shimmered in his hands, but already its light was growing duller, as the first crystal had dulled after it was found. There was much Jem might have said to his guardian. Questions, accusations, hovered on his lips. It came to him that really he was quite entitled to ask just who this strange lord might be.

In the event he only murmured, 'My lord, there were times when it seemed you barely trusted me.'

Lord Empster turned. Drawing on his pipe, he looked towards the altar. He spoke quietly, but still his words echoed in the Temple.

'No more, Jemany, no more. I was fearful of your untried powers, and sought delays – I was wrong. I sought to break you from the attachments of the past – I was wrong. I failed to see that in this boy who stands beside you now, you should find a friend more steadfast than any other you shall ever meet.'

Jem clutched Rajal's hand. 'My brother.'

'Quite.' But Lord Empster did not smile. 'From now on we must work swiftly to assemble the Orokon. The danger which lies before us is immense, but the cost of failure ... well, Jemany, you have read The Burning Verses. Had Viana's people won their victory today, the evil which besets these lands would perhaps have been allayed for a time. The crystal, when it is found, unleashes a positive energy. Remember, Jemany, when you found the Crystal of Koros?'

It was Rajal who answered. 'Irion Day.'

'Quite,' Lord Empster said again. 'But today was different. When the first dragons appeared over the field, it seemed that Zenzau would triumph after all, but the energy was not strong enough. You could defeat the King and Queen of Swords, but no more. Already Toth's minions are working amongst us, bringing chaos and terror.'

'The blue dragon,' Rajal murmured.

'Dragon?' Jem looked between his two companions. 'Then it was all true, what happened over the battlefield?'

'Of course,' said Lord Empster. 'Truth slips easily through the gaps between dimensions. But the dragons were the reality, the essence that lay behind what happened today.'

Jem thought of Polty, but before he could ask his question, Lord Empster replied, 'Why, Jemany, is it not clear? As you have found your destiny, so he has found his. That young man is our implacable foe, and I am certain we shall see him again. But come.' Only now did the strange lord smile. 'This heathen Temple can be no place for a noble Ejlander and his young ward—' he looked at Rajal '—and his *two* young wards. My carriage awaits, and there is a long journey before us.'

'To Agondon?' said Jem.

'No, Jemany, you may never return there – not until your quest is over. We must make for the coast at once. Already it is not safe for us here, and now we must find the red crystal, the Crystal of Theron. At the coast, Captain Porlo's ship awaits. Tomorrow we sail for the burning southern lands of Unang Lia.'

'Captain Porlo? Unang Lia?' Excitement hammered in Jem's heart. Then came fear, as he thought again of the prophecy that held him in its grip.

His quest had barely begun!

They turned towards the doors. But one strange thing still had to happen before they could leave the Temple of Wrax. They had forgotten the Priestess, but still she remained in the glimmering shadows, unmoving, silent.

'Priestess?' Jem stepped towards her, but as he did so she fell forward suddenly, crumbling just as the mocking-tree had crumbled. For a terrible moment, Jem thought he had killed her.

But no: she had died already.

Lord Empster blew out a stream of smoke. 'Poor Hara! Her vigil is over. But she was weary of it, too weary, and we must not repine.'

'Hara?' said Rajal.

'Her true name – the name she bore in the Time of Juvescence, before she was entrusted with her terrible burden. *Ajl* is an old Zenzan word meaning *guardian*, no more. Priestess Ajl was but a projection of the mocking-tree. Its being was hers, and her being was the tree's. Now the tree is dead, the Priestess is dead, too. For as I say, she was really Hara – Hara, who was locked with the crystal inside the tree, after she was violated by the King of Swords.'

Jem looked down wonderingly at the dust at his feet. He would have suggested they gather it up – to scatter, perhaps, amidst the greenwood the Priestess had loved and worshipped – but now Lord Empster was striding towards the doorway, betraying more than a hint of impatience, speaking of the challenges that lay ahead. Jem concealed the crystal hurriedly inside his jacket, smiled at Rajal, and followed behind.

As the hatch in the great doors opened again, the dust that had once been Viana's Priestess stirred and blew across the stone-slabbed floor. Some of it whirled on to the altar, where a little mouse and a shiny-backed beetle scurried nervously back and forth, nibbling from time to time at two dog-eared playing-cards that lay, like remnants of an ended game, on the green baize beneath the dead, golden tree.

Here ends the Second Book of THE OROKON.
In the Third Book, *Sultan of the Moon and Stars*,
while new evils unfold in Agondon,
Jem's quest takes him to exotic lands.
But Cata is not far behind – and nor is Polty.